THE
CITY WATCH
TRILOGY

THE

CITY WATCH
TRILOGY

Terry Pratchett

VICTOR GOLLANCZ

LONDON

First published as one volume in Great Britain 1999
By Victor Gollancz Ltd
Orion House, 5 Upper St Martin's Lane, London WC2H 9EA

A catalogue record for this book is available
from the British Library

ISBN 0575 067985

Printed in Great Britain by Clays Ltd, St Ives plc

CONTENTS

Dedication

They may be called the Palace Guard, the City Guard or the Patrol. Whatever the name, their purpose in any work of heroic fantasy is identical: it is, round about Chapter Three (or ten minutes into the film) to rush into the room, attack the hero one at a time, and be slaughtered. No one ever asks them if they wanted to.

This book is dedicated to those fine men.

And also to Mike Harrison, Mary Gentle, Neil Gaiman and all the others who assisted with and laughed at the idea of L-space; too bad we never used Schrödinger's Paperback . . .

GUARDS! GUARDS!

This is where the dragons went.

They lie . . .

Not dead, not asleep. Not waiting, because waiting implies expectation. Possibly the word we're looking for here is . . .

. . . dormant.

And although the space they occupy isn't like normal space, nevertheless they are packed in tightly. Not a cubic inch there but is filled by a claw, a talon, a scale, the tip of a tail, so the effect is like one of those trick drawings and your eyeballs eventually realize that the space between each dragon is, in fact, another dragon.

They could put you in mind of a can of sardines, if you thought sardines were huge and scaly and proud and arrogant.

And presumably, somewhere, there's the key.

In another space entirely, it was early morning in Ankh-Morpork, oldest and greatest and grubbiest of cities. A thin drizzle dripped from the grey sky and punctuated the river mist that coiled among the streets. Rats of various species went about their nocturnal occasions. Under night's damp cloak assassins assassinated, thieves thieved, hussies hustled. And so on.

And drunken Captain Vimes of the Night Watch staggered slowly down the street, folded gently into the gutter outside the Watch House and lay there while, above him, strange letters made of light sizzled in the damp and changed colour . . .

The city wasa, wasa, wasa wossname. Thing. *Woman.* Thass what it was. Woman. Roaring, ancient, centuries old. Strung you along, let you fall in thingy, love, with her, then kicked you inna, inna, thingy. Thingy, in your mouth. Tongue. Tonsils. *Teeth.* That's what it, she, did. She wasa . . . thing, you know, lady dog. Puppy. Hen. *Bitch.* And then you hated her and, and just when you thought you'd got her, it, out of your, your, whatever, then she opened her great booming rotten heart to you, caught you off bal, bal, bal, thing. *Ance.* Yeah. Thassit. Never knew where where you stood. Lay. Only thing you were sure of, you couldn't let her go. Because, because she was yours, all you had, even in her gutters . . .

*

3

Damp darkness shrouded the venerable buildings of Unseen University, premier college of wizardry. The only light was a faint octarine flicker from the tiny windows of the new High Energy Magic building, where keen-edged minds were probing the very fabric of the universe, whether it liked it or not.

And there was light, of course, in the Library.

The Library was the greatest assemblage of magical texts anywhere in the multiverse. Thousands of volumes of occult lore weighted its shelves.

It was said that, since vast amounts of magic can seriously distort the mundane world, the Library did not obey the normal rules of space and time. It was said that it went on *forever*. It was said that you could wander for days among the distant shelves, that there were lost tribes of research students somewhere in there, that strange things lurked in forgotten alcoves and were preyed on by other things that were even stranger.*

Wise students in search of more distant volumes took care to leave chalk marks on the shelves as they roamed deeper into the fussy darkness, and told friends to come looking for them if they weren't back by supper.

And, because magic can only loosely be bound, the Library books themselves were more than mere pulped wood and paper.

Raw magic crackled from their spines, earthing itself harmlessly in the copper rails nailed to every shelf for that very purpose. Faint traceries of blue fire crawled across the bookcases and there was a sound, a papery whispering, such as might come from a colony of roosting starlings. In the silence of the night the books talked to one another.

There was also the sound of someone snoring.

The light from the shelves didn't so much illuminate as highlight the darkness, but by its violet flicker a watcher might just have identified an ancient and battered desk right under the central dome.

The snoring was coming from underneath it, where a piece of tattered blanket barely covered what looked like a heap of sandbags but was in fact an adult male orang-utan.

It was the Librarian.

---

* All this was untrue. The truth is that even big collections of ordinary books distort space, as can readily be proved by anyone who has been around a really old-fashioned secondhand bookshop, one of those that look as though they were designed by M. Escher on a bad day and has more staircases than storeys and those rows of shelves which end in little doors that are surely too small for a full sized human to enter. The relevant equation is: Knowledge = power = energy = matter = mass; a good bookshop is just a genteel Black Hole that knows how to read.

4

Not many people these days remarked upon the fact that he was an ape. The change had been brought about by a magical accident, always a possibility where so many powerful books are kept together, and he was considered to have got off lightly. After all, he was still basically the same shape. And he had been allowed to keep his job, which he was rather good at, although 'allowed' is not really the right word. It was the way he could roll his upper lip back to reveal more incredibly yellow teeth than any other mouth the University Council had ever seen before that somehow made sure the matter was never really raised.

But now there was another sound, the alien sound of a door creaking open. Footsteps padded across the floor and disappeared amongst the clustering shelves. The books rustled indignantly, and some of the larger grimoires rattled their chains.

The Librarian slept on, lulled by the whispering of the rain.

In the embrace of his gutter, half a mile away, Captain Vimes of the Night Watch opened his mouth and started to sing.

Now a black-robed figure scurried through the midnight streets, ducking from doorway to doorway, and reached a grim and forbidding portal. No mere doorway got that grim without effort, one felt. It looked as though the architect had been called in and given specific instructions. We want something eldritch in dark oak, he'd been told. So put an unpleasant gargoyle thing over the archway, give it a slam like the footfall of a giant and make it clear to everyone, in fact, that this isn't the kind of door that goes 'ding-dong' when you press the bell.

The figure rapped a complex code on the dark woodwork. A tiny barred hatch opened and one suspicious eye peered out.

'"The significant owl hoots in the night,"' said the visitor, trying to wring the rainwater out of its robe.

'"Yet many grey lords go sadly to the masterless men,"' intoned a voice on the other side of the grille.

'"Hooray, hooray for the spinster's sister's daughter,"' countered the dripping figure.

'"To the axeman, all supplicants are the same height."'

'"Yet verily, the rose is within the thorn."'

'"The good mother makes bean soup for the errant boy,"' said the voice behind the door.

There was a pause, broken only by the sound of the rain. Then the visitor said, 'What?'

'"The good mother makes bean soup for the errant boy."'

There was another, longer pause. Then the damp figure said,

'Are you sure the ill-built tower doesn't tremble mightily at a butterfly's passage?'

'Nope. Bean soup it is. I'm sorry.'

The rain hissed down relentlessly in the embarrassed silence.

'What about the cagèd whale?' said the soaking visitor, trying to squeeze into what little shelter the dread portal offered.

'What about it?'

'It should know nothing of the mighty deeps, if you must know.'

'*Oh*, the cagèd *whale. You* want the *Elucidated* Brethren of the Ebon Night. Three doors down.'

'Who're you, then?'

'We're the Illuminated and Ancient Brethren of Ee.'

'I thought you met over in Treacle Street,' said the damp man, after a while.

'Yeah, well. You know how it is. The fretwork club have the room Tuesdays. There was a bit of a mix-up.'

'Oh? Well, thanks anyway.'

'My pleasure.' The little door slammed shut.

The robed figure glared at it for a moment, and then splashed further down the street. There was indeed another portal there. The builder hadn't bothered to change the design much.

He knocked. The little barred hatch shot back.

'Yes?'

'Look, "The significant owl hoots in the night", all right?'

'"Yet many grey lords go sadly to the masterless men."'

'"Hooray, hooray for the spinster's sister's daughter", okay?'

'"To the axeman, all supplicants are the same height."'

'"Yet verily, the rose is within the thorn." It's pissing down out here. You do *know* that, don't you?'

'Yes,' said the voice, in the tones of one who indeed does know it, and is not the one standing in it.

The visitor sighed.

'"The cagèd whale knows nothing of the mighty deeps,"' he said. 'If it makes you any happier.'

'"The ill-built tower trembles mightily at a butterfly's passage."'

The supplicant grabbed the bars of the window, pulled himself up to it, and hissed: 'Now let us in, I'm soaked.'

There was another damp pause.

'These deeps . . . did you say mighty or nightly?'

'Mighty, I said. *Mighty* deeps. On account of being, you know, deep. It's me, Brother Fingers.'

'It sounded like nightly to me,' said the invisible doorkeeper cautiously.

6

'Look, do you want the bloody book or not? I don't have to do this. I could be at home in bed.'

'You *sure* it was mighty?'

'Listen, I know how deep the bloody deeps are all right,' said Brother Fingers urgently. 'I knew how mighty they were when you were a perishing neophyte. Now will you open this door?'

'Well . . . all right.'

There was the sound of bolts sliding back. Then the voice said, 'Would you mind giving it a push? The Door of Knowledge Through Which the Untutored May Not Pass sticks something wicked in the damp.'

Brother Fingers put his shoulder to it, forced his way through, gave Brother Doorkeeper a dirty look, and hurried within.

The others were waiting for him in the Inner Sanctum, standing around with the sheepish air of people not normally accustomed to wearing sinister hooded black robes. The Supreme Grand Master nodded at him.

'Brother Fingers, isn't it?'

'Yes, Supreme Grand Master.'

'Do you have that which you were sent to get?'

Brother Fingers pulled a package from under his robe.

'Just where I said it would be,' he said. 'No problem.'

'Well done, Brother Fingers.'

'Thank you, Supreme Grand Master.'

The Supreme Grand Master rapped his gavel for attention. The room shuffled into some sort of circle.

'I call the Unique and Supreme Lodge of the Elucidated Brethren to order,' he intoned. 'Is the Door of Knowledge sealed fast against heretics and knowlessmen?'

'Stuck solid,' said Brother Doorkeeper. 'It's the damp. I'll bring my plane in next week, soon have it—'

'All right, all *right*,' said the Supreme Grand Master testily. 'Just a yes would have done. Is the triple circle well and truly traced? Art all here who Art Here? And it be well for an knowlessman that he should not be here, for he would be taken from this place and his gaskin slit, his moules shown to the four winds, his welchet torn asunder with many hooks and his figgin placed upon a spike *yes what is it?*'

'Sorry, did you say *Elucidated* Brethren?'

The Supreme Grand Master glared at the solitary figure with its hand up.

'Yea, the Elucidated Brethren, guardian of the sacred knowledge since a time no man may wot of—'

'Last February,' said Brother Doorkeeper helpfully. The

Supreme Grand Master felt that Brother Doorkeeper had never really got the hang of things.

'Sorry. Sorry. Sorry,' said the worried figure. 'Wrong society, I'm afraid. Must have taken a wrong turning. I'll just be going, if you'll excuse me . . .'

'And his figgin placed upon a spike,' repeated the Supreme Grand Master pointedly, against a background of damp wooden noises as Brother Doorkeeper tried to get the dread portal open. 'Are we quite finished? Any more knowlessmen happened to drop in on their way somewhere else?' he added with bitter sarcasm. 'Right. Fine. *So* glad. I suppose it's too much to ask if the Four Watchtowers are secured? Oh, good. And the Trouser of Sanctity, has anyone bothered to shrive it? Oh, you did. Properly? I'll check, you know . . . all right. And have the windows been fastened with the Red Cords of Intellect, in accordance with ancient prescription? Good. Now perhaps we can get on with it.'

With the slightly miffed air of one who has run their finger along a daughter-in-law's top shelf and found against all expectation that it is sparkling clean, the Grand Master got on with it.

What a shower, he told himself. A bunch of incompetents no other secret society would touch with a ten-foot Sceptre of Authority. The sort to dislocate their fingers with even the simplest secret handshake.

But incompetents with possibilities, nevertheless. Let the other societies take the skilled, the hopefuls, the ambitious, the self-confident. He'd take the whining resentful ones, the ones with a bellyful of spite and bile, the ones who knew they could make it big if only they'd been given the chance. Give him the ones in which the floods of venom and vindictiveness were dammed up behind thin walls of ineptitude and low-grade paranoia.

And stupidity, too. They've all sworn the oath, he thought, but not a man jack of 'em has even asked what a figgin is.

'Brethren,' he said. 'Tonight we have matters of profound importance to discuss. The good governance, nay, the very future of Ankh-Morpork lies in our hands.'

They leaned closer. The Supreme Grand Master felt the beginnings of the old thrill of power. They were hanging on his words. This was a feeling worth dressing up in bloody silly robes for.

'Do we not well know that the city is in thrall to corrupt men, who wax fat on their ill-gotten gains, while better men are held back and forced into virtual servitude?'

'We certainly do!' said Brother Doorkeeper vehemently, when they'd had time to translate this mentally. 'Only last week, down

8

at the Bakers' Guild, I tried to point out to Master Critchley that—'

It wasn't eye contact, because the Supreme Grand Master had made sure the Brethren's hoods shrouded their faces in mystic darkness, but nevertheless he managed to silence Brother Doorkeeper by dint of sheer outraged silence.

'Yet it was not always thus,' the Supreme Grand Master continued. 'There was once a golden age, when those worthy of command and respect were justly rewarded. An age when Ankh-Morpork wasn't simply a big city but a great one. An age of chivalry. An age when – yes, Brother Watchtower?'

A bulky robed figure lowered its hand. 'Are you talking about when we had kings?'

'Well done, Brother,' said the Supreme Grand Master, slightly annoyed at this unusual evidence of intelligence. 'And—'

'But that was all sorted out hundreds of years ago,' said Brother Watchtower. 'Wasn't there this great battle, or something? And since then we've just had the ruling lords, like the Patrician.'

'Yes, very good, Brother Watchtower.'

'There aren't any more kings, is the point I'm trying to make,' said Brother Watchtower helpfully.

'As Brother Watchtower says, the line of—'

'It was you talking about chivalry that give me the clue,' said Brother Watchtower.

'Quite so, and—'

'You get that with kings, chivalry,' said Brother Watchtower happily. 'And knights. And they used to have these—'

'*However*,' said the Supreme Grand Master sharply, 'it may well be that the line of the kings of Ankh is not as defunct as hitherto imagined, and that progeny of the line exists even now. Thus my researches among the ancient scrolls do indicate.'

He stood back expectantly. There didn't seem to be the effect he'd expected, however. Probably they can manage 'defunct', he thought, but I ought to have drawn the line at 'progeny'.

Brother Watchtower had his hand up again.

'Yes?'

'You saying there's some sort of heir to the throne hanging around somewhere?' said Brother Watchtower.

'This may be the case, yes.'

'Yeah. They do that, you know,' said Brother Watchtower knowledgeably. 'Happens all the time. You read about it. Skions, they're called. They go lurking around in the distant wildernesses for ages, handing down the secret sword and birthmark and so forth from generation to generation. Then just when the old kingdom needs them, they turn up and turf out any usurpers that happen to be around. And then there's general rejoicing.'

The Supreme Grand Master felt his own mouth drop open. He hadn't expected it to be as easy as this.

'Yes, all right,' said a figure the Supreme Grand Master knew to be Brother Plasterer. 'But so what? Let's say a skion turns up, walks up to the Patrician, says "What ho, I'm king, here's the birthmark as per spec, now bugger off". What's he got then? Life expectancy of maybe two minutes, that's what.'

'You don't *listen*,' said Brother Watchtower. 'The thing is, the skion has to arrive when the kingdom is threatened, doesn't he? Then everyone can see, right? Then he gets carried off to the palace, cures a few people, announces a half-holiday, hands round a bit of treasure, and Bob's your uncle.'

'He has to marry a princess, too,' said Brother Doorkeeper. 'On account of him being a swineherd.'

They looked at him.

'Who said anything about him being a swineherd?' said Brother Watchtower. 'I never said he was a swineherd. What's this about swineherds?'

'He's got a point, though,' said Brother Plasterer. 'He's generally a swineherd or a forester or similar, your basic skion. It's to do with being in wossname. Cognito. They've got to appear to be of, you know, humble origins.'

'Nothing special about humble origins,' said a very small Brother, who seemed to consist entirely of a little perambulatory black robe with halitosis. 'I've got lots of humble origins. In my family we thought swineherding was a posh job.'

'But your family doesn't have the blood of kings, Brother Dunnykin,' said Brother Plasterer.

'We might of,' said Brother Dunnykin sulkily.

'Right, then,' said Brother Watchtower grudgingly. 'Fair enough. But at the essential moment, see, your genuine kings throw back their cloak and say "Lo!" and their essential kingnessness shines through.'

'How, exactly?' said Brother Doorkeeper.

'—*might of got the blood of kings*,' muttered Brother Dunnykin. '*Got no right saying I might not have got the blood of*—'

'Look, it just does, okay? You just know it when you see it.'

'But before that they've got to save the kingdom,' said Brother Plasterer.

'Oh, yes,' said Brother Watchtower heavily. 'That's the main thing, is that.'

'What from, then?'

10

'—*got as much right as anyone to might have the blood of kings*—'

'The Patrician?' said Brother Doorkeeper.

Brother Watchtower, as the sudden authority on the ways of royalty, shook his head.

'I dunno that the Patrician is a threat, exactly,' he said. 'He's not your actual tyrant, as such. Not as bad as some we've had. I mean, he doesn't actually *oppress*.'

'I get oppressed all the time,' said Brother Doorkeeper. 'Master Critchley, where I work, he oppresses me morning, noon and night, shouting at me and everything. And the woman in the vegetable shop, she oppresses me all the time.'

'That's right,' said Brother Plasterer. 'My landlord oppresses me something wicked. Banging on the door and going on and on about all the rent I allegedly owe, which is a total lie. And the people next door oppress me all night long. I tell them, I work all day, a man's got to have some time to learn to play the tuba. That's oppression, that is. If I'm not under the heel of the oppressor, I don't know who is.'

'Put like that,' said Brother Watchtower slowly, 'I reckon my brother-in-law is oppressing me all the time with having this new horse and buggy he's been and bought. *I* haven't got one. I mean, where's the justice in that? I bet a king wouldn't let that sort of oppression go on, people's wives oppressing 'em with why haven't they got a new coach like our Rodney and that.'

The Supreme Grand Master listened to this with a slightly light-headed feeling. It was as if he'd known that there were such things as avalanches, but had never dreamed when he dropped the little snowball on top of the mountain that it could lead to such astonishing results. He was hardly having to egg them on at all.

'I bet a king'd have something to say about landlords,' said Brother Plasterer.

'And he'd outlaw people with showy coaches,' said Brother Watchtower. 'Probably bought with stolen money, too, I reckon.'

'I think,' said the Supreme Grand Master, tweaking things a little, 'that a wise king would only, as it were, outlaw showy coaches for the *undeserving*.'

There was a thoughtful pause in the conversation as the assembled Brethren mentally divided the universe into the deserving and the undeserving, and put themselves on the appropriate side.

'It'd be only fair,' said Brother Watchtower slowly. 'But Brother Plasterer was right, really. I can't see a skion manifesting his destiny just because Brother Doorkeeper thinks the woman in the vegetable shop keeps giving him funny looks. No offence.'

'*And* bloody short weight,' said Brother Doorkeeper. 'And she—'

'Yes, yes, yes,' said the Supreme Grand Master. 'Truly the right-thinking folk of Ankh-Morpork are beneath the heel of the oppressors. However, a king generally reveals himself in rather more dramatic circumstances. Like a war, for example.'

Things were going well. Surely, for all their self-centred stupidity, one of them would be bright enough to make the suggestion?

'There used to be some old prophecy or something,' said Brother Plasterer. 'My grandad told me.' His eyes glazed with the effort of dramatic recall. '"Yea, the king will come bringing Law and Justice, and know nothing but the Truth, and Protect and Serve the People with his Sword." You don't all have to look at me like that, I didn't make it up.'

'Oh, we *all* know *that* one. And a fat lot of good that'd be,' said Brother Watchtower. 'I mean, what does he do, ride in with Law and Truth and so on like the Four Horsemen of the Apocalypse? Hallo everyone,' he squeaked, 'I'm the king, and that's Truth over there, watering his horse. Not very practical, is it? Nah. You can't trust old legends.'

'Why not?' said Brother Dunnykin, in a peeved voice.

'"Cos they're legendary. That's how you can tell,' said Brother Watchtower.

'Sleeping princesses is a good one,' said Brother Plasterer. 'Only a king can wake 'em up.'

'Don't be daft,' said Brother Watchtower severely. 'We haven't got a king, so we can't have princesses. Stands to reason.'

'Of course, in the *old* days it was easy,' said Brother Doorkeeper happily.

'Why?'

'He just had to kill a dragon.'

The Supreme Grand Master clapped his hands together and offered a silent prayer to any god who happened to be listening. He'd been right about these people. Sooner or later their rambling little minds took them where you wanted them to go.

'What an interesting idea,' he trilled.

'Wouldn't work,' said Brother Watchtower dourly. 'There ain't no big dragons now.'

'There could be.'

The Supreme Grand Master cracked his knuckles.

'Come again?' said Brother Watchtower.

'I said there could be.'

There was a nervous laugh from the depths of Brother Watchtower's cowl.

'What, the real thing? Great big scales and wings?'

'Yes.'

'Breath like a blast furnace.'

'Yes.'

'Them big claw things on its feet?'

'Talons? Oh, yes. As many as you want.'

'What do you mean, as many as I want?'

'I would hope it's self-explanatory, Brother Watchtower. If you want dragons, you can have dragons. *You* can bring a dragon here. Now. Into the city.'

'Me?'

'All of you. I mean us,' said the Supreme Grand Master.

Brother Watchtower hesitated. 'Well, I don't know if that's a very good—'

'And it would obey your every command.'

That stopped them. That pulled them up. That dropped in front of their weaselly little minds like a lump of meat in a dog pound.

'Can you just repeat that?' said Brother Plasterer slowly.

'You can control it. You can make it do whatever you want.'

'What? A real dragon?'

The Supreme Grand Master's eyes rolled in the privacy of his hood.

'Yes, a real one. Not a little pet swamp dragon. The genuine article.'

'But I thought they were, you know . . . miffs.'

The Supreme Grand Master leaned forward.

'They were myths and they were real,' he said loudly. 'Both a wave and a particle.'

'You've lost me there,' said Brother Plasterer.

'I will demonstrate, then. The book please, Brother Fingers. Thank you. Brethren, I must tell you that when I was undergoing my tuition by the Secret Masters—'

'The what, Supreme Grand Master?' said Brother Plasterer.

'Why don't you listen? You never *listen*. He said the Secret Masters!' said Brother Watchtower. 'You know, the venerable sages what live on some mountain and secretly run everything and taught him all this lore and that, and can walk on fires and that. He told us last week. He's going to teach us, aren't you, Supreme Grand Master,' he finished obsequiously.

'Oh, the *Secret* Masters,' said Brother Plasterer. 'Sorry. It's these mystic hoods. Sorry. Secret. I remember.'

But when I rule the city, the Supreme Grand Master said to himself, there is going to be none of this. I shall form a new secret society of keen-minded and intelligent men, although not too intelligent of course, not *too* intelligent. And we will overthrow the cold tyrant and we will usher in a new age of enlightenment and fraternity and humanism and Ankh-Morpork will become a Utopia and people like Brother Plasterer will be roasted over slow fires if I have any say in the matter, which I will. *And* his figgin.*

'When I was, as I said, undergoing my tuition by the Secret Masters—' he continued.

'That was where they told you you had to walk on ricepaper, wasn't it,' said Brother Watchtower conversationally. 'I always thought that was a good bit. I've been saving it off the bottom of my macaroons ever since. Amazing, really. I can walk on it no trouble. Shows what being in a proper secret society does for you, does that.'

When he is on the griddle, the Supreme Grand Master thought, Brother Plasterer will not be lonely.

'Your footfalls on the road of enlightenment are an example to us all, Brother Watchtower,' he said. 'If I may continue, however – among the many secrets—'

'—from the Heart of Being—' said Brother Watchtower approvingly.

'—from the Heart, as Brother Watchtower says, of Being, was the current location of the noble dragons. The belief that they died out is quite wrong. They simply found a new evolutionary niche. And they can be summoned from it. This book – ' he flourished it – 'gives specific instructions.'

'It's just in a book?' said Brother Plasterer.

'No ordinary book. This is the only copy. It has taken me years to track it down,' said the Supreme Grand Master. 'It's in the handwriting of Tubal de Malachite, a great student of dragon lore. His actual handwriting. He summoned dragons of all sizes. And so can you.'

There was another long, awkward silence.

'Um,' said Brother Doorkeeper.

'Sounds a bit like, you know . . . *magic* to me,' said Brother Watchtower, in the nervous tone of the man who has spotted which cup the pea is hidden under but doesn't like to say. 'I mean, not wishing to question your supreme wisdomship and that, but . . . well . . . you know . . . magic . . .'

His voice trailed off.

'Yeah,' said Brother Plasterer uncomfortably.

---

* A figgin is defined in the *Dictionary of Eye-Watering Words* as 'a small short-crust pasty containing raisins'. The Dictionary would have been invaluable for the Supreme Grand Master when he thought up the Society's oaths, since it also includes welchet ('a type of waistcoat worn by certain clock-makers'), gaskin ('a shy, grey-brown bird of the coot family'), and moules ('a game of skill and dexterity, involving tortoises').

'It's, er, the wizards, see,' said Brother Fingers. 'You prob'ly dint know this, when you was banged up with them venerable herberts on their mountain, but the wizards round here come down on you like a ton of bricks if they catches you doin' anything like that.'

'Demarcation, they call it,' said Brother Plasterer. 'Like, I don't go around fiddling with the mystic interleaved wossnames of causality, and they don't do any plastering.'

'I fail to see the problem,' said the Supreme Grand Master. In fact, he saw it all too clearly. This was the last hurdle. Help their tiny little minds over this, and he held the world in the palm of his hand. Their stupefyingly unintelligent self-interest hadn't let him down so far, surely it couldn't fail him now . . .

The Brethren shuffled uneasily. Then Brother Dunnykin spoke.

'Huh. *Wizards.* What do they know about a day's work?'

The Supreme Grand Master breathed deeply. *Ah . . .*

The air of mean-minded resentfulness thickened noticeably.

'Nothing, and that's a fact,' said Brother Fingers. 'Goin' around with their noses in the air, too good for the likes a'us. I used to see 'em when I worked up the University. Backsides a mile wide, I'm telling you. Catch 'em doing a job of honest toil?'

'Like thieving, you mean?' said Brother Watchtower, who had never liked Brother Fingers much.

'O'course, they *tell* you,' Brother Fingers went on, pointedly ignoring the comment, 'that you shouldn't go round doin' magic on account of only them knowin' about not disturbin' the universal harmony and whatnot. Load of rubbish, in my opinion. '

'We-ell,' said Brother Plasterer, 'I dunno, really. I mean, you get the mix wrong, you just got a lot of damp plaster round your ankles. But you get a bit of magic wrong, and they say ghastly things comes out the woodwork and stitches you *right* up.'

'Yeah, but it's the wizards that say that,' said Brother Watchtower thoughtfully. 'Never could stand them myself, to tell you the truth. Could be they're on to a good thing and don't want the rest of us to find out. It's only waving your arms and chanting, when all's said and done.'

The Brethren considered this. It sounded plausible. If *they* were on to a good thing, *they* certainly wouldn't want anyone else muscling in.

The Supreme Grand Master decided that the time was ripe.

'Then we are agreed, brethren? You are prepared to practise magic?'

'Oh, *practise*,' said Brother Plaster, relieved. 'I don't mind *practising*. So long as we don't have to do it for real—'

The Supreme Grand Master thumped the book.

15

'I mean carry out real spells! Put the city back on the right lines! Summon a dragon!' he shouted.

They took a step back. Then Brother Doorkeeper said, 'And then, if we get this dragon, the rightful king'll turn up, just like that?'

'Yes!' said the Supreme Grand Master.

'I can see that,' said Brother Watchtower supportively. 'Stands to reason. Because of destiny and the gnomic workings of fate.'

There was a moment's hesitation, and then a general nodding of cowls. Only Brother Plasterer looked vaguely unhappy.

'We-ell,' he said. 'It won't get out of hand, will it?'

'I assure you, Brother Plasterer, that you can give it up any time you like,' said the Supreme Grand Master smoothly.

'Well . . . all right,' said the reluctant Brother. 'Just for a bit, then. Could we get it to stay here long enough to burn down, for example, any oppressive vegetable shops?'

Ah . . .

He'd won. There'd be dragons again. And a king again. Not like the old kings. A king who would do what he was told.

'That', said the Supreme Grand Master, 'depends on how much help you can be. We shall need, initially, any items of magic you can bring . . .'

It might not be a good idea to let them see that the last half of de Malachite's book was a charred lump. The man was clearly not up to it.

He could do a lot better. And absolutely no-one would be able to stop him.

Thunder rolled . . .

It is said that the gods play games with the lives of men. But what games, and why, and the identities of the actual pawns, and what the game is, and what the rules are – who knows?

Best not to speculate.

Thunder rolled. . . .

It rolled a six.

Now pull back briefly from the dripping streets of Ankh-Morpork, pan across the morning mists of the Disc, and focus in again on a young man heading for the city with all the openness, sincerity and innocence of purpose of an iceberg drifting into a major shipping lane.

The young man is called Carrot. This is not because of his hair, which his father has always clipped short for reasons of Hygiene. It is because of his shape.

It is the kind of tapering shape a boy gets through clean living, healthy eating, and good mountain air in huge lungfuls. When he flexes his shoulder muscles, other muscles have to move out of the way first.

He is also bearing a sword presented to him in mysterious circumstances. Very mysterious circumstances. Surprisingly, therefore, there is something very unexpected about this sword. It isn't magical. It hasn't got a name. When you wield it you don't get a feeling of power, you just get blisters; you could believe it was a sword that had been used so much that it had ceased to be anything other than a quintessential sword, a long piece of metal with very sharp edges. And it hasn't got destiny written all over it.

It's practically unique, in fact.

Thunder rolled.

The gutters of the city gurgled softly as the detritus of the night was carried along, in some cases protesting feebly.

When it came to the recumbent figure of Captain Vimes, the water diverted and flowed around him in two streams. Vimes opened his eyes. There was a moment of empty peace before memory hit him like a shovel.

It had been a bad day for the Watch. There had been the funeral of Herbert Gaskin, for one thing. Poor old Gaskin. He had broken one of the fundamental rules of being a guard. It wasn't the sort of rule that someone like Gaskin could break twice. And so he'd been lowered into the sodden ground with the rain drumming on his coffin and no-one present to mourn him but the three surviving members of the Night Watch, the most despised group of men in the entire city. Sergeant Colon had been in tears. Poor old Gaskin.

Poor old Vimes, Vimes thought.

Poor old Vimes, here in gutter. But that's where he started. Poor old Vimes, with the water swirling in under breastplate. Poor old Vimes, watching rest of gutter's contents ooze by. Prob'ly even poor old Gaskin has got better view now, he thought.

Lessee . . . he'd gone off after the funeral and got drunk. No, not drunk, another word, ended with 'er'. Drunker, that was it. Because world all twisted up and wrong, like distorted glass, only came back into focus if you looked at it through bottom of bottle.

Something else now, what was it.

Oh, yes. Night-time. Time for duty. Not for Gaskin, though. Have to get new fellow. New fellow coming anyway, wasn't that it?

Some stick from the hicks. Written letter. Some tick from the shicks . . .

Vimes gave up, and slumped back. The gutter continued to swirl.

Overhead, the lighted letters fizzed and flickered in the rain.

It wasn't only the fresh mountain air that had given Carrot his huge physique. Being brought up in a gold mine run by dwarfs and working a twelve-hour day hauling wagons to the surface must have helped.

He walked with a stoop. What will do *that* is being brought up in a gold mine run by dwarfs who thought that five feet was a good height for a ceiling.

He'd always known he was different. More bruised for one thing. And then one day his father had come up to him or, rather, come up to his waist, and told him that he was not, in fact, as he had always believed, a dwarf.

It's a terrible thing to be nearly sixteen and the wrong species.

'We didn't like to say so before, son,' said his father. 'We thought you'd grow out of it, see.'

'Grow out of what?' said Carrot.

'Growing. But now your mother thinks, that is, we *both* think, it's time you went out among your own kind. I mean, it's not fair, keeping you cooped up here without company of your own height.' His father twiddled a loose rivet on his helmet, a sure sign that he was worried. 'Er,' he added.

'But *you're* my kind!' said Carrot desperately.

'In a manner of speaking, yes,' said his father. 'In another manner of speaking, which is a rather more precise and accurate manner of speaking, no. It's all this genetics business, you see. So it might be a very good idea if you were to go out and see something of the world.'

'What, for good?'

'Oh, no! No. Of course not. Come back and visit whenever you like. But, well, a lad your age, stuck down here . . . It's not right. You know. I mean. Not a child any more. Having to shuffle around on your knees most of the time, and everything. It's not right.'

'What is my own kind, then?' said Carrot, bewildered.

The old dwarf took a deep breath. 'You're human,' he said.

'What, like Mr Varneshi?' Mr Varneshi drove an ox-cart up the mountain trails once a week, to trade things for gold. 'One of the Big People?'

'You're six foot six, lad. He's only five foot.' The dwarf twiddled the loose rivet again. 'You see how it is.'

18

'Yes, but – but maybe I'm just tall for my height,' said Carrot desperately. 'After all, if you can have short humans, can't you have tall dwarfs?'

His father patted him companionably on the back of the knees.

'You've got to face facts, boy. You'd be much more at home up on the surface. It's in your blood. The roof isn't so low, either.' You can't keep knocking yourself out on the sky, he told himself.

'Hold on,' said Carrot, his honest brow wrinkling with the effort of calculation. 'You're a dwarf, right? And mam's a dwarf. So I should be a dwarf, too. Fact of life.'

The dwarf sighed. He'd hoped to creep up on this, over a period of months maybe, sort of break it to him gently, but there wasn't any time any more.

'Sit down, lad,' he said. Carrot sat.

'The thing is,' he said wretchedly, when the boy's big honest face was a little nearer his own, 'we found you in the woods one day. Toddling about near one of the tracks . . . um.' The loose rivet squeaked. The king plunged on.

'Thing is, you see . . . there were these carts. On fire, as you might say. And dead people. Um, yes. Extremely dead people. Because of bandits. It was a bad winter that winter, there were all sorts coming into the hills . . . So we took you in, of course, and then, well, it was a long winter, like I said, and your mam got used to you, and, well, we never got around to asking Varneshi to make enquiries. That's the long and the short of it.'

Carrot took this fairly calmly, mostly because he didn't understand nearly all of it. Besides, as far as he was aware, being found toddling in the woods was the normal method of childbirth. A dwarf is not considered old enough to have the technical processes explained to him* until he has reached puberty.'†

'All right, dad,' he said, and leaned down so as to be level with the dwarf's ear. 'But you know, me and – you know Minty Rock-smacker? She's really beautiful, dad, got a beard as soft as a, a, a very soft thing – we've got an understanding, and – '

'Yes,' said the dwarf, coldly. 'I know. Her father's had a word with me.' So did her mother with your mother, he added silently, and then *she* had a word with me. Lots of words.

It's not that they don't like you, you're a steady lad and a fine worker, you'd make a good son-in-law. *Four* good sons-in-law. That's the trouble. And she's only sixty, anyway. It's not proper. It's not right.

---

* The pronoun is used by dwarfs to indicate both sexes. All dwarfs have beards and wear up to twelve layers of clothing. Gender is more or less optional.

† i.e., about 55.

He'd heard about children being reared by wolves. He wondered whether the leader of the pack ever had to sort out something tricky like this. Perhaps he'd have to take him into a quiet clearing somewhere and say, Look, son, you might have wondered why you're not as hairy as everyone else . . .

He'd discussed it with Varneshi. A good solid man, Varneshi. Of course, he'd known the man's father. And his grandfather, now he came to think about it. Humans didn't seem to last long, it was probably all the effort of pumping blood up that high.

'Got a problem there, king.* Right enough,' the old man had said, as they shared a nip of spirits on a bench outside Shaft #2.

'He's a good lad, mind you,' said the king. 'Sound character. Honest. Not exactly brilliant, but you tell him to do something, he don't rest until he's done it. Obedient.'

'You could chop his legs off,' said Varneshi.

'It's not his legs that's going to be the problem,' said the king darkly.

'Ah. Yes. Well, in *that* case you could—'

'No.'

'No,' agreed Varneshi, thoughtfully. 'Hmm. Well, then what you should do is, you should send him away for a bit. Let him mix a bit with humans.' He sat back. 'What you've got here, king, is a duck,' he added, in knowledgeable tones.

'I don't think I should tell him that. He's refusing to believe he's a human as it is.'

'What I mean is, a duck brought up among chickens. Well-known farmyard phenomenon. Finds it can't bloody well peck and doesn't know what swimming is.' The king listened politely. Dwarfs don't go in much for agriculture. 'But you send him off to see a lot of other ducks, let him get his feet wet, and he won't go running around after bantams any more. And Bob's your uncle.'

Varneshi sat back and looked rather pleased with himself.

When you spend a large part of your life underground, you develop a very literal mind. Dwarfs have no use for metaphor and simile. Rocks are hard, the darkness is dark. Start messing around with descriptions like that and you're in big trouble, is their motto. But after two hundred years of talking to humans the king had, as it were, developed a painstaking mental toolkit which was nearly adequate for the job of understanding them.

'Surely Bjorn Stronginthearm is my uncle,' he pointed out, slowly.

'Same thing.'

* Lit. *dezka-knik*, 'mine supervisor'.

20

There was a pause while the king subjected this to careful analysis.

'You're saying,' he said, weighing each word, 'that we should send Carrot away to be a duck among humans because Bjorn Stronginthearm is my uncle.'

'He's a fine lad. Plenty of openings for a big strong lad like him,' said Varneshi.

'I have heard that dwarfs go off to work in the Big City,' said the king uncertainly. 'And they send back money to their families, which is very commendable and proper.'

'There you are then. Get him a job in, in – ' Varneshi sought for inspiration – 'in the Watch, or something. My great-grandfather was in the Watch, you know. Fine job for a big lad, my grandad said.'

'What is a Watch?' said the king.

'Oh,' said Varneshi, with the vagueness of someone whose family for the last three generations hadn't travelled more than twenty miles, 'they goes about making sure people keep the laws and do what they're told.'

'That is a very proper concern,' said the king who, since he was usually the one doing the telling, had very solid views about people doing what they were told.

'Of course, they don't take just anyone,' said Varneshi, dredging the depths of his recollection.

'I should think not, for such an important task. I shall write to their king.'

'I don't think they have a king there,' said Varneshi. 'Just some man who tells them what to do.'

The king of the dwarfs took this calmly. This seemed to be about ninety-seven per cent of the definition of kingship, as far as he was concerned.

Carrot took the news without fuss, just as he took instructions about re-opening Shaft # 4 or cutting timber for shoring props. All dwarfs are by nature dutiful, serious, literate, obedient and thoughtful people whose only minor failing is a tendency, after one drink, to rush at enemies screaming 'Arrrrrrgh!' and axing their legs off at the knee. Carrot saw no reason to be any different. He would go to this city – whatever *that* was – and have a man made of him.

They took only the finest, Varneshi had said. A watchman had to be a skilled fighter and clean in thought, word and deed. From the depths of his ancestral anecdotage the old man had dragged tales of moonlight chases across rooftops, and tremendous battles

21

with miscreants which, of course, his great-grandad had won despite being heavily outnumbered.

Carrot had to admit it sounded better than mining.

After some thought, the king wrote to the ruler of Ankh-Morpork, respectfully asking if Carrot could be considered for a place amongst the city's finest.

Letters rarely got written in that mine. Work stopped and the whole clan had sat around in respectful silence as his pen scrittered across the parchment. His aunt had been sent up to Varneshi's to beg his pardon but could he see his way clear to sparing a smidgen of wax. His sister had been sent down to the village to ask Mistress Garlick the witch how you stopped spelling recommendation.

Months had gone by.

And then there'd been the reply. It was fairly grubby, since mail in the Ramtops was generally handed to whoever was going in more or less the right direction, and it was also fairly short. It said, baldly, that his application was accepted, and would he present himself for duty immediately.

'Just like that?' he said. 'I thought there'd be tests and things. To see if I was suitable.'

'You're my son,' said the king. 'I told them that, see. Stands to reason you'll be suitable. Probably officer material.'

He'd pulled a sack from under his chair, rummaged around in it and presented Carrot with a length of metal, more a sword than a saw but only just.

'This might rightly belong to you,' he said. 'When we found the . . . carts, this was the only thing left. The bandits, you see. Just between you and me – ' he beckoned Carrot closer – 'we had a witch look at it. In case it was magic. But it isn't. Quite the most unmagical sword she'd ever seen, she said. They normally have a bit, see, on account of it's like magnetism, I suppose. Got quite a nice balance, though.'

He handed it over.

He rummaged around some more. 'And then there's this.' He held up a shirt. 'It'll protect you.'

Carrot fingered it carefully. It was made from the wool of Ramtop sheep, which had all the warmth and softness of hog bristles. It was one of the legendary woolly dwarf vests, the kind of vest that needs hinges.

'Protect me from what?' he said.

'Colds, and so on,' said the king. 'Your mother says you've got to wear it. And, er . . . that reminds me. Mr Varneshi says he'd like you to drop in on the way down the mountain. He's got something for you.'

His father and mother had waved him out of sight. Minty didn't. Funny, that. She seemed to have been avoiding him lately.

He'd taken the sword, slung on his back, sandwiches and clean underwear in his pack, and the world, more or less, at his feet. In his pocket was the famous letter from the Patrician, the man who ruled the great fine city of Ankh-Morpork.

At least, that's how his mother had referred to it. It certainly had an important-looking crest at the top, but the signature was something like 'Lupin Squiggle, Sec'y, pp'.

Still, if it wasn't actually *signed* by the Patrician then it had certainly been written by someone who worked for him. Or in the same building. Probably the Patrician had at least *known* about the letter. In general terms. Not *this* letter, perhaps, but probably he knew about the existence of letters in general.

Carrot walked steadfastly down the mountain paths, disturbing clouds of bumblebees. After a while he unsheathed the sword and made experimental stabs at felonious tree stumps and unlawful assemblies of stinging nettles.

Varneshi was sitting outside his hut, threading dried mushrooms on a string.

'Hello, Carrot,' he said, leading the way inside. 'Looking forward to the city?'

Carrot gave this due consideration.

'No,' he said.

'Having second thoughts, are you?'

'No. I was just walking along,' said Carrot honestly. 'I wasn't thinking about anything much.'

'Your dad give you the sword, did he?' said Varneshi, rummaging on a fetid shelf.

'Yes. And a woolly vest to protect me against chills.'

'Ah. Yes, it can be very damp down there, so I've heard. Protection. Very important. 'He turned around and added, dramatically, '*This* belonged to my great-grandfather.'

It was a strange, vaguely hemispherical device surrounded by straps.

'It's some sort of sling?' said Carrot, after examining it in polite silence.

Varneshi told him what it was.

'Codpiece like in fish?' said Carrot, mystified.

'No. It's for the fighting,' mumbled Varneshi. 'You should wear it all the time. Protects your vitals, like.'

Carrot tried it on.

23

'It's a bit small, Mr Varneshi.'

'That's because you don't wear it on your head, you see.'

Varneshi explained some more, to Carrot's mounting bewilderment and, subsequently, horror. 'My great-grandad used to say,' Varneshi finished, 'that but for this I wouldn't be here today.'

'What did he mean by that?'

Varneshi's mouth opened and shut a few times. 'I've no idea,' he said, spinelessly.

Anyway, the shameful thing was now at the very bottom of Carrot's pack. Dwarfs didn't have much truck with things like that. The ghastly preventative represented a glimpse into a world as alien as the backside of the moon.

There had been another gift from Mr Varneshi. It was a small but very thick book, bound in a leather that had become like wood over the years.

It was called: The Laws And Ordinances of The Cities of Ankh And Morpork.

'This belonged to my great-grandad as well,' he said. 'This is what the Watch has to know. You have to know all the laws,' he said virtuously, 'to be a good officer.'

Perhaps Varneshi should have recalled that, in the whole of Carrot's life, no-one had ever really lied to him or given him an instruction that he wasn't meant to take quite literally. Carrot solemnly took the book. It would never have occurred to him, if he was going to be an officer of the Watch, to be less than a good one.

It was a five hundred mile journey and, surprisingly, quite uneventful. People who are rather more than six feet tall and nearly as broad across the shoulders often have uneventful journeys. People jump out at them from behind rocks then say things like, 'Oh. Sorry. I thought you were someone else.'

He'd spent most of the journey reading.

And now Ankh-Morpork was before him.

It was a little disappointing. He'd expected high white towers rearing over the landscape, and flags. Ankh-Morpork didn't rear. Rather, it sort of skulked, clinging to the soil as if afraid someone might steal it. There were no flags.

There was a guard on the gate. At least, he was wearing chainmail and the thing he was propped up against was a spear. He had to be a guard.

Carrot saluted him and presented the letter. The man looked at it for some time.

'Mm?' he said, eventually.

'I think I've got to see Lupin Squiggle Sec'y pp,' said Carrot.

'What's the pp for?' said the guard suspiciously.

'Could it be Pretty Promptly?' said Carrot, who had wondered about this himself.

'Well, I don't know about any Sec'y,' said the guard. 'You want Captain Vimes of the Night Watch.'

'And where is he based?' said Carrot, politely.

'At this time of day I'd try The Bunch of Grapes in Easy Street,' said the guard. He looked Carrot up and down. 'Joining the watch, are you?'

'I hope to prove worthy, yes,' said Carrot.

The guard gave him what could loosely be called an old-fashioned look. It was practically neolithic.

'What was it you done?' he said.

'I'm sorry?' said Carrot.

'You must of done something,' said the guard.

'My father wrote a letter,' said Carrot proudly. 'I've been volunteered.'

'Bloody hellfire,' said the guard.

Now it was night again, and beyond the dread portal:

'Are the Wheels of Torment duly spun?' said the Supreme Grand Master.

The Elucidated Brethren shuffled around their circle.

'Brother Watchtower?' said the Supreme Grand Master.

'Not my job to spin the Wheels of Torment,' muttered Brother Watchtower. ''s Brother Plasterer's job, spinning the Wheels of Torment—'

'No it bloody well isn't, it's my job to oil the Axles of the Universal Lemon,' said Brother Plasterer hotly. 'You always say it's *my* job—'

The Supreme Grand Master sighed in the depths of his cowl as yet another row began. From this dross he was going to forge an Age of Rationality?

'Just shut up, will you?' he snapped. 'We don't really need the Wheels of Torment tonight. Stop it, the pair of you. Now, Brethren – you have all brought the items as instructed?'

There was a general murmuring.

'Place them in the Circle of Conjuration,' said the Supreme Grand Master.

It was a sorry collection. Bring magical things, he'd said. Only Brother Fingers had produced anything worthwhile. It looked like some sort of altar ornament, best not to ask from where. The Supreme Grand Master stepped forward and prodded one of the other things with his toe.

'What,' he said, 'is this?'

''s a amulet,' muttered Brother Dunnykin. ''s very powerful. Bought it off a man. Guaranteed. Protects you against crocodile bites.'

'Are you sure you can spare it?' said the Supreme Grand Master. There was a dutiful titter from the rest of the Brethren.

'Less of that, brothers,' said the Grand Master, spinning around. 'Bring magical things, I said. Not cheap jewellery and rubbish! Good grief, this city is lousy with magic!' He reached down. 'What are these things, for heaven's sake?'

'They're stones,' said Brother Plasterer uncertainly.

'I can see that. Why're they magical?'

Brother Plasterer began to tremble. 'They've got holes in them, Supreme Grand Master. Everyone knows that stones with holes in them are magical.'

The Supreme Grand Master walked back to his place on the circle. He threw his arms up.

'Right, fine, okay,' he said wearily. 'If that's how we're going to do it, that's how we're going to do it. If we get a dragon six inches long we'll *all* know the reason why. Won't we, Brother Plasterer. Brother Plasterer? Sorry. I didn't hear what you said? Brother Plasterer?'

'I said yes, Supreme Grand Master,' whispered Brother Plasterer.

'Very well. So long as that's *quite* understood.' The Supreme Grand Master turned and picked up the book.

'And now,' he said, 'if we are all quite ready . . .'

'Um.' Brother Watchtower meekly raised his hand.

'Ready for what, Supreme Grand Master?' he said.

'For the summoning, of course. Good grief, I should have thought—'

'But you haven't told us what we're supposed to *do*, Supreme Grand Master,' whined Brother Watchtower.

The Grand Master hesitated. This was quite true, but he wasn't going to admit it.

'Well, of course,' he said. 'It's obvious. You have to focus your concentration. Think hard about dragons,' he translated. 'All of you.'

'That's all, is it?' said Brother Doorkeeper.

'Yes.'

'Don't we have to chant a mystic prune or something?'

The Supreme Grand Master stared at him. Brother Doorkeeper managed to look as defiant in the face of oppression as an anony-

26

mous shadow in a black cowl could look. He hadn't joined a secret society not to chant mystic runes. He'd been looking forward to it.

'You can if you like,' said the Supreme Grand Master. 'Now, I want you – *yes, what is it, Brother Dunnykin?*'

The little Brother lowered his hand. 'Don't know any mystic prunes, Grand Master. Not to what you might call chant . . .'

'Hum!'

He opened the book.

He'd been rather surprised to find, after pages and pages of pious ramblings, that the actual Summoning itself was one short sentence. Not a chant, not a brief piece of poetry, but a mere assemblage of meaningless syllables. De Malachite said they caused interference patterns in the waves of reality, but the daft old fool was probably making it up as he went along. That was the trouble with wizards, they had to make everything look difficult. All you really needed was willpower. And the Brethren had a lot of that. Small-minded and vitriolic willpower, yes, lousy with malignity maybe, but still powerful enough in its way . . .

They'd try nothing fancy this time round. Somewhere inconspicuous . . .

Around him the Brethren were chanting what each man considered, according to his lights, to be something mystical. The general effect was actually quite good, if you didn't listen to the words.

The words. Oh, yes . . .

He looked down, and spoke them aloud.

Nothing happened.

He blinked.

When he opened his eyes again he was in a dark alley, his stomach was full of fire, and he was very angry.

It was about to be the worst night of his life for Zebbo Mooty, Thief Third Class, and it wouldn't have made him any happier to know that it was also going to be the last one. The rain was keeping people indoors, and he was way behind on his quota. He was, therefore, a little less cautious than he might otherwise have been.

In the night time streets of Ankh-Morpork caution is an absolute. There is no such thing as moderately cautious. You are either very cautious, or you are dead. You might be walking around and breathing, but you're dead, just the same.

He heard the muffled sounds coming from the nearby alley, slid his leather-bound cosh from his sleeve, waited until the victim was almost turning the corner, sprang out, said 'Oh, shi—' and died.

It was a most unusual death. No-one else had died like that for hundreds of years.

The stone wall behind him glowed cherry red with heat, which gradually faded into darkness.

He was the first to see the Ankh-Morpork dragon. He derived little comfort from knowing this, however, because he was dead.

'—t,' he said, and his disembodied self looked down at the small heap of charcoal which, he knew with an unfamiliar sort of certainty, was what he had just been disembodied from. It was a strange sensation, seeing your own mortal remains. He didn't find it as horrifying as he would have imagined if you'd asked him, say, ten minutes ago. Finding that you are dead is mitigated by also finding that there really is a you who can find you dead.

The alley opposite was empty again.

'That was really strange,' said Mooty.

EXTREMELY UNUSUAL, CERTAINLY.

'Did you see that? What was it?' Mooty looked up at the dark figure emerging from the shadows. 'Who're you, anyway?' he added suspiciously.

GUESS, said the voice.

Mooty peered at the hooded figure.

'Cor!' he said. 'I thought you dint turn up for the likes o' me.'

I TURN UP FOR EVERYONE.

'I mean in . . . person, sort of thing.'

SOMETIMES. ON SPECIAL OCCASIONS.

'Yeah, well,' said Mooty, 'this is one of them, all right! I mean, it looked like a bloody dragon! What's a man to do? You don't expect to find a dragon around the corner!'

AND NOW, IF YOU WOULD CARE TO STEP THIS WAY . . . said Death, laying a skeletal hand on Mooty's shoulder.

'Do you know, a fortune teller once told me I'd die in my bed, surrounded by grieving great-grandchildren,' said Mooty, following the stately figure. 'What do you think of that, eh?'

I THINK SHE WAS WRONG.

'A bloody dragon,' said Mooty. 'Fire breathing, too. Did I suffer much?'

NO. IT WAS PRACTICALLY INSTANTANEOUS.

'That's good. I wouldn't like to think I'd suffered much.' Mooty looked around him. 'What happens now?' he said.

Behind them, the rain washed the little heap of black ash into the mud.

*

The Supreme Grand Master opened his eyes. He was lying on his back. Brother Dunnykin was preparing to give him the kiss of life. The mere thought was enough to jerk anyone from the borders of consciousness.

He sat up, trying to shed the feeling that he weighed several tons and was covered in scales.

'We did it,' he whispered. 'The dragon! It came! I felt it!'

The Brethren glanced at one another.

'We never saw nothing,' said Brother Plasterer.

'I might of seen something,' said Brother Watchtower loyally.

'No, not *here*,' snapped the Supreme Grand Master. 'You hardly want it to materialize *here*, do you? It was out there, in the city. Just for a few seconds . . .'

He pointed. 'Look!'

The Brethren turned around guiltily, expecting at any moment the hot flame of retribution.

In the centre of the circle the magic items were gently crumbling to dust. Even as they watched, Brother Dunnykin's amulet collapsed.

'Sucked dry,' whispered Brother Fingers. 'I'll be damned!'

'Three dollars that amulet cost me,' muttered Brother Dunnykin.

'But it proves it works,' said the Supreme Grand Master. 'Don't you see, you fools? It works! We *can* summon dragons!'

'Could be a bit expensive in magical items,' said Brother Fingers doubtfully.

'—*three dollars, it was. No rubbish*—'

'Power,' growled the Supreme Grand Master, 'does not come cheap.'

'Very true,' nodded Brother Watchtower. 'Not cheap. Very true.' He looked at the little heap of exhausted magic again. 'Cor,' he said. 'We did it, though, dint we! We only went and bloody well did some magic, right?'

'See?' said Brother Fingers. 'I *tole* you there was nothin' to it.'

'You all did exceptionally well,' said the Supreme Grand Master encouragingly.

'—*should've been six dollars, but he said he'd cut his own throat and sell it me for three dollars*—'

'Yeah,' said Brother Watchtower. 'We got the hang of it all right! Dint hurt a bit. We done real magic! And dint get et by tooth fairies from out of the woodwork either, Brother Plasterer, I couldn't help noticing.'

The other Brethren nodded. Real magic. Nothing to it. Everyone had just better *watch out*.

'Hang on, though,' said Brother Plasterer. 'Where's this dragon *gone*? I mean, did we really summon it or not?'

'Fancy you asking a silly question like that,' said Brother Watchtower doubtfully.

The Supreme Grand Master brushed the dust off his mystic robe.

'We summoned it,' he said, 'and it came. But only as long as the magic lasted. Then it went back. If we want it to stay longer, we need more magic. Understand? And that is what we must get.'

'*—three dollars I shan't see again in a hurry—*'

'Shut up!'

Dearest Father [wrote Carrot] Well, here I am in Ankh-Morpork. It is not like at home. I think it must have changed a bit since Mr Varneshi's great-grandfather was here. I don't think people here know Right from Wrong.

I found Captain Vimes in a common ale-house. I remembered what you said about a good dwarf not going into such places, but since he did not come out, I went in. He was lying with his head on the table. When I spoke to him, he said, pull the other one, kid, it has got bells on. I believe he was the worse for drink. He told me to find a place to stay and report to Sgt Colon at the Watch House tonight. He said, anyone wanting to join the guard needed their head examined.

Mr Varneshi did not mention this. Perhaps it is done for reasons of Hygiene.

I went for a walk. There are many people here. I found a place, it is called The Shades. Then I saw some men trying to rob a young Lady. I set about them. They did not know how to fight properly and one of them tried to kick me in the Vitals, but I was wearing the Protective as instructed and he hurt himself. Then the Lady came up to me and said, Was I Interested in Bed. I said yes. She took me to where she lived, a boarding house, I think it is called. It is run by a Mrs Palm. The Lady whose purse it was, she is called Reet, said, You should of seen him, there were 3 of them, it was amazing. Mrs Palm said, It is on the house. She said, what a big Protective. So I went upstairs and fell asleep, although it is a very noisy place. Reet woke me up once or twice to say, Do you want anything, but they had no apples. So I have fallen on my Feet, as they say here but, I don't see how that is possible because, if you fall you fall off your Feet, it is Common Sense.

There is certainly a lot to do. When I went to see the Sgt I saw a place called, The Thieves' Guild!! I asked Mrs Palm and she said, Of course. She said the leaders of the Thieves in the City meet there. I went to the Watch House and met Sgt Colon, a very fat man, and when I told him about the Thieves' Guild he said, Don't be A Idiot. I do not think he is serious. He says, Don't you worry about Thieves' Guilds, This is all what you have to do, you walk along the Streets at Night, shouting, It's Twelve O'clock and All's Well. I said, What if it is not all well, and he said, You bloody well find another street.

This is not Leadership.

I have been given some chain mail. It is rusty and not well made.

They give you money for being a guard. It is, 20 dollars a month. When I get it I will send you it.

I hope you are all well and that Shaft # 5 is now open. This afternoon I will go and look at the Thieves' Guild. It is disgraceful. If I do something about it, it will be a Feather in my Cap. I am getting the Hang of how they talk here already. Your loving son, Carrot.

PS. Please give all my love to Minty. I really miss her.

Lord Vetinari, the Patrician of Ankh-Morpork, put his hand over his eyes.

'He did what?'

'I was *marched* through the streets,' said Urdo van Pew, currently President of the Guild of Thieves, Burglars and Allied Trades. 'In broad daylight! With my hands tied together!' He took a few steps towards the Patrician's severe chair of office, waving a finger.

'You know very well that we have kept within the Budget,' he said. 'To be *humiliated* like that! Like a common criminal! There had better be a *full* apology,' he said, 'or you will have another strike on your hands. We will be driven to it, despite our natural civic responsibilities,' he added.

It was the finger. The finger was a mistake. The Patrician was staring coldly at the finger. Van Pew followed his gaze, and quickly lowered the digit. The Patrician was not a man you shook a finger at unless you wanted to end up being able to count only to nine.

'And you say this was one person?' said Lord Vetinari.

'Yes! That is—' Van Pew hesitated.

It did sound weird, now he came to tell someone.

'But there are hundreds of you in there,' said the Patrician calmly. 'Thick as, you should excuse the expression, thieves.'

Van Pew opened and shut his mouth a few times. The honest answer would have been: yes, and if anyone had come sidling in and skulking around the corridors it would have been the worse for them. It was the way he strode in as if he owned the place that fooled everyone. That and the fact that he kept hitting people and telling them to Mend their Ways.

The Patrician nodded.

'I shall deal with the matter momentarily,' he said. It was a good word. It always made people hesitate. They were never quite sure whether he meant he'd deal with it *now*, or just deal with it *briefly*. And no-one ever dared ask.

Van Pew backed down.

'A full apology, mark you. I have a position to maintain.' he added.

'Thank you. Do not let me detain you,' said the Patrician, once again giving the language his own individual spin.

'Right. Good. Thank you. Very well,' said the thief.

'After all, you have such a lot of work to do,' Lord Vetinari went on.

'Well, of course this is the case.' The thief hesitated. The Patrician's last remark had barbs on it. You found yourself waiting for him to strike.

'Er,' he said, hoping for a clue.

'With so much business being conducted, that is.'

Panic took over the thief's features. Randomized guilt flooded his mind. It wasn't a case of what had he done, it was a question of what the Patrician had found out about. The man had eyes everywhere, none of them so terrifying as the icy blue ones just above his nose.

'I, er, don't quite follow . . .' he began.

'Curious choice of targets.' The Patrician picked up a sheet of paper. 'For example, a crystal ball belonging to a fortune teller in Sheer Street. A small ornament from the temple of Offler the Crocodile God. And so on. Gewgaws.'

'I am afraid I really don't know—' said the head thief. The Patrician leaned forward.

'No *unlicensed* thieving, surely?' he said.*

'I shall look into it directly!' stuttered the head thief. 'Depend upon it!'

The Patrician gave him a sweet smile. 'I'm sure I can,' he said. 'Thank you for coming to see me. Don't hesitate to leave.'

The thief shuffled out. It was always like this with the Patrician, he reflected bitterly. You came to him with a perfectly reasonable

---

* One of the remarkable innovations introduced by the Patrician was to make the Thieves' Guild *responsible* for theft, with annual budgets, forward planning and, above all, rigid job protection. Thus, in return for an agreed average level of crime per annum, the thieves themselves saw to it that unauthorized crime was met with the full force of Injustice, which was generally a stick with nails in it.

complaint. Next thing you knew, you were shuffling out backwards, bowing and scraping, relieved simply to be getting away. You had to hand it to the Patrician, he admitted grudgingly. If you didn't, he sent men to come and take it away.

When he'd gone Lord Vetinari rang the little bronze bell that summoned his secretary. The man's name, despite his handwriting, was Lupine Wonse. He appeared, pen poised.

You could say this about Lupine Wonse. He was neat. He always gave the impression of just being completed. Even his hair was so smoothed-down and oiled it looked as though it had been painted on.

'The Watch appears to be having some difficulty with the Thieves' Guild,' said the Patrician. 'Van Pew has been in here claiming that a member of the Watch arrested him.'

'What for, sir?'

'Being a thief, apparently.'

'A member of the *Watch*?' said the secretary.

'I know. But just sort it out, will you?'

The Patrician smiled to himself.

It was always hard to fathom Lord Vetinari's idiosyncratic sense of humour, but a vision of the red-faced, irate head thief kept coming back to him.

One of the Patrician's greatest contributions to the reliable operation of Ankh-Morpork had been, very early in his administration, the legalizing of the ancient Guild of Thieves. Crime was always with us, he reasoned, and therefore, if you were going to have crime, it at least should be *organized* crime.

And so the Guild had been encouraged to come out of the shadows and build a big Guildhouse, take their place at civic banquets, and set up their training college with day-release courses and City and Guilds certificates and everything. In exchange for the winding down of the Watch, they agreed, while trying to keep their faces straight, to keep crime levels to a level to be determined annually. That way, everyone could plan ahead, said Lord Vetinari, and part of the uncertainty had been removed from the chaos that is life.

And then, a little while later, the Patrician summoned the leading thieves again and said, oh, by the way, there was something else. What was it, now? Oh, yes . . .

I know who you are, he said. I know where you live. I know what kind of horse you ride. I know where your wife has her hair done. I know where your lovely children, how old are they now, my, doesn't time fly, I know where they play. So you won't forget about what we agreed, will you? And he smiled.

So did they, after a fashion.

And in fact it had turned out very satisfactorily from everyone's point of view. It took the head thieves a very little time to grow paunches and start having coats-of-arms made and meet in a proper building rather than smoky dens, which no-one had liked much. A complicated arrangement of receipts and vouchers saw to it that, while everyone was eligible for the attentions of the Guild, no-one had too much, and this was very acceptable – at least to those citizens who were rich enough to afford the quite reasonable premiums the Guild charged for an uninterrupted life. There was a strange foreign word for this: *inn-sewer-ants*. No-one knew exactly what it had originally meant. but Ankh-Morpork had made it its own.

The Watch hadn't liked it, but the plain fact was that the thieves were far better at controlling crime than the Watch had ever been. After all, the Watch had to work twice as hard to cut crime just a little, whereas all the Guild had to do was to work less.

And so the city prospered, while the Watch had dwindled away, like a useless appendix, into a handful of unemployables who no-one in their right mind could ever take seriously.

The last thing anyone wanted them to do was get it into their heads to fight crime. But seeing the head thief discommoded was always worth the trouble, the Patrician felt.

Captain Vimes knocked very hesitantly at the door, because each tap echoed around his skull.

'Enter.'

Vimes removed his helmet, tucked it under his arm and pushed the door open. Its creak was a blunt saw across the front of his brain.

He always felt uneasy in the presence of Lupine Wonse. Come to that, he felt uneasy in the presence of Lord Vetinari – but that was different, that was down to *breeding*. And ordinary fear, of course. Whereas he'd known Wonse since their childhood in the Shades. The boy had shown promise even then. He was never a gang leader. Never a gang leader. Hadn't got the strength or stamina for that. And, after all, what was the point in being the gang leader? Behind every gang leader were a couple of lieutenants bucking for promotion. Being a gang leader is not a job with long-term prospects. But in every gang there is a pale youth who's allowed to stay because he's the one who comes up with all the clever ideas, usually to do with old women and unlocked shops; this was Wonse's natural place in the order of things.

34

Vimes had been one of the middle rankers, the falsetto equivalent of a yes-man. He remembered Wonse as a skinny little kid, always tagging along behind in hand-me-down pants with the kind of odd skipping run he'd invented to keep up with the bigger boys, and forever coming up with fresh ideas to stop them idly ganging up on him, which was the usual recreation if nothing more interesting presented itself. It was superb training for the rigours of adulthood, and Wonse became good at it.

Yes, they'd both started in the gutter. But Wonse had worked his way up whereas, as he himself would be the first to admit, Vimes had merely worked his way *along*. Every time he seemed to be getting anywhere he spoke his mind, or said the wrong thing. Usually both at once.

That was what made him uncomfortable around Wonse. It was the ticking of the bright clockwork of ambition.

Vimes had never mastered ambition. It was something that happened to other people.

'Ah, Vimes.'

'Sir,' said Vimes woodenly. He didn't try to salute in case he fell over. He wished he'd had time to drink dinner.

Wonse rummaged in the papers of his desk.

'Strange things afoot, Vimes. Serious complaint about you, I'm afraid,' he said. Wonse didn't wear glasses. If he *had* worn glasses, he'd have peered at Vimes over the top of them.

'Sir?'

'One of your Night Watch men. Seems he arrested the head of the Thieves' Guild.'

Vimes swayed a little and tried hard to focus. He wasn't ready for this sort of thing.

'Sorry, sir,' he said. 'Seem to have lost you there.'

'I *said*, Vimes, that one of your men arrested the head of the Thieves' Guild.'

'One of my men?'

'*Yes.*'

Vimes's scattered brain cells tried valiantly to regroup. 'A member of the *Watch*?' he said.

Wonse grinned mirthlessly. 'Tied him up and left him in front of the palace. There's a bit of a stink about it, I'm afraid. There was a note ... ah ... here it is ... "This man is charged with, Conspiracy to commit Crime, under Section 14(iii) of the General Felonies Act, 1678, by me, Carrot Ironfoundersson."'

Vimes squinted at him.

'Fourteen eye-eye-eye?'

'Apparently,' said Wonse.

'What does that mean?'

'I really haven't the faintest notion,' said Wonse drily. 'And what about the name . . . Carrot?'

'But we don't do things like that!' said Vimes. 'You can't go around arresting the Thieves' Guild. I mean, we'd be at it all day!'

'Apparently this Carrot thinks otherwise.'

The captain shook his head, and winced. 'Carrot? Doesn't ring a bell.' The tone of blurred conviction was enough even for Wonse, who was momentarily taken aback.

'He was quite—' The secretary hesitated. 'Carrot, Carrot,' he said. *'I've* heard the name before. Seen it written down.' His face went blank. 'The volunteer, that was it! Remember me showing you?'

Vimes stared at him. 'Wasn't there a letter from, I don't know, some dwarf—?'

'All about serving the community and keeping the streets safe, that's right. Begging that his son would be found suitable for a humble position in the Watch.' The secretary was rummaging among his files.

'What'd he done?' said Vimes.

'Nothing. That was it. Not a blessed thing.'

Vimes's brow creased as his thoughts shaped themselves around a new concept.

'A *volunteer?*' he said.

'Yes.'

'He didn't have to join?'

'He *wanted* to join. And you said it must be a joke, and I said we ought to try and get more ethnic minorities into the Watch. You remember?'

Vimes tried to. It wasn't easy. He was vaguely aware that he drank to forget. What made it rather pointless was that he couldn't remember what it was he was forgetting any more. In the end he just drank to forget about drinking.

A trawl of the chaotic assortment of recollections that he didn't even try to dignify any more by the name of memory produced no clue.

'Do I?' he said helplessly.

Wonse folded his hands on the desk and leaned forward.

'Now look, Captain,' he said. 'Lordship wants an explanation. I don't want to have to tell him the captain of the Night Watch hasn't the faintest idea what goes on among the men under, if I may use the term loosely, his command. That sort of thing only leads to trouble, questions asked, that sort of thing. We don't want that, do we. Do we?'

'No, sir,' Vimes muttered. A vague recollection of someone earnestly talking to him in the Bunch of Grapes was bobbing guiltily at the back of his mind. Surely that hadn't been a dwarf? Not unless the qualification had been radically altered, at any rate.

'Of course we don't,' said Wonse. 'For old times' sake. And so on. So I'll think of something to tell him and you, Captain, will make a point of finding out what's going on and putting a stop to it. Give this dwarf a short lesson in what it means to be a guard, all right?'

'Haha,' said Vimes dutifully.

'I'm sorry?' said Wonse.

'Oh. Thought you made an ethnic joke, there. Sir.'

'Look, Vimes, I'm being very understanding. In the circumstances. Now, I want you to get out there and sort this out. Do *you* understand?'

Vimes saluted. The black depression that always lurked ready to take advantage of his sobriety moved in on his tongue.

'Right you are, Mr Secretary,' he said. 'I'll see to it that he learns that arresting thieves is against the law.'

He wished he hadn't said that. If he didn't say things like that he'd have been better off now, Captain of the *Palace* Guard, a big man. Giving him the Watch had been the Patrician's little joke. But Wonse was already reading a new document on his desk. If he noticed the sarcasm, he didn't show it.

Dearest Mother [Carrot wrote] it has been a much better day. I went into the Thieves' Guild and arrested the chief Miscreant and dragged him to the Patrician's Palace. No more trouble from him, I fancy. And Mrs Palm says I can stay in the attic because, it is always useful to have a man around the place. This was because, in the night, there were men the Worse for Drink making a Fuss in one of the Girl's Rooms, and I had to speak to them and they Showed Fight and one of them tried to hurt me with his knee but I had the Protective and Mrs Palm says he has broken his Patella but I needn't pay for a new one.

I do not understand some of the Watch duties. I have a partner, his name is Nobby. He says I am too keen. He says I have got a lot to learn. I think this is true, because, I have only got up to Page 326 in, The Laws and Ordinances of the Cities of Ankh and Morpork. Love to all, Your Son, Carrot.

PS. Love to Minty.

*

37

It wasn't just the loneliness, it was the back-to-front way of living. That was it, thought Vimes.

The Night Watch got up when the rest of the world was going to bed, and went to bed when dawn drifted over the landscape. You spent your whole time in the damp, dark streets, in a world of shadows. The Night Watch attracted the kind of people who for one reason or another were inclined to that kind of life.

He reached the Watch House. It was an ancient and surprisingly large building, wedged between a tannery and a tailor who made suspicious leather goods. It must have been quite imposing once, but quite a lot of it was now uninhabitable and patrolled only by owls and rats. Over the door a motto in the ancient tongue of the city was now almost eroded by time and grime and lichen, but could just be made out:

FABRICATI DIEM, PVNC

It translated – according to Sergeant Colon, who had served in foreign parts and considered himself an expert on languages – as 'To Protect and to Serve'.

Yes. Being a guard must have meant something, once.

Sergeant Colon, he thought, as he stumbled into the musty gloom. Now there was a man who liked the dark. Sergeant Colon owed thirty years of happy marriage to the fact that Mrs Colon worked all day and Sergeant Colon worked all night. They communicated by means of notes. He got her tea ready before he left at night, she left his breakfast nice and hot in the oven in the mornings. They had three grown-up children, all born, Vimes had assumed, as a result of extremely persuasive handwriting.

And Corporal Nobbs . . . well, anyone like Nobby had unlimited reasons for not wishing to be seen by other people. You didn't have to think hard about *that*. The only reason you couldn't say that Nobby was close to the animal kingdom was that the animal kingdom would get up and walk away.

And then, of course, there was himself. Just a skinny, unshaven collection of bad habits marinated in alcohol. And that was the Night Watch. Just the three of them. Once there had been dozens, hundreds. And now – just three.

Vimes fumbled his way up the stairs, groped his way into his office, slumped into the primeval leather chair with its prolapsed stuffing, scrabbled at the bottom drawer, grabbed bottle, bit cork, tugged, spat out cork, drank. Began his day.

The world swam into focus.

Life is just chemicals. A drop here, a drip there, everything's changed. A mere dribble of fermented juices and suddenly you're going to live another few hours.

Once, in the days when this had been a respectable district, some hopeful owner of the tavern next door had paid a wizard a considerable sum of money for an illuminated sign, every letter a different colour. Now it worked erratically and sometimes short-circuited in the damp. At the moment the E was a garish pink and flashed on and off at random.

Vimes had grown accustomed to it. It seemed like part of life.

He stared at the flickering play of light on the crumbling plaster for a while, and then raised one sandalled foot and thumped heavily on the floorboards, twice.

After a few minutes a distant wheezing indicated that Sergeant Colon was climbing the stairs.

Vimes counted silently. Colon always paused for six seconds at the top of the flight to get some of his breath back.

On the seventh second the door opened. The sergeant's face appeared around it like a harvest moon.

You could describe Sergeant Colon like this: he was the sort of man who, if he took up a military career, would automatically gravitate to the post of sergeant. You couldn't imagine him ever being a corporal. Or, for that matter, a captain. If he didn't take up a military career, then he looked cut out for something like, perhaps, a sausage butcher; some job where a big red face and a tendency to sweat even in frosty weather were practically part of the specification.

He saluted and, with considerable care, placed a scruffy piece of paper on Vimes's desk and smoothed it out.

'Evenin', Captain,' he said. 'Yesterday's incident reports, and that. Also, you owe fourpence to the Tea Club.'

'What's this about a dwarf, Sergeant?' said Vimes abruptly.

Colon's brow wrinkled. 'What dwarf?'

'The one who's just joined the Watch. Name of – ' Vimes hesitated – 'Carrot, or something.'

'Him?' Colon's mouth dropped open. 'He's a *dwarf*? I always said you couldn't trust them little buggers! He fooled me all right, Captain, the little sod must of lied about his height!' Colon was a sizeist, at least when it came to people smaller than himself.

'Do you know he arrested the President of the Thieves' Guild this morning?'

'What for?'

'For being president of the Thieves' Guild, it seems.'

The sergeant looked puzzled. 'Where's the crime in that?'

'I think perhaps I had better have a word with this Carrot,' said Vimes.

'Didn't you see him, sir?' said Colon. 'He said he'd reported to you, sir.'

'I, uh, must have been busy at the time. Lot on my mind,' said Vimes.

'Yes, sir,' said Colon, politely. Vimes had just enough self-respect left to look away and shuffle the strata of paperwork on his desk.

'We've got to get him off the streets as soon as possible,' he muttered. 'Next thing you know he'll be bringing in the chief of the Assassins' Guild for bloody well killing people! Where is he?'

'I sent him out with Corporal Nobbs, Captain. I said he'd show him the ropes, sort of thing.'

'You sent a raw recruit out with *Nobby?*' said Vimes wearily.

Colon stuttered. 'Well, sir, experienced man, I thought, Corporal Nobbs could teach him a lot—'

'Let's just hope he's a slow learner,' said Vimes, ramming his brown iron helmet on his head. 'Come on.'

When they stepped out of the Watch House there was a ladder against the tavern wall. A bulky man at the top of it swore under his breath as he wrestled with the illuminated sign.

'It's the E that doesn't work properly,' Vimes called up.

'What?'

'The E. And the T sizzles when it rains. It's about time it was fixed.'

'Fixed? Oh. Yes. Fixed. That's what I'm doing all right. Fixing.'

The Watch men splashed off through the puddles. Brother Watchtower shook his head slowly, and turned his attention once again to his screwdriver.

Men like Corporal Nobbs can be found in every armed force. Although their grasp of the minutiae of the Regulations is usually encyclopedic, they take good care never to be promoted beyond, perhaps, corporal. He tended to speak out of the corner of his mouth. He smoked incessantly but the weird thing, Carrot noticed, was that any cigarette smoked by Nobby became a dog-end almost instantly but *remained* a dog-end indefinitely or until lodged behind his ear, which was a sort of nicotine Elephant's Graveyard. On the rare occasions he took one out of his mouth he held it cupped in his hand.

He was a small, bandy-legged man, with a certain resemblance to a chimpanzee who never got invited to tea parties.

His age was indeterminate. But in cynicism and general world weariness, which is a sort of carbon dating of the personality, he was about seven thousand years old.

'A cushy number, this route,' he said, as they strolled along a damp street in the merchants' quarter. He tried a doorhandle. It was locked. 'You stick with me,' he added, 'and I'll see you're all right. Now, you try the handles on the other side of the street.'

'Ah. I understand, Corporal Nobbs. We've got to see if anyone's left their store unlocked,' said Carrot.

'You catch on fast, son.'

'I hope I can apprehend a miscreant in the act,' said Carrot zealously.

'Er, yeah,' said Nobby, uncertainly.

'But if we find a door unlocked I suppose we must summon the owner,' Carrot went on. 'And one of us would have to stay to guard things, right?'

'Yeah?' Nobby brightened. 'I'll do that,' he said. 'Don't you worry about it. Then you could go and find the victim. Owner, I mean.'

He tried another doorknob. It turned under his grip.

'Back in the mountains,' said Carrot, 'if a thief was caught, he was hung up by the—'

He paused, idly rattling a doorknob.

Nobby froze.

'By the what?' he said, in horrified fascination.

'Can't remember now,' said Carrot. 'My mother said it was too good for them, anyway. Stealing is Wrong.'

Nobby had survived any number of famous massacres by not being there. He let go of the doorknob, and gave it a friendly pat.

'Got it!' said Carrot. Nobby jumped.

'Got what?' he shouted.

'I remember what we hang them up by,' said Carrot

'Oh,' said Nobby weakly. 'Where?'

'We hang them up by the town hall,' said Carrot. 'Sometimes for days. They don't do it again, I can tell you. And Bjorn Strongin-thearm's your uncle.'

Nobby leaned his pike against the wall and fumbled a fag-end from the recesses of his ear. One or two things, he decided, needed to be sorted out.

'Why did you have to become a guard, lad?' he said.

'Everyone keeps on asking me that,' said Carrot. 'I didn't have to. I wanted to. It will make a Man of me.'

Nobby never looked anyone directly in the eye. He stared at Carrot's right ear in amazement.

'You mean you ain't running away from anything?' he said.

'What would I want to run away from anything for?'

Nobby floundered a bit. 'Ah. There's always something. Maybe – maybe you was wrongly accused of something. Like, maybe,' he grinned, 'maybe the stores was mysteriously short on certain items and you was unjustly blamed. Or certain items was found in your kit and you never knew how they got there. That sort of thing. You can tell old Nobby. Or,' he nudged Carrot, 'p'raps it was something else, eh? *Shershay la fem*, eh? Got a girl into trouble?'

'I—' Carrot began, and then remembered that, yes, one should tell the truth, even to odd people like Nobby who didn't seem to know what it was. And the truth was that he was always getting Minty in trouble, although exactly how and why was a bit of a mystery. Just about every time he left after paying calls on her at the Rocksmacker cave, he could hear her father and mother shouting at her. They were always very polite to him, but somehow merely being seen with him was enough to get Minty into trouble.

'Yes,' he said.

'Ah. Often the case,' said Nobby wisely.

'All the time,' said Carrot. 'Just about every night, really.'

'Blimey,' said Nobby, impressed. He looked down at the Protective. 'Is that why they make you wear that, then?'

'What do you mean?'

'Well, don't worry about it,' said Nobby. 'Everyone's got their little secret. Or big secret, as it might be. Even the captain. He's only with us because he was Brung Low by a Woman. That's what the sergeant says. Brung low.'

'Goodness,' said Carrot. It sounded painful.

'But I reckon it's 'cos he speaks his mind. Spoke it once too often to the Patrician, I heard. Said the Thieves' Guild was nothing but a pack of thieves, or something. That's why he's with us. Dunno, really.' He looked speculatively at the pavement and then said: 'So where're you staying, lad?'

'There's a lady called Mrs Palm—' Carrot began.

Nobby choked on some smoke that went the wrong way.

'In the Shades?' he wheezed. 'You're staying *there*?'

'Oh, yes.'

'Every *night*?'

'Well, every day, really. Yes.'

'And you've come here to have a man made of you?'

'Yes!'

'I don't think I should like to live where you come from,' said Nobby.

'Look,' said Carrot, thoroughly lost, 'I came because Mr Varneshi said it was the finest job in the world, upholding the law and everything. That's right, isn't it?'

'Well, er,' said Nobby. 'As to that . . . I mean, upholding the Law . . . I mean, *once*, yes, before we had all the Guilds and stuff . . .

the law, sort of thing, ain't really, I mean, these days, everything's more . . . oh, I dunno. Basically you just ring your bell and keep your head down.'

Nobby sighed. Then he grunted, snatched his hourglass from his belt, and peered in at the rapidly-draining sand grains. He put it back, pulled the leather muffler off his bell's clapper, and shook it once or twice, not very loudly.

'Twelve of the clock,' he muttered, 'and all's well.'

'And that's it, is it?' said Carrot, as the tiny echoes died away

'More or less. More or less.' Nobby took a quick drag on his dog-end.

'Just that? No moonlight chases across rooftops? No swinging on chandeliers? Nothing like that?' said Carrot.

'Shouldn't think so,' said Nobby fervently. 'I never done anything like that. No-one ever said anything to me about that.' He snatched a puff on the cigarette. 'A man could catch his death of cold, chasing around on rooftops. I reckon I'll stick to the bell, if it's all the same to you.'

'Can I have a go?' said Carrot.

Nobby was feeling unbalanced. It can be the only reason why he made the mistake of wordlessly handing Carrot the bell.

Carrot examined it for a few seconds. Then he waved it vigorously over his head.

'*Twelve o'clock!*' he bellowed. '*And all's weeeeelllll!*'

The echoes bounced back and forth across the street and finally were overwhelmed by a horrible, thick silence. Several dogs barked somewhere in the night. A baby started crying.

'Ssshh!' hissed Nobby.

'Well, it *is* all well, isn't it?' said Carrot.

'It won't be if you keep on ringing that bloody bell! Give it here.'

'I don't understand!' said Carrot. 'Look, I've got this book Mr Varneshi gave me—' He fumbled for the Laws and Ordinances.

Nobby glanced at them, and shrugged. 'Never heard of 'em,' he said. 'Now just shut up your row. You don't want to go making a din like that. You could attract all sorts. Come on, this way.'

He grabbed Carrot's arm and bustled him along the street.

'What sorts?' protested Carrot as he was pushed determinedly forward.

'Bad sorts,' muttered Nobby.

'But we're the *Watch*!'

'Damn right! And we don't want to go tangling with people like that! Remember what happened to Gaskin!'

'I don't remember what happened to Gaskin!' said Carrot, totally bewildered. 'Who's Gaskin?'

'Before your time,' mumbled Nobby. He deflated a bit. 'Poor bugger. Could of happened to any of us.' He looked up and glared at Carrot. 'Now stop all this, you hear? It's getting on my nerves. Moonlight bloody chases, my bum!'

He stalked along the street. Nobby's normal method of locomotion was a kind of sidle, and the combination of stalking and sidling at the same time created a strange effect, like a crab limping.

'But, but,' said Carrot, 'in this book it says—'

'I don't want to know from no book,' growled Nobby.

Carrot looked utterly crestfallen.

'But it's the Law—' he began.

He was nearly terminally interrupted by an axe that whirred out of a low doorway beside him and bounced off the opposite wall. It was followed by sounds of splintering timber and breaking glass.

'Hey, Nobby!' said Carrot urgently, 'There's a fight going on!'

Nobby glanced at the doorway. 'O'*course* there is,' he said. 'It's a dwarf bar. Worst kind. You keep out of there, kid. Them little buggers like to trip you up and then kick twelve kinds of shit out of you. You come along o'Nobby and he'll – '

He grabbed Carrot's treetrunk arm. It was like trying to tow a building.

Carrot had gone pale.

'Dwarfs *drinking*? And *fighting*?' he said.

'You bet,' said Nobby. 'All the time. And they use the kind of language I wouldn't even use to my own dear mother. You don't want to mix it with them, they're a poisonous bunch of – *don't go in there!*'

No-one knows why dwarfs, who at home in the mountains lead quiet, orderly lives, forget it all when they move to the big city. Something comes over even the most blameless iron-ore miner and prompts him to wear chain-mail all the time, carry an axe, change his name to something like Grabthroat Shinkicker and drink himself into surly oblivion.

It's probably because they *do* live such quiet and orderly lives back home. After all, probably the first thing a young dwarf wants to do when he hits the big city after seventy years of working for his father at the bottom of a pit is have a big drink and then hit someone.

The fight was one of those enjoyable dwarfish fights with about a hundred participants and one hundred and fifty alliances. The screams, oaths and the ringing of axes on iron helmets mingled

44

with the sounds of a drunken group by the fireplace who – another dwarfish custom – were singing about gold.

Nobby bumped into the back of Carrot, who was watching the scene with horror.

'Look, it's like this every night in here,' said Nobby. 'Don't interfere, that's what the sergeant says. It's their ethnic folkways, or somethin'. You don't go messin' with ethnic folkways.'

'But, but,' Carrot stuttered, 'these are my *people*. Sort of. It's shameful, acting like this. What must everyone think?'

'We think they're mean little buggers,' said Nobby. 'Now, *come on!*'

But Carrot had waded into the scuffling mass. He cupped his hands around his mouth and bellowed something in a language Nobby didn't understand. Practically any language including his native one would have fitted that description, but in this case it was Dwarfish.

'*Gr'duzk! Gr'dazk! aaK'zt ezem ke bur'k tze tzim?*'*

The fighting stopped. A hundred bearded faces glared up at Carrot's stooped figure, their annoyance mingled with surprise.

A battered tankard bounced off his breastplate. Carrot reached down and picked up a struggling figure, without apparent effort.

'*J'uk, ydtruz-t'rud-eztuza, hudr'zd dezek drez'huk, huzukruk't b'tduz g'ke'k me'ek b'tdv'z't be'tk kce'drutk ke'hkt'd. aaDb'thuk?*'†

No dwarf had ever heard so many Old Tongue words from the mouth of anyone over four feet high. They were astonished.

Carrot lowered the offending dwarf to the floor. There were tears in his eyes.

'You're dwarfs!' he said. 'Dwarfs shouldn't be acting like this! Look at you all. Aren't you ashamed?'

One hundred bone-hard jaws dropped.

'I mean, *look* at you!' Carrot shook his head. 'Can you imagine what your poor, white-bearded old mother, slaving away back in her little hole, wondering how her son is getting on tonight, can you imagine what she'd think if she saw you now? Your own dear mothers, who first showed you how to use a pickaxe—'

Nobby, standing by the doorway in terror and amazement, was aware of a growing chorus of nose-blowings and muffled sobs as

---

* Lit: 'Good day! Good day! What is all of this that is going on here (in this place)?'

† 'Listen, sunshine [lit: 'the stare of the great hot eye in the sky whose fiery gaze penetrates the mouth of the cavern'] I don't want to have to give anyone a smacking, so if you play B'tduz[1] with me, I'll play B'tduz with you. Okay?'[2]

[1] A popular dwarfish game which consists of standing a few feet apart and throwing large rocks at one another's head.

[2] Lit: 'All correctly beamed and propped?'

Carrot went on: '—she's probably thinking, I expect he's having a quiet game of dominoes or something—'

A nearby dwarf, wearing a helmet encrusted with six-inch spikes, started to cry gently into his beer.

'And I bet it's a *long time* since any of you wrote her a letter, too, and you promised to write every week—'

Nobby absent-mindedly took out a grubby handkerchief and passed it to a dwarf who was leaning against the wall, shaking with grief.

'Now, then,' said Carrot kindly. 'I don't want to be hard on anyone, but I shall be coming past here every night from now on and I shall expect to see proper standards of dwarf behaviour. I know what it's like when you're far from home, but there's no excuse for this sort of thing.' He touched his helmet. '*G'hruk, t'uk.*'*

He gave them all a bright smile and half-walked, half-crouched out of the bar. As he emerged into the street Nobby tapped him on the arm.

'Don't you ever do anything like that to me again,' he fumed. 'You're in the City Watch! Don't give me any more of this law business!'

'But it is very important,' said Carrot seriously, trotting after Nobby as he sidled into a narrower street.

'Not as important as stayin' in one piece,' said Nobby. 'Dwarf bars! If you've got any sense, my lad, you'll come in here. And shut up.'

Carrot stared up at the building they had reached. It was set back a little from the mud of the street. The sounds of considerable drinking were coming from inside. A battered sign hung over the door. It showed a drum.

'A tavern, is it?' said Carrot, thoughtfully. 'Open at this hour?'

'Don't see why not,' said Nobby, pushing open the door. 'Damn useful idea. The Mended Drum.'

'And more drinking?' Carrot thumbed hastily through the book.

'I hope so,' said Nobby. He nodded to the troll which was employed by the Drum as a splatter.† 'Evenin', Detritus. Just showing the new lad the ropes.'

The troll grunted, and waved a crusted arm.

The inside of the Mended Drum is now legendary as the most famous disreputable tavern on the Discworld, and such a feature of the city that, after recent unavoidable redecorations, the new

---

* 'Evening, all.' (Lit: 'Felicitations to all present at the closing of the day'.)
† Like a bouncer, but trolls use more force.

owner spent days recreating the original patina of dirt, soot and less identifiable substances on the walls and imported a ton of pre-rotted rushes for the floor. The drinkers were the usual bunch of heroes, cut throats, mercenaries, desperadoes and villains, and only microscopic analysis could have told which was which. Thick coils of smoke hung in the air, perhaps to avoid touching the walls.

The conversation dipped fractionally as the two guards wandered in, and then rose to its former level. A couple of cronies waved to Nobby.

He realized that Carrot was busy.

'What you doin'?' he said. 'And no talkin' about mothers, right?'

'I'm taking notes,' said Carrot, grimly. 'I've got a notebook.'

'That's the ticket,' said Nobby. 'You'll like this place. I comes here every night for my supper.'

'How do you spell "contravention"?' said Carrot, turning over a page.

'I don't,' said Nobby, pushing through the crowds. A rare impulse to generosity lodged in his mind. 'What d'you want to drink?'

'I don't think that would be very appropriate,' said Carrot. 'Anyway, Strong Drink is a Mocker.'

He was aware of a penetrating stare in the back of his neck, and turned and looked into the big, bland and gentle face of an orang-utan.

It was seated at the bar with a pint mug and a bowl of peanuts in front of it. It tilted its glass amicably towards Carrot and then drank deeply and noisily by apparently forming its lower lip into a sort of prehensile funnel and making a noise like a canal being drained.

Carrot nudged Nobby.

'There's a monk—' he began.

'Don't say it!' said Nobby urgently. 'Don't say the word! It's the Librarian. Works up at the University. Always comes down here for a nightcap of an evening.'

'And people don't object?'

'Why should they?' said Nobby. 'He always stands his round, just like everyone else.'

Carrot turned and looked at the ape again. A number of questions pressed for attention, such as: where does it keep its money? The Librarian caught his gaze, misinterpreted it, and gently pushed the bowl of peanuts towards him.

Carrot pulled himself to his full impressive height and consulted his notebook. The afternoon spent reading *The Laws and Ordinances* had been well spent.

'Who is the owner, proprietor, lessee, or landlord of these premises?' he said to Nobby.

'Wassat?' said the small guard. 'Landlord? Well, I suppose Charley here is in charge tonight. Why?' He indicated a large, heavy-set man whose face was a net of scars; its owner paused in the act of spreading the dirt more evenly around some glasses by means of a damp cloth, and gave Carrot a conspiratorial wink.

'Charley, this is Carrot,' said Nobby. 'He's stopping along of Rosie Palm's.'

'What, every night?' said Charley.

Carrot cleared his throat.

'If you are in charge,' he intoned, 'then it is my duty to inform you that you are under arrest.'

'A rest of what, friend?' said Charley, still polishing.

'Under *arrest*,' said Carrot, 'with a view to the presentation of charges to whit 1)(i) that on or about 18th Grune, at a place called the Mended Drum, Filigree Street, you did a) serve or b) did cause to serve alcoholic beverages after the hours of 12 (twelve) midnight, contrary to the provisions of the Public Ale Houses (Opening) Act of 1678, and 1)(ii) on or about 18th Grune, at a place called the Mended Drum, Filigree Street, you did serve or did cause to serve alcoholic beverages in containers other than of a size and capacity laid down by aforesaid Act, and 2)(i) that on or about 18th Grune, at a place called the Mended Drum, Filigree Street, you did allow customers to carry unsheathed edge weapons of a length greater than 7 (seven) inches, contrary to Section Three of said Act and 2)(ii) that on or about 18th Grune, at a place called the Mended Drum, Filigree Street, you did serve alcoholic beverages in premises apparently unlicensed for the sale and/or consumption of said beverages, contrary to Section Three of the aforesaid Act.'

There was dead silence as Carrot turned over another page, and went on: 'It is also my duty to inform you that it is my intention to lay evidence before the Justices with a view to the consideration of charges under the Public Foregatherings (Gambling) Act, 1567, the Licensed Premises (Hygiene) Acts of 1433, 1456, 1463, 1465, er, and 1470 through 1690, and also – ' he glanced sideways at the Librarian, who knew trouble when he heard it coming and was hurriedly trying to finish his drink – 'the Domestic and Domesticated Animals (Care and Protection) Act, 1673.'

The silence that followed held a rare quality of breathless anticipation as the assembled company waited to see what would happen next.

Charley carefully put down the glass, whose smears had been buffed up to a brilliant shine, and looked down at Nobby.

Nobby was endeavouring to pretend that he was totally alone and had no connection whatsoever with anyone who might be standing next to him and coincidentally wearing an identical uniform.

'What'd he mean, Justices?' he said to Nobby. 'There ain't no Justices.'

Nobby gave a terrified shrug.

'New, is he?' said Charley.

'Make it easy on yourself,' said Carrot.

'This is nothing personal, you understand,' said Charley to Nobby. 'It's just a wossname. Had a wizard in here the other night talking about it. Sort of bendy educational thing, you know?' He appeared to think for a moment. '*Learning curve*. That was it. It's a learning curve. Detritus, get your big stony arse over here a moment.'

Generally, about this time in the Mended Drum, someone throws a glass. And, in fact, this now happened.

Captain Vimes ran up Short Street – the longest in the city, which shows the famous Morpork subtle sense of humour in a nutshell – with Sergeant Colon stumbling along behind, protesting.

Nobby was outside the Drum, hopping from one foot to another. In times of danger he had a way of propelling himself from place to place without apparently moving through the intervening space which could put any ordinary matter transporter to shame. ''E's fighting in there!' he stuttered, grabbing the captain's arm.

'All by himself?' said the captain.

'No, with everyone!' shouted Nobby, hopping from one foot to the other.

'Oh.'

Conscience said: There's three of you. He's wearing the same uniform. He's one of your *men*. Remember poor old Gaskin.

Another part of his brain, the hated, despicable part which had nevertheless enabled him to survive in the Guards these past ten years, said: It's rude to butt in. We'll wait until he's finished, and then ask him if he wants any assistance. Besides, it isn't Watch policy to interfere in fights. It's a lot simpler to go in afterwards and arrest anyone recumbent.

There was a crash as a nearby window burst outwards and deposited a stunned fighter on the opposite side of the street.

'I think,' said the captain carefully, 'that we'd better take prompt action.'

'That's right,' said Sgt Colon, 'a man could get hurt standing here.'

They sidled cautiously a little way down the street, where the sound of splintering wood and breaking glass wasn't so overpowering, and carefully avoided one another's eyes. There was the occasional scream from within the tavern, and every now and again a mysterious ringing noise, as though someone was hitting a gong with their knee.

They stood in a little pool of embarrassed silence.

'You had your holidays this year, Sergeant?' said Captain Vimes eventually, rocking back and forth on his heels.

'Yessir. Sent the wife to Quirm last month, sir, to see her aunt.'

'Very nice at this time of year, I'm told.'

'Yessir.'

'All the geraniums and whatnot.'

A figure tumbled out of an upper window and crumpled on the cobbles.

'That's where they've got the floral sundial, isn't it?' said the captain desperately.

'Yessir. Very nice, sir. All done with little flowers, sir.'

There was a sound like something hitting something else repeatedly with something heavy and wooden. Vimes winced.

'I don't think he'd of been *happy* in the Watch, sir,' said the sergeant, in a kindly voice.

The door of the Mended Drum had been torn off during riots so often that specially-tempered hinges had recently been installed, and the fact that the next tremendous crash tore the whole door and doorframe out of the wall only showed that quite a lot of money had been wasted. A figure in the midst of the wreckage tried to raise itself on its elbows, groaned, and slumped back.

'Well, it would seem that it's all—' the captain began, and Nobby said: 'It's that bloody troll!'

'What?' said Vimes.

'It's the troll! The one they have on the door!'

They advanced with extreme caution.

It was, indeed, Detritus the splatter.

It is very difficult to hurt a creature that is, to all intents and purposes, a mobile stone. Someone seemed to have managed it, though. The fallen figure was groaning like a couple of bricks being crushed together.

'That's a turnup for the books,' said the sergeant vaguely. All three of them turned and peered at the brightly-lit rectangle where the doorway had been. Things had definitely quietened down a bit in there.

'You don't think,' said the sergeant, 'that he's *winning*, do you?'

The captain thrust out his jaw. 'We owe it to our colleague and fellow officer,' he said, 'to find out.'

There was a whimper from behind them. They turned and saw Nobby hopping on one leg and clutching a foot.

'What's up with you, man?' said Vimes.

Nobby made agonized noises.

Sergeant Colon began to understand. Although cautious obsequiousness was the general tenor of Watch behaviour, there wasn't one member of the entire squad who hadn't, at some time, been at the wrong end of Detritus's fists. Nobby had merely tried to play catch-up in the very best traditions of policemen everywhere.

'He went and kicked him inna rocks, sir,' he said.

'Disgraceful,' said the captain vaguely. He hesitated. 'Do trolls *have* rocks?' he said.

'Take it from me, sir.'

'Good grief,' Vimes said. 'Dame Nature moves in strange ways, doesn't she.'

'Right you are, sir,' said the sergeant obediently.

'And now,' said the captain, drawing his sword, 'forward!'

'Yessir.'

'This means you too, Sergeant,' the captain added.

'Yessir.'

It was possibly the most circumspect advance in the history of military manoeuvres, right down at the bottom end of the scale that things like the Charge of the Light Brigade are at the top of.

They peered cautiously around the ravished doorway.

There were a number of people sprawled across the tables, or what remained of the tables. Those who were still conscious looked unhappy about it.

Carrot stood in the middle of the floor. His rusty chain mail was torn, his helmet was missing, he was swaying a little from side to side and one eye was already starting to swell, but he recognized the captain, dropped the feebly-protesting customer he was holding, and threw a salute.

'Beg to report thirty-one offences of Making an Affray, sir, and fifty-six cases of Riotous Behaviour, forty-one offences of Obstructing an Officer of the Watch in the Execution of his Duty, thirteen offences of Assault with a Deadly Weapon, six cases of Malicious Lingering, and – and – Corporal Nobby hasn't even shown me one rope yet—'

He fell backwards, breaking a table.

Captain Vimes coughed. He wasn't at all sure what you were supposed to do next. As far as he knew, the Watch had never been in this position before.

'I think you should get him a drink, Sergeant,' he said.

'Yessir.'

'And get me one, too.'

'Yessir.'

'Have one yourself, why don't you.'

'Yessir.'

'And you, Corporal, will you please – *what* are you doing?'

'Searchingthebodiesir,' said Nobby quickly, straightening up. 'For incriminating evidence, and that.'

'In their money pouches?'

Nobby thrust his hands behind his back. 'You never know, sir,' he said.

The sergeant had located a miraculously unbroken bottle of spirits in the wreckage and forced a lot of its contents between Carrot's lips.

'What we going to do with all this lot, Captain?' he said over his shoulder.

'I haven't the faintest idea,' said Vimes, sitting down. The Watch jail was just about big enough for six very small people, which were usually the only sort to be put in it. Whereas these—

He looked around him desperately. There was Nork the Impaler, lying under a table and making bubbling noises. There was Big Henri. There was Grabber Simmons, one of the most feared bar-room fighters in the city. All in all, there were a lot of people it wouldn't pay to be near when they woke up.

'We could cut their froats, sir,' said Nobby, veteran of a score of residual battlefields. He had found an unconscious fighter who was about the right size and was speculatively removing his boots, which looked quite new and about the right size.

'That would be entirely wrong,' said Vimes. He wasn't sure how you actually went about cutting a throat. It had never hitherto been an option.

'No,' he said, 'I think perhaps we'll let them off with a caution.'

There was a groan from under the bench.

'Besides,' he went on quickly, 'we should get our fallen comrade to a place of safety as soon as possible.'

'Good point,' said the sergeant. He took a swig of the spirits, for the sake of his nerves.

The two of them managed to sling Carrot between them and guide his wobbling legs up the steps. Vimes, collapsing under the weight, looked around for Nobby.

'Corporal Nobbs,' he rasped, 'why are you kicking people when they're down?'

'Safest way, sir,' said Nobby.

Nobby had long ago been told about fighting fair and not striking a fallen opponent, and had then given some creative thought to how these rules applied to someone four feet tall with the muscle tone of an elastic band.

'Well, stop it. I want you to caution the felons,' said the captain.

'How, sir?'

'Well, you—' Captain Vimes stopped. He was blowed if he knew. He'd never done it.

'Just do it,' he snapped. 'Surely I don't have to tell you everything?'

Nobby was left alone at the top of the stairs. A general muttering and groaning from the floor indicated that people were waking up. Nobby thought quickly. He shook an admonitory cheese-straw of a finger.

'Let that be a lesson to you,' he said. '*Don't do it again.*'

And ran for it.

Up in the darkness of the rafters the Librarian scratched himself reflectively. Life was certainly full of surprises. He was going to watch developments with interest. He shelled a thoughtful peanut with his feet, and swung away into the darkness.

The Supreme Grand Master raised his hands.

'Are the Thuribles of Destiny ritually chastised, that Evil and Loose Thinking may be banished from this Sanctified Circle?'

'Yep.'

The Supreme Grand Master lowered his hands.

'Yep?' he said.

'Yep,' said Brother Dunnykin happily. 'Done it myself.'

'You are *supposed* to say "Yea, O Supreme One",' said the Supreme Grand Master. 'Honestly, I've told you enough times, if you're not all going to enter into the spirit of the thing—'

'Yes, you listen to what the Supreme Grand Master tells you,' said Brother Watchtower, glaring at the errant Brother.

'I spent hours chastising them thuribles,' muttered Brother Dunnykin.

'Carry on, O Supreme Grand Master,' said Brother Watchtower.

'Very well, then,' said the Grand Master. 'Tonight we'll try another experimental summoning. I trust you have obtained suitable raw material, brothers?'

'—scrubbed and scrubbed, not that you get any thanks—'

'All sorted out, Supreme Grand Master,' said Brother Watchtower.

It was, the Grand Master conceded, a slightly better collection. The Brothers had certainly been busy. Pride of place was given to an illuminated tavern sign whose removal, the Grand Master thought, should have merited some sort of civic award. At the moment the E was a ghastly pink and flashed on and off at random.

'*I* got that,' said Brother Watchtower proudly. 'They thought I was mending it or something, but I took my screwdriver and I—'

'Yes, well done,' said the Supreme Grand Master. 'Shows initiative.'

'*Thank* you, Supreme Grand Master,' beamed Brother Watchtower.

'*—knuckles rubbed raw, all red and cracked. Never even got my three dollars back, either, no-one as much as says—*'

'And now,' said the Supreme Grand Master, taking up the book, 'we will begin to commence. Shut up, Brother Dunnykin.'

Every town in the multiverse has a part that is something like Ankh-Morpork's Shades. It's usually the oldest part, its lanes faithfully following the original tracks of medieval cows going down to the river, and they have names like the Shambles, the Rookery, Sniggs Alley . . .

Most of Ankh-Morpork is like that in any case. But the Shades was even more so, a sort of black hole of bred-in-the-brickwork lawlessness. Put it like this: even the *criminals* were afraid to walk the streets. The Watch didn't set foot in it.

They were accidentally setting foot in it now. Not very reliably. It had been a trying night, and they had been steadying their nerves. They were now so steady that all four were relying on the other three to keep them upright and steer.

Captain Vimes passed the bottle back to the sergeant.

'Shame on, on, on,' he thought for a bit, 'you,' he said. 'Drun' in fron' of a super, super, superererer ofisiler.'

The sergeant tried to speak, but could only come out with a series of esses.

'Put yoursel' onna charge,' said Captain Vimes, rebounding off a wall. He glared at the brickwork. 'This wall assaulted me,' he declared. 'Hah! Think you're tough, eh! Well, 'm a ofisler of, of, of the Law, I'llhaveyouknow, and we don' take any, any, any.'

He blinked slowly, once or twice.

'What's it we don' take any of, Sar'nt?' he said.

'Chances, sir?' said Colon.

'No, no, no. S'other stuff. Never mind. Anyway, we don' take any of, of, of *it* from anyone.' Vague visions were trotting through his mind, of a room full of criminal types, people that had jeered at him, people whose very existence had offended and taunted him for years, lying around and groaning. He was a little unclear how it had happened, but some almost forgotten part of him, some much younger Vimes with a bright shining breastplate and big hopes, a Vimes he thought the alcohol had long ago drowned, was suddenly restless.

'Shallie, shallie, shallie tell you something, Sarn't?' he said.

'Sir?' The four of them bounced gently off another wall and began another slow crabwise waltz across the alley.

'This city. This city. This city, Sar'nt. This city is a, is a, is a Woman, Sarn't. So t'is. A Woman, Sarn't. Ancient raddled old beauty, Sarn't. Butifyoufallinlovewithher, then, then, then shekicksyouinnateeth – '

''s woman?' said Colon.

He screwed up his sweating face with the effort of thought.

''s eight miles wide, sir. 's gotta river in it. Lots of, of houses and stuff, sir,' he reasoned.

'Ah. Ah. Ah.' Vimes waggled an unsteady finger at him. 'Never, never, never said it wasa *small* woman, did I. Be fair.' He waved the bottle. Another random thought exploded in the froth of his mind.

'We showed 'em, anyway,' he said excitedly, as the four of them began an oblique shuffle back to the opposite wall. 'Showed them, dint we? Taught thema forget they won't lesson inna hurry, eh?'

'S'right,' said the sergeant, but not very enthusiastically. He was still wondering about his superior officer's sex life.

But Vimes was in the kind of mood that didn't need encouragement.

'Hah!' he shouted, at the dark alleyways. 'Don' like it, eh? Taste of your, your, your own medicine thingy. Well, now you can bootle in your trems!' He threw the empty bottle into the air.

'Two o'clock!' he yelled. 'And all's weeeellll!'

Which was astonishing news to the various shadowy figures who had been silently shadowing the four of them for some time. Only sheer puzzlement had prevented them making their attentions sharp and plain. These people are clearly guards, they were thinking, they've got the right helmets and everything, and yet here they are in the Shades. So they were being watched with the fascination that a pack of wolves might focus on a handful of sheep who had not only trotted into the clearing, but were making playful butts and baa-ing noises; the outcome was, of course, going to be mutton but in the meantime inquisitiveness gave a stay of execution.

Carrot raised his muzzy head.

'Where're we?' he groaned.

'On our way home,' said the sergeant. He looked up at the pitted, worm-eaten and knife-scored sign above them. 'We're jus' goin' down, goin' down, goin' down – ' he squinted – 'Sweetheart Lane.'

'Sweetheart Lane s'not on the way home,' slurred Nobby. 'We wouldn't wanta go down Sweetheart Lane, it's in the Shades. Catch us goin' down Sweetheart Lane—'

There was a crowded moment in which realisation did the icy work of a good night's sleep and several pints of black coffee. The three of them, by unspoken agreement, clustered up towards Carrot.

'What we gonna *do*, Captain?' said Colon.

'Er. We could call for help,' said the captain uncertainly.

'What, *here*?'

'You've got a point.'

'I reckon we must of turned left out of Silver Street instead of right,' quavered Nobby.

'Well, that's one mistake we won't make again in a hurry,' said the captain. Then he wished he hadn't.

They could hear footsteps. Somewhere off to their left, there was a snigger.

'We must form a square,' said the captain. They all tried to form a point.

'Hey! What was that?' said Sergeant Colon.

'What?'

'There it was again. Sort of a leathery sound.'

Captain Vimes tried not to think about hoods and garrotting.

There were, he knew, many gods. There was a god for every trade. There was a beggars' god, a whores' goddess, a thieves' god, probably even an assassins' god.

He wondered whether there was, somewhere in that vast pantheon, a god who would look kindly on hard-pressed and fairly innocent law-enforcement officers who were quite definitely about to die.

There probably wasn't, he thought bitterly. Something like that wasn't *stylish* enough for gods. Catch any god worrying about any poor sod trying to do his best for a handful of dollars a month. Not them. Gods went overboard for smart bastards whose idea of a day's work was prising the Ruby Eye of the Earwig King out of its socket, not for some unimaginative sap who just pounded the pavement every night . . .

'More sort of slithery,' said the sergeant, who liked to get things right.

And then there was a sound—

—perhaps a volcanic sound, or the sound of a boiling geyser, but at any rate a long, dry *roar* of a sound, like the bellows in the forges of the Titans—

—but it was not so bad as the light, which was blue-white and the sort of light to print the pattern of your eyeballs' blood vessels on the back of the inside of your skull.

They both went on for hundreds of years and then, instantly, stopped.

The dark aftermath was filled with purple images and, once the ears regained an ability to hear, a faint, clinkery sound.

The guards remained perfectly still for some time.

'Well, well,' said the captain weakly.

After a further pause he said, very clearly, every consonant slotting perfectly into place, 'Sergeant, take some men and investigate that, will you?'

'Investigate what, sir?' said Colon, but it had already dawned on the captain that if the sergeant took some men it would leave him, Captain Vimes, all alone.

'No, I've a better idea. We'll all go,' he said firmly. They all went.

Now that their eyes were used to the darkness they could see an indistinct red glow ahead of them.

It turned out to be a wall, cooling rapidly. Bits of calcined brickwork were falling off as they contracted, making little pinging noises.

That wasn't the worst bit. The worst bit was what was on the wall.

They stared at it.

They stared at it for a long time.

It was only an hour or two till dawn, and no-one even suggested trying to find their way back in the dark. They waited by the wall. At least it was warm.

They tried not to look at it.

Eventually Colon stretched uneasily and said, 'Chin up, Captain. It could have been worse.'

Vimes finished the bottle. It didn't have any effect. There were some types of sobriety that you just couldn't budge.

'Yes,' he said. 'It could have been us.'

The Supreme Grand Master opened his eyes.

'Once again,' he said, 'we have achieved success.'

The Brethren burst into a ragged cheer. The Brothers Watchtower and Fingers linked arms and danced an enthusiastic jig in their magic circle.

The Supreme Grand Master took a deep breath.

First the carrot, he thought, and now the stick. He *liked* the stick.

'Silence!' he screamed.

'Brother Fingers, Brother Watchtower, cease this shameful display!' he screeched. 'The rest of you, be silent!'

They quietened down, like rowdy children who have just seen the teacher come into the room. Then they quietened down a lot more, like children who have just seen the teacher's *expression*.

The Supreme Grand Master let this sink in, and then stalked along their ragged ranks.

'I suppose,' he said, 'that we think we've done some magic, do we? *Hmm*? Brother Watchtower?'

Brother Watchtower swallowed. 'Well, er, you *said* we were, er, I mean—'

'*You haven't done ANYTHING yet!*'

'Well, er, no, er—' Brother Watchtower trembled.

'Do *real* wizards leap about after a tiny spell and start chanting "Here we go, here we go, here we go", Brother Watchtower? *Hmm?*'

'Well, we were sort of—'

The Supreme Grand Master spun on his heel.

'And do they keep looking apprehensively at the woodwork, Brother Plasterer?'

Brother Plasterer hung his head. He hadn't realized anyone had noticed.

When the tension was twanging satisfactorily, like a bowstring, the Supreme Grand Master stood back.

'Why do I bother?' he said, shaking his head. 'I could have chosen *anyone*. I could have picked the *best*. But I've got a bunch of *children*.'

'Er, honest,' said Brother Watchtower, 'we was making an effort, I mean, we was really concentrating. Weren't we, lads?'

'Yes,' they chorused. The Supreme Grand Master glared at them.

'There's no room in this Brotherhood for Brothers who are not behind us all the way,' he warned.

With almost visible relief the Brethren, like panicked sheep who see that a hurdle has been opened in the fold, galloped towards the opening.

'No worries about that, your supremity,' said Brother Watchtower fervently.

'Commitment must be our watchword!' said the Supreme Grand Master.

'Watchword. Yeah,' said Brother Watchtower. He nudged Brother Plasterer, whose eyes had strayed to the skirting board again.

'Wha? Oh. Yeah. Watchword. Yeah,' said Brother Plasterer.

'And trust and fraternity,' said the Supreme Grand Master.

'Yeah. And them, too,' said Brother Fingers.

'*So,*' said the Supreme Grand Master, 'if there be any one here not anxious, yea, *eager* to continue in this great work, let him step forward now.'

No-one moved.

They're hooked. Ye gods, I'm good at this, thought the Supreme Grand Master. I can play on their horrible little minds like a xylophone. It's amazing, the sheer power of mundanity. Who'd have thought that weakness could be a greater force than strength? But you have to know how to direct it. And I do.

'Very well, then,' he said. 'And now, we will repeat the Oath.'

He led their stumbling, terrified voices through it, noting with approval the strangled way they said 'figgin'. And he kept one eye on Brother Fingers, too.

He's slightly brighter than the others, he thought. Slightly less gullible, at least. Better make sure I'm always the last to leave. Don't want any clever ideas about following me home.

You need a special kind of mind to rule a city like Ankh-Morpork, and Lord Vetinari had it. But then, he was a special kind of person.

He baffled and infuriated the lesser merchant princes, to the extent that they had long ago given up trying to assassinate him and now merely jockeyed for position amongst themselves. Anyway, any assassin who tried to attack the Patrician would be hard put to it to find enough flesh to insert the dagger.

While other lords dined on larks stuffed with peacocks' tongues, Lord Vetinari considered that a glass of boiled water and half a slice of dry bread was an elegant sufficiency.

It was exasperating. He appeared to have no vice that anyone could discover. You'd have thought, with that pale, equine face, that he'd incline towards stuff with whips, needles, and young women in dungeons. The other lords could have accepted that. Nothing wrong with whips and needles, in moderation. But the Patrician apparently spent his evenings studying reports and, on special occasions, if he could stand the excitement, playing chess.

He wore black a lot. It wasn't particularly impressive black, such as the best assassins wore, but the sober, slightly shabby black of a man who doesn't want to waste time in the mornings wondering what to wear. And you had to get up very early in the morning to get the better of the Patrician; in fact, it was wiser not to go to bed at all.

But he was popular, in a way. Under his hand, for the first time in a thousand years, Ankh-Morpork *operated*. It might not be fair or just or particularly democratic, but it worked. He tended it as one tends a topiary bush, encouraging a growth here, pruning an errant twig there. It was said that he would tolerate absolutely anything apart from anything that threatened the city,* and here it was . . .

He stared at the stricken wall for a long time, while the rain dripped off his chin and soaked his clothes. Behind him, Wonse hovered nervously.

Then one long, thin, blue-veined hand reached out and the fingertips traced the shadows.

Well, not so much shadows, more a series of silhouettes. The outline was very distinct. Inside, there was the familiar pattern of brickwork. Outside, though, something had fused the wall in a rather nice ceramic substance, giving the ancient flettons a melted, mirror-like finish.

The shapes outlined in brickwork showed a tableau of six men frozen in an attitude of surprise. Various upraised hands had quite clearly been holding knives and cutlasses.

The Patrician looked down silently on the pile of ash at his feet. A few streaks of molten metal might once have been the very same weapons that were now so decisively etched into the wall.

'Hmm,' he said.

Captain Vimes respectfully led him across the lane and into Fast Luck Alley, where he pointed out Exhibit A, to whit . . .

'Footprints,' he said. 'Which is stretching it a bit, sir. They're more what you'd call claws. One might go so far as to say talons.'

The Patrician stared at the prints in the mud. His expression was quite unreadable.

'I see,' he said eventually. 'And do you have an opinion about all this, Captain?'

The captain did. In the hours until dawn he'd had all sorts of opinions, starting with a conviction that it had been a big mistake to be born.

* And mime artists. It was a strange aversion, but there you are. Anyone in baggy trousers and a white face who tried to ply their art anywhere within Ankh's crumbling walls would very quickly find themselves in a scorpion pit, on one wall of which was painted the advice: Learn The Words.

And then the grey light had filtered even into the Shades, and he was still alive and uncooked, and had looked around him with an expression of idiot relief and seen, not a yard away, these footprints. That had not been a good moment to be sober.

'Well, sir,' he said, 'I know that dragons have been extinct for thousands of years, sir—'

'Yes?' The Patrician's eyes narrowed.

Vimes plunged on. 'But, sir, the thing is, do *they* know? Sergeant Colon said he heard a leathery sound just before, just before, just before the, er . . . offence.'

'So you think an extinct, and indeed a possibly entirely mythical, dragon flew into the city, landed in this narrow alley, incinerated a group of criminals, and then flew away?' said the Patrician. 'One might say, it was a very public-spirited creature.'

'Well, when you put it like that—'

'If I recall, the dragons of legend were solitary and rural creatures who shunned people and dwelt in forsaken, out of the way places,' said the Patrician. 'They were hardly *urban* creatures.'

'No, sir,' said the captain, repressing a comment that if you wanted to find a really forsaken, out of the way place then the Shades would fit the bill pretty well.

'Besides,' said Lord Vetinari, 'one would imagine that someone would have noticed, wouldn't you agree?'

The captain nodded at the wall and its dreadful frieze. 'Apart from them, you mean, sir?'

'In my opinion,' said Lord Vetinari, 'it's some kind of warfare. Possibly a rival gang has hired a wizard. A little local difficulty.'

'Could be linked to all this strange thieving, sir,' volunteered Wonse.

'But there's the footprints, sir,' said Vimes doggedly.

'We're close to the river,' said the Patrician. 'Possibly it was, perhaps, a wading bird of some sort. A mere coincidence,' he added, 'but I should cover them over, if I were you. We don't want people getting the wrong idea and jumping to silly conclusions, do we?' he added sharply

Vimes gave in.

'As you wish, sir,' he said, looking at his sandals.

The Patrician patted him on the shoulder.

'Never mind,' he said. 'Carry on. Good show of initiative, that man. Patrolling in the Shades, too. Well done.'

He turned, and almost walked into the wall of chain mail that was Carrot.

To his horror, Captain Vimes saw his newest recruit point politely to the Patrician's coach. Around it, fully-armed and wary, were six members of the Palace Guard, who straightened up and took a wary interest. Vimes disliked them intensely. They had plumes on their helmets. He hated plumes on a guard.

He heard Carrot say, 'Excuse me, sir, is this your coach, sir?' and the Patrician looked him blankly up and down and said, 'It is. Who are you, young man?'

Carrot saluted. 'Lance-constable Carrot, sir.'

'Carrot, Carrot. That name rings a bell.'

Lupine Wonse, who had been hovering behind him, whispered in the Patrician's ear. His face brightened. 'Ah, the young thief-taker. A little error there, I think, but commendable. No person is above the law, eh?'

'No, sir,' said Carrot.

'Commendable, commendable,' said the Patrician. 'And now, gentlemen—'

'About your coach, sir,' said Carrot doggedly, 'I couldn't help noticing that the front offside wheel, contrary to the—'

He's going to arrest the Patrician, Vimes told himself, the thought trickling through his brain like an icy rivulet. He's actually going to arrest the Patrician. The supreme ruler. He's going to arrest him. This is what he's actually going to do. The boy doesn't know the meaning of the word 'fear'. Oh, wouldn't it be a good idea if he knew the meaning of the word 'survival' . . .

And I can't get my jaw muscles to move.

We're all dead. Or worse, we're all detained at the Patrician's pleasure. And as we all know, he's seldom that pleased.

It was at this precise moment that Sergeant Colon earned himself a metaphorical medal.

'Lance-constable Carrot!' he shouted. 'Attention! Lance-constable Carrot, abou-uta turna! Lance-constable Carrot, qui-uck marcha!'

Carrot brought himself to attention like a barn being raised and stared straight ahead with a ferocious expression of acute obedience.

'Well done, that man,' said the Patrician thoughtfully, as Carrot strode stiffly away. 'Carry on, Captain. And do come down heavily on any silly rumours about dragons, right?'

'Yes, sir,' said Captain Vimes.

'Good man.'

The coach rattled off, the bodyguard running alongside.

Behind him, Captain Vimes was only vaguely aware of the sergeant yelling at the retreating Carrot to stop.

He was thinking.

He looked at the prints in the mud. He used his regulation pike, which he knew was exactly seven feet long, to measure their size and the distance between them. He whistled under his breath. Then, with considerable caution, he followed the alley around the corner; it led to a small, padlocked and dirt-encrusted door in the back of a timber warehouse.

There was something very wrong, he thought.

The prints come out of the alley, but they don't go in. And we don't often get any wading birds in the Ankh, mainly because the pollution would eat their legs away and anyway, it's easier for them to walk on the surface.

He looked up. A myriad washing lines criss-crossed the narrow rectangle of the sky as efficiently as a net.

So, he thought, something big and fiery came out of this alley but didn't come into it.

And the Patrician is very worried about it.

I've been told to forget about it.

He noticed something else at the side of the alley, and bent down and picked up a fresh, empty peanut shell.

He tossed it from hand to hand, staring at nothing.

Right now, he needed a drink. But perhaps it ought to wait.

The Librarian knuckled his way urgently along the dark aisles between the slumbering bookshelves.

The rooftops of the city belonged to him. Oh, assassins and thieves might make use of them, but he'd long ago found the forest of chimneys, buttresses, gargoyles and weathervanes a convenient and somehow comforting alternative to the streets.

At least, up until now.

It had seemed amusing and instructive to follow the Watch into the Shades, an urban jungle which held no fears for a 300-lb ape. But now the nightmare he had seen while brachiating across a dark alley would, if he had been human, have made him doubt the evidence of his own eyes.

As an ape, he had no doubts whatsoever about his eyes and believed them all the time.

Right now he wanted to concentrate them urgently on a book that might hold a clue. It was in a section no-one bothered with much these days; the books in there were not really magical. Dust lay accusingly on the floor.

Dust with footprints in it.

'Oook?' said the Librarian, in the warm gloom.

He proceeded cautiously now, realising with a sense of inevitability that the footprints seemed to have the same destination in mind as he did.

He turned a corner and there it was.

The section.

The bookcase.

The shelf.

The gap.

There are many horrible sights in the multiverse. Somehow, though, to a soul attuned to the subtle rhythms of a library, there are few worse sights than a hole where a book ought to be.

Someone had stolen a book.

In the privacy of the Oblong Office, his personal sanctum, the Patrician paced up and down. He was dictating a stream of instructions.

'And send some men to paint that wall,' he finished.

Lupine Wonse raised an eyebrow.

'Is that wise, sir?' he said.

'You don't think a frieze of ghastly shadows will cause comment and speculation?' said the Patrician sourly.

'Not as much as fresh paint in the Shades,' said Wonse evenly.

The Patrician hesitated a moment. 'Good point,' he snapped. 'Have some men demolish it.'

He reached the end of the room, spun on his heel, and stalked up it again. Dragons! As if there were not enough important, enough *real* things to take up his time.

'Do you believe in dragons?' he said.

Wonse shook his head. 'They're impossible, sir.'

'So I've heard,' said Lord Vetinari. He reached the opposite wall, turned.

'Would you like me to investigate further?' said Wonse.

'Yes. Do so.'

'And I shall ensure the Watch take great care,' said Wonse.

The Patrician stopped his pacing. 'The Watch? The Watch? My dear chap, the Watch are a bunch of incompetents commanded by a drunkard. It's taken me years to achieve it. The last thing we need to concern ourselves with is the Watch.'

He thought for a moment. 'Ever seen a dragon, Wonse? One of the big ones, I mean? Oh, they're impossible. You said.'

'They're just legend, really. Superstition,' said Wonse.

'Hmm,' said the Patrician. 'And the thing about legends, of course, is that they are legendary.'

'Exactly, sir.'

'Even so—' The Patrician paused, and stared at Wonse for some time. 'Oh, well,' he said. 'Sort it out. I'm not having any of this dragon business. It's the type of thing that makes people restless. Put a stop to it.'

When he was alone he stood and looked out gloomily over the twin city. It was drizzling again.

Ankh-Morpork! Brawling city of a hundred thousand souls! And, as the Patrician privately observed, ten times that number of actual people. The fresh rain glistened on the panorama of towers and rooftops, all unaware of the teeming, rancorous world it was dropping into. Luckier rain fell on upland sheep, or whispered gently over forests, or pattered somewhat incestuously into the sea. Rain that fell on Ankh-Morpork, though, was rain that was in trouble. They did terrible things to water, in Ankh-Morpork. Being drunk was only the start of its problems.

The Patrician liked to feel that he was looking out over a city that worked. Not a beautiful city, or a renowned city, or a well-drained city, and certainly not an architecturally favoured city; even its most enthusiastic citizens would agree that, from a high point of vantage, Ankh-Morpork looked as though someone had tried to achieve in stone and wood an effect normally associated with the pavements outside all-night takeaways.

But it worked. It spun along cheerfully like a gyroscope on the lip of a catastrophe curve. And this, the Patrician firmly believed, was because no one group was ever powerful enough to push it over. Merchants, thieves, assassins, wizards – all competed energetically in the race without really realizing that it needn't be a race at all, and certainly not trusting one another enough to stop and wonder who had marked out the course and was holding the starting flag.

The Patrician disliked the word 'dictator'. It affronted him. He never told anyone what to do. He didn't have to, that was the wonderful part. A large part of his life consisted of arranging matters so that this state of affairs continued.

Of course, there were various groups seeking his overthrow, and this was right and proper and the sign of a vigorous and healthy society. No-one could call him unreasonable about the matter. Why, hadn't he founded most of them himself? And what was so beautiful was the way in which they spent nearly all their time bickering with one another.

Human nature, the Patrician always said, was a marvellous thing. Once you understood where its levers were.

He had an unpleasant premonition about this dragon business. If ever there was a creature that didn't have any obvious levers, it was a dragon. It would have to be sorted out.

The Patrician didn't believe in unnecessary cruelty.* He did not believe in pointless revenge. But he was a great believer in the need for things to be sorted out.

Funnily enough, Captain Vimes was thinking the same thing. He found he didn't like the idea of citizens, even of the Shades, being turned into a mere ceramic tint.

And it had been done in front of the Watch, more or less. As if the Watch didn't matter, as if the Watch was just an irrelevant detail. That was what rankled.

Of course, it was true. That only made it worse.

What was making him even angrier was that he had disobeyed orders. He had scuffed up the tracks, certainly. But in the bottom drawer of his ancient desk, hidden under a pile of empty bottles, was a plaster cast. He could feel it staring at him through three layers of wood.

He couldn't imagine what had got into him. And now he was going even further out on to the limb.

He reviewed his, for want of a better word, troops. He'd asked the senior pair to turn up in plain clothes. This meant that Sergeant Colon, who'd worn uniform all his life, was looking red-faced and uncomfortable in the suit he wore for funerals. Whereas Nobby—

'I wonder if I made the word "plain" clear enough?' said Captain Vimes.

'It's what I wear outside work, guv,' said Nobby reproachfully.

'Sir,' corrected Sergeant Colon.

'My voice is in plain clothes too,' said Nobby. 'Initiative, that is.'

Vimes walked slowly around the corporal.

'And your plain clothes do not cause old women to faint and small boys to run after you in the street?' he said.

Nobby shifted uneasily. He wasn't at home with irony.

'No, sir, guv,' he said. 'It's all the go, this style.'

This was broadly true. There was a current fad in Ankh for big, feathered hats, ruffs, slashed doublets with gold frogging, flared pantaloons and boots with ornamental spurs. The trouble was, Vimes reflected, that most of the fashion-conscious had more body to go between these component bits, whereas all that could be said of Corporal Nobbs was that he was in there somewhere.

It might be advantageous. After all, absolutely no-one would

---

* While being bang alongside the idea of necessary cruelty, of course.

ever believe, when they saw him coming down the street, that here was a member of the Watch trying to look inconspicuous.

It occurred to Vimes that he knew absolutely nothing about Nobbs outside working hours. He couldn't even remember where the man lived. All these years he'd known the man and he'd never realized that, in his secret private life, Corporal Nobbs was a bit of a peacock. A very *short* peacock, it was true, a peacock that had been hit repeatedly with something heavy, perhaps, but a peacock nonetheless. It just went to show, you never could tell.

He brought his attention back to the business in hand.

'I want you two,' he said to Nobbs and Colon, 'to mingle unobtrusively, or obtrusively in your case, Corporal Nobbs, with people tonight and, er, see if you can detect anything unusual.'

'Unusual like what?' said the sergeant.

Vimes hesitated. He wasn't exactly sure himself. 'Anything,' he said, 'pertinent.'

'Ah.' The sergeant nodded wisely. 'Pertinent. Right.'

There was an awkward silence.

'Maybe people have seen weird things," said Captain Vimes. 'Or perhaps there have been unexplained fires. Or footprints. You know,' he finished, desperately, 'signs of dragons.'

'You mean, like, piles of gold what have been slept on,' said the sergeant.

'And virgins being chained to rocks,' said Nobbs, knowingly.

'I can see you're experts,' sighed Vimes. 'Just do the best you can.'

'This mingling,' said Sergeant Colon delicately, 'it would involve going into taverns and drinking and similar, would it?'

'To a certain extent,' said Vimes.

'Ah,' said the sergeant, happily.

'In moderation.'

'Right you are, sir.'

'And at your own expense.'

'Oh.'

'But before you go,' said the captain, 'do either of you know anyone who might *know* anything about dragons? Apart from sleeping on gold and the bit with the young women, I mean.'

'Wizards would,' volunteered Nobby.

'Apart from wizards,' said Vimes firmly. You couldn't trust wizards. Every guard knew you couldn't trust wizards. They were even worse than civilians.

Colon thought about it. 'There's always Lady Ramkin,' he said. 'Lives in Scoone Avenue. Breeds swamp dragons. You know, the little buggers people keep as pets?'

'Oh, her,' said Vimes gloomily. 'I think I've seen her around. The one with the "Whinny If You Love Dragons" sticker on the back of her carriage?'

'That's her. She's mental,' said Sergeant Colon. 'What do you want *me* to do, sir?' said Carrot.

'Er. You have the most important job,' said Vimes hurriedly. 'I want you to stay here and watch the office.'

Carrot's face broadened in a slow, unbelieving grin.

'You mean I'm left in *charge*, sir?' he said.

'In a manner of speaking,' said Vimes. 'But you're not allowed to arrest anyone, understand?' he added quickly.

'Not even if they're breaking the law, sir?'

'Not even then. Just make a note of it.'

'I'll read my book, then,' said Carrot. 'And polish my helmet.'

'Good boy,' said the captain. It should be safe enough, he thought. No-one ever comes in here, not even to report a lost dog. No-one ever thinks about the Watch. You'd have to be really out of touch to go to the Watch for help, he thought bitterly.

Scoone Avenue was a wide, tree-lined, and incredibly select part of Ankh, high enough above the river to be away from its all-pervading smell. People in Scoone Avenue had old money, which was supposed to be much better than new money, although Captain Vimes had never had enough of either to spot the difference. People in Scoone Avenue had their own personal bodyguards. People in Scoone Avenue were said to be so aloof they wouldn't even talk to the gods. This was a slight slander. They *would* talk to gods, if they were well-bred gods of decent family.

Lady Ramkin's house was not hard to find. It commanded an outcrop that gave it a magnificent view of the city, if that was your idea of a good time. There were stone dragons on the gatepost, and the gardens had an unkempt overgrown look. Statues of Ramkins long gone loomed up out of the greenery Most of them had swords and were covered in ivy up to the neck.

Vimes sensed that this was not because the garden's owner was too poor to do anything about it, but rather that the garden's owner thought there were much more important things than ancestors, which was a pretty unusual point of view for an aristocrat.

They also apparently thought that there were more important things than property repair. When he rang the bell of the rather pleasant old house itself, in the middle of a flourishing rhododendron forest, several bits of the plaster facade fell off.

That seemed to be the only effect, except that something round the back of the house started to howl. Some *things*.

It started to rain again. After a while Vimes felt the dignity of his position and cautiously edged around the building, keeping well back in case anything else collapsed.

He reached a heavy wooden gate in a heavy wooden wall. In contrast with the general decrepitude of the rest of the place, it seemed comparatively new and very solid.

He knocked. This caused another fusillade of strange whistling noises.

The door opened. Something dreadful loomed over him.

'Ah, good man. Do you know anything about mating?' it boomed.

It was quiet and warm in the Watch House. Carrot listened to the hissing of sand in the hourglass and concentrated on buffing up his breastplate. Centuries of tarnish had given up under his cheerful onslaught. It gleamed.

You knew where you were with a shiny breastplate. The strangeness of the city, where they had all these laws and concentrated on ignoring them, was too much for him. But a shiny breastplate was a breastplate well shined.

The door opened. He peered across the top of the ancient desk. There was no-one there.

He tried a few more industrious rubs.

There was the vague sound of someone who had got fed up with waiting. Two purple-fingernailed hands grasped the edge of the desk, and the Librarian's face rose slowly into view like an early-morning coconut.

'Oook,' he said.

Carrot stared. It had been explained to him carefully that, contrary to appearances, laws governing the animal kingdom did not apply to the Librarian. On the other hand, the Librarian himself was never very interested in obeying the laws governing the human kingdom, either. He was one of those little anomalies you have to build around.

'Hallo,' said Carrot uncertainly. ('Don't call him "boy" or pat him, that always gets him annoyed.')

'Oook.'

The Librarian prodded the desk with a long, many-jointed finger.

'What?'

'*Oook.*'

'Sorry?'

The Librarian rolled his eyes. It was strange, he felt, that so-called intelligent dogs, horses and dolphins never had any difficulty indicating to humans the vital news of the moment, e.g., that the three children were lost in the cave, or the train was about to take the line leading to the bridge that had been washed away or similar, while he, only a handful of chromosomes away from wearing a vest, found it difficult to persuade the average human to came in out of the rain. You just couldn't talk to some people.

'*Oook!*' he said, and beckoned.

'I can't leave the office,' said Carrot. 'I've had Orders.'

The Librarian's upper lip rolled back like a blind.

'Is that a smile?' said Carrot. The Librarian shook his head.

'Someone hasn't committed a crime, have they?' said Carrot.

'Oook.'

'A bad crime?'

'Oook! '

'Like murder?'

'Eeek.'

'Worse than murder?'

'*Eeek!* The Librarian knuckled over to the door and bounced up and down urgently.

Carrot gulped. Orders were orders, yes, but this was something else. The people in this city were capable of anything.

He buckled on his breastplate, screwed his sparkling helmet on to his head, and strode towards the door.

Then he remembered his responsibilities. He went back to the desk, found a scrap of paper, and painstakingly wrote: *Out Fighting Crime. Pleass Call Again Later. Thankyou.*

And *then* he went out on to the streets, untarnished and unafraid.

The Supreme Grand Master raised his arms.

'Brethren,' he said, 'let us begin . . .'

It was so easy. All you had to do was channel that great septic reservoir of jealousy and cringing resentment that the Brothers had in such abundance, harness their dreadful mundane unpleasantness which had a force greater in its way than roaring evil, and then open your own mind . . .

. . . into the place where the dragons went.

Vimes found himself grabbed by the arm and pulled inside. The heavy door shut behind him with a definite click.

'It's Lord Mountjoy Gayscale Talonthrust III of Ankh,' said the apparition, which was dressed in huge and fearsomely-padded armour. 'You know, I really don't think he can cut the mustard.'

'He can't?' said Vimes, backing away.

'It really needs two of you.'

'It does, doesn't it,' whispered Vimes, his shoulder blades trying to carve their way out through the fence.

'Could you oblige?' boomed the thing.

'What?'

'Oh, don't be squeamish, man. You just have to help him up into the air. It's me who has the tricky part. I know it's cruel, but if he can't manage it tonight then he's for the choppy-chop. Survival of the fittest and all that, don't you know.'

Captain Vimes managed to get a grip on himself. He was clearly in the presence of some sex-crazed would-be murderess, insofar as any gender could be determined under the strange lumpy garments. If it wasn't female, then references to 'it's me who has the tricky part' gave rise to mental images that would haunt him for some time to come. He knew the rich did things differently, but this was going too far.

'Madam,' he said coldly, 'I am an officer of the Watch and I must warn you that the course of action you are suggesting breaks the laws of the city – ' and also of several of the more strait-laced gods, he added silently – 'and I must advise you that his Lordship should be released unharmed immediately—'

The figure stared at him in astonishment.

'Why?' it said. 'It's my bloody dragon.'

'Have another drink, not-Corporal Nobby?' said Sergeant Colon unsteadily.

'I do not mind if I do, not-Sgt Colon,' said Nobby.

They were taking inconspicuosity seriously. That ruled out most of the taverns on the Morpork side of the river, where they were very well known. Now they were in a rather elegant one in downtown Ankh, where they were being as unobtrusive as they knew how. The other drinkers thought they were some kind of cabaret.

'I was thinking,' said Sgt Colon.

'What?'

'If we bought a bottle or two, we could go home and then we'd be really inconspicuous.'

Nobby gave this some thought.

'But he said we've got to keep our ears open,' he said. 'We're supposed to, what he said, detect anything.'

'We can do that at my house,' said Sgt Colon. 'We could listen all night, really hard.'

'Tha's a good point,' said Nobby. In fact, it sounded better and better the more he thought about it.

'But first,' he announced, 'I got to pay a visit.'

'Me too,' said the sergeant. 'This detecting business gets to you after a while, doesn't it.'

They stumbled out into the alley behind the tavern. There was a full moon up, but a few rags of scruffy cloud were drifting across it. The pair inconspicuously bumped into one another in the darkness.

'Is that you, Detector Sergeant Colon?' said Nobby.

'Tha's right! Now, can you detect the door to the privy, Detector Corporal Nobbs? We're looking for a short, dark door of mean appearance, ahahaha.'

There were a couple of clanks and a muffled swear-word from Nobby as he staggered across the alley, followed by a yowl when one of Ankh-Morpork's enormous population of feral cats fled between his legs.

'Who loves you, pussycat?' said Nobby under his breath.

'Needs must, then,' said Sgt Colon, and faced a handy corner.

His private musings were interrupted by a grunt from the corporal.

'You there, Sgt?'

'*Detector* Sergeant to you, Nobby,' said Sgt Colon pleasantly.

Nobby's tone was urgent and suddenly very sober. 'Don't piss about, Sergeant, I just saw a dragon fly over!'

'I've seen a horsefly,' said Sgt Colon, hiccuping gently. 'And I've seen a housefly. I've even seen a greenfly. But I ain't never seen a dragon fly.'

'Of course you have, you pillock,' said Nobby urgently. 'Look, I'm not messing about! He had wings on him like, like, like great big wings!'

Sergeant Colon turned majestically. The corporal's face had gone so white that it showed up in the darkness.

'Honest, Sergeant!'

Sgt Colon turned his eyes to the damp sky and the rain-washed moon.

'All right,' he said, 'show me.'

There was a slithering noise behind him, and a couple of roof tiles smashed on to the street.

He turned. And there, on the roof, was the dragon.

'There's a dragon on the roof!' he warbled. 'Nobby, it's a *dragon* on the roof! What shall I do, Nobby? There's a dragon on the roof. It's looking right at me, Nobby!'

'For a start, you could do your trousers up,' said Nobby, from behind the nearest wall.

Even shorn of her layers of protective clothing, Lady Sybil Ramkin was still toweringly big. Vimes knew that the barbarian hublander folk had legends about great chain-mailed, armour-bra'd, carhorse-riding maidens who swooped down on battlefields and carried off dead warriors on their cropper to a glorious roistering afterlife, while singing in a pleasing mezzo-soprano. Lady Ramkin could have been one of them. She could have led them. She could have carried off a *battalion*. When she spoke, every word was like a hearty slap on the back and clanged with the aristocratic self-assurance of the totally well-bred. The vowel sounds alone would have cut teak.

Vimes's ragged forebears were used to voices like that, usually from heavily-armoured people on the back of a war charger telling them why it would be a jolly good idea, don'tcherknow, to charge the enemy and hit them for six. His legs wanted to stand to attention.

Prehistoric men would have worshipped her, and in fact had amazingly managed to carve lifelike statues of her thousands of years ago. She had a mass of chestnut hair; a wig, Vimes learned later. No-one who had much to do with dragons kept their own hair for long.

She also had a dragon on her shoulder. It had been introduced as Talonthrust Vincent Wonderkind of Quirm, referred to as Vinny, and seemed to be making a large contribution to the unusual chemical smell that pervaded the house. This smell permeated everything. Even the generous slice of cake she offered him tasted of it.

'The, er, shoulder . . . it looks . . . very nice,' he said, desperate to make conversation.

'Rubbish,' said her ladyship. 'I'm just training him up because shoulder-sitters fetch twice the price.'

Vimes murmured that he had occasionally seen society ladies with small, colourful dragons on their shoulders, and thought it looked very, er, nice.

'Oh, it *sounds* nice,' she said. 'I'll grant you. Then they realize it means sootburns, frizzled hair and crap all down their back. Those talons dig in, too. And then they think the thing's getting too big and smelly and next thing you know it's either down to the

Morpork Sunshine Sanctuary for Lost Dragons or the old heave-ho into the river with a rope round your neck, poor little buggers.' She sat down, arranging a skirt that could have made sails for a small fleet. 'Now then. *Captain* Vimes, was it?'

Vimes was at a loss. Ramkins long-dead stared down at him from ornate frames high on the shadowy walls. Between, around and under the portraits were the weapons they'd presumably used, and had used well and often by the look of them. Suits of armour stood in dented ranks along the walls. Quite a number, he couldn't help noticing, had large holes in them. The ceiling was a faded riot of moth-eaten banners. You did not need forensic examination to understand that Lady Ramkin's ancestors had never shirked a fight.

It was amazing that she was capable of doing something so unwarlike as having a cup of tea.

'My forebears,' she said, following his hypnotized gaze. 'You know, not one Ramkin in the last thousand years has died in his bed.'

'Yes, ma'am?'

'Source of family pride, that.'

'Yes, ma'am.'

'*Quite* a few of them have died in other people's, of course.'

Captain Vimes's teacup rattled in its saucer. 'Yes, ma'am,' he said.

'Captain is *such* a dashing title, I've always thought.' She gave him a bright, brittle smile. 'I mean, colonels and so on are always so stuffy, majors are pompous, but one always feels somehow that there is something delightfully *dangerous* about a captain. What was it you had to show me?'

Vimes gripped his parcel like a chastity belt.

'I wondered,' he faltered, 'how big swamp . . . er . . .'

He stopped. Something dreadful was happening to his lower regions.

Lady Ramkin followed his gaze. 'Oh, take no notice of him,' she said cheerfully. 'Hit him with a cushion if he's a bother.'

A small elderly dragon had crawled out from under his chair and placed its jowly muzzle in Vimes's lap. It stared up at him soulfully with big brown eyes and gently dribbled something quite corrosive, by the feel of it, over his knees. And it stank like the ring around an acid bath.

'That's Dewdrop Mabelline Talonthrust the First,' said her ladyship. 'Champion and sire of champions. No fire left now, poor soppy old thing. He likes his belly rubbed.'

Vimes made surreptitiously vicious jerking motions to dislodge the old dragon. It blinked mournfully at him with rheumy eyes and rolled back the corner of its mouth, exposing a picket fence of soot-blackened teeth.

'Just push him off if he's a nuisance,' said Lady Ramkin cheerfully. 'Now then, what was it you were asking?'

'I was wondering how big swamp dragons grow?' said Vimes, trying to shift position. There was a faint growling noise.

'You came all the way up here to ask me that? Well . . . I seem to recall Gayheart Talonthrust of Ankh stood fourteen thumbs high, toe to matlock,' mused Lady Ramkin.

'Er . . .'

'About three foot six inches,' she added kindly.

'No bigger than that?' said Vimes hopefully. In his lap the old dragon began to snore gently.

'Golly, no. He was a bit of a freak, actually. Mostly they don't get much bigger than eight thumbs.'

Captain Vimes's lips moved in hurried calculation. 'Two feet?' he ventured.

'Well done. That's the cobbs, of course. The hens are a bit smaller.'

Captain Vimes wasn't going to give in. 'A cobb would be a male dragon?' he said.

'Only after the age of two years,' said Lady Ramkin triumphantly. 'Up to the age of eight months he's a pewmet, then he's a cock until fourteen months, and then he's a snood – '

Captain Vimes sat entranced, eating the horrible cake, britches gradually dissolving, as the stream of information flooded over him; how the males fought with flame but in the laying season only the hens* breathed fire, from the combustion of complex intestinal gases, to incubate the eggs which needed such a fierce temperature, while the males gathered firewood; a group of swamp dragons was a *slump* or an *embarrassment*; a female was capable of laying up to three clutches of four eggs every year, most of which were trodden on by absent-minded males; and that dragons of both sexes were vaguely uninterested in one another, and indeed everything except firewood, except for about once every two months when they became as single-minded as a buzzsaw.

He was helpless to prevent himself being taken out to the kennels at the back, outfitted from neck to ankle in leather armour faced with steel plates, and ushered into the long low building where the whistling had come from.

The temperature was terrible, but not as bad as the cocktail of

---

* Only until their third clutch, of course. After that they're dams.

75

smells. He staggered aimlessly from one metal-lined pen to another, while pear-shaped, squeaking little horrors with red eyes were introduced as 'Moonpenny Duchess Marchpaine, who's gravid at the moment' and 'Moonmist Talonthrust II, who was Best of Breed at Pseudopolis last year'. Jets of pale green flame played across his knees.

Many of the stalls had rosettes and certificates pinned over them.

'And this one, I'm afraid, is Goodboy Bindle Featherstone of Quirm,' said Lady Ramkin relentlessly.

Vimes stared groggily over the charred barrier at the small creature curled up in the middle of the floor. It bore about the same resemblance to the rest of them as Nobby did to the average human being. Something in its ancestry had given it a pair of eyebrows that were about the same size as its stubby wings, which could never have supported it in the air. Its head was the wrong shape, like an anteater. It had nostrils like jet intakes. If it ever managed to get airborne the things would have the drag of twin parachutes.

It was also turning on Captain Vimes the most silently intelligent look he'd ever had from any animal, including Corporal Nobbs.

'It happens,' said Lady Ramkin sadly. 'It's all down to genes, you know.'

'It is?' said Vimes. Somehow, the creature seemed to be concentrating all the power its siblings wasted in flame and noise into a stare like a thermic lance. He couldn't help remembering how much he'd wanted a puppy when he was a little boy. Mind you, they'd been starving – anything with meat on it would have done.

He heard the dragon lady say, 'One tries to breed for a good flame, depth of scale, correct colour and so on. One just has to put up with the occasional total whittle.'

The little dragon turned on Vimes a gaze that would be guaranteed to win it the award for Dragon the Judges would Most Like to Take Home and Use as A Portable Gas Lighter.

Total whittle, Vimes thought. He wasn't sure of the precise meaning of the word, but he could hazard a shrewd guess. It sounded like whatever it was you had left when you had extracted everything of any value whatsoever. Like the Watch, he thought. Total whittles, every one of them. And just like him. It was the saga of his life.

'That's Nature for you,' said her ladyship. 'Of course I wouldn't *dream* of breeding from him, but he wouldn't be able to anyway.'

'Why not?' said Vimes.

'Because dragons have to mate in the air and he'll never be able to fly with those wings, I'm afraid. I'll be sorry to lose the bloodline, naturally. His sire was Brenda Rodley's Treebite Brightscale. Do you know Brenda?'

'Er, no,' said Vimes. Lady Ramkin was one of those people who assumed that everyone else knew everyone one knew.

'Charming gel. Anyway, his brothers and sisters are shaping up very well.'

Poor little bastard, thought Vimes. That's Nature for you in a nutshell. Always dealing off the bottom of the pack.

No wonder they call her a *mother* . . .

'You said you had something to show me,' Lady Ramkin prompted.

Vimes wordlessly handed her the parcel. She slipped off her heavy mittens and unwrapped it.

'Plaster cast of a footprint,' she said, baldly. 'Well?'

'Does it remind you of anything?' said Vimes.

'Could be a wading bird.'

'Oh.' Vimes was crestfallen.

Lady Ramkin laughed. 'Or a really big dragon. Got it out of a museum, did you?'

'No. I got it off the street this morning.'

'Ha? Someone's been playing tricks on you, old chap.'

'Er. There was, er, circumstantial evidence.'

He told her. She stared at him.

'*Draco nobilis*,' she said hoarsely.

'Pardon?' said Vimes.

'*Draco nobilis*. The Noble dragon. As opposed to these fellows – ' she waved a hand in the direction of the massed ranks of whistling lizards – '*Draco vulgaris*, the lot of them. But the big ones are all gone, you know. This really is a nonsense. No two ways about it. All gone. Beautiful things, they were. Weighed tons. Biggest things ever to fly. No-one knows how they did it.'

And then they realized.

It was suddenly very quiet.

All along the rows of kennels, the dragons were silent, bright-eyed and watchful. They were staring at the roof.

Carrot looked around him. Shelves stretched away in every direction. On those shelves, books. He made a calculated guess.

'This is the Library, isn't it?' he said.

The Librarian maintained his gentle but firm grip on the boy's hand and led him along the maze of aisles.

'Is there a body?' said Carrot. There'd have to be. Worse than murder! A body in a library. It could lead to anything.

The ape eventually padded to a halt in front of a shelf no different than, it seemed, a hundred others. Some of the books were chained up. There was a gap. The Librarian pointed to it.

'Oook.'

'Well, what about it? A hole where a book should be.'

'Oook.'

'A book has been taken. A book has been taken? You summoned the Watch,' Carrot drew himself up proudly, 'because someone's taken a *book*? You think that's worse than murder?'

The Librarian gave him the kind of look other people would reserve for people who said things like 'What's so bad about genocide?'

'This is practically a criminal offence, wasting Watch time,' said Carrot. 'Why don't you just tell the head wizards, or whoever they are?'

'Oook.' The Librarian indicated with some surprisingly economical gestures that most wizards would not find their own bottoms with both hands.

'Well, I don't see what we can do about it,' said Carrot. 'What's the book called?'

The Librarian scratched his head. This one was going to be tricky. He faced Carrot, put his leather-glove hands together, then folded them open.

'*I know* it's a book. What's its name?'

The Librarian sighed, and held up a hand.

'Four words?' said Carrot. 'First word.' The ape pinched two wrinkled fingers together. 'Small word? A. The. Fo—'

'Oook!'

'The? The. Second word . . . third word? Small word. The? A? To? Of? Fro – Of? Of. The something Of something. Second word. What? Oh. First syllable. Fingers? Touching your fingers. Thumbs.'

The orang-utan growled and tugged theatrically at one large hairy ear.

'Oh, *sounds* like. Fingers? Hand? Adding up. Sums. Cut off. Smaller word . . . Sum. Sum! Second syllable. Small. Very small syllable. A. In. Un. On. On! Sum. On. Sum On. Summon! Summon-*er*? Summon-*ing*? Summoning. Summoning. The Summoning of Something. This is fun, isn't it! Fourth word. Whole word—'

He peered intently as the Librarian gyrated mysteriously.

'Big thing. Huge big thing. Flapping. Great big flapping leaping thing. Teeth. Huffing. Blowing. Great big huge blowing flapping thing.' Sweat broke out on Carrot's forehead as he tried obediently to understand. 'Sucking fingers. Sucking fingers thing. Burnt. Hot. Great big hot blowing flapping thing . . .'

The Librarian rolled his eyes. Homo sapiens? You could keep it.

The great dragon danced and spun and trod the air over the city. Its colour was moonlight, gleaming off its scales. Sometimes it would twist and glide with deceptive speed over the rooftops for the sheer joy of existing.

And it was all wrong, Vimes thought. Part of him was marvelling at the sheer beauty of the sight, but an insistent, weaselly little group of brain cells from the wrong side of the synapses was scrawling its graffiti on the walls of wonderment.

It's a bloody great lizard, they jeered. Must weigh tons. Nothing that big can fly, not even on beautiful wings. And what is a flying lizard doing with great big scales on its back?

Five hundred feet above him a lance of blue-white flame roared into the sky.

It can't *do* something like that! It'd burn its own lips off!

Beside him Lady Ramkin stood with her mouth open. Behind her, the little caged dragons yammered and howled.

The great beast turned in the air and swooped over the rooftops. The flame darted out again. Below it, yellow flames sprang up. It was done so quietly and stylishly that it took Vimes several seconds to realize that several buildings had in fact been set on fire.

'Golly!' said Lady Ramkin. 'Look! It's using the thermals! That's what the fire is for!' She turned to Vimes, her eyes hopelessly aglow. 'Do you realise we're very probably seeing something that no-one has seen for centuries?'

'Yes, it's a bloody flying alligator setting fire to my city!' shouted Vimes.

She wasn't listening to him. 'There must be a breeding colony somewhere,' she said. 'After all this time! Where do you think it lives?'

Vimes didn't know. But he swore to himself that he would find out, and ask it some very serious questions.

'One egg,' breathed the breeder. 'Just let me get my hands on one egg . . .'

Vimes stared at her in genuine astonishment. It dawned on him that he was very probably a flawed character.

Below them, another building exploded into flame.

'How far exactly,' he said, speaking very slowly and carefully, as to a child, 'did these things fly?'

'They're very territorial animals,' murmured her ladyship. 'According to legend, they—'

Vimes realized he was in for another dose of dragon lore. 'Just give me the facts, m'lady,' he said impatiently.

'Not very far, really,' she said, slightly taken aback.

'Thank you very much, ma'am, you've been very helpful,' muttered Vimes, and broke into a run.

Somewhere in the city. There was nothing outside for miles except low fields and swamp. It had to be living somewhere in the city.

His sandals flapped on the cobbles as he hurtled down the streets. Somewhere in the city! Which was totally ridiculous, of course. Totally ridiculous and impossible.

He didn't deserve this. Of all the cities in all the world it could have flown into, he thought, it's flown into mine . . .

By the time he reached the river the dragon had vanished. But a pall of smoke was hanging over the streets and several human bucket chains had been formed to pass lumps of the river to the stricken buildings.* The job was considerably hampered by the droves of people streaming out of the streets, carrying their possessions. Most of the city was wood and thatch, and they weren't taking any chances.

In fact the danger was surprisingly small. Mysteriously small, when you came to think about it.

Vimes had surreptitiously taken to carrying a notebook these days, and he had noted the damage as if the mere act of writing it down somehow made the world a more understandable place.

Itym: Ae Coache House (belonging to an inoffensive businessman, who'd seen his new carriage go up in flames).

Itym: Ae smalle vegettable shope (with pin-point accuracy).

Vimes wondered about that. He'd bought some apples in there once, and there didn't appear to be anything about it that a dragon could possibly take offence at.

Still, very considerate of the dragon, he thought as he made his way to the Watch House. When you think of all the timber yards, hayricks, thatched roofs and oil stores it could have hit by chance,

---

* The Guild of Fire Fighters had been outlawed by the Patrician the previous year after many complaints. The point was that, if you bought a contract from the Guild, your house would be protected against fire. Unfortunately, the general Ankh-Morpork ethos quickly came to the fore and fire fighters would tend to go to prospective clients' houses in groups, making loud comments like 'Very inflammable looking place, this' and 'Probably go up like a firework with just one carelessly-dropped match, know what I mean?'

it's managed to really frighten everyone without actually harming the city.

Rays of early morning sunlight were piercing the drifts of smoke as he pushed open the door. This was home. Not the bare little room over the candlemaker's shop in Wixon's Alley, where he slept, but this nasty brown room that smelt of unswept chimneys, Sgt Colon's pipe, Nobby's mysterious personal problem and, latterly, Carrot's armour polish. It was almost like home.

No-one else was there. He wasn't entirely surprised. He clumped up to his office and leaned back in his chair, whose cushion would have been thrown out of its basket in disgust by an incontinent dog, pulled his helmet over his eyes, and tried to think.

No good rushing about. The dragon had vanished in all the smoke and confusion, as suddenly as it had come. Time for rushing about soon enough. The important thing was working out where to rush to . . .

He'd been right. Wading bird! But where did you start looking for a bloody great dragon in a city of a million people?

He was aware that his right hand, entirely unbidden, had pulled open the bottom drawer, and three of his fingers, acting on sealed orders from his hindbrain, had lifted out a bottle. It was one of those bottles that emptied themselves. Reason told him that sometimes he must occasionally start one, break the seal, see amber liquid glistening all the way up to the neck. It was just that he couldn't remember the sensation. It was as if the bottles arrived two-thirds empty . . .

He stared at the label. It seemed to be Jimkin Bearhugger's Old Selected Dragon's Blood Whiskey. Cheap and powerful, you could light fires with it, you could clean spoons. You didn't have to drink much of it to be drunk, which was just as well.

It was Nobby who shook him awake with the news that there was a dragon in the city, and also that Sgt Colon had had a nasty turn. Vimes sat and blinked owlishly while the words washed around him. Apparently having a fire-breathing lizard focusing interestedly on one's nether regions from a distance of a few feet can upset the strongest constitution. An experience like that could leave a lasting mark on a person.

Vimes was still digesting this when Carrot turned up with the Librarian swinging along behind him.

'Did you see it? Did you see it?' he said.

'We all saw it,' said Vimes.

'I know all about it!' said Carrot triumphantly. 'Someone's brought it here with magic. Someone's stolen a book out of the Library and guess what it's called?'

'Can't even begin to,' said Vimes weakly.

'It's called *The Summoning of Dragons*!'

'Oook,' confirmed the Librarian.

'Oh? What's it about?' said Vimes. The Librarian rolled his eyes.

'It's about how to summon dragons. By magic!'

'Oook.'

'And that's illegal, that is!' said Carrot happily. 'Releasing Feral Creatures upon the Streets, contrary to the Wild Animals (Public—'

Vimes groaned. That meant wizards. You got nothing but trouble with wizards.

'I suppose,' he said, 'there wouldn't be another copy of this book around, would there?'

'Oook.' The Librarian shook his head.

'And you wouldn't happen to know what's in it?' Vimes sighed. 'What? Oh. Four words,' he said wearily. 'First word. Sounds like. Bend. Bough? Sow, cow, how . . . How. Second word. Small word. The, a, to . . . To. Yes, *understood*, but I meant in any kind of detail? No. I see.'

'What're we going to do now, sir?' said Carrot anxiously.

'It's out there,' intoned Nobby. 'Gone to ground, like, during the hours of daylight. Coiled up in its secret lair, on top of a great hoard of gold, dreamin' ancient reptilian dreams fromma dawna time, waitin' for the secret curtains of the night, when once more it will sally forth—' He hesitated and added sullenly, 'What're you all looking at me like that for?'

'Very poetic,' said Carrot.

'Well, everyone knows the real old dragons used to go to sleep on a hoard of gold,' said Nobby. 'Well known folk myth.'

Vimes looked blankly into the immediate future. Vile though Nobby was, he was also a good indication of what was going through the mind of the average citizen. You could use him as a sort of laboratory rat to forecast what was going to happen next.

'I expect you'd be really interested in finding out where that hoard is, wouldn't you?' said Vimes experimentally.

Nobby looked even more shifty than usual. 'Well, Cap'n, I was thinking of having a bit of a look around. You know. When I'm off duty, of course,' he added virtuously.

'Oh, dear,' said Captain Vimes.

He lifted up the empty bottle and, with great care, put it back in the drawer.

*

The Elucidated Brethren were nervous. A kind of fear crackled from brother to brother. It was the fear of someone who, having cheerfully experimented with pouring the powder and wadding the ball, has found that pulling the trigger had led to a godawful bang and pretty soon someone is bound to come and see who's making all the noise.

The Supreme Grand Master knew that he had them, though. Sheep and lamb, sheep and lamb. Since they couldn't do anything much worse than they had already done they might as well press on and damn the world, and pretend they'd wanted it like this all along. Oh, the joy of it . . .

Only Brother Plasterer was actually happy.

'Let that be a lesson to all oppressive vegetable sellers,' he kept saying.

'Yes, er,' said Brother Doorkeeper. 'Only, the thing is, there's no chance of us sort of accidentally summoning the dragon *here*, is there?'

'I – that is, *we* – have it under perfect control,' said the Supreme Grand Master smoothly. 'The power is ours. I can assure you.'

The Brothers cheered up a little bit.

'And now,' the Supreme Grand Master continued, 'there is the matter of the king.'

The Brothers looked solemn, except for Brother Plasterer.

'Have we found him, then?' he said. 'That's a stroke of luck.'

'You never listen, do you?' snapped Brother Watchtower. 'It was all explained last week, we don't go around *finding* anyone, we *make* a king.'

'I thought he was supposed to turn up. 'Cos of destiny.'

Brother Watchtower sniggered. 'We sort of help Destiny along a bit.'

The Supreme Grand Master smiled in the depths of his robe. It was amazing, this mystic business. You tell them a lie, and then when you don't need it any more you tell them another lie and tell them they're progressing along the road to wisdom. Then instead of laughing they follow you even more, hoping that at the heart of all the lies they'll find the truth. And bit by bit they accept the unacceptable. Amazing.

'Bloody hell, that's clever,' said Brother Doorkeeper. 'How do we do that, then?'

'Look, the Supreme Grand Master said what we do, we find some handsome lad who's good at taking orders, he kills the dragon, and Bob's your uncle. Simple. Much more *intelligent* than waitin' for a so-called real king.'

'But—' Brother Plasterer seemed deep in the toils of cerebration, 'if *we* control the dragon, and we *do* control the dragon, right? Then we don't need anyone killing it, we just stop summoning it, and everyone'll be happy, right?'

'Ho yes,' said Brother Watchtower nastily, 'I can just see it, can you? We just trot out, say "Hello, we won't set fire to your houses any more, aren't we nice", do we? The whole point about the thing with the king is that he'll be a, a sort of—'

'Undeniably potent and romantic symbol of absolute authority,' said the Supreme Grand Master smoothly.

'That's it,' said Brother Watchtower. 'A potent authority.'

'Oh, I *see*,' said Brother Plasterer. 'Right. Okay. That's what the king'll be.'

'That's it,' said Brother Watchtower.

'No-one going to argue with a potent authority, are they?'

'Too right,' said Brother Watchtower.

'Stroke of luck, then, finding the true king right now,' said Brother Plasterer. 'Million to one chance, really.'

'We *haven't* found the right king. We don't *need* the right king,' said the Supreme Grand Master wearily. 'For the last time! I've just found us a likely lad who looks good in a crown and can take orders and knows how to flourish a sword. Now just *listen . . .*'

Flourishing, of course, was important. It didn't have much to do with wielding. Wielding a sword, the Supreme Grand Master considered, was simply the messy business of dynastic surgery. It was just a matter of thrust and cut. Whereas a king had to flourish one. It had to catch the light in just the right way, leaving watchers in no doubt that here was Destiny's chosen. He'd taken a long time preparing the sword and shield. It had been very expensive. The shield shone like a dollar in a sweep's earhole but the sword, the sword was magnificent . . .

It was long and shiny. It looked like something some genius of metalwork – one of those little Zen guys who works only by the light of dawn and can beat a club sandwich of folded steels into something with the cutting edge of a scalpel and the stopping-power of a sex-crazed rhinoceros on bad acid – had made and then retired in tears because he'd never, ever, do anything so good again. There were so many jewels on the hilt it had to be sheathed in velvet, you had to look at it through smoked glass. Just laying a hand on it practically conferred kingship.

As for the lad . . . he was a distant cousin, keen and vain, and stupid in a passably aristocratic way. Currently he was under guard in a distant farmhouse, with an adequate supply of drink and several young ladies, although what the boy seemed most interested in was mirrors. Probably hero material, the Supreme Grand Master thought glumly.

'I suppose,' said Brother Watchtower, 'that he *isn't* the real air to the throne?'

'What do you mean?' said the Supreme Grand Master.

'Well, you know how it is. Fate plays funny tricks. Haha. It'd be a laugh, wouldn't it,' said Brother Watchtower, 'if this lad turned out to be the real king. After all this trouble—'

'*There is no real king any more!*' snapped the Supreme Grand Master. 'What do you expect? Some people wandering in the wilderness for hundreds and hundreds of years, patiently handing down a sword and a birthmark? Some sort of *magic?*' He spat the word. He'd make use of magic, means to an end, end justifies means and so forth, but to go around believing it, believing it had some sort of moral force, like logic, made him wince. 'Good grief, man, be logical! Be rational. Even if any of the old royal family survived, the blood line'd be so watered down by now that there must be thousands of people who lay claim to the throne. Even – ' he tried to think of the least likely claimant – 'even someone like Brother Dunnykin.' He stared at the assembled Brethren. 'Don't see him here tonight, by the way.'

'Funny thing, that,' said Brother Watchtower thoughtfully. 'Didn't you hear?'

'What?'

'He got bitten by a crocodile on his way home last night. Poor little bugger.'

'*What?*'

'Million to one chance. It'd escaped from a menagerie, or something, and was lying low in his back yard. He went to feel under his doormat for his doorkey and it had him by the funes.'* Brother Watchtower fumbled under his robe and produced a grubby brown envelope. 'We're having a whip-round to buy him some grapes and that, I don't know whether you'd like to, er . . .'

'Put me down for three dollars,' said the Supreme Grand Master.

Brother Watchtower nodded. 'Funny thing,' he said, 'I already have.'

Just a few more nights, thought the Supreme Grand Master. By tomorrow the people'll be so desperate, they'd crown even a one-legged troll if he got rid of the dragon. And we'll have a king, and he'll have an advisor, a trusted man, of course, and this stupid rabble can go back to the gutter. No more dressing up, no more ritual.

---

* A species of geranium.

No more summoning the dragon.

I can give it up, he thought. I can give it up any time I like.

The streets outside the Patrician's palace were thronged. There was a manic air of carnival. Vimes ran a practised eye over the assortment before him. It was the usual Ankh-Morpork mob in times of crisis; half of them were here to complain, a quarter of them were here to watch the other half, and the remainder were here to rob, importune or sell hot-dogs to the rest. There were a few new faces, though. There were a number of grim men with big swords slung over their shoulders and whips slung on their belts, striding through the crowds.

'News spreads quick, don't it,' observed a familiar voice by his ear. 'Morning, Captain.'

Vimes looked into the grinning, cadaverous face of Cut-me-own-Throat Dibbler, purveyor of absolutely anything that could be sold hurriedly from an open suitcase in a busy street and was guaranteed to have fallen off the back of an oxcart.

'Morning, Throat,' said Vimes absently. 'What're you selling?'

'Genuine article, Captain.' Throat leaned closer. He was the sort of person who could make 'Good morning' sound like a once-in-a-lifetime, never-to-be-repeated offer. His eyes swivelled back and forth in their sockets, like two rodents trying to find a way out. 'Can't afford to be without it,' he hissed. 'Anti-dragon cream. Personal guarantee: if you're incinerated you get your money back, no quibble.'

'What you're saying,' said Vimes slowly, 'if I understand the wording correctly, is that if I am baked alive by the dragon you'll return the money?'

'Upon personal application,' said Cut-me-own-Throat. He unscrewed the lid from a jar of vivid green ointment and thrust it under Vimes's nose. 'Made from over fifty different rare spices and herbs to a recipe known only to a bunch of ancient monks what live on some mountain somewhere. One dollar a jar, and I'm cutting my own throat. It's a public service, really,' he added piously.

'You've got to hand it to those ancient monks, brewing it up so quickly,' said Vimes.

'Clever buggers,' agreed Cut-me-own-Throat. 'It must be all that meditation and yak yogurt.'

'So what's happening, Throat?' said Vimes. 'Who're all the guys with the big swords?'

'Dragon hunters, Capt'n. The Patrician announced a reward of fifty thousand dollars to anyone who brings him the dragon's head. Not attached to the dragon, either; he's no fool, that man.'

'What?'

'That's what he said. It's all written on posters.'

'Fifty thousand dollars!'

'Not chicken feed, eh?'

'More like dragon fodder,' said Vimes. It'd bring trouble, you mark his words. 'I'm amazed you're not grabbing a sword and joining in.'

'I'm more in what you might call the service sector, Cap'n.' Throat looked both ways conspiratorially, and then passed Vimes a slip of parchment.

It said:

Anti-dragon mirror shields A$ 500

Portable lair detectors A$250

Dragon-piercing arrows A$100 per each

Shovels A$5 Picks A$5 Sacks A$1

Vimes handed it back. 'Why the sacks?' he said.

'On account of the hoard,' said Throat.

'Oh, yes,' said Vimes gloomily. 'Of course.'

'Tell you what,' said Throat, 'tell you what. For our boys in brown, ten percent off.'

'And you're cutting your own throat, Throat?'

'Fifteen percent for officers!' urged Throat, as Vimes walked away. The cause of the slight panic in his voice was soon apparent. He had plenty of competition.

The people of Ankh-Morpork were not by nature heroic but were, by nature, salesmen. In the space of a few feet Vimes could have bought any number of magical weapons *Genuine certyfycate of orthenticity with everyone*, a cloak of invisibility – a good touch, he thought, and he was really impressed by the way the stallowner was using a mirror with no glass in it – and, by way of lighter relief, dragon biscuits, balloons and windmills on sticks. Copper bracelets guaranteed to bring relief from dragons were a nice thought.

There seemed to be as many sacks and shovels about as there were swords.

Gold, that was it. The hoard. Hah!

Fifty thousand dollars! An officer of the Watch earned thirty dollars a month and had to pay to have his own dents beaten out.

What he couldn't do with fifty thousand dollars . . .

Vimes thought about this for a while and then thought of the things he *could* do with fifty thousand dollars. There were so many more of them, for a start.

He almost walked into a group of men clustered around a poster nailed to the wall. It declared, indeed, that the head of the dragon that had terrorized the city would be worth A$50,000 to the brave hero that delivered it to the palace.

One of the cluster, who from his size, weaponry and that way he was slowly tracing the lettering with his finger Vimes decided was a leading hero, was doing the reading for the others.

'—to ter-her pal-ack-ee,' he concluded.

'Fifty thousand,' said one of them reflectively, rubbing his chin.

'Cheap job,' said the intellectual. 'Well below the rate. Should be half the kingdom and his daughter's hand in marriage.'

'Yes, but he ain't a king. He's a Patrician.'

'Well, half his Patrimony or whatever. What's his daughter like?'

The assembled hunters didn't know.

'He's not married,' Vimes volunteered. 'And he hasn't got a daughter.'

They turned and looked him up and down. He could see the disdain in their eyes. They probably got through dozens like him every day. 'Not got a daughter?' said one of them. 'Wants people to kill dragons and he hasn't got a daughter?'

Vimes felt, in an odd way, that he ought to support the lord of the city. 'He's got a little dog that he's very fond of,' he said helpfully.

'Bleeding disgusting, not even having a daughter,' said one of the hunters. 'And what's fifty thousand dollars these days? You spend that much in nets.'

'S'right,' said another. 'People think it's a fortune, but they don't reckon on, well, it's not pensionable, there's all the medical expenses, you've got to buy and maintain your own gear—'

'—wear and tear on virgins—' nodded a small fat hunter.

'Yeah, and then there's . . . what?'

'My speciality is unicorns,' the hunter explained, with an embarrassed smile.

'Oh, right.' The first speaker looked like someone who'd always been dying to ask the question. 'I thought they were very rare these days.'

'You're right there. You don't see many unicorns, either,' said the unicorn hunter. Vimes got the impression that, in his whole life, this was his only joke.

'Yeah, well. Times are hard,' said the first speaker sharply.

'Monsters are getting more uppity, too,' said another. 'I heard where this guy, he killed this monster in this lake, no problem, stuck its arm up over the door—'

'Pour encourjay lays ortras,' said one of the listeners.

'Right, and you know what? Its mum come and complained. Its actual mum come right down to the hall next day and *complained*. Actually *complained*. That's the respect you get.'

'The females are always the worst,' said another hunter gloomily. 'I knew this cross-eyed gorgon once, oh, she was a terror. Kept turning her own nose to stone.'

'It's *our* arses on the line every time,' said the intellectual. 'I mean, I wish I had a dollar for every horse I've had eaten out from underneath me.'

'Right. Fifty thousand dollars? He can stuff it.'

'Yeah.'

'Right. Cheapskate.'

'Let's go and have a drink.'

'Right.'

They nodded in righteous agreement and strode off towards the Mended Drum, except for the intellectual, who sidled uneasily back to Vimes.

'What sort of dog?' he said.

'What?' said Vimes.

'I said, what sort of dog?'

'A small wire-haired terrier, I think,' said Vimes.

The hunter thought about this for some time. 'Nah,' he said eventually, and hurried off after the others.

'He's got an aunt in Pseudopolis, I believe,' Vimes called after him.

There was no response. The captain of the Watch shrugged, and carried on through the throng to the Patrician's palace . . .

. . . where the Patrician was having a difficult lunchtime.

'Gentlemen!' he snapped. 'I really don't see what else there is to do!'

The assembled civic leaders muttered amongst themselves.

'At times like this it's traditional that a hero comes forth,' said the President of the Guild of Assassins. 'A dragon slayer. Where is he, that's what I want to know? Why aren't our schools turning out young people with the kind of skills society needs?'

'Fifty thousand dollars doesn't sound much,' said the Chairman of the Guild of Thieves.

'It may not be much to you, my dear sir, but it is all the city can afford,' said the Patrician firmly.

'If it doesn't afford any more than that I don't think there'll *be* a city for long,' said the thief.

'And what about trade?' said the representative of the Guild of Merchants. 'People aren't going to sail here with a cargo of rare comestibles just to have it incinerated, are they?'

'Gentlemen! Gentlemen!' The Patrician raised his hands in a conciliatory fashion. 'It seems to me,' he went on, taking advantage of the brief pause, 'that what we have here is a strictly *magical* phenomenon. I would like to hear from our learned friend on this point. Hmm?'

Someone nudged the Archchancellor of Unseen University, who had nodded off.

'Eh? What?' said the wizard, startled into wakefulness.

'We were wondering,' said the Patrician loudly, 'what you were intending to do about this dragon of yours?'

The Archchancellor was old, but a lifetime of survival in the world of competitive wizardry and the byzantine politics of Unseen University meant that he could whip up a defensive argument in a split second. You didn't remain Archchancellor for long if you let *that* sort of ingenuous remark whizz past your ear.

'*My* dragon?' he said.

'It's well known that the great dragons are extinct,' said the Patrician brusquely. 'And, besides, their natural habitat was definitely rural. So it seems to me that this one must be mag—'

'With respect, Lord Vetinari,' said the Archchancellor, 'it has often been *claimed* that dragons are extinct, but the current evidence, if I may make so bold, tends to cast a certain doubt on the theory. As to habitat, what we are seeing here is simply a change of behaviour pattern, occasioned by the spread of urban areas into the countryside which has led many hitherto rural creatures to adopt, nay in many cases to positively embrace, a more municipal mode of existence, and many of them thrive on the new opportunities thereby opened to them. For example, foxes are always knocking over my dustbins.'

He beamed. He'd managed to get all the way through it without actually needing to engage his brain.

'Are you saying,' said the assassin slowly, 'that what we've got here is the first *civic* dragon?'

'That's evolution for you,' said the wizard, happily. 'It should do well, too,' he added. 'Plenty of nesting sites, and a more than adequate food supply.'

Silence greeted this statement, until the merchant said, 'What exactly is it that they *do* eat?'

The thief shrugged. 'I seem to recall stories about virgins chained to huge rocks,' he volunteered.

'It'll starve round here, then,' said the assassin. 'We're on loam.'

'They used to go around ravening,' said the thief. 'Dunno if that's any help . . .'

'Anyway,' said the leader of the merchants, 'it seems to be your problem again, my lord.'

Five minutes later the Patrician was striding the length of the Oblong Office, fuming.

'They were laughing at me,' said the Patrician. 'I could tell!'

'Did you suggest a working party?' said Wonse.

'Of course I did! It didn't do the trick this time. You know, I really am inclined to increase the reward money.'

'I don't think that would work, my lord. Any proficient monster slayer knows the rate for the job.'

'Ha! Half the kingdom,' muttered the Patrician.

'And your daughter's hand in marriage,' said Wonse.

'I suppose an aunt isn't acceptable?' the Patrician said hopefully.

'Tradition demands a daughter, my lord.'

The Patrician nodded gloomily.

'Perhaps we can buy it off,' he said aloud. 'Are dragons intelligent?'

'I believe the word traditionally is "cunning", my lord,' said Wonse. 'I understand they have a liking for gold.'

'Really? What do they spend it on?'

'They sleep on it, my lord.'

'What, do you mean in a mattress?'

'No, my lord. On *it*.'

The Patrician turned this fact over in his mind. 'Don't they find it rather knobbly?' he said.

'So I would imagine, sir. I don't suppose anyone has ever asked.'

'Hmm. Can they talk?'

'They're apparently good at it, my lord.'

'Ah. Interesting.'

The Patrician was thinking: if it can talk, it can negotiate. If it can negotiate, then I have it by the short – by the small scales, or whatever it is they have.

'And they are said to be silver tongued,' said Wonse. The Patrician leaned back in his chair.

'Only silver?' he said.

There was the sound of muted voices in the passageway outside and Vimes was ushered in.

'Ah, Captain,' said the Patrician, 'what progress?'

'I'm sorry, my lord?' said Vimes, as the rain dripped off his cape.

'Towards apprehending this dragon,' said the Patrician firmly.

'The wading bird?' said Vimes.

'You know very well what I mean,' said Vetinari sharply.

'Investigations are in hand,' said Vimes automatically.

The Patrician snorted. 'All you have to do is find its lair,' he said. 'Once you have the lair, you have the dragon. That's obvious. Half the city seems to be looking for it.'

'If there is a lair,' said Vimes.

Wonse looked up sharply.

'Why do you say that?'

'We are considering a number of possibilities,' said Vimes woodenly.

'If it has no lair, where does it spend its days?' said the Patrician.

'Inquiries are being pursued,' said Vimes.

'Then pursue them with alacrity. And find the lair,' said the Patrician sourly.

'Yes, sir. Permission to leave, sir?'

'Very well. But I shall expect progress by tonight, do you understand?'

Now why did I wonder if it has a lair? Vimes thought, as he stepped out into the daylight and the crowded square. Because it didn't look real, that's why. If it isn't real, it doesn't need to do anything we expect. How can it walk out of an alley it didn't go into?

Once you've ruled out the impossible then whatever is left, however improbable, must be the truth. The problem lay in working out what was impossible, of course. That was the trick, all right.

There was also the curious incident of the orang-utan in the night-time . . .

By day the Library buzzed with activity. Vimes moved through it diffidently. Strictly speaking, he could go anywhere in the city, but the University had always held that it fell under thaumaturgical law and he felt it wouldn't be wise to make the kind of enemies where you were lucky to end up the same temperature, let alone the same shape.

He found the Librarian hunched over his desk. The ape gave him an expectant look.

'Haven't found it yet. Sorry,' said Vimes. 'Enquiries are continuing. But there is a little help you can give me.'

'Oook?'

'Well, this is a magical library, right? I mean, these books are sort of intelligent, isn't that so? So I've been thinking: I bet if I got in here at night, they'd soon kick up a fuss. Because they don't know me. But if they *did* know me, they'd probably not mind. So whoever took the book would have to be a wizard, wouldn't they? Or someone who works for the University, at any rate.'

The Librarian glanced from side to side, then grasped Vimes's hand and led him into the seclusion of a couple of bookshelves. Only then did he nod his head.

'Someone they know?'

A shrug, and then another nod.

'That's why you told us, is it?'

'Oook.'

'And not the University Council?'

'Oook.'

'Any idea who it is?'

The Librarian shrugged, a decidedly expressive gesture for a body which was basically a sack between a pair of shoulderblades.

'Well, it's something. Let me know if any other strange things happen, won't you?' Vimes looked up at the banks of shelves. 'Stranger than usual, I mean.'

'Oook.'

'Thank you. It's a pleasure to meet a citizen who regards it as their duty to assist the Watch.'

The Librarian gave him a banana.

Vimes felt curiously elated as he stepped out into the city's throbbing streets again. He was definitely detecting things. They were little bits of things, like a jigsaw. No one of them made any real sense, but they all hinted at a bigger picture. All he needed to do was find a corner, or a bit of an edge . . .

He was pretty certain it wasn't a wizard, whatever the Librarian might think. Not a proper, paid-up wizard. This sort of thing wasn't their style.

And there was, of course, this business about the lair. The most sensible course would be to wait and see if the dragon turned up tonight, and try and see *where*. That meant a high place. Was there some way of detecting dragons themselves? He'd had a look at Cut-me-own-Throat Dibbler's dragon detectors, which consisted solely of a piece of wood on a metal stick. When the stick was burned through, you'd found your dragon. Like a lot of Cut-me-own-Throat's devices, it was completely efficient in its own special way while at the same time being totally useless.

There had to be a better way of finding the thing than waiting until your fingers were burned off.

*

The setting sun spread out on the horizon like a lightly-poached egg.

The rooftops of Ankh-Morpork sprouted a fine array of gargoyles even in normal times, but now they were alive with as ghastly an array of faces as ever were seen outside a woodcut about the evils of gin-drinking among the non-woodcut-buying classes. Many of the faces were attached to bodies holding a fearsome array of homely weapons that had been handed down from generation to generation for centuries, often with some force.

From his perch on the roof of the Watch House Vimes could see the wizards lining the rooftops of the University, and the gangs of opportunist hoard-researchers waiting in the streets, shovels at the ready. If the dragon really did have a bed somewhere in the city, then it would be sleeping on the floor tomorrow.

From somewhere below came the cry of Cut-me-own-Throat Dibbler, or one of his colleagues, selling hot sausages. Vimes felt a sudden surge of civic pride. There had to be something right about a citizenry which, when faced with catastrophe, thought about selling sausages to the participants.

The city waited. A few stars came out.

Colon, Nobby and Carrot were also on the roof. Colon was sulking because Vimes had forbidden him to use his bow and arrow.

These weren't encouraged in the city, since the heft and throw of a longbow's arrow could send it through an innocent bystander a hundred yards away rather than the innocent bystander at whom it was aimed.

'That's right,' said Carrot, 'the Projectile Weapons (Civic Safety) Act, 1634.'

'Don't you keep on quoting all that sort of stuff,' snapped Colon. 'We don't *have* any of them laws any more! That's all old stuff! It's all more wossname now. Pragmatic.'

'Law or no law,' said Vimes, '*I* say put it away.'

'But Captain, I was a dab hand at this!' protested Colon. 'Anyway,' he added peevishly, 'a lot of other people have got them.'

That was true enough. Neighbouring rooftops bristled like hedgehogs. If the wretched thing turned up, it was going to think it was flying through solid wood with slots in it. You could almost feel sorry for it.

'I said put it away,' said Vimes. 'I'm not having my guards shooting citizens. So put it away.'

'That's very true,' said Carrot. 'We're here to protect and to serve, aren't we, Captain.'

Vimes gave him a sidelong look. 'Er.' he said. 'Yeah. Yes. That's right.'

On the roof of her house on the hill, Lady Ramkin adjusted a rather inadequate folding chair on the roof, arranged the telescope, coffee flask and sandwiches on the parapet in front of her, and settled down to wait. She had a notebook on her knee.

Half an hour went by. Hails of arrows greeted a passing cloud, several unfortunate bats, and the rising moon.

'Bugger this for a game of soldiers,' said Nobby, eventually. 'It's been scared off.'

Sgt Colon lowered his pike. 'Looks like it,' he conceded.

'And it's getting chilly up here,' said Carrot. He politely nudged Captain Vimes, who was slumped against the chimney, staring moodily into space.

'Maybe we ought to be getting down, sir?' he said. 'Lots of people are.'

'Hmm?' said Vimes, without moving his head.

'Could be coming on to rain, too,' said Carrot.

Vimes said nothing. For some minutes he had been watching the Tower of Art, which was the centre of Unseen University and reputedly the oldest building in the city. It was certainly the tallest. Time, weather and indifferent repairs had given it a gnarled appearance, like a tree that has seen too many thunderstorms.

He was trying to remember its shape. As is the case with many things that are totally familiar, he hadn't really looked at it for years. Now he was trying to convince himself that the forest of little turrets and crenellations at its top looked just the same tonight as they had done yesterday

It was giving him some difficulty.

Without taking his eyes off it, he grabbed Sgt Colon's shoulder and gently pointed him in the right direction.

He said, 'Can you see anything odd about the top of the tower?'

Colon stared up for a while, and then laughed nervously. 'Well, it looks like there's a dragon sitting on it, doesn't it?'

'Yes. That's what I thought.'

'Only, only, only when you sort of look properly, you can see it's just made up out of shadows and clumps of ivy and that. I mean, if you half-close one eye, it looks like two old women and a wheelbarrow.'

Vimes tried this. 'Nope,' he said. 'It still looks like a dragon. A huge one. Sort of hunched up, and looking down. Look, you can see its wings folded up.'

'Beg pardon, sir. That's just a broken turret giving the effect.'

They watched it for a while.

Then Vimes said, 'Tell me, Sergeant – I ask in a spirit of pure inquiry – what do you think's causing the effect of a pair of huge wings unfurling?'

Colon swallowed.

'I think that's caused by a pair of huge wings, sir,' he said.

'Spot on, Sergeant.'

The dragon dropped. It wasn't a swoop. It simply kicked away from the top of the tower and half-fell, half-flew straight downwards, disappearing from view behind the University buildings.

Vimes caught himself listening for the thump.

And then the dragon was in view again, moving like an arrow, moving like a shooting star, moving like something that has somehow turned a thirty-two feet per second per second plummet into an unstoppable upward swoop. It glided over the rooftops at little more than head height, all the more horrible because of the sound. It was as though the air was slowly and carefully being torn in half.

The Watch threw themselves flat. Vimes caught a glimpse of huge, vaguely horse-like features before it slid past.

'Sodding arseholes,' said Nobby, from somewhere in the guttering.

Vimes redoubled his grip on the chimney and pulled himself upright. 'You are in uniform, Corporal Nobbs,' he said, his voice hardly shaking at all.

'Sorry, Captain. Sodding arseholes, *sir.*'

'Where's Sergeant Colon?'

'Down here, sir. Holding on to this drainpipe, sir.'

'Oh, for goodness sake. Help him up, Carrot.'

'Gosh,' said Carrot, 'look at it go!'

You could tell the position of the dragon by the rattle of arrows across the city, and by the screams and gurgles of all those hit by the misses and ricochets.

'He hasn't even flapped his wings yet!' shouted Carrot, trying to stand on the chimney pot. 'Look at him *go!*'

It shouldn't be that *big*, Vimes told himself, watching the huge shape wheel over the river. It's as long as a street!

There was a puff of flame above the docks, and for a moment the creature passed in front of the moon. *Then* it flapped its wings, once, with a sound like the damp hides of a pedigree herd being slapped across a cliff.

It turned in a tight circle, pounded the air a few times to build up speed, and came back.

When it passed over the Watch House it coughed a column of

spitting white fire. Tiles under it didn't just melt, they erupted in red-hot droplets. The chimney stack exploded and rained bricks across the street.

Vast wings hammered at the air as the creature hovered over the burning building, fire spearing down on what rapidly became a glowing heap. Then, when all that was left was a spreading puddle of melted rock with interesting streaks and bubbles in it, the dragon raised itself with a contemptuous flick of its wings and soared away and upwards, over the city.

Lady Ramkin lowered her telescope and shook her head slowly.

'That's not right,' she whispered. 'That's not right at *all*. Shouldn't be able to do anything like *that*.'

She raised the lens again and squinted, trying to see what was on fire. Down below, in their long kennels, the little dragons howled.

Traditionally, upon waking from blissfully uneventful insensibility, you ask: 'Where am I?' It's probably part of the racial consciousness or something.

Vimes said it.

Tradition allows a choice of second lines. A key point in the selection process is an audit to see that the body has all the bits it remembers having yesterday.

Vimes checked.

Then comes the tantalizing bit. Now that the snowball of consciousness is starting to roll, is it going to find that it's waking up inside a body lying in a gutter with something multiple, the noun doesn't matter after an adjective like 'multiple', nothing good ever follows 'multiple', or is it going to be a case of crisp sheets, a soothing hand, and a businesslike figure in white pulling open the curtains on a bright new day? Is it all over, with nothing worse to look forward to now than weak tea, nourishing gruel, short, strengthening walks in the garden and possibly a brief platonic love affair with a ministering angel, or was this all just a moment's blackout and some looming bastard is now about to get down to real business with the thick end of a pickaxe helve? Are there, the consciousness wants to know, going to be grapes?

At this point some outside stimulus is helpful. 'It's going to be all right' is favourite, whereas 'Did anyone get his number?' is definitely a bad sign; either, however, is better than 'You two hold his hands behind his back'.

In fact someone said, 'You were nearly a goner there, Captain.'

The pain sensations, which had taken advantage of Vimes's unconscious state to bunk off for a metaphorical quick cigarette, rushed back.

Vimes said, 'Arrgh.' Then he opened his eyes.

There was a ceiling. This ruled out one particular range of unpleasant options and was very welcome. His blurred vision also revealed Corporal Nobbs, which was less so. Corporal Nobbs proved nothing; you could be *dead* and see something like Corporal Nobbs.

Ankh-Morpork did not have many hospitals. All the Guilds maintained their own sanitariums, and there were a few public ones run by the odder religious organisations, like the Balancing Monks, but by and large medical assistance was nonexistent and people had to die inefficiently, without the aid of doctors. It was generally thought that the existence of cures encouraged slackness and was in any case probably against Nature's way.

'Have I already said "Where am I?"' said Vimes faintly.

'Yes.'

'Did I get an answer?'

'Dunno where this place is, Captain. It belongs to some posh bint. She said to bring you up here.'

Even though Vimes's mind appeared to be full of pink treacle he nevertheless grabbed two clues and wrestled them together. The combination of 'rich' and 'up here' meant something. So did the strange chemical smell in the room, which even overpowered Nobby's more everyday odours.

'We're not talking about Lady Ramkin, are we?' he said cautiously.

'You could be right. Great big biddy. Mad for dragons.' Nobby's rodent face broke into the most horribly knowing grin Vimes had ever seen. 'You're in her bed,' he said.

Vimes peered around him, feeling the first overtures of a vague panic. Because now that he could halfway focus, he could see a certain lack of bachelor sockness about the place. There was a faint hint of talcum powder.

'Bit of a boodwah,' said Nobby, with the air of a connoisseur.

'Hang on, hang on a minute,' said Vimes. 'There was this dragon. It was right over us . . .'

The memory rose up and hit him like a zombie with a grudge.

'You all right, Captain?'

—the talons, outspread, wide as a man's reach; the boom and thump of the wings, bigger than sails; the stink of chemicals, the gods alone knew what sort . . .

It had been so close he could see the tiny scales on its legs and the red gleam in its eyes. They were more than just reptile eyes. They were eyes you could drown in.

And the breath, so hot that it wasn't like fire at all, but something almost solid, not burning things but smashing them apart . . .

On the other hand, he was here and alive. His left side felt as though it had been hit with an iron bar, but he was quite definitely alive.

'What happened?' he said.

'It was young Carrot,' said Nobby. 'He grabbed you and the sergeant and jumped off the roof just before it got us.'

'My side hurts. It must have got me,' said Vimes.

'No, I reckon that was where you hit the privy roof,' said Nobby. 'And then you rolled off and hit the water butt.'

'What about Colon? Is he hurt?'

'Not hurt. Not exactly *hurt*. He landed more sort of softly. Him being so heavy, he went *through* the roof. Talk about a short sharp shower of—'

'And then what happened?'

'Well, we sort of made you comfy, and then everyone went blundering about and shouting for the sergeant. Until they found out where he was, o'course, then they just stood where they were and shouted. And then this woman come running up yelling,' said Nobby.

'This is Lady Ramkin you're referring to?' said Vimes coldly. His ribs were aching really magnificently now.

'Yeah. Big fat party,' said Nobby, unmoved. 'Cor, she can't half boss people about! "Oh, the poor dear man, you must bring him up to my house this instant." So we did. Best place, too. Everyone's running around down in the city like chickens with their heads cut off.'

'How much damage did it do?'

'Well, after you were out of it the wizards hit it with fireballs. It didn't like that at all. Just seemed to make it stronger and angrier. Took out the University's entire Widdershins wing.'

'And—?'

'That's about it, really. It flamed a few more things, and then it must of flown away in all the smoke.'

'No-one saw where it went?'

'If they did, they ain't saying.' Nobby sat back and leered. 'Disgusting, really, her livin' in a room like this. She's got pots of money, sarge says, she's got no call livin' in ordinary rooms. What's the good of not wanting to be poor if the rich are allowed to go round livin' in ordinary rooms? Should be marble.' He sniffed.

'Anyway, she said I was to fetch her when you woke up. She's feeding her dragons now. Odd little buggers, aren't they. It's amazing she's allowed to keep 'em.'

'What do you mean?'

'You know. Tarred with the same brush, and that.'

When Nobby had shambled out Vimes took another look around the room. It did, indeed, lack the gold leaf and marble that Nobby felt was compulsory for people of a high station in life. All the furniture was old, and the pictures on the wall, though doubtless valuable, looked the sort of pictures that are hung on bedroom walls because people can't think of anywhere else to put them. There were also a few amateurish watercolours of dragons. All in all, it had the look about it of a room that is only ever occupied by one person, and has been absent-mindedly moulded around them over the years, like a suit of clothes with a ceiling.

It was clearly the room of a woman, but one who had cheerfully and without any silly moping been getting on with her life while all that soppy romance stuff had been happening to other people somewhere else, and been jolly grateful that she had her health.

Such clothing as was visible had been chosen for sensible hard-wearing qualities, possibly by a previous generation by the look of it, rather than its use as light artillery in the war between the sexes. There were bottles and jars neatly arranged on the dressing table, but a certain severity of line suggested that their labels would say things like 'Rub on nightly' rather than 'Just a dab behind the ears'. You could imagine that the occupant of this room had slept in it all her life and had been called 'my little girl' by her father until she was forty.

There was a big sensible blue dressing gown hanging behind the door. Vimes knew, without even looking, that it would have a rabbit on the pocket.

In short, it was the room of a woman who never expected that a man would ever see the inside of it.

The bedside table was piled high with papers. Feeling guilty, but doing it anyway, Vimes squinted at them.

Dragons was the theme. There were letters from the Cavern Club Exhibitions Committee and the Friendly Flamethrowers League. There were pamphlets and appeals from the Sunshine Sanctuary for Sick Dragons – 'Poor little VINNY's fires were nearly Damped after Five years' Cruel Use as a Paint-Stripper, but now—' And there were requests for donations, and talks, and things that added up to a heart big enough for the whole world, or at least that part of it that had wings and breathed fire.

If you let your mind dwell on rooms like this, you could end up being oddly sad and full of a strange, diffuse compassion which would lead you to believe that it might be a good idea to wipe out the whole human race and start again with amoebas.

Beside the drift of paperwork was a book. Vimes twisted painfully and looked at the spine. It said: *Diseases of the Dragon*, by Sybil Deidre Olgivanna Ramkin.

He turned the stiff pages in horrified fascination. They opened into another world, a world of quite stupefying problems. Slab Throat. The Black Tups. Dry Lung. Storge. Staggers, Heaves, Weeps, Stones. It was amazing, he decided after reading a few pages, that a swamp dragon ever survived to see a second sunrise. Even walking across a room must be reckoned a biological triumph.

The painstakingly-drawn illustrations he looked away from hurriedly. You could only take so much innards.

There was a knock at the door.

'I say? Are you decent?' Lady Ramkin boomed cheerfully.

'Er—'

'I've brought you something jolly nourishing.'

Somehow Vimes imagined it would be soup. Instead it was a plate stacked high with bacon, fried potatoes and eggs. He could hear his arteries panic just by looking at it.

'I've made a bread pudding, too,' said Lady Ramkin, slightly sheepishly. 'I don't normally cook much, just for myself. You know how it is, catering for one.'

Vimes thought about the meals at his lodgings. Somehow the meat was always grey, with mysterious tubes in it.

'Er,' he began, not used to addressing ladies from a recumbent position in their own beds. 'Corporal Nobbs tells me—'

'And what a colourful little man Nobby is!' said Lady Ramkin.

Vimes wasn't certain he could cope with this.

'Colourful?' he said weakly.

'A real character. We've been getting along famously.'

'You have?'

'Oh, yes. What a great fund of anecdotes he has.'

'Oh, yes. He's got that all right.' It always amazed Vimes how Nobby got along with practically everyone. It must, he'd decided, have something to do with the common denominator. In the entire world of mathematics there could be no denominator as common as Nobby.

'Er,' he said, and then found he couldn't leave this strange new byway, 'you don't find his language a bit, er, ripe?'

'Salty,' corrected Lady Ramkin cheerfully. 'You should have heard my father when he was annoyed. Anyway, we found we've

got a lot in common. It's an amazing coincidence, but my grandfather once had his grandfather whipped for malicious lingering. '

That must make them practically family, Vimes thought.
Another stab of pain from his stricken side made him wince.

'You've got some very bad bruising and probably a cracked rib or
two,' she said. 'If you roll over I'll put some more of this on.' Lady
Ramkin flourished a jar of yellow ointment.

Panic crossed Vimes's face. Instinctively, he raised the sheets up
around his neck.

'Don't play silly buggers, man,' she said. 'I shan't see anything I
haven't seen before. One backside is pretty much like another. It's
just that the ones I see generally have tails on. Now roll over and
up with the nightshirt. It belonged to my grandfather, you know.'

There was no resisting that tone of voice. Vimes thought about
demanding that Nobby be brought in as a chaperon, and then
decided that would be even worse.

The cream burned like ice.

'What *is* it?'

'All kinds of stuff. It'll reduce the bruising and promote the
growth of healthy scale.'

'What?'

'Sorry. Probably not scale. Don't look so worried. I'm almost
positive about that. Okay, all done.' She gave him a slap on the
rump.

'Madam, I am Captain of the Night Watch,' said Vimes, knowing
it was a bloody daft thing to say even as he said it.

'Half naked in a lady's bed, too,' said Lady Ramkin, unmoved.
'Now sit up and eat your tea. We've got to get you good and
strong.'

Vimes's eyes filled with panic.

'Why?' he said.

Lady Ramkin reached into the pocket of her grubby jacket.

'I made some notes last night,' she said. 'About the dragon.'

'Oh, the dragon.' Vimes relaxed a bit. Right now the dragon
seemed a much safer prospect.

'And I did a bit of working out, too. I'll tell you this: it's a very
odd beast. It shouldn't be able to get airborne.'

'You're right there.'

'If it's built like swamp dragons, it should weigh about twenty
tons. Twenty tons! It's impossible. It's all down to weight and
wingspan ratios, you see.'

'I saw it drop off the tower like a swallow.'

'I know. It should have torn its wings off and left a bloody great
hole in the ground,' said Lady Ramkin firmly. 'You can't muck

about with aerodynamics. You can't just scale up from small to big and leave it at that, you see. It's all a matter of muscle power and lifting surfaces.'

'I *knew* there was something wrong,' said Vimes, brightening up. 'And the flame, too. Nothing goes around with that kind of heat inside it. How do swamp dragons manage it?'

'Oh, that's just chemicals,' said Lady Ramkin dismissively. 'They just distill something flammable from whatever they've eaten and ignite the flame just as it comes out of the ducts. They never actually have fire inside them, unless they get a case of blowback.'

'What happens then?'

'You're scraping dragon off the scenery,' said Lady Ramkin cheerfully. 'I'm afraid they're not very well-designed creatures, dragons.'

Vimes listened.

They would never have survived at all except that their home swamps were isolated and short of predators. Not that a dragon made good eating, anyway – once you'd taken away the leathery skin and the enormous flight muscles, what was left must have been like biting into a badly-run chemical factory. No wonder dragons were always ill. They relied on permanent stomach trouble for supplies of fuel. Most of their brain power was taken up with controlling the complexities of their digestion, which could distill flame-producing fuels from the most unlikely ingredients. They could even rearrange their internal plumbing overnight to deal with difficult processes. They lived on a chemical knife-edge the whole time. One misplaced hiccup and they were geography.

And when it came to choosing nesting sites, the females had all the common sense and mothering instinct of a brick.

Vimes wondered why people had been so worried about dragons in the olden days. If there was one in a cave near you, all you had to do was wait until it self-ignited, blew itself up, or died of acute indigestion.

'You've really studied them, haven't you,' he said.

'Someone ought to.'

'But what about the big ones?'

'Golly, yes. They're a great mystery, you know,' she said, her expression becoming extremely serious.

'Yes, you said.'

'There are legends, you know. It seems as though one species of dragon started to get bigger and bigger and then . . . just vanished.'

'Died out, you mean?'

'No . . . they turned up, sometimes. From somewhere. Full of vim and vigour. And then, one day, they stopped coming at all.' She gave Vimes a triumphant look. 'I think they found somewhere where they could really *be*.'

'Really be what?'

'Dragons. Where they could really fulfil their potential. Some other dimension or something. Where the gravity isn't so strong, or something.'

'I thought when I saw it,' said Vimes, 'I thought, you can't have something that flies *and* has scales like that.'

They looked at each other.

'We've got to find it in its lair,' said Lady Ramkin.

'No bloody flying newt sets fire to *my* city,' said Vimes.

'Just think of the contribution to dragon lore,' said Lady Ramkin.

'Listen, if anyone ever sets fire to this city, it's going to be *me*.'

'It's an amazing opportunity. There's so many questions . . .'

'You're right there.' A phrase of Carrot's crossed Vimes's mind. 'It can help us with our enquiries,' he suggested.

'But in the morning,' said Lady Ramkin firmly.

Vimes's look of bitter determination faded.

'I shall sleep downstairs, in the kitchen,' said Lady Ramkin cheerfully. 'I usually have a camp bed made up down there when it's egg-laying time. Some of the females always need assistance. Don't you worry about me.'

'You're being very helpful,' Vimes muttered.

'I've sent Nobby down to the city to help the others set up your headquarters,' said Lady Ramkin.

Vimes had completely forgotten the Watch House. 'It must have been badly damaged,' he ventured.

'Totally destroyed,' said Lady Ramkin. 'Just a patch of melted rock. So I'm letting you have a place in Pseudopolis Yard.'

'Sorry?'

'Oh, my father had property all over the city,' she said. 'Quite useless to me, really. So I told my agent to give Sergeant Colon the keys to the old house in Pseudopolis Yard. It'll do it good to be aired.'

'But that area – I mean, there's real cobbles on the streets – the rent alone, I mean, Lord Vetinari won't—'

'Don't you worry about it,' she said, giving him a friendly pat. 'Now, you really ought to get some sleep.'

Vimes lay in bed, his mind racing. Pseudopolis Yard was on the Ankh side of the river, in quite a high-rent district. The sight of Nobby or Sergeant Colon walking down the street in daylight would probably have the same effect on the area as the opening of a plague hospital.

He dozed, gliding in and out of a sleep where giant dragons pursued him waving jars of ointment . . .

And awoke to the sound of a mob.

Lady Ramkin drawing herself up haughtily was not a sight to forget, although you could try. It was like watching continental drift in reverse as various sub-continents and islands pulled themselves together to form one massive, angry protowoman.

The broken door of the dragon house swung on its hinges. The inmates, already as highly strung as a harp on amphetamines, were going mad. Little gouts of flame burst against the metal plates as they stampeded back and forth in their pens.

'Hwhat,' she said, 'is the meaning of this?'

If a Ramkin had ever been given to introspection she'd have admitted that it wasn't a very original line. But it was handy. It did the job. The reason that cliches become cliches is that they are the hammers and screwdrivers in the toolbox of communication.

The mob filled the broken doorway. Some of it was waving various sharp implements with the up-and-down motion proper to rioters.

'Worl,' said the leader, 'it's the dragon, innit?'

There was a chorus of muttered agreement.

'Hwhat about it?' said Lady Ramkin.

'Worl. It's been burning the city. They don't fly far. You got dragons here. Could be one of them, couldn't it?'

'Yeah.'

'S'right. '

'*QED.*'*

'So what we're going to do is, we're going to put 'em down.'

'S'right.'

'Yeah.'

'*Pro bono publico.*'

Lady Ramkin's bosom rose and fell like an empire. She reached out and grabbed the dunging fork from its hook on the wall.

'One step nearer, I warn you, and you'll be sorry,' she said.

The leader looked beyond her to the frantic dragons.

'Yeah?' he said, nastily. 'And what'll you do, eh?'

Her mouth opened and shut once or twice. 'I shall summon the Watch!' she said at last.

The threat did not have the effect she had expected. Lady

---

* Some rioters can be quite well-educated.

Ramkin had never paid much attention to those bits of the city that didn't have scales on.

'Well, that's too bad,' said the leader. 'That's really worrying, you know that? Makes me go all weak at the knees, that does.'

He extracted a lengthy cleaver from his belt. 'And now you just stand aside, lady, because—'

A streak of green fire blasted out of the back of the shed, passed a foot over the heads of the mob. and burned a charred rosette in the woodwork over the door.

Then came a voice that was a honeyed purr of sheer deadly menace.

'This is Lord Mountjoy Quickfang Winterforth IV, the hottest dragon in the city. It could burn your head clean off.'

Captain Vimes limped forward from the shadows.

A small and extremely frightened golden dragon was clamped firmly under one arm. His other hand held it by the tail.

The rioters watched it, hypnotized.

'Now I know what you're thinking,' Vimes went on, softly. 'You're wondering, after all this excitement, has it got enough flame left? And, y'know, I ain't so sure myself . . .'

He leaned forward, sighting between the dragon's ears, and his voice buzzed like a knife blade:

'What you've got to ask yourself is: Am I feeling lucky?'

They swayed backwards as he advanced.

'Well?' he said. '*Are* you feeling lucky?'

For a few moments the only sound was Lord Mountjoy Quickfang Winterforth IV's stomach rumbling ominously as fuel sloshed into his flame chambers.

'Now look, er,' said the leader, his eyes fixed hypnotically on the dragon's head, 'there's no call for anything like that—'

'In fact he might just decide to flare off all by himself,' said Vimes. 'They have to do it to stop the gas building up. It builds up when they get nervous. And, y'know, I reckon you've made them all pretty nervous now.'

The leader made what he hoped was a vaguely conciliatory gesture, but unfortunately did it with the hand that was still holding a knife.

'Drop it,' said Vimes sharply, 'or you're history.'

The knife clanged on the flagstones. There was a scuffle at the back of the crowd as a number of people, metaphorically speaking, were a long way away and knew nothing about it.

'But before the rest of you good citizens disperse quietly and go about your business,' said Vimes meaningfully, 'I suggest you look hard at these dragons. Do any of them look sixty feet long? Would

you say they've got an eighty-foot wingspan? How hot do they flame, would you say?'

'Dunno,' said the leader.

Vimes raised the dragon's head slightly. The leader rolled his eyes.

'Dunno, sir,' he corrected.

'Do you want to find out?'

The leader shook his head. But he did manage to find his voice.

'Who are you, anyway?' he said.

Vimes drew himself up. 'Captain Vimes, City Watch,' he said.

This met with almost complete silence. The exception was the cheerful voice, somewhere in the back of the crowd, which said: 'Night shift, is it?'

Vimes looked down at his nightshirt. In his hurry to get off his sickbed he'd shuffled hastily into a pair of Lady Ramkin's slippers. For the first time he saw they had pink pompoms on them.

And it was at this moment that Lord Mountjoy Quickfang Winterforth IV chose to belch.

It wasn't another stab of roaring fire. It was just a near-invisible ball of damp flame which rolled over the mob and singed a few eyebrows. But it definitely made an impression.

Vimes rallied magnificently. They couldn't have noticed his brief moment of sheer horror.

'That one was just to get your attention,' he said, poker-faced. 'The next one will be a little lower.'

'Er,' said the leader. 'Right you are. No problem. We were just going anyhow. No big dragons here, right enough. Sorry you've been troubled.'

'Oh, no,' said Lady Ramkin triumphantly. 'You don't get away *that* easily!' She reached up on to a shelf and produced a tin box. It had a slot in the lid. It rattled. On the side was the legend: *The Sunshine Sanctuary for Sick Dragons.*

The initial whip-round produced four dollars and thirty-one pence. After Captain Vimes gestured pointedly with the dragon, a further twenty-five dollars and sixteen pence were miraculously forthcoming. Then the mob fled.

'We made a profit on the day, anyway,' said Vimes, when they were alone again.

'That was jolly brave of you!'

'Let's just hope it doesn't catch on,' said Vimes, gingerly putting the exhausted dragon back in its pen. He felt quite light-headed.

Once again he was aware of eyes staring fixedly at him. He glanced sideways into the long, pointed face of Goodboy Bindle

Featherstone, rearing up in a pose best described as The Last Puppy in the Shop.

To his astonishment, he found himself reaching over and scratching it behind its ears, or at least behind the two spiky things at the sides of its head which were presumably its ears. It responded with a strange noise that sounded like a complicated blockage in a brewery. He took his hand away hurriedly.

'It's all right,' said Lady Ramkin. 'It's his stomachs rumbling. That means he likes you.'

To his amazement, Vimes found that he was rather pleased about this. As far as he could recall. nothing in his life before had thought him worth a burp.

'I thought you were, er, going to get rid of him,' he said.

'I suppose I shall have to,' she said. 'You know how it is, though. They look up at you with those big, soulful eyes—'

There was a brief, mutual, awkward silence.

'How would it be if I—'

'You don't think you might like—'

They stopped.

'It'd be the least I could do,' said Lady Ramkin.

'But you're already giving us the new headquarters and everything!'

'That was simply my duty as a good citizen,' said Lady Ramkin. 'Please accept Goodboy as, as a *friend*.'

Vimes felt that he was being inched out over a very deep chasm on a very thin plank.

'I don't even know what they eat,' he said.

'They're omnivores, actually,' she said. 'They eat everything except metal and igneous rocks. You can't be finicky, you see, when you evolve in a swamp.'

'But doesn't he need to be taken for walks? Or flights, or whatever?'

'He seems to sleep most of the time.' She scratched the ugly thing on top of its scaly head. 'He's the most relaxed dragon I've ever bred, I must say.'

'What about, er, you know?' He indicated the dunging fork.

'Well, it's mainly gas. Just keep him somewhere well ventilated. You haven't got any valuable carpets, have you? It's best not to let them lick your face, but they can be trained to control their flame. They're very helpful for lighting fires.'

Goodboy Bindle Featherstone curled up amidst a barrage of plumbing noises.

They've got eight stomachs, Vimes remembered; the drawings in the book had been very detailed. And there's lots of other stuff like fractional-distillation tubes and mad alchemy sets in there.

No swamp dragon could ever terrorize a kingdom, except by accident. Vimes wondered how many had been killed by enterprising heroes. It was terribly cruel to do something like that to creatures whose only crime was to blow themselves absent-mindedly to pieces in mid-air, which was not something any individual dragon made a habit of. It made him quite angry to think about it. A race of, of *whittles*, that's what dragons were. Born to lose. Live fast, die wide. Omnivores or not, what they must *really* live on was their nerves, flapping apologetically through the world in mortal fear of their own digestive system. The family would be just getting over father's explosion, and some twerp in a suit of armour would come plodding into the swamp to stick a sword into a bag of guts that was only one step away from self-destruction in any case.

Huh. It'd be interesting to see how the great dragon slayers of the past stood up to the *big* dragon. Armour? Best not to wear it. It'd all be the same in any case, and at least your ashes wouldn't come prepackaged in their own foil.

He stared and stared at the malformed little thing, and the idea that had been knocking for attention for the last few minutes finally gained entrance. Everyone in Ankh-Morpork wanted to find the dragon's lair. At least, wanted to find it empty. Bits of wood on a stick wouldn't do it, he was certain. But, as they said, set a thief . . .*

He said, 'Could one dragon sniff out another? I mean, follow a scent?'

Dearest Mother [wrote Carrot] Talk about a Turn Up for the Books. Last night the dragon burned up our Headquarters and Lo and Behold we have been given a better one, it is in a place called Pseudopolis Yard, opposite the Opera House. Sgt Colon said we have gone Up in the World and has told Nobby not to try to sell the furnishings. Going Up in the World is a metaphor, which I am learning about, it is like Lying but more decorative. There are proper carpets to spit on. Twice today groups of people have tried to search the cellars here for the dragon, it is amazing. And digging up people's privies and poking into attics, it is like a Fever. One thing is, people haven't got time for much else, and Sgt Colon says, when

---

* The phrase 'Set a thief to catch a thief' had by this time (after strong representations from the Thieves' Guild) replaced a much older and quintessentially Ankh-Morporkian proverb, which was 'Set a deep hole with spring-loaded sides, tripwires, whirling knife blades driven by water power, broken glass and scorpions, to catch a thief.'

you go out on your Rounds and shout Twelve of the Clock and All's Well while a dragon is melting the street you feel a bit of a Burke.

I have moved out of Mrs Palm's because, there are dozens of bedrooms here. It was sad and they made me a cake but I think it is for the best, although Mrs Palm never charged me rent which was very nice of her considering she is a widow with so many fine daughters to bring up plus dowries ekcetra.

Also I have made friends with this ape who keeps coming round to see if we have found his book. Nobby says it is a flea-ridden moron because it won 18d off him playing Cripple Mr Onion, which is a game of chance with cards which I do not play, I have told Nobby about the Gambling (Regulation) Acts, and he said Piss off, which I think is in violation of the Decency Ordinances of 1389 but I have decided to use my Discretion.

Capt Vimes is ill and is being looked after by a Lady. Nobby says it is well known she is Mental, but Sgt Colon says its just because of living in a big house with a lot of dragons but she is worth a Fortune and well done to the Capt for getting his feet under the table. I do not see what the furniture has to do with it. This morning I went for a walk with Reet and showed her many interesting examples of the ironwork to be found in the city. She said it was very interesting. She said I was quite different to anyone she's ever met. Your loving son, Carrot. X

PS I hope Minty is keeping well.

He folded the paper carefully and shoved it into the envelope.

'Sun's going down,' said Sergeant Colon.

Carrot looked up from his sealing wax.

'That means it will be night soon,' Colon went on, accurately.

'Yes, Sergeant.'

Colon ran a finger round his collar. His skin was impressively pink, the result of a morning's scrubbing, but people were still staying at a respectful distance.

Some people are born to command. Some people achieve command. And others have command thrust upon them, and the sergeant was now included in this category and wasn't very happy about it.

Any minute now, he knew, he was going to have to say that it was time they went out on patrol. He didn't want to go out on patrol. He wanted to find a nice sub-basement somewhere. But *nobblyess obligay* – if he was in charge, he had to do it.

It wasn't the loneliness of command that was bothering him. It was the being-fried-alive of command that was giving him problems.

He was also pretty sure that unless they came up with something about this dragon very soon then the Patrician was going to be unhappy. And when the Patrician was unhappy, he became very democratic. He found intricate and painful ways of spreading that unhappiness as far as possible. Responsibility, the sergeant thought, was a terrible thing. So was being horribly tortured. As far as he could see, the two facts were rapidly heading towards one another.

And thus he was terribly relieved when a small coach pulled up outside the Yard. It was very old, and battered. There was a faded coat of arms on the door. Painted on the back, and rather newer, was the little message: *Whinny If You Love Dragons.*

Out of it, wincing as he got down, stepped Captain Vimes. Following him was the woman known to the sergeant as Mad Sybil Ramkin. And finally, hopping down obediently on the end of its lead, was a small—

The sergeant was too nervous to take account of actual size.

'Well, I'll be mogadored! They've only gone and caught it!'

Nobby looked up from the table in the corner where he was continually failing to learn that it is almost impossible to play a game of skill and bluff against an opponent who smiles all the time. The Librarian took advantage of the diversion to help himself to a couple of cards off the bottom of the pack.

'Don't be daft. That's just a swamp dragon,' said Nobby. 'She's all right, is Lady Sybil. A real lady.'

The other two guards turned and stared at him. This was Nobby talking.

'You two can bloody well stop that,' he said. 'Why shouldn't I know a lady when I sees one? She give me a cup of tea in a cup fin as paper and a silver spoon in it,' he said, speaking as one who had peeped over the plateau of social distinction. '*And* I give it back to her, so you can stop looking at me like that!'

'What is it you actually *do* on your evenings off?' said Colon.

'No business of yourn.'

'Did you really give the spoon back?' said Carrot.

'Yes I bloody well did!' said Nobby hotly.

'Attention, lads,' said the sergeant, flooded with relief.

The other two entered the room. Vimes gave his men his usual look of resigned dismay.

'My squad,' he mumbled.

'Fine body of men,' said Lady Ramkin. 'The good old rank and file, eh?'

'The rank, anyway,' said Vimes.

Lady Ramkin beamed encouragingly. This led to a strange

shuffling among the men. Sergeant Colon, by dint of some effort, managed to make his chest stick out more than his stomach. Carrot straightened up from his habitual stoop. Nobby vibrated with soldierly bearing, hands thrust straight down by his sides, thumbs pointing sharply forward, pigeon chest inflated so much that his feet were in danger of leaving the ground.

'I always think we can all sleep safer in my bed knowing that these brave men are watching over us,' said Lady Ramkin, walking sedately along the rank, like a treasure galleon running ahead of a mild breeze. 'And who is this?'

It is difficult for an orang-utan to stand to attention. Its body can master the general idea, but its skin can't. The Librarian was doing his best, however, standing in a sort of respectful heap at the end of the line and maintaining the kind of complex salute you can only achieve with a four-foot arm.

''E's plain clothes, ma'am,' said Nobby smartly. 'Special Ape Services.'

'Very enterprising. Very enterprising indeed,' said Lady Ramkin. 'How long have you been an ape, my man?'

'Oook.'

'Well done.' She turned to Vimes, who was definitely looking incredulous.

'A credit to you,' she said. 'A fine body of men—'

'Oook. '

'—anthropoids,' corrected Lady Ramkin, with barely a break in the flow.

For a moment the rank felt as though they had just returned from single-handedly conquering a distant province. They felt, in fact, tremendously bucked-up, which was how Lady Ramkin would almost certainly have put it and which was definitely several letters of the alphabet away from how they normally felt. Even the Librarian felt favoured, and for once had let the phrase 'my men' pass without comment.

A trickling noise and a strong chemical smell prompted them to look around.

Goodboy Bindle Featherstone was squatting with an air of sheepish innocence alongside what was not so much a stain on the carpet as a hole in the floor. A few wisps of smoke were curling up from the edges.

Lady Ramkin sighed.

'Don't you worry, ma'am,' volunteered Nobby cheerfully. 'Soon have that cleaned up.'

'I'm afraid they're often like that when they're excited,' she said.

'Fine specimen you got there, ma'am,' Nobby went on, revelling in the new-found experience of social intercourse.

'It's not mine,' she said. 'It belongs to the captain now. Or all of you, perhaps. A sort of mascot. His name is Goodboy Bindle Featherstone.'

Goodboy Bindle Featherstone bore up stoically under the weight of the name, and sniffed a table leg.

'He looks more like my brother Errol,' said Nobby, playing the cheeky chirpy lovable city sparrow card for all it was worth. 'Got the same pointed nose, excuse me for saying so, milady.'

Vimes looked at the creature, which was investigating its new environment, and knew that it was now, irrevocably, an Errol. The little dragon took an experimental bite out of the table, chewed it for a few seconds, spat it out, curled up and went to sleep.

'He ain't going to set fire to anything, is he?' said the sergeant anxiously.

'I don't think so. He doesn't seem to have worked out what his flame ducts are for yet,' said Lady Ramkin.

'You can't teach him anything about relaxing, though,' said Vimes. 'Anyway, men . . .'

'Oook.'

'I wasn't talking to you, sir. What's this doing here?'

'Er,' said Sergeant Colon hurriedly, 'I, er . . . with you being away and all, and us likely to be short-handed . . . Carrot here says it's all according to the law and that . . . I swore him in, sir. The ape, sir.'

'Swore him in what, Sergeant?' said Vimes.

'As Special Constable, sir,' said Colon, blushing. 'You know, sir. Sort of citizen's Watch.'

Vimes threw up his hands. 'Special? Bloody *unique!*'

The Librarian gave Vimes a big smile.

'Just temporarily, sir. For the duration, like,' said Colon pleadingly. 'We could do with the help, sir, and . . . well, he's the only one who seems to like us . . .'

'I think it's a *frightfully* good idea,' said Lady Ramkin. 'Well done, that ape.'

Vimes shrugged. The world was mad enough already, what could make it worse?

'Okay,' he said. 'Okay! I give in. Fine! Give him a badge, although I'm damned if I know where he'll wear it! Fine! Yes! Why not?'

'You all right, Captain?' said Colon, all concern.

'Fine! Fine! Welcome to the new Watch!' snapped Vimes, striding vaguely around the room. 'Great! After all, we pay peanuts, don't we, so we might as well employ mon—'

The sergeant's hand slapped respectfully across Vimes's mouth.

'Er, just one thing, Captain,' said Colon urgently, to Vimes's astonished eyes. 'You don't use the "M" word. Gets right up his nose, sir. He can't help it, he loses all self-control. Like a red rag to a wossname, sir. "Ape" is all right, sir, but not the "M" word. Because, sir, when he gets angry he doesn't just go and sulk, sir, if you get my drift. He's no trouble at all apart from that, sir. All right? Just don't say monkey. Ohshit.'

The Brethren were nervous.

He'd heard them talking. Things were moving too fast for them. He thought he'd led them into the conspiracy a bit at a time, never giving them more truth than their little brains could cope with, but he'd still overestimated them. A firm hand was needed. Firm but fair.

'Brothers,' said the Supreme Grand Master, 'are the Cuffs of Veracity duly enhanced?'

'What?' said Brother Watchtower vaguely. 'Oh. The Cuffs. Yeah. Enhanced. Right.'

'And the Martlets of Beckoning, are they fittingly divested?'

Brother Plasterer gave a guilty start. 'Me? What? Oh. Fine, no problem. Divested. Yes.'

The Supreme Grand Master paused.

'Brothers,' he said softly. 'We are so *near*. Just once more. Just a few *hours*. Once more and the world is *ours*. Do you *understand*, Brothers?'

Brother Plasterer shuffled a foot.

'Well,' he said. 'I mean, of course. Yes. No fears about that. Behind you one hundred and ten percent—'

He's going to say *only*, thought the Supreme Grand Master.

'—only—'

Ah.

'—we, that is, all of us, we've been . . . odd, really, you feel so different, don't you, after summoning the dragon, sort of—'

'Cleaned out,' said Brother Plasterer helpfully.

'—yes, like it's sort of – ' Brother Watchtower struggled with the serpents of self-expression – 'taking something out of you . . .'

'Sucked dry,' said Brother Plasterer.

'Yes, like he said, and we . . . well, it's maybe it's a bit risky . . .'

'Like stuff's been dragged from your actual living brain by eldritch creatures from the Beyond,' said Brother Plasterer.

'I'd have said more like a bit of a sick headache, myself,' said Brother Watchtower helplessly. 'And we was wondering, you know,

114

about all this stuff about cosmic balance and that, because, well, look what happened to poor old Dunnykin. Could be a bit of a judgement. Er.'

'It was just a maddened crocodile hidden in a flower bed,' said the Supreme Grand Master. 'It could have happened to anyone. I understand your feelings, however.'

'You do?' said Brother Watchtower.

'Oh, yes. They're only natural. All the greatest wizards feel a little ill-at-ease before undertaking a great work such as this.' The Brethren preened themselves. Great wizards. That's us. Yeah. 'But in a few hours it'll be over, and I am sure that the king will reward you handsomely. The future will be glorious.'

This normally did the trick. It didn't appear to be working this time.

'But the dragon—' Brother Watchtower began.

'There won't *be* any dragon! We won't need it. Look,' said the Supreme Grand Master, 'it's quite simple. The lad will have a marvellous sword. Everyone *knows* kings have marvellous swords—'

'This'd be the marvellous sword you've been telling us about, would it?' said Brother Plasterer.

'And when it touches the dragon,' said the Supreme Grand Master, 'it'll be . . . *foom!*'

'Yeah, they do that,' said Brother Doorkeeper. 'My uncle kicked a swamp dragon once. He found it eating his pumpkins. Damn thing nearly took his leg off.'

The Supreme Grand Master sighed. A few more hours, yes, and then no more of this. The only thing he hadn't decided was whether to let them alone – who'd believe them, after all? – or send the Guard to arrest them for being terminally stupid.

'No,' he said patiently, 'I mean the dragon will vanish. We'll have sent it back. End of dragon.'

'Won't people be a bit suspicious?' said Brother Plasterer. 'Won't they expect lumps of dragon all over the place?'

'No,' said the Supreme Grand Master triumphantly, 'because one touch from the Sword of Truth and Justice will totally destroy the Spawn of Evil!'

The Brethren stared at him.

'That's what they'll believe, anyway,' he added. 'We can provide a bit of mystic smoke at the time.'

'Dead easy, mystic smoke,' said Brother Fingers.

'No bits, then?' said Brother Plasterer, a shade disappointed.

Brother Watchtower coughed. 'Dunno if people will accept that,' he said. 'Sounds a bit too neat, like.'

'Listen,' snapped the Supreme Grand Master, 'they'll accept anything! They'll see it *happen*! People will be so keen to see the boy win, they won't think twice about it! Depend upon it! Now . . . let us commence . . .'

He concentrated.

Yes, it was easier. Easier every time. He could feel the scales, feel the rage of the dragon as he reached into *the place where the dragons went* and took control.

This was power, and it was his.

Sergeant Colon winced. 'Ow.'

'Don't be a big softy,' said Lady Ramkin cheerfully, tightening the bandage with a well-practised skill handed down through many generations of Ramkin womenfolk. 'He hardly touched you.'

'And he's *very sorry*,' said Carrot sharply. 'Show the sergeant how sorry you are. Go on.'

'Oook,' said the Librarian, sheepishly.

'Don't let him kiss me!' squeaked Colon.

'Do you think picking someone up by their ankles and bouncing their head on the floor comes under the heading of Striking a Superior Officer?' said Carrot.

'I'm not pressing charges, me,' said the sergeant hurriedly.

'Can we get on?' said Vimes impatiently. 'We're going to see if Errol can sniff out the dragon's lair. Lady Ramkin thinks it's got to be worth a try.'

'You mean set a deep hole with spring-loaded sides, tripwires, whirling knife blades driven by water power, broken glass and scorpions, to catch a thief, Captain?' said the sergeant doubtfully. 'Ow!'

'Yes, we don't want to lose the scent,' said Lady Ramkin. 'Stop being a big baby, Sergeant.'

'Brilliant idea about using Errol, ma'am, if I may make so bold,' said Nobby, while the sergeant blushed under his bandage.

Vimes was not certain how long he would be able to put up with Nobby the social mountaineer.

Carrot said nothing. He was gradually coming to terms with the fact that he probably wasn't a dwarf, but dwarf blood flowed in his veins in accordance with the famous principle of morphic resonance, and his borrowed genes were telling him that nothing was going to be that simple. Finding a hoard even when the dragon wasn't at home was pretty risky. Anyway, he was certain he'd know if there was one around. The presence of large amounts of gold always made a dwarf's palms itch, and his weren't itching.

'We'll start by that wall in the Shades,' said the captain.

Sergeant Colon glanced sideways at Lady Ramkin, and found it impossible to show cowardice in the face of the supportive. He contented himself with, 'Is that wise, Captain?'

'Of course it isn't. If we were wise, we wouldn't be in the Watch.'

'I say! All this is tremendously exciting,' said Lady Ramkin.

'Oh, I don't think you should come, m'lady—' Vimes began.

'*Sybil*, please!—'

'—it's a very disreputable area, you see.'

'But I'm sure I shall be perfectly safe with your men,' she said. 'I'm sure vagabonds just *melt* away when they see you.'

That's dragons, thought Vimes. They melt away when they see dragons, and just leave their shadows on the wall. Whenever he felt that he was slowing down, or that he was losing interest, he remembered those shadows, and it was like having dull fire poured down his backbone. Things like that shouldn't be allowed to happen. Not in my city.

In fact the Shades were not a problem. Many of its denizens were out hoard-hunting anyway, and those that remained were far less inclined than hitherto to lurk in dark alleys. Besides, the more sensible of them recognized that Lady Ramkin, if waylaid, would probably tell them to pull up their socks and not be silly, in a voice so used to command that they would probably find themselves doing it.

The wall hadn't been knocked down yet and still bore its grisly fresco. Errol sniffed around it, trotted up the alley once or twice, and went to sleep.

'Dint work,' said Sergeant Colon.

'Good idea, though,' said Nobby loyally.

'It could be all the rain and people walking about, I suppose,' said Lady Ramkin.

Vimes scooped up the dragon. It had been a vain hope anyway. It was just better to be doing something than nothing.

'We'd better get back,' he said. 'The sun's gone down.'

They walked back in silence. The dragon's even tamed the Shades, Vimes thought. It's taken over the whole city, even when it isn't here. People'll start tying virgins to rocks any day now.

It's a metaphor of human bloody existence, a dragon. And if that wasn't bad enough, it's also a bloody great hot flying thing.

He pulled out the key to the new headquarters. While he was fumbling in the lock, Errol woke up and started to yammer.

'Not now,' Vimes said. His side twinged. The night had barely started and already he felt too tired.

A slate slid down the roof and smashed on the cobbles beside him.

'Captain,' hissed Sergeant Colon.

'What?'

'It's on the roof, Captain.'

Something about the sergeant's voice got through to Vimes. It wasn't excited. It wasn't frightened. It just had a tone of dull, leaden terror.

He looked up. Errol started to bounce up and down under his arm.

The dragon – *the* dragon – was peering down interestedly over the guttering. Its face alone was taller than a man. Its eyes were the size of very large eyes, coloured a smouldering red and filled with an intelligence that had nothing to do with human beings. It was far older, for one thing. It was an intelligence that had already been long basted in guile and marinated in cunning by the time a group of almost-monkeys were wondering whether standing on two legs was a good career move. It wasn't an intelligence that had any truck with, or even understood, the arts of diplomacy.

It wouldn't play with you, or ask you riddles. But it understood all about arrogance and power and cruelty and if it could possibly manage it, it would burn your head off. Because it liked to.

It was even more angry than usual at the moment. It could sense something behind its eyes. A tiny, weak, *alien* mind, bloated with self-satisfaction. It was infuriating, like an unscratchable itch. It was making it do things it didn't want to do . . . and stopping it from doing things it wanted to do very much.

Those eyes were, for the moment, focused on Errol, who was going frantic. Vimes realized that all that stood between him and a million degrees of heat was the dragon's vague interest in why Vimes had a smaller dragon under his arm.

'Don't make any sudden moves,' said Lady Ramkin's voice behind him. 'And don't show fear. They can always tell when you're afraid.'

'Is there any other advice you can offer at this time?' said Vimes slowly, trying to speak without moving his lips.

'Well, tickling them behind their ears often works.'

'Oh,' said Vimes weakly.

'And a good sharp "no!" and taking away their food bowl.'

'Ah?'

'And hitting them on the nose with a roll of paper is what I do in *extreme* cases.'

In the slow, brightly-outlined, desperate world Vimes was now inhabiting, which seemed to revolve around the craggy nostrils a few metres away from him, he became aware of a gentle hissing sound.

The dragon was taking a deep breath.

The intake of air stopped. Vimes looked into the darkness of the flame ducts and wondered whether he'd see anything, whether there'd be some tiny white glow or something, before fiery oblivion swept over him.

At that moment a horn rang out.

The dragon raised its head in a puzzled way and made a noise that sounded vaguely interrogative without being in any way a word.

The horn rang out again. The noise seemed to have a number of echoes that lived a life of their own. It sounded like a challenge. If that wasn't what it was, then the horn blower was soon going to be in trouble, because the dragon gave Vimes a smouldering look, unfolded its enormous wings, leapt heavily into the air and, against all the rules of aeronautics, flew slowly away in the direction of the sound.

Nothing in the world should have been able to fly like that. The wings thumped up and down with a noise like potted thunder, but the dragon moved as though it was idly sculling through the air. If it stopped flapping, the movement suggested, it would simply glide to a halt. It floated, not flew. For something the size of a barn with an armour-plated hide, it was a pretty good trick.

It passed over their heads like a barge, heading for the Plaza of Broken Moons.

'Follow it!' shouted Lady Ramkin.

'That's not right, it flying like that. I'm pretty sure there's something in one of the Witchcraft Laws,' said Carrot, taking out his notebook. 'And it's damaged the roof. It's really piling up the offences, you know.'

'You all right, Captain?' said Sergeant Colon.

'I could see right up its nose,' said Captain Vimes dreamily. His eyes focused on the worried face of the sergeant. 'Where's it gone?' he demanded. Colon pointed along the street.

Vimes glowered at the shape disappearing over the rooftops.

'Follow it!' he said.

The horn sounded again.

Other people were hurrying towards the plaza. The dragon drifted ahead of them like a shark heading towards a wayward airbed, its tail flicking slowly from side to side.

'Some loony is going to fight it!' said Nobby.

'I thought someone would have a go,' said Colon. 'Poor bugger'll be baked in his own armour.'

This seemed to be the opinion of the crowds lining the plaza. The people of Ankh-Morpork had a straightforward, no-nonsense approach to entertainment, and while they were looking forward to seeing a dragon slain, they'd be happy to settle instead for seeing someone being baked alive in his own armour. You didn't get the chance every day to see someone baked alive in their own armour. It would be something for the children to remember.

Vimes was jostled and bounced around by the crowd as more people flooded into the plaza behind them.

The horn sounded a third challenge.

'That's a slug-horn, that is,' said Colon knowledgeably. 'Like a tocsin, only deeper.'

'You sure?' said Nobby.

'Yep.'

'It must have been a bloody big slug.'

'Peanuts! Figgins! Hot sausages!' whined a voice behind them. 'Hello, lads. Hallo, Captain Vimes! In at the death, eh? Have a sausage. On the house.'

'What's going on, Throat?' said Vimes, clinging to the vendor's tray as more people spilled around them.

'Some kid's ridden into the city and said he'd kill the dragon,' said Cut-me-own-Throat. 'Got a magic sword, he says.'

'Has he got a magic skin?'

'You've got no romance in your soul, Captain,' said Throat, removing a very hot toasting fork from the tiny frying pan on his tray and applying it gently to the buttock of a large woman in front of him. 'Stand aside, madam, commerce *is* the lifeblood of the city, thank you very much. O'course,' he continued, 'by rights there should be a maiden chained to a rock. Only the aunt said no. That's the trouble with some people. No sense of tradition. This lad says he's the rightful air, too.'

Vimes shook his head. The world was definitely going mad around him. 'You've lost me there,' he said.

'Air,' said Throat patiently. 'You know. Air to the throne.'

'What throne?'

'The throne of Ankh.'

'*What throne of Ankh?*'

'You know. Kings and that.' Throat looked reflective. 'Wish I knew what his bloody name is,' he said. 'I put an order in to Igneous the Troll's all-night wholesale pottery for three gross of coronation mugs and it's going to be a right pain, painting all the names in afterwards. Shall I put you down for a couple, Cap'n? To you ninety pence, and that's cutting me own throat.'

Vimes gave up, and shoved his way back through the throng using Carrot as a lighthouse. The lance-constable loomed over the crowd, and the rest of the rank had anchored themselves to him.

'It's all gone mad,' he shouted. 'What's going on, Carrot?'

'There's a lad on a horse in the middle of the plaza,' said Carrot. 'He's got a glittery sword, you know. Doesn't seem to be doing much at the moment, though.'

Vimes fought his way into the lee of Lady Ramkin.

'Kings,' he panted. 'Of Ankh. And Thrones. Are there?'

'What? Oh, yes. There used to be,' said Lady Ramkin. 'Hundreds of years ago. Why?'

'Some kid says he's heir to the throne!'

'That's right,' said Throat, who'd followed Vimes in the hope of clinching a sale. 'He made a big speech about how he was going to kill the dragon, overthrow the usurpers and right all wrongs. Everyone cheered. Hot sausages, two for a dollar, made of genuine pig, why not buy one for the lady?'

'Don't you mean pork, sir?' said Carrot warily, eyeing the glistening tubes.

'Manner of speaking, manner of speaking,' said Throat quickly. 'Certainly your actual pig products. Genuine pig.'

'Everyone cheers any speech in this city,' growled Vimes. 'It doesn't mean anything!'

'Get your pig sausages, five for two dollars!' said Throat, who never let a conversation stand in the way of trade. 'Could be good for business, could monarchy. Pig sausages! Pig sausages! Inna bun! And righting all wrongs, too. Sounds like a solid idea to me. With onions!'

'Can I press you to a hot sausage, ma'am?' said Nobby.

Lady Ramkin looked at the tray around Throat's neck. Thousands of years of good breeding came to her aid and there was only the faintest suggestion of horror in her voice when she said, 'My, they look good. What splendid foodstuffs.'

'Are they made by monks on some mystic mountain?' said Carrot.

Throat gave him an odd look. 'No,' he said patiently, 'by pigs.'

'What wrongs?' said Vimes urgently. 'Come on, tell me. What wrongs is he going to right?'

'We-ell,' said Throat, 'there's, well, taxes. That's wrong, for a start.' He had the grace to look slightly embarrassed. Paying taxes was something that, in Throat's world. happened only to other people.

'That's right,' said an old woman next to him. 'And the gutter of

121

my house leaks something dreadful and the landlord won't do nothing. That's wrong.'

'And premature baldness,' said the man in front of her. 'That's wrong, too.' Vimes's mouth dropped open.

'Ah. Kings can cure that, you know,' said another protomonarchist knowingly.

'As a matter of fact,' said Throat, rummaging in his pack, 'I've got one bottle left of this astonishing ointment what is made – ' he glared at Carrot – 'by some ancient monks who live on a mountain—'

'And they can't answer back, you know,' the monarchist went on. 'That's how you can tell they're royal. Completely incapable of it. It's to do with being gracious.'

'Fancy,' said the leaky-guttering woman.

'Money, too,' said the monarchist, enjoying the attention. 'They don't carry it. That's how you can always tell a king.'

'Why? It's not that heavy,' said the man whose remaining hair was spread across the dome of his head like the remnant of a defeated army. '*I* can carry hundreds of dollars, no problem.'

'You probably get weak arms, being a king,' said the woman wisely. 'Probably with the waving.'

'I've always thought,' said the monarchist, pulling out a pipe and beginning to fill it with the ponderous air of one who is going to deliver a lecture, 'that one of the major problems of being a king is the risk of your daughter getting a prick.'

There was a thoughtful pause.

'And falling asleep for a hundred years,' the monarchist went on stolidly.

'Ah,' said the others, unaccountably relieved.

'And then there's wear and tear on peas,' he added.

'Well, there would be,' said the woman, uncertainly.

'Having to sleep on them all the time,' said the monarchist.

'Not to mention hundreds of mattresses.'

'Right.'

'Is that so? I think I could get 'em for him wholesale,' said Throat. He turned to Vimes, who had been listening to all this with leaden depression. 'See, Captain? And you'd be in the *royal* guard, I expect. Get some plumes in your helmet.'

'Ah, pageantry,' said the monarchist, pointing with his pipe. 'Very important. Lots of spectacles.'

'What, free?' said Throat.

'We-ell, I think maybe you have to pay for the frames,' said the monarchist.

'You're all bloody mad!' shouted Vimes. 'You don't know anything about him and he hasn't even won yet!'

'Bit of a formality, I expect,' said the woman.

'It's a fire-breathing dragon!' screamed Vimes, remembering those nostrils. 'And he's just a guy on a horse, for heaven's sake!'

Throat prodded him gently in the breastplate. 'You got no soul, Cap'n,' he said. 'When a stranger comes into the city under the thrall of the dragon and challenges it with a glittery sword, weeell, there's only one outcome, ain't there? It's probably destiny. '

'Thrall?' shouted Vimes. '*Thrall?* You thieving bugger, Throat, you were flogging cuddly dragon dolls yesterday!'

'That's was just business, Cap'n. No need to get excited about it,' said Throat pleasantly.

Vimes went back to the rank in a gloomy rage. Say what you liked about the people of Ankh-Morpork, they had always been staunchly independent, yielding to no man their right to rob, defraud, embezzle and murder on an equal basis. This seemed absolutely right, to Vimes's way of thinking. There was no difference at all between the richest man and the poorest beggar, apart from the fact that the former had lots of money, food, power, fine clothes, and good health. But at least he wasn't any *better*. Just richer, fatter, more powerful, better dressed and healthier. It had been like that for hundreds of years.

'And now they get one sniff of an ermine robe and they go all gooey,' he muttered.

The dragon was circling the plaza slowly and warily. Vimes craned to see over the heads in front of him.

In the same way that various predators have the silhouette of their prey almost programmed into their genes, it was possible that the shape of someone on a horse holding a sword clicked a few tumblers in a dragon's brain. It was showing keen but wary interest.

Back in the crowd, Vimes shrugged. 'I didn't even know we were a kingdom.'

'Well, we haven't been for ages,' said Lady Ramkin. 'The kings got thrown out, and jolly good job too. They could be quite frightful.'

'But you're, well, from a pos – from a high-born family,' he said. 'I should have thought you'd be all for kings.'

'Some of them were fearful oiks, you know,' she said airily. 'Wives all over the place, and chopping people's heads off, fighting pointless wars, eating with their knife, chucking half-eaten chicken legs over their shoulders, that sort of thing. Not *our* sort of people at all.'

The plaza went quiet. The dragon had flapped slowly to the far end and was almost stationary in the air, apart from the slow beating of its wings.

Vimes felt something claw gently at his back, and then Errol was on his shoulder, gripping with his hind claws. His stubby wings were beating in time with those of the bigger specimen. He was hissing. His eyes were fixed on the hovering bulk.

The boy's horse jigged nervously on the plaza's flagstones as he dismounted, flourished the sword and turned to face the distant enemy.

He certainly looks confident, Vimes told himself. On the other hand, how does the ability to slay dragons fit you for kingship in this day and age?

It was certainly a very *shiny* sword. You had to admit that.

And now it was two of the clock the following morning. And all was well, apart from the rain. It was drizzling again.

There are some towns in the multiverse which think they know how to have a good time. Places like New Orleans and Rio reckon they not only know how to push the boat out but set fire to the harbour as well; but compared to Ankh-Morpork with its hair down they're a Welsh village at 2pm on a wet Sunday afternoon.

Fireworks banged and sparkled in the damp air over the turbid mud of the river Ankh. Various domesticated animals were being roasted in the streets. Dancers conga'd from house to house, often managing to pick up any loose ornaments while doing so. There was a lot of quaffing going on. People who in normal circumstances would never think of doing it were shouting 'Hurrah'.

Vimes stalked gloomily through the crowded streets, feeling like the only pickled onion in a fruit salad. He'd given the rank the evening off.

He wasn't feeling at all royalist. He didn't think he had anything against kings as such, but the sight of *Ankh-Morporkians* waving flags was mysteriously upsetting. That was something only silly subject people did, in other countries. Besides, the idea of royal plumes in his hat revolted him. He'd always had a thing about plumes. Plumes sort of, well, bought you off, told everyone that you didn't belong to yourself. And he'd feel like a bird. It'd be the last straw.

His errant feet led him back to the Yard. After all, where else was there? His lodgings were depressing and his landlady had complained about the holes which, despite much shouting, Errol kept making in the carpet. And the smell Errol made. And Vimes couldn't drink in a tavern tonight without seeing things that would upset him even more than the things he normally saw when he was drunk.

It was nice and quiet, although the distant sounds of revelry could be heard through the window.

Errol scrambled down from his shoulder and started to eat the coke in the fireplace.

Vimes sat back and put his feet up.

What a day! And what a fight! The dodging, the weaving, the shouts of the crowd, the young man standing there looking tiny and unprotected, the dragon taking a deep breath in a way now very familiar to Vimes . . .

And not flaming. That had surprised Vimes. It had surprised the crowd. It had certainly surprised the dragon, which had tried to squint at its own nose and clawed desperately at its flame ducts. It had remained surprised right up to the moment when the lad ducked in under one claw and thrust the sword home.

And then a thunderclap.

You'd have thought there'd have been some bits of dragon left, really.

Vimes pulled a scrap of paper towards him. He looked at the notes he'd made yesterday:

Itym: Heavy draggon, but yet it can flye right welle;
Itym: The fyre be main hot, yet issueth from ane living Thinge;
Itym: The Swamp dragons be right Poor Thinges, yet this
  monstrous Form waxeth full mightily;
Itym: From whence it cometh none knowe, nor wither it goeth,
  nor where it bideth betweentimes;
Itym: Whyfore did it burneth so neatlie?

He pulled the pen and ink towards him and, in a slow round hand, added:

Itym: Can a draggon be destroyed into utterlye noethinge?

He thought for a while, and continued:

Itym: Whyfore did it Explode that noone may find it, search they
  greatly?

A puzzler, that. Lady Ramkin said that when a swamp dragon exploded there was dragon everywhere. And this one had been a damn great thing. Admittedly its insides must have been an alchemical nightmare, but the citizens of Ankh-Morpork should still have been spending the night shovelling dragon off the streets. No-one seemed to have bothered about this. The purple smoke was quite impressive, though.

Errol finished off the coke and started on the fire irons. So far this evening he had eaten three cobblestones, a doorknob, something unidentifiable he'd found in the gutter and, to general astonishment, three of Cut-me-own-Throat's sausages made of genuine pork organs. The crunching of the poker going down mingled with the patter of rain on the windows.

Vimes stared at the paper again and then wrote:

Itym: How can Kinges come of noethinge?

He hadn't even seen the lad close to. He looked personable enough, not exactly a great thinker, but definitely the kind of profile you wouldn't mind seeing on your small change. Mind you, after killing the dragon he could have been a cross-eyed goblin for all that it mattered. The mob had borne him in triumph to the Patrician's palace.

Lord Vetinari had been locked up in his own dungeons. He hadn't put up much fight, apparently. Just smiled at everyone and went quietly.

What a happy coincidence for the city that, just when it needed a champion to kill the dragon, a king came forth.

Vimes turned this thought over for a while. Then he turned it back to front. He picked up the quill and wrote:

Itym: What a happy chance it be, for a lad that would be Kinge, that there be a Draggon to slae to prove beyond doubt his boney fiddes.

It was a lot better than birthmarks and swords, that was for sure.

He twiddled the quill for a while, and then doodled:

Itym: The draggon was not a Mechanical devise, yette surely no wizzard has the power to create a beaste of that mag. magg. maggnyt. Size.
Itym: Whye, in the Pinche, could it not Flame?
Itym: Where did it come from?
Itym: Where did it goe?

The rain pounded harder on the window. The sounds of celebration became distinctly damp, and then faded completely. There was a murmur of thunder.

Vimes underlined *goe* several times. After further consideration he added two more question marks: ??

After staring at the effect for some time he rolled the paper into a ball and threw it into the fireplace, where it was fielded and swallowed by Errol.

There had been a crime. Senses Vimes didn't know he possessed, ancient policeman's senses, prickled the hairs on his neck and told him there had been a crime. It was probably such an odd crime that it didn't figure anywhere in Carrot's book, but it had been committed all right. A handful of high-temperature murders was only the start of it. He'd find it, and give it a name.

Then he stood up, took his leather rain cape from its hook behind the door, and stepped out into the naked city.

This is where the dragons went.

They lie . . .

Not dead, not asleep. Not waiting, because waiting implies expectation. Possibly the word we're looking for here is . . .

. . . *angry*.

It could remember the feel of real air under its wings, and the sheer pleasure of the flame. There had been empty skies above and an interesting world below, full of strange running creatures. Existence had a different texture there. A better texture.

And just when it was beginning to enjoy it, it had been crippled, stopped from flaming and whipped back, like some hairy canine mammal.

The world had been taken away from it.

In the reptilian synapses of the dragon's mind the suggestion was kindled that, just possibly, it could get the world back. It had been summoned, and disdainfully banished again. But perhaps there was a trail, a scent, a thread which would lead it to the sky . . .

Perhaps there was a pathway of thought itself . . .

It recalled a mind. The peevish voice, so full of its own diminutive importance, a mind almost like that of a dragon, but on a tiny, tiny scale.

Aha.

It stretched its wings.

Lady Ramkin made herself a cup of cocoa and listened to the rain gurgling in the pipes outside.

She slipped off the hated dancing shoes, which even she was prepared to concede were like a pair of pink canoes. But *nobblyess obligay,* as the funny little sergeant would say, and as the last representative of one of Ankh-Morpork's oldest families she'd had to go to the victory ball to show willing.

Lord Vetinari seldom had balls. There was a popular song about it, in fact. But now it was going to be balls all the way.

She couldn't stand balls. For sheer enjoyment it wasn't a patch on mucking out dragons. You knew where you were, mucking out dragons. You didn't get hot and pink and have to eat silly things on sticks, or wear a dress that made you look like a cloud full of cherubs. Little dragons didn't give a damn what you looked like so long as there was a feeding bowl in your hands.

Funny, really. She'd always thought it took weeks, *months,* to organize a ball. Invitations, decorations, sausages on poles, ghastly chickeny mixture to force into those little pastry cases. But it had all been done in a matter of hours, as if someone had been expecting it. One of the miracles of catering, obviously.

She'd even danced with the, for want of a better word, new king, who had said some polite words to her although they had been rather muffled.

And a coronation tomorrow. You'd have thought it'd take months to sort out.

She was still musing on that as she mixed the dragons' late night feed of rock oil and peat, spiked with flowers of sulphur. She didn't bother to change out of the ballgown but slipped the heavy apron over the top, donned the gloves and helmet, pulled the visor down over her face and ran, clutching the feed buckets, through the driving rain to the shed.

She knew it as soon as she opened the door. Normally the arrival of food would be greeted with hoots and whistles and brief bursts of flame.

The dragons, each in its pen, were sitting up in attentive silence and staring up through the roof.

It was somehow scary. She clanged the buckets together.

'No need to be afraid, nasty big dragon all gone!' she said brightly. 'Get stuck in to this, you people!'

One or two of them gave her a brief glance, and then went back to their—

What? They didn't seem to be frightened. Just very, very attentive. It was like a vigil. They were waiting for something to happen.

The thunder muttered again.

A couple of minutes later she was on her way down into the damp city.

*

128

There are some songs which are never sung sober. 'Nellie Dean' is one. So is any song beginning 'As I was a walking . . .' In the area around Ankh-Morpork, the favoured air is 'A Wizard's Staff Has A Knob On The End'.

The rank were drunk. At least, two out of three of the rank were drunk. Carrot had been persuaded to try a shandy and hadn't liked it much. He didn't know all the words, either, and many of the ones he did know he didn't understand.

'Oh, I *see*,' he said eventually. 'It's a sort of humorous play on words, is it?'

'You know,' said Colon wistfully, peering into the thickening mists rolling in off the Ankh, 's'at times like this I wish old—'

'You're not to say it,' said Nobby, swaying a little. 'You agreed, we wouldn't say nothing, it's no good talking about it.'

'It was his favourite song,' said Colon sadly. 'He was a good light tenor.'

'Now, *Sarge*—'

'He was a righteous man, our Gaskin,' said Colon.

'We couldn't of helped it,' said Nobby sulkily.

'We could have,' said Colon. 'We could have run faster.'

'What happened, then?' said Carrot.

'He died,' said Nobby, 'in the hexecution of his duty.'

'I *told* him,' said Colon, taking a swig at the bottle they had brought along to see them through the night, 'I *told* him. Slow down, I said. You'll do yourself a mischief, I said. I don't know what got into him, running ahead like that.'

'I blame the Thieves' Guild,' said Nobby. 'Allowing people like that on the streets—'

'There was this bloke we saw done a robbery one night,' said Colon miserably. 'Right in front of us! And Captain Vimes, he said Come On, and we run, only the point is you shouldn't run too fast, see. Else you might catch them. Leads to all sorts of problems, catching people—'

'They don't like it,' said Nobby. There was a mutter of thunder, and a flurry of rain.

'They don't like it,' agreed Colon. 'But Gaskin went and forgot, he ran on, went round the corner and, well, this bloke had a couple of mates waiting—'

'It was his heart really,' said Nobby.

'Well. Anyway. And there he was,' said Colon. 'Captain Vimes was very upset about it. You shouldn't run fast in the Watch, lad,' he said solemnly. 'You can be a fast guard or you can be an old guard, but you can't be a fast old guard. Poor old Gaskin.'

'It didn't ought to be like that,' said Carrot.

Colon took a pull at the bottle.

'Well, it is,' he said. Rain bounced on his helmet and trickled down his face.

'But it didn't ought to be,' said Carrot flatly.

'But it is,' said Colon.

Someone else in the city was also ill at ease. He was the Librarian.

Sergeant Colon had given him a badge. The Librarian turned it round and round in his big gentle hands, nibbling at it.

It wasn't that the city suddenly had a king. Orangs are traditionalists, and you couldn't get more traditional than a king. But they also liked things neat, and things weren't neat. Or, rather, they were *too* neat. Truth and reality were never as neat as this. Sudden heirs to ancient thrones didn't grow on trees, and he should know.

Besides, no-one was looking for his book. That was human priorities for you.

The book was the key to it. He was sure of that. Well, there was one way to find out what was in the book. It was a perilous way, but the Librarian ambled along perilous ways all day.

In the silence of the sleeping library he opened his desk and removed from its deepest recesses a small lantern carefully built to prevent any naked flame being exposed. You couldn't be too careful with all this paper around . . .

He also took a bag of peanuts and, after some thought, a large ball of string. He bit off a short length of the string and used it to tie the badge around his neck, like a talisman. Then he tied one end of the ball to the desk and, after a moment's contemplation, knuckled off between the bookshelves, paying out the string behind him.

Knowledge equals power . . .

The string was important. After a while the Librarian stopped. He concentrated all his powers of librarianship.

Power equals energy . . .

People were stupid, sometimes. They thought the Library was a dangerous place because of all the magical books, which was true enough, but what made it really one of the most dangerous places there could ever be was the simple fact that it was a library.

Energy equals matter . . .

He swung into an avenue of shelving that was apparently a few feet long and walked along it briskly for half an hour.

Matter equals mass.

And mass distorts space. It distorts it into polyfractal L-space.

So, while the Dewey system has its fine points, when you're

setting out to look something up in the multidimensional folds of L-space what you really need is a ball of string.

Now the rain was trying hard. It glistened off the flagstones in the Plaza of Broken Moons, littered here and there with torn bunting, flags, broken bottles and the occasional regurgitated supper. There was still plenty of thunder about, and a green, fresh smell in the air. A few shreds of mist from the Ankh hovered over the stones. It would be dawn soon.

Vimes's footsteps echoed wetly from the surrounding buildings as he picked his way across the plaza. The boy had stood *here*.

He peered through the mist shreds at the surrounding buildings, getting his bearings. So the dragon had been hovering – he paced forward – *here*.

'And,' said Vimes, 'this is where it was killed.'

He fumbled in his pockets. There were all sorts of things in there – keys, bits of string, corks. His finger closed on a stub end of chalk.

He knelt down. Errol jumped off his shoulder and waddled away to inspect the detritus of the celebration. He always sniffed everything before he ate it, Vimes noticed. It was a bit of a puzzle why he bothered, because he always ate it anyway.

Its head had been about, let's see, *here*.

He walked backwards, dragging the chalk over the stones, progressing slowly over the damp, empty square like an ancient worshipper treading a maze. Here a wing, curving away towards a tail which stretched out to *here*, change hands, now head for the other wing . . .

When he finished he walked to the centre of the outline and ran his hands over the stones. He realized he was half-expecting them to be warm.

Surely there should be something. Some, oh, he didn't know, some grease or something, some crispy fried dragon lumps.

Errol started eating a broken bottle with every sign of enjoyment.

'You know what I think?' said Vimes. 'I think it went somewhere.'

Thunder rolled again.

'All right, all right,' muttered Vimes. 'It was just a thought. It wasn't that dramatic.'

Errol stopped in mid-crunch.

Very slowly, as though it was mounted on very smooth, well-oiled bearings, the dragon's head turned to face upwards.

What it was staring at intently was a patch of empty air. There wasn't much else you could say about it.

Vimes shivered under his cape. This was daft.

'Look, don't muck about,' he said. 'There's nothing there.'

Errol started to tremble.

'It's just the rain,' said Vimes. 'Go on, finish your bottle. *Nice bottle.*'

A thin, worried keening noise broke from the dragon's mouth.

'I'll show you,' said Vimes. He cast around and spotted one of Throat's sausages, cast aside by a hungry reveller who had decided he was never going to be *that* hungry. He picked it up.

'Look,' he said, and threw it upwards.

He felt sure, watching its trajectory, that it ought to have fallen back to the ground. It shouldn't have fallen *away*, as if he'd dropped it neatly into a tunnel in the sky. And the tunnel shouldn't have been looking back at him.

Vivid purple lightning lashed from the empty air and struck the houses on the near side of the plaza, skittering across the walls for several yards before winking out with a suddenness that almost denied that it had ever happened at all.

Then it erupted again, this time hitting the rimward wall. The light broke where it hit into a network of searching tendrils spreading across the stones.

The third attempt went upwards, forming an actinic column that eventually rose fifty or sixty feet in the air, appeared to stabilize, and started to spin slowly.

Vimes felt that a comment was called for. He said: 'Arrgh.'

As the light revolved it sent out thin zigzag streamers that jittered away across the rooftops, sometimes dipping, sometimes doubling back. *Searching.*

Errol ran up Vimes's back in a flurry of claws and fastened himself firmly on his shoulder. The excruciating agony recalled to Vimes that there was something he should be doing. Was it time to scream again? He tried another 'Arrgh'. No, probably not.

The air started to smell like burning tin.

Lady Ramkin's coach rattled into the plaza making a noise like a roulette wheel and pounded straight for Vimes, stopping in a skid that sent it juddering around in a semi-circle and forced the horses either to face the other way or plait their legs. A furious vision in padded leather, gauntlets, tiara and thirty yards of damp pink tulle leaned down towards him and screamed: 'Come on, you bloody idiot!'

One glove caught him under his unresisting shoulder and hauled him bodily on to the box.

'And stop screaming!' the phantom ordered, focusing generations of natural authority into four syllables. Another shout spurred the horses from a bewildered standing start to a full gallop.

The coach bounced away over the flagstones. An exploratory tendril of flickering light brushed the reins for a moment and then lost interest.

'I suppose you haven't got any idea what's happening?' shouted Vimes, against the crackling of the spinning fire.

'Not the foggiest!'

The crawling lines spread like a web over the city, growing fainter with distance. Vimes imagined them creeping through windows and sneaking under doors.

'It looks as though it's searching for something!' he shouted.

'Then getting away before it finds it is a first-class idea, don't you think?'

A tongue of fire hit the dark Tower of Art, slid blindly down its ivy-grown flanks, and disappeared through the dome of Unseen University's Library.

The other lines blinked out.

Lady Ramkin brought the coach to a halt at the far side of the square.

'What does it want the Library for?' she said, frowning.

'Maybe it wants to look something up?'

'Don't be silly,' she said breezily. 'There's just a lot of books in there. What would a flash of lightning want to read?'

'Something very short?'

'I really think you could try to be a bit more help.'

The line of light exploded into an arc between the Library's dome and the centre of the plaza and hung in the air, a band of brilliance several feet across.

Then, in a sudden rush, it became a sphere of fire which grew swiftly to encompass almost all the plaza, vanished suddenly, and left the night full of ringing, violet shadows.

And the plaza full of dragon.

Who would have thought it? So much power, so close at hand. The dragon could feel the magic flowing into it, renewing it from second to second, in defiance of all boring physical laws. This wasn't the poor fare it had been given before. This was the right stuff. There was no end to what it could do, with power like this.

But first it had to pay its respects to certain people . . .

It sniffed the dawn air. It was searching for the stink of minds.

Noble dragons don't have friends. The nearest they can get to the idea is an enemy who is still alive.

The air became very still, so still that you could almost hear the slow fall of dust. The Librarian swung on his knuckles between the endless bookshelves. The dome of the Library was still overhead but then, it always was.

It seemed quite logical to the Librarian that, since there were aisles where the shelves were on the outside then there should be other aisles in the space between the books themselves, created out of quantum ripples by the sheer weight of words. There were certainly some odd sounds coming from the other side of some shelving, and the Librarian knew that if he gently pulled out a book or two he would be peeking into different libraries under different skies.

Books bend space and time. One reason the owners of those aforesaid little rambling, poky second-hand bookshops always seem slightly unearthly is that many of them really *are*, having strayed into this world after taking a wrong turning in their own bookshops in worlds where it is considered commendable business practice to wear carpet slippers all the time and open your shop only when you feel like it. You stray into L-space at your peril.

Very senior librarians, however, once they have proved themselves worthy by performing some valiant act of librarianship, are accepted into a secret order and are taught the raw arts of survival beyond the Shelves We Know. The Librarian was highly skilled in all of them, but what he was attempting now wouldn't just get him thrown out of the Order but probably out of life itself.

All libraries everywhere are connected in L-space. All libraries. Everywhere. And the Librarian, navigating by booksign carved on shelves by past explorers, navigating by smell, navigating even by the siren whisperings of nostalgia, was heading purposely for one very special one.

There was one consolation. If he got it wrong, he'd never know it.

Somehow the dragon was worse on the ground. In the air it was an elemental thing, graceful even when it was trying to burn you to your boots. On the ground it was just a damn great animal.

It's huge head reared against the grey of dawn, turning slowly.

Lady Ramkin and Vimes peered cautiously from behind a water-trough. Vimes had his hand clamped over Errol's muzzle. The little dragon was whimpering like a kicked puppy, and fighting to get away.

'It's a magnificent brute,' said Lady Ramkin, in what she probably thought was a whisper.

'I do wish you wouldn't keep saying that,' said Vimes.

There was a scraping noise as the dragon dragged itself over the stones.

'I *knew* it wasn't killed,' growled Vimes. 'There were no bits. It was too neat. It was sent somewhere by some sort of magic, I bet. Look at it. It's bloody impossible! It needs magic to keep it alive!'

'What do you mean?' said Lady Ramkin, not tearing her gaze from its armoured flanks.

What did he mean? What *did* he mean? He thought fast.

'It's just not physically possible, that's what I mean,' he said. 'Nothing that heavy should be able to fly, or breathe fire like that. I told you.'

'But it looks real enough. I mean, you'd expect a magical creature to be, well, gauzy.'

'Oh, it's real. It's real all right,' said Ramkin bitterly. 'But supposing it needs magic like we need, like we need . . . sunlight? Or food.'

'It's a thaumivore, you mean?'

'I just think it eats magic, that's all,' said Vimes, who had not had a classical education. 'I mean, all these little swamp dragons, always on the point of extinction, suppose one day back in prehistoric times some of them found out how to use magic?'

'There used to be a lot of natural magic around once,' said Lady Ramkin thoughtfully.

'There you are, then. After all, creatures use the air and the sea. I mean, if there's a natural resource around, something's going to use it, aren't they? Then it wouldn't matter about bad digestion and weight and wing size and so on, because the magic would take care of it. Wow!'

But you'd need a *lot*, he thought. He wasn't certain how much magic you'd need to change the world enough to let tons of armoured carcass flit around the sky like a swallow, but he'd bet it was lots.

All those thefts. Someone'd been feeding the dragon.

He looked at the bulk of the Unseen University Library of magic books, the greatest accumulation of distilled magical power on the Discworld.

And now the dragon had learned how to feed itself.

He became terribly aware that Lady Ramkin had moved, and

saw to his horror that she was striding towards the dragon, chin stuck out like an anvil.

'What the hell are you doing?' he whispered loudly.

'If it's descended from the swamp dragons then *I* can probably control it,' she called back. 'You have to look them in the eye and use a no-nonsense tone of voice. They can't resist a stern human voice. They don't have the willpower, you know. They're just big softies.'

To his shame, Vimes realized that his legs were going to have nothing to do with any mad dash to drag her back. His pride didn't like that, but his body pointed out that it wasn't his pride that stood a very reasonable chance of being thinly laminated to the nearest building. Through ears burning with embarrassment he heard her say: 'Bad boy!'

The echoes of that stern injunction rang out across the plaza.

Oh gods, he thought, is that how you train a dragon? Point them at the melted patch on the floor and threaten to rub their nose in it?

He risked a peep over the horsetrough.

The dragon's head was swinging around slowly, like a crane jib. It had some difficulty focusing on her, right below it. Vimes could see the great red eyes narrow as the creature tried to squint down the length of its own nose. It looked puzzled. He wasn't surprised.

'Sit!' bellowed Lady Ramkin, in a tone so undisobeyable that even Vimes felt his legs involuntarily sag. 'Good boy! I think I may have a lump of coke somewhere—' She patted her pockets.

Eye contact. That was the important thing. She really, Vimes thought, shouldn't have looked down even for a moment.

The dragon raised one talon in a leisurely fashion and pinned her to the ground.

As Vimes half-rose in horror Errol escaped from his grip and cleared the trough in one leap. He bounced across the plaza in a series of wing-whirring arcs, mouth gaping, emitting wheezing burps, trying to flame.

He was answered with a tongue of blue-white fire that melted a streak of bubbling rock several yards long but failed to strike the challenger. It was hard to pick him out of the air because, quite clearly, even Errol didn't know where he was going to be, or what way up he was going to be when he got there. His only hope at this point lay in movement, and he vaulted and spun between the increasingly furious bursts of fire like a scared but determined random particle.

The great dragon reared up with the sound of a dozen anchor chains being thrown into a corner, and tried to bat the tormenter out of the air.

Vimes's legs gave in at that point and decided that they might allow themselves to be heroic legs for a while. He scurried across the intervening space, sword at the ready for what good it might do, grabbed Lady Ramkin by an arm and a handful of bedraggled ballgown, and swung her on to his shoulder.

He got several yards before the essential bad judgement of this move dawned on him.

He went 'Gngh'. His vertebrae and knees were trying to fuse into one lump. Purple spots flashed on and off in front of his eyes. On top of it all, something unfamiliar but apparently made of whalebone was poking sharply into the back of his neck.

He managed a few more steps by sheer momentum, knowing that when he stopped he was going to be utterly crushed. The Ramkins hadn't bred for beauty, they'd bred for healthy solidity and big bones, and they'd got very good at it over the centuries.

A gout of livid dragonfire crackled into the flagstones a few feet away.

Afterwards he wondered if he'd only imagined leaping several inches into the air and covering the rest of the distance to the horsetrough at a respectable run. Perhaps, in extremis, everyone learned the kind of instant movement that was second nature to Nobby. Anyway, the horsetrough was behind him and Lady Ramkin was in his arms, or at least was pinning his arms to the ground. He managed to free them and tried to massage a bit of life back. What did you do next? She didn't seem to be injured. He recalled something about loosening a person's clothing, but in Lady Ramkin's case that might be dangerous without special tools.

She solved the immediate problem by grabbing the edge of the trough and hauling herself upright.

'*Right*,' she said, 'it's the slipper for you—' Her eyes focused on Vimes for the first time.

'What the hell's going on—' she began again, and then caught the scene over his shoulder.

'Oh *sod*,' she said. 'Pardon my Klatchian.'

Errol was running out of energy. The stubby wings were indeed incapable of real flight, and he was remaining airborne solely by flapping madly, like a chicken. The great talons swished through the air. One of them caught one of the plaza's fountains, and demolished it.

The next one swatted Errol neatly.

He shot over Vimes's head in a straight rising line, hit a roof behind him, and slid down it.

'You've got to catch him!' shouted Lady Vimes. 'You must! It's vital!'

Vimes stared at her, and then dived forward as Errol's pear-shaped body slithered over the edge of the roof and dropped. He was surprisingly heavy.

'Thank goodness,' said Lady Ramkin, struggling to her feet. 'They explode so easily, you know. It could have been very dangerous.'

They remembered the other dragon. It wasn't the exploding sort. It was the killing-people kind. They turned, slowly.

The creature loomed over them, sniffed and then, as if they were of no importance at all, turned away. It sprang ponderously into the air and, with one slow flap of its wings, began to scull leisurely away down the plaza and up and into the mists that were rolling over the city.

Vimes was currently more concerned with the smaller dragon in his hands. Its stomach was rumbling alarmingly. He wished he'd paid more attention to the book on dragons. Was a stomach noise like this a sign they were about to explode, or was the point you had to watch out for the point when the rumbling stopped?

'We've got to follow it!' said Lady Ramkin. 'What happened to the carriage?'

Vimes waved a hand vaguely in the direction that, as far as he could tell, the horses had taken in their panic.

Errol sneezed a cloud of warm gas that smelled worse than something walled up in a cellar, pawed the air weakly, licked Vimes's face with a tongue like a hot cheese-grater, struggled out of his arms and trotted away.

'Where's he off to?' boomed Lady Ramkin, emerging from the mists dragging the horses behind her. They didn't want to come, their hooves were scraping up sparks, but they were fighting a losing battle.

'He's still trying to challenge it!' said Vimes. 'You'd think he'd give in, wouldn't you?'

'They fight like blazes,' said Lady Ramkin, as he climbed on to the coach. 'It's a matter of making your opponent explode, you see.'

'I thought, in Nature, the defeated animal just rolls on its back in submission and that's an end of it,' said Vimes, as they clattered after the disappearing swamp dragon.

'Wouldn't work with dragons,' said Lady Ramkin. 'Some daft creature rolls on its back, you disembowel it. That's how they look at it. Almost human, really.'

The clouds were clustered thickly over Ankh-Morpork. Above them, the slow golden sunlight of the Discworld unrolled.

The dragon sparkled in the dawn as it trod the air joyously, doing impossible turns and rolls for the sheer delight of it. Then it remembered the business of the day.

They'd had the *presumption* to summon it . . .

Below it, the rank wandered from side to side up the Street of Small Gods. Despite the thick fog it was beginning to get busy.

'What d'you call them things, like thin stairs?' said Sergeant Colon.

'Ladders,' said Carrot.

'Lot of 'em about,' said Nobby. He mooched over to the nearest one, and kicked it.

'Oi!' A figure struggled down, half buried in a string of flags.

'What's going on?' said Nobby.

The flag bearer looked him up and down.

'Who wants to know, tiddler?' he said.

'Excuse me, we do,' said Carrot, looming out of the fog like an iceberg. The man gave a sickly grin.

'Well, it's the coronation, isn't it,' he said. 'Got to get the streets ready for the coronation. Got to have the flags up. Got to get the old bunting out, haven't we?'

Nobby gave the dripping finery a jaundiced look. 'Doesn't look that old to me,' he said. 'It looks new. What're them fat saggy things on that shield?'

'Those are the royal hippos of Ankh,' said the man proudly. 'Reminders of our noble heritage.'

'How long have we had a noble heritage, then?' said Nobby.

'Since yesterday, of course.'

'You can't have a heritage in a day,' said Carrot. 'It has to last a long time.'

'If we haven't got one,' said Sergeant Colon, 'I bet we'll soon have had one. My wife left me a note about it. All these years, and she turns out to be a monarchist.' He kicked the pavement viciously. 'Huh!' he said. 'A man knocks his pipes out for thirty years to put a bit of meat on the table, but all she's talking about is some boy who gets to be king for five minutes' work. Know what was for my tea last night? Beef dripping sandwiches!'

This did not have the expected response from the two bachelors.

'Cor!' said Nobby.

'*Real* beef dripping?' said Carrot. 'The kind with the little crunchy bits on top? And shiny blobs of fat?'

'Can't remember when I last addressed the crust on a bowl of dripping,' mused Nobby, in a gastronomic heaven. 'With just a bit of salt and pepper, you've got a meal fit for a k—'

'Don't even say it,' warned Colon.

'The best bit is when you stick the knife in and crack the fat and all the browny gold stuff bubbles up,' said Carrot dreamily. 'A moment like that is worth a ki—'

'Shutup! Shutup!' shouted Colon. 'You're just – *what the hell was that?*'

They felt the sudden downdraught, saw the mist above them roll into coils that broke against the house walls. A blast of colder air swept along the street, and was gone.

'It was like something gliding past, up there somewhere,' said the sergeant. He froze. 'Here, you don't think—?'

'We saw it killed, didn't we?' said Nobby urgently.

'We saw it *vanish*,' said Carrot.

They looked at one another, alone and damp in the mist-shrouded street. There could be anything up there. The imagination peopled the dank air with terrible apparitions. And what was worse was the knowledge that Nature might have done an even better job.

'Nah,' said Colon. 'It was probably just some . . . some big wading bird. Or something.'

'Isn't there anything we should do?' said Carrot.

'Yes,' said Nobby. 'We should go away quickly. Remember Gaskin.'

'Maybe it's another dragon,' said Carrot. 'We should warn people and—'

'No,' said Sergeant Colon vehemently, 'because, Ae, they wouldn't believe us and, Bee, we've got a king now. 'S his job, dragons.'

'S'right,' said Nobby. 'He'd probably be really angry. Dragons are probably, you know, royal animals. Like deer. A man could probably have his tridlins plucked just for thinking about killing one, when there's a king around.'*

'Makes you glad you're common,' said Colon.

'Commoner,' corrected Nobby.

'That's not a very civic attitude—' Carrot began. He was interrupted by Errol.

The little dragon came trotting up the middle of the street, stumpy tail high, his eyes fixed on the clouds above him. He went right by the rank without giving them any attention at all.

'What's up with him?' said Nobby.

A clatter behind them introduced the Ramkin coach.

'Men?' said Vimes hesitantly, peering through the fog.

'Definitely,' said Sergeant Colon.

---

* Tridlins: A short and unnecessary religious observance performed daily by the Holy Balancing Dervishes of Otherz, according to the *Dictionary of Eye-WateringWords.*

'Did you see a dragon go past? Apart from Errol?'

'Well, er,' said the sergeant, looking at the other two. 'Sort of, sir. Possibly. It might of been.'

'Then don't stand there like a lot of boobies,' said Lady Ramkin. 'Get in! Plenty of room inside!'

There was. When it was built, the coach had probably been the marvel of the day, all plush and gilt and tasselled hangings. Time, neglect and the ripping out of the seats to allow its frequent use to transport dragons to shows had taken their toll, but it still reeked of privilege, style and, of course, dragons.

'What do you think you're doing?' said Colon, as it rattled off through the fog.

'Wavin',' said Nobby, gesturing graciously to the billows around them.

'Disgusting, this sort of thing, really,' mused Sergeant Colon. 'People goin' around in coaches like this when there's people with no roof to their heads.'

'It's Lady Ramkin's coach,' said Nobby. 'She's all right.'

'Well, yes, but what about her ancestors, eh? You don't get big houses and carriages without grindin' the faces of the poor a bit.'

'You're just annoyed because your missus has been embroidering crowns on her undies,' said Nobby.

'That's got nothing to do with it,' said Sergeant Colon indignantly. 'I've always been very firm on the rights of man.'

'And dwarf,' said Carrot.

'Yeah, right,' said the sergeant uncertainly. 'But all this business about kings and lords, it's against basic human dignity. We're all born equal. It makes me sick.'

'Never heard you talk like this before, Frederick,' said Nobby.

'It's Sergeant Colon to you, Nobby.'

'Sorry, Sergeant.'

The fog itself was shaping up to be a real Ankh-Morpork autumn gumbo.* Vimes squinted through it as the droplets buckled down to a good day's work soaking him to the skin.

'I can just make him out,' he said. 'Turn left here.'

'Any ideas where we are?' said Lady Ramkin.

'Business district somewhere,' said Vimes shortly. Errol's progress was slowing a bit. He kept looking up and whining.

'Can't see a damn thing above us in this fog,' he said. 'I wonder if—'

---

* Like a pea-souper, only much thicker, fishier, and with things in it you'd probably rather not know about.

The fog, as if in acknowledgement, lit up. Ahead of them it blossomed like a chrysanthemum and made a noise like 'whoomph'.

'Oh, no,' moaned Vimes. 'Not again!'

'Are the Cups of Integrity well and truly suffused?' intoned Brother Watchtower.

'Aye, suffused full well.'

'The Waters of the World, are they Abjured?

'Yea, abjured full mightily.'

'Have the Demons of Infinity been bound with many chains?'

'Damn,' said Brother Plasterer, 'there's always something.'

Brother Watchtower sagged. 'Just once it would be nice if we could get the ancient and timeless rituals right, wouldn't it. You'd better get on with it.'

'Wouldn't it be quicker, Brother Watchtower, if I just did it twice next time?' said Brother Plasterer.

Brother Watchtower gave this some grudging consideration. It seemed reasonable.

'All right,' he said. 'Now get back down there with the others. And you should call me Acting Supreme Grand Master, understand?'

This did not meet with what he considered to be a proper and dignified reception among the brethren.

'No-one said anything to us about you being Acting Supreme Grand Master,' muttered Brother Doorkeeper.

'Well, that's all you know because I bloody well am because Supreme Grand Master asked me to open the Lodge on account of him being delayed with all this coronation work,' said Brother Watchtower haughtily. 'If that doesn't make me Acting Supreme Grand bloody Master I'd like to know what does, all right?'

'I don't see why,' muttered Brother Doorkeeper. 'You don't have to have a grand title like that. You could just be called something like, well . . . Rituals Monitor.'

'Yeah,' said Brother Plasterer. 'Don't see why you should give yourself airs. You ain't even been taught the ancient and mystic mysteries by monks, or anything.'

'We've been hanging around for hours, too,' said Brother Doorkeeper. 'That's not right. I thought we'd get rewarded—'

Brother Watchtower realized that he was losing control. He tried wheedling diplomacy.

'I'm sure Supreme Grand Master will be along directly,' he said. 'Let's not spoil it all now, eh? Lads? Arranging that fight with the dragon and everything, getting it all off right, that was something, wasn't it? We've been through a lot, right? It's worth waiting just a bit longer, okay?'

The circle of robed and cowled figures shuffled in grudging agreement.

'Okay.'

'Fair enough.'

'Yeah.'

CERTAINLY.

'Okay.'

'If you say so.'

It began to creep over Brother Watchtower that something wasn't right, but he couldn't quite put a name to it.

'Uh,' he said. 'Brothers?'

They, too, shifted uneasily. Something in the room was setting their teeth on edge. There was an atmosphere.

'Brothers,' repeated Brother Watchtower, trying to reassert himself, 'we are *all* here, aren't we?'

There was a worried chorus of agreement

'Of course we are.'

'What's the matter?'

'Yes!'

YES.

'Yes. '

There it was again, a subtle wrongness about things that you couldn't quite put your finger on because your finger was too scared. But Brother Watchtower's troublesome thoughts were interrupted by a scrabbling sound on the roof. A few nubs of plaster dropped into the circle.

'Brothers?' repeated Brother Watchtower nervously.

Now there was one of those silent sounds, a long, buzzing silence of extreme concentration and just possibly the indrawing of breath into lungs the size of haystacks. The last rats of Brother Watchtower's self-confidence fled the sinking ship of courage.

'Brother Doorkeeper, if you could just unbolt the dread portal—' he quavered.

And then there was light.

There was no pain. There was no time.

Death strips away many things, especially when it arrives at a temperature hot enough to vaporize iron, and among them are your illusions. The immortal remains of Brother Watchtower watched the dragon flap away into the fog, and then looked down at the congealing puddle of stone, metal and miscellaneous trace elements that was all that remained of the secret headquarters. And of its occupants, he realized in the dispassionate way that is part of being dead. You go through your whole life and end up a smear swirling around like cream in a coffee cup. Whatever the gods' games were, they played them in a damn mysterious way.

He looked up at the hooded figure beside him.

'We never intended this,' he said weakly. 'Honestly. No offence. We just wanted what was due to us.'

A skeletal hand patted him on the shoulder, not unkindly.

And Death said, CONGRATULATIONS.

Apart from the Supreme Grand Master, the only Elucidated Brother to be away at the time of the dragon was Brother Fingers. He'd been sent out for some pizzas. Brother Fingers was always the one sent out for takeaway food. It was cheaper. He'd never bothered to master the art of paying for things.

When the guards rolled up just behind Errol, Brother Fingers was standing with a stack of cardboard boxes in his hands and his mouth open.

Where the dread portal should have been was a warm melted patch of assorted substances.

'Oh, my goodness,' said Lady Ramkin.

Vimes slid down from the coach and tapped Brother Fingers on the shoulder.

'Excuse me, sir,' he said, 'did you by any chance see what—'

When Brother Fingers turned towards him his face was the face of a man who has hang-glided over the entrance to Hell. He kept opening and shutting his mouth but no words were coming out.

Vimes tried again. The sheer terror frozen in Brother Fingers's expression was getting to him.

'If you would be so kind to accompany me to the Yard,' said Vimes, 'I have reason to believe that you—' He hesitated. He wasn't entirely certain what it was that he had reason to believe. But the man was clearly guilty. You could tell just by looking at him. Not, perhaps, guilty of anything specific. Just guilty in general terms.

'Mmmmmuh,' said Brother Fingers.

Sergeant Colon gently lifted the lid of the top box.

'What do you make of it, Sergeant?' said Vimes, stepping back.

'Er. It looks like a Klatchian Hots with anchovies, sir,' said Sergeant Colon knowledgeably.

'I mean the man,' said Vimes wearily.

'Nnnnn,' said Brother Fingers.

Colon peered under the hood. 'Oh, I know him, sir,' he said. 'Bengy "Lightfoot" Boggis, sir. He's a capo de monty in the Thieves'

Guild. I know him of old, sir. Sly little bugger. Used to work at the University.'

'What, as a wizard?' said Vimes.

'Odd job man, sir. Gardening and carpentry and that.'

'Oh. *Did* he?'

'Can't we do something for the poor man?' said Lady Ramkin.

Nobby saluted smartly. 'I could kick him in the bollocks for you if you like, m'lady.'

'Dddrrr,' said Brother Fingers, beginning to shake uncontrollably, while Lady Ramkin smiled the iron-hard blank smile of a high-born lady who is determined not to show that she has understood what has just been said to her.

'Put him in the coach, you two,' said Vimes. 'If it's all right with you, Lady Ramkin—'

'—Sybil—' corrected Lady Ramkin. Vimes blushed, and plunged on – 'it might be a good idea to get him indoors. Charge him with the theft of one book, to whit, *The Summoning of Dragons*.'

'Right you are, sir,' said Sergeant Colon. 'The pizzas're getting cold, too. You know how the cheese goes all manky when it gets cold.'

'And no kicking him, either,' Vimes warned. 'Not *even* where it doesn't show. Carrot, you come with me.'

'DDddrrraa,' Brother Fingers volunteered.

'And take Errol,' added Vimes. 'He's driving himself mad here. Game little devil, I'll give him that.'

'Marvellous, when you come to think about it,' said Colon.

Errol was trotting up and down in front of the ravaged building, whining.

'Look at him,' said Vimes. 'Can't wait to get to grips.' His gaze found itself drawn, as though by wires, up to the rolling clouds of fog.

It's in there somewhere, he thought.

'What we going to do now, sir?' said Carrot, as the carriage rattled off.

'Not nervous, are you?' said Vimes.

'No, sir.'

The way he said it jogged something in Vimes's mind.

'No,' he said, 'you're not, are you? I suppose it's being brought up by the dwarfs that did it. You've got no imagination.'

'I'm sure I try to do my best, sir,' said Carrot firmly.

'Still sending all your pay home to your mother?'

'Yes, sir.'

'You're a good boy.'

'Yessir So what are we going to do, Captain Vimes?' Carrot repeated.

Vimes looked around him. He walked a few aimless, exasperated steps. He spread his arms wide and then flopped them down by his sides.

'How should I know?' he said. 'Warn people, I guess. We'd better get over to the Patrician's palace. And then—'

There were footsteps in the fog. Vimes stiffened, put his finger to his lips and pulled Carrot into the shelter of a doorway.

A figure loomed out of the billows.

Another one of 'em, thought Vimes. Well, there's no law about wearing long black robes and deep cowls. There could be dozens of perfectly innocent reasons why this person is wearing long black robes and a deep cowl and standing in front of a melted-down house at dawn.

Perhaps I should ask him to name just one.

He stepped out.

'Excuse me, sir—' he began.

The cowl swung around. There was a hiss of indrawn breath.

'I just wonder if you would mind – *after him, lance-constable!*'

The figure had a good start. It scuttled along the street and had reached the corner before Vimes was halfway there. He skidded around it in time to see a shape vanish down an alley.

Vimes realized he was running alone. He panted to a halt and looked back just in time to see Carrot jog gently around the corner.

'What's wrong?' he wheezed.

'Sergeant Colon said I wasn't to run,' said Carrot.

Vimes looked at him vaguely. Then slow comprehension dawned.

'Oh,' he said. 'I, er, see. I don't think he meant in *every* circumstance, lad.' He stared back into the fog. 'Not that we had much of a chance in this fog and these streets.'

'Might have been just an innocent bystander, sir,' said Carrot.

'What, in Ankh-Morpork?'

'Yes, sir.'

'We should have grabbed him, then, just for the rarity value,' said Vimes.

He patted Carrot on the shoulder. 'Come on. We'd better get along to the Patrician's palace.'

'The King's palace,' corrected Carrot.

'What?' said Vimes, his train of thought temporarily shunted.

'It's the King's palace now,' said Carrot. Vimes squinted sideways at him.

He gave a short, mirthless laugh.

'Yeah, that's right,' he conceded. 'Our dragon-killing king. Well done that man.' He sighed. 'They're not going to like this.'

They didn't. None of them did.

The first problem was the palace guard.

Vimes had never liked them. They'd never liked *him*. Okay, so maybe the rank were only one step away from petty scofflaws, but in Vimes's professional opinion the palace guard these days were only one step away from being the worst criminal scum the city had ever produced. A step further *down*. They'd have to *reform* a bit before they could even be considered for inclusion in the Ten Most Unwanted list.

They were rough. They were tough. They weren't the sweepings off the gutter, they were what you still found sticking to the gutter when the gutter sweepers had given up in exhaustion. They had been extremely well-paid by the Patrician, and presumably were extremely well-paid by someone else now, because when Vimes walked up to the gates a couple of them stopped lounging against the walls and straightened up while still maintaining just the right amount of psychological slouch to cause maximum offence.

'Captain Vimes,' said Vimes, staring straight ahead. 'To see the king. It's of the utmost importance.'

'Yeah? Well, it'd have to be,' said a guard. 'Captain Slimes, was it?'

'Vimes,' said Vimes evenly. 'With a Vee.'

One of the guards nodded to his companion.

'Vimes,' he said. 'With a Vee.'

'Fancy,' said the other guard.

'It's most urgent,' said Vimes, maintaining a wooden expression. He tried to move forward.

The first guard sidestepped neatly and pushed him sharply in the chest.

'No-one is going nowhere,' he said. 'Orders of the king, see? So you can push off back to your pit, Captain Vimes with a Vee.'

It wasn't the words which made up Vimes's mind. It was the way the other man sniggered.

'Stand aside,' he said.

The guard leaned down. 'Who's going to make me,' he rapped on Vimes's helmet, 'copper?'

There are times when it is a veritable pleasure to drop the bomb right away.

'Lance-constable Carrot, I want you to charge these men,' said Vimes.

Carrot saluted. 'Very good, sir,' he said, and turned and trotted smartly back the way they had come.

'Hey!' shouted Vimes, as the boy disappeared around a corner.

'That's what I like to see,' said the first guard, leaning on his spear. 'That's a young man with initiative, that young man. A bright lad. He doesn't want to stop along here and have his ears twisted off. That's a young man who's going to go a long way, if he's got any sense.'

'Very sensible,' said the other guard.

He leaned the spear against the wall.

'You Watch men make me want to throw up,' he said conversationally. 'Poncing around all the time, never doing a proper job of work. Throwing your weight about as if you counted for something. So me and Clarence are going to show you what *real* guarding is all about, isn't that right?'

I could just about manage one of them, Vimes thought as he took a few steps backward. If he was facing the other way, at least.

Clarence propped his spear against the gateway and spat on his hands.

There was a long, terrifying ululation. Vimes was amazed to realize it wasn't coming from him.

Carrot appeared around the corner at a dead run. He had a felling axe in either hand.

His huge leather sandals flapped on the cobblestones as he bounded closer, accelerating all the time. And all the time there was this cry, *deedahdeedahdeedah*, like something caught in a trap at the bottom of a two-tone echo canyon.

The two palace guards stood rigid with astonishment.

'I should duck, if I was you,' said Vimes from near ground level.

The two axes left Carrot's hands and whirred through the air making a noise like a brace of partridges. One of them hit the palace gate, burying half the head in the woodwork. The other one hit the shaft of the first one, and split it. Then Carrot arrived.

Vimes went and sat down on a nearby bench for a while, and rolled himself a cigarette.

Eventually he said, 'I think that's about enough, constable. I think they'd like to come quietly now.'

'Yes, sir. What are they accused of, sir?' said Carrot, holding one limp body in either hand.

'Assaulting an officer of the Watch in the execution of his duty and . . . oh, yes. Resisting arrest.'

'Under Section (vii) of the Public Order Act of 1457?' said Carrot.

'Yes,' said Vimes solemnly. 'Yes. Yes, I suppose so.'

'But they didn't resist very much, sir,' Carrot pointed out.

'Well, *attempting* to resist arrest. I should just leave them over by the wall until we come back. I don't expect they'll want to go anywhere.'

'Right you are, sir.'

'Don't hurt them, mind,' said Vimes. 'You mustn't hurt prisoners.'

'That's right, sir,' said Carrot, conscientiously. 'Prisoners once Charged have Rights, sir. It says so in the Dignity of Man (Civic Rights) Act of 1341. I keep telling Corporal Nobbs. They have Rights, I tell him. This means you do not Put the Boot in.'

'Very well put, constable.'

Carrot looked down. 'You have the right to remain silent,' he said. 'You have the right not to injure yourself falling down the steps on the way to the cells. You have the right not to jump out of high windows. You do not have to say anything, you see, but anything you do say, well, I have to take it down and it might be used in evidence.' He pulled out his notebook and licked his pencil. He leaned down further.

'Pardon?' he said. He looked up at Vimes.

'How do you spell "groan", sir?' he said.

'G-R-O-N-E, I think.'

'Very good, sir.'

'Oh, and constable?'

'Yes, sir?'

'Why the axes?'

'They *were* armed, sir. I got them from the blacksmith in Market Street, sir. I said you'd be along later to pay for them.'

'And the cry?' said Vimes weakly.

'Dwarfish war yodel, sir,' said Carrot proudly.

'It's a *good* cry,' said Vimes, picking his words with care. 'But I'd be grateful if you'd warn me first another time, all right?'

'Certainly, sir.'

'In writing, I think.'

The Librarian swung on. It was slow progress, because there were things he wasn't keen on meeting. Creatures evolve to fill every niche in the environment, and some of those in the dusty immensity of L-space were best avoided. They were much more unusual than ordinary unusual creatures.

Usually he could forewarn himself by keeping a careful eye on the kickstool crabs that grazed harmlessly on the dust. When they were spooked, it was time to hide. Several times he had to flatten himself against the shelves as a thesaurus thundered by. He waited patiently as a herd of Critters crawled past, grazing on the contents of the choicer books and leaving behind them piles of small slim volumes of literary criticism. And there were other things, things which he hurried away from and tried not to look hard at . . .

And you had to avoid cliches at all costs.

He finished the last of his peanuts atop a stepladder, which was browsing mindlessly off the high shelves.

The territory definitely had a familiar feel, or at least he got the feeling that it would eventually be familiar. Time had a different meaning in L-space.

There were shelves whose outline he felt he knew. The book titles, while still unreadable, held a tantalizing hint of legibility. Even the musty air had a smell he thought he recognized.

He shambled quickly along a side passage, turned the corner and, with only the slightest twinge of disorientation, shuffled into that set of dimensions that people, because they don't know any better, think of as normal.

He just felt extremely hot and his fur stood straight out from his body as temporal energy gradually discharged.

He was in the dark.

He extended one arm and explored the spines of the books by his side. Ah. Now he knew where he was.

He was home.

He was home a week ago.

It was essential that he didn't leave footprints. But that wasn't a problem. He shinned up the side of the nearest bookcase and, under the starlight of the dome, hurried onwards.

Lupine Wonse glared up, red-eyed, from the heap of paperwork on his desk. No-one in the city knew anything about coronations. He'd had to make it up as he went along. There should be plenty. Of things to wave, he knew that.

'Yes?' he said, abruptly.

'Er, there's a Captain Vimes to see you,' said the flunkey.

'Vimes of the Watch?'

'Yes, sir. Says it's of the utmost importance.'

Wonse looked down his list of other things that were also of the utmost importance. Crowning the king, for one thing. The high priests of fifty-three religions were all claiming the honour. It was going to be a scrum. And then there were the crown jewels.

Or rather, there *weren't* the crown jewels. Somewhere in the preceding generations the crown jewels had disappeared. A jeweller in the Street of Cunning Artificers was doing the best he could in the time with gilt and glass.

Vimes could wait.

'Tell him to come back another day,' said Wonse.

'Good of you to see us,' said Vimes, appearing in the doorway. Wonse glared at him.

'Since you're here . . .' he said. Vimes dropped his helmet on Wonse's desk in what the secretary thought was an offensive manner, and sat down.

'Take a seat,' said Wonse.

'Have you had breakfast yet?' said Vimes.

'Now really—' Wonse began.

'Don't worry,' said Vimes cheerfully. 'Constable Carrot will go and see what's in the kitchens. This chap will show him the way.'

When they had gone Wonse leaned across the drifts of paperwork.

'There had better,' he said, 'be a very good reason for—'

'The dragon is back,' said Vimes.

Wonse stared at him for a while.

Vimes stared back.

Wonse's senses came back from whatever corners they'd bounced into.

'You've been drinking, haven't you,' he said.

'No. The dragon is *back*.'

'Now, look—' Wonse began.

'I saw it,' said Vimes flatly.

'A dragon? You're sure?'

Vimes leaned across the desk. 'No! I could be bloody mistaken!' he shouted. 'It may have been something else with sodding great big claws, huge leathery wings and hot, fiery breath! There must be masses of things like that!'

'But we all saw it killed!' said Wonse.

'I don't know what *we* saw!' said Vimes, 'But I know what *I* saw!'

He leaned back, shaking. He was suddenly feeling extremely tired.

'Anyway,' he said, in a more normal voice, 'it's flamed a house in Bitwash Street. Just like the other ones.'

'Any of them get out?'

Vimes put his head in his hands. He wondered how long it was since he'd last had any sleep, proper sleep, the sort with sheets. Or food, come to that. Was it last night, or the night before? Had he ever, come to think of it, ever slept at all in all his life? It didn't seem like it. The arms of Morpheus had rolled up their sleeves and were giving the back of his brain a right pummelling, but bits were fighting back. Any of them get . . .?

'Any of who?' he said.

'The people in the house, of course,' said Wonse. 'I assume there were people in it. At night, I mean.'

'Oh? Oh. Yes. It wasn't like a normal house. I think it was some sort of secret society thing,' Vimes managed. Something was clicking in his mind, but he was too tired to examine it.

'Magic, you mean?'

'Dunno,' said Vimes. 'Could be. Guys in robes.'

He's going to tell me I've been overdoing it, he said. He'll be right, too.

'Look,' said Wonse, kindly. 'People who mess around with magic and don't know how to control it, well, they can blow themselves up and—'

'Blow themselves up?'

'And you've had a busy few days,' said Wonse soothingly. 'If I'd been knocked down and almost burned alive by a dragon I expect I'd be seeing them all the time.'

Vimes stared at him with his mouth open. He couldn't think of anything to say. Whatever stretched and knotted elastic had been driving him along these last few days had gone entirely limp.

'You don't think you've been overdoing it, do you?' said Wonse.

Ah, thought Vimes. Jolly good.

He slumped forward.

The Librarian leaned cautiously over the top of the bookcase and unfolded an arm into the darkness.

There it was.

His thick fingernails grasped the spine of the book, pulled it gently from its shelf and hoisted it up. He raised the lantern carefully.

No doubt about it. *The Summoning of Dragons.* Single copy, first edition, slightly foxed and extremely dragoned.

He set the lamp down beside him, and began to read the first page.

'Mmm?' said Vimes, waking up.

'Brung you a nice cup of tea, Cap'n,' said Sergeant Colon. 'And a figgin.'

Vimes looked at him blankly.

'You've been asleep,' said Sergeant Colon helpfully. 'You was spark out when Carrot brought you back.'

Vimes looked around at the now-familiar surroundings of the Yard. 'Oh,' he said.

'Me and Nobby have been doing some *detectoring*,' said Colon. 'You know that house that got melted? Well, no-one lives there. It's just rooms that get hired out. So we found out who hires them. There's a caretaker who goes along every night to put the chairs away and lock up. He wasn't half creating about it being burned down. You know what caretakers are like.'

He stood back, waiting for the applause.

'Well done,' said Vimes dutifully, dunking the figgin into the tea.

'There's three societies use it,' said Colon. He extracted his notebook. 'To wit, viz, The Ankh-Morpork Fine Art Appreciation Society, hem hem, the Morpork Folk-Dance and Song Club, and the Elucidated Brethren of the Ebon Night.'

'Why hem hem?' said Vimes.

'Well, you know. Fine *Art*. It's just men paintin' pictures of young wimmin in the nudd. The altogether,' explained Colon the connoisseur. 'The caretaker told me. Some of them don't even have any paint on their brushes, you know. Shameful.'

There must be a million stories in the naked city, thought Vimes. So why do I always have to listen to ones like these?

'When do they meet?' he said.

'Mondays, 7.30, admission ten pence,' said Colon, promptly. 'As for the folk-dance people – well, no problem there. You know you always wondered what Corporal Nobbs does on his evenings off?'

Colon's face split into a watermelon grin.

'No!' said Vimes incredulously. 'Not Nobby?'

'Yep!' said Colon, delighted at the result.

'What, jumping about with bells on and waving his hanky in the air?'

'He says it is important to preserve old folkways,' said Colon.

'Nobby? Mr Steel-toecaps-in-the-groin, I-was-just-checking-the-doorhandle-and-it-opened-all-by-itself?'

'Yeah! Funny old world, ain't it? He was very bashful about it.'

'Good grief,' said Vimes.

'It just goes to show, you never can tell,' said Colon. 'Anyway, the caretaker said the Elucidated Brethren always leave the place in a mess. Scuffed chalk marks on the floor, he said. And they never put the chairs back properly or wash out the tea urn. They've been meeting a lot lately, he said. The nuddy wimmin painters had to meet somewhere else last week.'

'What did you do with our suspect?' said Vimes.

'Him? Oh, he done a runner, Captain,' said the sergeant, looking embarrassed.

'Why? He didn't look in any shape to run anywhere.'

'Well, when we got back here, we sat him down by the fire and wrapped him up because he kept on shivering,' said Sergeant Colon, as Vimes buckled his armour on.

'I hope you didn't eat his pizzas.'

'Errol et 'em. It's the cheese, see, it goes all—'

'Go on.'

'Well,' said Colon awkwardly, 'he kept on shivering, sort of thing, and groaning on about dragons and that. We felt sorry for him, to tell the truth. And then he jumps up and runs out of the door for no reason at all.'

Vimes glanced at the sergeant's big, open, dishonest face.

'No reason?' he prompted.

'*Well*, we decided to have a bite, so I sent Nobby out to the baker's, see, and, well, we fought the prisoner ought to have something to eat . . .'

'Yes?' said Vimes encouragingly.

'*Well*, when Nobby asked him if he wanted his figgin toasted, he just give a scream and ran off.'

'Just that?' said Vimes. 'You didn't threaten him in any way?'

'Straight up, Captain. Bit of a mystery, if you ask me. He kept going on about someone called Supreme Grand Master.'

'Hmm.' Vimes glanced out of the window. Grey fog lagged the world with dim light. 'What time is it?' he said.

'Five of the clock, sir.'

'Right. Well, before it gets dark—'

Colon gave a cough. 'In the morning, sir. This is tomorrow, sir.'

'You let me sleep all *day*?'

'Didn't have the heart to wake you up, sir. No dragon activity, if that's what you're thinking. Dead quiet all round, in fact.'

Vimes glared at him and threw the window open.

The fog rolled in, in a slow, yellow-edged waterfall.

'We reckon it must of flown away,' said Colon's voice, behind him.

Vimes stared up into the heavy, rolling clouds.

'Hope it clears up for the coronation,' Colon went on, in a worried voice. 'You all right, sir?'

It hasn't flown away, Vimes thought. Why should it fly away? We can't hurt it, and it's got everything it wants right here. It's up there somewhere.

'You all right, sir?' Colon repeated.

It's got to be up high somewhere, in the fog. There's all kinds of towers and things.

'What time's the coronation, Sergeant?' he said.

'Noon, sir. And Mr Wonse has sent a message about how you're to be in your best armour among all the civic leaders, sir.'

'Oh, has he?'

'And Sergeant Hummock and the day squad will be lining the route, sir.'

'What with?' said Vimes vaguely, watching the skies.

'Sorry, sir?'

Vimes squinted upwards to get a better view of the roof. 'Hmm?' he said.

'I said they'll be lining the route, sir,' said Sergeant Colon.

'It's up there, Sergeant,' said Vimes. 'I can practically smell it.'

'Yes, sir,' said Colon obediently.

'It's deciding what to do next.'

'Yes, sir?'

'They're not unintelligent, You know. They just don't think like us.

'Yes, sir.'

'So be damned to any lining of the route. I want you three up on roofs, understand?'

'Yes, si— what?'

'Up on the roofs. Up high. When it makes its move, I want us to be the first to know.'

Colon tried to indicate by his expression that *he* didn't.

'Do you think that's a good idea, sir?' he ventured.

Vimes gave him a blank look. 'Yes, Sergeant, I do. It was one of mine,' he said coldly. 'Now go and see to it.'

When he was left to himself Vimes washed and shaved in cold water, and then rummaged in his campaign chest until he unearthed his ceremonial breastplate and red cloak. Well, the cloak had been red *once*, and still was, here and there, although most of it resembled a small net used very successfully for catching moths. There was also a helmet, defiantly without plumes, from which the molecule-thick gold leaf had long ago peeled.

He'd started saving up for a new cloak, once. Whatever had happened to the money?

There was no-one in the guardroom. Errol lay in the wreckage of the fourth fruit box Nobby had scrounged for him. The rest had all been eaten, or had dissolved.

In the warm silence the everlasting rumbling of his stomach sounded especially loud. Occasionally he whimpered.

Vimes scratched him vaguely behind the ears.

'What's up with you, boy?' he said.

The door creaked open. Carrot came in, saw Vimes hunkered down by the ravaged box, and saluted.

'We're a bit worried about him, Captain,' he volunteered. 'He hasn't eaten his coal. Just lies there twitching and whining all the time. You don't think something's wrong with him, do you?'

'Possibly,' said Vimes. 'But having something wrong with them is quite normal for a dragon. They always get over it. One way or another.'

Errol gave him a mournful look and closed his eyes again. Vimes pulled his scrap of blanket over him.

There was a squeak. He fished around beside the dragon's shivering body, pulled out a small rubber hippo, stared at it in surprise and then gave it one or two experimental squeezes.

'I thought it would be something for him to play with,' said Carrot, slightly shamefaced.

'You bought him a little toy?'

'Yes, sir.'

'What a kind thought.'

Vimes hoped Carrot hadn't noticed the fluffy ball tucked into the back of the box. It had been quite expensive.

He left the two of them and stepped into the outside world.

There was even more bunting now. People were beginning to line the main streets, even though there were hours to wait. It was still very depressing.

He felt an appetite for once, one that it'd take more than a drink or two to satisfy. He strolled along for breakfast at Harga's House of Ribs, the habit of years, and got another unpleasant surprise. Normally the only decoration in there was on Sham Harga's vest and the food was good solid stuff for a cold morning, all calories and fat and protein and maybe a vitamin crying softly because it was all alone. Now laboriously-made paper streamers crisscrossed the room and he was confronted with a crayonned menu in which the words 'Coronasion' and 'Royall' figured somewhere on every crooked line.

Vimes pointed wearily at the top of the menu.

'What's this?' he said.

Harga peered at it. They were alone in the grease-walled cafe. 'It says "Bye Royarl Appointmente", Captain,' he said proudly.

'What's it mean?'

Harga scratched his head with a ladle. 'What it means is,' he said, 'if the king comes in here, he'll like it.'

'Have you got anything that isn't too aristocratic for me to eat, then?' said Vimes sourly, and settled for a slice of plebeian fried bread and a proletarian steak cooked so rare you could still hear it bray. Vimes ate it at the counter.

A vague scraping noise disturbed his thoughts. 'What're you doing?' he said.

Harga looked up guiltily from his work behind the counter.

'Nothing, Cap'n,' he said. He tried to hide the evidence behind him when Vimes glared over the knife-chewed woodwork.

'Come on, Sham. You can show me.'

Harga's beefy hands came reluctantly into view.

'I was only scraping the old fat out of the pan,' he mumbled.

'I see. And how long have we known each other, Sham?' said Vimes, with terrible kindness.

'Years, Cap'n,' said Harga. 'You bin coming in here nearly every day, reg'lar. One of my best customers.'

Vimes leaned over the counter until his nose was level with the squashy pink thing in the middle of Harga's face.

'And in all that time, have you *ever* changed the fat?' he demanded.

Harga tried to back away. 'Well—'

'It's been like a friend to me, that old fat,' said Vimes. 'There's little black bits in there I've grown to know and love. It's a meal in itself. And you've cleaned out the coffee jug, haven't you. I can tell. This is love-in-a-canoe coffee if ever I tasted it. The other stuff had *flavour.*'

'Well, I thought it was time—'

'*Why?*'

Harga let the pan fall from his pudgy fingers. 'Well, I thought, if the king should happen to come in—'

'You're all *mad!*'

'But, Cap'n—'

Vimes's accusing finger buried itself up to the second joint in Harga's expansive vest.

'You don't even know the wretched fellow's name!' he shouted.

Harga rallied. 'I do, Cap'n,' he stuttered. 'Course I do. Seen it on the decorations and everything. He's called Rex Vivat.'

Very gently, shaking his head in despair, crying in his heart for the essential servility of mankind, Vimes let him go.

In another time and place, the Librarian finished reading. He'd reached the end of the text. Not the end of the book – there was plenty more book. It had been scorched beyond the point of legibility, though.

Not that the last few unburned pages were very easy to read. The author's hand had been shaking, he'd been writing fast, and he'd blotted a lot. But the Librarian had wrestled with many a terrifying text in some of the worst books ever bound, words that tried to read you as you read them, words that writhed on the page. At least these weren't words like that. These were just the words of a man frightened for his life. A man writing a dreadful warning.

It was a page a little back from the burned section that drew the Librarian's eye. He sat and stared at it for some time.

Then he stared at the darkness.

It was *his* darkness. He was asleep out there somewhere. Somewhere out there a thief was heading for this place, to steal this book. And then someone would read this book, read these words, and do it anyway.

His hands itched.

All he had to do was hide the book, or drop on to the thief's head and unscrew it by the ears.

He stared into the darkness again . . .

But that would be interfering with the course of history. Horrible things could happen. The Librarian knew all about this sort of thing, it was part of what you had to know before you were allowed into L-space. He'd seen pictures in ancient books. Time could bifurcate, like a pair of trousers. You could end up in the wrong leg, living a life that was actually happening in the *other* leg, talking to people who weren't in your leg, walking into walls that weren't there any more. Life could be horrible in the wrong trouser of Time.

Besides, it was against Library rules.* The assembled Librarians of Time and Space would certainly have something to say about it if he started to tinker with causality.

He closed the book carefully and tucked it back into the shelf. Then he swung gently from bookcase to bookcase until he reached the doorway. For a moment he stopped and looked down at his own sleeping body. Perhaps he wondered, briefly, whether to wake himself up, have a little chat, tell himself that he had friends and not to worry. If so, he must have decided against it. You could get yourself into a lot of trouble that way.

Instead he slipped out of the door, and lurked in the shadows, and followed the hooded thief when it came out clutching the book, and waited near the dread portal in the rain until the Elucidated Brethren had met and, when the last one left, followed him to his home, and murmured to himself in anthropoid surprise . . .

---

* The three rules of the Librarians of Time and Space are: 1) Silence; 2) Books must be returned no later than the last date shown; and 3) Do not interfere with the nature of causality.

And then ran back to his Library and the treacherous pathways of L-space.

By mid-morning the streets were packed, Vimes had docked Nobby a day's salary for waving a flag, and an air of barbed gloom settled over the Yard, like a big black cloud with occasional flashes of lightning in it.

'"Get up in a high place",' muttered Nobby. 'That's all very well to say.'

'I was looking forward to lining the streets,' said Colon. 'I'd have got a good view.'

'You were going on about privilege and the rights of man the other night,' said Nobby accusingly.

'Yes, well, one of the privileges and rights of this man is getting a good view,' said the sergeant. 'That's all I'm saying.'

'I've never seen the captain in such a filthy temper,' said Nobby. 'I liked it better when he was on the drink. I reckon he's—'

'You know, I think Errol is really ill,' said Carrot.

They turned towards the fruit basket.

'He's very hot. And his skin looks all shiny.'

'What's the right temperature for a dragon?' said Colon.

'Yeah. How do you take it?' said Nobby.

'I think we ought to ask Lady Ramkin to have a look at him,' said Carrot. 'She knows about these things.'

'No, she'll be getting ready for the coronation. We shouldn't go disturbing her,' said Colon. He stretched out his hand to Errol's quivering flanks. 'I used to have a dog that – arrgh! That's not hot, that's boiling!'

'I've offered him lots of water and he just won't touch it. What are you *doing* with that kettle, Nobby?'

Nobby looked innocent. 'Well, I thought we might as well make a cup of tea before we go out. It's a shame to waste—'

'Take it off him!'

Noon came. The fog didn't lift but it did thin a bit, to allow a pale yellow haze where the sun should have been.

Although the passage of years had turned the post of Captain of the Watch into something rather shabby, it still meant that Vimes was entitled to a seat at official occasions. The pecking order had moved it, though, so that now he was in the lowest tier on the rickety bleachers between the Master of the Fellowship of Beggars and the head of the Teachers' Guild. He didn't mind that. Anything was better than the top row, among the Assassins, Thieves, Merchants and all the other things that had floated to the top of society. He never knew what to talk about. Anyway, the teacher was restful company since he didn't do much but clench and unclench his hands occasionally, and whimper.

'Something wrong with your neck, Captain?' said the chief beggar politely, as they waited for the coaches.

'What?' said Vimes distractedly.

'You keep on staring upwards,' said the beggar.

'Hmm? Oh. No. Nothing wrong,' said Vimes.

The beggar wrapped his velvet cloak around him.

'You couldn't by any chance spare – ' he paused, calculating a sum in accordance with his station – 'about three hundred dollars for a twelve-course civic banquet, could you?'

'No.'

'Fair enough. Fair enough,' said the chief beggar amiably. He sighed. It wasn't a rewarding job, being chief beggar. It was the differentials that did for you. Low-grade beggars made a reasonable enough living on pennies, but people tended to look the other way when you asked them for a sixteen-bedroom mansion for the night.

Vimes resumed his study of the sky.

Up on the dais the High Priest of Blind Io, who last night by dint of elaborate ecumenical argument and eventually by a club with nails in it had won the right to crown the king, fussed over his preparations. By the small portable sacrificial altar a tethered billy goat was peacefully chewing the cud and possibly thinking, in Goat: What a lucky billy goat I am, to be given such a good view of the proceedings. This is going to be something to tell the kids.

Vimes scanned the diffused outlines of the nearest buildings.

A distant cheering suggested that the ceremonial procession was on its way.

There was a scuffle of activity around the dais as Lupine Wonse chivvied a scramble of servants who rolled a purple carpet down the steps.

Across the square, amongst the ranks of Ankh-Morpork's faded aristocracy, Lady Ramkin's face tilted upwards.

Around the throne, which had been hastily created out of wood and gold foil, a number of lesser priests, some of them with slight head wounds, shuffled into position.

Vimes shifted in his seat, aware of the sound of his own heartbeat, and glared at the haze over the river.

. . . and saw the wings.

*

160

Dear Mother and Father [wrote Carrot, in between staring dutifully into the fog] Well, the town is *On Fate* for the coronation,
which is more complicated than at home, and now I am on Day
duty as well. This is a shame because, I was going to watch the
Coronation with Reet, but it does not do to complain. I must go
now because we are expecting a dragon any minute although it
does not exist really. Your loving son, Carrot.

PS. Have you seen anything of Minty lately?

'You idiot!'

'Sorry,' said Vimes. 'Sorry.'

People were climbing back into their seats, many of them giving
him furious looks. Wonse was white with fury.

'How could you have been so *stupid?*' he raged.

Vimes stared at his own fingers.

'I thought I saw—' he began.

'It was a *raven!* You know what ravens are? There must be
hundreds of them in the city!'

'In the fog, you see, the size wasn't easy to—' Vimes mumbled.

'And poor Master Greetling, you ought to have known what loud
noises do to him!' The head of the Teachers' Guild had to be led
away by some kind people.

'Shouting out like that!' Wonse went on.

'Look, I said I'm sorry! It was an honest mistake!'

'I've had to hold up the procession and everything!'

Vimes said nothing. He could feel hundreds of amused or unsym-
pathetic eyes on him.

'Well,' he muttered, 'I'd better be getting back to the Yard—'

Wonse's eyes narrowed. 'No,' he snapped. 'But you can go home,
if you like. Or anywhere your *fancies* take you. Give me your
badge.'

'Huh?'

Wonse held out his hand.

'Your badge,' he repeated.

'My badge?'

'That's what I said. I want to keep you out of trouble.'

Vimes looked at him in astonishment. 'But it's my *badge!*'

'And you're going to give it to me,' said Wonse grimly. 'By order
of the king.'

'What d'you mean? He doesn't even know!' Vimes heard the
wailing in his own voice.

Wonse scowled. 'But he will,' he said. 'And I don't expect he'll
even bother to appoint a successor.'

Vimes slowly unclipped the verdigrised disc of copper, weighed it in his hand, and then tossed it to Wonse without a word.

For a moment he considered pleading, but something rebelled. He turned, and stalked off through the crowd.

So that was it.

As simple as that. After half a lifetime of service. No more City Watch. Huh. Vimes kicked at the pavement. It'd be some sort of Royal Guard now.

With plumes in their damn helmets.

Well, he'd had enough. It wasn't a proper life anyway, in the Watch. You didn't meet people in the best of circumstances. There must be hundreds of other things he could do, and if he thought for long enough he could probably remember what some of them were.

Pseudopolis Yard was off the route of the procession, and as he stumbled into the Watch House he could hear the distant cheering beyond the rooftops. Across the city the temple gongs were being sounded.

Now they are ringing the gongs, thought Vimes, but soon they will – they will – they will *not* be ringing the gongs. Not much of an aphorism, he thought, but he could work on it. He had the time, now.

Vimes noticed the mess.

Errol had started eating again. He'd eaten most of the table, the grate, the coal scuttle, several lamps and the squeaky rubber hippo. Now he lay in his box again, skin twitching, whimpering in his sleep.

'A right mess you've made,' said Vimes enigmatically. Still, at least *he* wouldn't have to tidy it up.

He opened his desk drawer.

Someone had eaten into that, too. All that was left was a few shards of glass.

Sergeant Colon hauled himself on to the parapet around the Temple of Small Gods. He was too old for this sort of thing. He'd joined for the bell ringing, not sitting around on high places waiting for dragons to find him.

He got his breath back, and peered through the fog.

'Anyone human still up here?' he whispered.

Carrot's voice sounded dead and featureless in the dull air.

'Here I am, Sergeant,' he said.

'I was just checking if you were still here,' said Colon.

'I'm still here, Sergeant,' said Carrot, obediently.

Colon joined him.

'Just checking you were not et,' he said, trying to grin.

'I haven't been et,' said Carrot.

'Oh,' said Colon. 'Good, then.' He tapped his fingers on the damp stonework, feeling he ought to make his position absolutely clear.

'Just checking,' he repeated. 'Part of my duty, see. Going around, sort of thing. It's not that I'm frightened of being up on the roofs by myself, you understand. Thick up here, isn't it.'

'Yes, Sergeant.'

'Everything all okay?' Nobby's muffled voice sidled its way through the thick air, quickly followed by its owner.

'Yes, Corporal,' said Carrot.

'What you doing up here?' Colon demanded.

'I was just coming up to check Lance-constable Carrot was all right,' said Nobby innocently. 'What were *you* doing, Sergeant?'

'We're all all right,' said Carrot, beaming. 'That's good, isn't it.'

The two NCOs shifted uneasily and avoided looking at one another. It seemed like a long way back to their posts, across the damp, cloudy and, above all, *exposed* rooftops.

Colon made an executive decision.

'Sod this,' he said, and found a piece of fallen statuary to sit on. Nobby leaned on the parapet and winkled a damp dog-end from the unspeakable ashtray behind his ear.

'Heard the procession go by,' he observed. Colon filled his pipe, and struck a match on the stone beside him.

'If that dragon's alive,' he said, blowing out a plume of smoke and turning a small patch of fog into smog, 'then it'll have got the hell away from here, I'm telling you. Not the right sort of place for dragons, a city,' he added, in the tones of someone doing a great job of convincing himself. 'It'll have gone off to somewhere where there's high places and plenty to eat, you mark my words.'

'Somewhere like the city, you mean?' said Carrot.

'Shut up,' said the other two in unison.

'Chuck us the matches, Sergeant,' said Nobby.

Colon tossed the bundle of evil yellow-headed lucifers across the leads. Nobby struck one, which was immediately blown out. Shreds of fog drifted past him.

'Wind's getting up,' he observed.

'Good. Can't stand this fog,' said Colon. 'What was I saying?'

'You were saying the dragon'll be miles away,' prompted Nobby.

'Oh. Right. Well, it stands to reason, doesn't it? I mean, I wouldn't hang around here if I could fly away. If I could fly, I wouldn't be sitting on a roof on some manky old statue. If I could fly, I'd—'

'What statue?' said Nobby, cigarette halfway to his mouth.

'This one,' said Colon, thumping the stone. 'And don't try to give me the willies, Nobby. You know there's hundreds of mouldy old statues up on Small Gods.'

'No I don't,' said Nobby. 'What I do know is, they were all taken down last month when they releaded the roof. There's just the roof and the dome and that's it. You have to take notice of little things like that,' he added, 'when you're detectoring.'

In the damp silence that followed Sergeant Colon looked down at the stone he was sitting on. It had a taper, and a scaly pattern, and a sort of indefinable tail-like quality. Then he followed its length up and into the rapidly-thinning fog.

On the dome of Small Gods the dragon raised its head, yawned, and unfolded its wings.

The unfolding wasn't a simple operation. It seemed to go on for some time, as the complex biological machinery of ribs and pleats slid apart. Then, with wings outstretched, the dragon yawned, took a few steps to the edge of the roof, and launched itself into the air.

After a while a hand appeared over the edge of the parapet. It flailed around for a moment until it got a decent grip.

There was a grunt. Carrot hauled himself back on to the roof and pulled the other two up behind him. They lay flat out on the leads, panting. Carrot observed the way that the dragon's talons had scored deep grooves in the metal. You couldn't help noticing things like that.

'Hadn't,' he panted, 'hadn't we better warn people?'

Colon dragged himself forward until he could look across the city.

'I don't think we need bother,' he said. 'I think they'll soon find out.'

The High Priest of Blind Io was stumbling over his words. There had never been an official coronation service in Ankh-Morpork, as far as he could find out. The old kings had managed quite well with something on the lines of: 'We hath got the crown, i'faith, and we will kill any whoreson who tries to take it away, by the Lord Harry.' Apart from anything else, this was rather short. He'd spent a long time drafting something longer and more in keeping with the spirit of the times, and was having some trouble remembering it.

He was also being put off by the goat, which was watching him with loyal interest.

164

'Get *on* with it!' Wonse hissed, from his position behind the throne.

'All in good time,' the high priest hissed back. 'This is a coronation, I'll have you know. You might try to show a little respect.'

'Of course I'm showing respect! Now get on—'

There was a shout, off to the right. Wonse glared into the crowd. 'It's that Ramkin woman,' he said. 'What's she up to?'

People around her were chattering excitedly now. Fingers pointed all the same way, like a small fallen forest. There were one or two screams, and then the crowd moved like a tide.

Wonse looked along the wide Street of Small Gods.

It wasn't a raven out there. Not this time.

The dragon flew slowly, only a few feet above the ground. wings sculling gracefully through the air.

The flags that crisscrossed the street were caught up and snapped like so much cobweb, piling up on the creature's spine plates and flapping back along the length of its tail.

It flew with head and neck fully extended, as if the great body was being towed like a barge. The people on the street yelled and fought one another for the safety of doorways. It paid them no attention.

It should have come roaring, but the only sounds were the creaking of wings and the snapping of banners.

It *should* have come roaring. Not like this, not slowly and deliberately, giving terror time to mature. It should have come threatening. Not promising.

It should have come roaring, not flying gently to the accompaniment of the zip and zing of merry bunting.

Vimes pulled open the other drawer of his desk and glared at the paperwork, such as there was of it. There wasn't really much in there that he could call his own. A scrap of sugar bag reminded him that he now owed the Tea Kitty six pence.

Odd. He wasn't angry yet. He would be later on, of course. By evening he'd be furious. Drunk and furious. But not yet. Not yet. It hadn't really sunk in, and he knew he was just going through the motions as a preventative against thinking.

Errol stirred sluggishly in his box, raised his head and whined.

'What's the matter, boy?' said Vimes, reaching down. 'Upset stomach?'

The little dragon's skin was moving as though heavy industry was being carried on inside. Nothing in *Diseases of the Dragon* said anything about *this*. From the swollen stomach came sounds like a distant and complicated war in an earthquake zone.

That surely wasn't right. Sybil Ramkin said you had to pay great attention to a dragon's diet, since even a minor stomach upset would decorate the walls and ceiling with pathetic bits of scaly skin. But in the past few days . . . well, there had been cold pizzas, and the ash from Nobby's horrible dog-ends, and all-in-all Errol had eaten more or less what he liked. Which was just about everything, to judge by the room. Not to mention the contents of the bottom drawer.

'We really haven't looked after you very well, have we?' said Vimes. 'Treated you like a dog, really.' He wondered what effect squeaky rubber hippos had on the digestion.

Vimes became slowly aware that the distant cheering had turned to screams.

He stared vaguely at Errol, and then smiled an incredibly evil smile and stood up.

There were sounds of panic and the mob on the run.

He placed his battered helmet on his head and gave it a jaunty tap. Then, humming a mad little tune, he sauntered out of the building.

Errol remained quite still for a while and then, with extreme difficulty, half-crawled and half-rolled out of his box. Strange messages were coming from the massive part of his brain that controlled his digestive system. It was demanding certain things that he couldn't put a name to. Fortunately it was able to describe them in minute detail to the complex receptors in his enormous nostrils. They flared, subjecting the air of the room to an intimate examination. His head turned, triangulating.

He pulled himself across the floor and began to eat, with every sign of enjoyment, Carrot's tin of armour polish.

People streamed past Vimes as he strolled up the Street of Small Gods. Smoke rose into the air from the Plaza of Broken Moons.

The dragon squatted in the middle of it, on what remained of the coronation dais. It had a self-satisfied expression.

There was no sign of the throne, or of its occupant, although it was possible that complicated forensic examination of the small pile of charcoal in the wrecked and smouldering woodwork might offer some clue.

Vimes caught hold of an ornamental fountain to steady himself as the crowds stampeded by. Every street out of the plaza was packed with struggling bodies. Not noisy ones, Vimes noticed. People weren't wasting their breath with screaming any more. There was just this solid, deadly determination to be somewhere else.

The dragon spread its wings and flapped them luxuriously. The people at the rear of the crowd took this as a signal to climb up the backs of the people in front of them and run for safety from head to head.

Within a few seconds the square was empty of all save the stupid and the terminally bewildered. Even the badly trampled were making a spirited crawl for the nearest exit.

Vimes looked around him. There seemed to be a lot of fallen flags, some of which were being eaten by an elderly goat which couldn't believe its luck. He could distantly see Cut-me-own-Throat on his hands and knees, trying to restore the contents of his tray.

By Vimes's side a small child waved a flag hesitantly and shouted 'Hurrah'.

Then everything went quiet.

Vimes bent down.

'I think you should be going home,' he said.

The child squinted up at him.

'Are you a Watch man?' it said.

'No,' said Vimes. 'And yes.'

'What happened to the king, Watch man?'

'Er. I think he's gone off for a rest,' said Vimes.

'My auntie said I shouldn't talk to Watch men,' said the child.

'Do you think it might be a good idea to go home and tell her how obedient you've been, then?' said Vimes.

'My auntie said, if I was naughty, she'd put me on the roof and call the dragon,' said the child, conversationally. 'My auntie said it eats you all up starting with the legs, so's you can see what's happening.'

'Why don't you go home and tell your auntie she's acting in the best traditions of Ankh-Morpork child-rearing?' said Vimes. 'Go on. Run along.'

'It crunches up all your bones,' said the child happily. 'And when it gets to your head, it—'

'Look, it's up there!' shouted Vimes. 'The great big dragon that crunches you up! Now go *home*!'

The child looked up at the thing perched on the crippled dais.

'I haven't seen it crunch anyone yet,' it complained.

'Push off or you'll feel the back of my hand,' said Vimes.

This seemed to fit the bill. The child nodded understandingly.

'Right. Can I shout hurrah again?'

'If you like,' said Vimes.

'Hurrah.'

So much for community policing, Vimes thought. He peered out from behind the fountain again.

A voice immediately above him rumbled, 'Say what you like, I still swear it's a magnificent specimen.'

Vimes's gaze travelled upwards until it crested the edge of the fountain's top bowl.

'Have you noticed,' said Sybil Ramkin, hauling herself upright by a piece of eroded statuary and dropping down in front of him, 'how every time we meet, a dragon turns up?' She gave him an arch smile. 'It's a bit like having your own tune. Or something.'

'It's just sitting there,' said Vimes hurriedly. 'Just looking around. As if it's waiting for something to happen.'

The dragon blinked with Jurassic patience.

The roads off the square were packed with people. That's the Ankh-Morpork instinct, Vimes thought. Run away, and then stop and see if anything interesting is going to happen to other people.

There was a movement in the wreckage near the dragon's front talon, and the High Priest of Blind Io staggered to his feet, dust and splinters cascading from his robes. He was still holding the ersatz crown in one hand.

Vimes watched the old man look upwards into a couple of glowing red eyes a few feet away.

'Can dragons read minds?' whispered Vimes.

'I'm sure mine understand every word I say,' hissed Lady Ramkin. 'Oh, no! The silly old fool is giving it the crown!'

'But isn't that a smart move?' said Vimes. 'Dragons like gold. It's like throwing a stick for a dog, isn't it?'

'Oh dear,' said Sybil Ramkin. 'It might not, you know. Dragons have such sensitive mouths.'

The great dragon blinked at the tiny circle of gold. Then, with extreme delicacy, it extended one metre-long claw and hooked the thing out of the priest's trembling fingers.

'What d'you mean, sensitive?' said Vimes, watching the claw travel slowly towards the long, horse-like face.

'A really incredible sense of taste. They're so, well, chemically orientated.'

'You mean it can probably *taste* gold?' whispered Vimes, watching the crown being carefully licked.

'Oh, certainly. And smell it.'

Vimes wondered what the chances were of the crown being made of gold. Not high, he decided. Gold foil over copper, perhaps. Enough to fool human beings. And then he wondered what someone's reaction would be if they were offered sugar which turned out, once you'd put three spoonfuls in your coffee, to be salt.

The dragon removed the claw from its mouth in one graceful movement and caught the high priest, who was just sneaking away, a blow which knocked him high into the air. When he was screaming at the top of the arc the great mouth came around and – 'Gosh!' said Lady Ramkin.

There was a groan from the watchers.

'The *temperature* of the thing!' said Vimes. 'I mean, nothing left! Just a wisp of smoke!'

There was another movement in the rubble. Another figure pulled itself upright and leaned dazedly against a broken spar.

It was Lupine Wonse, under a coating of soot.

Vimes watched him look up into a pair of nostrils the size of drain-covers.

Wonse broke into a run. Vimes wondered what it felt like, running away from something like that, expecting any minute your backbone to reach, very briefly, a temperature somewhere beyond the vaporization point of iron. He could guess.

Wonse made it halfway across the square before the dragon darted forward with surprising agility for such a bulk and snatched him up. The talon swept on upward until the struggling figure was being held a few feet from the dragon's face.

It appeared to examine him for some time, turning him this way and that. Then, moving on its three free legs and flapping its wings occasionally to help with its balance, it trotted away across the plaza and headed towards the – what once had *been* the Patrician's palace. To what once had been the king's palace, too.

It ignored the frightened spectators silently pressing themselves against the walls. The arched gateway was shouldered aside with depressing ease. The doors themselves, tall and iron-bound and solid, lasted a surprising ten seconds before collapsing into a heap of glowing ash.

The dragon stepped through.

Lady Ramkin turned in astonishment. Vimes had started to laugh.

There was a manic edge to it and there were tears in his eyes, but it was still laughter. He laughed and laughed until he slid gently down the edge of the fountain, his legs splaying out in front of him.

'Hooray, hooray, hooray!' he giggled, almost choking.

'What on earth d'you mean?' Lady Ramkin demanded.

'Put out more flags! Blow the cymbals, roast the tocsin! We've crowned it! We've got a king after all! What ho!'

'Have you been drinking?' she snapped.

'Not yet!' sniggered Vimes. 'Not yet! But I will be!'

He laughed on, knowing that when he stopped black depression was going to drop on him like a lead souffle. But he could see the future stretching out ahead of them . . .

. . . after all, it was definitely *noble*. And it didn't carry money, and it couldn't answer back. It could certainly do something for the inner cities, too. Like torching them to the bedrock.

We'll really do it, he thought. That's the Ankh-Morpork way. If you can't beat it or corrupt it, you pretend it was your idea in the first place.

Vivat Draco.

He became aware that the small child had wandered up again. It waved its flag gently at him and said, 'Can I shout hurrah again now?'

'Why not?' said Vimes. 'Everyone else will.'

From the palace came the muffled sounds of complicated destruction . . .

Errol pulled a broomstick across the floor with his mouth and, whimpering with effort, hauled it upright. After a lot more whimpering and several false starts he managed to winkle the end of it between the wall and the big jar of lamp oil.

He paused for a moment, breathing like a bellows, and pushed.

The jar resisted for a moment, rocked back and forth once or twice, and then fell over and smashed on the flagstones. Crude, very badly-refined oil spread out in a black puddle.

Errol's huge nostrils twitched. Somewhere in the back of his brain unfamiliar synapses clicked like telegraph keys. Great balks of information flooded down the thick nerve cord to his nose, carrying inexplicable information about triple bonds, alkanes and geometric isomerism. However, almost all of it missed the small part of Errol's brain that was used for being Errol.

All he knew was that he was suddenly very, very thirsty.

Something major was happening in the palace. There was the occasional crash of a floor or thump of a falling ceiling . . .

In his rat-filled dungeon, behind a door with more locks than a major canal network, the Patrician of Ankh-Morpork lay back and grinned in the darkness.

*

Outside, bonfires flared in the dusk.

Ankh-Morpork was celebrating. No-one was quite sure why, but they'd worked themselves up for a celebration tonight, barrels had been broached, oxen had been put on spits, one paper hat and celebratory mug had been issued per child, and it seemed a shame to waste all that effort. Anyway, it had been a very interesting day, and the people of Ankh-Morpork set great store by entertainment.

'The way I see it,' said one of the revellers, halfway through a huge greasy lump of half-raw meat, 'a dragon as king mightn't be a bad idea. When you think it through, is what I mean.'

'It definitely looked very gracious,' said the woman to his right, as if testing the idea. 'Sort of, well, sleek. Nice and smart. Not scruffy. Takes a bit of a pride in itself.' She glared at some of the younger revellers further down the table. 'The trouble with people today is they don't take pride in themselves.'

'And there's foreign policy, of course,' said a third, helping himself to a rib. 'When you come to think about it.'

'What d'you mean?'

'Diplomacy,' said the rib-eater, flatly.

They thought about it. And then you could see them turning the idea around and thinking about it the other way, in a polite effort to see what the hell he was getting at.

'Dunno,' said the monarchical expert slowly. 'I mean, your actual dragon, it's got these, basically, two sort of ways of negotiation. Hasn't it? I mean, it's either roasting you alive, or it isn't. Correct me if I'm wrong,' he added.

'That's my point. I mean, let's say the ambassador from Klatch comes along, you know how arrogant that lot are, suppose he says: we want this, we want that, we want the other thing. Well,' he said, beaming at them, 'what *we* say is, shut your face unless you want to go home in a jar.'

They tried out this idea for mental fit. It had that certain something.

'They've got a big fleet, Klatch,' said the monarchist uncertainly. 'Could be a bit risky, roasting diplomats. People see a pile of charcoal come back on the boat, they tend to look a bit askance.'

'Ah, *then* we say, Ho there, Johnny Klatchian, you no like-um, big fella lizard belong-sky bake mud hut belong-you pretty damn chop-chop.'

'We could really say that?'

'Why not? *And* then we say, send plenty tribute toot sweet.'

'I never did like them Klatchians,' said the woman firmly. 'The stuff they eat! It's disgustin'. And gabblin' away all the time in their heathen lingo . . .'

In the shadows, a match flared.

Vimes cupped his hands around the flame, sucked on the foul tobacco, tossed the match into the gutter and slouched off down the damp, puddle-punctuated alley.

If there was anything that depressed him more than his own cynicism, it was that quite often it still wasn't as cynical as real life.

We've got along with the other guys for centuries, he thought. Getting along has practically been all our foreign policy. Now I think I've just heard us declare war on an ancient civilisation that we've always got along with, more or less, even if they do talk funny. And after that, the world. What's worse, we'll probably win.

Similar thoughts, although with a different perspective, were going through the minds of the civic leaders of Ankh-Morpork when, next morning, each received a short note bidding them to be at the palace for a working lunch, by order.

It didn't say whose order. Or, they noted, whose lunch.

Now they were assembled in the antechamber.

And there had been changes. It had never been what you might call a select place. The Patrician had always felt that if you made people comfortable they might want to stay. The furniture had been a few very elderly chairs and, around the walls, portraits of earlier city rulers holding scrolls and things.

The chairs were still there. The portraits were not. Or, rather, the stained and cracked canvases were piled in a corner, but the gilt frames were gone.

The councillors tried to avoid one another's faces, and sat tapping their fingers on their knees.

Finally a couple of very worried-looking servants opened the doors to the main hall. Lupine Wonse lurched through.

Most of the councillors had been up all night anyway, trying to formulate some kind of policy *vis-à-vis* dragons, but Wonse looked as though he hadn't been to sleep in years. His face was the colour of a fermented dishcloth. Never particularly well-padded, he now looked like something out of a pyramid.

'Ah,' he intoned. 'Good. Are you all here? Then perhaps you would step this way, gentlemen.'

'Er,' said the head thief, 'the note mentioned lunch?'

'Yes?' said Wonse.

'With a *dragon?*'

'Good grief, you don't think it would eat you, do you?' said Wonse. 'What an idea!'

172

'Never crossed me mind,' said the head thief, relief blowing from his ears like steam. 'The very idea. Haha.'

'Haha,' said the chief merchant.

'Hoho,' said the head assassin. 'The very idea.'

'No, I expect you're all far too stringy,' said Wonse. 'Haha.'

'Haha.'

'Ahaha.'

'Hoho.' The temperature lowered by several degrees.

'So if you would kindly step this way?'

The great hall had changed. For one thing, it was a great deal greater. Several walls had been knocked into adjoining rooms, and the ceiling and several storeys of upper rooms had been entirely removed. The floor was a mass of rubble except in the middle of the room, which was a heap of gold—

Well, gold*ish*. It looked as though someone had scoured the palace for anything that shone or glittered. There were the picture frames, and the gold thread out of tapestries, and silver, and the occasional gem. There were also tureens from the kitchens, candlesticks, warming pans, fragments of. mirror. Sparkly stuff.

The councillors were not in a position to pay much attention to this, however, because of what was hanging above their heads.

It looked like the biggest badly-rolled cigar in the universe, if the biggest badly-rolled cigar in the universe was in the habit of hanging upside down. Two talons could be dimly seen gripping the dark rafters.

Halfway between the glittering heap and the doorway a small table had been laid. The councillors noted without much surprise that the familiar ancient silverware was missing. There were china plates, and cutlery that looked as though it had very recently been whittled from bits of wood. Wonse took a seat at the head of the table and nodded to the servants.

'Please be seated, gentlemen,' he said. 'I am sorry things are a little . . . different, but the king hopes you will bear with it until matters can be more suitably organized.'

'The, er,' said the head merchant.

'The king,' repeated Wonse. His voice sounded one dribble away from madness.

'Oh. The king. Right,' said the merchant. From where he was sitting he had a good view of the big hanging thing. There seemed to be some movement there, some trembling in the great folds that wrapped it. 'Long life to him, say I,' he added quickly.

The first course was soup with dumplings in it. Wonse didn't have any. The rest of them ate in a terrified silence broken only by the dull chiming of wood on china.

'There are certain matters of decree to which the king feels your assent would be welcome,' said Wonse, eventually. 'A pure formality, of course, and I am sorry to bother you with such petty detail.'

The big bundle appeared to sway in the breeze.

'No trouble at all,' squeaked the head thief.

'The king graciously desires it to be known,' said Wonse, 'that it would be pleased to receive coronation gifts from the population at large. Nothing complex, of course. Simply any precious metals or gems they might have by them and can easily spare. I should stress, by the way, that this is by no means compulsory. Such generosity as he is confident of expecting should be an entirely voluntary act.'

The chief assassin looked sadly at the rings on his fingers, and sighed. The head merchant was already resignedly unshipping his gilt chain of office from around his neck.

'Why, gentlemen!' said Wonse. 'This is most unexpected!'

'Um,' said the Archchancellor of Unseen University. 'You will be – that is, I am sure the king is aware that, traditionally, the University is exempt from all city levies and taxes . . .'

He stifled a yawn. The wizards had spent the night directing their best spells against the dragon. It was like punching fog.

'My dear sir, this is no levy,' protested Wonse. 'I hope that nothing I have said would lead you to expect anything like that. Oh, no! No. Any tribute should be, as I said, entirely voluntary. I hope that is absolutely clear.'

'As crystal,' said the head assassin, glaring at the old wizard. 'And these entirely voluntary tributes we are about to make, they go—?'

'On the hoard,' said Wonse.

'Ah.'

'While I am positive the people of the city will be very generous indeed once they fully understand the situation,' said the head merchant, 'I am sure the king will understand that there is very little gold in Ankh-Morpork?'

'Good point,' said Wonse. 'However, the king intends to pursue a vigorous and dynamic foreign policy which should remedy matters.'

'Ah,' the councillors chorused, rather more enthusiastically this time.

'For example,' Wonse went on, 'the king feels that our legitimate interests in Quirm, Sto Lat, Pseudopolis and Tsort have been seriously compromised in recent centuries. This will be speedily corrected and, gentlemen, I can assure you that treasure will positively flow into the city from those anxious to enjoy the king's protection.'

The head assassin glanced at the hoard. A very definite idea formed in his mind as to where all that treasure would end up. You had to admire the way dragons knew how to put the bite on. It was practically human.

'Oh,' he said.

'Of course, there will probably be other acquisitions in the way of land, property and so forth, and the king wishes it to be fully understood that loyal Privy Councillors will be richly rewarded. '

'And, er,' said the head assassin, who was beginning to feel that he had got a firm grip on the nature of the king's mental processes, 'no doubt the, er—'

'Privy Councillors,' said Wonse.

'No doubt they will respond with even greater generosity in the matter of, for example, treasure?'

'I am sure such considerations haven't crossed the king's mind,' said Wonse, 'but the point is very well made.'

'I thought it would be.'

The next course was fat pork, beans and floury potatoes. More, as they couldn't help noticing, fattening food.

Wonse had a glass of water.

'Which brings us on to a further matter of some delicacy which I am sure that well-travelled, broadminded gentlemen such as your-selves will have no difficulty in accepting,' he said. The hand holding the glass was beginning to shake.

'I hope it will also be understood by the population at large, especially since the king will undoubtedly be able to contribute in so many ways to the well-being and defence of the city. For example, I am sure that the people will rest more contentedly in their beds knowing that the dr— the king is tirelessly protecting them from harm. There can, however, be ridiculous ancient . . . prejudices . . . which will only be eradicated by ceaseless work . . . on the part of all men of good will.'

He paused, and looked at them. The head assassin said later that he had looked into the eyes of many men who, obviously, were very near death, but he had never looked into eyes that were so clearly and unmistakably looking back at him from the slopes of Hell. He hoped he would never, he said, ever have to look into eyes like that again.

'I am referring,' said Wonse, each word coming slowly to the surface like bubbles in some quicksand, 'to the matter of . . . the king's . . . diet.'

There was a terrible silence. They heard the faint rustle of wings behind them, and the shadows in the corners of the hall grew darker and seemed to close in.

'Diet,' said the head thief, in a hollow voice.

'Yes,' said Wonse. His voice was almost a squeak. Sweat was dripping down his face. The head assassin had once heard the word 'rictus' and wondered when you should use it correctly to describe someone's expression, and now he knew. That was what Wonse's face had become; it was the ghastly rictus of someone trying not to hear the words his own mouth was saying.

'We, er, we thought,' said the head assassin, very carefully, 'that the dr— the king, well, must have been arranging matters for himself, over the weeks.'

'Ah, but poor stuff, you know. Poor stuff. Stray animals and so forth,' said Wonse, staring hard at the tabletop. 'Obviously, as king, such makeshifts are no longer appropriate.'

The silence grew and took on a texture. The councillors thought hard, especially about the meal they had just eaten. The arrival of a huge trifle with a lot of cream on it only served to concentrate their minds.

'Er,' said the head merchant, 'how often is the king hungry?'

'All the time,' said Wonse, 'but it eats once a month. It is really a ceremonial occasion.'

'Of course,' said the head merchant. 'It would be.'

'And, er,' said the head assassin, 'when did the king last, er, eat?'

'I'm sorry to say it hasn't eaten properly ever since it came here,' said Wonse.

'Oh.'

'You must understand,' said Wonse, fiddling desperately with his wooden cutlery, 'that merely waylaying people like some common assassin—'

'Excuse *me*—' the head assassin began.

'Some common murderer, I mean – there is no . . . satisfaction there. The whole essence of the king's feeding is that it should be, well . . . an act of bonding between king and subjects. It is, it is perhaps a living allegory. Reinforcing the close links between the crown and the community,' he added.

'The precise nature of the meal—' the head thief began, almost choking on the words. 'Are we talking about young maidens here?'

'Sheer prejudice,' said Wonse. 'The age is immaterial. Marital status is, of course, of importance. And social class. Something to do with flavour, I believe.' He leaned forward, and now his voice was pain-filled and urgent and, they felt, genuinely his own for the first time. 'Please consider it!' he hissed. 'After all, just one a month! In exchange for so much! The families of people of use to the king, Privy Councillors such as yourselves, would not, of course, even be considered. And when you think of all the alternatives . . .'

They didn't think about all the alternatives. It was enough to think about just one of them.

The silence purred at them as Wonse talked. They avoided one another's faces, for fear of what they might see mirrored there. Each man thought: one of the others is bound to say something soon, some protest, and then I'll murmur agreement, not actually *say* anything, I'm not as stupid as that, but definitely murmur very firmly, so that the others will be in no doubt that I thoroughly disapprove, because at a time like this it behooves all decent men to nearly stand up and be almost heard . . .

But no-one said anything. The cowards, each man thought.

And no-one touched the pudding, or the brick-thick chocolate mints served afterwards. They just listened in flushed, gloomy horror as Wonse's voice droned on, and when they were dismissed they tried to leave as separately as possible, so that they didn't have to talk to one another.

Except for the head merchant, that is. He found himself leaving the palace with the chief assassin, and they strolled side by side, minds racing. The chief merchant tried to look on the bright side; he was one of those men who organise sing-songs when things go drastically wrong.

'Well, well,' he said. 'So we're privy councillors now. Just fancy.'

'Hmm,' said the assassin.

'I wonder what's the difference between ordinary councillors and privy councillors?' wondered the merchant aloud.

The assassin scowled at him. 'I think,' he said, 'it is because you're expected to eat shit.'

He turned the glare back on his feet again. What kept going through his mind were Wonse's last words, as he shook the secretary's limp hand. He wondered if anyone else had heard them. Unlikely . . . they'd been a shape rather than a sound. Wonse had simply moved his lips around them while staring fixedly at the assassin's moon-tanned face.

Help. Me.

The assassin shivered. Why him? As far as he could see there was only one kind of help he was qualified to give, and very few people ever asked for it for themselves. In fact, they usually paid large sums for it to be given as a surprise present to other people. He wondered what was happening to Wonse that made any alternative seem better . . .

*

177

Wonse sat alone in the dark, ruined hall. Waiting.

He could try running. But it'd find him again. It'd always be able to find him. It could smell his mind.

Or it would flame him. That was worse. Just like the Brethren. *Perhaps* it was an instantaneous death, it *looked* an instantaneous death, but Wonse lay awake at night wondering whether those last micro-seconds somehow stretched to a subjective, white-hot eternity, every tiny part of your body a mere smear of plasma and you, there, alive in the middle of it all . . .

Not you. I would not flame you.

It wasn't telepathy. As far as Wonse had always understood it, telepathy was like hearing a voice in your head.

This was like hearing a voice in your body. His whole nervous system twanged to it, like a bow.

Rise.

Wonse jerked to his feet, overturning the chair and banging his legs on the table. When that voice spoke, he had as much control over his body as water had over gravity.

Come.

Wonse lurched across the floor.

The wings unfolded slowly, with the occasional creak, until they filled the hall from side to side. The tip of one smashed a window, and stuck out into the afternoon air.

The dragon slowly, sensuously, stretched out its neck and yawned. When it had finished, it brought its head around until it was a few inches in front of Wonse's face.

What does voluntary mean?

'It, er, it means doing something of your own free will,' said Wonse.

But they have no *free will! They will increase my hoard, or I will flame them!*

Wonse gulped. 'Yes,' he said, 'but you mustn't—'

The silent roar of fury spun him around.

There is nothing I mustn't!

'No, no, no!' squeaked Wonse, clutching his head. 'I didn't mean that! Believe me! This way is better, that's all! Better and safer!'

None can defeat me!

'This is certainly the case—'

None can control me!

Wonse flung up his finger-spread hands in a conciliatory fashion. 'Of course, of course,' he said. 'But there are ways and ways, you know. Ways and ways. All the roaring and flaming, you see, you don't need it . . .'

Foolish ape! How else can I make them do my bidding?

Wonse put his hands behind his back.

'They'll do it of their own free will,' he said. 'And in time, they'll come to believe it was their own idea. It'll be a tradition. Take it from me. We humans are adaptable creatures.'

The dragon gave him a long, blank stare.

'In fact,' said Wonse, trying to keep the trembling out of his voice, 'before too long, if someone comes along and tells them that a dragon king is a bad idea, they'll kill him themselves.'

The dragon blinked.

For the first time Wonse could remember, it seemed uncertain.

'I know people, you see,' said Wonse, simply.

The dragon continued to pin him with its gaze.

If you are lying . . . it thought, eventually.

'You know I can't. Not to you.'

And they really act like this?

'Oh, yes. All the time. It's a basic human trait.'

Wonse knew the dragon could read at least the upper levels of his mind. They resonated in terrible harmony. And he could see the mighty thoughts behind the eyes in front of him.

The dragon was horrified.

'I'm sorry,' said Wonse weakly. 'That's just how we are. It's all to do with survival, I think.'

There will be no mighty warriors sent to kill me? it thought, almost plaintively.

'I don't think so.'

No heroes?

'Not any more. They cost too much.'

But I will be eating people!

Wonse whimpered.

He felt the sensation of the dragon rummaging around in his mind, trying to find a clue to understanding. He half-saw, half-sensed the flicker of random images, of dragons, of the mythical age of reptiles and – and here he felt the dragon's genuine astonishment – of some of the less commendable areas of human history, which were most of it. And after the astonishment came the baffled anger. There was practically nothing the dragon could do to people that they had not, sooner or later, tried on one another, often with enthusiasm.

You have the effrontery to be squeamish, it thought at him. *But we were dragons. We were supposed to be cruel, cunning, heartless and terrible. But this much I can tell you, you ape –* the great face pressed even closer, so that Wonse was staring into the pitiless depths of its eyes – *we never burned and tortured and ripped one another apart and called it morality.*

The dragon stretched its wings again, once or twice, and then dropped heavily on to the tawdry assortment of mildly precious things. Its claws scrabbled at the pile. It sneered.

A three-legged lizard wouldn't hoard this lot, it thought.

'There will be better things,' whispered Wonse, temporarily relieved at the change in direction.

There had better be.

'Can I-t–' Wonse hesitated – 'can I ask you a question?'

Ask.

'You don't *need* to eat people, surely? I think that's the only problem from people's point of view, you see,' he added, his voice speeding up to a gabble. 'The treasure and everything, that doesn't have to be a problem, but if it's just a matter of, well, protein, then perhaps it has occurred to a powerful intellect such as your own that something less controversial, like a cow, might—'

The dragon breathed a horizontal streak of fire that calcined the opposite wall.

Need? Need? it roared, when the sound had died away. *You talk to me of need? Isn't it the tradition that the finest flower of woman-hood should be sent to the dragon to ensure peace and prosperity?*

'But, you see, we have always been moderately peaceful and reasonably prosperous—'

DO YOU WANT THIS STATE OF AFFAIRS TO CONTINUE?

The force of the thought drove Wonse to his knees.

'Of course,' he managed.

The dragon stretched its claws luxuriantly.

Then the need is not mine, it is yours, it thought.

Now get out of my sight.

Wonse sagged as it left his mind.

The dragon slithered over the cut-price hoard, leapt up on to the ledge of one of the hall's big windows, and smashed the stained glass with its head. The multicoloured image of a city father cascaded into the other debris below.

The long neck stretched out into the early evening air, and turned like a seeking needle. Lights were coming on across the city. The sound of a million people being alive made a muted, deep thrumming.

The dragon breathed deeply, joyfully.

Then it hauled the rest of its body on to the ledge, shouldered the remains of the window's frame aside, and leapt into the sky.

'What is it?' said Nobby.

It was vaguely round, of a woodish texture, and when struck made a noise like a ruler plucked over the edge of a desk.

Sergeant Colon tapped it again.

'I give in,' he said.

Carrot proudly lifted it out of the battered packaging.

'It's a cake,' he said, shoving both hands under the thing and raising it with some difficulty. 'From my mother.' He managed to put it on the table without trapping his fingers.

'Can you eat it?' said Nobby. 'It's taken months to get here. You'd think it would go stale.'

'Oh, it's to a special dwarfish recipe,' said Carrot. 'Dwarfish cakes don't go stale.'

Sergeant Colon gave it another sharp rap. 'I suppose not,' he conceded.

'It's incredibly sustaining,' said Carrot. 'Practically magical. The secret has been handed down from dwarf to dwarf for centuries. One tiny piece of this and you won't want anything to eat all day.'

'Get away?' said Colon.

'A dwarf can go hundreds of miles with a cake like this in his pack,' Carrot went on.

'I bet he can,' said Colon gloomily, 'I bet all the time he'd be thinking, "Bloody hell, I hope I can find something else to eat soon, otherwise it's the bloody cake again."'

Carrot, to whom the word irony meant something to do with metal, picked up his pike and after a couple of impressive rebounds managed to cut the cake into approximately four slices.

'There we are,' he said cheerfully. 'One for each of us, and one for the captain.' He realized what he had said. 'Oh. Sorry.'

'Yes,' said Colon flatly.

They sat in silence for a moment.

'I *liked* him,' said Carrot. 'I'm sorry he's gone.'

There was some more silence, very similar to the earlier silence but even deeper and more furrowed with depression.

'I expect you'll be made captain now,' said Carrot.

Colon started. 'Me? I don't want to be captain! I can't do the thinking. It's not worth all that thinking, just for another nine dollars a month.'

He drummed his fingers on the table.

'Is that all he got?' said Nobby. 'I thought officers were rolling in it.'

'Nine dollars a month,' said Colon. 'I saw the pay scales once. Nine dollars a month and two dollars plumes allowance. Only he never claimed that bit. Funny, really.'

'He wasn't the plumes type,' said Nobby.

'You're right,' said Colon. 'The thing about the captain, see, I

read this book once . . . you know we've all got alcohol in our bodies
. . . sort of *natural* alcohol? Even if you never touch a drop in your
life, your body sort of makes it anyway . . . but Captain Vimes, see,
he's one of those people whose body doesn't do it naturally. Like,
he was born two drinks below normal.'

'Gosh,' said Carrot.

'Yes . . . so, when he's sober, he's *really* sober. Knurd, they call
it. You know how you feel when you wake up if you've been on the
piss all night, Nobby? Well, he feels like that *all the time.*'

'Poor bugger,' said Nobby. 'I never realized. No wonder he's
always so gloomy.'

'So he's always trying to catch up, see. It's just that he doesn't
always get the dose right. And, of course – ' Colon glanced at Carrot
– 'he was brung low by a woman. Mind you, just about anything
brings him low.'

'So what do *we* do now, Sergeant?' said Nobby.

'And do you think he'd mind if we eat his cake?' said Carrot
wistfully. 'It'd be a shame to let it go stale.'

Colon shrugged.

The older men sat in miserable silence as Carrot macerated his
way through the cake like a bucket-wheel rockcrusher in a chalk
pit. Even if it had been the lightest of soufflés they wouldn't have
had any appetite.

They were contemplating life without the captain. It was going
to be bleak, even without dragons. Say what you liked about
Captain Vimes, he'd had style. It was a cynical, black-nailed style,
but he'd had it and they didn't. He could read long words and add
up. Even that was style, of a sort. He even got drunk in style.

They'd been trying to drag the minutes out, trying to stretch out
the time. But the night had come.

There was no hope for them.

They were going to have to go out on the streets.

It was six of the clock. And all wasn't well.

'I miss Errol, too,' said Carrot.

'He was the captain's, really,' said Nobby. 'Anyway, Lady
Ramkin'll know how to look after him.'

'It's not as though we could leave anything around, either,' said
Colon. 'I mean, even the lamp oil. He even drank the lamp oil.'

'And mothballs,' said Nobby. 'A whole box of mothballs. Why
would anyone want to eat mothballs? And the kettle. And sugar.
He was a devil for sugar.'

'He was nice, though,' said Carrot. 'Friendly.'

'Oh, I'll grant you,' said Colon. 'But it's not right, really, a pet
where you have to jump behind a table every time it hiccups.'

'I shall miss his little face,' said Carrot.

Nobby blew his nose, loudly.

It was echoed by a hammering on the door. Colon jerked his head. Carrot got up and opened it.

A couple of members of the palace guard were waiting with arrogant impatience. They stepped back when they saw Carrot, who had to bend a bit to see under the lintel; bad news like Carrot travels fast.

'We've brung you a proclamation,' said one of them. 'You've got to—'

'What's all that fresh paint on your breastplate?' said Carrot politely. Nobby and the sergeant peered around him.

'It's a dragon,' said the younger of the guards.

'*The* dragon,' corrected his superior.

''Ere, I know you,' said Nobby. 'You're Skully Maltoon. Used to live in Mincing Street. Your mum made cough sweets, din't she, and fell in the mixture and died. I never have a cough sweet but I think of your mum.'

'Hello, Nobby,' said the guard, without enthusiasm.

'I bet your old mum'd be proud of you, you with a *dragon* on your vest,' said Nobby conversationally. The guard gave him a look made of hatred and embarrassment.

'And new plumes on your hat, too,' Nobby added sweetly.

'*This here is a proclamation what you are commanded to read,*' said the guard loudly. 'And post up on street corners also. By order.'

'Whose?' said Nobby.

Sergeant Colon grabbed the scroll in one ham-like fist.

'Where As,' he read slowly, tracing the lettering with a hesitant finger, 'It hathe Pleas-Sed the Der-Rer-Aa-Ger – the dragon, Ker-Ii – king of kings and Aa-Ber-Ess-Uh-Ler – ' sweat beaded on the broad pink cliff of his forehead – 'absolute, that is, Rer-Uh-Ler-Eh-Rer, ruler of—'

He lapsed into the tortured silence of academia, his fingertip jerking slowly down the parchment.

'No,' he said at last. 'That's not right, is it? It's not going to eat someone?'

'Consume,' said the older guard.

'It's all part of the social . . . social contract,' said his assistant woodenly. 'A small price to pay, I'm sure you will agree, for the safety and protection of the city.'

'From what?' said Nobby. 'We've never had an enemy we couldn't bribe or corrupt.'

'Until now,' said Colon darkly.

183

'You catch on fast,' said the guard. 'So you're going to broadcast it. On pain of pain.'

Carrot peered over Colon's shoulder.

'What's a virgin?' he said.

'An unmarried girl,' said Colon quickly.

'What, like my friend Reet?' said Carrot, horrified.

'Well, no,' said Colon.

'She's not married, you know. None of Mrs Palm's girls are married.'

'Well, yes,' said Colon.

'Well, then,' said Carrot, with an air of finality. 'We're not having any of *that* kind of thing, I hope.'

'People won't stand for it,' said Colon. 'You mark my words.'

The guards stepped back, out of range of Carrot's rising wrath.

'They can please themselves,' said the senior guard. 'But if you don't proclaim it, you can try explaining things to His Majesty.'

They hurried off.

Nobby darted out into the street. 'Dragon on your vest!' he shouted. 'If your old mum knew about this she'd turn in her vat, you goin' around with a dragon on your vest!'

Colon wandered back to the table and spread out the scroll.

'Bad business,' he mumbled.

'It's already killed people,' said Carrot. 'Contrary to sixteen separate Acts in Council.'

'Well, yes. But that was just like, you know, the hurry-burly of this and that,' said Colon. 'Not that it wasn't bad, I mean, but people sort of *participating*, just handing over some slip of a girl and standing round watching as if it's all proper and legal, that's much worse.'

'I reckon it all depends on your point of view,' said Nobby thoughtfully.

'What d'you mean?'

'Well, from the point of view of someone being burned alive, it probably doesn't matter much,' said Nobby philosophically.

'People won't stand for it, I said,' said Colon, ignoring this. 'You'll see. They'll march on the palace, and what will the dragon do then, eh?'

'Burn 'em all,' said Nobby promptly.

Colon looked puzzled. 'It wouldn't do that, would it?' he said.

'Don't see what's to prevent it, do you?' said Nobby. He glanced out of the doorway. 'He was a good lad, that boy. Used to run errands for my grandad. Who'd have thought he'd go around with a dragon on his chest . . .'

'What are we going to *do*, Sergeant?' said Carrot.

'I don't want to be burned alive,' said Sergeant Colon. 'My wife'd give me hell. So I suppose we've got to wossname, proclaim it. But don't worry, lad,' he said, patting Carrot on one muscular arm and repeating, as if he hadn't quite believed himself the first time, 'it won't come to that. People'll never stand for it.'

Lady Ramkin ran her hands over Errol's body.

'Damned if I know what's going on in there,' she said. The little dragon tried to lick her face. 'What's he been eating?'

'The last thing, I think, was a kettle,' said Vimes.

'A kettle of what?'

'No. A kettle. A black thing with a handle and spout. He sniffed it for ages, then he ate it.'

Errol grinned weakly at him, and belched. They both ducked.

'Oh, and then we found him eating soot out of the chimney,' Vimes went on, as their heads rose again over the railings.

They leaned back over the reinforced bunker that was one of Lady Ramkin's sickbay pens. It had to be reinforced. Usually one of the first things a sick dragon did was lose control of its digestive processes.

'He doesn't look sick, exactly,' she said. 'Just fat.'

'He whines a lot. And you can sort of see things moving under his skin. You know what I think? You know you said they can rearrange their digestive system?'

'Oh, yes. All the stomachs and pancreatic crackers can be hooked up in various ways, you see. To take advantage—'

'Of whatever they can find to make flame with,' said Vimes. 'Yes. I think he's trying to make some sort of very hot flame. He wants to challenge the big dragon. Every time it takes to the air he just sits there whining.'

'And doesn't explode?'

'Not that we've noticed. I mean, I'm sure if he did, we'd spot it.'

'He just eats indiscriminately?'

'Hard to be sure. He sniffs everything, and eats most things. Two gallons of lamp oil, for example. Anyway, I can't leave him down there. We can't look after him properly. It's not as if we need to find out where the dragon is now,' he added bitterly.

'I think you're being a bit silly about all this,' she said, leading the way back to the house.

'Silly? I was sacked in front of all those people!'

'Yes, but it was all a misunderstanding, I'm sure.'

'*I* didn't misunderstand it!'

'Well, I think you're just upset because you're impotent.'

Vimes's eyes bulged. 'Whee?' he said.

'Against the dragon,' Lady Ramkin went on, quite unconcerned. 'You can't do anything about it.'

'I reckon this damn city and the dragon just about deserve one another,' said Vimes.

'People are frightened. You can't expect much of people when they're so frightened.' She touched him gingerly on his arm. It was like watching an industrial robot being expertly manipulated to grasp an egg gently.

'Not everyone's as brave as you,' she added, timidly.

'Me?'

'The other week. When you stopped them killing my dragons.'

'Oh, *that*. That's not bravery. Anyway, that was just people. People are easier. I'll tell you one thing for nothing, I'm not looking up that dragon's nose again. I wake up at days thinking about that.'

'Oh.' She seemed deflated. 'Well, if you're sure . . . I've got a lot of friends, you know. If you need any help, you've only got to say. The Duke of Sto Helit is looking for a guard captain, I'm sure. I'll write you a letter. You'll like them, they're a very nice young couple.'

'I'm not sure what I shall do next,' said Vimes, more gruffly than he intended. 'I'm considering one or two offers.'

'Well, of course. I'm sure you know best.'

Vimes nodded.

Lady Ramkin twisted her handkerchief round and round in her hands.

'Well, then,' she said.

'Well,' said Vimes.

'I, er, expect you'll be wanting to be off, then.'

'Yes, I expect I had better be going.'

There was a pause. Then they both spoke at once.

'It's been very—'

'I'd just like to say—'

'Sorry.'

'Sorry.'

'No, you were speaking.'

'No, sorry, you were saying?'

'Oh.' Vimes hesitated. 'I'll be off, then.'

'Oh. Yes.' Lady Ramkin gave him a washed-out smile. 'Can't keep all these offers waiting, can you,' she said.

She thrust out a hand. Vimes shook it carefully.

'So I'll just be going, then,' he said.

'Do call again,' said Lady Ramkin, more coldly, 'if you are ever in this area. And so on. I'm sure Errol would like to see you.'

'Yes. Well. Goodbye, then.'

'Goodbye, Captain Vimes.'

He stumbled out of the door and walked hurriedly down the dark, overgrown path. He could feel her gaze on the back of his neck as he did so or, at least, he told himself that he could. She'd be standing in the doorway, nearly blocking out the light. Just watching me. But I'm not going to look back, he thought. That would be a really silly thing to do. I mean, she's a lovely person, she's got a lot of common sense and an enormous personality, but really . . .

I'm not going to look back, even if she stands there while I walk all the way down the street. Sometimes you have to be cruel to be kind.

So when he heard the door shut when he was only halfway down the drive he suddenly felt very, very angry, as if he had just been robbed.

He stood still and clasped and unclasped his hands in the darkness. He wasn't Captain Vimes any more, he was Citizen Vimes, which meant that he could do things he'd once never dreamt of doing. Perhaps he could go and smash some windows.

No, that wouldn't be any good. He wanted more than that. To get rid of that bloody dragon, to get his job back, to get his hands on whoever was behind all this, to forget himself just once and hit someone until he was exhausted . . .

He stared at nothing. Down below the city was a mass of smoke and steam. He wasn't thinking of that, though.

He was thinking of a running man. And, further back in the fuddled mists of his life, a boy running to keep up.

And under his breath he said, 'Any of them get out?'

Sergeant Colon finished the proclamation and looked around at the hostile crowd.

'Don't blame me,' he said. 'I just read the things. I don't write 'em.'

'That's human sacrifice, that is,' said someone.

'There's nothing wrong with human sacrifice,' said a priest.

'Ah, *per say*,' said the first speaker quickly. 'For proper religious reasons. And using condemned criminals and so on.* But that's

---

* A number of religions in Ankh-Morpork still practised human sacrifice, except that they didn't really need to practise any more because they had got so good at it. City law said that only condemned criminals should be used, but that was all right because in most of the religions refusing to volunteer for sacrifice was an offence punishable by death.

different from bunging someone to a dragon just because it's feeling peckish.'

'That's the spirit!' said Sergeant Colon.

'Taxes is one thing, but eating people is another.'

'Well said!'

'If we all say we won't put up with it, what can the dragon do?'

Nobby opened his mouth. Colon clamped a hand over it and raised a triumphant fist in the air.

'It's just what I've always said,' he said. 'The people united can never be ignited!'

There was a ragged cheer.

'Hang on a minute,' said a small man, slowly. 'As far as we know, the dragon's only good at one thing. It flies around the city setting fire to people. I'm not actually certain what is being proposed that would stop it doing this.'

'Yes, but if we *all* protest—' said the first speaker, his voice modulated with uncertainty.

'It can't burn *everybody*,' said Colon. He decided to play his new ace again and added, proudly, 'The people united can never be ignited!' There was rather less of a cheer this time. People were reserving their energy for worrying.

'I'm not exactly sure I understand why not. Why can't it burn everyone and fly off to another city?'

'Because . . .'

'The hoard,' said Colon. 'It needs people to bring it treasure.'

'Yeah.'

'Well, maybe, but how many, exactly?'

'What?'

'How many people? Out of the whole city, I mean. Perhaps it won't need to burn the whole city down, just some bits. Do we know what bits?'

'Look, this is getting silly,' said the first speaker. 'If we go around looking at the problems the whole time, we'll never do anything.'

'It just pays to think things through first, that's all I'm saying. Such as, what happens even if we beat the dragon?'

'Oh, come on!' said Sergeant Colon.

'No, seriously. What's the alternative?'

'A human being, for a start!'

'Please yourself,' said the little man primly. 'But I reckon one person a month is pretty good compared to some rulers we've had. Anyone remember Nersh the Lunatic? Or Giggling Lord Smince and his Laugh-A-Minute Dungeon?'

The was a certain amount of mumbling of the 'he's got a point' variety.

'But they got overthrown!' said Colon.

'No they didn't. They were assassinated.'

'Same thing,' said Colon. 'I mean, no-one's going to assassinate the dragon. It'd take more than a dark night and a sharp knife to see it off, I know that.'

I can see what the captain means, he thought. No wonder he always has a drink after he thinks about things. We always beat ourselves before we even start. Give any Ankh-Morpork man a big stick and he'll end up clubbing himself to death.

'Look here, you mealy-mouthed little twerp,' said the first speaker, picking up the little one by his collar and curling his free hand into a fist, 'I happen to have three daughters, and I happen to not want any of them et, thank you very much.'

'Yes, and the people united . . . will . . . never . . . be . . .'

Colon's voice faltered. He realised that the rest of the crowd were all staring upward.

The bugger, he thought, as rationality began to drain away. It must have flannel feet.

The dragon shifted its position on the ridge of the nearest house, flapped its wings once or twice, yawned, and then stretched its neck down into the street.

The man blessed with daughters stood, with his fist upraised, in the centre of a rapidly expanding circle of bare cobbles. The little man wriggled out of his frozen grasp and darted into the shadows.

It suddenly seemed that no man in the entire world was so lonely and without friends.

'I see,' he said quietly. He scowled up at the inquisitive reptile. In fact it didn't seem particularly belligerent. It was looking at him with something approaching interest.

'I don't care!' he shouted, his voice echoing from wall to wall in the silence. 'We defy you! If you kill me, you might as well kill all of us!'

There was some uneasy shuffling of feet amongst those sections of the crowd who didn't feel that this was absolutely axiomatic.

'We can resist you, you know!' growled the man. 'Can't we, everyone. What was that slogan about being united, Sergeant?'

'Er,' said Colon, feeling his spine turn to ice.

'I warn you, dragon, the human spirit is—'

They never found out what it was, or at least what *he* thought it was, although possibly in the dark hours of a sleepless night some of them might have remembered the subsequent events and formed a pretty good and gut-churning insight, to whit, that one of the things sometimes forgotten about the human spirit is that while it is, in the right conditions, noble and brave and wonderful, it is also, when you get right down to it, only human.

The dragon flame caught him full on the chest. For a moment he was visible as a white-hot outline before the neat, black remains spiralled down into a little puddle of melting cobbles.

The flame vanished.

The crowd stood like statues, not knowing if it was staying put or running that would attract more attention.

The dragon stared down, curious to see what they were going to do next.

Colon felt that, as the only civic official present, it was up to him to take charge of the situation. He coughed.

'Right, then,' he said, trying to keep the squeak out of his voice. 'If you would just move along there, ladies and gentlemen. Move along, now. Move along. Let's be having you, please.'

He waved his arms in a vague gesture of authority as the people shuffled nervously away. Out of the corner of his eye he saw red flames behind the rooftops, and sparks spiralling in the sky.

'Haven't you got any homes to go to?' he croaked.

The Librarian knuckled out into the Library of the here and now. Every hair on his body bristled with rage.

He pushed open the door and swung out into the stricken city.

Someone out there was about to find that their worst nightmare was a maddened Librarian.

With a badge.

The dragon swooped leisurely back and forth over the night-time city, barely flapping its wings. It didn't need to. The thermals were giving it the lift it needed.

There were fires all over Ankh-Morpork. So many bucket chains had formed between the river and various burning buildings that buckets were getting misdirected and hijacked. Not that you really needed a bucket to pick up the turbid waters of the river Ankh – a net was good enough.

Downstream, teams of smoke-stained people worked feverishly to close the huge, corroded gates under the Brass Bridge. They were Ankh-Morpork's last defence against fire, since then the Ankh had no outlet and gradually, oozingly, filled the space between the walls. A man could suffocate under it.

The workers on the bridge were the ones who couldn't or

wouldn't run. Many others were teeming through the gates of the city and heading out across the chilly, mist-wreathed plains.

But not for long. The dragon, looping and curving gracefully above the devastation, glided out over the walls. After a few seconds the guards saw actinic fire stab down through the mists. The tide of humanity flowed back, with the dragon hovering over it like a sheepdog. The fires of the stricken city glowed redly off the underside of its wings.

'Got any suggestions about what we do next, Sergeant?' said Nobby.

Colon didn't reply. I wish Captain Vimes were here, he thought. He wouldn't have known what to do either, but he's got a much better vocabulary to be baffled in.

Some of the fires went out as the rising waters and the confused tangle of fire chains did their work. The dragon didn't appear to be inclined to start any more. It had made its point.

'I wonder who it'll be,' said Nobby.

'What?' said Carrot.

'The sacrifice, I mean.'

'Sergeant said people wouldn't put up with it,' said Carrot stoically.

'Yeah, well. Look at it this way: if you say to people, what's it to be, either your house burned down around you or some girl you've probably never met being eaten, well they might get a bit thoughtful. Human nature, see.'

'I'm sure a hero will turn up in time,' said Carrot. 'With some new sort of weapon, or something. And strike at its voonerable spot.'

There was the silence of sudden intense listening.

'What's one of them?' said Nobby.

'A spot. Where it's voonerable. My grandad used to tell me stories. Hit a dragon in its voonerables, he said, and you've killed it.'

'Like kicking it in the wossnames?' said Nobby, interestedly.

'Dunno. I suppose so. Although, Nobby, I've told you before it is not right to—'

'And where's the spot, like?'

'Oh, a different place on each dragon. You wait till it flies over and then you say, there's the voonerable spot, and then you kill it,' said Carrot. 'Something like that.'

Sergeant Colon stared blankly into space.

'Hmm,' said Nobby.

They watched the panorama of panic for a while. Then Sergeant Colon said, 'You sure about the voonerables?'

'Yes. Oh, yes.'

'I wish you hadn't been, lad.'

They looked at the terrified city again.

'You know,' said Nobby, 'you always told me you used to win prizes for archery in the army, Sergeant. You said you had a lucky arrow, you always made sure you got your lucky arrow back, you said you—'

'All right! All right! But this isn't the same thing, is it? Anyway, I'm not a hero. Why should I do it?'

'Captain Vimes pays us thirty dollars a month,' said Carrot.

'Yes,' said Nobby, grinning, 'and *you* get five dollars extra responsibility allowance.'

'But Captain Vimes has gone,' said Colon wretchedly.

Carrot looked at him sternly. 'I am sure,' he said, 'that if he were here, he'd be the first to—'

Colon waved him into silence. 'That's all very well,' he said. 'But what if I miss?'

'Look on the bright side,' said Nobby. 'You'll probably never know it.'

Sergeant Colon's expression mutated into an evil, desperate grin. '*We'll* never know it, you mean,' he said.

'What?'

'If you think I'm standing on some rooftop on my tod, you can think again. I order you to accompany me. Anyway,' he added, 'you get one dollar responsibility allowance, too.'

Nobby's face twisted in panic. 'No I don't!' he croaked. 'Captain Vimes said he was docking it for five years for being a disgrace to the species!'

'Well, you might just get it back. Anyway, you know all about voonerables. I've watched you fight.'

Carrot saluted smartly. 'Permission to volunteer, sir,' he said. 'And I only get twenty dollars a month training pay and I don't mind at all, sir.'

Sergeant Colon cleared his throat. Then he straightened the hang of his breastplate. It was one of those with astonishingly impressive pectoral muscles embossed upon it. His chest and stomach fitted into it in the same way that jelly fits into a mould.

What would Captain Vimes do now? Well, he'd have a drink. But if he didn't have a drink, what would he do?

'What we need,' he said slowly, 'is a Plan.'

That sounded good. That sentence alone sounded worth the pay. If you had a Plan, you were halfway there.

And already he thought he could hear the cheering of crowds.

They were lining the streets, and they were throwing flowers, and he was being carried triumphantly through the grateful city.

The drawback was, he suspected, that he was being carried in an urn.

Lupine Wonse padded along the draughty corridors to the Patrician's bedroom. It had never been a sumptuous apartment at best, and contained little more than a narrow bed and a few battered cupboards. It looked even worse now, with one wall gone. Sleepwalk at night now and you could step right into the vast cavern that was the Great Hall.

Even so, he shut the door behind him for a semblance of privacy. Then, cautiously and with many nervous glances at the great space beyond, he knelt down in the centre of the floor and pried up a board.

A long black robe was dragged into view. Then Wonse reached further down into the dusty space between the floors and rummaged around. He rummaged still further. Then he lay down and stuck both arms into the gap and flailed desperately.

A book sailed across the room and hit him in the back of the head.

'Looking for this, were you?' said Vimes.

He stepped out of the shadows.

Wonse was on his knees, his mouth opening and shutting.

What's he going to say, Vimes thought. Is it going to be: *I know what this looks like*, or will it be: *How did you get in here*, or maybe it'll be: *Listen, I can explain everything.* I wish I had a loaded dragon in my hands right now.

Wonse said, 'Okay. Clever of you to guess.'

Of course, that was always an outside chance, Vimes added.

'Under the floorboards,' he said aloud. 'First place anyone'd look. Rather foolish, that was.'

'I know. I suppose he didn't think anyone would be searching,' said Wonse, standing up and brushing the dust off himself.

'I'm sorry?' said Vimes pleasantly.

'Vetinari. You know how he was for scheming and things. He was involved in most of the plots against himself, that was how he ran things. He enjoyed it. Obviously he called it up and couldn't control it. Something even more cunning than he was.'

'So what were you doing?' said Vimes.

'I wondered if it might be possible to reverse the spell. Or maybe call up another dragon. They'd fight then.'

'A sort of balance of terror, you mean?' said Vimes.

'Could be worth a try,' said Wonse earnestly. He took a few steps closer. 'Look, about your job, I know we were both a bit over-wrought at the time, so of course if you want it back there'll be no prob—'

'It must have been terrible,' said Vimes. 'Imagine what must have gone through his mind. He called it up, and then found it wasn't just some sort of tool but a real thing with a mind of its own. A mind just like his, but with all the brakes off. You know, I wouldn't mind betting that at the start he really thought that what he was doing was all for the best. He must have been insane. Sooner or later, anyway.'

'Yes,' said Wonse hoarsely. 'It must have been terrible.'

'Ye gods, but I'd like to get my hands on him! All those years I've known the man, and I'd never realized . . .'

Wonse said nothing.

'Run,' said Vimes softly.

'What?'

'Run. I want to see you run.'

'I don't underst—'

'I saw someone run away, the night the dragon flamed that house. I remember thinking at the time that he moved in a funny way, sort of bounding along. And then the other day I saw you running away from the dragon. Could almost have been the same man, I thought. Skipping, almost. Like someone running to keep up. *Any of them get out, Wonse?*'

Wonse waved a hand in what he might have thought was a nonchalant way. 'That's just ridiculous, that's not proof,' he said.

'I noticed you sleep in here now,' said Vimes. 'I suppose the *king* likes to have you handy, does he?'

'You've got no proof at all,' whispered Wonse.

'Of course I haven't. The way someone runs. The eager tone of voice. That's all. But that doesn't matter, does it? Because it wouldn't matter even if I *did* have proof,' said Vimes. 'There's no-one to take it to. And you can't give me my job back.'

'I can!' said Wonse. 'I can, and you needn't just be captain—'

'You can't give me my job back,' repeated Vimes. 'It was never yours to take away. I was never an officer of the city, or an officer of the king, or an officer of the Patrician. I was an officer of the law. It might have been corrupted and bent, but it was law, of a sort. There isn't any law now except: "you'll get burned alive if you don't watch out". Where's the place in there for me?'

Wonse darted forward and grabbed him by the arm.

'But you can help me!' he said. 'There may be a way to destroy the dragon, d'you see, or at least we can help people, channel things to mitigate the worst of it, somehow find a meeting point—'

Vimes's blow caught Wonse on the cheek and spun him around.

'The dragon's *here*,' he snapped. 'You can't channel it or persuade it or negotiate with it. There's no truce with dragons. You brought it here and we're stuck with it, you *bastard*.'

Wonse lowered his hand from the bright white mark where the punch had connected.

'What are you going to do?' he said.

Vimes didn't know. He'd thought of a dozen ways that the thing could go, but the only one that was really suitable was killing Wonse. And, face to face, he couldn't do it.

'That's the trouble with people like you,' said Wonse, getting up. 'You're always against anything attempted for the betterment of mankind, but you never have any proper plans of your own. Guards! Guards!'

He grinned maniacally at Vimes.

'Didn't expect that, did you?' he said. 'We've still got guards here, you know. Not so many, of course. Not many people want to come in.'

There were footsteps in the passage outside and four of the palace guards padded in, swords drawn.

'I wouldn't put up a fight, if I were you,' Wonse went on. 'They're desperate and uneasy men. But very highly paid.'

Vimes said nothing. Wonse was a gloater. You always stood a chance with gloaters. The old Patrician had never been a gloater, you could say that for him. If he wanted you dead, you never even heard about it.

The thing to do with gloaters was play the game according to the rules.

'You'll never get away with it,' he said.

'You're right. You're absolutely right. But never is a long time,' said Wonse. '*None* of us get away with anything for that long.'

'You shall have some time to reflect on this,' he said and nodded to the guards. 'Throw him in the *special* dungeon. And then go about that other little task.'

'Er,' said the leader of the guards, and hesitated.

'What's the matter, man?'

'You, er, want us to attack him?' said the guard miserably. Thick though the palace guard were, they were as aware as everyone else of the conventions, and when guards are summoned to deal with one man in overheated circumstances it's not a good time for them. The bugger's bound to be heroic, he was thinking. This guard was not looking forward to a future in which he was dead.

'Of course, you idiot!'

'But, er, there's only one of him,' said the guard captain.

'And he's smilin',' said a man behind him.

'Prob'ly goin' to swing on the chandeliers any minute,' said one of his colleagues. 'And kick over the table, and that.'

'He's not even armed!' shrieked Wonse.

'Worst kind, that,' said one of the guards, with deep stoicism. 'They leap up, see, and grab one of the ornamental swords behind the shield over the fireplace.'

'Yeah,' said another, suspiciously. 'And then they chucks a chair at you.'

'There's no fireplace! There's no sword! There's only him! Now *take* him!' screamed Wonse.

A couple of guards grabbed Vimes tentatively by the shoulders.

'You're not going to do anything heroic, are you?' whispered one of them.

'Wouldn't know where to start,' he said.

'Oh. Right.'

As Vimes was hauled away he heard Wonse breaking into insane laughter. They always did, your gloaters.

But he was correct about one thing. Vimes didn't have a plan. He hadn't thought much about what was going to happen next. He'd been a fool, he told himself, to think that you just had a confrontation and that was the end of it.

He also wondered what the other task was.

The palace guards said nothing, but stared straight ahead and marched him down, across the ruined hall, and through the wreckage of another corridor to an ominous door. They opened it, threw him in, and marched away.

And no-one, absolutely no-one, noticed the thin, leaf-like thing that floated gently down from the shadows of the roof, tumbling over and over in the air like a sycamore seed, before landing in the tangled gewgaws of the hoard.

It was a peanut shell.

It was the silence that awoke Lady Ramkin. Her bedroom looked out over the dragon pens, and she was used to sleeping to the susurration of rustling scales, the occasional roar of a dragon flaming in its sleep, and the keening of the gravid females. Absence of any sound at all was like an alarm clock.

She had cried a bit before going to sleep, but not much, because it was no use being soppy and letting the side down. She lit the lamp, pulled on her rubber boots, grabbed the stick which might be all that stood between her and theoretical loss of virtue, and hurried down through the shadowy house. As she crossed the damp lawn to the kennels she was vaguely aware that something was happening down in the city, but dismissed it as not currently worth thinking about. Dragons were more important.

She pushed open the door.

Well, they were still there. The familiar stink of swamp dragons, half pond mud and half chemical explosion, gusted out into the night.

Each dragon was balancing on its hind legs in the centre of its pen, neck arched, staring with ferocious intensity at the roof.

'Oh,' she said. 'Flying around up there again, is it? Showing off. Don't you worry about it, children. Mummy's here.'

She put the lamp on a high shelf and stamped along to Errol's pen.

'Well now, my lad,' she began, and stopped.

Errol was stretched out on his side. A thin plume of grey smoke was drifting from his mouth, and his stomach expanded and contracted like a bellows. And his skin from the neck down was an almost pure white.

'I think if I ever rewrite *Diseases* you'll get a whole chapter all to yourself,' she said quietly, and unbolted the gate of the pen. 'Let's see if that nasty temperature has gone down, shall we?'

She reached out to stroke his skin and gasped. She pulled the hand back hurriedly and watched the blisters form on her fingertips.

Errol was so cold he burned.

As she stared at him the small round marks that her warmth had melted filmed over with frozen air.

Lady Ramkin sat back on her haunches.

'Just what kind of dragon *are* you—?' she began.

There was the distant sound of a knock at the front door of the house. She hesitated for a moment, then blew out the lamp, crept heavily along the length of the kennels and pulled aside the scrap of sacking over the window.

The first light of dawn showed her the silhouette of a guardsman on her doorstep, the plumes of his helmet blowing in the breeze.

She bit her lip in panic, scuttled back to the door, fled across the lawn and dived into the house, taking the stairs three at a time.

'Stupid, stupid,' she muttered, realizing the lamp was back downstairs. But no time for that. By the time she went and got it, Vimes might have gone away.

Working by feel and memory in the gloom she found her best wig and rammed it on her head. Somewhere among the ointments and dragon remedies on her dressing table was something called, as far as she could remember, *Dew of the Night* or some such unsuitable name, a present long ago from a thoughtless nephew. She tried several bottles before she found something that, by the smell of it, was probably the one. Even to a nose which had long ago shut down most of its sensory apparatus in the face of the overpoweringness of dragons, it seemed, well, more *potent* than she remembered. But apparently men liked that kind of thing. Or so she had read. Damn nonsense, really. She twitched the top hem of her suddenly far too sensible nightshirt into a position which, she hoped, revealed without actually exposing, and hurried back down the stairs.

She stopped in front of the door, took a deep breath, twisted the handle and realized even as she pulled the door open that she should have taken the rubber boots off—

'Why, Captain,' she said winsomely, 'this *is* a *who the hell are you?*'

The head of the palace guard took several steps backwards and, because he was of peasant stock, made a few surreptitious signs to ward off evil spirits. They clearly didn't work. When he opened his eyes again the thing was still there, still bristling with rage, still reeking of something sickly and fermented, still crowned with a skewed mass of curls, still looming behind a quivering bosom that made the roof of his mouth go dry—

He'd heard about these sort of things. Harpies, they were called. What had it done with Lady Ramkin?

The sight of the rubber boots had him confused, though. Legends about harpies were short on references to rubber boots.

'Out with it, fellow,' Lady Ramkin boomed, hitching up her nightie to a more respectable neckline. 'Don't just stand there opening and shutting your mouth. What d'you want?'

'Lady Sybil Ramkin?' said the guard, not in the polite way of someone seeking mere confirmation but in the incredulous tones of someone who found it very hard to believe the answer could be 'yes'.

'Use your eyes, young man. Who d'you think I am?'

The guard pulled himself together.

'Only I've got a summons for Lady Sybil Ramkin,' he said uncertainly.

Her voice was withering. 'What do you mean, a summons?'

'To attend upon the palace, you see.'

'I can't imagine why that is necessary at this time in the morning,' she said, and made to slam the door. It wouldn't shut, though, because of the sword point jammed into it at the last moment.

'If you *don't* come,' said the guard, 'I have been ordered to take steps.'

The door shot back and her face pressed against his, almost knocking him unconscious with the scent of rotting rose petals.

'If you think you'll lay a hand on me—' she began.

The guard's glance darted sideways, just for a moment, to the dragon kennels. Sybil Ramkin's face went pale.

'You wouldn't!' she hissed.

He swallowed. Fearsome though she was, she was only human. She could only bite your head off metaphorically. There were, he told himself, far worse things than Lady Ramkin although, admittedly, they weren't three inches from his nose at this point in time.

'Take steps,' he repeated, in a croak.

She straightened up, and eyed the row of guards behind him.

'I see,' she said coldly. 'That's the way, is it? Six of you to fetch one feeble woman. Very well. You will, of course, allow me to fetch a coat. It is somewhat chilly.'

She slammed the door.

The palace guards stamped their feet in the cold and tried not to look at one another. This obviously wasn't the way you went around arresting people. They weren't *allowed* to keep you waiting on the doorstep, this wasn't the way the world was supposed to work. On the other hand, the only alternative was to go in there and drag her out, and it wasn't one anyone could summon any enthusiasm for. Besides, the guard captain wasn't sure he had enough men to drag Lady Ramkin anywhere. You'd need teams of thousands, with log rollers.

The door creaked open again, revealing only the musty darkness of the hall within.

'Right, men—' said the captain, uneasily.

Lady Ramkin appeared. He got a brief, blurred vision of her bounding through the doorway, screaming, and it might well have been the last thing he remembered if a guard hadn't had the presence of mind to trip her up as she hurtled down the steps. She plunged forward, cursing, ploughed into the overgrown lawn, hit her head on a crumbling statue of an antique Ramkin, and slid to a halt.

The double-handed broadsword she had been holding landed beside her, bolt upright, and vibrated to a standstill.

After a while one of the guards crept forward cautiously and tested the blade with his finger.

'Bloody hell,' he said, in a voice of mixed horror and respect. 'And the dragon wants to eat *her*?'

'Fits the bill,' said the captain. 'She's got to be the highest-born lady in the city. I don't know about maiden,' he added, 'and right at this minute I'm not going to speculate. Someone go and fetch a cart.'

He fingered his ear, which had been nicked by the tip of the sword. He was not, by nature, an unkind man, but at this moment he was certain that he would prefer the thickness of a dragon's hide between himself and Sybil Ramkin when she woke up.

'Weren't we supposed to kill her pet dragons, sir?' said another guard. 'I thought Mr Wonse said something about killing all the dragons.'

'That was just a threat we were supposed to make,' said the captain.

The guard's brow furrowed. 'You sure, sir? I thought—'

The captain had had enough of this. Screaming harpies and broadswords making a noise like tearing silk in the air beside him had severely ruined his capacity for seeing the other fellow's point of view.

'Oh, you *thought*, did you?' he growled. 'A thinker, are you? Do you think you'd be suitable for another posting, then? *City* guard, maybe? They're full of thinkers, they are.'

There was an uncomfortable titter from the rest of the guards.

'If you'd *thought*,' added the captain sarcastically, 'you'd have thought that the king is hardly going to want other dragons dead, is he? They're probably distant relatives or something. I mean, it wouldn't want us to go around killing its own kind, would it?'

'Well, sir, *people* do, sir,' said the guard sulkily.

'Ah, well,' said the captain. 'That's different.' He tapped the side of his helmet meaningfully. 'That's 'cos we're intelligent.'

Vimes landed in damp straw and also in pitch darkness, although after a while his eyes became accustomed to the gloom and he could make out the walls of the dungeon.

It hadn't been built for gracious living. It was basically just a space containing all the pillars and arches that supported the palace. At the far end a small grille high on the wall let in a mere suspicion of grubby, second-hand light.

There was another square hole in the floor. It was also barred. The bars were quite rusty, though. It occurred to Vimes that he could probably work them loose eventually, and then all he would have to do was slim down enough to go through a nine-inch hole.

What the dungeon did *not* contain was any rats, scorpions, cockroaches or snakes. It had *once* contained snakes, it was true, because Vimes's sandals crunched on small, long white skeletons.

He crept cautiously along one damp wall, wondering where the rhythmic scraping sound was coming from. He rounded a squat pillar, and found out.

The Patrician was shaving, squinting into a scrap of mirror propped against the pillar to catch the light. No, Vimes realized, not propped. Supported, in fact. By a rat. It was a large rat, with red eyes.

The Patrician nodded to him without apparent surprise.

'Oh,' he said. 'Vimes, isn't it? I heard you were on the way down. Jolly good. You had better tell the kitchen staff – ' and here Vimes realized that the man was speaking to the rat – 'that there will be two for lunch. Would you like a beer, Vimes?'

'What?' said Vimes.

'I imagine you would. Pot luck, though, I am afraid. Skrp's people are bright enough, but they seem to have a bit of a blind spot when it comes to labels on bottles.'

Lord Vetinari patted his face with a towel and dropped it on the floor. A grey shape darted from the shadows and dragged it away down the floor grille.

Then he said, 'Very well, Skrp. You may go.' The rat twitched its whiskers at him, leaned the mirror against the wall, and trotted off.

'You're waited on by *rats?*' said Vimes.

'They help out, you know. They're not really very efficient, I'm afraid. It's their paws.'

'But, but, but,' said Vimes. 'I mean, how?'

'I suspect Skrp's people have tunnels that extend into the University,' Lord Vetinari went on. 'Although I think they were probably pretty bright to start with.'

At least Vimes understood that bit. It was well known that thaumic radiations affected animals living around the Unseen University campus, sometimes prodding them towards minute analogues of human civilization and even mutating some of them into entirely new and specialized species, such as the .303 bookworm and the wallfish. And, as the man said, rats were quite bright to start with.

'But they're helping you?' Said Vimes.

'Mutual. It's mutual. Payment for services rendered, you might say,' said the Patrician, sitting down on what Vimes couldn't help noticing was small velvet cushion. On a low shelf, so as to be handy, were a notepad and a neat row of books.

'How can you help rats, sir?' he said weakly.

'Advice. I advise them, you know.' The Patrician leaned back. 'That's the trouble with people like Wonse,' he said. 'They never know when to stop. Rats, snakes *and* scorpions. It was sheer bedlam in here when I came. The rats were getting the worst of it, too.'

And Vimes thought he was beginning to get the drift.

'You mean you sort of trained them?' he said.

'Advised. Advised. I suppose it's a knack,' said Lord Vetinari modestly.

Vimes wondered how it was done. Did the rats side with the scorpions against the snakes and then, when the snakes were beaten, invite the scorpions to a celebratory slap-up meal and eat them? Or were individual scorpions hired with large amounts of, oh, whatever it was scorpions ate, to sidle up to selected leading snakes at night and sting them?

He remembered hearing once about a man who, locked up in a cell for years, trained little birds and created a sort of freedom. And he thought of ancient sailors, shorn of the sea by old age and infirmity, who spent their days making big ships in little bottles.

Then he thought of the Patrician, robbed of his city, sitting cross-legged on the grey floor in the dim dungeon and recreating it around him, encouraging in miniature all the little rivalries, power struggles and factions. He thought of him as a sombre, brooding statue amid paving stones alive with slinking shadows and sudden, political death. It had probably been easier than ruling Ankh, which had larger vermin who didn't have to use both hands to carry a knife.

There was a clink over by the drain. Half a dozen rats appeared, dragging something wrapped in a cloth. They rathandled it past the grille and, with great effort, hauled it to the Patrician's feet. He leaned down and undid the knot.

'We seem to have cheese, chicken legs, celery, a piece of rather stale bread and a nice bottle, oh, a nice bottle apparently of Merckle and Stingbat's Very Famous Brown Sauce. *Beer*, I said, Skrp.' The leading rat twitched its nose at him. 'Sorry about this, Vimes. They can't read, you see. They don't seem to get the hang of the concept. But they're very good at listening. They bring me all the news.'

'I see you're very comfortable here,' said Vimes weakly.

'Never build a dungeon you wouldn't be happy to spend the night in yourself,' said the Patrician, laying out the food on the cloth.

'The world would be a happier place if more people remembered that.'

'We all thought you had built secret tunnels and suchlike,' said Vimes.

'Can't imagine why,' said the Patrician. 'One would have to keep on running. So inefficient. Whereas here I am at the hub of things. I hope you understand that, Vimes. Never trust any ruler who puts his faith in tunnels and bunkers and escape routes. The chances are that his heart isn't in the job.'

'Oh.'

He's in a dungeon in his own palace with a raving lunatic in charge upstairs, and a dragon burning the city, and he thinks he's got the world where he wants it. It must be something about high office. The altitude sends people mad.

'You, er, you don't mind if I have a look around, do you?' he said.

'Feel free,' said the Patrician.

Vimes paced the length of the dungeon and checked the door. It was heavily barred and bolted, and the lock was massive.

Then he tapped the walls in what might possibly be hollow places. There was no doubt that it was a well-built dungeon. It was the kind of dungeon you'd feel good about having dangerous criminals put in. Of course, in those circumstances you'd prefer there to be no trapdoors, hidden tunnels or secret ways of escape.

These weren't those circumstances. It was amazing what several feet of solid stone did to your sense of perspective.

'Do guards come in here?' he demanded.

'Hardly ever,' said the Patrician, waving a chicken leg. 'They don't bother about feeding me, you see. The idea is that one should moulder. In fact,' he said, 'up 'til recently I used to go to the door and groan a bit every now and then, just to keep them happy.'

'They're bound to come in and check, though?' said Vimes hopefully.

'Oh, I don't think we should tolerate that,' said the Patrician.

'How are you going to prevent them?'

Lord Vetinari gave him a pained look.

'My dear Vimes,' he said, 'I thought you were an observant man. Did you look at the door?'

'Of course I did,' said Vimes, and added, 'sir. It's bloody massive.'

'Perhaps you should have another look?'

Vimes gaped at him, and then stamped across the floor and glared at the door. It was one of the popular dread portal variety, all bars and bolts and iron spikes and massive hinges. No matter how long he looked at it, it didn't become any less massive. The lock was one of those dwarfish-made buggers that it'd take years to pick. All in all, if you had to have a symbol for something totally immovable, that door was your man.

The Patrician appeared alongside him in heart-stopping silence.

'You see,' he said, 'it's always the case, is it not, that should a city be overtaken by violent civil unrest the current ruler is thrown into the dungeons? To a certain type of mind that is so much more satisfying than mere execution.'

'Well, okay, but I don't see—' Vimes began.

'And you look at this door and what you see is a really strong cell door, yes?'

'Of course. You've only got to look at the bolts and—'

'You know, I'm really rather pleased,' said Lord Vetinari quietly.

Vimes stared at the door until his eyebrows ached. And then, just as random patterns in cloud suddenly, without changing in any way, become a horse's head or a sailing ship, he saw what he'd been looking at all along.

A sense of terrifying admiration overcame him.

He wondered what it was like in the Patrician's mind. All cold and shiny, he thought, all blued steel and icicles and little wheels clicking along like a huge clock. The kind of mind that would carefully consider its own downfall and turn it to advantage.

It was a perfectly normal dungeon door, but it all depended on your sense of perspective.

In this dungeon the Patrician could hold off the world.

All that was on the outside was the lock.

All the bolts and bars were on the inside.

The rank clambered awkwardly across the damp rooftops as the morning mist was boiled off by the sun. Not that there would be any clear air today – sticky swathes of smoke and stale steam wreathed the city and filled the air with the sad smell of dampened cinders.

'What is this place?' said Carrot, helping the others along a greasy walkway.

Sergeant Colon looked around at the forest of chimneys.

'We're just above Jimkin Bearhugger's whisky distillery,' he said. 'On a direct line, see, between the palace and the plaza. It's bound to fly over here.'

Nobby looked wistfully over the side of the building.

'I bin in there once,' he said. 'Checked the door one dark night and it just come open in my hand.'

'Eventually, I expect,' said Colon sourly.

'Well, I had to go in, din't I, to check there was no miscreanting going on. Amazing place in there. All pipes and stuff. And the smell!'

'"Every bottle matured for up to seven minutes",' quoted Colon. '"Ha' a drop afore ye go", it says on the label. Damn right, too. I had a drop once, and I went all day.'

He knelt down and unwrapped the long sacking package he had been manhandling, with extreme difficulty, during the climb. This revealed a longbow of ancient design and a quiver of arrows.

He picked up the bow slowly, reverentially, and ran his pudgy fingers along it.

'You know,' he said quietly, 'I was damn good with this, when I were a lad. The captain should of let me have a go the other night.'

'You keep on telling us,' said Nobby unsympathetically.

'Well, I used to win prizes.' The sergeant unwound a new bowstring, looped it around one end of the bow, stood up, pressed down, grunted a bit . . .

'Er. Carrot?' he said, slightly out of breath.

'Yes, Sarge?'

'You any good at stringing bows?'

Carrot grasped the bow, compressed it easily, and slipped the other end of the string into place.

'That's a good start, Sarge,' said Nobby.

'Don't you be sarcastic with me, Nobby! It ain't strength, it's keenness of eye and steadiness of hand what counts. Now you pass me an arrow. Not that one!'

Nobby's fingers froze in the act of grasping a shaft.

'That's my *lucky* arrow!' spluttered Colon. 'None of you is to touch my lucky arrow!'

'Looks just like any other bloody arrow to me, Sarge,' said Nobby mildly.

'That's the one I shall use for the actual wossname, the coup de grass,' said Colon. 'Never let me down, my lucky arrow didn't. Hit whatever I shot at. Hardly even had to aim. If that dragon's got any voonerables, that arrow'll find 'em.'

He selected an identical-looking but presumably less lucky arrow and nocked it. Then he looked around the rooftops with a speculative eye.

'Better get my hand in,' he muttered. 'Of course, once you learn you never forget, it's like riding a – riding a – riding something you never forget being able to ride.'

He pulled the bowstring back to his ear, and grunted.

'Right,' he wheezed, as his arm trembled with the tension like a branch in a gale. 'See the roof of the Assassins' Guild over there?'

They peered through the grubby air.

'Right, then,' said Colon. 'And do you see the weathervane on it? Do you see it?'

Carrot glanced at the arrowhead. It was weaving back and forth in a series of figure-eights.

'It's a long way off, Sarge,' said Nobby doubtfully.

'Never you mind me, you keep your eyes on the weathervane,' groaned the sergeant.

They nodded. The weathervane was in the shape of a creeping man with a big cloak; his outstretched dagger was always turned to stab the wind. At this distance, though, it was tiny.

'*Okay*,' panted Colon. 'Now, d'you see the man's eye?'

'Oh, come *on*,' said Nobby.

'Shutup, shutup, shutup!' groaned Colon. 'Do you see it, I said!'

'I think *I* can see it, Sarge,' said Carrot loyally.

'Right. Right,' said the sergeant, swaying backwards and forwards with effort. 'Right. Good lad. Okay. Now keep an eye on it, right?'

He grunted, and loosed the arrow.

Several things happened so fast that they will have to be recounted in stop-motion prose. Probably the first was the bowstring slapping into the soft inner part of Colon's wrist, causing him to scream and drop the bow. This had no effect on the path of the arrow, which was already flying straight and true towards a gargoyle on the rooftop just across the road. It hit it on the ear, bounced, ricocheted off a wall six feet away, and headed back towards Colon apparently at a slightly increased speed, going past his ear with a silky humming noise.

It vanished in the direction of the city walls.

After a while Nobby coughed and gave Carrot a look of innocent inquiry.

'About how big,' he said, 'is a dragon's voonerables, roughly?'

'Oh, it can be a tiny spot,' said Carrot helpfully.

'I was sort of afraid of that,' said Nobby. He wandered to the edge of the roof, and pointed downwards. 'There's a pond just here,' he said. 'They use it for cooling water in the stills. I reckon it's pretty deep, so after the sergeant has shot at the dragon we can jump in it. What d'you say?'

'Oh, but we don't need to do that,' said Carrot. 'Because the sergeant's lucky arrow would of hit the spot and the dragon'll be dead, so we won't have anything to worry about.'

'Granted, granted,' said Nobby hurriedly, looking at Colon's scowling face. 'But just in case, you know, if by a million-to-one chance he misses – I'm not saying he will, mark you, you just have to think of all eventualities – if, by incredible bad luck, he doesn't quite manage to hit the voonerable dead on, then your dragon is going to lose his rag, right, and it's probably a good idea to not be here. It's a long shot, I know. Call me a worry-wart if you like. That's all I'm saying.'

Sergeant Colon adjusted his armour haughtily.

'When you really need them the most,' he said, 'million-to-one chances *always* crop up. Well-known fact.'

'The sergeant is right, Nobby,' said Carrot virtuously. 'You know that when there's just one chance which might just work – well, it works. Otherwise there'd be no – ' he lowered his voice – 'I mean, it stands to reason, if last desperate chances didn't work, there'd be no . . . well, the gods wouldn't let it be any other way. They wouldn't.'

As one man, the three of them turned and looked through the murky air towards the hub of the Discworld, thousands of miles away. Now the air was grey with old smoke and mist shreds, but on a clear day it was possible to see Cori Celesti, home of the gods. *Site* of the home of the gods, anyway. They lived in Dunmanifestin, the stuccoed Valhalla, where the gods faced eternity with the kind of minds that were at a loss to know what to do to pass a wet afternoon. They played games with the fates of men, it was said. Exactly what game they thought they were playing at the moment was anyone's guess.

But of course there were rules. Everyone knew there were rules. They just had to hope like Hell that the gods knew the rules, too.

'It's got to work,' mumbled Colon. 'I'll be using my lucky arrow 'n all. You're right. Last hopeless chances have got to work. Nothing makes any sense otherwise. You might as well not be alive.'

Nobby looked down at the pond again. After a moment's hesitation Colon joined him. They had the speculative faces of men who had seen many things, and knew that while you could of course depend on heroes, and kings, and ultimately on gods, you could *really* depend on gravity and deep water.

'Not that we'll need it,' said Colon virtuously.

'Not with your lucky arrow,' said Nobby.

'That's right. But, just out of interest, how far down is it, d'you think?' said Colon.

'About thirty feet, I'd say. Give or take.'

'Thirty feet.' Colon nodded slowly. 'That's what I'd reckon. And it's deep, is it?'

'Very deep, I've heard.'

'I'll take your word for it. It looks pretty mucky. I'd hate to have to jump in it. '

Carrot slapped him cheerfully on the back, nearly pushing him over, and said, 'What's up, Sarge? Do you want to live for ever?'

'Dunno. Ask me again in five hundred years.'

'It's a good job we've got your lucky arrow, then!' said Carrot.

'Hmm?' said Colon, who seemed to be in a miserable daydream world of his own.

'I mean, it's a good job we've got a last desperate million-to-one chance to rely on, or we'd really be in trouble!'

'Oh, yes,' said Nobby sadly. 'Lucky old us.'

The Patrician lay back. A couple of rats dragged a cushion under his head.

'Things are rather bad outside, I gather,' he said.

'Yes,' said Vimes bitterly. 'You're right. You're the safest man in the city.'

He wedged another knife in a crack in the stones and tested his weight carefully, while Lord Vetinari looked on with interest. He'd managed to get six feet off the floor and up to a level with the grille.

Now he started to hack at the mortar around the bars.

The Patrician watched him for a while, and then took a book off the little shelf beside him. Since the rats couldn't read the library he'd been able to assemble was a little baroque, but he was not a man to ignore fresh knowledge. He found his bookmark in the pages of *Lacemaking Through the Ages*, and read a few pages.

After a while he found it necessary to brush a few crumbs of mortar off the book, and looked up.

'Are you achieving success?' he inquired politely.

Vimes gritted his teeth and hacked away. Outside the little grille was a grubby courtyard, barely lighter than the cell. There was a midden in one corner, but currently it looked very attractive. More attractive than the dungeon, at any rate. An honest midden was preferable to the way Ankh-Morpork was going these days. It was probably allegorical, or something.

He stabbed, stabbed, stabbed. The knife blade twanged and shook in his hand.

The Librarian scratched his armpits thoughtfully. He was facing problems of his own.

He had come here full of rage against book thieves and that rage still burned. But the seditious thought had occurred to him that, although crimes against books were the worst kind of crimes, revenge ought, perhaps, to be postponed.

It occurred to him that, while of course what humans chose to do to one another was all one to him, there were certain activities that should be curtailed in case the perpetrators got over-confident and started doing things like that to books, too.

The Librarian stared at his badge again, and gave it a gentle nibble in the optimistic hope that it had become edible. No doubt about it, he had a Duty to the captain.

The captain had always been kind to him. And the captain had a badge, too.

Yes.

There were times when an ape had to do what a man had to do . . .

The orang-utan threw a complex salute and swung away into the darkness.

The sun rose higher, rolling through the mists and stale smoke like a lost balloon.

The rank sat in the shade of a chimney stack, waiting and killing time in their various ways. Nobby was thoughtfully probing the contents of a nostril, Carrot was writing a letter home, and Sergeant Colon was worrying.

After a while he shifted his weight uneasily and said, 'I've fought of a problem.'

'Wassat, Sarge?' said Carrot.

Sergeant Colon looked wretched. '*Weeell*, what if it's not a million-to-one chance?' he said.

Nobby stared at him.

'What d'you mean?' he said.

'Well, all *right*, last desperate million-to-one chances always work, right, no problem, but . . . well, it's pretty wossname, specific. I mean, isn't it?'

'You tell me,' said Nobby.

'What if it's just a thousand-to-one chance?' said Colon agonisedly.

'What?'

'Anyone ever heard of a thousand-to-one shot coming up?'

Carrot looked up. 'Don't be daft, Sergeant,' he said. 'No-one ever saw a thousand-to-one chance come up. The odds against it are – ' his lips moved – 'millions to one.'

'Yeah. Millions,' agreed Nobby.

'So it'd only work if it's your actual million-to-one chance,' said the sergeant.

'I suppose that's right,' said Nobby.

'So 999,943-to-one, for example—' Colon began.

Carrot shook his head. 'Wouldn't have a hope. No-one ever said, "It's a 999,943-to-one chance but it might just work."'

They stared out across the city in the silence of ferocious mental calculation.

'We could have a real problem here,' said Colon eventually.

Carrot started to scribble furiously. When questioned, he explained at length about how you found the surface area of a dragon and then tried to estimate the chances of an arrow hitting any one spot.

'Aimed, mind,' said Sergeant Colon. 'I *aim*.'

Nobby coughed.

'In that case it's got to be a lot less than a million-to-one chance,' said Carrot. 'It could be a hundred-to-one. If the dragon's flying slowly and it's a big spot, it could be practically a certainty.'

Colon's lips shaped themselves around the phrase, *It's a certainty but it might just work*. He shook his head. 'Nah,' he said.

'So what we've got to do, then,' said Nobby slowly, 'is adjust the odds . . .'

Now there was a shallow hole in the mortar near the middle bar. It wasn't much, Vimes knew, but it was a start.

'You don't require assistance, by any chance?' said the Patrician.

'No.'

'As you wish.'

The mortar was half-rotted, but the bars had been driven deep into the rock. Under their crusting of rust there was still plenty of iron. It was a long job, but it was something to do and required a blessed absence of thought. They couldn't take it away from him. It was a good, clean challenge; you knew if you went on chipping away, you'd win through eventually.

It was the 'eventually' that was the problem. Eventually Great A'Tuin would reach the end of the universe. Eventually the stars would go out. Eventually Nobby might have a bath, although that would probably involve a radical rethinking of the nature of Time.

He hacked at the mortar anyway, and then stopped as something small and pale fell down outside, quite slowly.

'Peanut shell?' he said.

The Librarian's face, surrounded by the inner-tube jowls of the Librarian's head, appeared upside down in the barred opening, and gave him a grin that wasn't any less terrible for being the wrong way up.

'Oook?'

The orang-utan flopped down off the wall, grabbed a couple of bars, and pulled. Muscles shunted back and forward across its barrel chest in a complex pavane of effort. The mouthful of yellow teeth gaped in silent concentration.

There were a couple of dull 'thungs' as the bars gave up and broke free. The ape flung them aside and reached into the gaping hole. Then the longest arms of the Law grabbed the astonished Vimes under his shoulders and pulled him through in one movement.

The rank surveyed their handiwork.

'Right,' said Nobby. 'Now, what are the chances of a man standing on one leg with his hat on backwards and a handkerchief in his mouth hitting a dragon's voonerables?'

'Mmph,' said Colon.

'It's pretty long odds,' said Carrot. 'I reckon the hanky is a bit over the top, though.'

Colon spat it out. 'Make up your minds,' he said. 'Me leg's going to sleep.'

Vimes picked himself up off the greasy cobbles and stared at the Librarian. He was experiencing something which had come as a shock to many people, usually in much more unpleasant circumstances such as a brawl started in the Mended Drum when the ape wanted a bit of peace and quiet to enjoy a reflective pint, which was this: the Librarian might look like a stuffed rubber sack, but what it was stuffed with was muscle.

'That was amazing,' was all he could find to say. He looked down at the twisted bars, and felt his mind darken. He grabbed the bent metal. 'You don't happen to know where Wonse is, do you?' he added.

'Eeek!' The Librarian thrust a tattered piece of parchment under his nose. 'Eeek!'

Vimes read the words.

It hathe pleased ... whereas ... at the stroke of noone ... a maiden pure, yet high born ... compact between ruler and ruled ...

'In my city!' he growled. 'In my bloody city!'

He grabbed the Librarian by two handfuls of chest hair and pulled him up to eye height.

'What time is it?' he shouted.

'Oook!'

A long red-haired arm unfolded itself upwards. Vimes's gaze followed the pointing finger. The sun definitely had the look of a heavenly body that was nearly at the crest of its orbit and looking forward to a long, lazy coasting towards the blankets of dusk . . .

'I'm not bloody well going to have it, understand?' Vimes shouted, shaking the ape back and forth.

'Oook,' the Librarian pointed out, patiently.

'What? Oh. Sorry.' Vimes lowered the ape, who wisely didn't make an issue of it because a man angry enough to lift 300 lbs of orang-utan without noticing is a man with too much on his mind.

Now he was staring around the courtyard.

'Any way out of here?' he said. 'Without climbing the walls, I mean.'

He didn't wait for an answer but loped around the walls until he reached a narrow, grubby door, and kicked it open. It hadn't been locked anyway, but he kicked it just the same. The Librarian trailed along behind, swinging on his knuckles.

The kitchen on the other side of the door was almost deserted, the staff having finally lost their nerve and decided that all prudent chefs refrained from working in an establishment where there was a mouth bigger than they were. A couple of palace guards were eating a cold lunch.

'Now,' said Vimes, as they half-rose, 'I don't want to have to—'

They didn't seem to want to listen. One of them reached for a crossbow.

'Oh, the hell with it.' Vimes grabbed a butcher's knife from a block beside it and threw it.

There is an art in throwing knives and, even then, you need the right kind of knife. Otherwise it does just what this one did, which is miss completely.

The guard with the bow leaned sideways, righted himself, and found that a purple fingernail was gently blocking the firing mechanism. He looked around. The Librarian hit him right on top of his helmet.

The other guard shrank back, waving his hands frantically.

'Nonono!' he said. 'It's a misunderstanding! What was it you said you didn't want to have to do? Nice monkey!'

'Oh, dear,' said Vimes. '*Wrong!*'

He ignored the terrified screaming and rummaged through the debris of the kitchen until he came up with a cleaver. He'd never felt really at home with swords, but a cleaver was a different matter. A cleaver had weight. It had purpose. A sword might have a certain nobility about it, unless it was the one belonging for example to Nobby, which relied on rust to hold it together, but what a cleaver had was a tremendous ability to cut things up.

He left the biology lesson – that no monkey was capable of bouncing someone up and down by their ankles – found a likely door, and hurried through it. This took him outside again, into the big cobbled area that surrounded the palace. Now he could get his bearings, now he could . . .

There was a boom in the air above him. A gale blew *downwards*, knocking him over.

The King of Ankh-Morpork, wings outspread, glided across the sky and settled for a moment on the palace gateway, talons gouging long scars in the stone as it caught its balance. The sun glittered off its arched back as it stretched its neck, roared a lazy billow of flames, and sprang into the air again.

Vimes made an animal – a mammalian animal – noise in the back of his throat, and ran out into the empty streets.

Silence filled the ancestral home of the Ramkins. The front door swung back and forth on its hinges, letting in the common, badly-brought up breeze which wandered through the deserted rooms, gawping and looking for dust on the top of the furniture. It wound up the stairs and banged through the door of Sybil Ramkin's bedroom, rattling the bottles on the dressing table and riffling through the pages of *Diseases of the Dragon*.

A really fast reader could have learned the symptoms of everything from Abated Heels to Zigzag Throat.

And down below, in the low, warm and foul-smelling shed that housed the swamp dragons, it seemed that Errol had got them all. Now he sat in the centre of his pen, swaying and moaning softly. White smoke rolled slowly from his ears and drifted towards the floor. From somewhere inside his swollen stomach came complex explosive hydraulic noises, as though desperate teams of gnomes were trying to drive a culvert through a cliff in a thunderstorm.

His nostrils flared, turning more or less of their own volition.

The other dragons craned over the pen walls, watching him cautiously.

There was another distant gastric roar. Errol shifted painfully.

The dragons exchanged glances. Then, one by one, they lay down carefully on the floor and put their paws over their eyes.

*

Nobby put his head on one side.

'It looks promising,' he said critically. 'We might be nearly there. I reckon the chances of a man with soot on his face, his tongue sticking out, standing on one leg and singing *The Hedgehog Song* ever hitting a dragon's voonerables would be . . . what'd you say, Carrot?'

'A million to one, I reckon,' said Carrot virtuously.

Colon glared at them.

'Listen, lads,' he said, 'you're not winding me up, are you?'

Carrot looked down at the plaza below them.

'Oh, bloody hell,' he said softly.

'Wassat?' said Colon urgently, looking around.

'They're chaining a woman to a rock!'

The rank stared over the parapet. The huge and silent crowd that lined the plaza stared too, at a white figure struggling between half a dozen palace guards.

'Wonder where they got the rock from?' said Colon. 'We're on loam here, you know.'

'Fine strapping wench, whoever she is,' said Nobby approvingly, as one of the guards wheeled off bow-legged and collapsed. 'That's one lad who won't know what to do with his evenin's for a few weeks. Got a mean right knee, so she has.'

'Anyone we know?' said Colon.

Carrot squinted.

'It's Lady Ramkin!' he said, his mouth dropping open.

'Never!'

'He's right. In a nightie,' said Nobby.

'The buggers!' Colon snatched up his bow and fumbled for an arrow. 'I'll give 'em voonerables! Well-spoken lady like her, it's a disgrace!'

'Er,' said Carrot, who had glanced over his shoulder. 'Sergeant?'

'This is what it comes to!' muttered Colon. 'Decent women can't walk down the street without being eaten! Right, you bastards, you're . . . you're *geography*—'

'Sergeant!' Carrot repeated urgently.

'It's history, not geography,' said Nobby. 'That's what you're supposed to say. History. "You're history!" you say.'

'Well, whatever,' snapped Colon. 'Let's see how—'

'*Sergeant!*'

Nobby was looking behind them, too.

'Oh, shit,' he said.

'Can't miss,' muttered Colon, taking aim.

'*Sergeant!*'

'Shut up, you two, I can't concentrate when you keep shout—'
'Sergeant, *it's coming!*'

The dragon accelerated.

The drunken rooftops of Ankh-Morpork blurred as it passed over, wings sneering at the air. Its neck stretched out straight ahead, the pilot flames of its nostrils streamed behind it, the sound of its flight panned across the sky.

Colon's hands shook. The dragon seemed to be aiming at his throat, and it was moving too fast, far too fast . . .

'This is it!' said Carrot. He glanced towards the Hub, in case any gods had forgotten what they were there for, and added, speaking slowly and distinctly, 'It's a million-to-one-chance, but it might just work!'

'Fire the bloody thing!' screamed Nobby.

'Picking my spot, lad, picking my spot,' quavered Colon. 'Don't you worry, lads, I told you this is my lucky arrow. First-class arrow, this arrow, had it since I was a lad, you'd be amazed at the things I shot at with this, don't you worry.'

He paused, as the nightmare bore down on him on wings of terror.

'Er, Carrot?' he said meekly.

'Yes, Sarge?'

'Did your old grandad ever say what a voonerable spot *looks* like?'

And then the dragon wasn't approaching any more, it was there, passing a few feet overhead, a streaming mosaic of scales and noise, filling the entire sky.

Colon fired.

They watched the arrow rise straight and true.

Vimes half-ran, half-staggered over the damp cobbles, out of breath and out of time.

It can't be like this, he thought wildly. The hero always cuts it fine, but he always get there just in the nick of time. Only the nick of time was probably five minutes ago.

And I'm not a hero. I'm out of condition, and I need a drink, and I get a handful of dollars a month without plumes allowance. That's not hero's pay. Heroes get kingdoms and princesses, and they take regular exercise, and when they smile the light glints off their teeth, *ting*. The bastards.

Sweat stung his eyes. The rush of adrenaline that had carried him out of the palace had spent itself, and was now exacting its inevitable toll.

He stumbled to a halt, and grabbed a wall to keep him upright while he gasped for air. And thus he saw the figures on the rooftop.

Oh, no! he thought. They're not heroes either! What do they think they're playing at?

It was a million-to-one chance. And who was to say that, somewhere in the millions of other possible universes, it might not have worked?

That was the sort of thing the gods really liked. But Chance, who sometimes can overrule even the gods, has 999,999 casting votes.

In *this* universe, for example, the arrow bounced off a scale and clattered away into oblivion.

Colon stared as the dragon's pointed tail passed overhead.

'It . . . missed . . . ' he mouthed.

'But it couldn't of missed!' He stared red-eyed at the other two. 'It was a sodding last desperate million-to-one chance!'

The dragon twisted its wings, swung its huge bulk around on a pivot of air, and bore down on the roof.

Carrot grabbed Nobby around the waist and laid a hand on Colon's shoulder.

The sergeant was weeping with rage and frustration.

'Million-to-bloody-one last desperate bloody chance!'

'Sarge—'

The dragon flamed.

It was a beautifully controlled line of plasma. It went through the roof like butter.

It cut through stairways.

It crackled into ancient timbers and made them twist like paper. It sliced into pipes.

It punched through floor after floor like the fist of an angry god and, eventually, reached the big copper vat containing a thousand gallons of freshly-made mature whisky-type spirit.

It burned into that, too.

Fortunately, the chances of anyone surviving the ensuing explosion were exactly a million-to-one.

*

The fireball rose like a – well, a rose. A huge orange rose, streaked with yellow. It took the roof with it and wrapped it around the astonished dragon, lifting it high into the air in a boiling cloud of broken timber and bits of piping.

The crowd watched in bemusement as the superhot blast flung it into the sky and barely noticed Vimes as he pushed his way, wheezing and crying, through the press of bodies.

He shouldered past a row of palace guards and shambled as fast as he could across the flagstones. No-one was paying him much attention at the moment.

He stopped.

It wasn't a rock, because Ankh-Morpork was on loam. It was just some huge remnant of mortared masonry, probably thousands of years old, from somewhere in the city foundations. Ankh-Morpork was so old now that what it was built on, by and large, was Ankh-Morpork.

It had been dragged into the centre of the plaza, and Lady Sybil Ramkin had been chained to it. She appeared to be wearing a nightie and huge rubber boots. By the look of her she had been in a fight, and Vimes felt a momentary pang of sympathy for whoever else had been involved. She gave him a look of pure fury.

'You!'

'*You!*'

He waved the cleaver vaguely.

'But why you—?' he began.

'Captain Vimes,' she said sharply, 'you will oblige me by not waving that thing about and you will start putting it to its proper use!'

Vimes wasn't listening.

'Thirty dollars a month!' he muttered. 'That's what they died for! Thirty dollars! And I docked some from Nobby. I had to, didn't I? I mean, that man could make a *melon* go rusty!'

'Captain Vimes!'

He focused on the cleaver.

'Oh,' he said. 'Yes. Right!'

It was a good steel cleaver, and the chains were elderly and rather rusty iron. He hacked away, raising sparks from the masonry.

The crowd watched in silence, but several palace guards hurried towards him.

'What the hell do you think you're doing?' said one of them, who didn't have much imagination.

'What the hell do you think *you're* doing?' Vimes growled, looking up.

They stared at him.

'What?'

Vimes took another hack at the chains. Several loops tinkled to the ground.

'Right, you've asked for—' one of the guards began. Vimes's elbow caught him under his rib cage; before he collapsed, Vimes's foot kicked savagely at the other one's kneecaps, bringing his chin down ready for another stab with the other elbow.

'Right,' said Vimes absently. He rubbed the elbow. It was sheer agony.

He moved the cleaver to his other hand and hammered at the chains again, aware at the back of his mind that more guards were hurrying up, but with that special kind of run that guards had. He knew it well. It was the run that said, there's a dozen of us, let someone else get there first. It said, he looks ready to kill, no-one's paying me to get killed, maybe if I run slowly enough he'll get away . . .

No point in spoiling a good day by catching someone.

Lady Ramkin shook herself free. A ragged cheer went up and started to grow in volume. Even in their current state of mind, the people of Ankh-Morpork always appreciated a performance.

She grabbed a handful of chain and wrapped it around one pudgy fist.

'Some of those guards don't know how to treat—' she began.

'No time, no time,' said Vimes, grabbing her arm. It was like trying to drag a mountain.

The cheering stopped, abruptly.

There was a sound behind Vimes. It was not, particularly, a loud noise. It just had a peculiarly nasty carrying quality. It was the click of four sets of talons hitting the flagstones at the same time.

Vimes looked around and up.

Soot clung to the dragon's hide. A few pieces of charred wood had lodged here and there, and were still smouldering. The magnificent bronze scales were streaked with black.

It lowered its head until Vimes was a few feet away from its eyes, and tried to focus on him.

Probably not worth running, Vimes told himself. It's not as if I've got the energy anyway.

He felt Lady Ramkin's hand engulf his.

'Jolly well done,' she said. 'It nearly worked.'

*

Charred and blazing wreckage rained down around the distillery. The pond was a swamp of debris, covered with a coating of ash. Out of it, dripping slime, rose Sergeant Colon.

He clawed his way to the bank and pulled himself up, like some sea-dwelling lifeform that was anxious to get the whole evolution thing over with in one go.

Nobby was already there, spread out like a frog, leaking water. 'Is that you, Nobby?' said Sergeant Colon anxiously.

'It's me, Sergeant.'

'I glad about that, Nobby,' said Colon fervently.

'I wish it wasn't me, Sergeant.'

Colon tipped the water out of his helmet, and then paused.

'What about young Carrot?' he said.

Nobby pushed himself up on his elbows, groggily.

'Dunno,' he said. 'One minute we were on the roof, next minute we were jumping.'

They both looked at the ashen waters of the pond.

'I suppose,' said Colon slowly, 'he can swim?'

'Dunno. He never said. Not much to swim in, up in the mountains. When you come to think about it,' said Nobby.

'But perhaps there were limpid blue pools and deep mountain streams,' said the sergeant hopefully. 'And icy tarns in hidden valleys and that. Not to mention subterranean lakes. He'd be bound to have learned. In and out of the water all day, I expect.'

They stared at the greasy grey surface.

'It was probably that Protective,' said Nobby. 'P'raps it filled with water and dragged him down.'

Colon nodded gloomily.

'I'll hold your helmet,' said Nobby, after a while.

'But I'm your superior officer!'

'Yes,' said Nobby reasonably, 'but if you get stuck down there, you're going to want your best man up here, ready to rescue you, aren't you?'

'That's ... reasonable,' said Colon eventually. 'That's a good point. '

'Right, then.'

'Drawback is, though . . .'

'What?'

'. . . I can't swim,' Colon said.

'How did you get out of that, then?'

Colon shrugged. 'I'm a natural floater.'

Their eyes, once again, turned to the dankness of the pond. Then Colon stared at Nobby. Then Nobby, very slowly, unbuckled his helmet.

'There isn't someone still in there, is there?' said Carrot, behind them.

They looked around. He hoicked some mud out of an ear. Behind him the remains of the brewery smouldered.

'I thought I'd better nip out quickly, see what was going on,' he said brightly, pointing to a gate leading out of the yard. It was hanging by one hinge.

'Oh,' said Nobby weakly. 'Jolly good.'

'There's an alley out there,' said Carrot.

'No dragons in it, are there?' said Colon suspiciously.

'No dragons, no humans. There's no-one around,' said Carrot impatiently. He drew his sword. 'Come on!' he said.

'Where to?' said Nobby. He'd pulled a damp butt from behind his ear and was looking at it with an expression of deepest sorrow. It was obviously too far gone. He tried to light it anyway.

'We want to fight the dragon, don't we?' said Carrot.

Colon shifted uncomfortably. 'Yes, but aren't we allowed to go home for a change of clothes first?'

'And a nice warm drink?' said Nobby.

'And a meal,' said Colon. 'A nice plate of—'

'You should be ashamed of yourselves,' said Carrot. 'There's a lady in distress and a dragon to fight and all you can think of is food and drink!'

'Oh, I'm not just thinking about food and drink,' said Colon.

'We could be all that stands between the city and total destruction!'

'Yes, but—' Nobby began.

Carrot drew his sword and waved it over his head.

'Captain Vimes would have gone!' he said. 'All for one!'

He glared at them, and rushed out of the yard.

Colon gave Nobby a sheepish look.

'Young people today,' he said.

'All for one what?' said Nobby.

The sergeant sighed. 'Come on, then.'

'Oh, all right.'

They staggered out into the alley. It was empty.

'Where'd he go?' said Nobby.

Carrot stepped out of the shadows, grinning all over his face.

'Knew I could rely on you,' he said. 'Follow me!'

'Something odd about that boy,' said Colon, as they limped after him. 'He always manages to persuade us to follow him, have you noticed?'

'All for one what?' said Nobby.

'Something about the voice, I reckon.'

'Yes, but all for one what?'

The Patrician sighed and, carefully marking his place, laid aside his book. To judge from the noise there seemed to be an awful lot of excitement going on out there. It was highly unlikely any palace guards would be around, which was just as well. The guards were highly-trained men and it would be a shame to waste them.

He would need them later on.

He padded over to the wall and pushed a small block that looked exactly like all the other small blocks. No other small block, however, would have caused a section of flagstone to grind ponderously aside.

There was a carefully chosen assortment of stuff in there – iron rations, spare clothes, several small chests of precious metals and jewels, tools. And there was a key. Never build a dungeon you couldn't get out of.

The Patrician took the key and strolled over to the door. As the wards of the lock slid back in their well-oiled grooves he wondered, again, whether he should have told Vimes about the key. But the man seemed to have got so much satisfaction out of breaking out. It would probably have been positively bad for him to have told him about the key. Anyway, it would have spoiled his view of the world. He needed Vimes and his view of the world.

Lord Vetinari swung the door open and, silently, strode out into the ruins of his palace.

They trembled as, for the second time in a couple of minutes, the city rocked.

The dragon kennels exploded. The windows blew out. The door left the wall ahead of a great billow of black smoke and sailed into the air, tumbling slowly, to plough into the rhododendrons.

Something very energetic and hot was happening in that building. More smoke poured out, thick and oily and solid. One of the walls folded in on itself, and then another one toppled sluggishly on to the lawn.

Swamp dragons shot determinedly out of the wreckage like champagne corks, wings whirring frantically.

Still the smoke unrolled. But there was something in there, some point of fierce white light that was gently rising.

It disappeared from view as it passed a stricken window, and then, with a piece of roof tile still spinning on the top of his head,

Errol climbed above his own smoke and ascended into the skies of Ankh-Morpork.

The sunlight glinted off his silver scales as he hovered about a hundred feet up, turning slowly, balancing nicely on his own flame . . .

Vimes, awaiting death on the plaza, realised that his mouth was hanging open. He shut it again.

There was absolutely no sound in the city now but the noise of Errol's ascent.

They can rearrange their own plumbing, Vimes told himself bemusedly. To suit circumstances. He's made it work in reverse. But his thingys, his genes . . . surely he must have been halfway to it anyway. No wonder the little bugger has got such stubby wings. His body must have known he wasn't going to need them, except to steer.

Good grief. I'm watching the first ever dragon to flame *backwards*.

He risked a glance immediately above him. The great dragon was frozen, its enormous bloodshot eyes concentrating on the tiny creature.

With a challenging roar of flame and a pummelling of air the King of Ankh-Morpork rose, all thought of mere humans forgotten.

Vimes turned sharply to Lady Ramkin.

'How do they fight?' he said urgently. 'How do dragons fight?'

'I – that is, well, they just flap at each other and blow flame,' she said. 'Swamp dragons, that is. I mean, who's ever seen a noble dragon fight?' She patted her nightie. 'I must take some notes, I've got my memo book somewhere . . .'

'In your *nightshirt?*'

'It's amazing how ideas come to one in bed, I've always said.'

Flames roared into the space where Errol had been, but he wasn't there. The king tried to spin in mid-air. The little dragon circled in an easy series of smoke rings, weaving a cat's cradle in the sky with the huge adversary gyrating helplessly in the middle. More flames, hotter and longer, stabbed at him and missed.

The crowd watched in breathless silence.

''allo, Captain,' said an ingratiating voice.

Vimes looked down. A small and stagnant pond disguised as Nobby grinned sheepishly up at him.

'I thought you were dead!' he said.

'We're not,' said Nobby.

'Oh. Good.' There didn't seem much else to say.

'What do you reckon on the fight, then?'

Vimes looked back up. Smoke trails spiralled across the city.

'I'm afraid it's not going to work,' said Lady Ramkin. 'Oh. Hallo, Nobby.'

'Afternoon, ma'am,' said Nobby, touching what he thought was his forelock.

'What d'you mean, it's not going to work?' said Vimes. 'Look at him go! It hasn't hit him yet!'

'Yes, but his flame has touched it several times. It doesn't seem to have any effect. It's not hot enough, I think. Oh, he's dodging well. But he's got to be lucky every time. *It* has only got to be lucky once.'

The meaning of this sank in.

'You mean,' said Vimes, 'all this is just – just *show*? He's just doing it to *impress*?'

''S'not his fault,' said Colon, materializing behind them. 'It's like dogs, innit? Doesn't really dawn on the poor little bugger that he's up against a big one. He's just ready for a scrap.'

Both dragons appeared to realise that the fight was the well-known Klatchian standoff. With another smoke ring and a billow of white flame they parted and retreated a few hundred yards.

The king hovered, flapping its wings quickly. Height. That was the thing. When dragon fought dragon, height was always the thing . . .

Errol balanced on his flame. He seemed to be thinking.

Then he nonchalantly kicked his back legs out as though hovering on your own stomach gases was something dragons had mastered over millions of years, somersaulted, and fled. For a moment he was visible as a silver streak, and then he was out over the city walls and gone.

A groan followed him. It came from ten thousand throats.

Vimes threw up his hands.

'Don't you worry, guv,' said Nobby quickly. 'He's – he's probably gone to, to have a drink. Or something. Maybe it's the end of round one. Or something.'

'I mean, he ate our kettle and everything,' said Colon uncertainly. 'He wouldn't just run away after eating a kettle. Stands to reason. Anyone who could eat a kettle wouldn't run away from *anything*.'

'And my armour polish,' said Carrot. 'It was nearly a whole dollar for the tin.'

'There you are then,' said Colon. 'It's like I said.'

'Look,' said Vimes, as patiently as he could manage. 'He's a nice dragon, I liked him as much as you, a very nice little chap, but he's just done the sensible thing, for gods' sake, he's not going to get burned to bits just to save us. Life just doesn't work like that. You might as well face it.'

Overhead the great dragon strutted through the air and flamed a nearby tower. It had won.

'I've never seen that before,' said Lady Ramkin. 'Dragons normally fight to the death.'

'At last they've bred one who's sensible,' said Vimes morosely. 'Let's be honest: the chances of a dragon the size of Errol beating something that big are a million-to-one.'

There was one of those silences you get after one clear bright note has been struck and the world pauses.

The rank looked at one another.

'Million-to-one?' asked Carrot nonchalantly.

'Definitely,' said Vimes. 'Million-to-one.'

The rank looked at one another again.

'Million-to-one,' said Colon.

'Million-to-one,' agreed Nobby.

'That's right,' said Carrot. 'Million-to-one.'

There was another high-toned silence. The members of the rank were wondering who was going to be the first to say *it*.

Sergeant Colon took a deep breath.

'But it might just work,' he said.

'What are you talking about?' snapped Vimes. 'There's no—'

Nobby nudged him urgently in the ribs and pointed out across the plains.

There *was* a column of black smoke out there. Vimes squinted. Running ahead of the smoke, speeding over the cabbage fields and closing fast, was a silvery bullet.

The great dragon had seen it too. It flamed defiance and climbed for extra height, mashing the air with its enormous wings.

Now Errol's flame was visible, so hot as to be almost blue. The landscape rolled away underneath him at an impossible speed, and he was accelerating.

Ahead of him the king extended its claws. It was almost grinning.

Errol's going to hit it, Vimes thought. Gods help us all, it'll be a fireball.

Something odd was happening out in the fields. A little way behind Errol the ground appeared to be ploughing itself up, throwing cabbage stalks into the air. A hedgerow erupted in a shower of sawdust . . .

Errol passed silently over the city walls, nose up, wings folded down to tiny flaps, his body honed to a mere cone with a flame at one end. His opponent blew out a tongue of fire; Vimes watched

Errol, with a barely noticeable flip of a wing stub, roll easily out of its path. And then he was gone, speeding out towards the sea in the same eerie silence.

'He miss—' Nobby began.

The air ruptured. An endless thunderclap of noise dragged across the city, smashing tiles, toppling chimneys. In mid-air, the king was picked up, flattened out and spun like a top in the sonic wash. Vimes, his hands over his own ears, saw the creature flame desperately as it turned and became the centre of a spiral of crazy fire.

Magic crackled along its wings. It screamed like a distressed foghorn. Then, shaking its head dazedly, it began to glide in a wide circle.

Vimes groaned. It had survived something that tore masonry apart. What did you have to *do* to beat it? You can't fight it, he thought. You can't burn it, you can't smash it. There's nothing you can do to it.

The dragon landed. It wasn't a perfect landing. A perfect landing wouldn't have demolished a row of cottages. It was slow, and it seemed to go on for a long time and rip up a considerable stretch of city.

Wings flapping aimlessly, neck waving and spraying random flame, it ploughed on through a debris of beams and thatch. Several fires started up along the trail of destruction.

Finally it came to rest at the end of the furrow, almost invisible under a heap of former architecture.

The silence that it left was broken only by the shouts of someone trying to organize yet another bucket chain from the river to douse the fires.

Then people started to move.

From the air Ankh-Morpork must have looked like a disturbed anthill, with streams of dark figures flowing towards the wreck of the dragon.

Most of them had some kind of weapon.

Many of them had spears.

Some of them had swords.

All of them had one aim in mind.

'You know what?' said Vimes aloud. 'This is going to be the world's first democratically killed dragon. One man, one stab.'

'Then you've got to stop them. You can't let them kill it!' said Lady Ramkin.

Vimes blinked at her.

'Pardon?' he said.

'It's wounded!'

'Lady, that was the intention, wasn't it? Anyway, it's only stunned,' said Vimes.

'I mean you can't let them kill it like *this*,' said Lady Ramkin insistently. 'Poor thing!'

'What do you want to do, then?' demanded Vimes, his temper unravelling. 'Give it a strengthening dose of tar oil and a nice comfy basket in front of the stove?'

'It's butchery!'

'Suits me fine!'

'But it's a dragon! It's just doing what a dragon does! It never would have come here if people had left it alone!'

Vimes thought: it was about to eat her, and she can still think like this. He hesitated. Perhaps that *did* give you the right to an opinion . . .

Sergeant Colon sidled up as they glared, white-faced, at one another, and hopped desperately from one squelching foot to the other.

'You better come at once, Captain,' he said. 'It's going to be bloody murder!'

Vimes waved a hand at him. 'As far as I'm concerned,' he mumbled, avoiding Sybil Ramkin's glare, 'it's got it coming to it.'

'It's not that,' said Colon. 'It's Carrot. He's arrested the dragon.'

Vimes paused.

'What do you mean, *arrested*?' he said. 'You don't mean what I think you mean, do you?'

'Could be, sir,' said Colon uncertainly. 'Could be. He was up on the rubble like a shot, sir, grabbed it by a wing and said "You're *nicked*, chummy", sir. Couldn't believe it, sir. Sir, the thing is . . .'

'Well?'

The sergeant hopped from one foot to the other. 'You know you said prisoners weren't to be molested, sir . . .'

It was quite a large and heavy roof timber and it scythed quite slowly through the air, but when it hit people they rolled backwards and stayed hit.

'Now *look*,' said Carrot, hauling it in and pushing back his helmet, 'I don't want to have to tell anyone again, right?'

Vimes shouldered his way through the dense crowd, staring at the bulky figure atop the mound of rubble and dragon. Carrot turned slowly, the roof beam held like a staff. His gaze was like a lighthouse beam. Where it fell, the crowd lowered their weapons and looked merely sullen and uncomfortable.

'I must warn you,' Carrot went on, 'that interfering with an officer in the execution of his duty is a serious offence. And I shall come down like a ton of bricks on the very next person who throws a stone.'

A stone bounced off the back of his helmet. There was a barrage of jeers.

'Let us at it!'

'That's right!'

'We don't want guards ordering us about!'

'Quis custodiet custard?'

'Yeah? Right!'

Vimes pulled the sergeant towards him. 'Go and organize some rope. Lots of rope. As thick as possible. I suppose we can – oh, tie its wings together, maybe, and bind up its mouth so it can't flame.'

Colon peered at him.

'Are you serious, sir? We're really going to *arrest* it?'

'Do it!'

It's *been* arrested, he thought, as he pushed his way forward. Personally I would have preferred it to drop in the sea, but it's been arrested and now we've got to deal with it or let it go free.

He felt his own feelings about the bloody thing evaporate in the face of the mob. What could you do with it? Give it a fair trial, he thought, and then execute it. Not kill it. That's what heroes do out in the wilderness. You can't think like that in cities. Or rather, you *can*, but if you're going to then you might as well burn the whole place down right now and start again. You ought to do it . . . well, by the book.

That's it. We tried everything else. Now we might as well try and do it by the book.

Anyway, he added mentally, that's a city guard up there. We've got to stick together. Nobody else will have anything to do with us.

A burly figure in front of him drew back an arm with a halfbrick in it.

'Throw that brick and you're a dead man,' said Vimes, and then ducked and pushed his way through the press of people while the would-be thrower looked around in amazement.

Carrot half-raised his club in a threatening gesture as Vimes climbed up the rubble pile.

'Oh, hello, Captain Vimes,' he said, lowering it, 'I have to report I have arrested this—'

'Yes, I can see,' said Vimes. 'Did you have any suggestions about what we do next?'

'Oh, yes, sir. I have to read it its rights, sir,' said Carrot.

'I mean apart from that.'

'Not really, sir.'

Vimes looked at those parts of the dragon still visible under the rubble. How *could* you kill one of these? You'd have to spend a day at it.

A lump of rock ricocheted off his breastplate.

'Who did that?'

The voice lashed out like a whip.

The crowd went quiet.

Sybil Ramkin scrambled up on the wreckage, eyes afire, and glared furiously at the mob.

'I said,' she said, 'who did that? If the person who did it does not own up I shall be *extremely* angry! Shame on you all!'

She had their full attention. Several people holding stones and things let them drop quietly to the ground.

The breeze flapped the remnants of her nightshirt as her Ladyship took up a new haranguing position.

'Here is the *gallant* Captain Vimes—'

'Oh gods,' said Vimes in a small voice, and pulled his helmet down over his eyes.

'—and his *dauntless* men, who have taken the *trouble* to come here today, to save your—'

Vimes gripped Carrot's arm and manoeuvred him down the far side of the heap.

'You all right, Captain?' said the lance-constable. 'You've gone all red.'

'Don't *you* start,' snapped Vimes. 'It's bad enough getting all those leers from Nobby and the sergeant.'

To his astonishment Carrot patted him companionably on the shoulder.

'I know how it is,' he said sympathetically. 'I had this girl back home, her name was Minty, and her father—'

'Look, for the last time, there is absolutely *nothing* between—' Vimes began.

There was a rattle beside them. A small avalanche of plaster and thatch rolled down. The rubble heaved, and opened one eye. One big black pupil floating in a bloodshot glow tried to focus on them.

'We must be mad,' said Vimes.

'Oh, no, sir,' said Carrot. 'There's plenty of precedents. In 1135 a hen was arrested for crowing on Soul Cake Thursday. And during the regime of Psychoneurotic Lord Snapcase a colony of bats was executed for persistent curfew violations. That was in 1401. August, I think. Great days for the law, they were,' said Carrot dreamily. 'In 1321, you know, a small cloud was prosecuted for covering the sun during the climax of Frenzied Earl Hargath's investiture ceremony.'

'I hope Colon gets a move on with—' Vimes stopped. He had to know. *'How?'* he said. 'What can you do to a cloud?'

'The Earl sentenced it to be stoned to death,' said Carrot. 'Apparently thirty-one people were killed.' He pulled out his notebook and glared at the dragon.

'Can it hear us, do you think?' he said.

'I suppose so.'

'Well, then.' Carrot cleared his throat and turned back to the stunned reptile. 'It is my duty to warn you that you are to be reported for consideration of prosecution on some or all of the following counts, to whit: One, (One) i, that on or about 18th Grune last, in a place known as Sweetheart Lane, the Shades, you did unlawfully vent flame in a manner likely to cause grievous bodily harm, in contravention of Clause Seven of the Industrial Processes Act, 1508; AND THAT, One, (One) ii, that on or about 18th Grune last, in a place known as Sweetheart Lane, the Shades, you caused or did cause to cause the death of six persons unknown—'

Vimes wondered how long the rubble would hold the creature down. Several weeks would be necessary, if the length of the charge sheet was anything to go by.

The crowd went silent. Even Sybil Ramkin was standing in astonishment.

'What's the matter?' said Vimes to the upturned faces. 'Haven't you ever seen a dragon being arrested before?

'—Sixteen (Three) ii, on the night of Grune 24th last, you did flame or cause to flame those premises known as the Old Watch House, Ankh-Morpork, valued at two hundred dollars; AND THAT, Sixteen (Three) iii, on the night of Grune 24th last, upon being apprehended by an officer of the Watch in the execution of his duty—'

'I think we should hurry up,' whispered Vimes. 'It's getting rather restive. Is all this necessary?'

'Well, I believe one can summarize,' said Carrot. 'In exceptional circumstances, according to Bregg's Rules for—'

'It may come as a surprise, but these *are* exceptional circumstances, Carrot,' said Vimes. 'And they're going to be really *astonishingly* exceptional if Colon doesn't hurry up with that rope.'

More rubble moved as the dragon strained to get up. There was a thump as a heavy beam was shouldered aside. The crowd began to run for it.

It was at this point that Errol came back over the rooftops in a series of minor explosions, leaving a trail of smoke rings. Dipping low, he buzzed the crowd and sent the front rank stumbling backwards.

He was also wailing like a foghorn.

Vimes grabbed Carrot and stumbled down the heap as the king started to scrabble desperately to get free.

'He's come back for the kill!' he shouted. 'It probably took him all this time just to slow down!'

Now Errol was hovering over the fallen dragon, and hooting shrilly enough to bust bottles.

The great dragon stuck its head up in a cascade of plaster dust. It opened its mouth but, instead of the lance of white fire that Vimes tensed himself to expect, it merely made a noise like a kitten. Admittedly a kitten shouting into a tin bath at the bottom of a cave, but still a kitten.

Broken spars fell aside when the huge creature got unsteadily to its feet. The great wings opened, showering the surrounding streets with dust and bits of thatch. Some of it clanged off the helmet of Sergeant Colon, hurrying back with what looked like a small washing line coiled over his arm.

'You're letting it get up!' Vimes shouted, pushing the sergeant to safety. 'You're not supposed to let it get up, Errol! Don't let it get up!'

Lady Ramkin frowned. 'That's not right,' she said. 'They never usually fight like that. The winner usually kills the loser.'

'Right on!' shouted Nobby.

'And then half the time he explodes with the excitement in any case.'

'Look, it's *me*!' Vimes yelled, as Errol hovered unconcernedly over the scene. 'I bought you the fluffy ball! The one with the bell in it! You can't do this to us!'

'No, wait a minute,' said Lady Ramkin, laying a hand on his arm. 'I'm not sure we haven't got hold of the wrong end of the stick here—'

The great dragon leapt into the air and brought its wings down with a *whump* that flattened a few more buildings. The huge head swung around, the bleary eyes caught sight of Vimes.

There seemed to be some thought going on inside them.

Errol arced across the sky and hovered protectively in front of the captain, facing the thing down. For a moment it looked as though he might be turned into a small flying charcoal biscuit, and then the dragon lowered its gaze in a slightly embarrassed way and started to rise.

It climbed in a wide spiral, gathering speed as it did so. Errol went with it, orbiting the huge body like a tug around a liner.

'It's – it's as though he's *fussing* over it,' said Vimes.

'Add up the bastard!' shouted Nobby enthusiastically.

'Total, Nobby,' said Colon. 'You mean "total".'

Vimes felt Lady Ramkin's gaze on the back of his neck. He looked at her expression.

Realization dawned. 'Oh,' he said.

Lady Ramkin nodded.

'Really?' said Vimes.

'Yes,' she said. 'I really ought to have thought of it before. It was such a hot flame, of course. And they're always so much more territorial than the males.'

'Why don't you fight the bastard!' shouted Nobby, at the dwindling dragons.

'Bitch, Nobby,' said Vimes quietly. 'Not bastard. Bitch.'

'Why don't you fi—what?'

'It's a member of the female gender,' explained Lady Ramkin.

'What?'

'We meant that if you tried your favourite kick, Nobby, it wouldn't work,' said Vimes.

'It's a *girl*,' translated Lady Ramkin.

'But it's sodding *enormous*!' said Nobby.

Vimes coughed urgently. Nobby's rodent eyes slid sideways to Sybil Ramkin, who blushed like a sunset.

'A fine figure of a dragon, I mean,' he said quickly.

'Er. Wide, egg-bearing hips,' said Sergeant Colon anxiously.

'Statueskew,' Nobby added fervently.

'Shut up,' said Vimes. He brushed the dust off the remains of his uniform, adjusted the hang of his breastplate, and set his helmet on squarely. He patted it firmly. This wasn't where it ended, he knew that. This was where it all got started.

'You men come with me. Come on, hurry! While everyone's still watching them,' he added.

'But what about the king?' said Carrot. 'Or queen? Or whatever it is now?'

Vimes stared at the rapidly shrinking shapes. 'I really don't know,' he said. 'That's up to Errol, I suppose. We've got other things to do.'

Colon saluted, still fighting for breath. 'Where we going, sir?' he managed.

'To the palace. Any of you still got a sword?'

'You can use mine, Captain,' said Carrot. He handed it over.

'Right,' said Vimes quietly. He glared at them. 'Let's go.'

*

The rank trailed behind Vimes through the stricken streets.

He started to walk faster. The rank started to trot to keep up.

Vimes began to trot to keep ahead.

The rank broke into a canter.

Then, as if on an unspoken word of command, they broke into a run.

Then into a gallop.

People scurried away as they rattled past. Carrot's enormous sandals hammered on the cobbles. Sparks flew up from the scads of Nobby's boots. Colon ran quietly for such a fat man, as fat men often do, face locked in a scowl of concentration.

They pounded along the Street of Cunning Artificers, turned into Hogsback Alley, emerged into the Street of Small Gods and thundered towards the palace. Vimes kept barely in the lead, mind currently empty of everything except the need to run and run.

At least, nearly everything. But his head buzzed and resonated manically with those of all city guards everywhere, all the pavement-pounding meatheads in the multiverse who had ever, just occasionally, tried to do what was Right.

Far ahead of them a handful of palace guards drew their swords, took a second look, thought better of it, darted back inside the wall and started to close the gates. They clanged together as Vimes arrived.

He hesitated, panting for breath, and looked at the massive things. The ones that the dragon had burned had been replaced by gates even more forbidding. From behind them came the sound of bolts sliding back.

This was no time for half measures. He was a captain, godsdammit. An officer. Things like this didn't present a problem for an officer. Officers had a tried and tested way of solving problems like this. It was called a sergeant.

'Sergeant Colon!' he snapped, his mind still buzzing with universal policemanhood, 'shoot the lock off!'

The sergeant hesitated. 'What, sir? With a bow and arrow, sir?'

'I mean—' Vimes hesitated. 'I mean, open these gates!'

'Sir!' Colon saluted. He glared at the gates for a moment. 'Right!' he barked. 'Lance-constable Carrot, one stepa forwarda, *take*! Lance-constable Carrot, inna youra owna timer! Open these gatesa!'

'Yes, sir!'

Carrot stepped forward, saluted, folded an enormous hand into a fist and rapped gently on the woodwork.

'Open up,' he said, 'in the name of the Law!'

There was some whispering on the other side of the gates, and eventually a small hatch halfway up the door slid open a fraction and a voice said, 'Why?'

'Because if you don't it will be Impeding an Officer of the Watch in the Execution of his Duty, which is punishable by a fine of not less than thirty dollars, one month's imprisonment, or being remanded in custody for social inquiry reports and half an hour with a red-hot poker,' said Carrot.

There was some more muffled whispering, the sound of bolts being drawn, and then the gates opened about halfway.

There was no-one visible on the other side.

Vimes put a finger to his lips. He motioned Carrot towards one gate and dragged Nobby and Colon to the other.

'Push,' he whispered. They pushed, hard. There was a sudden eruption of pained cursing from behind the woodwork.

'Run!' shouted Colon.

'No!' shouted Vimes. He walked around the gate. Four semi-crushed palace guards glowered at him.

'No,' he said. 'No more running. I want these men arrested.'

'You wouldn't dare,' said one of the men. Vimes peered at him.

'Clarence, isn't it?' he said. 'With a C. Well, Clarence with a C, watch my lips. Either you can be charged with Aiding and Abetting or – ' he leaned closer, and glanced meaningfully at Carrot – 'with an axe.'

'Swivel on that one, doggybag!' added Nobby, jumping from one foot to the other in vicious excitement.

Clarence's little piggy eyes glared at the looming bulk that was Carrot, and then at Vimes's face. There was absolutely no mercy there. He appeared to reach a reluctant decision.

'Jolly good,' said Vimes. 'Lock them in the gatehouse, Sergeant.'

Colon drew his bow and squared his shoulders. 'You heard the Man,' he rasped. 'One false move and you're . . . you're – ' he took a desperate stab at it – 'you're Home Economics!'

'Yeah! Slam 'em up in the banger!' shouted Nobby. If worms could turn, Nobby was revolving at generating speeds. 'Douche-balls!' he sneered, at their retreating backs.

'Aiding and Abetting what, Captain?' said Carrot, as the weapon-less guards trooped away. 'You have to aid and abet something.'

'I think in this case it will just be generalized abetting,' said Vimes. 'Persistent and reckless abetment.'

'Yeah,' said Nobby. 'Can't stand abettors. Slimebreaths!'

Colon handed Captain Vimes the guardhouse key. 'It's not very secure in there, Captain,' he said. 'They'll be able to break out eventually.'

'I hope so,' said Vimes, 'because the very first drain we come to, you're going to drop the key down it. Everyone here? Right. Follow me.'

Lupine Wonse scurried along the ruined corridors of the palace, *The Summoning of Dragons* under one arm, the glittering royal sword grasped uncertainly in one hand.

He halted, panting, in a doorway.

Not a lot of his mind was currently in a state sane enough to have proper thoughts, but the small part that was still in business kept insisting that it couldn't have seen what it had seen or heard what it had heard.

Someone was following him.

And he'd seen Vetinari walking through the palace. He *knew* the man was securely put away. The lock was completely unpickable. He remembered the Patrician being absolutely insistent that it be an unpickable lock when it was installed.

There was movement in the shadows at the end of the passage. Wonse gibbered a bit, fumbled with the doorhandle beside him, darted in, slammed the door and leaned against it, fighting for breath.

He opened his eyes.

He was in the old private audience room. The Patrician was sitting in his old seat, one leg crossed on the other, watching him with mild interest.

'Ah, Wonse,' he said.

Wonse jumped, scrabbled at the doorhandle, leapt into the corridor and ran for it until he reached the main staircase, rising now through the ruins of the central palace like a forlorn corkscrew. Stairs – height – high ground – defence. He ran up them three at a time.

All he needed was a few minutes of peace. *Then* he'd show them.

The upper floors were more full of shadows. What they were short on was structural strength. Pillars and walls had been torn out by the dragon as it built its cave. Rooms gaped pathetically on the edge of the abyss. Dangling shreds of wall-hanging and carpet flapped in the wind from the smashed windows. The floor sprang and wobbled like a trampoline as Wonse scurried across it. He struggled to the nearest door.

'That was commendably fast,' said the Patrician.

Wonse slammed the door in his face and ran, squeaking, down a corridor.

Sanity took a brief hold. He paused by a statue. There was no sound, no hurrying footsteps, no whirr of hidden doors. He gave the statue a suspicious look and prodded it with the sword.

When it failed to move he opened the nearest door and slammed it behind him, found a chair and wedged it under the handle. This was one of the upper state rooms, bare now of most of its furnishings, and lacking its fourth wall. Where it should have been was just the gulf of the cavern.

The Patrician stepped out of the shadows.

'Now you have got it out of your system—' he said.

Wonse spun around, sword raised.

'You don't really exist,' he said. 'You're a – a ghost, or something.'

'I believe this is not the case,' said the Patrician.

'You can't stop me! I've got some magic stuff left, I've got the book!' Wonse took a brown leather bag out of his pocket. 'I'll bring back another one! You'll see!'

'I urge you not to,' said Lord Vetinari mildly.

'Oh, you think you're so clever, so in-control, so *swave*, just because I've got a sword and you haven't! Well, I've got more than that, I'll have you know,' said Wonse triumphantly. 'Yes! I've got the palace guards on my side! They follow me, not you! No-one likes you, you know. No-one *ever* liked you.'

He swung the sword so that its needle point was a foot from the Patrician's thin chest.

'So it's back to the cells for you,' he said. 'And this time I'll make *sure* you stay there. Guards! Guards!'

There was the clatter of running feet outside. The door rattled, the chair shook. There was a moment's silence, and then door and chair erupted in splinters.

'Take him away!' screamed Wonse. 'Fetch more scorpions! Put him in . . . *you're not the—*'

'Put the sword down,' said Vimes, while behind him Carrot picked bits of door out of his fist.

'Yeah,' said Nobby, peering around the captain. 'Up against the wall and spread 'em, motherbreath!'

'Eh? What's he supposed to spread?' whispered Sergeant Colon anxiously.

Nobby shrugged. 'Dunno,' he said. 'Everything, I reckon. Safest way.'

Wonse stared at the rank in disbelief.

'Ah, Vimes,' said the Patrician. 'You will—'

'Shut up,' said Vimes calmly. 'Lance-constable Carrot?'

'Sir!'

'Read the prisoner his rights.'

'Yes, sir.' Carrot produced his notebook, licked his thumb, flicked through the pages.

'Lupine Wonse,' he said, 'AKA Lupin Squiggle Sec'y PP—'

'Wha?' said Wonse.

'—currently domiciled in the domicile known as The Palace, Ankh-Morpork, it is my duty to inform you that you have been arrested and will be charged with – ' Carrot gave Vimes an agonised look – 'a number of offences of murder by means of a blunt instrument, to whit, a dragon, and many further offences of generalized abetting, to be more specifically ascertained later. You have the right to remain silent. You have the right not to be summarily thrown into a piranha tank. You have the right to trial by ordeal. You have the—'

'This is madness,' said the Patrician calmly.

'I thought I told you to shut up!' snapped Vimes, spinning around and shaking a finger under the Patrician's nose.

'Tell me, Sarge,' whispered Nobby, 'do you think we're going to *like* it in the scorpion pit?'

'—say anything, er, but anything you do say will be written down, er, here, in my notebook, and, er, may be used in evidence—'

Carrot's voice trailed into silence.

'Well, if this pantomime gives you any pleasure, Vimes,' said the Patrician eventually, 'take him down to the cells. I'll deal with him in the morning.'

Wonse made no signal. There was no scream or cry. He just rushed at the Patrician, sword raised.

Options flickered across Vimes's mind. In the lead came the suggestion that standing back would be a good plan, let Wonse do it, disarm him afterwards, let the city clean itself up. Yes. A good plan.

And it was therefore a total mystery to him why he chose to dart forward, bringing Carrot's sword up in a half-baked attempt at blocking the stroke . . .

Perhaps it was something to do with doing it by the book.

There was a clang. Not a particularly loud one. He felt something bright and silver whirr past his ear and strike the wall.

Wonse's mouth fell open. He dropped the remnant of his sword and backed away, clutching *The Summoning*.

'You'll be sorry,' he hissed. 'You'll all be *very sorry!*'

He started to mumble under his breath.

Vimes felt himself trembling. He was pretty certain he knew what had zinged past his head, and the mere thought was making his hands sweat. He'd come to the palace ready to kill and there'd been this *minute*, just this *minute*, when for once the world had seemed to be operating properly and he was in charge of it and now, now all he wanted was a drink. And a nice week's sleep.

'Oh, give *up*!' he said. 'Are you going to come quietly?'

The mumbling went on. The air began to feel hot and dry.

Vimes shrugged. 'That's it, then,' he said, and turned away. 'Throw the book at him, Carrot.'

'Right, sir.'

Vimes remembered too late.

Dwarfs have trouble with metaphors.

They also have a very good aim.

The Laws and Ordinances of Ankh and Morpork caught the secretary on the forehead. He blinked, staggered, and stepped backwards.

It was the longest step he ever took. For one thing, it lasted the rest of his life.

After several seconds they heard him hit, five storeys below.

After several more seconds their faces appeared over the edge of the ravaged floor.

'What a way to go,' said Sergeant Colon.

'That's a fact,' said Nobby, reaching up to his ear for a dog-end.

'Killed by a wossname. A metaphor.'

'Dunno,' said Nobby. 'Looks like the ground to me. Got a light, Sarge?'

'That was right, wasn't it, sir?' said Carrot anxiously. 'You said to—'

'Yes, yes,' said Vimes. 'Don't worry.' He reached down with a shaking hand, picked up the bag Wonse had been holding, and tipped out a pile of stones. Every one had a hole in it. Why? he thought.

A metallic noise behind him made him look around. The Patrician was holding the remains of the royal sword. As the captain watched, the man wrenched the other half of the sword out of the far wall. It was a clean break.

'Captain Vimes,' he said.

'Sir?'

'That sword, if you please?'

Vimes handed it over. He couldn't, right now, think of anything else to do. He was probably due for a scorpion pit of his very own as it was.

Lord Vetinari examined the rusty blade carefully.

'How long have you had this, Captain?' he said mildly.

'Isn't mine, sir. Belongs to Lance-constable Carrot, sir.'

'Lance—?'

'Me, sir, your graciousness,' said Carrot, saluting.

'Ah.'

The Patrician turned the blade over and over slowly, staring at it as if fascinated. Vimes felt the air thicken, as though history was clustering around this point, but for the life of him he couldn't think why. This was one of those points where the Trousers of Time bifurcated themselves, and if you weren't careful you'd go down the wrong leg—

Wonse arose in a world of shades, icy confusion pouring into his mind. But all he could think of at the moment was the tall cowled figure standing over him.

'I thought you were all dead,' he mumbled. It was strangely quiet and the colours around him seemed washed-out, muted. Something was very wrong. 'Is that you, Brother Doorkeeper?' he ventured.

The figure reached out.

METAPHORICALLY, it said.

—and the Patrician handed the sword to Carrot.

'Very well done, young man,' he said. 'Captain Vimes, I suggest you give your men the rest of the day off.'

'Thank you, sir,' said Vimes. 'Okay, lads. You heard his lordship.'

'But not you, Captain. We must have a little talk.'

'Yes, sir?' said Vimes innocently.

The rank scurried out, giving Vimes sympathetic and sorrowful glances.

The Patrician walked to the edge of the floor and looked down.

'Poor Wonse,' he said.

'Yes, sir.' Vimes stared at the wall.

'I would have preferred him alive, you know.'

'Sir?'

'Misguided, yes, but a useful man. His head could have been of further use to me.'

'Yes, sir.'

'The rest, of course, we could have thrown away.'

'Yes, sir.'

'That was a joke, Vimes.'

'Yes, sir.'

'The chap never grasped the idea of secret passages, mind you.'

'No, sir.'

'That young fellow. Carrot, you called him?'

'Yes, sir.'

'Keen fellow. Likes it in the Watch?'

'Yes, sir. Right at home. sir.'

'You saved my life.'

'Sir?'

'Come with me.'

He stalked away through the ruined palace, Vimes trailing behind, until he reached the Oblong Office. It was quite tidy. It had escaped most of the devastation with nothing more than a layer of dust. The Patrician sat down, and suddenly it was as if he'd never left. Vimes wondered if he ever had.

He picked up a sheaf of papers and brushed the plaster off them.

'Sad,' he said. 'Lupine was such a tidy-minded man.'

'Yes, sir.'

The Patrician steepled his hands and looked at Vimes over the top of them.

'Let me give you some advice, Captain,' he said.

'Yes, sir?'

'It may help you make some sense of the world.'

'Sir.'

'I believe you find life such a problem because you think there are the good people and the bad people,' said the man. 'You're wrong, of course. There are, always and only, the bad people, *but some of them are on opposite sides.*'

He waved his thin hand towards the city and walked over to the window.

'A great rolling sea of evil,' he said, almost proprietorially. 'Shallower in some places, of course, but deeper, oh, so much *deeper* in others. But people like you put together little rafts of rules and vaguely good intentions and say, this is the opposite, this will triumph in the end. Amazing!' He slapped Vimes good-naturedly on the back.

'Down there,' he said, 'are people who will follow any dragon, worship any god, ignore any iniquity. All out of a kind of humdrum, everyday badness. Not the really high, creative loathesomeness of the great sinners, but a sort of mass-produced darkness of the soul. Sin, you might say, without a trace of originality. They accept evil not because they say *yes*, but because they don't say *no*. I'm sorry if this offends you,' he added, patting the captain's shoulder, 'but you fellows really need us.'

'Yes, sir?' said Vimes quietly.

'Oh, yes. We're the only ones who know how to make things work. You see, the only thing the good people are good at is overthrowing the bad people. And you're *good* at that, I'll grant you. But the trouble is that it's the *only* thing you're good at. One day it's the ringing of the bells and the casting down of the evil tyrant, and the next it's everyone sitting around complaining that ever since the tyrant was overthrown no-one's been taking out the trash. Because the bad people know how to *plan*. It's part of the specification, you might say. Every evil tyrant has a plan to rule the world. The good people don't seem to have the knack.'

'Maybe. But you're wrong about the rest!' said Vimes. 'It's just because people are afraid, and alone—' He paused. It sounded pretty hollow, even to him.

He shrugged. 'They're just people,' he said. 'They're just doing what people do. Sir.'

Lord Vetinari gave him a friendly smile.

'Of course, of course,' he said. 'You have to believe that, I appreciate. Otherwise you'd go quite mad. Otherwise you'd think you're standing on a feather-thin bridge over the vaults of Hell. Otherwise existence would be a dark agony and the only hope would be that there is no life after death. I quite understand.'

He looked at his desk, and sighed. 'And now,' he said, 'there is such a lot to do. I'm afraid poor Wonse was a good servant but an inefficient master. So you may go. Have a good night's sleep. Oh, and do bring your men in tomorrow. The city must show its gratitude.'

'It must *what*?' said Vimes.

The Patrician looked at a scroll. Already his voice was back to the distant tones of one who organizes and plans and controls.

'Its gratitude,' he said. 'After every triumphant victory there must be heroes. It is essential. Then everyone will know that everything has been done properly.'

He glanced at Vimes over the top of the scroll.

'It's all part of the natural order of things,' he said.

After a while he made a few pencil annotations to the paper in front of him and looked up.

'I said,' he said, 'that you may go.'

Vimes paused at the door.

'Do you believe all that, sir?' he said. 'About the endless evil and the sheer blackness?'

'Indeed, indeed,' said the Patrician, turning over the page. 'It is the only logical conclusion.'

'But you get out of bed every morning, sir?'

'Hmm? Yes? What is your point?'

'I'd just like to know *why*, sir.'

'Oh, do go away, Vimes. There's a good fellow.'

*

240

In the dark and draughty cave hacked from the heart of the palace the Librarian knuckled across the floor. He clambered over the remains of the sad hoard and looked down at the splayed body of Wonse.

Then he reached down, very gently, and prised *The Summoning of Dragons* from the stiffening fingers. He blew the dust off it. He brushed it tenderly, as if it was a frightened child.

He turned to climb down the heap, and stopped. He bent down again, and carefully pulled another book from among the glittering rubble. It wasn't one of his, except in the wide sense that all books came under his domain. He turned a few pages carefully.

'Keep it,' said Vimes behind him. 'Take it away. Put it somewhere.'

The orang-utan nodded at the captain, and rattled down the heap. He tapped Vimes gently on the kneecap, opened *The Summoning of Dragons*, leafed through its ravaged pages until he found the one he'd been looking for, and silently passed the book up.

Vimes squinted at the crabbed writing.

Yet draggons are notte liken unicornes, I willen. They dwellyth in some Realm definèd bye thee Fancie of the Wille and, thus, it myte bee thate whomsoever calleth upon them, and giveth them theyre patheway unto thys worlde, calleth theyre Owne dragon of the Mind.

Yette, I trow, the Pure in Harte maye stille call a Draggon of Power as a Forse for Goode in thee worlde, and this ane nighte the Grate Worke will commence. All hathe been prepared I hath laboured most mytily to be a Worthie Vessle . . .

A realm of fancy, Vimes thought. That's where they went, then. Into our imaginations. And when we call them back we shape them, like squeezing dough into pastry shapes. Only you don't get gingerbread men, you get what you are. Your own darkness, given shape . . .

Vimes read it through again, and then looked at the following pages.

There weren't many. The rest of the book was a charred mass.

Vimes handed it back to the ape.

'What kind of a man was de Malachite?' he said.

The Librarian gave this the consideration due from someone who knew the *Dictionary of City Biography* by heart. Then he shrugged.

'Particularly holy?' said Vimes.

The ape shook his head.

'Well, noticeably evil, then?'

241

The ape shrugged, and shook his head again.

'If I were you,' said Vimes, 'I'd put that book somewhere very safe. And the book of the Law with it. They're too bloody dangerous.'

'Oook.'

Vimes stretched. 'And now,' he said, 'let's go and have a drink.'

'Oook.'

'But just a small one.'

'Oook.'

'And you're paying.'

'Eeek.'

Vimes stopped and stared down at the big, mild face.

'Tell me,' he said. 'I've always wanted to know . . . is it *better*, being an ape?'

The Librarian thought about it. 'Oook,' he said.

'Oh. Really?' said Vimes.

It was next day. The room was wall-to-wall with civic dignitaries. The Patrician sat on his severe chair, surrounded by the Council. Everyone present was wearing the shiny waxen grins of those bent on good works.

Lady Sybil Ramkin sat off to one side, wearing a few acres of black velvet. The Ramkin family jewels glittered on her fingers, neck and in the black curls of today's wig. The total effect was striking, like a globe of the heavens.

Vimes marched the rank to the centre of the hall and stamped to a halt with his helmet under his arm, as per regulations. He'd been amazed to see that even Nobby had made an effort – the suspicion of shiny metal could be seen here and there on his breastplate. And Colon was wearing an expression of almost constipated importance. Carrot's armour gleamed.

Colon ripped off a textbook salute for the first time in his life.

'All present and correct, sah!' he barked.

'Very good, Sergeant,' said Vimes coldly. He turned to the Patrician and raised an eyebrow politely.

Lord Vetinari gave a little wave of his hand.

'Stand easy, or whatever it is you chaps do,' he said. 'I'm sure we needn't wait on ceremony here. What do you say, Captain?'

'Just as you like, sir,' said Vimes.

'Now, men,' said the Patrician, leaning forward, 'we have heard some remarkable accounts of your magnificent efforts in defence of the city . . .'

Vimes let his mind wander as the golden platitudes floated past.

For a while he derived a certain amount of amusement from watching the faces of the Council. A whole sequence of expressions drifted across them as the Patrician spoke. It was, of course, vitally important that there be a ceremony like this. Then the whole thing could be neat and *settled*. And forgotten. Just another chapter in the long and exciting history of eckcetra, eckcetra. Ankh-Morpork was good at starting new chapters.

His trawling gaze fell on Lady Ramkin. She winked. Vimes's eyes swivelled front again, his expression suddenly as wooden as a plank.

'. . . token of our gratitude,' the Patrician finished, sitting back.

Vimes realized that everyone was looking at him.

'Pardon?' he said.

'I *said*, we have been trying to think of some suitable recompense, Captain Vimes. Various public-spirited citizens – ' the Patrician's eyes took in the Council and Lady Ramkin – 'and, of course, myself, feel that an appropriate reward is due.'

Vimes still looked blank.

'Reward?' he said.

'It *is* customary for such heroic endeavour,' said the Patrician, a little testily.

Vimes faced forward again. 'Really haven't thought about it, sir,' he said. 'Can't speak for the men, of course.'

There was an awkward pause. Out of the corner of his eye Vimes was aware of Nobby nudging the sergeant in the ribs. Eventually Colon stumbled forward and ripped off another salute. 'Permission to speak, sir,' he muttered.

The Patrician nodded graciously.

The sergeant coughed. He removed his helmet and pulled out a scrap of paper.

'Er,' he said. 'The thing is, saving your honour's presence, we think, you know, what with saving the city and everything, or sort of, or, what I mean is . . . we just had a go, you see, man on the spot and that sort of thing . . . the thing is, we reckon we're entitled. If you catch my drift.'

The assembled company nodded. This was exactly how it should be.

'Do go on,' said the Patrician.

'So we, like, put our heads together,' said the sergeant. 'A bit of a cheek, I know . . .'

'Please carry *on*, Sergeant,' said the Patrician. 'You needn't keep stopping. We are well aware of the *magnitude* of the matter. '

'Right, sir. Well, sir. First, it's the wages.'

'The wages?' said Lord Vetinari. He stared at Vimes, who stared at nothing.

The sergeant raised his head. His expression was the determined expression of a man who is going to see it through.

'Yes, sir,' he said. 'Thirty dollars a month. It's not right. We think –' he licked his lips and glanced behind him at the other two, who were making vague encouraging motions – 'we think a basic rate of, er, thirty-five dollars? A month?' He stared at the Patrician's stony expression. 'With increments as per rank? We thought five dollars.'

He licked his lips again, unnerved by the Patrician's expression. 'We won't go below four,' he said. 'And that's flat. Sorry, your Highness, but there it is.'

The Patrician glanced again at Vimes's impassive face, then looked back at the rank.

'That's *it*?' he said.

Nobby whispered in Colon's ear and then darted back. The sweating sergeant gripped his helmet as though it was the only real thing in the world.

'There was another thing, your reverence,' he said.

'Ah.' The Patrician smiled knowingly.

'There's the kettle. It wasn't much good anyway, and then Errol et it. It was nearly two dollars.' He swallowed. 'We could do with a new kettle, if it's all the same, your lordship.'

The Patrician leaned forward, gripping the arms of his chair.

'I want to be clear about this,' he said coldly. 'Are we to believe that you are asking for a petty wage increase and a domestic utensil?'

Carrot whispered in Colon's other ear.

Colon turned two bulging, watery-rimmed eyes to the dignitaries. The rim of his helmet was passing through his fingers like a millwheel.

'Well,' he began, 'sometimes, we thought, you know, when we has our dinner break, or when it's quite, like, at the end of a watch as it may be, and we want to relax a bit, you know, wind down . . .' His voice trailed away.

'Yes?'

Colon took a deep breath.

'I suppose a dartboard would be out of the question—?'

The thunderous silence that followed was broken by an erratic snorting.

Vimes's helmet dropped out of his shaking hand. His breastplate wobbled as the suppressed laughter of the years burst out in great

244

uncontrollable eruptions. He turned his face to the row of councillors and laughed and laughed until the tears came.

Laughed at the way they got up, all confusion and outraged dignity.

Laughed at the Patrician's carefully immobile expression.

Laughed for the world and the saving of souls.

Laughed and laughed, and laughed until the tears came.

Nobby craned up to reach Colon's ear.

'*I told you*,' he hissed. 'I *said* they'd never wear it. I *knew* a dartboard'd be pushing our luck. You've upset 'em all now.'

Dear Mother and Father [wrote Carrot] You will never guess, I have been in the Watch only a few weeks and, already I am to be a full Constable. Captain Vimes said, the Patrician himself said I was to be One, and that also he hoped I should have a long and successful career in the Watch as well and, he would follow it with special interest. Also my wages are to go up by ten dollars and we had a special bonus of twenty dollars that Captain Vimes paid for out of his own pocket, Sgt Colon said. Please find money enclosed. I am keeping a little bit by though because I went to see Reet and Mrs Palm said all the girls had been following my career with Great Interest as well and I am to come to dinner on my night off. Sgt Colon has been telling me about how to start courting, which is very interesting and not at all complicated it appears. I arrested a dragon but it got away. I hope Mr Varneshi is well.

I am as happy as anyone can be in the whole world.

Your son, Carrot.

Vimes knocked on the door.

An effort had been made to spruce up the Ramkin mansion, he noticed. The encroaching shrubbery had been pitilessly hacked back. An elderly workman atop a ladder was nailing the stucco back on the walls while another, with a spade, was rather arbitrarily defining the line where the lawn ended and the old flower beds had begun.

Vimes stuck his helmet under his arm, smoothed back his hair, and knocked. He'd considered asking Sergeant Colon to accompany him, but had brushed the idea aside quickly. He couldn't have tolerated the sniggering. Anyway, what was there to be afraid of? He'd stared into the jaws of death three times; four, if you included telling Lord Vetinari to shut up.

To his amazement the door was eventually opened by a butler so elderly that he might have been resurrected by the knocking.

'Yerss?' he said.

'Captain Vimes, City Watch,' said Vimes.

The man looked him up and down.

'Oh, yes,' he said. 'Her ladyship did say. I believe her ladyship is with her dragons,' he said. 'If you like to wait in 'ere, I will—'

'I know the way,' said Vimes, and set off around the overgrown path.

The kennels were a ruin. An assortment of battered wooden boxes were lying around under an oilcloth awning. From their depths a few sad swamp dragons whiffled a greeting at him.

A couple of women were moving purposefully among the boxes. Ladies, rather. They were far too untidy to be mere women. No ordinary women would have dreamed of looking so scruffy; you needed the complete self-confidence that comes with knowing who your great-great-great-great-grandfather was before you could wear clothes like that. But they were, Vimes noticed, incredibly good clothes, or had been once; clothes bought by one's parents, but so expensive and of such good quality that they never wore out and were handed down, like old china and silverware and gout.

Dragon breeders, he thought. You can tell. There's something about them. It's the way they wear their silk scarves, old tweed coats and granddad's riding boots. And the smell, of course.

A small wiry woman with a face like old saddle leather caught sight of him.

'Ah,' she said, 'you'll be the gallant captain.' She tucked an errant strand of white hair back under a headscarf and extended a veiny brown hand. 'Brenda Rodley. That's Rosie Devant-Molei. She runs the Sunshine Sanctuary, you know.' The other woman, who had the build of someone who could pick up carthorses in one hand and shoe them with the other, gave him a friendly grin.

'Samuel Vimes,' said Vimes weakly.

'My father was a Sam,' said Brenda vaguely. 'You can always trust a Sam, he said.' She shooed a dragon back into its box. 'We're just helping Sybil. Old friends, you know. The collection's all to blazes, of course. They're all over the city, the little devils. I dare say they'll come back when they're hungry, though. What a bloodline, eh?'

'I'm sorry?'

'Sybil reckons he was a sport, but I say we should be able to breed back into the line in three or four generations. I'm famed for my stud, you know,' she said. 'That'd be something, though. A whole new type of dragon.'

Vimes thought of supersonic contrails cries-crossing the sky.

'Er,' he said. 'Yes.'

'Well, we must get on.'

'Er, isn't Lady Ramkin around?' said Vimes. 'I got this message that it was essential, she said, for me to come here.'

'She's indoors somewhere,' said Miss Rodley. 'Said she had something important to see to. Oh, do be careful with that one, Rose, you silly gel!'

'More important than *dragons*?' said Vimes.

'Yes. Can't think what's come over her.' Brenda Rodley fished in the pocket of an oversized waistcoat. 'Nice to have met you, Captain. Always good to meet new members of the Fancy. Do drop in any time you're passing, I'd be only too happy to show you around.' She extracted a grubby card and pressed it into his hand. 'Must be off now, we've heard that some of them are trying to build nests on the University tower. Can't have that. Must get 'em down before it gets dark.'

Vimes squinted at the card as the women crunched off down the drive, carrying nets and ropes.

It said: *Brenda, Lady Rodley. The Dower House, Quirm Castle, Quirm.* What it meant, he realized, was that striding away down the path like an animated rummage stall was the dowager Duchess of Quirm, who owned more country than you could see from a very high mountain on a very clear day. Nobby would not have approved. There seemed to be a special kind of poverty that only the very, very rich could possibly afford . . .

That was how you got to be a power in the land, he thought. You never cared a toss about whatever anyone else thought and you were never, ever, uncertain about anything.

He padded back to the house. A door was open. It led into a large but dark and musty hall. Up in the gloom the heads of dead animals haunted the walls. The Ramkins seemed to have endangered more species than an ice age.

Vimes wandered aimlessly through another mahogany archway.

It was a dining room, containing the kind of table where the people at the other end are in a different time zone. One end had been colonized by silver candlesticks.

It was laid for two. A battery of cutlery flanked each plate. Antique wineglasses sparkled in the candlelight.

A terrible premonition took hold of Vimes at the same moment as a gust of *Captivation*, the most expensive perfume available anywhere in Ankh-Morpork, blew past him.

'Ah, Captain. So nice of you to come.'

Vimes turned around slowly, without his feet appearing to move.

Lady Ramkin stood there, magnificently.

Vimes was vaguely aware of a brilliant blue dress that sparkled in the candlelight, a mass of hair the colour of chestnuts, a slightly anxious face that suggested that a whole battalion of skilled painters and decorators had only just dismantled their scaffolding and gone home, and a faint creaking that said underneath it all mere corsetry was being subjected to the kind of tensions more usually found in the heart of large stars.

'I, er,' he said. 'If you, er. If you'd said, er. I'd, er. Dress more suitable, er. Extremely, er. Very. Er.'

She bore down upon him like a glittering siege engine.

In a sort of dream he allowed himself to be ushered to a seat. He must have eaten, because servants appeared out of nowhere with things stuffed with other things, and came back later and took the plates away. The butler reanimated occasionally to fill glass after glass with strange wines. The heat from the candles was enough to cook by. And all the time Lady Ramkin talked in a bright and brittle way – about the size of the house, the responsibilities of a huge estate, the feeling that it was time to take One's Position in Society More Seriously, while the setting sun filled the room with red and Vimes's head began to spin.

Society, he managed to think, didn't know what was going to hit it. Dragons weren't mentioned once, although after a while something under the table put its head on Vimes's knee and dribbled.

Vimes found it impossible to contribute to the conversation. He felt outflanked, beleaguered. He made one sally, hoping maybe to reach high ground from which to flee into exile.

'Where do you think they've gone?' he said.

'Where what?' said Lady Ramkin, temporarily halted.

'The dragons. You know. Errol and his wi— female.'

'Oh, somewhere isolated and rocky, I should imagine,' said Lady Ramkin. 'Favourite country for dragons.'

'But it – *she's* a magical animal,' said Vimes. 'What'll happen when the magic goes away?'

Lady Ramkin gave him a shy smile.

'Most people seem to manage,' she said.

She reached across the table and touched his hand.

'Your men think you need looking after,' she said meekly.

'Oh. Do they?' said Vimes.

'Sergeant Colon said he thought we'd get along like a *maison en Flambé*.'

'Oh. Did he?'

'And he said something else,' she said. 'What was it, now? Oh, yes: "It's a million to one chance",' said Lady Ramkin, 'I think he said, "but it might just work".'

She smiled at him.

And then it arose and struck Vimes that, in her own special category, she was quite beautiful; this was the category of all the women, in his entire life, who had ever thought he was worth smiling at. She couldn't do worse, but then, he couldn't do better. So maybe it balanced out. She wasn't getting any younger but then, who was? And she had style and money and common-sense and self-assurance and all the things that he didn't, and she had opened her heart, and if you let her she could engulf you; the woman was a city.

And eventually, under siege, you did what Ankh-Morpork had always done – unbar the gates, let the conquerors in, and make them your own.

How did you start? She seemed to be expecting something.

He shrugged, and picked up his wine glass and sought for a phrase. One crept into his wildly resonating mind.

'Here's looking at you, kid,' he said.

The gongs of various midnights banged out the old day.

(. . . and further towards the Hub, where the Ramtop Mountains joined the forbidding spires of the central massif, where strange hairy creatures roamed the eternal snows, where blizzards howled around the freezing peaks, the lights of a lone lamasery shone out over the high valleys. In the courtyard a couple of yellow-robed monks stacked the last case of small green bottles on to a sleigh, ready for the first leg of the incredibly difficult journey down to the distant plains. The box was labelled, in careful brush-strokes, 'Mstr. C.M.O.T. Dibbler, Ankh-Morpork'.

'You know, Lobsang,' said one of them, 'one cannot help wondering what it is he does with this stuff.')

Corporal Nobbs and Sergeant Colon lounged in the shadows near the Mended Drum, but straightened up as Carrot came out bearing a tray. Detritus the troll stepped aside respectfully.

'Here we are, lads,' said Carrot. 'Three pints. On the house.'

'Bloody hell, I never thought you'd do it,' said Colon, grasping a handle. 'What did you say to him?'

'I just explained how it was the duty of all good citizens to help the guard at all times,' said Carrot innocently, 'and I thanked him for his co-operation.'

'Yeah, and the rest,' said Nobby.

'No, that was all I said.'

'Then you must have a really convincing tone of voice.'

'Ah. Well, make the most of it, lads, while it lasts,' said Colon.

They drank thoughtfully. It was a moment of supreme peace, a few minutes snatched from the realities of real life. It was a brief bite of stolen fruit and enjoyed as such. No-one in the whole city seemed to be fighting or stabbing or making affray and, just for now, it was possible to believe that this wonderful state of affairs might continue.

And even if it didn't, then there were memories to get them through. Of running, and people getting out of the way. Of the looks on the faces of the horrible palace guard. Of, when all the thieves and heroes and gods had failed, of *being there*. Of nearly doing things nearly right.

Nobby shoved the pot on a convenient window sill, stamped some life back into his feet and blew on his fingers. A brief fumble in the dark recesses of his ear produced a fragment of cigarette.

'What a time, eh?' said Colon contentedly, as the flare of a match illuminated the three of them.

The others nodded. Yesterday seemed like a lifetime ago, even now. But you could never forget something like that, no matter who else did, no matter what happened from now on.

'If I never see any bloody king it'll be too soon,' said Nobby.

'I don't reckon he was the right king, anyway,' said Carrot. 'Talking of kings: anyone want a crisp?'

'There's no right kings,' said Colon, but without much rancour. Ten dollars a month was going to make a big difference. Mrs Colon was acting very differently towards a man bringing home another ten dollars a month. Her notes on the kitchen table were a lot more friendly.

'No, but I mean, there's nothing special about having an ancient sword,' said Carrot. 'Or a birthmark. I mean, look at me. I've got a birthmark on my arm.'

'My brother's got one, too,' said Colon. 'Shaped like a boat.'

'Mine's more like a crown thing,' said Carrot.

'Oho, that makes you a king, then,' grinned Nobby. 'Stands to reason.'

'I don't see why. My brother's not an admiral,' said Colon reasonably.

'And I've got this sword,' said Carrot.

He drew it. Colon took it from his hand, and turned it over and over in the light from the flare over the Drum's door. The blade was dull and short, and notched like a saw. It was well-made and there might have been an inscription on it once, but it had long ago been worn into indecipherability by sheer use.

'It's a nice sword,' he said thoughtfully. 'Well-balanced.'

'But not one for a king,' said Carrot. 'Kings' swords are big and shiny and magical and have jewels on and when you hold them up they catch the light, *ting*.'

'*Ting*,' said Colon. 'Yes. I suppose they have to, really.'

'I'm just saying you can't go round giving people thrones just because of stuff like that,' said Carrot. 'That's what Captain Vimes said.'

'Nice job, mind,' said Nobby. 'Good hours, kinging.'

'Hmm?' Colon had momentarily been lost in a little world of speculation. Real kings had shiny swords, obviously. Except, except, except maybe your *real* real king of, like, days of yore, he would have a sword that didn't sparkle one bit but was bloody efficient at cutting things. Just a thought.

'I say kinging's a good job,' Nobby repeated. 'Short hours.'

'Yeah. Yeah. But not long days,' said Colon. He gave Carrot a thoughtful look.

'Ah. There's that, of course.'

'Anyway, my father says being king's too much like hard work,' said Carrot. 'All the surveying and assaying and everything.' He drained his pint. 'It's not the kind of thing for the likes of us. Us – ' he looked proudly – 'guards. You all right, Sergeant?'

'Hmm? What? Oh. Yes.' Colon shrugged. What about it, anyway? Maybe things turned out for the best. He finished the beer. 'Best be off,' he said. 'What time was it?'

'About twelve o'clock,' said Carrot.

'Anything else?'

Carrot gave it some thought. 'And all's well?' he said.

'Right. Just testing.'

'You know,' said Nobby, 'the way you say it, lad, you could almost believe it was true.'

Let the eye of attention pull back . . .

This is the Disc, world and mirror of worlds, borne through space on the back of four giant elephants who stand on the back of Great A'Tuin the Sky Turtle. Around the Rim of this world the ocean pours off endlessly into the night. At its Hub rises the ten-mile spike of the Cori Celesti, on whose glittering summit the gods play games with the fates of men . . .

. . . if you know what the rules are, and who are the players.

On the far edge of the Disc the sun was rising. The light of the morning began to flow across the patchwork of seas and continents, but it did so slowly, because light is tardy and slightly heavy in the presence of a magical field.

On the dark crescent, where the old light of sunset had barely drained from the deepest valleys, two specks, one big, one small, flew out of the shadow, skimmed low across the swells of the Rim ocean, and struck out determinedly over the totally unfathomable, star-dotted depths of space.

Perhaps the magic would last. Perhaps it wouldn't. But then, what does?

MEN AT ARMS

Corporal Carrot, Ankh-Morpork City Guard (Night Watch), sat down in his nightshirt, took up his pencil, sucked the end for a moment, and then wrote:

'Dearest Mume and Dad,
                               'Well here is another fine Turnup for the Books, for I have been made Corporal!! It means another Five Dollars a month plus also I have a new jerkin with, two stripes upon it as well. And a new copper badge! It is a Great responsibility!! This is all because we have got new recruits because the Patrician who, as I have formerly vouchsafed is the ruler of the city, has agreed the Watch must reflect the ethnic makeup of the City—'

Carrot paused for a moment and stared out of the small dusty bedroom window at the early evening sunlight sidling across the river. Then he bent over the paper again.

'—which I do not Fulley understand but must have something to do with the dwarf Grabpot Thundergust's Cosmetic Factory. Also, Captain Vimes of who I have often written to you of is, leaving the Watch to get married and Become a Fine Gentleman and, I'm sure we wish him All the Best, he taught me All I Know apart, from the things I taught myself. We are clubbing together to get him a Surprise Present, I thought one of those new Watches that don't need demons to make them go and we could inscribe on the back something like "A Watch from, your Old Freinds in the Watch", this is a pune or Play on Words. We do not know who will be the new Captain, Sgt. Colon says he will Resign if it's him, Cpl. Nobbs—'

Carrot stared out of the window again. His big honest forehead wrinkled with effort as he tried to think of something positive to say about Corporal Nobbs.

'—is more suited in his current Roll, and I have not been in the Watch long enough. So we shall just have to wait and See—'

*

It began, as many things do, with a death. And a burial, on a spring morning, with mist on the ground so thick that it poured into the grave and the coffin was lowered into cloud.

A small greyish mongrel, host to so many assorted doggy diseases that it was surrounded by a cloud of dust, watched impassively from the mound of earth.

Various elderly female relatives cried. But Edward d'Eath didn't cry, for three reasons. He was the eldest son, the thirty-seventh Lord d'Eath, and it was Not Done for a d'Eath to cry; he was – just, the diploma still had the crackle in it – an Assassin, and Assassins didn't cry at a death, otherwise they'd never be stopping; and he was angry. In fact, he was enraged.

Enraged at having to borrow money for this poor funeral. Enraged at the weather, at this common cemetery, at the way the background noise of the city didn't change in any way, even on such an occasion as this. Enraged at history. It was never meant to be like this.

It shouldn't have *been* like this.

He looked across the river to the brooding bulk of the Palace, and his anger screwed itself up and became a lens.

Edward had been sent to the Assassins' Guild because they had the best school for those whose social rank is rather higher than their intelligence. If he'd been trained as a Fool, he'd have invented satire and made dangerous jokes about the Patrician. If he'd been trained as a Thief,* he'd have broken into the Palace and stolen something very valuable from the Patrician.

However . . . he'd been sent to the Assassins . . .

That afternoon he sold what remained of the d'Eath estates, and enrolled again at the Guild school.

For the post-graduate course.

He got full marks, the first person in the history of the Guild ever to do so. His seniors described him as a man to watch – and, because there was something about him that made even Assassins uneasy, preferably from a long way away.

In the cemetery the solitary gravedigger filled in the hole that was the last resting place of d'Eath senior.

He became aware of what seemed to be thoughts in his head. They went something like this:

Any chance of a bone? No, no, sorry, bad taste there, forget I mentioned it. You've got beef sandwiches in your wossname, lunch-

---

* But no *gentleman* would *dream* of being trained as a Thief.

box thingy, though. Why not give one to the nice little doggy over there?

The man leaned on his shovel and looked around.

The grey mongrel was watching him intently.

It said, 'Woof?'

It took Edward d'Eath five months to find what he was looking for. The search was hampered by the fact that he did not *know* what he was looking for, only that he'd know it when he found it. Edward was a great believer in Destiny. Such people often are.

The Guild library was one of the largest in the city. In certain specialized areas it was *the* largest. These areas mainly had to do with the regrettable brevity of human life and the means of bringing it about.

Edward spent a lot of time there, often at the top of a ladder, often surrounded by dust.

He read every known work on armaments. He didn't know what he was looking for and he found it in a note in the margin of an otherwise very dull and inaccurate treatise on the ballistics of crossbows. He copied it out, carefully.

Edward spent a lot of time among history books as well. The Assassins' Guild was an association of gentlemen of breeding, and people like that regard the whole of recorded history as a kind of stock book. There were a great many books in the Guild library, and a whole portrait gallery of kings and queens,* and Edward d'Eath came to know their aristocratic faces better than he did his own. He spent his lunch hours there.

It was said later that he came under bad influences at this stage. But the secret of the history of Edward d'Eath was that he came under no outside influences at all, unless you count all those dead kings. He just came under the influence of himself.

That's where people get it wrong. Individuals aren't naturally paid-up members of the human race, except biologically. They need to be bounced around by the Brownian motion of society, which is a mechanism by which human beings constantly remind one another that they are ... well ... human beings. He was also spiralling inwards, as tends to happen in cases like this.

He'd had no plan. He'd just retreated, as people do when they feel under attack, to a more defensible position, i.e. the past, and then something happened which had the same effect on Edward as

---

* Often with discreet plaques under them modestly recording the name of the person who'd killed them. This was the *Assassins'* portrait gallery, after all.

finding a plesiosaur in his goldfish pond would on a student of ancient reptiles.

He'd stepped out blinking in the sunlight one hot afternoon, after a day spent in the company of departed glory, and had seen the face of the past strolling by, nodding amiably to people.

He hadn't been able to control himself. He'd said, 'Hey, you! Who are y-ou?'

The past had said, 'Corporal Carrot, sir. Night Watch. Mr d'Eath, isn't it? Can I help you?'

'What? No! No. Be about your b-usiness!'

The past nodded and smiled at him, and strolled on, into the future.

Carrot stopped staring at the wall.

> 'I have expended three dollars on an iconograph box which, is a thing with a browned inside that paints pictures of thing's, this is all the Rage these days. Please find enclosed pictures of my room and my freinds in the Watch, Nobby is the one making the Humerous Gesture but he is a Rough Diamond and a good soul deep down.'

He stopped again. Carrot wrote home at least once a week. Dwarfs generally did. Carrot was two metres tall but he'd been brought up as a dwarf, and then further up as a human. Literary endeavour did not come easily to him, but he persevered.

'The weather,' he wrote, very slowly and carefully, 'continues Very Hot . . .'

Edward could not believe it. He checked the records. He double-checked. He asked questions and, because they were innocent enough questions, people gave him answers. And finally he took a holiday in the Ramtops, where careful questioning led him to the dwarf mines around Copperhead, and thence to an otherwise unremarkable glade in a beech wood where, sure enough, a few minutes of patient digging unearthed traces of charcoal.

He spent the whole day there. When he'd finished, carefully replacing the leafmould as the sun went down, he was quite certain.

Ankh-Morpork had a king again.

And this was *right*. And it was *fate* that had let Edward recognize this *just* when he'd got his Plan. And it was *right* that it was *Fate*, and the city would be *Saved* from its ignoble present by its

glorious past. He had the *Means*, and he had the *end*. And so on
. . . Edward's thoughts often ran like this.

He could think in *italics*. Such people need watching.
Preferably from a safe distance.

'I was Interested in your letter where you said people have been
coming and asking about me, this is Amazing, I have been here
hardly Five Minutes and already I am Famus.

'I was very pleased to hear about the opening of #7 shaft. I
don't mind Telling You that although, I am very happy here I
miss the Good Times back Home. Sometimes on my day Off I go
and, sit in the Cellar and hit my head with an axe handle but, it
is Not the Same.

'Hoping this finds you in Good Health, Yrs. faithfully,
      'Your loving son, adopted,
                    Carrot.'

He folded the letter up, inserted the iconographs, sealed it with
a blob of candle wax pressed into place with his thumb, and put it
in his pants pocket. Dwarf mail to the Ramtops was quite reliable.
More and more dwarfs were coming to work in the city, and
because dwarfs are very conscientious many of them sent money
home. This made dwarf mail just about as safe as anything, since
their mail was closely guarded. Dwarfs are very attached to gold.
Any highwayman demanding 'Your money or your life' had better
bring a folding chair and packed lunch and a book to read while
the debate goes on.

Then Carrot washed his face, donned his leather shirt and
trousers and chainmail, buckled on his breastplate and, with his
helmet under his arm, stepped out cheerfully, ready to face whatever the future would bring.

This was another room, somewhere else.

It was a poky room, the plaster walls crumbling, the ceilings
sagging like the underside of a fat man's bed. And it was made
even more crowded by the furniture.

It was old, good furniture, but this wasn't the place for it. It
belonged in high echoing halls. Here, it was crammed. There were
dark oak chairs. There were long sideboards. There was even a
suit of armour. There was barely room for the half dozen or so
people who sat at the huge table. There was barely room for the
table.

A clock ticked in the shadows.

The heavy velvet curtains were drawn, even though there was still plenty of daylight left in the sky. The air was stifling, both from the heat of the day and the candles in the magic lantern.

The only illumination was from the screen which, at that moment, was portraying a very good profile of Corporal Carrot Ironfoundersson.

The small but very select audience watched it with the carefully blank expressions of people who are half convinced that their host is several cards short of a full deck but are putting up with it because they've just eaten a meal and it would be rude to leave too soon.

'Well?' said one of them. 'I think I've seen him walking around the city. So? He's just a watchman, Edward.'

'Of course. It is essential that he should be. A humble station in life. It all fits the classic p-attern.' Edward d'Eath gave a signal. There was a click as another glass slide was slotted in. '*This* one was not p-ainted from life. King P-paragore. Taken from an old p-ainting. This one' – *click!* – 'is King Veltrick III. From another p-portrait. This one is Queen Alguinna IV . . . note the line of the chin? This one' – *click!* – 'is a sevenpenny p-iece from the reign of Webblethorpe the Unconscious, note again the detail of the chin and general b-bone structure, and this' – *click!* – 'is . . . an upside d-own picture of a vase of flowers. D-elphiniums, I believe. Why is this?'

'Er, sorry, Mr Edward, I 'ad a few glass plates left and the demons weren't tired and—'

'Next slide, please. And then you may leave us.'

'Yes, Mr Edward.'

'Report to the d-uty torturer.'

'Yes, Mr Edward.'

Click!

'And this is a rather good – well done, Bl-enkin – image of the bust of Queen Coanna.'

'Thank you, Mr Edward.'

'More of her face would have enabled us to be certain of the likeness, however. There is sufficient, I believe. You may go, Bl-enkin.'

'Yes, Mr Edward.'

'A little something off the ears, I th-ink.'

'Yes, Mr Edward.'

The servant respectfully shut the door behind him, and then went down to the kitchen shaking his head sadly. The d'Eaths hadn't been able to afford a family torturer for years. For the boy's sake he'd just have to do the best he could with a kitchen knife.

The visitors waited for the host to speak, but he didn't seem about to do so, although it was sometimes hard to tell with Edward. When he was excited, he suffered not so much from a speech impediment as from misplaced pauses, as if his brain were temporarily putting his mouth on hold.

Eventually, one of the audience said: 'Very well. So what is your point?'

'You've seen the likeness. Isn't it ob-vious?'

'Oh, come now—'

Edward d'Eath pulled a leather case towards him and began undoing the thongs.

'But, but the boy was adopted by Discworld dwarfs. They found him as a baby in the forests of the Ramtop mountains. There were some b-urning wagons, corpses, that sort of thing. B-andit attack, apparently. The dwarfs found a sword in the wreckage. He has it now. A very *old* sword. And it's always sharp.'

'So? The world is full of old swords. *And* grindstones.'

'This one had been very well hidden in one of the carts, which had broken up. Strange. One would expect it to be ready to hand, yes? To be used? In b-andit country? And then the boy grows up and, and ... Fate ... conspires that he and his sword come to Ankh-Morpork, where he is currently a watchman in the Night Watch. I couldn't believe it!'

'That's still not—'

Edward raised his hand a moment, and then pulled out a package from the case.

'I made careful enq-uiries, you know, and was able to find the place where the attack occurred. A most careful search of the ground revealed old cart n-ails, a few copper coins and, in some charcoal ... this.'

They craned to see.

'Looks like a ring.'

'Yes. It's, it's, it's superficially d-iscoloured, of course, otherwise someone would have spot-ted it. Probably secreted somewhere on a cart. I've had it p-artly cleaned. You can just read the inscription. Now, *here* is an ill-ustrated inventory of the royal jewellery of Ankh done in AM 907, in the reign of King Tyrril. May I, please, may I draw your a-ttention to the small wedding ring in the b-ottom left-hand corner of the page? You will see that the artist has hel-pfully drawn the inscription.'

It took several minutes for everyone to examine it. They were naturally suspicious people. They were all descendants of people for whom suspicion and paranoia had been prime survival traits.

Because they were all aristocrats. Not one among them did not know the name of his or her great-great-great-grandfather and what embarrassing disease he'd died of.

They had just eaten a not-very-good meal which had, however, included some ancient and worthwhile wines. They'd attended because they'd all known Edward's father, and the d'Eaths were a fine old family, if now in very reduced circumstances.

'So you see,' said Edward proudly, 'the evidence is overwhelming. We have a king!'

His audience tried to avoid looking at another's faces.

'I thought you'd be pl-eased,' said Edward.

Finally, Lord Rust voiced the unspoken consensus. There was no room in those true-blue eyes for pity, which was not a survival trait, but sometimes it was possible to risk a little kindness.

'Edward,' he said, 'the last king of Ankh-Morpork died centuries ago.'

'Executed by t-raitors!'

'Even if a descendant could still be found, the royal blood would be somewhat watered down by now, don't you think?'

'The royal b-lood *cannot* be wa-tered down!'

Ah, thought Lord Rust. So he's *that* kind. Young Edward thinks the touch of a king can cure scrofula, as if royalty was the equivalent of a sulphur ointment. Young Edward thinks that there is no lake of blood too big to wade through to put a rightful king on a throne, no deed too base in defence of a crown. A romantic, in fact.

Lord Rust was not a romantic. The Rusts had adapted well to Ankh-Morpork's post-monarchy centuries by buying and selling and renting and making contacts and doing what aristocrats have always done, which is trim sails and survive.

'Well, maybe,' he conceded, in the gentle tones of someone trying to talk someone else off a ledge, 'but we must ask ourselves: does Ankh-Morpork, at this point in time, *require* a king?'

Edward looked at him as though he were mad.

'Need? *Need*? While our fair city languishes under the heel of the ty-rant?'

'Oh. You mean Vetinari.'

'Can't you see what he's done to this city?'

'He *is* a very unpleasant, jumped-up little man,' said Lady Selachii, 'but I would not say he actually *terrorizes* much. Not as such.'

'You have to hand it to him,' said Viscount Skater, 'the city operates. More or less. Fellas and whatnot do things.'

'The streets are safer than they used to be under Mad Lord Snapcase,' said Lady Selachii.

'Sa-fer? Vetinari set up the Thieves' Guild!' shouted Edward.

'Yes, yes, of course, very reprehensible, certainly. On the other hand, a modest annual payment and one walks in safety . . .'

'He always says,' said Lord Rust, 'that if you're going to have crime, it might as well be organized crime.'

'Seems to me,' said Viscount Skater, 'that all the Guild chappies put up with him because anyone else would be worse, yes? We've certainly had some . . . difficult ones. Anyone remember Homicidal Lord Winder?'

'Deranged Lord Harmoni,' said Lord Monflathers.

'Laughing Lord Scapula,' said Lady Selachii. 'A man with a *very* pointed sense of humour.'

'Mind you, Vetinari . . . there's something not entirely . . .' Lord Rust began.

'I know what you mean,' said Viscount Skater. 'I don't like the way he always knows what you're thinking before you think it.'

'Everyone knows the Assassins have set *his* fee at a million dollars,' said Lady Selachii. 'That's how much it would cost to have him killed.'

'One can't help feeling,' said Lord Rust, 'that it would cost a lot more than that to make sure he stayed dead.'

'Ye gods! What happened to pride? What happened to honour?'

They perceptibly jumped as the last Lord d'Eath thrust himself out of his chair.

'Will you listen to yourselves? Please? Look at you. What man among you has not seen his family name degraded since the days of the kings? Can't you remember the men your forefathers were?' He strode rapidly around the table, so that they had to turn to watch him. He pointed an angry finger.

'You, Lord Rust! Your ancestor was cr-eated a Baron after singlehandedly killing thirty-seven Klatchians while armed with nothing more than a p-in, isn't that so?'

'Yes, but—'

'You, sir . . . Lord Monflathers! The first Duke led six hundred men to a glorious and epic de-feat at the Battle of Quirm! Does that mean n-othing? And you, Lord Venturii, and you, Sir George . . . sitting in Ankh in your old houses with your old names and your old money, while Guilds – *Guilds*! Ragtags of tradesmen and merchants! – Guilds, I say, have a voice in the r-unning of the city!'

He reached a bookshelf in two strides and threw a huge leather-bound book on to the table, where it upset Lord Rust's glass.

'*Twurp's P-eerage*,' he shouted. 'We all have pages in there! We *own* it. But this man has you mesmerized! I assure you he is flesh and blood, a mere mortal! No one dares remove him because they th-ink it will make things a little worse for themselves! Ye g-ods!'

His audience looked glum. It was all true, of course . . . if you put it that way. And it didn't sound any better coming from a wild-eyed, pompous young man.

'Yes, yes, the good old days. Towerin' spires and pennants and chivalry and all that,' said Viscount Skater. 'Ladies in pointy hats. Chappies in armour bashin' one another and whatnot. But, y'know, we have to move with the times—'

'It was a golden age,' said Edward.

My god, thought Lord Rust. He actually *does* believe it.

'You see, dear boy,' said Lady Selachii, 'a few chance likenesses and a piece of jewellery – that doesn't really add up to much, does it?'

'My nurse told me,' said Viscount Skater, 'that a *true* king could pull a sword from a stone.'

'Hah, yes, and cure dandruff,' said Lord Rust. 'That's just a legend. That's not *real*. Anyway, I've always been a bit puzzled about that story. What's so hard about pulling a sword out of a stone? The real work's already been done. You ought to make yourself useful and find the man who put the sword in the stone in the first place, eh?'

There was a sort of relieved laughter. That's what Edward remembered. It all ended up in laughter. Not exactly at *him*, but he was the type of person who always takes laughter personally.

Ten minutes later, Edward d'Eath was alone.

They're being so *nice* about it. Moving with the times! He'd expected more than that of them. A lot more. He'd dared to hope that they might be inspired by his lead. He'd pictured himself at the head of an army—

Blenkin came in at a respectful shuffle.

'I saw 'em all off, Mr Edward,' he said.

'Thank you, Blenkin. You may clear the table.'

'Yes, Mr Edward.'

'Whatever happened to honour, Blenkin?'

'Dunno, sir. I never took it.'

'They didn't want to listen.'

'No, sir.'

'They didn't want to l-isten.'

Edward sat by the dying fire, with a dog-eared copy of Thigh-biter's *The Ankh-Morpork Succesfion* open on his lap. Dead kings and queens looked at him reproachfully.

And there it might have ended. In fact it did end there, in millions of universes. Edward d'Eath grew older and obsession turned to a sort of bookish insanity of the gloves-with-the-fingers-cut-out and carpet slippers variety, and became an expert on royalty although no one ever knew this because he seldom left his rooms. Corporal Carrot became Sergeant Carrot and, in the full-ness of time, died in uniform aged seventy in an unlikely accident involving an anteater.

In a million universes, Lance-Constables Cuddy and Detritus didn't fall through the hole. In a million universes, Vimes didn't find the pipes. (In one strange but theoretically possible universe the Watch House was redecorated in pastel colours by a freak whirlwind, which also repaired the door latch and did a few other odd jobs around the place.) In a million universes, the Watch failed.

In a million universes, this was a very short book.

Edward dozed off with the book on his knees and had a dream. He dreamed of glorious struggle. Glorious was another important word in his personal vocabulary, like honour.

If traitors and dishonourable men would not see the truth then he, Edward d'Eath, was the finger of Destiny.

The problem with Destiny, of course, is that she is often not careful where she puts her finger.

Captain Sam Vimes, Ankh-Morpork City Guard (Night Watch), sat in the draughty anteroom to the Patrician's audience chamber with his best cloak on and his breastplate polished and his helmet on his knees.

He stared woodenly at the wall.

He ought to be happy, he told himself. And he was. In a way. Definitely. Happy as anything.

He was going to get married in a few days.

He was going to stop being a guard.

He was going to be a gentleman of leisure.

He took off his copper badge and buffed it absent-mindedly on the edge of his cloak. Then he held it up so that the light glinted off the patina'd surface. AMCW No.177. He sometimes wondered how many other guards had had the badge before him.

Well, now someone was going to have it after him.

This is Ankh-Morpork, Citie of One Thousand Surprises (according to the Guild of Merchants' guidebook). What more need be said? A sprawling place, home to a million people, greatest of cities on the

Discworld, located on either side of the river Ankh, a waterway so muddy that it looks as if it is flowing upside down.

And visitors say: how does such a big city exist? What keeps it going? Since it's got a river you can chew, where does the drinking water come from? What is, in fact, the basis of its civic economy? How come it, against all probability, *works*?

Actually, visitors don't often say this. They usually say things like 'Which way to the, you know, the . . . er . . . you know, the young ladies, right?'

But if they started thinking with their brains for a little while, that's what they'd be thinking.

The Patrician of Ankh-Morpork sat back on his austere chair with the sudden bright smile of a very busy person at the end of a crowded day who's suddenly found in his schedule a reminder saying: 7.00–7.05, Be Cheerful and Relaxed and a People Person.

'Well, of course I was very saddened to receive your letter, captain . . .'

'Yes, sir,' said Vimes, still as wooden as a furniture warehouse.

'*Please* sit down, captain.'

'Yes, sir.' Vimes remained standing. It was a matter of pride.

'But of course I quite understand. The Ramkin country estates are very extensive, I believe. I'm sure Lady Ramkin will appreciate your strong right hand.'

'Sir?' Captain Vimes, while in the presence of the ruler of the city, always concentrated his gaze on a point one foot above and six inches to the left of the man's head.

'And of course you will be quite a rich man, captain.'

'Yes, sir.'

'I hope you have thought about that. You will have new responsibilities.'

Yes, sir.'

It dawned on the Patrician that he was working on both ends of this conversation. He shuffled through the papers on his desk.

'And of course I shall have to promote a new chief officer for the Night Watch,' said the Patrician. 'Have you any suggestions, captain?'

Vimes appeared to descend from whatever cloud his mind had been occupying. This was *guard work*.

'Well, not Fred Colon . . . He's one of Nature's sergeants . . .'

*

Sergeant Colon, Ankh-Morpork City Guard (Night Watch) surveyed the bright faces of the new recruits.

He sighed. He remembered his first day. Old Sergeant Wimbler. What a tartar! Tongue like a whiplash! If the old boy had lived to see *this* . . .

What was it called? Oh, yeah. Affirmative action hirin' procedure, or something. Silicon Anti-Defamation League had been going on at the Patrician, and now—

'Try it one more time, Lance-Constable Detritus,' he said. 'The trick is, you stops your hand just above your ear. Now, just get up off the floor and try salutin' one more time. Now, then . . . Lance-Constable Cuddy?'

'Here!'

'Where?'

'In front of you, sergeant.'

Colon looked down and took a step back. The swelling curve of his more than adequate stomach moved aside to reveal the upturned face of Lance-Constable Cuddy, with its helpful intelligent expression and one glass eye.

'Oh. Right.'

'I'm taller than I look.'

Oh, gods, thought Sergeant Colon wearily. Add 'em up and divide by two and you've got two normal men, except normal men don't join the Guard. A troll and a dwarf. And that ain't the worst of it—

Vimes drummed his fingers on the desk.

'Not Colon, then,' he said. 'He's not as young as he was. Time he stayed in the Watch House, keeping up on the paperwork. Besides, he's got a lot on his plate.'

'Sergeant Colon has always had a lot on his plate, I should say,' said the Patrician.

'With the new recruits, I mean,' said Vimes, meaningfully. 'You remember, sir?'

The ones you told me I had to have? he added in the privacy of his head. They weren't to go in the *Day* Watch, of course. And those bastards in the Palace Guard wouldn't take them, either. Oh, no. Put 'em in the Night Watch, because it's a joke anyway and no one'll really see 'em. No one important, anyway.

Vimes had only given in because he knew it wouldn't be his problem for long.

It wasn't as if he was speciesist, he told himself. But the Watch was a job for men.

'How about Corporal Nobbs?' said the Patrician.

'Nobby?'

They shared a mental picture of Corporal Nobbs.

'No.'

'No.'

'Then of course there is,' the Patrician smiled, 'Corporal Carrot. A fine young man. Already making a name for himself, I gather.'

'That's . . . true,' said Vimes.

'A further promotion opportunity, perhaps? I would value your advice.'

Vimes formed a mental picture of Corporal Carrot—

'This,' said Corporal Carrot, 'is the Hubwards Gate. To the whole city. Which is what we guard.'

'What from?' said Lance-Constable Angua, the last of the new recruits.

'Oh, you know. Barbarian hordes, warring tribesmen, bandit armies . . . that sort of thing.'

'What? Just *us*?'

'Us? Oh, no!' Carrot laughed. 'That'd be silly, wouldn't it? No, if you see anything like that, you just ring your bell as hard as you like.'

'What happens then?'

'Sergeant Colon and Nobby and the rest of 'em will come running along just as soon as they can.'

Lance-Constable Angua scanned the hazy horizon.

She smiled.

Carrot blushed.

Constable Angua had mastered saluting first go. She wouldn't have a full uniform yet, not until someone had taken a, well, let's face it, a *breastplate* along to old Remitt the armourer and told him to beat it out really well *here* and *here*, and no helmet in the world would cover all that mass of ash-blonde hair but, it occurred to Carrot, Constable Angua wouldn't need any of that stuff really. People would be queuing up to get arrested.

'So what do we do now?' she said.

'Proceed back to the Watch House, I suppose,' said Carrot. 'Sergeant Colon'll be reading out the evening report, I expect.'

She'd mastered 'proceeding', too. It's a special walk devised by beat officers throughout the multiverse – a gentle lifting of the instep, a careful swing of the leg, a walking pace that can be kept up hour after hour, street after street. Lance-Constable Detritus wasn't going to be ready to learn 'proceeding' for some time, or at least until he stopped knocking himself out every time he saluted.

'Sergeant Colon,' said Angua. 'He was the fat one, yes?'

'That's right.'

'Why has he got a pet monkey?'

'Ah,' said Carrot. 'I think it is Corporal Nobbs to whom you refer . . .'

'It's human? He's got a face like a join-the-dots puzzle!'

'He does have a very good collection of boils, poor man. He does tricks with them. Just never get between him and a mirror.'

Not many people were on the streets. It was too hot, even for an Ankh-Morpork summer. Heat radiated from every surface. The river slunk sullenly in the bottom of its bed, like a student around 11 a.m. People with no pressing business out of doors lurked in cellars and only came out at night.

Carrot moved through the baking streets with a proprietorial air and a slight patina of honest sweat, occasionally exchanging a greeting. Everyone knew Garrot. He was easily recognizable. No one else was about two metres tall with flame-red hair. Besides, he walked as if he owned the city.

'Who was that man with the granite face I saw in the Watch House?' said Angua, as they proceeded along Broad Way.

'That was Detritus the troll,' said Carrot. 'He used to be a bit of a criminal, but now he's courting Ruby she says he's got to—'

'No, that *man*,' said Angua, learning as had so many others that Carrot tended to have a bit of trouble with metaphors. 'Face like thu – face like someone very disgruntled.'

'Oh, that was Captain Vimes. But he's never *been* gruntled, I think. He's retiring at the end of the week, and getting married.'

'Doesn't look very happy about it,' said Angua.

'Couldn't say.'

'I don't think he likes the new recruits.'

The other thing about Constable Carrot was that he was incapable of lying.

'Well, he doesn't like trolls much,' he said. 'We couldn't get a word out of him all day when he heard we had to advertise for a troll recruit. And then we had to have a dwarf, otherwise they'd be trouble. I'm a dwarf, too, but the dwarfs here don't believe it.'

'You don't say?' said Angua, looking up at him.

'My mother had me by adoption.'

'Oh. Yes, but I'm not a troll *or* a dwarf,' said Angua sweetly.

'No, but you're a w—'

Angua stopped. 'That's it, is it? Good grief! This *is* the Century of the Fruitbat, you know. Ye gods, does he really think like that?'

'He's a bit set in his ways.'

'Congealed, I should think.'

'The Patrician said we had to have a bit of representation from the minority groups,' said Carrot.

'Minority groups!'

'Sorry. Anyway, he's only got a few more days—'

There was a splintering noise across the street. They turned as a figure sprinted out of a tavern and hared away up the street, closely followed – at least for a few steps – by a fat man in an apron.

'Stop! Stop! Unlicensed thief!'

'Ah,' said Carrot. He crossed the road, with Angua padding along behind him, as the fat man slowed to a waddle.

''Morning, Mr Flannel,' he said. 'Bit of trouble?'

'He took seven dollars and I never saw no Thief Licence!' said Mr Flannel. 'What you going to do about it? I pay my taxes!'

'We shall be hotly in pursuit any moment,' said Carrot calmly, taking out his notebook. 'Seven dollars, was it?'

'At least fourteen.'

Mr Flannel looked Angua up and down. Men seldom missed the opportunity.

'Why's she got a helmet on?' he said.

'She's a new recruit, Mr Flannel.'

Angua gave Mr Flannel a smile. He stepped back.

'But she's a—'

'Got to move with the times, Mr Flannel,' said Carrot, putting his notebook away.

Mr Flannel drew his mind back to business.

'In the meantime, there's eighteen dollars of mine that I won't see again,' he said sharply.

'Oh, *nil desperandum*, Mr Flannel, *nil desperandum*,' said Carrot cheerfully. 'Come, Constable Angua. Let us proceed upon our inquiries.'

He proceeded off, with Flannel staring at them with his mouth open.

'Don't forget my twenty-five dollars,' he shouted.

'Aren't you going to *chase* the man?' said Angua, running to keep up.

'No point,' said Carrot, stepping sideways into an alley that was so narrow as to be barely visible. He strolled between the damp, moss-grown walls, in deep shadow.

'Interesting thing,' he said. 'I bet there's not many people know that you can get to Zephire Street from Broad Way. You ask anyone. They'll say you can't get out of the other end of Shirt Alley.

But you can because, all you do, you go up Mormius Street, and then you can squeeze between these bollards *here* into Borborygmic Lane – good, aren't they, very good iron – and here we are in Whilom Alley—'

He wandered to the end of the alley and stood listening for a while.

'What are we waiting for?' said Angua.

There was the sound of running feet. Carrot leaned against the wall, and stuck out one arm into Zephire Street There was a thud. Carrot's arm didn't move an inch. It must have been like running into a girder.

They looked down at the unconscious figure. Silver dollars rolled across the cobbles.

'Oh dear, oh dear, oh dear,' said Carrot. 'Poor old Here'n'now. He *promised* me he was going to give it up, too. Oh well . . .'

He picked up a leg.

'How much money?' he said.

'Looks like three dollars,' said Angua.

'Well done. The exact amount.'

'No, the shopkeeper said—'

'Come on. Back to the Watch House. Come on, Here'n'now. It's your lucky day.'

'Why is it his lucky day?' said Angua. 'He was *caught*, wasn't he?'

'Yes. By us. Thieves' Guild didn't get him first. They aren't so kind as us.'

Here'n'now's head bounced from cobblestone to cobblestone.

'Pinching three dollars and then trotting straight home,' sighed Carrot. 'That's Here'n'now. Worst thief in the world.'

'But you said Thieves' Guild—'

'When you've been here a while, you'll understand how it all works,' said Carrot. Here'n'now's head banged on the kerb. 'Eventually,' Carrot added. 'But it all does work. You'd be amazed. It all works. I wish it didn't. But it does.'

While Here'n'now was being mildly concussed on the way to the safety of the Watch's jail, a clown was being killed.

He was ambling along an alley with the assurance of one who is fully paid up this year with the Thieves' Guild when a hooded figure stepped out in front of him.

'Beano?'

'Oh, hello . . . it's Edward, right?'

The figure hesitated.

'I was just going back to the Guild,' said Beano.

The hooded figure nodded.

'Are you OK?' said Beano.

'I'm sorry about th-is,' it said. 'But it is for the good of the city. It is nothing p-ersonal.'

He stepped behind the clown. Beano felt a crunch, and then his own personal internal universe switched off.

Then he sat up.

'Ow,' he said, 'that hur—'

But it didn't.

Edward d'Eath was looking down at him with a horrified expression.

'Oh . . . I didn't mean to hit you that hard! I only wanted you out of the way!'

'Why'd you have to hit me at all?'

And then the feeling stole over Beano that Edward wasn't exactly looking at him, and certainly wasn't talking to him.

He glanced at the ground, and experienced that peculiar sensation known only to the recently dead – horror at what you see lying in front of you, followed by the nagging question: so who's doing the looking?

KNOCK KNOCK.

He looked up.

'Who's there?'

DEATH.

'Death who?'

There was a chill in the air. Beano waited. Edward was frantically patting his face . . . well, what until recently had been his face.

I WONDER . . . CAN WE START AGAIN? I DON'T SEEM TO HAVE THE HANG OF THIS.

'Sorry?' said Beano.

'I'm s-orry!' moaned Edward, 'I meant it for the best!'

Beano watched his murderer drag his . . . *the* . . . body away.

'Nothing personal, he says,' he said. 'I'm glad it wasn't anything personal. I should hate to think I've just been killed because it was *personal*.'

IT'S JUST THAT IT HAS BEEN SUGGESTED THAT I SHOULD BE MORE OF A PEOPLE PERSON.

'I mean, *why*? I thought we were getting on really well. It's very hard to make friends in my job. In your job too, I suppose.'

BREAK IT TO THEM GENTLY AS IT WERE.

'One minute walking along, the next minute dead. Why?'

THINK OF IT MORE AS BEING . . . DIMENSIONALLY DISADVANTAGED.

The shade of Beano the clown turned to Death.

'What *are* you talking about?'

YOU'RE DEAD.

'Yes. I know.' Beano relaxed, and stopped wondering too much about events in an increasingly irrelevant world. Death found that people often did, after the initial confusion. After all, the worst had already happened. At least . . . with any luck.

IF YOU WOULD CARE TO FOLLOW ME . . .

'Will there be custard pies? Red noses? *Juggling*? Are there likely to be baggy trousers?'

No.

Beano had spent almost all his short life as a clown. He smiled grimly, under his make-up.

'I *like* it.'

Vimes's meeting with the Patrician ended as all such meetings did, with the guest going away in possession of an unfocused yet nagging suspicion that he'd only just escaped with his life.

Vimes trudged on to see his bride-to-be. He knew where she would be found.

The sign scrawled across the big double gates in Morphic Street said: Here be Dragns.

The brass plaque *beside* the gates said: The Ankh-Morpork Sunshine Sanctuary for Sick Dragons.

There was a small and hollow and pathetic dragon made out of papier-mâché and holding a collection box, chained very heavily to the wall, and bearing the sign: Don't Let My Flame Go Out.

This was where Lady Sybil Ramkin spent most of her days.

She was, Vimes had been told, the richest woman in Ankh-Morpork. In fact she was richer than all the other women in Ankh-Morpork rolled, if that were possible, into one.

It was going to be a strange wedding, people said. Vimes treated his social superiors with barely concealed distaste, because the women made his head ache and the men made his fists itch. And Sybil Ramkin was the last survivor of one of the oldest families in Ankh. But they'd been thrown together like twigs in a whirlpool, and had yielded to the inevitable . . .

When he was a little boy, Sam Vimes had thought that the very rich ate off gold plates and lived in marble houses.

He'd learned something new: the very *very* rich could afford to be poor. Sybil Ramkin lived in the kind of poverty that was only available to the very rich, a poverty approached from the other side. Women who were merely well-off saved up and bought dresses made of silk edged with lace and pearls, but Lady Ramkin was so rich she could afford to stomp around the place in rubber boots and a tweed skirt that had belonged to her mother. She was so rich she could afford to live on biscuits and cheese sandwiches. She was so rich she lived in three rooms in a thirty-four-roomed mansion; the rest of them were full of very expensive and very *old* furniture, covered in dust sheets.

The reason that the rich were so rich, Vimes reasoned, was because they managed to spend less money.

Take boots, for example. He earned thirty-eight dollars a month plus allowances. A really good pair of leather boots cost fifty dollars. But an *affordable* pair of boots, which were sort of OK for a season or two and then leaked like hell when the cardboard gave out, cost about ten dollars. Those were the kind of boots Vimes always bought, and wore until the soles were so thin that he could tell where he was in Ankh-Morpork on a foggy night by the feel of the cobbles.

But the thing was that *good* boots lasted for years and years. A man who could afford fifty dollars had a pair of boots that'd still be keeping his feet dry in ten years' time, while a poor man who could only afford cheap boots would have spent a hundred dollars on boots in the same time *and would still have wet feet*.

This was the Captain Samuel Vimes 'Boots' theory of socio-economic unfairness.

The point was that Sybil Ramkin hardly ever had to buy anything. The mansion was full of this big, solid furniture, bought by her ancestors. It never wore out. She had whole boxes full of jewellery which just seemed to have accumulated over the centuries. Vimes had seen a wine cellar that a regiment of speleologists could get so happily drunk in that they wouldn't mind that they'd got lost without trace.

Lady Sybil Ramkin lived quite comfortably from day to day by spending, Vimes estimated, about half as much as he did. But she spent a lot more on dragons.

The Sunshine Sanctuary for Sick Dragons was built with very, very thick walls and a very, very lightweight roof, an idiosyncrasy of architecture normally only found elsewhere in firework factories.

And *this* is because the natural condition of the common swamp dragon is to be chronically ill, and the natural state of an unhealthy dragon is to be laminated across the walls, floor and ceiling of whatever room it is in. A swamp dragon is a badly run, dangerously unstable chemical factory one step from disaster. One quite small step.

It has been speculated that its habit of exploding violently when angry, excited, frightened or merely plain bored is a developed survival trait* to discourage predators. Eat dragons, it proclaims, and you'll have a case of indigestion to which the term 'blast radius' will be appropriate.

Vimes therefore pushed the door open carefully. The smell of dragons engulfed him. It was an unusual smell, even by Ankh-Morpork standards – it put Vimes in mind of a pond that had been used to dump alchemical waste for several years and then drained.

Small dragons whistled and yammered at him from pens on either side of the path. Several excited gusts of flame sizzled the hair on his bare shins.

He found Sybil Ramkin with a couple of the miscellaneous young women in breeches who helped run the Sanctuary; they were generally called Sara or Emma, and all looked exactly the same to Vimes. They were struggling with what seemed to be an irate sack. She looked up as he approached.

'Ah, here's Sam,' she said. 'Hold this, there's a lamb.'

The sack was thrust into his arms. At the same moment a talon ripped out of the bottom of the sack and scraped down his breast-plate in a spirited attempt to disembowel him. A spiky-eared head thrust its way out of the other end, two glowing red eyes focused on him briefly, a tooth-serrated mouth gaped open and a gush of evil-smelling vapour washed over him.

Lady Ramkin grabbed the lower jaw triumphantly, and thrust the other arm up to the elbow down the little dragon's throat.

'Got you!' She turned to Vimes, who was still rigid with shock. 'Little devil wouldn't take his limestone tablet. Swallow. *Swallow!* there! Who's a good boy then? You can let him go now.'

The sack slipped from Vimes's arms.

'Bad case of Flameless Gripe,' said Lady Ramkin. 'Hope we've got it in time—'

The dragon ripped its way out of the sack and looked around for something to incinerate. Everyone tried to get out of the way.

Then its eyes crossed, and it hiccuped.

The limestone tablet *pinged* off the opposite wall.

'*Everybody down!*'

They leapt for such cover as was provided by a watertrough and a pile of clinkers.

The dragon hiccuped again, and looked puzzled.

Then it exploded.

---

* From the point of view of the species as a whole. Not from the point of view of the dragon now landing in small pieces around the landscape.

They stuck their heads up when the smoke had cleared and looked down at the sad little crater.

Lady Ramkin took a handkerchief out of a pocket of her leather overall and blew her nose.

'Silly little bugger,' she said. 'Oh, well. How are you, Sam? Did you go to see Havelock?'

Vimes nodded. Never in his life, he thought, would he get used to the idea of the Patrician of Ankh-Morpork having a first name, or that anyone could ever know him well enough to call him by it.

'I've been thinking about this dinner tomorrow night,' he said desperately. 'You know, I really don't think I can—'

'Don't be silly,' said Lady Ramkin. 'You'll enjoy it. It's time you met the Right People. You know that.'

He nodded mournfully.

'We shall expect you up at the house at eight o'clock, then,' she said. 'And don't look like that. It'll help you *tremendously*. You're far too good a man to spend his nights traipsing around dark wet streets. It's time you got on in the world.'

Vimes wanted to say that he *liked* traipsing around dark wet streets, but it would be no use. He *didn't* like it much. It was just what he'd always done. He thought about his badge in the same way he thought about his nose. He didn't love it or hate it. It was just his badge.

'So just you run along. It'll be terrific fun. Have you got a handkerchief?'

Vimes panicked.

'What?'

'Give it to me.' She held it close to his mouth. 'Spit . . .' she commanded.

She dabbed at a smudge on his cheek. One of the Interchangeable Emmas gave a giggle that was just audible. Lady Ramkin ignored it.

'There,' she said. 'That's better. Now off you go and keep the streets safe for all of us. And if you want to do something *really* useful, you could find Chubby.'

'Chubby?'

'He got out of his pen last night.'

'A dragon?'

Vimes groaned, and pulled a cheap cigar out of his pocket. Swamp dragons were becoming a minor nuisance in the city. Lady Ramkin got very angry about it. People would buy them when they were six inches long and a cute way of lighting fires and then, when they were burning the furniture and leaving corrosive holes in the carpet, the floor and the cellar ceiling underneath it, they'd be shoved out to fend for themselves.

'We rescued him from a blacksmith in Easy Street,' said Lady Ramkin. 'I said, "My good man, you can use a forge like everyone else". Poor little thing.'

'Chubby,' said Vimes. 'Got a light?'

'He's got a blue collar,' said Lady Ramkin.

'Right, yes.'

'He'll follow you like a lamb if he thinks you've got a charcoal biscuit.'

'Right.' Vimes patted his pockets.

'They're a little bit over-excited in this heat.'

Vimes reached down into a pen of hatchlings and picked up a small one, which flapped its stubby wings excitedly. It spurted a brief jet of blue flame. Vimes inhaled quickly.

'Sam, I really wish you wouldn't do that.'

'Sorry.'

'So if you could get young Carrot and that *nice* Corporal Nobbs to keep an eye out for—'

'No problem.'

For some reason Lady Sybil, keen of eye in every other respect, persisted in thinking of Corporal Nobbs as a cheeky, lovable rascal. It had always puzzled Sam Vimes. It must be the attraction of opposites. The Ramkins were more highly bred than a hilltop bakery, whereas Corporal Nobbs had been disqualified from the human race for shoving.

As he walked down the street in his old leather and rusty mail, with his helmet screwed on his head, and the feel of the cobbles through the worn soles of his boots telling him he was in Acre Alley, no one would have believed that they were looking at a man who was very soon going to marry the richest woman in Ankh-Morpork.

Chubby was not a happy dragon.

He missed the forge. He'd quite liked it in the forge. He got all the coal he could eat and the blacksmith hadn't been a particularly unkind man. Chubby had not demanded much out of life, and had got it.

Then this large woman had taken him away and put him in a pen. There had been other dragons around. Chubby didn't particularly like other dragons. And people'd given him unfamiliar coal.

He'd been quite pleased when someone had taken him out of the pen in the middle of the night. He'd thought he was going back to the blacksmith.

Now it was dawning on him that this was not happening. He was in a box, he was being bumped around, and now he was getting angry . . .

Sergeant Colon fanned himself with his clipboard, and then glared at the assembled guards.

He coughed.

'Right then, people,' he said. 'Settle down.'

'We are settled down, Fred,' said Corporal Nobbs.

'That's Sergeant to you, Nobby,' said Sergeant Colon.

'What do we have to sit down for anyway? We didn't used to do all this. I feel a right berk, sitting down listenin' to you goin' on about—'

'We got to do it proper, now there's more of us,' said Sergeant Colon. 'Right! Ahem. Right. OK. We welcome to the guard today Lance-Constable Detritus – *don't salute!* – and Lance-Constable Cuddy, also Lance-Constable Angua. We hope you will have a long and – what's that you've got there, Cuddy?'

'What?' said Cuddy, innocently.

'I can't help noticing that you still has got there what appears to be a double-headed throwing axe, lance-constable, despite what I vouchsafed to you earlier re Guard rules.'

'Cultural weapon, sergeant?' said Cuddy hopefully.

'You can leave it in your locker. Guards carry one sword, short, and one truncheon.'

With the exception of Detritus, he added mentally. Firstly, because even the longest sword nestled in the troll's huge hand like a toothpick, and secondly, because until they'd got this saluting business sorted out he wasn't about to see a member of the Watch nail his own hand to his own ear. He'd have a truncheon, and like it. Even then, he'd probably beat himself to death.

Trolls and dwarfs! Dwarfs and trolls! He didn't deserve it, not at his time of life. And that wasn't the worst of it.

He coughed again. When he read from his clipboard, it was in the sing-song voice of someone who learned his public speaking at school.

'Right,' he said again, a little uncertainly. 'So. Says here—'

'Sergeant?'

'Now wh— Oh, it's you, Corporal Carrot. Yes?'

'Aren't you forgetting something, sergeant?' said Carrot.

'I dunno,' said Colon cautiously. 'Am I?'

'About the recruits, sarge. Something they've got to take?' Carrot prompted.

Sergeant Colon rubbed his nose. Let's see . . . they had, as per standing orders, taken and signed for one shirt (mail, chain) one helmet, iron and copper, one breastplate, iron (except in the case of Lance-Constable Angua, who'd need to be fitted special, and Lance-Constable Detritus, who'd signed for a hastily adapted piece of armour which had once belonged to a war elephant), one truncheon, oak, one emergency pike or halberd, one crossbow, one hourglass, one short sword (except for Lance-Constable Detritus) and one badge, office of, Night Watchman's, copper.

'I think they've got the lot, Carrot,' he said. 'All signed for. Even Detritus got someone to make an X for him.'

'They've got to take the oath, sarge.'

'Oh. Er. Have they?'

'Yes, sarge. It's the law.'

Sergeant Colon looked embarrassed. It probably was the law, at that. Carrot was much better at this sort of thing. He knew the laws of Ankh-Morpork by heart. He was the only person who did. All Colon knew was that *he'd* never taken an oath when he joined, and as for Nobby, the best he'd ever get to an oath was something like 'bugger this for a game of soldiers'.

'All right, then,' he said. 'You've all, er, got to take the oath . . . eh . . . and Corporal Carrot will show you how. Did you take the, er, oath when you joined us, Carrot?'

'Oh, yes, sarge. Only no one asked me, so I gave it to myself, quiet like.'

'Oh? Right. Carry on, then.'

Carrot stood up and removed his helmet. He smoothed down his hair. Then he raised his right hand.

'Raise your right hands, too,' he said. 'Er . . . that's the one nearest Lance-Constable Angua, Lance-Constable Detritus. And repeat after me . . .' He closed his eyes and his lips moved for a moment, as though he was reading something off the inside of his skull.

'"I comma square bracket recruit's name square bracket comma" . . .'

He nodded at them. 'You say it.'

They chorused a reply. Angua tried not to laugh.

'" . . . do solemnly swear by square bracket recruit's deity of choice square bracket . . ."'

Angua couldn't trust herself to look at Carrot's face.

'" . . . to uphold the Laws and Ordinances of the city of Ankh-Morpork, serve the public truft comma and defend the fubjects of

His ftroke Her bracket delete whichever is inappropriate bracket Majefty bracket name of reigning monarch bracket . . ."'

Angua tried to look at a point behind Carrot's ear. On top of everything else, Detritus' patient monotone was already several dozen words behind everyone else.

'" . . . without fear comma favour comma or thought of perfonal rafety semi-colon to purfue evildoers and protect the innocent comma laying down my life if necefsary in the caufe of said duty comma so help me bracket aforefaid deity bracket full stop Gods Save the King stroke Queen bracket delete whichever is inappropriate bracket full stop."'

Angua subsided gratefully, and then *did* see Carrot's face. There were unmistakable tears trickling down his cheek.

'Er . . . right, . . . that's it, then, thank you,' said Sergeant Colon, after a while.

'—*pro-tect the in-no-cent com-ma*—'

'In your own time, Lance-Constable Detritus.'

The sergeant cleared his throat and consulted the clipboard again.

'Now, Grabber Hoskins has been let out of jail again, so be on the look out, you know what he's like when he's had his celebratory drink, and bloody Coalface the troll beat up four men last night—'

'—*in the caufe of said du-ty com-ma*—"

'Where's Captain Vimes?' demanded Nobby. 'He should be doing this.'

'Captain Vimes is . . . sorting things out,' said Sergeant Colon. ''S'not easy, learning civilianing. Right.' He glanced at his clipboard again, and back to the guardsmen. Men . . . hah.

His lips moved as he counted. There, sitting between Nobby and Constable Cuddy, was a very small, raggedy man, whose beard and hair were so overgrown and matted together that he looked like a ferret peering out of a bush.

'—*me brack-et af-ore-said de-it-y brack-et full stop.*'

'Oh, no,' he said. 'What're you doing here, Here'n'now? Thank you, Detritus – *don't salute* – you can sit down now.'

'Mr Carrot brings me in,' said Here'n'now.

'Protective custody, sarge,' said Carrot.

'*Again?*' Colon unhooked the cell keys from their nail over the desk and tossed them to the thief. 'All right. Cell Three. Take the keys in with you, we'll holler if we need 'em back.'

'You're a toff, Mr Colon,' said Here'n'now, wandering down the steps to the cells.

Colon shook his head.

'Worst thief in the world,' he said.

'He doesn't look that good,' said Angua.

'No, I mean the *worst*,' said Colon. 'As in "not good at it".'

'Remember when he was going to go all the way up to Dunman-ifestin to steal the Secret of Fire from the gods?' said Nobby.

'And I said "but we've *got* it, Here'n'now, we've had it for thousands of years,"' said Carrot. 'And *he* said, "that's right, so it has antique value".'*

'Poor old chap,' said Sergeant Colon. 'OK. What else have we got . . . yes, Carrot?'

'Now, they've got to take the King's Shilling,' said Carrot.

'Right. Yes. OK.' Colon fished in his pocket, and took out three sequin-sized Ankh-Morpork dollars, which had about the gold content of seawater. He tossed them one at a time to the recruits.

'This is called the King's Shilling,' he said, glancing at Carrot. 'Dunno why. You gotta get give it when you join. Regulations, see. Shows you've joined.' He looked embarrassed for a moment, and then coughed. 'Right. Oh, yeah. Loada roc—some trolls,' he corrected himself, 'got some kind of march down Short Street. Lance-Constable Detritus – *don't let him salute*! Right. What's this about, then?'

'It Troll New Year,' said Detritus.

'Is it? S'pose we got to learn about this sort of thing now. And says here there's this gritsuc—this dwarf rally or something—'

'Battle of Koom Valley Day,' said Constable Cuddy. 'Famous victory over the trolls.' He looked smug, insofar as anything could be seen behind the beard.

'Yeah? From ambush,' grunted Detritus, glowering at the dwarf.

'What? It was the trolls—' Cuddy began.

'Shut up,' said Colon. 'Look, it says here . . . says here they're marching . . . says here they're marching *up* Short Street.' He turned the paper over. 'Is this right?'

'Trolls going one way, dwarfs going the other?' said Carrot.

'Now *there's* a parade you don't want to miss,' said Nobby.

'What's wrong?' said Angua.

Carrot waved his hands vaguely in the air. 'Oh, dear. It's going to be dreadful. We must do something.'

'Dwarfs and trolls get along like a house on fire,' said Nobby. 'Ever been in a burning house, miss?'

Sergeant Colon's normally red face had gone pale pink. He buckled on his sword belt and picked up his truncheon.

---

* Fingers-Mazda, the first thief in the world, stole fire from the gods. But he was unable to fence it. It was too hot.†

† He got really burned on that deal.

'Remember,' he said, 'let's be careful out there.'

'Yeah,' said Nobby, 'let's be careful to stay in here.'

To understand why dwarfs and trolls don't like each other you have to go back a long way.

They get along like chalk and cheese. Very like chalk and cheese, really. One is organic, the other isn't, and also smells a bit cheesy. Dwarfs make a living by smashing up rocks with valuable minerals in them and the silicon-based lifeform known as trolls are, basically, rocks with valuable minerals in them. In the wild they also spend most of the daylight hours dormant, and that's not a situation a rock containing valuable minerals needs to be in when there are dwarfs around. And dwarfs hate trolls because, after you've just found an interesting seam of valuable minerals, you don't like rocks that suddenly stand up and tear your arm off because you've just stuck a pick-axe in their ear.

It was a state of permanent inter-species vendetta and, like all good vendettas, didn't really need a reason any more. It was enough that it had always existed.* Dwarfs hated trolls because trolls hated dwarfs, and vice versa.

The Watch lurked in Three Lamps Alley, which was about halfway down Short Street. There was a distant crackle of fireworks. Dwarfs let them off to drive away evil mine spirits. Trolls let them off because they tasted nice.

'Don't see why we can't let 'em fight it out amongst themselves and then arrest the losers,' said Corporal Nobbs. 'That's what we always used to do.'

'The Patrician gets really shirty about ethnic trouble,' said Sergeant Colon moodily. 'He gets really sarcastic about it.'

A thought struck him. He brightened up a little bit.

'Got any ideas, Carrot?' he said.

A second thought struck him. Carrot was a simple lad.

'Corporal Carrot?'

'Sarge?'

'Sort this lot out, will you?'

Carrot peered around the corner at the advancing walls of trolls and dwarfs. They'd already seen each other.

'Right you are, sergeant,' he said. 'Lance-Constables Cuddy and Detritus – *don't salute!* – you come with me.'

'You can't let him go out there!' said Angua. 'It's certain death!'

---

* The Battle of Koom Valley is the only one known to history where both sides ambushed each other.

'Got a real sense o'duty, that boy,' said Corporal Nobbs. He took a minute length of dog-end from behind his ear and struck a match on the sole of his boot.

'Don't worry, miss,' said Colon. 'He—'

'Lance-Constable,' said Angua.

'What?'

'Lance-Constable,' she repeated. 'Not miss. Carrot says I don't have any sex while I'm on duty.'

To the background of Nobby's frantic coughing, Colon said, very quickly, 'What I mean *is*, lance-constable, young Carrot's got krisma. Bags of krisma.'

'Krisma?'

'Bags of it.'

The jolting had stopped. Chubby was really annoyed now. Really, really annoyed.

There was a rustling noise. A piece of sacking moved aside and there, staring at Chubby, was another male dragon.

It looked annoyed.

Chubby reacted in the only way he knew how.

Carrot stood in the middle of the street, arms folded, while the two new recruits stood just behind him, trying to keep an eye on both approaching marches at the same time.

Colon thought Carrot was simple. Carrot often struck people as simple. And he was.

Where people went wrong was thinking that simple meant the same thing as stupid.

Carrot was not stupid. He was direct, and honest, and good-natured and honourable in all his dealings. In Ankh-Morpork this would normally have added up to 'stupid' in any case and would have given him the survival quotient of a jellyfish in a blast furnace, but there were a couple of other factors. One was a punch that even trolls had learned to respect. The other was that Carrot was genuinely, almost supernaturally, likeable. He got on well with people, even while arresting them. He had an exceptional memory for names.

For most of his young life he'd lived in a small dwarf colony where there were hardly any other people to know. Then, suddenly, he was in a huge city, and it was as if a talent had been waiting to unfold. And was still unfolding.

He waved cheerfully at the approaching dwarfs.

''Morning Mr Cumblethigh! 'Morning, Mr Stronginthearm!'

Then he turned and waved at the leading troll. There was a muffled 'pop' as a firework went off.

''Morning, Mr Bauxite!'

He cupped his hands.

'If you could all just stop and listen to me—' he bellowed.

The two marches *did* stop, with some hesitation and a general piling up of the people in the back. It was that or walk over Carrot.

If Carrot did have a minor fault, it lay in not paying attention to small details around him when his mind was on other things. So the whispered conversation behind his back was currently escaping him.

'—*hah! It was too an ambush! And your mother was an ore—*'

'Now then, gentlemen,' said Carrot, in a reasoned and amiable voice, 'I'm sure there's no need for this belligerent manner—'

'—*you ambush us too! my great-great-grandfather he at Koom Valley, he tell me!*'

'—in our fair city on such a lovely day. I must ask you as good citizens of Ankh-Morpork—'

'—*yeah? you even know who your father is, do you?*'

'—that, while you must certainly celebrate your proud ethnic folkways, to profit by the example of my fellow officers here, who have sunk their ancient differences—'

'—*I smash you head, you roguesome dwarfs!*'

'—for the greater benefit of—'

'—*I could take you with one hand tied behind my back!*'

'—the city, whose badge they are—'

'—*you get opportunity! I tie BOTH hands behind you back!*'

'—proud and privileged to wear.'

'Aargh!'

'Ooow!'

It dawned on Carrot that hardly anyone was paying any attention to him. He turned.

Lance-Constable Cuddy was upside down, because Lance-Constable Detritus was trying to bounce him on the cobbles by his helmet, although Lance-Constable Cuddy was putting the position to good effect by gripping Lance-Constable Detritus around the knee and trying to sink his teeth into Lance-Constable Detritus' ankle.

The opposing marchers watched in fascination.

'We should do something!' said Angua, from the guards' hiding place in the alley.

'Weeell,' said Sergeant Colon, slowly, 'it's always very tricky, ethnic.'

'Can put a foot wrong very easily,' said Nobby. 'Very thin-skinned, your basic ethnic.'

'Thin-skinned? They're trying to *kill* one another!'

'It's cultural,' said Sergeant Colon, miserably. 'No sense us tryin' to force our culture on 'em, is there? That's speciesist.'

Out in the street, Corporal Carrot had gone very red in the face.

'If he lays a finger on either of 'em, with all their friends watching,' said Nobby, 'the plan is, we run away like hell—'

Veins stood out on Carrot's mighty neck. He stuck his hands on his waist and bellowed:

'Lance-Constable Detritus! Salute!'

They'd spent hours trying to teach him. Detritus' brain took some time to latch on to an idea, but once it was there, it didn't fade away fast.

He saluted.

His hand was full of dwarf.

So he saluted while holding Lance-Constable Cuddy, swinging him up and over like a small angry club.

The sound of their helmets meeting echoed off the buildings, and it was followed a moment later by the crash of them both hitting the ground.

Carrot prodded them with the toe of his sandal.

Then he turned and strode towards the dwarf marchers, shaking with anger.

In the alleyway, Sergeant Colon started to suck the rim of his helmet out of terror.

'You've got *weapons*, haven't you?' snarled Carrot at a hundred dwarfs. 'Own up! If the dwarfs who've got weapons don't drop them right this minute the entire parade, and I mean the *entire* parade, will be put in the cells! I'm serious about this!'

The dwarfs in the front row took a step backwards. There was a desultory tinkle of metallic objects hitting the ground.

'*All* of them,' said Carrot menacingly. 'That includes you with the black beard trying to hide behind Mr Hamslinger! I can *see* you, Mr Stronginthearm! Put it *down*. No one's amused!'

'He's going to die, isn't he,' said Angua, quietly.

'Funny, that,' said Nobby. 'If *we* was to try it, we'd be little bits of mince. But it seems to work for him.'

'Krisma,' said Sergeant Colon, who was having to lean on the wall.

'Do you mean charisma?' said Angua.

'Yeah. One of them things. Yeah.'

'How does he manage it?'

'Dunno,' said Nobby. 'S'pose he's an easy lad to like?'

Carrot had turned on the trolls, who were smirking at the dwarfs' discomfiture.

'And as for you,' he said, 'I shall definitely be patrolling around Quarry Lane tonight, and I won't be seeing any trouble. Will I?'

There was a shuffling of huge oversized feet, and a general muttering.

Carrot cupped his hand to his ear.

'I couldn't quite hear,' he said.

There was a louder mutter, a sort of toccata scored for one hundred reluctant voices on the theme of 'Yes, Corporal Carrot.'

'Right. Now off you go. And let's have no more of this nonsense, there's good chaps.'

Carrot brushed the dust off his hands and smiled at everyone. The trolls looked puzzled. In theory, Carrot was a thin film of grease on the street. But somehow it just didn't seem to be happening . . .

Angua said, 'He just called a hundred trolls "good chaps". Some of them are just down off the mountains! Some of them have got *lichen* on them!'

'Smartest thing on a troll,' said Sergeant Colon.

And then the world exploded.

The Watch had left before Captain Vimes got back to Pseudopolis Yard. He plodded up the stairs to his office, and sat down in the sticky leather chair. He gazed blankly at the wall.

He *wanted* to leave the Guard. Of course he did.

It wasn't what you could call a way of life. Not *life*.

Unsocial hours. Never being certain from one day to the next what the Law actually was, in this pragmatic city. No home life, to speak of. Bad food, eaten when you could; he'd even eaten some of Cut-Me-Own-Throat Dibbler's sausages-in-a-bun before now. It always seemed to be raining or baking hot. No friends, except for the rest of the squad, because they were the only people who lived in *your* world.

Whereas in a few days he would, as Sergeant Colon had said, be on the gravy boat. Nothing to do all day but eat his meals and ride around on a big horse shouting orders at people.

At times like this the image of old Sergeant Kepple floated across his memory. He'd been head of the Watch when Vimes was a recruit. And, soon afterwards, he retired. They'd all clubbed together and bought him a cheap watch, one of those that'd keep going for a few years until the demon inside it evaporated.

Bloody stupid idea, Vimes thought moodily, staring at the wall.

Bloke leaves work, hands in his badge and hourglass and bell, and what'd we get him? A watch.

But he'd still come in to work the next day, with his new watch. To show everyone the ropes, he said; to tidy up a few loose ends, haha. See you youngsters don't get into trouble, haha. A month later he was bringing the coal in and sweeping the floor and running errands and helping people write reports. He was still there five years later. He was still there six years later, when one of the Watch got in early and found him lying on the floor . . .

And it emerged that no one, *no one*, knew where he lived, or even if there was a Mrs Kepple. They had a whip-round to bury him, Vimes remembered. There were just guards at the funeral . . .

Come to think of it, there were always just guards at a guard's funeral.

Of course it wasn't like that now. Sergeant Colon had been happily married for years, perhaps because he and his wife arranged their working lives so that they only met occasionally, normally on the doorstep. But she left him decent meals in the oven, and there was clearly something there; they'd got grand-children, even, so obviously there had been times when they'd been unable to avoid each other. Young Carrot had to fight young women off with a stick. And Corporal Nobbs . . . well, he probably made his own arrangements. He was said to have the body of a twenty-five year old, although no one knew where he kept it.

The point was that everyone else had someone, even if in Nobby's case it was probably against their will.

So, Captain Vimes, what is it really? Do you care for her? Don't worry too much about love, that's a dicey word for the over-forties. Or are you just afraid of becoming some old man dying in the groove of his life and buried out of pity by a bunch of youngsters who never knew you as anything other than some old fart who always seemed to be around the place and got sent out to bring back the coffee and hot figgins and was laughed at behind his back?

He'd wanted to avoid that. And now Fate was handing him a fairy tale.

Of course he'd known she was rich. But he hadn't expected the summons to Mr Morecombe's office.

Mr Morecombe had been the Ramkins' family solicitor for a long time. Centuries, in fact. He was a vampire.

Vimes disliked vampires. Dwarfs were law-abiding little buggers when they were sober, and even trolls were all right if you kept them where you could see them. But all the undead made his neck itch. Live and let live was all very well, but there was a problem right there, when you thought about it logically . . .

Mr Morecombe was scrawny, like a tortoise, and very pale. It had taken him ages to come to the point, and when it came the point nailed Vimes to his chair.

'*How* much?'

'Er. I believe I am right in saying the estate, including the farms, the areas of urban development, and the small area of unreal estate near the University, are together worth approximately . . . seven million dollars a year. Yes. Seven million at current valuation, I would say.'

'It's all *mine*?'

'From the hour of your wedding to Lady Sybil. Although she instructs me in this letter that you are to have access to all her accounts as of the present moment.'

The pearly dead eyes had watched Vimes carefully.

'Lady Sybil,' he said, 'owns approximately one-tenth of Ankh, and extensive properties in Morpork, plus of course considerable farm lands in—'

'But . . . but . . . we'll own them together . . .'

'Lady Sybil is very specific. She is deeding all the property to you as her husband. She has a somewhat . . . old-fashioned approach.' He pushed a folded paper across the table. Vimes took it, unfolded it, and stared.

'Should you predecease her, of course,' Mr Morecombe droned on, 'it will revert to her by common right of marriage. Or to any fruit of the union, of course.'

Vimes hadn't even said anything at that point. He'd just felt his mouth drop open and small areas of his brain fuse together.

'Lady Sybil,' said the lawyer, the words coming from far away, 'while not as young as she was, is a fine healthy woman and there is no reason why—'

Vimes had got through the rest of the interview on automatic.

He could hardly think about it now. When he tried, his thoughts kept skidding away. And, just as always happened when the world got too much for him, they skidded somewhere else.

He pulled open the bottom drawer of his desk and stared at the shiny bottle of Bearhugger's Very Fine Whiskey. He wasn't sure how it had got there. Somehow he'd never got around to throwing it out.

Start that again and you won't even see retirement. Stick to cigars.

He shut the drawer and leaned back, taking a half-smoked cigar from his pocket.

Maybe the guards weren't so good now anyway. Politics. Hah! Watchmen like old Kepple would turn in their graves if they knew that the Watch had taken on a w—

And the world exploded.

The window blew in, peppering the wall behind Vimes's desk with fragments and cutting one of his ears.

He threw himself to the floor and rolled under the desk.

Right, that did it! The alchemists had blown up their Guild House for the last time, if Vimes had anything to do with it . . .

But when he peered over the window sill he saw, across the river, the column of dust rising over the Assassins' Guild . . .

The rest of the Watch came trotting along Filigree Street as Vimes reached the Guild entrance. A couple of black-clad Assassins barred his way, in a polite manner which nevertheless indicated that impoliteness was a future option. There were sounds of hurrying feet behind the gates.

'You see this badge? You see it?' Vimes demanded.

'Nevertheless, this is Guild property,' said an Assassin.

'Let us in, in the name of the law!' bellowed Vimes.

The Assassin smiled nervously at him. 'The law is that *Guild* law prevails inside Guild walls,' he said.

Vimes glared at him. But it was true. The laws of the city, such as they were, stopped outside the Guild Houses. The Guilds had their own laws. The Guild owned the . . .

He stopped.

Behind him, Lance-Constable Angua reached down and picked up a fragment of glass.

Then she stirred the debris with her foot.

And then her gaze met that of a small, non-descript mongrel dog watching her very intently from under a cart. In fact non-descript was not what it was. It was very easy to descript. It looked like halitosis with a wet nose.

'Woof, woof,' said the dog, in a bored way. 'Woof, woof, woof, and growl, growl.'

The dog trotted into the mouth of an alleyway. Angua glanced around, and followed it. The rest of the squad were gathered around Vimes, who'd gone very quiet.

'Fetch me the Master of Assassins,' he said. 'Now!'

The young Assassin tried to sneer.

'Hah! Your uniform doesn't scare *me*,' he said.

Vimes looked down at his battered breastplate and worn mail.

'You're right,' he said. 'This is not a scary uniform. I'm sorry. Forward, Corporal Carrot and Lance-Constable Detritus.'

The Assassin was suddenly aware of the sunlight being blocked out.

'Now *these*, I think you'll agree,' said Vimes, from somewhere behind the eclipse, 'are scary uniforms.'

The Assassin nodded slowly. He hadn't asked for this. Usually there were never any guards outside the Guild. What would be the point? He had, tucked away in his exquisitely tailored black clothes, at least eighteen devices for killing people, but he was becoming aware that Lance-Constable Detritus had one on the end of each of his arms. Closer, as it were, to hand.

'I'll, er, I'll go and get the Master, then, shall I?' he said.

Carrot leaned down.

'Thank you for your co-operation,' he said gravely.

Angua watched the dog. The dog watched her.

She squatted on her haunches as it sat down and scratched an ear furiously.

Looking around carefully to make sure that no one could see them, she barked an inquiry.

'Don't bovver,' said the dog.

'You can *talk*?'

'Huh. *That* don't take much intelligence,' said the dog. 'And it don't take much intelligence to spot what *you* are, neither.'

Angua looked panicky.

'Where does it show?'

'It's the *smell*, girl. Din't you learn nuffin? Smelled you a mile orf. I thought, oh-ho, what's one of *them* doing in the Watch, eh?'

Angua waved a finger wildly.

'If you tell anyone—!'

The dog looked more pained than normal.

'No one'd listen,' it said.

'Why not?'

''Cos everyone knows dogs can't talk. They *hear* me, see, but unless things are really *tough* they just think they're thinking to 'emselves.' The little dog sighed. 'Trust me. I know what I'm talking about. I've read books. Well . . . chewed books.'

It scratched an ear again. 'Seems to me,' it said, 'we could help each other . . .'

'In what way?'

'Well, you could put me in the way of a pound of steak. That does wonders for my memory, steak. Makes it go clean away.'

Angua frowned.

'People don't like the word "blackmail",' she said.

'It ain't the only word they don't like,' said the dog. 'Take my case, now. I've got chronic intelligence. Is that any use to a dog? Did I ask for it? Not me. I just finds a cushy spot to spend my nights along at the High Energy Magic building at the University, no one told *me* about all this bloody magic leaking out the whole time, next thing I know I open me eyes, head starts fizzing like a dose of salts, oh-oh, thinks I, here we go again, hello abstract conceptualizing, intellectual development here we come . . . What bloody use is that to me? Larst time it happened, I ended up savin' the world from horrible wossnames from the Dungeon Dimensions, and did anyone say fanks? Wot a Good Dog, Give Him A Bone? Har har.' It held up a threadbare paw. 'My name's Gaspode. Something like this happens to me just about every week. Apart from that, I'm just a dog.'

Angua gave up. She grasped the moth-eaten limb and shook it.

'My name's Angua. You know what I am.'

'Forgotten it already,' said Gaspode.

Captain Vimes looked at the debris scattered across the courtyard from a hole in one of the ground-floor rooms. All the surrounding windows had broken, and there was a lot of glass underfoot. Mirror glass. Of course, assassins were notoriously vain, but mirrors would be in rooms, wouldn't they? You wouldn't expect a lot of glass outside. Glass got blown in, not out.

He saw Lance-Constable Cuddy bend down and pick up a couple of pulleys attached to a piece of rope, which was burned at one end.

There was a rectangle of card in the debris.

The hairs on the back of Vimes's hand prickled.

He sniffed rankness in the air.

Vimes would be the first to admit that he wasn't a good copper, but he'd probably be spared the chore because lots of other people would happily admit it for him. There was a certain core of stubborn bloody-mindedness there which upset important people, and anyone who upsets important people is automatically not a good copper. But he'd developed instincts. You couldn't live on the streets of a city all your life without them. In the same way that the whole jungle subtly changes at the distant approach of the hunter, there was an alteration in the feel of the city.

There was something happening here, something wrong, and he couldn't quite see what it was. He started to reach down—

'What is the meaning of this?'

Vimes straightened up. He did not turn around.

'Sergeant Colon, I want you to go back to the Watch House with Nobby and Detritus,' he said. 'Corporal Carrot and Lance-Constable Cuddy, you stay with me.'

'Yes, *sah!*' said Sergeant Colon, stamping heavily and ripping off a smart salute to annoy the Assassins. Vimes acknowledged it.

Then he turned around.

'Ah, Dr Cruces,' he said.

The Master of Assassins was white with rage, contrasting nicely with the extreme black of his clothing.

'No one sent for you!' he said. 'What gives you the right to be here, mister policeman? Walking around as if you own the place?'

Vimes paused, his heart singing. He savoured the moment. He'd like to take this moment and press it carefully in a big book, so that when he was old he could take it out occasionally and remember it.

He reached into his breastplate and pulled out the lawyer's letter.

'Well, if you would like the most fundamental reason,' he said, 'it is because I rather think I do.'

A man can be defined by the things he hates. There were quite a lot of things that Captain Vimes hated. Assassins were near the top of the list, just after kings and the undead.

He had to allow, though, that Dr Cruces recovered very quickly. He didn't explode when he read the letter, or argue, or claim it was a forgery. He simply folded it up, handed it back, and said, coldly, 'I see. The freehold, at least.'

'Quite so. Could you tell me what has been happening, please?'

He was aware of other senior Assassins entering the courtyard through the hole in the wall. They were very carefully looking at the debris.

Dr Cruces hesitated for a moment.

'Fireworks,' he said.

'What happened,' said Gaspode, 'was that someone put a dragon in a box right up against the wall inside the courtyard, right, and then they went and hid behind one of the statues and pulled a string and next minute – bang!'

'Bang?'

''S'right. Then our friend nips into the hole for a few seconds, right, comes out again, trots around the courtyard and next minute

there's Assassins everywhere and he's among 'em. What the hell.
Another man in black. No one notices, see?'

'You mean he's still in there?'

'How do I know? Hoods and cloaks, everyone in black . . .'

'How come you were able to see this?'

'Oh, I always nip into the Assassins' Guild on a Wednesday
night. Mixed grill night, see?' Gaspode sighed at Angua's blank
expression. 'The cook always does a mixed grill of a Wednesday
night. No one ever eats the black pudding. So it's round the
kitchens, see, woof woof, beg beg, who's a good boy then, look at
the little bugger, he looks as though he understands every word
I'm sayin', let's see what we've got here for a good doggy . . .'

He looked embarrassed for a moment.

'Pride is all very well, but a sausage is a sausage,' he said.

'Fireworks?' said Vimes.

Dr Cruces looked like a man grasping a floating log in a choppy
sea.

'Yes. Fireworks. Yes. For Founder's Day. Unfortunately someone
threw away a lighted match which ignited the box.' Dr Cruces
suddenly smiled. 'My dear Captain Vimes,' he said, clapping his
hands, 'much as I appreciate your concern, I really—'

'They were stored in that room over there?' said Vimes.

'Yes, but that's of no account—'

Vimes crossed to the hole in the wall and peered inside. A couple
of Assassins glanced at Dr Cruces and reached nonchalantly
towards various areas of their clothing. He shook his head. His
caution might have had something to do with the way Carrot put
his hand on the hilt of his sword, but it could also have been
because Assassins did have a certain code, after all. It was dishonourable to kill someone if you weren't being paid.

'It seems to be some kind of . . . museum,' said Vimes. 'Guild
memorabilia, that sort of thing?'

'Yes, exactly. Odd and ends. You know how they mount up over
the years.'

'Oh. Well, that all seems in order,' said Vimes. 'Sorry to have
troubled you, doctor. I will be going. I hope I have not inconvenienced you in any way.'

'Of course not! Glad to have been able to put your mind at rest.'

They were ushered gently yet firmly towards the gateway.

'I should clean up this glass,' said Captain Vimes, glancing at
the debris again. 'Someone could hurt themselves, all this glass
lying around. Wouldn't like to see one of your people get hurt.'

'We shall be doing it right this minute, captain,' said Dr Cruces.

'Good. Good. Thank you very much.' Captain Vimes paused at the doorway, and then thumped the palm of his hand on his forehead.

'Sorry, excuse me – mind like a sieve these days – what was it you said was stolen?'

Not a muscle, not a sinew moved on Dr Cruces's face.

'I didn't say anything was stolen, Captain Vimes.'

Vimes gaped at him for a moment.

'Right! Sorry! Of course, you didn't ... Apologies ... Work getting on top of me, I expect. I'll be going, then.'

The door slammed in his face.

'Right,' said Vimes.

'Captain, why—?' Carrot began. Vimes held up a hand.

'That wraps it up, then,' he said, slightly louder than necessary. 'Nothing to worry about. Let's get back to the Yard. Where's Lance-Constable Whatshername?'

'Here, captain,' said Angua, stepping out of the alley.

'Hiding, eh? And what's *that*?'

'Woof woof whine whine.'

'It's a little dog, captain.'

'Good grief.'

The clang of the big corroded Inhumation Bell echoed through the Assassins' Guild. Black-clad figures came running from all directions, pushing and shoving in their haste to get to the courtyard.

The Guild council assembled hurriedly outside Dr Cruces's office. His deputy, Mr Downey, knocked tentatively at the door.

'Come.'

The council filed in.

Cruces's office was the biggest room in the building. It always seemed wrong to visitors that the Assassins' Guild had such light, airy, well-designed premises, more like the premises of a gentlemen's club than a building where death was plotted on a daily basis.

Cheery sporting prints lined the walls, although the quarry was not, when you looked closely, stags or foxes. There were also group etchings – and, more recently, new-fangled iconographs – of the Guild, rows of smiling faces on black-clad bodies and the youngest members sitting cross-legged in front, one of them making a face.*

Down one side of the room was the big mahogany table where

---

* There's always one.

the elders of the Guild sat in weekly session. The other side of the room held Cruces's private library, and a small workbench. Above the bench was an apothecary cabinet, made up of hundreds of little drawers. The names on the drawer labels were in Assassins' code, but visitors from outside the Guild were generally sufficiently unnerved not to accept a drink.

Four pillars of black granite held up the ceiling. They had been carved with the names of noted Assassins from history. Cruces had his desk foursquare between them. He was standing behind it, his expression almost as wooden as the desk.

'I want a roll-call,' he snapped. 'Has anyone left the Guild?'

'No, sir.'

'How can you be so sure?'

'The guards on the roofs in Filigree Street say no one came in or went out, sir.'

'And who's watching *them*?'

'They're watching one another, sir.'

'Very well. Listen carefully. I want the mess cleaned up. If anyone needs to go outside the building, I want everyone watched. And then the Guild is going to be searched from top to bottom, do you understand?'

'What for, doctor?' said a junior lecturer in poisons.

'For . . . anything that is hidden. If you find anything and you don't know what it is, send for a council member immediately. And don't touch it.'

'But doctor, all sorts of things are hidden—'

'This will be different, do you understand?'

'No, sir.'

'Good. And no one is to speak to the wretched Watch about this. You, boy . . . bring me my hat.' Dr Cruces sighed. 'I suppose I shall have to go and tell the Patrician.'

'Hard luck, sir.'

The captain didn't say anything until they were crossing the Brass Bridge.

'Now then, Corporal Carrot,' he said, 'you know how I've always told you how observation is important?'

'Yes, captain. I have always paid careful attention to your remarks on the subject.'

'So what did you observe?'

'Someone'd smashed a mirror. Everyone knows Assassins like mirrors. But if it was a museum, why was there a mirror there?'

'Please, sir?'

'Who said that?'

'Down here, sir. Lance-Constable Cuddy.'

'Oh, yes. Yes?'

'I know a bit about fireworks, sir. There's a smell you get after fireworks. Didn't smell it, sir. Smelled something else.'

'Well . . . smelled, Cuddy.'

'And there were bits of burned rope and pulleys.'

'I smelled dragon,' said Vimes.

'Sure, captain?'

'Trust me.' Vimes grimaced. If you spent any time in Lady Ramkin's company, you soon found out what dragons smelled like. If something put its head in your lap while you were dining, you said nothing, you just kept passing it titbits and hoped like hell it didn't hiccup.

'There was a glass case in that room,' he said. 'It was smashed open. Hah! Something was stolen. There was a bit of card in the dust, but someone must have pinched it while old Cruces was talking to me. I'd give a hundred dollars to know what it said.'

'Why, captain?' said Corporal Carrot.

'Because that bastard Cruces doesn't want me to know.'

'I know what could have blown the hole open,' said Angua.

'What?'

'An exploding dragon.'

They walked in stunned silence.

'That could do it, sir,' said Carrot loyally. 'The little devils go bang at the drop of a helmet.'

'Dragon,' muttered Vimes. 'What makes you think it was a dragon, Lance-Constable Angua?'

Angua hesitated. 'Because a dog told me' was not, she judged, a career-advancing thing to say at this point.

'Woman's intuition?' she suggested.

'I *suppose*,' said Vimes, 'you wouldn't hazard an intuitive guess as to what was stolen?'

Angua shrugged. Carrot noticed how interestingly her chest moved.

'Something the Assassins wanted to keep where they could look at it?' she said.

'Oh, yes,' said Vimes. 'I suppose next you'll tell me this dog saw it all?'

'Woof?'

Edward d'Eath drew the curtains, bolted the door and leaned on it. It had been so easy!

He'd put the bundle on the table. It was thin, and about four feet long.

He unwrapped it carefully, and there . . . it . . . was.

It looked pretty much like the drawing. Typical of the man – a whole page full of meticulous drawings of crossbows, and this in the margin, as though it hardly mattered.

It was so simple! Why hide it away? Probably because people were afraid. People were always afraid of power. It made them nervous.

Edward picked it up, cradled it for a while, and found that it seemed to fit his arm and shoulder very snugly.

You're mine.

And that, more or less, was the end of Edward d'Eath. Something continued for a while, but what it was, and how it thought, wasn't entirely human.

It was nearly noon. Sergeant Colon had taken the new recruits down to the archery butts in Butts Treat.

Vimes went on patrol with Carrot.

He felt something inside him bubbling over. Something was brushing the tips of his corroded but nevertheless still-active instincts, trying to draw attention to itself. He had to be on the move. It was all that Carrot could do to keep up.

There were trainee Assassins in the streets around the Guild, still sweeping up debris.

'Assassins in daylight,' snarled Vimes. 'I'm amazed they don't turn to dust.'

'That's vampires, sir,' said Carrot.

'Hah! You're right. Assassins and licensed thieves and bloody vampires! You know, this was a great old city once, lad.'

Unconsciously, they fell into step . . . proceeding.

'When we had kings, sir?'

'Kings? Kings? Hell, no!'

A couple of Assassins looked around in surprise.

'I'll tell you,' said Vimes. 'A monarch's an absolute ruler, right? The head honcho—'

'Unless he's a queen,' said Carrot.

Vimes glared at him, and then nodded.

'OK, or the head honchette—'

'No, that'd only apply if she was a young woman. Queens tend to be older. She'd have to be a . . . a honcharina? No, that's for very young princesses. No. Um. A honchesa, I think.'

Vimes paused. There's something in the air in this city, he

297

thought. If the Creator had said, 'Let there be light' in Ankh-Morpork, he'd have got no further because of all the people saying 'What colour?'

'The supreme ruler, OK,' he said, starting to stroll forward again. 'OK.'

'But that's not right, see? One man with the power of life and death.'

'But if he's a good man—' Carrot began.

'What? *What*? OK. OK. Let's believe he's a good man. But his second-in-command – is he a good man too? You'd better hope so. Because *he's* the supreme ruler, too, in the name of the king. And the rest of the court . . . they've got to be good men. Because if just one of them's a bad man the result is bribery and patronage.'

'The Patrician's a supreme ruler,' Carrot pointed out. He nodded at a passing troll. 'G'day, Mr Carbuncle.'

'But he doesn't wear a crown or sit on a throne and he doesn't tell you it's *right* that he should rule,' said Vimes. 'I hate the bastard. But he's honest. Honest like a corkscrew.'

'Even so, a good man as king—'

'Yes? And then what? Royalty pollutes people's minds, boy. Honest men start bowing and bobbing just because someone's graddad was a bigger murdering bastard than theirs was. Listen! We probably had good kings, once! But kings breed other kings! And blood tells, and you end up with a bunch of arrogant, murdering bastards! Chopping off queens' heads and fighting their cousins every five minutes! And we had centuries of that! And then one day a man said "No more kings!" and we rose up and we fought the bloody nobles and we dragged the king off his throne and we dragged him into Sator Square and we chopped his bloody head off! Job well done!'

'Wow,' said Carrot. 'Who was he?'

'Who?'

'The man who said "No More Kings".'

People were staring. Vimes's face went from the red of anger to the red of embarrassment. There was little difference in the shading, however.

'Oh . . . he was Commander of the City Guard in those days,' he mumbled. 'They called him Old Stoneface.'

'Never heard of him,' said Carrot.

'He, er, doesn't appear much in the history books,' said Vimes. 'Sometimes there has to be a civil war, and sometimes, afterwards, it's best to pretend something didn't happen. Sometimes people have to do a job, and then they have to be forgotten. He wielded the axe, you know. No one else'd do it. It was a king's neck, after

298

all. Kings are,' he spat the word, '*special*. Even after they'd seen the . . . private rooms, and cleaned up the . . . bits. Even then. No one'd clean up the world. But he took the axe and cursed them all and did it.'

'What king was it?' said Carrot.

'Lorenzo the Kind,' said Vimes, distantly.

'I've seen his picture in the palace museum,' said Carrot. 'A fat old man. Surrounded by lots of children.'

'Oh yes,' said Vimes, carefully. 'He was very fond of children.'

Carrot waved at a couple of dwarfs.

'I didn't know this,' he said. 'I thought there was just some wicked rebellion or something.'

Vimes shrugged. 'It's in the history books, if you know where to look.'

'And that was the end of the kings of Ankh-Morpork.'

'Oh, there was a surviving son, I think. And a few mad relatives. They were banished. That's supposed to be a terrible fate, for royalty. I can't see it myself.'

'I think I can. And *you* like the city, sir.'

'Well, yes. But if it was a choice between banishment and having my head chopped off, just help me down with this suitcase. No, we're well rid of kings. But, I mean . . . the *city* used to work.'

'Still does,' said Carrot.

They passed the Assassins' Guild and drew level with the high, forbidding walls of the Fools' Guild, which occupied the other corner of the block.

'No, it just keeps going. I mean, look up there.'

Carrot obediently raised his gaze.

There was a familiar building on the junction of Broad Way and Alchemists. The façade was ornate, but covered in grime. Gargoyles had colonized it.

The corroded motto over the portico said 'NEITHER RAIN NOR SNOW NOR GLOM OF NIT CAN STAY THESE MEfsENGERS ABOT THIER DUTY' and in more spacious days that may have been the case, but recently someone had found it necessary to nail up an addendum which read:

> *DONT ARSK US ABOUT:*
> *rocks*
> *troll's with sticks*
> *All sorts of dragons*
> *Mrs Cake*
> *Huje green things with teeth*
> *Any kinds of black dogs with orange eyebrows*

Rains of spaniel's.
fog.
Mrs Cake

'Oh,' he said. 'The Royal Mail.'

'The Post Office,' corrected Vimes. 'My granddad said that once you could post a letter there and it'd be delivered within a month, without fail. You didn't have to give it to a passing dwarf and hope the little bugger wouldn't eat it before . . .'

His voice trailed off.

'Uh. Sorry. No offence meant.'

'None taken,' said Carrot cheerfully.

'It's not that I've got anything against dwarfs. I've always said you'd have to look very hard before you'd find a, a better bunch of highly skilled, law-abiding, hard-working—'

'—little buggers?'

'Yes. No!'

They proceeded.

'That Mrs Cake,' said Carrot, 'definitely a strong-minded woman, eh?'

'Too true,' said Vimes.

Something crunched under Carrot's enormous sandal.

'More glass,' he said. 'It went a long way, didn't it.'

'Exploding dragons! What an imagination the girl has.'

'Woof woof,' said a voice behind them.

'That damn dog's been following us,' said Vimes.

'It's barking at something on the wall,' said Carrot.

Gaspode eyed them coldly.

'Woof woof, bloody whine whine,' he said. 'Are you bloody blind or what?'

It was true that normal people couldn't hear Gaspode speak, because dogs *don't* speak. It's a well-known fact. It's well known at the organic level, like a lot of other well-known facts which over-rule the observations of the senses. This is because if people went around noticing everything that was going on all the time, no one would ever get anything done.* Besides, almost all dogs don't talk. Ones that do are merely a statistical error, and can therefore be ignored.

However, Gaspode had found he did tend to get heard on a subconscious level. Only the previous day someone had absent-mindedly kicked him into the gutter and had gone a few steps before they suddenly thought: I'm a bastard, what am I?

---

* This is *another* survival trait.

'There is something up there,' said Carrot. 'Look . . . something blue, hanging off that gargoyle.'

'Woof woof, *woof*! Would you *credit* it?'

Vimes stood on Carrot's shoulders and walked his hand up the wall, but the little blue strip was still out of reach.

The gargoyle rolled a stony eye towards him.

'Do you mind?' said Vimes. 'It's hanging on your ear . . .'

With a grinding of stone on stone, the gargoyle reached up a hand and unhooked the intrusive material.

'Thank you.'

'''on't ent-on it.'

Vimes climbed down again.

'You like gargoyles, don't you, captain,' said Carrot, as they strolled away.

'Yep. They may only be a kind of troll but they keep themselves to themselves and seldom go below the first floor and don't commit crimes anyone ever finds out about. My type of people.'

He unfolded the strip.

It was a collar or, at least, what remained of a collar – it was burnt at both ends. The word 'Chubby' was just readable through the soot.

'The devils!' said Vimes. 'They *did* blow up a dragon!'

The most dangerous man in the world should be introduced.

He has never, in his entire life, harmed a living creature. He has dissected a few, but only after they were dead,* and had marvelled at how well they'd been put together considering it had been done by unskilled labour. For several years he hadn't moved outside a large, airy room, but this was OK, because he spent most of his time inside his own head in any case. There's a certain type of person it's very hard to imprison.

He had, however, surmised that an hour's exercise every day was essential for a healthy appetite and proper bowel movements, and was currently sitting on a machine of his own invention.

It consisted of a saddle above a pair of treadles which turned, by means of a chain, a large wooden wheel currently held off the ground on a metal stand. Another, freewheeling, wooden wheel was positioned in front of the saddle and could be turned by means of a tiller arrangement. He'd fitted the extra wheel and tiller so

---

* Because he was an early form of free-thinking scientist, and did not believe that human beings had been created by some sort of divine being. Dissecting people when they were still alive tended to be a priestly preoccupation; they thought mankind *had* been created by some sort of divine being and wanted to have a closer look at His handiwork.

that he could wheel the entire thing over to the wall when he'd finished taking his exercise and, besides, it gave the whole thing a pleasing symmetry.

He called it 'the-turning-the-wheel-with-pedals-and-another-wheel-machine'.

Lord Vetinari was also at work.

Normally, he was in the Oblong Office or seated in his plain wooden chair at the foot of the steps in the palace of Ankh-Morpork; there was an ornate throne at the top of the steps, covered with dust. It was the throne of Ankh-Morpork and was, indeed, made of gold. He'd never dreamed of sitting on it.

But it was a nice day, so he was working in the garden.

Visitors to Ankh-Morpork were often surprised to find that there were some interesting gardens attached to the Patrician's Palace.

The Patrician was not a gardens kind of person. But some of his predecessors had been, and Lord Vetinari never changed or destroyed anything if there was no logical reason to do so. He maintained the little zoo, and the racehorse stable, and even recognized that the gardens themselves were of extreme historic interest because this was so obviously the case.

They had been laid out by Bloody Stupid Johnson.

Many great landscape gardeners have gone down in history and been remembered in a very solid way by the magnificent parks and gardens that they designed with almost god-like power and fore-sight, thinking nothing of making lakes and shifting hills and planting woodlands to enable future generations to appreciate the sublime beauty of wild Nature transformed by Man. There have been Capability Brown, Sagacity Smith, Intuition De Vere Slade-Gore . . .

In Ankh-Morpork, there was Bloody Stupid Johnson.

Bloody Stupid 'It Might Look A Bit Messy Now But Just You Come Back In Five Hundred Years' Time' Johnson. Bloody Stupid 'Look, The Plans Were The Right Way Round When I Drew Them' Johnson. Bloody Stupid Johnson, who had 2,000 tons of earth built into an artificial hillock in front of Quirm Manor because 'It'd drive me mad to have to look at a bunch of trees and mountains all day long, how about you?'

The Ankh-Morpork palace grounds were considered the high spot, if such it could be called, of his career. For example, they contained the ornamental trout lake, one hundred and fifty yards long and, because of one of those trifling errors of notation that were such a distinctive feature of Bloody Stupid's designs, one inch wide. It was the home of one trout, which was quite comfortable provided it didn't try to turn around, and had once featured an ornate fountain which, when first switched on, did nothing but groan ominously for five minutes and then fire a small stone cherub a thousand feet into the air.

It contained the hoho, which was like a haha only deeper. A haha is a concealed ditch and wall designed to allow landowners to look out across rolling vistas without getting cattle and inconvenient poor people wandering across the lawns. Under Bloody Stupid's errant pencil it was dug fifty feet deep and had claimed three gardeners already.

The maze was so small that people got lost looking *for* it.

But the Patrician rather liked the gardens, in a quiet kind of way. He had certain views about the mentality of most of mankind, and the gardens made him feel fully justified.

Piles of paper were stacked on the lawn around the chair. Clerks renewed them or took them away periodically. They were different clerks. All sorts and types of information flowed into the Palace, but there was only one place where it all came together, very much like strands of gossamer coming together in the centre of a web.

A great many rulers, good and bad and quite often dead, know what happened; a rare few actually manage, by dint of much effort, to know what's happening. Lord Vetinari considered both types to lack ambition.

'Yes, Dr Cruces,' he said, without looking up.

How the *hell* does he do it? Cruces wondered. I know I didn't make any noise . . .

'Ah, Havelock—' he began.

'You have something to tell me, doctor?'

'It's been . . . mislaid.'

'Yes. And no doubt you are anxiously seeking it. Very well. Good day.'

The Patrician hadn't moved his head the whole time. He hadn't even bothered to ask what it was. He bloody well knows, thought Cruces. How is it you can never tell him anything he doesn't know?

Lord Vetinari put down a piece of paper on one of the piles, and picked up another.

'You are still here, Dr Cruces.'

'I can assure you, m'Lord, that—'

'I'm sure you can. I'm sure you can. There is one question that intrigues me, however.'

'M'Lord?'

'Why was it in your Guild House to be stolen? I had been given to understand it had been destroyed. I'm quite sure I gave orders.'

This was the question the Assassin had been hoping would not be asked. But the Patrician was good at that game.

'Er. We – that is, my *predecessor* – thought it should serve as a warning and an example.'

The Patrician looked up and smiled brightly.

'Capital!' he said. 'I have always had a *great* belief in the effectiveness of examples. So I am sure you'll be able to sort this out with minimum inconvenience all round.'

'Certainly, m'Lord,' said the Assassin, glumly. 'But—'

Noon began.

Noon in Ankh-Morpork took some time, since twelve o'clock was established by consensus. Generally, the first bell to start was that one in the Teachers' Guild, in response to the universal prayers of its members. Then the water clock on the Temple of Small Gods would trigger the big bronze gong. The black bell in the Temple of Fate struck once, unexpectedly, but by then the silver pedal-driven carillon in the Fools' Guild would be tinkling, the gongs, bells and chimes of all the Guilds and temples would be in full swing, and it was impossible to tell them apart, except for the tongueless and magical octiron bell of Old Tom in the Unseen University clock tower, whose twelve measured silences temporarily overruled the din.

And finally, several strokes behind all the others, was the bell of the Assassins' Guild, which was always last.

Beside the Patrician, the ornamental sundial chimed twice and fell over.

'You were saying?' said the Patrician mildly.

'Captain Vimes,' said Dr Cruces. 'He's taking an interest.'

'Dear me. But it is his job.'

'Really? I must demand that you call him off!'

The words echoed around the garden. Several pigeons flew away.

'Demand?' said the Patrician, sweetly.

Dr Cruces backed and filled desperately. 'He is a servant after all,' he said. 'I see no reason why he should be allowed to involve himself in affairs that don't concern him.'

'I rather believe he thinks he's a servant of the law,' said the Patrician.

'He's a jack-in-office and an insolent upstart!'

'Dear me. I did not appreciate your strength of feeling. But since you demand it, I will bring him to heel without delay.'

'Thank you.'

'Don't mention it. Do not let me keep you.'

Dr Cruces wandered off in the direction of the Patrician's idle gesture.

Lord Vetinari bent over his paperwork again, and did not even look up when there was a distant, muffled cry. Instead, he reached down and rang a small silver bell.

A clerk hurried up.

'Go and fetch the ladder, will you, Drumknott?'he said. 'Dr Cruces seems to have fallen in the hoho.'

The back door to the dwarf Bjorn Hammerhock's workshop lifted off the latch and creaked open. He went to see if there was anyone there, and shivered.

He shut the door.

'Bit of a chilly breeze,' he said, to the room's other occupant. 'Still, we could do with it.'

The ceiling of the workshop was only about five feet above the floor. That was more than tall enough for a dwarf.

Ow, said a voice that no one heard.

Hammerhock looked at the thing clamped in the vice, and picked up a screwdriver.

Ow.

'Amazing,' he said. 'I *think* that moving this tube down the barrel forces the, er, six chambers to slide along, presenting a new one to the, er, firing hole. That seems clear enough. The triggering mechanism is really just a tinderbox device. The spring . . . *here* . . . has rusted through. I can easily replace that. You know,' he said, looking up, 'this is a very interesting device. With the chemicals in the tubes and all. Such a *simple* idea. Is it a clown thing? Some kind of automatic slap-stick?'

He sorted through a bin of metal offcuts to find a piece of steel, and then selected a file.

'I'd like to make a few sketches afterwards,' he said.

About thirty seconds later there was a *pop* and a cloud of smoke.

Bjorn Hammerhock picked himself up, shaking his head.

'That was lucky!' he said. 'Could have been a nasty accident there.' He tried to fan some of the smoke away, and then reached for the file again.

His hand went through it.

AHEM.

Bjorn tried again.

The file was as insubstantial as the smoke.

'What?'

AHEM.

The owner of the strange device was staring in horror at something on the floor. Bjorn followed his gaze.

'Oh,' he said. Realization, which had been hovering on the edge of Bjorn's consciousness, finally dawned. That was the thing about death. When it happened to you, you were among the first to know.

His visitor grabbed the device from the bench and rammed it into a cloth bag. Then he looked around wildly, picked up the corpse of Mr Hammerhock, and dragged it through the door towards the river.

There was a distant splash, or as close to a splash as you could get from the Ankh.

'Oh dear,' said Bjorn. 'And I can't swim, either.'

THAT WILL NOT, OF COURSE, BE A PROBLEM, said Death.

Bjorn looked at him.

'You're a lot shorter than I thought you'd be,' he said.

THIS IS BECAUSE I'M KNEELING DOWN, MR HAMMERHOCK.

'That damn thing *killed* me!'

YES.

'That's the first time anything like that has *ever* happened to me.'

TO ANYONE. BUT NOT, I SUSPECT, THE LAST TIME.

Death stood up. There was a clicking of knee joints. He no longer cracked his skull on the ceiling. There wasn't a ceiling any more. The room had gently faded away.

There were such things as dwarf gods. Dwarfs were not a naturally religious species, but in a world where pit props could crack without warning and pockets of fire damp could suddenly explode they'd seen the need for gods as the sort of supernatural equivalent of a hard hat. Besides, when you hit your thumb with an eight-pound hammer it's nice to be able to blaspheme. It takes a very special and strong-minded kind of atheist to jump up and down with their hand clasped under their other armpit and shout, 'Oh, random-fluctuations-in-the-space-time-continuum!' or 'Aaargh, primitive-and-outmoded-concept on a crutch!'

Bjorn didn't waste time asking questions. A lot of things become a shade urgent when you're dead.

'I believe in reincarnation,' he said.

I KNOW.

'I tried to live a good life. Does that help?'

THAT IS NOT UP TO ME. Death coughed. OF COURSE, . . . SINCE YOU BELIEVE IN REINCARNATION . . . YOU'LL BE BJORN AGAIN.

He waited.

'Yes. That's right,' said Bjorn. Dwarfs are known for their sense of humour, in a way. People point them out and say: 'Those little devils haven't *got* a sense of humour.'

306

UM. WAS THERE ANYTHING AMUSING IN THE STATEMENT I JUST MADE?

'Uh. No. No . . . I don't think so.'

IT WAS A PUN, OR PLAY ON WORDS. BJORN AGAIN.

'Yes?'

DID YOU NOTICE IT?

'I can't say I did.'

OH.

'Sorry.'

I'VE BEEN TOLD I SHOULD TRY TO MAKE THE OCCASION A LITTLE MORE ENJOYABLE.

'Bjorn again.'

YES.

'I'll think about it.'

THANK YOU.

'Hright,' said Sergeant Colon, 'this, men, is your truncheon, also nomenclatured your night stick or baton of office.' He paused while he tried to remember his army days, and brightened up.

'*Hand* you will look *after* hit,' he shouted. 'You will eat with hit, you will sleep with hit, you—'

''Scuse me.'

'Who said that?'

'Down here. It's me, Lance-Constable Cuddy.'

'Yes, pilgrim?'

'How do we eat with it, sergeant?'

Sergeant Colon's wound-up machismo wound down. He was suspicious of Lance-Constable Cuddy. He strongly suspected Lance-Constable Cuddy was a trouble-maker.

'What?'

'Well, do we use it as a knife or a fork or cut in half for chopsticks or what?'

'What are you talking about?'

'Excuse me, sergeant?'

'What *is* it, Lance-Constable Angua?'

'How exactly do we sleep with it, sir?'

'Well, I . . . I meant . . . *Corporal Nobbs, stop that sniggering right now!*' Colon adjusted his breastplate and decided to strike out in a new direction.

'Now, hwat we have 'ere is a puppet, mommet or heffigy' – indicating a vaguely humanoid shape made of leather and stuffed with straw, mounted on a stake – 'called by the hnickname of Harthur, weapons training, for the use hof. Forward, Lance-

Constable Angua. Tell me, Lance-Constable, do you think you could kill a man?'

'How long will I have?'

There was a pause while they picked up Corporal Nobbs and patted him on the back until he settled down.

'Very well,' said Sergeant Colon, 'what you must do now is take your truncheon like *so*, and on the command one, proceed smartly to Harthur and on the command two, tap him smartly upon the bonce. Hwun . . . two . . .'

The truncheon bounced off Arthur's helmet.

'Very good, only one thing wrong. Anyone tell me what it was?'

They shook their heads.

'From *behind*,' said Sergeant Colon. 'You hit 'em from *behind*. No sense in risking trouble, is there? Now you have a go, Lance-Constable Cuddy.'

'But sarge—'

'Do it.'

They watched.

'Perhaps we could fetch him a chair?' said Angua, after an embarrassing fifteen seconds.

Detritus sniggered.

'Him too *little* to be a guard,' he said.

Lance-Constable Cuddy stopped jumping up and down.

'Sorry, sergeant,' he said, 'this isn't how dwarfs do it, see?'

'It's how *guards* do it,' said Sergeant Colon. 'All right, Lance-Constable Detritus – *don't salute* – you give it a try.'

Detritus held the truncheon between what must technically be called thumb and forefinger, and smashed it over Arthur's helmet. He stared reflectively at the truncheon's stump. Then he bunched up his, for want of a better word, fist, and hammered Arthur over what was briefly its head until the stake was driven three feet into the ground.

'Now the dwarf, he can have a go,' he said.

There was another embarrassed five seconds. Sergeant Colon cleared his throat.

'Well, yes, I think we can consider him thoroughly apprehended,' he said. 'Make a note, Corporal Nobbs. Lance-Constable Detritus – *don't salute!* – deducted one dollar for loss of truncheon. And you're supposed to be able to ask 'em questions afterwards.'

He looked at the remains of Arthur.

'I think around about now is a good time to demonstrate the fine points of harchery,' he said.

*

308

Lady Sybil Ramkin looked at the sad strip of leather that was all that remained of the late Chubby.

'Who'd do something like this to a poor little dragon?' she said.

'We're trying to find out,' said Vimes. 'We . . . we think maybe he was tied up next to a wall and exploded.'

Carrot leaned over the wall of a pen.

'Coochee-coochee-coo?' he said. A friendly flame took his eyebrows off.

'I mean, he was as tame as anything,' said Lady Ramkin. 'Wouldn't hurt a fly, poor little thing.'

'How could someone make a dragon blow up?' said Vimes. 'Could you do it by giving it a kick?'

'Oh, yes,' said Sybil. 'You'd lose your leg, mind you.'

'Then it wasn't that. Any other way? So you wouldn't get hurt?'

'Not really. It'd be easier to make it blow itself up. Really, Sam, I don't like talking about—'

'I have to know.'

'Well . . . at this time of year the males fight. Make themselves look big, you know? That's why I always keep them apart.'

Vimes shook his head. 'There was only one dragon,' he said.

Behind them, Carrot leaned over the next pen, where a pear-shaped male dragon opened one eye and glared at him.

'Whosagoodboyden?' murmured Carrot. 'I'm sure I've got a bit of coal somewhere—'

The dragon opened the other eye, blinked, and then was fully awake and rearing up. Its ears flattened. Its nostrils flared. Its wings unfurled. It breathed in. From its stomach came the gurgle of rushing acids as sluices and valves were opened. Its feet left the floor. Its chest expanded—

Vimes hit Carrot at waist height, bearing him to the ground.

In its pen the dragon blinked. The enemy had mysteriously gone. Scared off!

It subsided, blowing off a huge flame.

Vimes unclasped his hands from his head and rolled over.

'What'd do you do that for, captain?' said Carrot. 'I wasn't—'

'It was attacking a dragon!' shouted Vimes. 'One that wouldn't back down!'

He pulled himself to his knees and tapped Carrot's breastplate.

'You polish that up real bright!' he said. 'You can see yourself in it. So can anything else!'

'Oh, yes, of course there's *that*,' said Lady Sybil. 'Everyone knows you should keep dragons away from mirrors—'

'Mirrors,' said Carrot. 'Hey, there were bits of—'

'Yes. He showed Chubby a mirror,' said Vimes.

'The poor little thing must have been trying to make himself bigger than himself,' said Carrot.

'We're dealing here,' said Vimes, 'with a twisted mind.'

'Oh, no! You think so?'

'Yes.'

'But . . . no . . . you can't be right. Because Nobby was with us all the time.'

'*Not* Nobby,' said Vimes testily. 'Whatever he might do to a dragon, I doubt if he'd make it explode. There's stranger people in this world than Corporal Nobbs, my lad.'

Carrot's expression slid into a rictus of intrigued horror.

'Gosh,' he said.

Sergeant Colon surveyed the butts. Then he removed his helmet and wiped his forehead.

'I think perhaps Lance-Constable Angua shouldn't have another go with the longbow until we've worked out how to stop her . . . her getting in the way.'

'Sorry, sergeant.'

They turned to Detritus, who was standing sheepishly behind a heap of broken longbows. Crossbows were out of the question. They sat in his massive hands like a hairpin. In theory the longbow would be a deadly weapon in his hands, just as soon as he mastered the art of when to let go.

Detritus shrugged.

'Sorry, mister,' he said. 'Bows aren't troll weapon.'

'Ha!' said Colon. 'As for you, Lance-Constable Cuddy—'

'Just can't get the hang of aiming, sergeant.'

'I thought dwarfs were famous for their skills in battle!'

'Yeah, but . . . not these skills,' said Cuddy.

'Ambush,' murmured Detritus.

Since he was a troll, the murmur bounced off distant buildings. Cuddy's beard bristled.

'You devious troll, I get my—'

'Well now,' said Sergeant Colon quickly, 'I think we'll stop training. You'll have to . . . sort of pick it up as you go along, all right?'

He sighed. He was not a cruel man, but he'd been either a soldier or a guard all his life, and he was feeling put-upon. Otherwise he wouldn't have said what he said next.

'I don't know, I really don't. Fighting among yourselves, smashing your own weapons . . . I mean, who do we think we're fooling?

Now, it's nearly noon, you take a few hours off, we'll see you again tonight. If you think it's worth turning up.'

There was a *spang*! noise. Cuddy's crossbow had gone off in his hand. The bolt whiffled past Corporal Nobbs's ear and landed in the river, where it stuck.

'Sorry,' said Cuddy.

'Tsk, tsk,' said Sergeant Colon.

That was the worst part. It would have been better all round if he'd called the dwarf some names. It would have been better if he'd made it seem that Cuddy was worth an insult.

He turned around and walked off towards Pseudopolis Yard.

They heard his muttered comment.

'What him say?' said Detritus.

'"A fine body of *men*",' said Angua, going red.

Cuddy spat on the ground, which didn't take long on account of its closeness. Then he reached under his cloak and produced, like a conjuror extracting a size 10 rabbit from a size 5 hat, his doubleheaded battle axe. And started to run.

By the time he reached the virginal target he was a blur. There was a rip and the dummy exploded like a nuclear haystack.

The other two wandered up and inspected the result, as pieces of chaff gently drifted to the ground.

'Yes, all right,' said Angua. 'But he did say you're supposed to be able to ask them questions afterwards.'

'He didn't say they've got to be able to answer them,' said Cuddy grimly.

'Lance-Constable Cuddy, deduct one dollar for target,' said Detritus, who already owed eleven dollars for bows.

'"If it's worth turning up"!' said Cuddy, losing the axe somewhere about his person again. 'Speciesist!'

'I don't think he meant it that way,' said Angua.

'Ho, it's all right for *you*,' said Cuddy.

'Why?'

''Cos you a *man*,' said Detritus.

Angua was bright enough to pause for a moment to think this over.

'A woman,' she said.

'Same thing.'

'Only in broad terms. Come on, let's go and have a drink . . .'

The transient moment of camaraderie in adversity completely evaporated.

'Drink with a troll?'

'Drink with a dwarf?'

'All right,' said Angua. 'How about *you* and *you* coming and having a drink with *me*?'

Angua removed her helmet and shook out her hair. Female trolls don't have hair, although the more fortunate ones are able to cultivate a fine growth of lichen, and a female dwarf is more likely to be complimented on the silkiness of her beard than on her scalp. But it was just possible the sight of Angua scraped little sparks off some shared, ancient, cosmic maleness.

'I haven't really had a chance to look around,' she said. 'But I saw a place in Gleam Street.'

Which meant that they had to cross the river, at least two of them trying to indicate to passers-by that they weren't with at least one of the other two. Which meant that, with desperate nonchalance, they were looking around.

Which meant that Cuddy saw the dwarf in the water.

If you could call it water.

If you could still call it a dwarf.

They looked down.

'You know,' said Detritus, after a while, 'that look like that dwarf who make weapons in Rime Street.'

'Bjorn Hammerhock?' said Cuddy.

'That the one, yeah.'

'It looks a *bit* like him,' Cuddy conceded, still talking in a cold flat voice, 'but not *exactly* like him.'

'What d'you mean?' said Angua.

'Because Mr Hammerhock,' said Cuddy, 'didn't have such a great big hole where his chest should be.'

Doesn't he ever sleep? thought Vimes. Doesn't the bloody man ever get his head down? Isn't there a room somewhere with a black dressing gown hanging on the door?

He knocked on the door of the Oblong Office.

'Ah, captain,' said the Patrician, looking up from his paperwork. 'You were commendably quick.'

'Was I?'

'You got my message?' said Lord Vetinari.

'No, sir. I've been . . . occupied.'

'Indeed. And what could occupy you?'

'Someone has killed Mr Hammerhock, sir. A big man in the dwarf community. He's been . . . shot with something, some kind of siege weapon or something, and dumped in the river. We've just fished him out. I was on the way to tell his wife. I think he lives in Treacle Street. And then I thought, since I was passing . . .'

'This is very unfortunate.'

'Certainly it was for Mr Hammerhock,' said Vimes.

The Patrician leaned back and stared at Vimes.

'Tell me,' he said, 'how was he killed?'

'I don't know. I've never seen anything like it . . . there was just a great big hole. But I'm going to find out what it was.'

'Hmm. Did I mention that Dr Cruces came to see me this morning?'

'No, sir.'

'He was very . . . concerned.'

'Yes, sir.'

'I think you upset him.'

'Sir?'

The Patrician seemed to be reaching a decision. His chair thumped forward.

'Captain Vimes—'

'Sir?'

'I know that you are retiring the day after tomorrow and feel, therefore, a little . . . restless. But while you are captain of the Night Watch I am asking you to follow two very specific instructions . . .'

'Sir?'

'You will cease *any* investigations connected with this theft from the Assassins' Guild. Do you understand? It is entirely Guild business.'

'Sir.' Vimes kept his face carefully immobile.

'I'm choosing to believe that the unspoken word in that sentence was a *yes*, captain.'

'Sir.'

'And that one, too. As for the matter of the unfortunate Mr Hammerhock . . . The body was discovered just a short while ago?'

'Yes, sir.'

'Then it's out of your jurisdiction, captain.'

'What? Sir?'

'The Day Watch can deal with it.'

'But we've *never* bothered with that hours-of-daylight jurisdiction stuff!'

'Nevertheless, in the current circumstances I shall instruct Captain Quirke to take over the investigation, if it turns out that one is necessary.'

If one is necessary. If people don't end up with half their chest gone by accident. Meteorite strike, perhaps, thought Vimes.

He took a deep breath and leaned on the Patrician's desk.

'Mayonnaise Quirke couldn't find his arse with an atlas! And he's got no idea about how to talk to dwarfs! He calls them gritsuckers! My men found the body! It's my jurisdiction!'

The Patrician glanced at Vimes's hands. Vimes removed them from the desk as if it had suddenly grown red-hot.

'Night Watch. That's what you are, captain. Your writ runs in the hours of darkness.'

'It's *dwarfs* we're talking about! If we don't get it right, they'll take the law into their own hands! That usually means chopping the head off the nearest troll! And you'll put *Quirke* on this?'

'I've given you an order, captain.'

'But—'

'You may go.'

'You can't—'

'I said you may *go*, Captain Vimes!'

'*Sir.*'

Vimes saluted. Then he turned about, and marched out of the room. He closed the door carefully, so that there was barely a click.

The Patrician heard him thump the wall outside. Vimes wasn't aware, but there were a number of barely perceptible dents in the wall outside the Oblong Office, their depths corresponding to his emotional state at the time.

By the sound of it, this one would need the services of a plasterer.

Lord Vetinari permitted himself a smile, although there was no humour in it.

The city *operated*. It was a self-regulating college of Guilds linked by the inexorable laws of mutual self-interest, and it *worked*. On average. By and large. Overall. Normally.

The last thing you needed was some Watchman blundering around upsetting things, like a loose . . . a loose . . . a loose siege catapult.

Normally.

Vimes seemed in a suitable emotional state. With any luck, the orders would have the desired effect . . .

There's a bar like it in every big city. It's where the coppers drink.

The Guard seldom drank in Ankh-Morpork's more cheerful taverns when they were off duty. It was too easy to see something that would put them back on duty again.* So they generally went to The Bucket, in Gleam Street. It was small and low-ceilinged,

* Suicide, for example. Murder was in fact a fairly uncommon event in Ankh-Morpork, but there were a lot of suicides. Walking in the night-time alleyways of The Shades was suicide. Asking for a short in a dwarf bar was suicide. Saying 'Got rocks in your head?' to a troll was suicide. You could commit suicide very easily, if you weren't careful.

and the presence of city guards tended to discourage other drinkers. But Mr Cheese, the owner, wasn't too worried about this. No one drinks like a copper who has seen too much to stay sober.

Carrot counted out his change on the counter.

'That's three beers, one milk, one molten sulphur on coke with phosphoric acid—'

'With umbrella in it,' said Detritus.

'—and A Slow Comfortable Double-Entendre with lemonade.'

'With a fruit salad in it,' said Nobby.

'Woof?'

'And some beer in a bowl,' said Angua.

'That little dog seems to have taken quite a shine to you,' said Carrot.

'Yes,' said Angua. 'I can't think why.'

The drinks were put in front of them. They stared at the drinks. They drank the drinks.

Mr Cheese, who knew coppers, wordlessly refilled the glasses and Detritus' insulated mug.

They stared at the drinks. They drank the drinks.

'You know,' said Colon, after a while, 'what gets me, what really *gets* me, is they just dumped him in the water. I mean, not even weights. Just dumped him. Like it didn't matter if he was found. You know what I mean?'

'What gets *me*,' said Cuddy, 'is that he was a dwarf.'

'What gets me is that he was murdered,' said Carrot.

Mr Cheese passed along the line again. They stared at the drinks. They drank the drinks.

Because the fact was that, despite all evidence to the contrary, murder was not a commonplace occurrence in Ankh-Morpork. There were, it was true, assassinations. And as aforesaid there were many ways one could inadvertently commit suicide. And there were occasional domestic fracas on a Saturday night as people sought a cheaper alternative to divorce. There were all these things, but at least they had a *reason*, however unreasonable.

'Big man in the dwarfs, was Mr Hammerhock,' said Carrot. 'A good citizen, too. Wasn't always stirring up old trouble like Mr Stronginthearm.'

'He's got a workshop in Rime Street,' said Nobby.

'Had,' said Sergeant Colon.

They stared at the drinks. They drank the drinks.

'What I want to know *is*,' said Angua, 'what put that hole in him?'

'Never see anything like that,' said Colon.

'Hadn't someone better go and tell Mrs Hammerhock?' said Angua.

'Captain Vimes is doing it,' said Carrot. 'He said he wouldn't ask anyone else to do it.'

'Rather him than me,' said Colon fervently. 'I wouldn't do that for a big clock. They can be fearsome when they're angry, those little buggers.'

Everyone nodded gloomily, including the little bugger and the bigger little bugger by adoption.

They stared at the drinks. They drank the drinks.

'Shouldn't we be finding out who did it?' said Angua.

'Why?' said Nobby.

She opened and shut her mouth once or twice, and finally came out with: 'In case they do it again?'

'It wasn't an assassination, was it?' said Cuddy.

'No,' said Carrot. 'They always leave a note. By law.'

They looked at the drinks. They drank the drinks.

'What a city,' said Angua.

'It all works, that's the funny thing,' said Carrot. 'D'you know, when I first joined the Watch I was so simple I arrested the head of the Thieves' Guild for thieving?'

'Sounds good to me,' said Angua.

'Got into a bit of trouble for that,' said Carrot.

'You see,' said Colon, 'thieves are *organized* here. I mean, it's *official*. They're *allowed* a certain amount of thieving. Not that they do much these days, mind you. If you pay them a little premium every year they give you a card and leave you alone. Saves time and effort all round.'

'And all thieves are members?' said Angua.

'Oh, *yes*,' said Carrot. 'Can't go thieving in Ankh-Morpork without a Guild permit. Not unless you've got a special talent.'

'Why? What happens? What *talent*?' she said.

'Well, like being able to survive being hung upside down from one of the gates with your ears nailed to your knees,' said Carrot.

Then Angua said: 'That's terrible.'

'Yes, I know. But the thing is,' said Carrot, 'the thing is: it works. The whole thing. Guilds and organized crimes and everything. It all seems to work.'

'Didn't work for Mr Hammerhock,' said Sergeant Colon.

They looked at their drinks. Very slowly, like a mighty sequoia beginning the first step towards resurrection as a million Save The Trees leaflets, Detritus toppled backwards with his mug still in his hand. Apart from the 90° change in position, he didn't move a muscle.

'It's the sulphur,' said Cuddy, without looking around. 'It goes right to their heads.'

Carrot thumped his fist on the bar.

We ought to do something!'

'We could nick his boots,' said Nobby.

'I mean about Mr Hammerhock.'

'Oh, yeah, yeah,' said Nobby. 'You sound like old Vimesy. If we was to worry about every dead body in this town—'

'But not like this!' snapped Carrot. 'Normally it's just . . . well . . . suicide, or Guild fighting, stuff like that. But he was just a dwarf! Pillar of the community! Spent all day making swords and axes and burial weapons and crossbows and torture implements! And then he's in the river with a great big hole in his chest! Who's going to do anything about it, if not us?'

'You been putting anything in your milk?' said Colon. 'Look, the dwarfs can sort it out. It's like Quarry Lane. Don't stick your nose where someone can pull it off and eat it.'

'We're the *City* Watch,' said Carrot. 'That doesn't mean just that part of the city who happens to be over four feet tall and made of flesh!'

'No dwarf did it,' said Cuddy, who was swaying gently. 'No troll, neither.' He tried to tap the side of his nose, and missed. 'The reason being, he still had all his arms and legs on.'

'Captain Vimes'll want it investigated,' said Carrot.

'Captain Vimes is trying to learn to be a civilian,' said Nobby.

'Well, I'm not going to—' Colon began, and got off his stool.

He hopped. He jumped up and down a bit, his mouth opening and shutting. Then the words managed to come out.

'My foot!'

'What about your foot?'

'Something stuck in it!'

He hopped backwards, clutching at one sandal, and fell over Detritus.

'You'd be amazed what can get stuck to your boots in this town,' said Carrot.

'There's something on the bottom of your sandal,' said Angua. 'Stop waving it about, you silly man.'

She drew her dagger.

'Bit of card or something. With a drawing pin in it. You picked it up somewhere. Probably took a while for you to tread it through . . . there.'

'Bit of card?' said Carrot.

'There's something written on it . . .' Angua scraped away the mud.

317

'What does that mean?' she said.

'I don't know. Something's gone, I suppose. Perhaps it's Mr Gonne's visiting card, whoever he is,' said Nobby. 'Who cares? Let's have ano—'

Carrot took the card and turned it over and over in his hands.

'Save the pin,' said Cuddy. 'You only get five of them for a penny. My cousin Gimick makes them.'

'This is important,' said Carrot, slowly. 'The captain ought to know about this. I think he was looking for it.'

'What's important about it?' said Sergeant Colon. 'Apart from my foot hurting like blazes.'

'I don't know. The captain'll know,' said Carrot stubbornly.

'You tell him, then,' said Colon. 'He's staying up at her ladyship's now.'

'Learning to be a gentleman,' said Nobby.

'I'm *going* to tell him,' said Carrot.

Angua glanced through the grubby window. The moon would be up soon. That was one trouble with cities. The damn thing could be lurking behind a tower if you weren't careful.

'And I'd better be getting back to my lodgings,' she said.

'I'll accompany you,' said Carrot, quickly. 'I ought to go and find Captain Vimes in any case.'

'It'll be out of your way . . .'

'Honestly, I'd like to.'

She looked at his earnest expression.

'I couldn't put you to the trouble,' she said.

'That's all right. I like walking. It helps me think.'

Angua smiled, despite her desperation.

They stepped out into the softer heat of the evening. Instinctively, Carrot settled into the policeman's pace.

'Very old street, this,' he said. 'They say there's an underground stream under it. I read that. What do you think?'

'Do you really like walking?' said Angua, falling into step.

'Oh, yes. There are many interesting byways and historical buildings to be seen. I often go for walks on my day off.'

She looked at his face. Ye gods, she thought.

'Why did you join the Watch?' she said.

'My father said it'd make a man of me.'

'It seems to have worked.'

'Yes. It's the best job there is.'

'Really?'

'Oh, yes. Do you know what "policeman" means?'

Angua shrugged. 'No.'

'It means "man of the *polis*". That's an old word for city.'

'Yes?'

'I read it in a book. Man of the city.'

She glanced sideways at him again. His face glowed in the light of a torch on the street corner, but it had some inner glow of its own.

He's *proud*. She remembered the oath.

Proud of being in the damn *Watch*, for gods' sake—

'Why did *you* join?' he said.

'Me? Oh, I . . . I like to eat meals and sleep indoors. Anyway, there isn't that much choice, is there? It was that or become . . . hah . . . a seamstress.'*

'And you're not very good at sewing?'

Angua's sharp glance saw nothing but honest innocence in his face.

'Yes,' she said, giving up, 'that's right. And then I saw this poster. "The City Watche Needs Men! Be A Man In The City Watche!" So I thought I'd give it a go. After all, I'd only have something to gain.'

She waited to see if he'd fail to pick this one up, too. He did.

'Sergeant Colon wrote the notice,' said Carrot. 'He's a fairly direct thinker.'

He sniffed.

'Can you smell something?' he said. 'Smells like . . . a bit like someone's thrown away an old privy carpet?'

'Oh, thank you very much,' said a voice very low down, somewhere in the darkness. 'Oh, yes. Thank you very much. That's very wossname of you. Old privy carpet. Oh, yes.'

'Can't smell anything,' Angua lied.

'Liar,' said the voice.

'Or hear anything.'

Captain Vimes's boots told him he was in Scoone Avenue. His feet were doing the walking of their own volition; his mind was somewhere else. In fact, some of it was dissolving gently in Jimkin Bearhugger's finest nectar.

---

* A survey by the Ankh-Morpork Guild of Merchants of tradespeople in the dock areas of Morpork found 987 women who gave their profession as 'seamstress'. Oh . . . and two needles.

If only they hadn't been so damn *polite*! There were a number of things he'd seen in his life which he'd always try, without success, to forget. Up until now he would have put, at the top of the list, looking at the tonsils of a giant dragon as it drew the breath intended to turn him into a small pile of impure charcoal. He still woke up sweating at the memory of the little pilot light. But he dreaded now that it was going to be replaced by the recollection of all those impassive dwarf faces, watching him politely, and the feeling that his words were dropping into a deep pit.

After all, what could he say? 'Sorry he's dead – and that's official. We're putting our worst men on the case'?

The late Bjorn Hammerhock's house had been full of dwarfs – silent, owlish, *polite* dwarfs. The news had got around. He wasn't telling anyone anything they didn't know. Many of them were holding weapons. Mr Stronginthearm was there. Captain Vimes had talked to him before about his speeches on the subject of the need for grinding all trolls in little bits and using them to make roads. But the dwarf wasn't saying anything now. He was just looking smug. There was an air of quiet, *polite* menace, that said: We'll listen to you. Then we'll do what we decide to do.

He hadn't even been sure which one was Mrs Hammerhock. They all looked alike to him. When she was introduced – helmeted, bearded – he'd got polite, non-committal answers. No, she'd locked his workshop and seemed to have mislaid the key. Thank you.

He'd tried to indicate as subtly as possible that a wholesale march on Quarry Lane would be frowned upon by the guard (probably from a vantage point at a safe distance) but hadn't the face to spell it out. He couldn't say: don't take matters into your own hands for the guard are mightily in pursuit of the wrongdoer, because he didn't have a clue where to start. Had your husband any enemies? Yes, someone put a huge great hole in him, but apart from *that*, did he have any enemies?

So he'd extracted himself with as much dignity as possible, which wasn't very much, and after a battle with himself which he'd lost, he'd picked up half a bottle of Bearhugger's Old Persnickety and wandered into the night.

Carrot and Angua reached the end of Gleam Street.

'Where are you staying?' said Carrot.

'Just down there.' She pointed.

'Elm Street? Not *Mrs Cake's*?'

'Yes. Why not? I just wanted a clean place, reasonably priced. What's wrong with that?'

'Well . . . I mean, I've nothing against Mrs Cake, a lovely woman, one of the best . . . but . . . well . . . you must have noticed . . .'

'Noticed what?'

'Well . . . she's not very . . . you know . . . *choosy*.'

'Sorry. I'm still not with you.'

'You must have seen some of the other guests? I mean, doesn't Reg Shoe still have lodgings there?'

'Oh, said Angua, 'you mean the zombie.'

'And there's a banshee in the attic.'

'Mr Ixolite. Yes.'

'And there's old Mrs Drull.'

'The ghoul. But she's retired. She does children's party catering now.'

'I mean, doesn't it strike you the place is a bit odd?'

'But the rates are reasonable and the beds are clean.'

'I shouldn't think anyone ever sleeps in them.'

'All *right*! I had to take what I could *get*!'

'Sorry. I know how it is. I was like that myself when I first arrived here. But my advice is to move out as soon as it's polite and find somewhere . . . well . . . more suitable for a young lady, if you know what I mean.'

'Not really. Mr Shoe even tried to help me upstairs with my stuff. Mind you, I had to help him upstairs with his arms afterwards. Bits fall off him all the time, poor soul.'

'But they're not really . . . our kind of people,' said Carrot wretchedly. 'Don't get me wrong. I mean . . . dwarfs? Some of my best friends are dwarfs. My *parents* are dwarfs. Trolls? No problem at *all* with trolls. Salt of the earth. Literally. Wonderful chaps under all that crust. But . . . undead . . . I just wish they'd go back to where they came from, that's all.'

'Most of them came from round here.'

'I just don't like 'em. Sorry.'

'I've got to go,' said Angua, coldly. She paused at the dark entrance of an alley.

'Right. Right,' said Carrot. 'Um. When shall I see you again?'

'Tomorrow. We're in the same job, yes?'

'But maybe when we're off duty we could take a—'

'Got to go!'

Angua turned and ran. The moon's halo was already visible over the rooftops of Unseen University.

'OK. Well. Right. Tomorrow, then,' Carrot called after her.

*

Angua could feel the world spinning as she stumbled through the shadows. She shouldn't have left it so long!

She stumbled out into a cross-street with a few people in it and managed to make it to an alley mouth, pawing at her clothes. . .

She was seen by Bundo Prung, recently expelled from the Thieves' Guild for unnecessary enthusiasm and conduct unbecoming in a mugger, and a desperate man. An isolated woman in a dark alley was just about what he felt he could manage.

He glanced around, and followed her in.

Silence followed, for about five seconds. Then Bundo emerged, very fast, and didn't stop running until he reached the docks, where a boat was leaving on the tide. He ran up the gangplank just before it was pulled up, and became a seaman, and died three years later when an armadillo fell on his head in a far-off country, and in all that time never said what he'd seen. But he did scream a bit whenever he saw a dog.

Angua emerged a few seconds later, and trotted away.

Lady Sybil Ramkin opened the door and sniffed the night air.

'Samuel Vimes! You're drunk!'

'Not yet! But I hope to be!' said Vimes, in cheerful tones.

'And you haven't changed out of your uniform!'

Vimes looked down, and then up again.

'That's right!' he said brightly.

'The guests will be here any minute. Go on up to your room. There's a tub drawn and Willikins has laid out a suit for you. Get along with you . . .'

'Jolly good!'

Vimes bathed in lukewarm water and a rosy alcoholic glow. Then he dried himself off as best he could and looked at the suit on the bed.

It had been made for him by the finest tailor in the city. Sybil Ramkin had a generous heart. She was a woman out for all she could give.

The suit was blue and deep purple, with lace on the wrists and at the throat. It was the height of fashion, he had been told. Sybil Ramkin wanted him to go up in the world. She'd never actually said it, but he knew she felt he was far too good to be a copper.

He stared at it in muzzy incomprehension. He'd never really worn a suit before. When he was a kid there'd been whatever rags could be tied on, and later on there'd been the leather knee britches and chainmail of the Watch – comfortable, practical clothes.

There was a hat with the suit. It had pearls on it.

Vimes had never worn any headgear before that hadn't been hammered out of one piece of metal.

The shoes were long and pointy.

He'd always worn sandals in the summer, and the traditional cheap boots in the winter.

Captain Vimes could just about manage to be an officer. He wasn't at all sure how to become a gentleman. Putting on the suit would seem to be part of it . . .

Guests were arriving. He could hear the crunch of carriage wheels on the driveway, and the flip-flop of the sedan-chair carriers.

He glanced out of the window. Scoone Avenue was higher than most of Morpork and offered unrivalled views of the city, if that was your idea of a good time. The Patrician's Palace was a darker shape in the dusk, with one lighted window high up. It was the centre of a well-lit area, which got darker and darker as the view widened and began to take in those parts of the city where you didn't light a candle because that was wasting good food. There was red torchlight around Quarry Lane . . . well, Trolls' New Year, understandable. And a faint glow over the High Energy Magic building at Unseen University; Vimes would arrest all wizards on suspicion of being too bloody clever by half. But more lights than you'd expect to see around Cable and Sheer, the part of the city that people like Captain Quirke referred to as 'tinytown' . . .

'Samuel!'

Vimes adjusted his cravat as best he could.

He'd faced trolls and dwarfs and dragons, but now he was having to meet an entirely new species. The rich.

It was always hard to remember, afterwards, how the world looked when she was *dans une certaine condition*, as her mother had delicately called it.

For example, she *remembered* seeing smells. The actual streets and buildings . . . they were there, of course, but only as a drab monochrome background against which the sounds and, yes, the smells seared like brilliant lines of . . . coloured fire and clouds of . . . well, of coloured smoke.

That was the point. That was where it all broke down. There were no proper words afterwards for what she heard and smelled. If you could see an eighth distinct colour just for a while, and then describe it back in the seven-coloured world, it'd have to be . . . 'something like a sort of greenish-purple'. Experience did not cross over well between species.

Sometimes, although not very often, Angua thought she was very lucky to get to see both worlds. And there was always twenty minutes after a Change when *all* the senses were heightened, so that the world glowed in every sensory spectrum like a rainbow. It was nearly worth it just for that.

There were varieties of werewolf. Some people merely had to shave every hour and wear a hat to cover the ears. They could pass for nearly normal.

But she could recognize them, nevertheless. Werewolves could spot another werewolf across a crowded street. There was something about the eyes. And, of course, if you had time, there were all sorts of other clues. Werewolves tended to live alone and take jobs that didn't bring them into contact with animals. They wore scent or aftershave a lot and tended to be very fastidious about their food. And kept diaries with the phases of the moon carefully marked in red ink.

It was no life, being a werewolf in the country. A stupid chicken went missing and you were a number one suspect. Everyone said it was better in the city.

It was certainly overpowering.

Angua could see several hours of Elm Street all in one go. The mugger's fear was a fading orange line. Carrot's trail was an expanding pale green cloud, with an edge that suggested he was slightly worried; there were additional tones of old leather and armour polish. Other trails, faint or powerful, cries-crossed the street.

There was one that smelled like an old privy carpet.

'Yo, bitch,' said a voice behind her.

She turned her head. Gaspode looked no better through canine vision, except that he was at the centre of a cloud of mixed odours.

'Oh. It's you.'

''S'right,' said Gaspode, feverishly scratching himself. He gave her a hopeful look. 'Just askin', you understand, just gettin' it over with right now, for the look of the thing, for wossname's sake as it might be, but I s'pose there's no chance of me sniffing—'

'None.'

'Just askin'. No offence meant.'

Angua wrinkled her muzzle.

'How come you smell so bad? I mean, you smelled bad enough when I was human, but now—'

Gaspode looked proud.

'Good, innit,' he said. 'It didn't just happen. I had to work at it. If you was a true dog, this'd be like really great aftershave. By the way, you want to get a collar, miss. No one bothers you if you've got a collar.'

'Thanks.'

Gaspode seemed to have something on his mind.

'Er . . . you don't rip hearts out, do you?'

'Not unless I want to,' said Angua.

'Right, right, right,' said Gaspode hurriedly. 'Where're you going?' He broke into a waddling, bow-legged trot to keep up with her.

'To have a sniff around Hammerhock's place. I didn't ask you to come.'

'Got nothing else to do,' said Gaspode. 'The House of Ribs don't put its rubbish out till midnight.'

'Haven't you got a home to go to?' said Angua, as they trotted under a fish-and-chip stall.

'Home? Me? Home? Yeah. Of course. No problemo. Laughing kids, big kitchen, three meals a day, humorous cat next door to chase, own blanket and spot by the fire, he's an old softy but we love him, ekcetera. No problem there. I just like to get out a bit,' said Gaspode.

'Only, I see *you* haven't got a collar.'

'It fell off.'

'Right?'

'It was the weight of all them rhinestones.'

'I expect it was.'

'They let me do pretty much as I like,' said Gaspode.

'I can see that.'

'Sometimes I don't go home for, oh, days at a time.'

'Right?'

'Weeks, sometimes.'

'Sure.'

'But they're always so glad to see me when I do,' said Gaspode.

'I thought you said you slept up at the University,' said Angua, as they dodged a cart in Rime Street.

For a moment Gaspode smelled uncertain, but he recovered magnificently.

'Yeah, right,' he said. 'We-ell, you know how it is, families . . . All them kids picking you up, giving you biscuits and similar, people pattin' you the whole time. Gets on yer nerves. So I sleeps up there quite often.'

'Right.'

'More often than not, point of fact.'

'Really?'

Gaspode whimpered a little.

'You want to be careful, you know. A young bitch like you can meet real trouble in this dog's city.'

They had reached the wooden jetty behind Hammerhock's workshop.

'How d'you—' Angua paused.

There was a mixture of smells here, but the overpowering one was as sharp as a saw.

'Fireworks?'

'And fear,' said Gaspode. 'Lots of fear.'

He sniffed the planks. 'Human fear, not dwarf. You can tell if it's dwarfs. It's the rat diet, see? Phew! Must have been real bad to stay this strong.'

'I smell one male human, one dwarf,' said Angua.

'Yeah. One dead dwarf.'

Gaspode stuck his battered nose along the line of the door, and snuffled noisily.

'There's other stuff,' he said, 'but it's a bugger what with the river so close and everything. There's oil and . . . grease . . . and all sorts – hey, where're you going?'

Gaspode trotted after her as Angua headed back to Rime Street, nose close to the ground.

'Following the trail.'

'What for? He won't thank you, you know.'

'Who won't?'

'Your young man.'

Angua stopped so suddenly that Gaspode ran into her.

'You mean Corporal Carrot? He's not my young man!'

'Yeah? I'm a dog, right? It's all in the nose, right? Smell can't lie. Pheremonies. It's the ole sexual alchemy stuff.'

'I've only known him a couple of nights!'

'Aha!'

'What do you mean, *aha?*'

'Nothing, nothing. Nothing wrong with it, anyway—'

'There isn't any *it* to be wrong!'

'Right, right. Not that it would be,' said Gaspode, adding hurriedly, 'even if there was. Everyone likes Corporal Carrot.'

'They do, don't they,' said Angua, her hackles settling down. 'He's very . . . likeable.'

'Even Big Fido only bit his hand when Carrot tried to pat him.'

'Who's Big Fido?'

'Chief Barker of the Dog Guild.'

'Dogs have got a Guild? Dogs? Pull one of the other ones, it's got bells on—'

'No, straight up. Scavenging rights, sunbathing spots, night-time barking duty, breeding rights, howling rotas . . . the whole bone of rubber.'

'Dog Guild,' snarled Angua sarcastically. 'Oh, yeah.'

'Chase a rat up a pipe in the wrong street and call me a liar. 'S'good job for you I'm around, else you could get into big trouble. There's big trouble for a dog in this town who ain't a Guild member. It's lucky for you,' said Gaspode, 'that you met me.'

'I suppose you're a big ma – dog in the Guild, yes?'

'Ain't a member,' said Gaspode smugly.

'How come you survive, then?'

'I can think on my paws, me. Anyway, Big Fido leaves me alone. I got the Power.'

'What power?'

'Never you mind. Big Fido . . . he's a friend o' mine.'

'Biting a man's arm for patting you doesn't sound very friendly.'

'Yeah? Last man who tried to pat Big Fido, they only ever found his belt buckle.'

'Yes?'

'And that was in a tree.'

'Where are we?'

'Not even a tree near here. What?'

Gaspode sniffed the air. His nose could read the city in a way reminiscent of Captain Vimes's educated soles.

'Junction of Scoone Avenue and Prouts,' he said.

'Trail's dying out. It's mixed up with too much other stuff.'

Angua sniffed around for a while. Someone had come up here, but too many people had crossed the trail. The sharp smell was still there, but only as suggestion in the welter of conflicting scents.

She was aware of an overwhelming smell of approaching soap. She'd noticed it before, but only as a woman and only as a faint whiff. As a quadruped, it seemed to fill the world.

Corporal Carrot was walking up the road, looking thoughtful. He wasn't looking where he was going, however, but he didn't need to. People stood aside for Corporal Carrot.

It was the first time she'd seen him through these eyes. Good grief. How did people not notice it? He walked through the city like a tiger through tall grass, or a hubland bear across the snow, wearing the landscape like a skin—

Gaspode glanced sideways. Angua was sitting on her haunches, staring.

'Yer tongue's hanging gut,' he said.

'What? . . . So? So what? That's natural. I'm panting.'

'Har, har.'

Carrot noticed them, and stopped.

'Why, it's the little mongrel dog,' he said.

'Woof, woof,' said Gaspode, his traitor tail wagging.

'I see *you've* got a lady friend, anyway,' said Carrot, patting him on the head and then absent-mindedly wiping his hand on his tunic.

'And, my word, what a splendid bitch,' he said. 'A Ramtop wolfhound, if I'm any judge.' He stroked Angua in a vague friendly way. 'Oh, well,' he said. 'This isn't getting any work done, is it?'

'Woof, whine, give the doggy a biscuit,' said Gaspode.

Carrot stood up and patted his pockets. 'I think I've got a piece of biscuit here – well, I could believe you understand every word I say . . .'

Gaspode begged, and caught the biscuit easily.

'Woof, woof, fawn, fawn,' he said.

Carrot gave Gaspode the slightly puzzled look that people always gave him when he said 'woof' instead of barking, nodded at Angua, and carried on towards Scoone Avenue and Lady Ramkin's house.

'There,' said Gaspode, crunching the stale biscuit noisily, 'goes a very nice boy. Simple, but nice.'

'Yes, he is simple, isn't he?' said Angua. 'That's what I first noticed about him. He's simple. And everything else here is complicated.'

'He was making sheep's eyes at you earlier,' said Gaspode. 'Not that I've got anything against sheep's eyes, mind you. If they're fresh.'

'You're disgusting.'

'Yeah, but at least I stay the same shape all month, no offence meant.'

'You're asking for a bite.'

'Oh, yeah,' moaned Gaspode. 'Yeah, you'll bite me. Aaargh. Oh, yes, that'll *really* worry me, that will. I mean, think about it. I've got so many dog diseases I'm only alive 'cos the little buggers are too busy fighting among 'emselves. I mean, I've even got Licky End, and you only get that if you're a pregnant sheep. Go on. Bite me. Change my life. Every time there's a full moon, suddenly I grow hair and yellow teeth and have to go around on all fours. Yes, I can see that making a big difference to my ongoing situation. Actually,' he said, 'I'm definitely on a losing streak in the hair department, so maybe a, you know, not the whole bite, maybe just a nibble—'

'Shut up.' At least *you've* got a lady friend, Carrot had said. As if there was something on his mind . . .

'A quick lick, even—'

'Shut up.'

'This unrest is all Vetinari's fault,' said the Duke of Eorle. 'The man has no style! So now, of course, we have a city where grocers have as much influence as barons. He even let the *plumbers* form a Guild! That's against nature, in my humble opinion.'

'It wouldn't be so bad if he set some kind of social example,' said Lady Omnius.

'Or even governed,' said Lady Selachii. 'People seem to be able to get away with anything.'

'I admit that the old kings were not necessarily *our* kind of people, towards the end,' said the Duke of Eorle, 'but at least they stood for something, in my humble opinion. We had a decent city in those days. People were more respectful and knew their place. People put in a decent day's work, they didn't laze around all the time. And we certainly didn't open the gates to whatever riff-raff was capable of walking through. And of course we also had law. Isn't that so, captain?'

Captain Samuel Vimes stared glassily at a point somewhere to the left and just above the speaker's left ear.

Cigar smoke hung almost motionless in the air. Vimes was dimly aware that he'd spent several hours eating too much food in the company of people he didn't like.

He longed for the smell of damp streets and the feel of the cobbles under his cardboard soles. A tray of post-prandial drinks was orbiting the table, but Vimes hadn't touched it, because it upset Sybil. And she tried not to show it, and that upset him even more.

The Bearhugger's had worn off. He hated being sober. It meant he started to think. One of the thoughts jostling for space was that there was no such thing as a humble opinion.

He hadn't had much experience with the rich and powerful. Coppers didn't, as a rule. It wasn't that they were less prone to commit crimes, it was just that the crimes they committed tended to be so far above the normal level of criminality that they were beyond the reach of men with bad boots and rusting mail. Owning a hundred slum properties wasn't a crime, although living in one was, almost. Being an Assassin – the Guild never actually *said* so, but an important qualification was being the son or daughter of a gentleman – wasn't a crime. If you had enough money, you could hardly commit crimes at all. You just perpetrated amusing little peccadilloes.

'And now everywhere you look it's uppity dwarfs and trolls and rude people,' said Lady Selachii. 'There's more dwarfs in Ankh-Morpork now than there are in any of their own cities, or whatever they call their holes.'

'What do you think, captain?' said the Duke of Eorle.

'Hmm?' Captain Vimes picked up a grape and started turning it over and over in his fingers.

'The current ethnic problem.'

'Are we having one?'

'Well, yes . . . Look at Quarry Lane. There's fighting there every night!'

'And they have absolutely no concept of religion!'

Vimes examined the grape minutely. What he wanted to say was: Of course they fight. They're *trolls*. Of course they bash one another with clubs – trollish is basically body language and, well, they like to shout. In fact, the only one who ever gives anyone any real trouble is that bastard Chrysoprase, and that's only because he apes humans and is a quick learner. As for religion, troll gods were hitting one another with clubs ten thousand years before we'd even stopped trying to eat rocks.

But the memory of the dead dwarf stirred something perverse in his soul.

He put the grape back on his plate.

'Definitely,' he said. 'In my view, the godless bastards should be rounded up and marched out of the city at spearpoint.'

There was a moment's silence.

'It's no more than they deserve,' Vimes added.

'Exactly! They're barely more than animals,' said Lady Omnius. Vimes suspected her first name was Sara.

'Have you noticed how massive their heads are?' said Vimes. 'That's really just rock. Very small brains.'

'And morally, of course . . .' said Lord Eorle.

There was a murmur of vague agreement. Vimes reached for his glass.

'Willikins, I don't think Captain Vimes wants any wine,' said Lady Ramkin.

'Wrong!' said Vimes cheerfully. 'And while we're on the subject, how about the dwarfs?'

'I don't know if anyone's noticed,' said Lord Eorle, 'but you certainly don't see as many dogs about as you used to.'

Vimes stared. It was true about the dogs. There didn't seem to be quite so many mooching around these days, that was a fact. But he'd visited a few dwarf bars with Carrot, and knew that dwarfs would indeed eat dog, but only if they couldn't get rat. And ten thousand dwarfs eating continuously with knife, fork and shovel wouldn't make a dent in Ankh-Morpork's rat population. It was a major feature in dwarfish letters back home: come on, everyone, and bring the ketchup.

'Notice how small their heads are?' he managed. 'Very limited cranial capacity, surely. Fact of measurement.'

'And you never see their women,' said Lady Sara Omnius. 'I find that very . . . suspicious. You know what they say about dwarfs,' she added darkly.

Vimes sighed. He was just about aware that you saw their women all the time, although they looked just like the male dwarfs. Surely *everyone* knew that, who knew anything about dwarfs?

'Cunning little devils too,' said Lady Selachii. 'Sharp as needles.'

'You know,' Vimes shook his head, 'you know, that's what's so damn annoying, isn't it? The way they can be so incapable of any rational thought and so bloody shrewd at the same time.'

Only Vimes saw the look Lady Ramkin flashed him. Lord Eorle stubbed out his cigar.

'They just move in and take over. And work away like ants all the time real people should be getting some sleep. It's not natural.'

Vimes's mind circled the comment and compared it to the earlier one about a decent day's work.

'Well, one of them won't be working so hard,' said Lady Omnius. 'My maid said one of them was found in the river this morning. Probably some tribal war or something.'

'Hah . . . it's a start, anyway,' said Lord Eorle, laughing. 'Not that anyone will notice one more or less.'

Vimes smiled brightly.

There was a wine bottle near his hand, despite Willikins's tactful best efforts to remove it. The neck looked invitingly grippable—

He was aware of eyes on him. He looked across the table into the face of a man who was watching him intently and whose last contribution to the conversation had been 'Could you be so kind as to pass me the seasonings, captain?' There was nothing remarkable about the face, except for the gaze – which was absolutely calm and mildly amused. It was Dr Cruces. Vimes had the strong impression that his thoughts were being read.

'Samuel!'

Vimes's hand stopped halfway to the bottle. Willikins was standing next to her ladyship.

'Apparently there's a young man at the door asking for you,' said Lady Ramkin. 'Corporal Carrot.'

'Gosh, this is exciting!' said Lord Eorle. 'Has he come to arrest us, do you think? Hahaha.'

'Ha,' said Vimes.

Lord Eorle nudged his partner.

'I expect that somewhere a crime is being committed,' he said.

'Yes,' said Vimes. 'Quite close, I think.'

Carrot was shown in, with his helmet under his arm at a respectful angle.

He gazed at the select company, licked his lips nervously, and saluted. Everyone was looking at him. It was hard not to notice Carrot in a room. There were bigger people than him in the city. He didn't loom. He just seemed, without trying, to distort things around him. Everything became background to Corporal Carrot.

'At ease, corporal,' said Vimes. 'What's up? I mean,' he added quickly, knowing Carrot's erratic approach to colourful language, 'what is the reason for you being here at this time?'

'Got something to show you, sir. Uh. Sir, I think it's from the Assass—'

'We'll just go and talk about it outside, shall we?' said Vimes. Dr Cruces hadn't twitched a muscle.

Lord Eorle sat back. 'Well, I must say I'm impressed,' he said. 'I'd always thought you Watchmen were a pretty ineffective lot, but I see you're pursuing your duty at all times. Always on the alert for the criminal mind, eh?'

'Oh, yes,' said Vimes. 'The criminal mind. Yes.'

The cooler air of the ancestral hallway came as a blessing. He leaned against the wall and squinted at the card.

'"Gonne"?'

'You know you said you saw something in the courtyard—' Carrot began.

'What's a gonne?'

'Maybe something *wasn't* in the Assassins' museum, and they put this sign on it?' said Carrot. 'You know, like "Removed for Cleaning"? They do that in museums.'

'No, I shouldn't think th— What do you know about museums, anyway?'

'Oh, well, sir,' said Carrot. 'I sometimes visit them on my day off. The one in the University, of course, and Lord Vetinari lets me look around the old Palace one, and then there's the Guild ones, they generally let me in if I ask nicely, and there's the dwarf museum off Rime Street—'

'Is there?' said Vimes, interested despite himself. He'd walked along Rime Street a thousand times.

'Yes, sir, just up Whirligig Alley.'

'Fancy that. What's in it?'

'Many interesting examples of dwarf bread, sir.'

Vimes thought about this for a moment. 'That's not important right now,' he said. 'This isn't how you spell gone, anyway.'

'Yes it is, sir,' said Carrot.

'I meant, it's not how gone is normally spelled.'

He flicked the card back and forth in his fingers.

'A man'd have to be a fool to break into the Assassins' Guild,' he said.

'Yes, sir.'

The anger had burned away the fumes. Once again he felt . . . not, not the thrill, that wasn't the right word . . . the *sense* of something. He still wasn't sure what it was. But it was there, waiting for him—

'Samuel Vimes, what's going on?'

Lady Ramkin shut the dining-room door behind her.

'I was watching you,' she said. 'You were being very rude, Sam.'

'I was trying not to be.'

'Lord Eorle is a very old friend.'

'Is he?'

'Well, I've known him a long time. I can't stand the man, actually. But you were making him look foolish.'

'He was making himself look foolish. I was merely helping.'

'But I've often heard you being . . . rude about dwarfs and trolls.'

'That's different. I've got a *right*. That idiot wouldn't know a troll if it walked over him.'

'Oh, he would know if a troll walked over him,' said Carrot, helpfully. 'Some of them weigh as much as—'

'What's so important, anyway?' said Lady Ramkin.

'We're . . . looking for whoever killed Chubby,' said Vimes.

Lady Ramkin's expression changed instantly.

'That's different, of course,' she said. 'People like that should be publicly flogged.'

Why did I say that? thought Vimes. Maybe because it's true. The . . . gonne . . . goes missing, next minute there's a little dwarf artificer thrown in the river with a nasty draught where his chest should be. They're linked. Now all I have to do is find the links . . .

'Carrot, can you come back with me to Hammerhock's?'

'Yes, captain. Why?'

'I want to see inside that workshop. And this time I've got a dwarf with me.'

More than that, he added, I've got Corporal Carrot. Everyone *likes* Corporal Carrot.

*

333

Vimes listened while the conversation droned on in dwarfish. Carrot seemed to be winning, but it was a near thing. The clan was giving in not because of reason, or in obedience to the law, but because . . . well . . . because it was Carrot who was asking.

Finally, the corporal looked up. He was sitting on a dwarf stool, so his knees practically framed his head.

'You have to understand, you see, that a dwarf's workshop is very important.'

'Right,' said Vimes. 'I understand.'

'And, er . . . you're a bigger.'

'Sorry?'

'A bigger. Bigger than a dwarf.'

'Ah.'

'Er. The inside of a dwarf's workshop is like . . . well, it's like the inside of his clothes, if you know what I mean. They say you can look, if I'm with you. But you mustn't touch anything. Er. They're not very happy about this, captain.'

A dwarf who was possibly Mrs Hammerhock produced a bunch of keys.

'I've always got on well with dwarfs,' said Vimes.

'They're not happy, sir. Um. They don't think we'll do any good.'

'We'll do our best!'

'Um. I didn't translate that properly. Um. They don't think *we're* any good. They don't mean to be offensive, sir. They just don't think we'll be allowed to get anywhere, sir.'

'Ow!'

'Sorry about that, captain,' said Carrot, who was walking like an inverted L. 'After you. Mind your head on the—'

'Ow!'

'Perhaps it'd be best if you sat down and I'll look around.'

The workshop was long and, of course, low, with another small door at the far end. There was a big workbench under a skylight. On the opposite wall was a forge and a tool rack. And a hole.

A chunk of plaster had fallen away a few feet above the ground, and cracks radiated away from the shattered brickwork underneath.

Vimes pinched the bridge of his nose. He hadn't found time to sleep today. That was another thing. He'd have to get used to sleeping when it was dark. He couldn't remember when he'd last slept at night.

He sniffed.

'I can smell fireworks,' he said.

'Could be from the forge,' said Carrot. 'Anyway, trolls and dwarfs have been letting fireworks off all over the city.'

Vimes nodded.

'All right,' he said, 'so what can we see?'

'Someone thumped the wall pretty hard just here,' said Carrot.

'Could have happened at any time,' said Vimes.

'No, sir, because there's the plaster dust underneath and a dwarf always keeps his workshop clean.'

'Really?'

There were various weapons, some of them half finished, on racks by the bench. Vimes picked up most of a crossbow.

'He did good work,' he said. 'Very good at mechanisms.'

'Well known for it,' said Carrot, poking around aimlessly on the bench. 'A very delicate hand. He made musical boxes for a hobby. Could never resist a mechanical challenge. Er. What are we looking for *actually*, sir?'

'Not sure. Now *this* is good . . .'

It was a war axe, and so heavy that Vimes's arm sagged. Intricate etched lines covered the blade. It must have represented weeks of work.

'Not your actual Saturday night special, eh?'

'Oh no,' said Carrot, 'that's a burial weapon.'

'I should think it is!'

'I mean, it's made to be buried with a dwarf. Every dwarf is buried with a weapon. You know? To take with him to . . . wherever he's going.'

'But it's fine workmanship! And it's got an edge like – aargh,' Vimes sucked his finger, 'like a razor.'

Carrot looked shocked. 'Of course. It'd be no good him facing them with an *inferior* weapon.'

'What them are you talking about?'

'Anything bad he encounters on his journey after death,' said Carrot, a shade awkwardly.

'Ah.' Vimes hesitated. This was an area in which he did not feel comfortable.

'It's an ancient tradition,' said Carrot.

'I thought dwarfs didn't believe in devils and demons and stuff like that.'

'That's true, but . . . we're not sure if they know.'

'Oh.'

Vimes laid down the axe and picked up something else from the work rack. It was a knight in armour, about nine inches high. There was a key in its back. He turned it, and then nearly dropped the thing when the figure's legs started to move. He put it down, and it began to march stiffly across the floor, waving its sword.

'Moves a bit like Colon, don't it,' said Vimes. 'Clockwork!'

'It's the coming thing,' said Carrot. 'Mr Hammerhock was good at that.'

Vimes nodded. 'We're looking for anything that shouldn't be here,' he said. 'Or something that should be and isn't. Is there anything missing?'

'Hard to say, sir. It isn't here.'

'What?'

'Anything that's missing, sir,' said Carrot conscientiously.

'I mean,' said Vimes, patiently, 'anything not here which you'd expect to find.'

'Well, he's got – he *had* – all the usual tools, sir. Nice ones, too. Shame, really.'

'What is?'

'They'll be melted down, of course.'

Vimes stared at the neat racks of hammers and files.

'Why? Can't some other dwarf use them?'

'What, use another dwarf's actual *tools*?' Carrot's mouth twisted in distaste, as though someone had suggested he wear Corporal Nobbs's old shorts. 'Oh, no, that's not . . . right. I mean, they're . . . part of him. I mean . . . someone else using them, after he's used them all these years, I mean . . . urrgh.'

'Really?'

The clockwork soldier marched under the bench.

'It'd feel . . . wrong,' said Carrot. 'Er. Yukky.'

'Oh.' Vimes stood up.

'Capt—'

'Ow!'

'—mind your head. Sorry.'

Rubbing his head with one hand, Vimes used the other to examine the hole in the plaster.

'There's . . . something in here,' he said. 'Pass me one of those chisels.'

There was silence.

'A chisel, please. If it makes you feel any better, we are trying to find out who killed Mr Hammerhock. All right?'

Carrot picked one up, but with considerable reluctance.

'This is Mr Hammerhock's chisel, this is,' he said reproachfully.

'Corporal Carrot, will you stop being a dwarf for two seconds? You're a guard! And give me the damn chisel! It's been a long day! Thank you!'

Vimes prised at the brickwork, and a rough disc of lead dropped into his hand.

'Slingshot?' said Carrot.

'No room in here,' said Vimes. 'Anyway, how the hell could it get this far into the wall?'

He slipped the disc into his pocket.

'That seems about it, thee,' he said, straightening up. 'We'd better – ow! – oh, fish out that clockwork soldier, will you? Better leave the place tidy.'

Carrot scrabbled in the darkness under the bench. There was a rustling noise.

'There's a piece of paper under here, sir.'

Carrot emerged, waving a small yellowing sheet. Vimes squinted at it.

'Looks like nonsense to me,' he said, eventually. 'It's not dwarfish, I know that. But these symbols – these things I've seen before. Or something like them.' He passed the paper back to Carrot. 'What can you make of it?'

Carrot frowned. 'I could make a hat,'he said, 'or a boat. Or a sort of chrysanthemum—'

'I mean the symbols. *These* symbols, just here.'

'Dunno, captain. They do look familiar, though. Sort of . . . like alchemists' writing?'

'Oh, no!' Vimes put his hands over his eyes. 'Not the bloody alchemists! Oh, no! Not that bloody gang of mad firework merchants! I can take the Assassins, but not those idiots! No! Please! What time is it?'

Carrot glanced at the hourglass on his belt. 'About half past eleven, captain.'

'Then I'm off to bed. Those clowns can wait until tomorrow. You could make me a happy man by telling me that this paper belonged to Hammerhock.'

'Doubt it, sir.'

'Me too. Come on. Let's go out through the back door.'

Carrot squeezed through.

'Mind your head, sir.'

Vimes, almost on his knees, stopped and stared at the doorframe.

'Well, corpora!,' he said eventually, 'we know it wasn't a troll that did it, don't we? Two reasons. One, a troll couldn't get through this door, it's dwarf sized.'

'What's the other reason, sir?'

Vimes carefully pulled something off a splinter on the low door lintel.

'The other reason, Carrot, is that trolls don't have hair.'

337

The couple of strands that had been caught in the grain of the beam were red and long. Someone had left them there inadvertently. Someone tall. Taller than a dwarf, anyway.

Vimes peered at them. They looked more like threads than hair. Fine red threads. Oh, well. A clue was a clue.

He carefully folded them up in a scrap of paper borrowed from Carrot's notebook, and handed them to the corporal.

'Here. Keep this safe.'

They crawled out into the night. There was a narrow, plank walkway attached to the walls, and beyond that was the river.

Vimes straightened up carefully.

'I don't like this, Carrot,' he said. 'There's something bad underneath all this.'

Carrot looked down.

'I mean, there are hidden things happening,' said Vimes, patiently.

'Yes, sir.'

'Let's get back to the Yard.'

They proceeded to the Brass Bridge, quite slowly, because Carrot cheerfully acknowledged everyone they met. Hard-edged ruffians, whose normal response to a remark from a Watchman would be genteelly paraphrased by a string of symbols generally found on the top row of a typewriter's keyboard, would actually smile awkwardly and mumble something harmless in response to his hearty, 'Good evening, Masher! Mind how you go!'

Vimes stopped halfway across the bridge to light his cigar, striking a match on one of the ornamental hippos. Then he looked down into the turbid waters.

'Carrot?'

'Yes, captain?'

'Do you think there's such a thing as a criminal mind?'

Carrot almost audibly tried to work this out.

'What ... you mean like ... Mr Cut-Me-Own-Throat Dibbler, sir?'

'He's not a criminal.'

'You *have* eaten one of his pies, sir?'

'I mean ... *yes* ... but ... he's just geographically divergent in the financial hemisphere.'

'Sir?'

'I mean he just disagrees with other people about the position of things. Like money. He thinks it should all be in his pocket. No, I meant—' Vimes closed his eyes, and thought about cigar smoke and flowing drink and laconic voices. There were people who'd steal money from people. Fair enough. That was just theft. But there were people who, with one easy word, would steal the humanity from people. That was something else.

The point was ... well, *he* didn't like dwarfs and trolls. But he didn't like anyone very much. The point was that he moved in their company every day, and he had a right to dislike them. The point was that no fat idiot had the right to say things like that.

He stared at the water. One of the piles of the bridge was right below him; the Ankh sucked and gurgled around it. Debris – baulks of timber, branches, rubbish – had piled up in a sort of sordid floating island. There was even fungus growing on it.

What he could do with right now was a bottle of Bearhugger's. The world swam into focus when you looked at it through the bottom of a bottle.

Something else swam into focus.

Doctrine of signatures, thought Vimes. That's what the herbalists call it. It's like the gods put a 'Use Me' label on plants. If a plant looks like a part of the body, it's good for ailments peculiar to that part. There's teethwort for teeth, spleenwort for ... spleens, eyebright for eyes ... there's even a toadstool called *Phallus impudicus*, and I don't know what *that's* for but Nobby is a big man for mushroom omelettes. Now ... either that fungus down there is *exactly* the medicine for hands, or ...

Vimes sighed.

'Carrot, can you go and get a boathook, please?'

Carrot followed his gaze.

'Just to the left of that log, Carrot.'

'Oh, no!'

'I'm afraid so. Haul it out, find out who he was, make out a report for Sergeant Colon.'

The corpse was a clown. Once Carrot had climbed down the pile and moved the debris aside, he floated face up, a big sad grin painted on his face.

'He's dead!'

'Catching, isn't it?'

Vimes looked at the grinning corpse. Don't investigate. Keep out of it. Leave it to the Assassins and bloody Quirke. These are your orders.

'Corporal Carrot?'

'Sir?'

These are your orders ...

Well, damn that. What did Vetinari think he was? Some kind of clockwork soldier?

'We're going to find out what's been going on here.'

'Yes, sir!'

'Whatever else happens. We're going to find out.'

The river Ankh is probably the only river in the universe on which the investigators can chalk the outline of the corpse.

'Dear Sgt Colon,
                    'I hope you are well. The weather is Fine. This is a corpse who, we fished out of the river last night but, we don't know who he is except he is a member of the Fools' Guild called Beano. He has been seriously hit on the back of the head and has been stuck under the bridge for some time, he is not a Pretty sight. Captain Vimes says to find out things. He says he thinks it is mixed up with the Murder of Mr Hammerhock. He says talk to the Fools. He says Do it. Also please find attached Piece of Paper. Captain Vimes says, try it out on the Alchemists—'

Sergeant Colon stopped reading for a while to curse all alchemists.

'—because it is Puzzling Evidence. Hoping this finds you in Good Health, Yours Faithfully, Carrot Ironfoundersson, (Cpl).'

The sergeant scratched his head. What the hell did that all mean?

Just after breakfast a couple of senior jesters from the Fools' Guild had come to pick up the corpse. Corpses in the river . . . well, there was nothing very unusual about that. But it wasn't the way clowns died, usually. After all, what did a clown have that was worth stealing? What sort of danger was a clown?

As for the alchemists, he was blowed if he was—

Of course, *he* didn't have to. He looked up at the recruits. They had to be good for something.

'Cuddy and Detritus – *don't salute!* – I've got a little job for you. Just take this piece of paper to the Alchemists' Guild, all right? And ask one of the loonies to tell you what he makes of it.'

'Where's the Alchemists' Guild, sergeant?' said Cuddy.

'In the Street of Alchemists, of course,' said Colon, 'at the moment. But I should run, if I was you.'

The Alchemists' Guild is opposite the Gamblers' Guild. Usually. Sometimes it's above it, or below it, or falling in bits around it.

The gamblers are occasionally asked why they continue to maintain an establishment opposite a Guild which accidentally blows up its Guild Hall every few months, and they say: 'Did you read the sign on the door when you came in?'

The troll and the dwarf walked towards it, occasionally barging into each other by deliberate accident.

'Anyway, you so clever, he gave paper to *me*?'

'Hah! Can you read it, then? Can you?'

'No, I tell you to read it. That called del-eg-ay-shun.'

'Hah! Can't read! Can't count! Stupid troll!'

'Not stupid!'

'Hah! Yes? Everyone knows trolls can't even count up to four!'*

'Eater of rats!'

'How many fingers am I holding up? You tell me, Mr Clever Rocks in the Head.'

'Many,' Detritus hazarded.

'Har har, no, five. You'll be in *big* trouble on payday. Sergeant Colon'll say, stupid troll, he won't know how many dollars I give him! Hah! How come you read the notice about joining the Watch, anyway? Got someone to read it to you?'

'How come *you* read notice? Get someone to hold you up?'

They walked into the door of the Alchemists' Guild.

'I knock. *My* job!'

'I'll knock!'

When Mr Sendivoge, the Guild secretary, opened the door it was to find a dwarf hanging on the knocker and being swung up and down by a troll. He adjusted his crash helmet.

'Yes?' he said.

Cuddy let go.

Detritus' massive brows knitted.

'Er. You loony bastard, what you make of this?' he said.

Sendivoge stared from Detritus to the paper. Cuddy was struggling to get around the troll, who was almost completely blocking the doorway.

'*What'd you go and call him that for?*'

'*Sergeant Colon, he said*—'

'I could make a hat out of it,' said Sendivoge, 'or a string of dollies, if I could get some scissors—'

'What my . . . colleague means, sir, is can you help us in our inquiries in re the writing on this alleged piece of paper here?' said Cuddy. 'That bloody hurt!'

---

* In fact, trolls traditionally count like this: one, two, three . . . *many*, and people assume this means they can have no grasp of higher numbers. They don't realize that many can *be* a number. As in: one, two, three, *many*, many-one, many-two, many-three, *many many*, many-many-one, many-many-two, many-many-three, *many many many*, many-many-many-one, many-many-many-two, many-many-many-three, *LOTS*.

Sendivoge peered at him.

'Are you Watchmen?' he said.

'I'm Lance-Constable Cuddy and this,' said Cuddy, gesturing upwards, 'is Lance-trying-to-be-Constable Detritus – *don't salu-* oh . . .'

There was a thump, and Detritus slumped sideways.

'Suicide squad, is he?' said the alchemist.

'He'll come round in a minute,' said Cuddy. 'It's the saluting. It's too much for him. You know trolls.'

Sendivoge shrugged and stared at the writing.

'Looks . . . familiar,' he said. 'Seen it somewhere before. Here . . . you're a dwarf, aren't you?'

'It's the nose, isn't it?' said Cuddy. 'It always gives me away.'

'Well, I'm sure we always try to be of help to the community,' said Sendivoge. 'Do come in.'

Cuddy's steel-tipped boots kicked Detritus back into semisensibility, and he lumbered after them.

'Why the, er, why the crash helmet, mister?' said Cuddy, as they walked along the corridor. All around them was the sound of hammering. The Guild was usually being rebuilt.

Sendivoge rolled his eyes.

'Balls,' he said, 'billiard balls, in fact.'

'I knew a man who played like that,' said Cuddy.

'Oh, no. Mr Silverfish is a good shot. That tends rather to be the problem, in fact.'

Cuddy looked at the crash helmet again.

'It's the ivory, you see.'

'Ah,' said Cuddy, not seeing, 'elephants?'

'Ivory *without* elephants. Transmuted ivory. Sound commercial venture.'

'I thought you were working on gold.'

'Ah, yes. Of course, you people know all about gold,' said Sendivoge.

'Oh, yes,' said Cuddy, reflecting on the phrase 'you people'.

'The gold,' said Sendivoge, thoughtfully, 'is turning out to be a bit tricky . . .'

'How long have you been trying?'

'Three hundred years.'

'That's a long time.'

'But we've been working on the ivory for only a week and it's going very well!' said the alchemist quickly. 'Except for some side effects which we'll doubtless soon be able to sort out.'

He pushed open a door.

It was a large room, heavily outfitted with the usual badly

ventilated furnaces, rows of bubbling crucibles, and one stuffed alligator. Things floated in jars. The air smelled of a limited life expectancy.

A lot of equipment had been moved away, however, to make room for a billiard table. Half a dozen alchemists were standing around it in the manner of men poised to run.

'It's the third this week,' said Sendivoge, gloomily. He nodded to a figure bent over a cue.

'Er, Mr Silverfish—' he began.

'Quiet! Game on!' said the head alchemist, squinting at the white ball.

Sendivoge glanced at the score rail.

'Twenty-one points,' he said. 'My word. Perhaps we're adding just the right amount of camphor to the nitro-cellulose after all—'

There was a click. The cue ball rolled away, bounced off the cushion—

—and then accelerated. White smoke poured off it as it bore down on an innocent cluster of red balls.

Silverfish shook his head.

'Unstable,' he said. 'Everybody *down!*'

Everyone in the room ducked, except for the two Watchmen, one of whom was in a sense pre-ducked and the other of whom was several minutes behind events.

The black ball took off on a column of flame, whiffled past Detritus' face trailing black smoke and then shattered a window. The green ball was staying in one spot but spinning furiously. The other balls cannoned back and forth, occasionally bursting into flame or caroming off the walls.

A red one hit Detritus between the eyes, curved back on to the table, holed itself in the middle pocket and then blew up.

There was silence, except for the occasional bout of coughing. Silverfish appeared through the oily smoke and, with a shaking hand, moved the score point one notch with the burning end of his cue.

'One,' he said. 'Oh well. Back to the crucible. Someone order another billiard table—'

''Scuse me,' said Cuddy, prodding him in the knee.

'Who's there?'

'Down here!'

Silverfish looked down.

'Oh. Are you a dwarf?'

Cuddy gave him a blank stare.

'Are you a giant?' he said.

'Me? Of course not!'

343

'Ah. Then I must be a dwarf, yes. And that's a troll behind me,' said Cuddy. Detritus pulled himself into something resembling attention.

'We've come to see if you can tell us what's on this paper,' said Cuddy.

'Yur,' said Detritus.

Silverfish looked at it.

'Oh, yes,' he said, 'some of old Leonard's stuff. Well?'

'Leonard?' said Cuddy. He glared at Detritus. 'Write this down,' he snapped.

'Leonard of Quirm,' said the alchemist.

Cuddy still looked lost.

'Never heard of him?' said Silverfish.

'Can't say I have, sir.'

'I thought everyone knew about Leonard da Quirm. Quite barmy. But a genius, too.'

'Was he an alchemist?'

Write this down, write this down . . . Detritus looked around blearily for a burnt bit of wood and a handy wall.

'Leonard? No. He didn't belong to a Guild. Or he belonged to all the Guilds, I suppose. He got around quite a bit. He *tinkered*, if you know what I mean?'

'No, sir.'

'He painted a bit, and messed about with mechanisms. Any old thing.'

Or a hammer and chisel even, thought Detritus.

'This,' said Silverfish, 'is a formula for . . . oh, well, I might as well tell you, it's hardly a big secret . . . it's a formula for what we called No.1 Powder. Sulphur, saltpetre and charcoal. You use it in fireworks. Any fool could make it up. But it looks odd because it's written back to front.'

'This sounds important,' hissed Cuddy to the troll.

'Oh, no. He always used to write back to front,' said Silverfish. 'He was odd like that. But very clever all the same. Haven't you seen his portrait of the Mona Ogg?'

'I don't think so.'

Silverfish handed the parchment to Detritus, who squinted at it as if he knew what it meant. Maybe he could write on this, he thought.

'The teeth followed you around the room. Amazing. In fact some people said they followed them *out* of the room and all the way down the street.'

'I think we should talk to Mr da Quirm,' said Cuddy.

'Oh, you could do that, you could do that, certainly,' said Silverfish. 'But he might not be in a position to listen. He disappeared a couple of years ago.'

... then when I find something to write with, thought Detritus, I have to find someone teach me how write ...

'Disappeared? How?' said Cuddy.

'We think,' said Silverfish, leaning closer, 'that he found a way of making himself invisible.'

'Really?'

'Because,' said Silverfish, nodding conspiratorially, *'no one's seen him.'*

'Ah,' said Cuddy. 'Er. This is just off of the top of my head, you understand, but I suppose he couldn't ... just have gone somewhere where you couldn't see him?'

'Nah, that wouldn't be like old Leonard. He wouldn't disappear. But he might vanish.'

'Oh.'

'He was a bit ... unhinged, if you know what I mean. Head too full of brains. Ha, I remember he had this idea once of getting lightning out of lemons! Hey, Sendivoge, you remember Leonard and his lightning lemons?'

Sendivoge made little circular motions alongside his head with one finger. 'Oh, yes. "If you stick copper and zinc rods in the lemon, hey presto, you get tame lightning." Man was an idiot!'

'Oh, not an idiot,' said Silverfish, picking up a billiard ball that had miraculously escaped the detonations. 'Just so sharp he kept cutting himself, as my granny used to say. Lightning lemons! Where's the sense in that? It was as bad as his "voices-in-the-sky" machine. I told him: Leonard, I said, what are wizards for, eh? There's perfectly normal magic available for that kind of thing. Lightning lemons? It'll be men with wings next! And you know what he said? You know what he said? He said: Funny you should say that ... Poor old chap.'

Even Cuddy joined in the laughter.

'And did you try it?' he said, afterwards.

'Try what?' said Silverfish.

'Har. Har. Har,' said Detritus, toiling behind the others.

'Putting the metal rods in the lemons?'

'Don't be a damn fool.'

'What dis letter mean?' said Detritus, pointing at the paper.

They looked.

'Oh, that's not a symbol,' said Silverfish. 'That's just old Leonard's way. He was always doodling in margins. Doodle, doodle, doodle. I told him: you should call yourself Mr Doodle.'

'I thought it was some alchemy thing,' said Cuddy. 'It looks a bit like a crossbow without the bow. And this word Ennogeht. What does that mean?'

'Search me. Sounds barbarian to me. Anyway . . . if that's all, officer . . . we've got some serious research to do,' said Silverfish, tossing the fake ivory ball up in the air and catching it again. 'We're not all daydreamers like poor old Leonard.'

'Ennogeht,' said Cuddy, turning the paper round and round. 'T-h-e-g-o-n-n-e—'

Silverfish missed the ball. Cuddy got behind Detritus just in time.

'I've done this before,' said Sergeant Colon, as he and Nobby approached the Fools' Guild. 'Keep up against the wall when I bangs the knocker, all right?'

It was shaped like a pair of artificial breasts, the sort that are highly amusing to rugby players and anyone whose sense of humour has been surgically removed. Colon gave it a quick rap and then flung himself to safety.

There was a whoop, a few honks on a horn, a little tune that someone somewhere must have thought was very jolly, a small hatch slid aside above the knocker and a custard pie emerged slowly, on the end of a wooden arm. Then the arm snapped and the pie collapsed in a little heap by Colon's foot.

'It's sad, isn't it?' said Nobby.

The door opened awkwardly, but only by a few inches, and a small clown stared up at him.

'I say, I say, I say,' it said, 'why did the fat man knock at the door?'

'I don't know,' said Colon automatically. 'Why *did* the fat man knock at the door?'

They stared at each other, tangled in the punchline.

'That's what I asked you,' said the clown reproachfully. He had a depressed, hopeless voice.

Sergeant Colon struck out towards sanity.

'Sergeant Colon, Night Watch,' he said, 'and this here is Corporal Nobbs. We've come to talk to someone about the man who . . . was found in the river, OK?'

'Oh. Yes. Poor Brother Beano. I suppose you'd better come in, thee,' said the clown.

Nobby was about to push at the door when Colon stopped him, and pointed wordlessly upwards.

'There seems to be a bucket of whitewash over the door,' he said.

'Is there?' said the clown. He was very small, with huge boots

346

that made him look like a capital L. His face was plastered with flesh-coloured make-up on which a big frown had been painted. His hair had been made from a couple of old mops, painted red. He wasn't fat, but a sort of hoop in his trousers was supposed to make him look amusingly overweight. A pair of rubber braces, so that his trousers bounced up and down when he walked, were a further component in the overall picture of a complete and utter twerp.

'Yes,' said Colon. 'There is.'

'Sure?'

'Positive.'

'Sorry about that,' said the clown. 'It's stupid, I know, but kind of traditional. Wait a moment.'

There were sounds of a stepladder being lugged into position, and various clankings and swearwords.

'All right, come on in.'

The clown led the way through the gatehouse. There was no sound but the flop-flop of his boots on the cobbles. Then an idea seemed to occur to him.

'It's a long shot, I know, but I suppose neither of you gentlemen'd like a sniff of my buttonhole?'

'No.'

'No.'

'No, I suppose not.' The clown sighed. 'It's not easy, you know. Clowning, I mean. I'm on gate duty 'cos I'm on probation.'

'You are?'

'I keep on forgetting: is it crying on the outside and laughing on the inside? I always get it mixed up.'

'About this Beano—' Colon began.

'We're just holding his funeral,' said the little clown. 'That's why my trousers are at half-mast.'

They stepped out into the sunlight again.

The inner courtyard was lined with clowns and fools. Bells tinkled in the breeze. Sunlight glinted off red noses and the occasional nervous jet of water from a fake buttonhole.

The clown ushered the guards into a line of fools.

'I'm sure Dr Whiteface will talk to you as soon as we've finished,' he said. 'My name's Boffo, by the way.' He held out his hand hopefully.

'Don't shake it,' Colon warned.

Boffo looked crestfallen.

A band struck up, and a procession of Guild members emerged from the chapel. A clown walked a little way ahead, carrying a small urn.

'This is very moving,' said Boffo.

On a dais on the opposite side of the quadrangle was a fat clown in baggy trousers, huge braces, a bow tie that was spinning gently in the breeze, and a top hat. His face had been painted into a picture of misery. He held a bladder on a stick.

The clown with the urn reached the dais, climbed the steps, and waited.

The band fell silent.

The clown in the top hat hit the urn-carrier about the head with the bladder – once, twice, three times . . .

The urn-bearer stepped forward, waggled his wig, took the urn in one hand and the clown's belt in the other and, with great solemnity, poured the ashes of the late Brother Beano into the other clown's trousers.

A sigh went up from the audience. The band struck up the clown anthem 'The March of the Idiots', and the end of the trombone flew off and hit a clown on the back of the head. He turned and swung a punch at the clown behind him, who ducked, causing a third clown to be knocked through the bass drum.

Colon and Nobby looked at one another and shook their heads.

Boffo produced a large red and white handkerchief and blew his nose with a humorous honking sound.

'Classic,' he said. 'It's what he would have wanted.'

'Have you any idea what happened?' said Colon.

'Oh, yes. Brother Grineldi did the old heel-and-toe trick and tipped the urn down—'

'I mean, why did Beano die?'

'Um. We think it was an accident,' said Boffo.

'An accident,' said Colon flatly.

'Yes. That's what Dr Whiteface thinks.' Boffo glanced upwards, briefly. They followed his gaze. The rooftops of the Assassins' Guild adjoined the Fools' Guild. It didn't do to upset neighbours like that, especially when the only weapon you had was a custard pie edged with short-crust pastry.

'That's what Dr Whiteface thinks,' said Boffo again, looking at his enormous shoes.

Sergeant Colon liked a quiet life. And the city could spare a clown or two. In his opinion, the loss of the whole boiling could only make the world a slightly happier place. And yet . . . and yet . . . honestly, he didn't know what had got into the Watch lately. It was Carrot, that was what it was. Even old Vimes had picked it up. We don't let things lie any more . . .

'Maybe he was cleaning a club, sort of thing, and it accidentally went off,' said Nobby. He'd caught it, too.

'No one'd want to kill young Beano,' said the clown, in a quiet voice. 'He was a friendly soul. Friends everywhere.'

'Almost everywhere,' said Colon.

The funeral was over. The jesters, jokers and clowns were going about their business, getting stuck in doorways on the way. There was much pushing and shoving and honking of noses and falling of prats. It was a scene to make a happy man slit his wrists on a fine spring morning.

'All I know is,' said Boffo, in a low voice, 'that when I saw him yesterday he was looking very . . . odd. I called out to him when he was going through the gates and—'

'How do you mean, odd?' said Colon. I am detectoring, he thought, with a faint touch of pride. People are Helping me with My Inquiries.

'Dunno. Odd. Not quite himself—'

'This was yesterday?'

'Oh, yes. In the morning. I know because the gate rota—'

'*Yesterday* morning?'

'That's what I said, mister. Mind you, we were all a bit nervous after the bang—'

'Brother Boffo!'

'Oh, no—' mumbled the clown.

A figure was striding towards them. A terrible figure.

No clowns were funny. That was the whole purpose of a clown. People laughed at clowns, but only out of nervousness. The point of clowns was that, after watching them, anything else that happened seemed enjoyable. It was nice to know there was someone worse off than you. Someone had to be the butt of the world.

But even clowns are frightened of something, and that is the white-faced clown. The one who never gets in the way of the custard. The one in the shiny white clothes, and the deadpan white make-up. The one with the little pointy hat and the thin mouth and the delicate black eyebrows.

Dr Whiteface.

'Who are these gentlemen?' he demanded.

'Er—' Boffo began.

'Night Watch, sir,' said Colon, saluting.

'And why are you here?'

'Investigating our inquiries as to the fatal demise of the clown Beano, sir,' said Colon.

'I rather think that is Guild business, sergeant. Don't you?'

'Well, sir, he *was* found in the—'

'I am sure it is something we don't need to bother the Watch with,' said Dr Whiteface.

349

Colon hesitated. He'd prefer to face Dr Cruces than this apparition. At least the Assassins were *supposed* to be unpleasant. Clowns were only one step away from mime artists, too.

'No, sir,' he said. 'It was obviously an accident, right?'

'Quite so. Brother Boffo will show you to the door,' said the head clown. 'And then,' he added, 'he will report to my office. Does he understand?'

'Yes, Dr Whiteface,' mumbled Boffo.

'What'll he do to you?' said Nobby, as they headed for the gate.

'Hat full of whitewash, probably,' said Boffo. 'Pie inna face if I'm lucky.'

He opened the wicket gate.

'A lot of us ain't happy about this,' he whispered. 'I don't see why those buggers should get away with it. We ought to go round to the Assassins and have it out with them.'

'Why the Assassins?' said Colon. 'Why would they kill a clown?'

Boffo looked guilty. 'I never said a thing!'

Colon glared at him. 'There's definitely something odd happening, Mr Boffo.'

Boffo looked around, as if expecting a vengeful custard pie at any moment.

'You find his nose,' he hissed. 'You just find his nose. His poor nose!'

The gate slammed shut.

Sergeant Colon turned to Nobby.

'Did exhibit A have a nose, Nobby?'

'Yes, Fred.'

'Then what was that about?'

'Search me.' Nobby scratched a promising boil. 'P'raps he meant a false nose. You know. Those red ones on elastic? The ones,' said Nobby, grimacing, 'they think are funny. He didn't have one.'

Colon rapped on the door, taking care to stand out of the way of any jolly amusing booby traps.

The hatch slid aside.

'Yes?' hissed Boffo.

'Did you mean his false nose?' said Colon.

'His real one! Now bugger off!'

The hatch snapped back.

'Mental,' said Nobby, firmly.

'Beano *had* a real nose. Did it look wrong to you?' said Colon.

'No. It had a couple of holes in it.'

'Well, I don't know about noses,' said Colon, 'but either Brother Boffo is dead wrong or there's something fishy going on.'

'Like what?'

'Well, Nobby, you're what I might call a career soldier, right?'
''S'right, Fred.'
'How many dishonourable discharges have you had?'
'Lots,' said Nobby, proudly. 'But I always puts a poultice on 'em.'
'You've been on a lot of battlefields, ain't you?'
'Dozens.'
Sergeant Colon nodded.
'So you've seen a lot of corpses, right, when you've been ministering to the fallen—'
Corporal Nobbs nodded. They both knew that 'ministering' meant harvesting any personal jewellery and stealing their boots. In many a faraway battlefield the last thing many a mortally wounded foeman ever saw was Corporal Nobbs heading towards him with a sack, a knife and a calculating expression.

'Shame to let good stuff go to waste,' said Nobby.
'So you've noticed how dead bodies get . . . deader,' said Sergeant Colon.
'Deader than dead?'
'You know. More corpsey,' said Sergeant Colon, forensic expert.
'Goin' stiff and purple and suchlike?'
'Right.'
'And then sort of manky and runny . . .'
'Yes, all right—'
'Makes it easier to get the rings off, mind you—'
'The *point* is, Nobby, that you can tell how old a corpse is. That clown, for e.g. You saw him, same as me. How long, would you say?'
'About 5′ 9″, I'd say. His boots didn't fit, I know that. Too floppy.'
'I meant how long he'd been dead.'
'Couple of days. You can tell because there's this—'
'So how come Boffo saw him yesterday morning?'
They strolled onwards.
'Bit of a poser, that is,' said Nobby.
'You're right. I expect the captain'll be very interested.'
'Maybe he was a zombie?'
'Shouldn't think so.'
'Never could stand zombies,' Nobby mused.
'Really?'
'It was always so hard to nick their boots.'
Sergeant Colon nodded at a passing beggar.
'You still doing the folk dancing on your nights off, Nobby?'
'Yes, Fred. We're practising "Gathering Sweet Lilacs" this week. There is a very complicated double crossover-step.'
'You're definitely a man of many parts, Nobby.'

'Only if I couldn't cut the rings off, Fred.'

'What I mean is, you presents an intriguing dichotomy.'

Nobby took a kick at a small scruffy dog.

'You been reading books again, Fred?'

'Got to improve my mind, Nobby. It's these new recruits. Carrot's got his nose in a book half the time, Angua knows words I has to look up, even the shortarse is brighter'n me. They keep on extracting the urine. I'm definitely a bit under-endowed in the head department.'

'You're brighter than Detritus,' said Nobby.

'That's what I tell myself. I say, "Fred, whatever happens, you're brighter than Detritus." But then I say, "Fred – so's *yeast.*"'

He turned away from the window.

So. The damn Watch!

That damn Vimes! *Exactly* the wrong man in the wrong place. Why didn't people learn from history? Treachery was in his very genes! How could a city run properly with someone like that, *poking* around? That wasn't what a Watch was for. Watchmen were supposed to do what they were told, and see to it that other people did too.

Someone like Vimes could upset things. Not because he was clever. A clever Watchman was a contradiction in terms. But sheer randomness might cause trouble.

The gonne lay on the table.

'What shall I do about Vimes?'

Kill him.

Angua woke up. It was almost noon, she was in her own bed at Mrs Cake's, and someone was knocking at the door.

'Mmm?' she said.

'Oi don't know. Shall I ask him to go away?' said a voice from around keyhole level.

Angua thought quickly. The other residents had warned her about this. She waited for her cue.

'Oh, thanks, love. Oi was forgetting,' said the voice.

You had to pick your time, with Mrs Cake. It was difficult, living in a house run by someone whose mind was only nominally attached to the present. Mrs Cake was a psychic.

'You've got your precognition switched on again, Mrs Cake,' said Angua, swinging her legs out of bed and rummaging quickly through the pile of clothes on the chair.

352

'Where'd we got to?' said Mrs Cake, still on the other side of the door.

'You just said, "I don't know, shall I ask him to go away?" Mrs Cake,' said Angua. Clothes! That was always the trouble! At least a male werewolf only had to worry about a pair of shorts and pretend he'd been on a brisk run.

'Right.' Mrs Cake coughed. '"There's a young man downstairs asking for you",' she said.

'"Who is it?",' said Angua.

There was a moment's silence.

'Yes, oi think that's all sorted gut,' said Mrs Cake. 'Sorry, dear. Oi get terrible headaches if'n people don't fill in the right bits. Are you human, dear?'*

'You can come in, Mrs Cake.'

It wasn't much of a room. It was mainly brown. Brown oilcloth flooring, brown walls, a picture over the brown bed of a brown stag being attacked by brown dogs on a brown moorland against a sky which, contrary to established meteorological knowledge, was brown. There was a brown wardrobe. Possibly, if you fought your way through the mysterious old coats† hanging in it, you'd break through into a magical fairyland full of talking animals and goblins, but it'd probably not be worth it.

Mrs Cake entered. She was a small fat woman, but made up for her lack of height by wearing a huge black hat; not the pointy witch variety, but one covered with stuffed birds, wax fruit and other assorted decorative items, all painted black. Angua quite liked her. The rooms were clean,‡ the rates were cheap, and Mrs Cake had a very understanding approach to people who lived slightly unusual lives and had, for example, an aversion to garlic. Her daughter was a werewolf and she knew all about the need for ground floor windows and doors with long handles that a paw could operate.

'He's got chainmail on,' said Mrs Cake. She was holding a bucket of gravel in either hand. 'He's got soap in his ears, too.'

'Oh. Er. Right.'

'Oi can tell 'im to bugger off if you like,' said Mrs Cake. 'That's what I allus does if the wrong sort comes round. Especially if they've got a stake. I can't be having with that sort of thing, people messing up the hallways, waving torches and stuff.'

'I think I know who it is,' said Angua. 'I'll see to it.'

---

* More usually a landlady would ask 'Are you decent?', but Mrs Cake knew her lodgers.
† Brown.
‡ And brown.

She tucked in her shirt.

'Pull the door to if you go out,' Mrs Cake called after her as she went out into the hall. 'Oi'm just off to change the dirt in Mr Winkins's coffin, on account of his back giving him trouble.'

'It looks like gravel to me, Mrs Cake.'

'Orthopaedic, see?'

Carrot was standing respectfully on the doorstep with his helmet under his arm and a very embarrassed expression on his face.

'Well?' said Angua, not unkindly.

'Er. Good morning. I thought, you know, perhaps, you not knowing very much about the city, really. I could, if you like, if you don't mind, not having to go on duty for a while . . . show you some of it . . .?'

For a moment Angua thought she'd contracted prescience from Mrs Cake. Various futures flitted across her imagination.

'I haven't had breakfast,' she said.

'They make a very good breakfast in Gimlet's dwarf delicatessen in Cable Street.'

'It's lunchtime.'

'It's breakfast time for the Night Watch.'

'I'm practically vegetarian.'

'He does a soya rat.'

She gave in. 'I'll fetch my coat.'

'Har, har,' said a voice, full of withering cynicism.

She looked down. Gaspode was sitting behind Carrot, trying to glare while scratching himself furiously.

'Last night we chased a cat up a tree,' said Gaspode. 'You and me, eh? We could make it. Fate has thrown us together, style of fing.'

'Go *away*.'

'Sorry?' said Carrot.

'Not you. That dog.'

Carrot turned.

'Him? Is he bothering you now? He's a nice little chap.'

'Woof, woof, biscuit.'

Carrot automatically patted his pocket.

'See?' said Gaspode. 'This boy is Mister Simple, am I right?'

'Do they let dogs in dwarf shops?' said Angua.

'No,' said Carrot.

'On a hook,' said Gaspode.

'Really? Sounds good to me,' said Angua. 'Let's go.'

'Vegetarian?' mumbled Gaspode, limping after them. 'Oh, my.'

'Shut up.'

'Sorry?' said Carrot.

'I was just thinking aloud.'

Vimes's pillow was cold and hard. He felt it gingerly. It was cold and hard because it was not a pillow but a table. His cheek appeared to be stuck to it, and he was not interested in speculating what with.

He hadn't even managed to take his armour off.

But he did manage to unstick one eye.

He'd been writing in his notebook. Trying to make sense of it all. And then he'd gone to sleep.

What time was it? No time to look back.

He traced out:

Stolen from Afsafsins' Guild: gonne – > Hammerhock killed.
Smell of fireworks. Lump of lead. Alchymical Symbols. 2nd body
in river. A clown. Where was his red nose? Gonne.

He stared at the scrawled notes.

I'm on the path, he thought. I don't have to know where it leads. I just have to follow. There's always a crime, if you look hard enough. And the Assassins are in this somewhere.

Follow every lead. Check every detail. Chip, chip away.

I'm hungry.

He staggered to his feet and looked at his face in the cracked mirror over the basin.

Events of the previous day filtered through the clogged gauze of memory. Central to all of them was the face of Lord Vetinari. Vimes grew angry just thinking about that. The cool way he'd told Vimes that he mustn't take an interest in the theft from—

Vimes stared at his reflection—

—something stung his ear and smashed the glass.

Vimes stared at the hole in the plaster, surrounded by the remains of a mirror frame. Around him, the mirror glass tinkled on to the floor.

Vimes stood stock still for a long moment.

Then his legs, reaching the conclusion that his brain was somewhere else, threw the rest of him on to the floor.

There was another tinkle and a half bottle of Bearhugger's exploded on the desk. Vines couldn't even remember buying it.

He scrambled forward on hands and knees and pulled himself upright alongside the window.

Images flashed through his mind. The dead dwarf. The hole in the wall . . .

A thought seemed to start in the small of his back and spread upwards to his brain. These were lath and plaster walls, and old ones at that; you could push a finger through them with a bit of effort. As for a lump of metal—

He hit the floor at the same time as a *pock* coincided with a hole punched through the wall on one side of the window. Plaster dust puffed into the air.

His crossbow was leaning against the wall. He wasn't an expert but, hells, who was? You pointed it and you fired it. He pulled it towards him, rolled on his back, stuck his foot in the stirrup and hauled on the string until it clicked into place.

Then he rolled back on to one knee and slotted a quarrel into the groove.

A catapult, that's what it was. It had to be. Troll-sized, perhaps. Someone up on the roof of the opera house or somewhere high . . .

Draw their fire, draw their fire . . . he picked up his helmet and balanced it on the end of another quarrel. The thing to do was crouch below the window and . . .

He thought for a moment. Then he shuffled across the floor to the corner, where there was a pole with a hook on the end. Once upon a time it had been used to open the upper windows, now long rusted shut.

He balanced his helmet on the end, wedged himself into the corner, and with a certain amount of effort moved the pole so that the helmet just showed over the window si . . .

Pock.

Splinters flew up from a point on the floor where it would undoubtedly have severely inconvenienced anyone lying on the boards cautiously raising a decoy helmet on a stick.

Vimes smiled. Someone was trying to kill him, and that made him feel more alive than he had done for days.

And they were also slightly less intelligent than he was. This is a quality you should always pray for in your would-be murderer.

He dropped the pole, picked up the crossbow, spun past the window, fired at an indistinct shape on the opera house roof opposite as if the bow could possibly carry across that range, leapt across the room and wrenched at the door. Something smashed into the doorframe as the door swung to behind him.

Then it was down the back stairs, out of the door, over the privy roof, into Knuckle Passage, up the back steps of Zorgo the Retro-phrenologist,* into Zorgo's operating room and over to the window.

---

* It works like this. Phrenology, as everyone knows, is a way of reading someone's character, aptitude and abilities by examining the bumps and hollows on their head.

Zorgo and his current patient looked at him curiously.

Pugnant's roof was empty. Vimes turned back and met a pair of puzzled gazes.

''Morning, Captain Vimes,' said the retrophrenologist, a hammer still upraised in one massive hand.

Vimes smiled manically.

'Just thought—' he began, and then went on, '—I saw an interesting rare butterfly on the roof over there.'

Troll and patient stared politely past him.

'But there wasn't,' said Vimes.

He walked back to the door.

'Sorry to have bothered you,' he said, and left.

Zorgo's patient watched him go with interest.

'Didn't he have a crossbow?' he said. 'Bit odd, going after interesting rare butterflies with a crossbow.'

Zorgo readjusted the fit of the grid on his patient's bald head.

'Dunno,' he said, 'I suppose it stops them creating all these damn thunderstorms.' He picked up the mallet again. 'Now, what were we going for today? Decisiveness, yes?'

'Yes. Well, no. Maybe.'

'Right.' Zorgo took aim. 'This,' he said with absolute truth, 'won't hurt a bit.'

It was more than just a delicatessen. It was a sort of dwarf community centre and meeting place. The babble of voices stopped when Angua entered, bending almost double, but started up again with slightly more volume and a few laughs when Carrot followed. He waved cheerfully at the other customers.

Then he carefully removed two chairs. It was just possible to sit upright if you sat on the floor.

'Very . . . nice,' said Angua. 'Ethnic.'

'I come in here quite a lot,' said Carrot. 'The food's good and, of course, it pays to keep your ear to the ground.'

'That'd certainly be easy here,' said Angua, and laughed.

'Pardon?'

'Well, I mean, the ground is . . . so much . . . closer . . .'

Therefore – according to the kind of logical thinking that characterizes the Ankh-Morpork mind – it should be possible to *mould* someone's character by *giving* them carefully graded bumps in all the right places. You can go into a shop and order an artistic temperament with a tendency to introspection and a side order of hysteria. What you actually *get* is hit on the head with a selection of different size mallets, but it creates employment and keeps the money in circulation, and that's the main thing.

She felt a pit opening wider with every word. The noise level had suddenly dropped again.

'Er,' said Carrot, staring fixedly at her. 'How can I put this? People are talking in Dwarfish . . . but they're listening in Human.'

'Sorry.'

Carrot smiled, and then nodded at the cook behind the counter and cleared his throat noisily.

'I think I might have a throat sweet somewhere—' Angua began.

'I was ordering breakfast,' said Carrot.

'You know the menu off by heart?'

'Oh, yes. But it's written on the wall as well.'

Angua turned and looked again at what she'd thought were merely random scratches.

'It's Oggham,' said Carrot. 'An ancient and poetic runic script whose origins are lost in the mists of time but it's thought to have been invented even before the Gods.'

'Gosh. What does it say?'

Carrot really cleared his throat this time.

> 'Soss, egg, beans and rat 12p
> Soss, rat and fried slice 10p
> Cream-cheese rat 9p
> Rat and beans 8p
> Rat and ketchup 7p
> Rat 4p'

'Why does ketchup cost almost as much as the rat?' said Angua.

'Have you tried rat without ketchup?' said Carrot. 'Anyway, I ordered you dwarf bread. Have you ever eaten dwarf bread?'

'No.'

'Everyone should try it once,' said Carrot. He appeared to consider this. 'Most people do,' he added.*

Three and a half minutes after waking up, Captain Samuel Vimes, Night Watch, staggered up the last few steps on to the roof of the

---

* Rat and cream cheese is only one of the famous Discworld dishes available in cosmopolitan Ankh-Morpork. According to the Guild of Merchants' publication *Wellcome to Ankh-Morpork, Citie of One Thousand Surprises*: 'Also to be bought in its well-stuffed emporia are Slumpie, Jammy Devils, Fikkun haddock, Distressed Pudding, Clooty Dumplings† and, not to be forgotten, the Knuckle Sandwich, made from finest pig knuckles. Not for something is it said, For a True Taste of Ankh-Morpork, Try a Knuckle Sandwich.'

† Not to be confused with the Scottish Clootie Dumpling, which is a kind of suet pudding full of fruit. The Ankh-Morpork version sits on the tongue like finest meringue, and on the stomach like a concrete bowling ball.

city's opera house, gasped for breath and threw up *allegro ma non troppo*.

Then he leaned against the wall, waving his crossbow vaguely in front of him.

There wasn't anyone else on the roof. There were just the leads, stretching away, drinking up the morning sunlight. It was already almost too hot to move.

When he felt a bit better he poked around among the chimneys and skylight. But there were a dozen ways down, and a thousand places to hide.

He could see right into his room from here. Come to that, he could see into the rooms of most of the city.

Catapult . . . no . . .

Oh, well. At least there'd been witnesses.

He walked to the edge of the roof, and peered over.

'Hello, there,' he said. He blinked. It was six storeys down, and not a sight to look at on a recently emptied stomach.

'Er . . . could you come up here, please?' he said.

''Ight oo are.'

Vimes stood back. There was a scrape of stone and a gargoyle pulled itself laboriously over the parapet, moving like a cheap stop-motion animation.

He didn't know much about gargoyles. Carrot had said something once about how marvellous it was, an urban troll species that had evolved a symbiotic relationship with gutters, and he had admired the way they funnelled run-off water into their ears and out through fine sieves in their mouths. They were probably the strangest species on the Disc.* You didn't get many birds nesting on buildings colonized by gargoyles, and bats tended to fly around them.

'What's your name, friend?'

''ornice-oggerooking-Oardway.'

Vimes's lips moved as he mentally inserted all those sounds unobtainable to a creature whose mouth was stuck permanently open. Cornice-overlooking-Broadway. A gargoyle's personal identity was intimately bound up with its normal location, like a limpet.

---

* Wrong. Vimes didn't travel much except on foot, and knew little of the Lancre Suicide Thrush, for example, or the Shadowing Lemma, which exists in only two dimensions and eats mathematicians, or the quantum weather butterfly. But it is possible that the strangest, and possibly saddest, species on Discworld is the hermit elephant. This creature, lacking the thick hide of its near relatives, lives in huts, moving up and building extensions as its size increases. It's not unknown for a traveller on the plains of Howondaland to wake up in the morning in the middle of a village that wasn't there the night before.

'Well now, Cornice,' he said, 'do you know who I am?'

'Oh,' said the gargoyle sullenly.

Vimes nodded. It sits up here in all weather straining gnats through its ears, he thought. People like that don't have a crowded address book. Even whelks get out more.

'I'm Captain Vimes of the Watch.'

The gargoyle pricked up its huge ears.

'Ar. Oo erk or Ister Arrot?'

Vimes worked this one out, too, and blinked.

'You know Corporal Carrot?'

'Oh, *Ess*. Air-ee-un owes Arrot.'

Vimes snorted. I grew up here, he thought, and when I walk down the street everyone says, 'Who's that glum bugger?' Carrot's been here a few months and *everyone* knows him. And he knows everyone. *Everyone* likes him. I'd be annoyed about that, if only he wasn't so likeable.

'You live right up here,' said Vimes, interested despite the more pressing problem on his mind, 'how come you know Arrot ... Carrot?'

'Ee cuns uk ere um-imes an awks oo ugg.'

'Uz ee?'

'Egg.'

'Did someone else come up here? Just now?'

'Egg.'

'Did you see who it was?'

'Oh. Ee oot izh oot on i ed. Ang et ogg a ire-erk. I or ing un ah-ay a-ong Or-oh-Ems Eet.'

Holofernes Street, Vimes translated. Whoever it was would be well away by now.

'Ee ad a ick,' Cornice volunteered. 'A ire-erk htick.'

'A what?'

'Ire-erk. Oo oh? Ang! Ock! Arks! Ockekts! Ang!'

'Oh, *fireworks*.'

'Egg. Aks ot I ed.'

'A firework stick? Like ... like a rocket stick?'

'Oh, ih-ee-ot! A htick, oo oint, ik koes ANG!'

'You point it and it goes bang?'

'Egg!'

Vimes scratched his head. Sounded like a wizard's staff. But they didn't go bang.

'Well ... thanks,' he said. 'You've been ... eh-ee elkfhull.'

He turned back towards the stairs.

Someone had tried to kill him.

And the Patrician had warned him against investigating the theft from the Assassins' Guild. *Theft*, he said.

Up until then, Vimes hadn't even been certain there *had* been a theft.

And then, of course, there are the laws of chance. They play a far greater role in police procedure than narrative causality would like to admit. For every murder solved by the careful discovery of a vital footprint or a cigarette end, a hundred failed to be resolved because the wind blew some leaves the wrong way or it didn't rain the night before. So many crimes are solved by a happy accident – by the random stopping of a car, by an overheard remark, by someone of the right nationality happening to be within five miles of the scene of the crime without an alibi . . .

Even Vimes knew about the power of chance.

His sandal clinked against something metallic.

'And this,' said Corporal Carrot, 'is the famous commemorative arch celebrating the Battle of Crumhorn. We won it, I think. It's got over ninety statues of famous soldiers. It's something of a landmark.'

'Should have put up a stachoo to the accountants,' said a doggy voice behind Angua. 'First battle in the universe where the enemy were persuaded to sell their weapons.'

'Where is it, then?' said Angua, still ignoring Gaspode.

'Ah. Yes. That's the problem,' said Carrot. 'Excuse me, Mr Scant. This is Mr Scant. Official Keeper of the Monuments. According to ancient tradition, his pay is one dollar a year and a new vest every Hogswatchday.'

There was an old man sitting on a stool at the road junction, with his hat over his eyes. He pushed it up.

'Afternoon, Mr Carrot. You'll be wanting to see the triumphal arch, will you?'

'Yes, please.' Carrot turned back to Angua. 'Unfortunately, the actual practical design was turned over to Bloody Stupid Johnson.'

The old man eventually produced a small cardboard box from a pocket, and reverentially took off the lid.

'Where is it?'

'Just there,' said Carrot. 'Behind that little bit of cotton wool.'

'Oh.'

'I'm afraid that for Mr Johnson accurate measurements were something that happened to other people.'

Mr Scant closed the lid.

'He also did the Quirm Memorial, the Hanging Gardens of Ankh, and the Colossus of Morpork,' said Carrot.

'The Colossus of Morpork?' said Angua.

Mr Scant held up a skinny finger. 'Ah,' he said. 'Don't go away.' He started to pat his pockets. 'Got 'im 'ere somewhere.'

'Didn't the man ever design anything useful?'

'Well, he did design an ornamental cruet set for Mad Lord Snapcase,' said Carrot, as they strolled away.

'He got that right?'

'Not exactly. But here's an interesting fact, four families live in a salt shaker and we use the pepper pot for storing grain.'

Angua smiled. Interesting facts. Carrot was full of interesting facts about Ankh-Morpork. Angua felt she was floating uneasily on a sea of them. Walking along a street with Carrot was like having three guided tours rolled into one.

'Now here,' said Carrot, 'is the Beggars' Guild. They're the oldest of the Guilds. Not many people know that.'

'Is that so?'

'People think it'd be the Fools or the Assassins. Ask anyone. They'll say "the oldest Guild in Ankh-Morpork is certainly the Fools' Guild or the Assassins' Guild". But they aren't. They're quite recent. But there's been a Beggars' Guild for centuries.'

'Really?' said Angua, weakly. In the last hour she'd learned more about Ankh-Morpork than any reasonable person wanted to know. She vaguely suspected that Carrot was trying to court her. But, instead of the usual flowers or chocolate, he seemed to be trying to gift-wrap a city.

And, despite all her better instincts, she was feeling jealous. Of a city! Ye gods, I've known him a couple of days!

It was the way he wore the place. You expected him any moment to break into the kind of song that has suspicious rhymes and phrases like 'my kind of town' and 'I wanna be a part of it' in it; the kind of song where people dance in the street and give the singer apples and join in and a dozen lowly matchgirls suddenly show amazing choreographical ability and everyone acts like cheery lovable citizens instead of the murderous, evil-minded, self-centred individuals they suspect themselves to be. But the point was that if Carrot had erupted into a song and dance, people *would* have joined in. Carrot could have jollied a circle of standing stones to form up behind him and do a rumba.

'There's some very interesting old statuary in the main court-yard,' he said. "Including a very good one of Jimi, the God of Beggars. I'll show you. They won't mind.'

He rapped on the door.

'You don't have to,' said Angua.

'It's no trouble—'

The door opened.

Angua's nostrils flared. There was a smell . . .

A beggar looked Carrot up and down. His mouth dropped open.

'It's Cumbling Michael, isn't it?' said Carrot, in his cheery way.

The door slammed.

'Well, that wasn't very friendly,' said Carrot.

'Stinks, don't it?' said a nasty little voice from somewhere behind Angua. While she was in no mood to acknowledge Gaspode, she found herself nodding. Although the beggars were an entire cocktail of odours the second biggest one was fear, and the biggest of all was blood. The scent of it made her want to scream.

There was a babble of voices behind the door, and it swung open again.

This time there was a whole crowd of beggars there. They were all staring at Carrot.

'All right, yer honour,' said the one hailed as Cumbling Michael, 'we give in. How did you know?'

'How did we know wh—' Carrot began, but Angua nudged him.

'Someone's been killed here,' she said.

'Who's she?' said Cumbling Michael.

'Lance-Constable Angua is a man of the Watch,' said Carrot.

'Har, har,' said Gaspode.

'I must say you people are getting better,' said Cumbling Michael. 'We only found the poor thing a few minutes ago.'

Angua could *feel* Carrot opening his mouth to say 'Who?' She nudged him again.

'You'd better take us to him,' she said.

He turned out to be—

—for one thing, he turned out to be a she. In a rag-strewn room on the top floor.

Angua knelt beside the body. It was very clearly a body now. It certainly wasn't a person. A person normally had more head on their shoulders.

'Why?' she said. 'Who'd do such a thing?'

Carrot turned to the beggars clustered around the doorway.

'Who was she?'

'Lettice Knibbs,' said Cumbling Michael. 'She was just the lady's maid to Queen Molly.'

Angua glanced up at Carrot.

'Queen?'

'They sometimes call the head beggar king or queen,' said Carrot. He was breathing heavily.

Angua pulled the maid's velvet cloak over the corpse.

'Just the maid,' she muttered.

There was a full-length mirror in the middle of the floor, or at least the frame of one. The glass was scattered like sequins around it.

So was the glass from a window pane.

Carrot kicked aside some shards. There was a groove in the floor, and something metallic embedded in it.

'Cumbling Michael, I need a nail and a length of string,' said Carrot, very slowly and carefully. His eyes never left the speck of metal. It was almost as if he expected it to do something.

'I don't think—' the beggar began.

Carrot reached out without turning his head and picked him up by his grubby collar without apparent effort.

'A length of string,' he repeated, 'and a nail.'

'Yes, Corporal Carrot.'

'And the rest of you, go away,' said Angua.

They goggled at her.

'Do it!' she shouted, clenching her fists. 'And stop staring at her!'

The beggars vanished.

'It'll take a while to get the string,' said Carrot, brushing aside some glass. 'They'll have to beg it off someone, you see.'

He drew his knife and started digging at the floorboards, with care. Eventually he excavated a metal slug, flattened slightly by its passage through the window, the mirror, the floorboards and certain parts of the late Lettice Knibbs that had never been designed to see daylight.

He turned it over and over in his hand.

'Angua?'

'Yes?'

'How did you know there was someone dead in here?'

'I . . . just had a feeling.'

The beggars returned, so unnerved that half a dozen of them were trying to carry one piece of string.

Carrot hammered the nail into the frame under the smashed pane to hold one end of the string. He stuck his knife in the groove and affixed the other end of the string to it. Then he lay down and sighted up the string.

'Good grief.'

'What is it?'

'It must have come from the roof of the opera house.'

'Yes? So?'

'That's more than two hundred yards away.'

'Yes?'

364

'The . . . thing went an inch into an oak floor.'

'Did you know the girl . . . at all?' said Angua, and felt embarrassed at asking.

'Not really.'

'I thought you knew everyone.'

'She was just someone I'd see around. The city's full of people who you just see around.'

'Why do beggars need servants?'

'*You don't think my hair gets like this by itself, dear, do you?*'

There was an apparition in the doorway. Its face was a mass of sores. There were warts, and *they* had warts, and *they* had hair on. It was possibly female, but it was hard to tell under the layers and layers of rags. The aforementioned hair looked as though it had been permed by a hurricane. With treacle on its fingers.

Then it straightened up.

'Oh. Corporal Carrot. Didn't know it was you.'

The voice was normal now, no trace of whine or wheedle. The figure turned and brought her stick down hard on something in the corridor.

'Naughty boy, Dribbling Sidney! You could have told I it were Corporal Carrot!'

'Arrgh!'

The figure strode into the room.

'And who's your ladyfriend, Mr Carrot?'

'This is Lance-Constable Angua. Angua, this is Queen Molly of the Beggars.'

For once, Angua noted, someone wasn't surprised to find a female in the Watch. Queen Molly nodded at her as one working woman to another. The Beggars' Guild was an equal-opportunity non-employer.

'Good day to you. You couldn't spare I ten thousand dollars for a small mansion, could you?'

'No.'

'Just asking.'

Queen Molly prodded at the gown.

'What was it, corporal?'

'I think it's a new kind of weapon.'

'We heard the glass smash and there she was,' said Molly. 'Why would anyone want to kill her?'

Carrot looked at the velvet cloak.

'Whose room is this?' he said.

'Mine. It's my dressing room.'

'Then whoever did it wasn't after her. He was after you, Molly. "Some in rags, and some in tags, and one in a velvet gown" . . . it's in your Charter, isn't it? Official dress of the chief beggar. She probably couldn't resist seeing what it looked like on her. Right gown, right room. Wrong person.'

Molly put her hand to her mouth, risking instant poisoning. 'Assassination?'

Carrot shook his head. 'That doesn't sound right. They like to do it up close. It's a caring profession,' he added, bitterly.

'What should I do?'

'Burying the poor thing would be a good start.' Carrot turned the metal slug over in his fingers. Then he sniffed it.

'Fireworks,' he said.

'Yes,' said Angua.

'And what are you going to do?' said Queen Molly. 'You're Watchmen, aren't you? What's happening? What are you going to do about it?'

Cuddy and Detritus were proceeding along Phedre Road. It was lined with tanneries and brick kilns and timber yards and was not generally considered a beauty spot which was why, Cuddy suspected, they'd been given it to patrol 'to get to know the city'. It got them out of the way. Sergeant Colon thought they made the place look untidy.

There was no sound but the clink of his boots and the thump of Detritus' knuckles on the ground.

Finally, Cuddy said: 'I just want you to know that I don't like being teamed up with you any more than you like being teamed up with me.'

'Right!'

'But if we're going to have to make the best of it, there'd better be some changes, OK?'

'Like what?'

'Like it's ridiculous you not even being able to count. I know trolls can count. Why can't you?'

'Can count!'

'How many fingers am I holding up, then?'

Detritus squinted.

'Two?'

'OK. *Now* how many fingers am I holding up?'

'Two . . . and one more . . .'

'So two and one more is . . .?'

Detritus looked panicky. This was calculus territory.

'Two and one more is three.'

'Two and one more is three.'

366

'Now how many?'

'Two and two.'

'That's *four*.'

'Four-er.'

'*Now* how many?'

Cuddy tried eight fingers. 'A twofour.'

Cuddy looked surprised. He'd expected 'many', or possibly 'lots'.

'What's a twofour?'

'A two and a two and a two and a two.'

Cuddy put his head on one side.

'Hmm,' he said. 'OK. A twofour is what we call an eight.'

'Ate.'

'You know,' said Cuddy, subjecting the troll to a long critical stare, 'you might not be as stupid as you look. This is not hard. Let's think about this. I mean . . . *I'll* think about this, and you can join in when you know the words.'

Vimes slammed the Watch House door behind him. Sergeant Colon looked up from his desk. He had a pleased expression.

'What's been happening, Fred?'

Colon took a deep breath.

'Interesting stuff, captain. Me and Nobby did some *detectoring* up at the Fools' Guild. I've writ it all down what we found out. It's all here. A proper report.'

'Fine.'

'All written down, look. Properly. Punctuation and everything.'

'Well done.'

'It's got commas and everything, look.'

'I'm sure I shall enjoy it, Fred.'

'And the – and Cuddy and Detritus have found out stuff, too. Cuddy's done a report, too. But it's not got so much punctuation as mine.'

'How long have I been asleep?'

'Six hours.'

Vimes tried to make mental space for all of this, and failed.

'I've got to get something inside me,' he said. 'Some coffee or something. And then the world will somehow be better.'

Anyone strolling along Phedre Road might have seen a troll and a dwarf apparently shouting at one another in excitement.

'A two-thirtytwo, and eight, and a one!'

'See? How many bricks in that pile?'

Pause.

'A sixteen, an eight, a four, a one!'

'Remember what I said about dividing by eight-and-two?'

Longer pause.

'Two-enty-nine . . .?'

'Right!'

'Right!'

'You can get there!'

'I can get there!'

'You're a natural at counting to two!'

'I'm a nat'ral at counting to two!'

'If you can count to two, you can count to anything!'

'If I can count to two, I can count to anything!'

'And then the world is your mollusc!'

'My mollusc! What's a mollusc?'

Angua had to scurry to keep up with Carrot.

'Aren't we going to look at the opera house?' she said.

'Later. Anyone up there'll be long gone by the time we get there. We must tell the captain.'

'You think she was killed by the same thing as Hammerhock?'

'Yes.'

'There are . . . niner birds.'

'That's right.'

'There are . . . one bridge.'

'Right.'

'There are . . . four-ten boats.'

'All right.'

'There are . . . one tousand. Three hundret. Six-ty. Four bricks.'

'OK.'

'There are—'

'I should give it a rest now. You don't want to wear everything out by counting—'

'There are – one running man . . .'

'What? Where?'

Sham Harga's coffee was like molten lead, but it had this in its favour: when you'd drunk it, there was this overwhelming feeling of relief that you'd got to the bottom of the cup.

'That,' said Vimes, 'was a bloody awful cup of coffee, Sham.'

'Right,' said Harga.

'I mean I've drunk a lot of bad coffee in my time but that, that was like having a saw dragged across my tongue. How long'd it been boiling?'

'What's today's date?' said Harga, cleaning a glass. He was generally cleaning glasses. No one ever found out what happened to the clean ones.

'August the fifteenth.'

'What year?'

Sham Harga smiled, or at least moved various muscles around his mouth. Sham Harga had run a successful eatery for many years by always smiling, never extending credit, and realizing that most of his customers wanted meals properly balanced between the four food groups: sugar, starch, grease and burnt crunchy bits.

'I'd like a couple of eggs,' said Vimes, 'with the yolks real hard but the whites so runny that they drip like treacle. And I want bacon, that special bacon all covered with bony nodules and dangling bits of fat. And a slice of fried bread. The kind that makes your arteries go clang just by looking at it.'

'Tough order,' said Harga.

'You managed it yesterday. And give me some more coffee. Black as midnight on a moonless night.'

Harga looked surprised. That wasn't like Vimes.

'How black's that, then?' he said.

'Oh, pretty damn black, I should think.'

'Not necessarily.'

'What?'

'You get more stars on a moonless night. Stands to reason. They show up more. It can be quite bright on a moonless night.'

Vimes sighed.

'An *overcast* moonless night?' he said.

Harga looked carefully at his coffee pot.

'Cumulus or cirro-nimbus?'

'I'm sorry? What did you say?'

'You gets city lights reflected off cumulus, because it's low lying, see. Mind you, you can get high-altitude scatter off the ice crystals in—'

'A moonless night,' said Vimes, in a hollow voice, 'that is as black as that coffee.'

'Right!'

'And a doughnut.' Vimes grabbed Harga's stained vest and pulled him until they were nose to nose. 'A doughnut as doughnutty as a doughnut made of flour, water, one large egg, sugar, a pinch of yeast, cinnamon to taste and a jam, jelly or rat filling depending on national or species preference, OK? Not as doughnutty as something in any way metaphorical. Just a doughnut. One doughnut.'

'A doughnut.'

'Yes.'

'You only had to say.'

Harga brushed off his vest, gave Vimes a hurt look, and went back into the kitchen.

'*Stop!* In the name of the law!'

'What the law's name, then?'

'How should I know!'

'Why we chasing him?'

'Because he's running away!'

Cuddy had only been a guard for a few days, but already he had absorbed one important and basic fact: it is almost impossible for anyone to be in a street without breaking the law. There are a whole quiverful of offences available to a policeman who wishes to pass the time of day with a citizen, ranging from Loitering with Intent through Obstruction to Lingering While Being the Wrong Colour/Shape/Species/Sex. It occurred briefly to him that anyone *not* making a dash for it when they saw Detritus knuckling along at high speed behind them was probably guilty of contravening the Being Bloody Stupid Act of 1581. But it was too late to take that into account. Someone was running, and they were chasing. They were chasing because he was running, and he was running because they were chasing.

Vimes sat down with his coffee and looked at the thing he'd picked up from the rooftop.

It looked like a short set of Pan pipes, provided Pan was restricted to six notes, all of them the same. They were made of steel, welded together. There was a strip of serrated metal along one side, like a flattened-out cogwheel, and the whole thing reeked of fireworks.

He laid it carefully beside his plate.

He read Sergeant Colon's report. Fred Colon had spent some time on it, probably with a dictionary. It went as follows:

'Report of Sgt. F. Colon. Approx. 10am today, Auguste 15, I proceeded in the company of Corporal, C. W. St. J. Nobbs, to the Guild of Fools and Joculators in God Street, whereupon we conversed with clown Boffo who said, clown Beano, the *corpus derelicti*, was definitely seen by him, clown Boffo, leaving the Guild the previous morning just after the explosion. {This is dead bent in my opinion, the reason being, the stiff was dead at least two days, Cpl. C. W. St. J. Nobbs agrees, so someone is telling meat pies, never trust anyone who falls on his arse for a living.} Whereupon Dr Whiteface met us, and, damn near gave us the *derriere velocite* out of the place. It seemed to us, viz, me and Cpl. C. W. St. J. Nobbs, that the Fools are worried that it might have been the Assassins, but we don't know why. Also, clown Boffo went on about us looking for Beano's nose, but he had a nose on when we saw him here, so we said to clown Boffo, did he mean a false nose, he said, no, a real one, bugger off. Whereupon we come back here.'

Vimes worked out what *derriere velocite* meant. The whole nose business looked like a conundrum wrapped up in an enigma, or at least in Sergeant Colon's handwriting, which was pretty much the same thing. Why be asked to look for a nose that wasn't lost? He looked at Cuddy's report, written in the careful angular handwriting of someone more used to runes. And sagas.

'Captain Vimes, this herewith is the chronicle of me, Lance-Constable Cvddy. Bright was the morning and high ovr hearts when we proceeded to the Alchemists Gvild, where events eventvated as I shall now sing. These inclvded exploding balls. As to the qvest vpon which we were sent, we were informed that the attached piece of paper [attached] is in the handwriting of Leonard of Qvirm, who vanished in mysteriovs circvmnstances. It is how to make a powder called No.1 powder, which is vsed in fireworks. Mr Silverfish the alchemist says any alchemists knows it. Also, in the margin of the paper, is a drawing of The Gonne, becavse I asked my covsin Grabpot abovt Leonard and he vsed to sell paints to Leonard and he recognized the writing and said Leonard always wrote backwards becavse he was a genivs. I have copied same herewith.'

Vimes laid the papers down and put the piece of metal on top of them.
Then he reached in his pocket and produced a couple of metal pellets.
A stick, the gargoyle had said.
Vimes looked at the sketch. It looked, as Cuddy had noted, like the stock of a crossbow with a pipe on the top of it. There were a

few sketches of strange mechanical devices alongside it, and a couple of the little six-pipe things. The whole drawing looked like a doodle. Someone, possibly this Leonard, had been reading a book about fireworks and had scribbled in the margins.

Fireworks.

Well . . . fireworks? But fireworks weren't a weapon. Crackers went bang. Rockets went up, more or less, but all you could be sure of them hitting was the sky.

Hammerhock was noted for his skill with mechanisms. That wasn't a major dwarfish attribute. People thought it was, but it wasn't. They were skilled with metal all right, and they made good swords and jewellery, but they weren't too *technical* when it came to things like cogwheels and springs. Hammerhock was unusual.

So . . .

Supposing there was a weapon. Supposing there was something about it that was different, strange, terrifying.

No, that couldn't be it. It'd either end up all over the place, or it'd be destroyed. It wouldn't end up in the Assassins' museum. What got put in museums? Things that hadn't worked, or had got lost, or ought to be remembered . . . so where's the sense in putting our firework *on show*?

There had been a lot of locks on the door. So . . . not a museum you just wandered into, then. Maybe you had to be a high-up Assassin, and one day one of the Guild leaders'd take you down there at dead, hah, of night, and say . . . and say . . .

For some reason the face of the Patrician loomed up at this point.

Once again Vimes felt the edge of something, some fundamental central thing . . .

'Where'd he go? Where'd he go?'

There was a maze of alleys around the doors. Cuddy leaned against a wall and fought for breath.

'There he go!' shouted Detritus. 'Along Whalebone Lane!'

He lumbered off in pursuit.

Vimes put down his coffee cup.

Whoever had shot those lead balls at him had been very accurate across several hundred yards, and had got off six shots faster than anyone could fire an arrow . . .

Vimes picked up the pipes. Six little pipes, six shots. And you could carry a pocketful of these things. You could shoot further, faster, more accurately than anyone else with any other kind of weapon . . .

So. A new *type* of weapon. Much, much faster than a bow. The Assassins wouldn't like that. They wouldn't like that *at all*. They weren't even keen on bows. The Assassins preferred to kill up close.

So they'd put the . . . the *gonne* safely under lock and key. The gods alone knew how they'd come by it in the first place. And a few senior Assassins would know about it. They'd pass on the secret: *beware of things like this . . .*

'Down there! He went into Grope Alley!'

'Slow down! Slow down!'

'Why?' said Detritus.

'It's a dead end.'

The two Watchmen lumbered to a halt.

Cuddy knew that he was currently the brains of the partnership, even though Detritus was presently counting, his face beaming with pride, the stones in the wall beside him.

Why had they chased someone halfway across the city? Because they'd run away. *No one* ran away from the Watch. Thieves just flashed their licences. Unlicensed thieves had nothing to fear from the Watch, since they'd saved up all their fear for the Thieves' Guild. Assassins always obeyed the letter of the law. And honest men didn't run away from the Watch.* Running away from the Watch was downright suspicious.

The origin of Grope Alley's name was fortunately lost in the celebrated mists of time, but it had come to be deserved. It had turned into a kind of tunnel as upper storeys were built out and over it, leaving a few inches of sky.

Cuddy peered around the corner, into the gloom.

Click. Click.

It came from deep in the darkness.

'Detritus?'

'Yeah?'

'Did he have any weapons?'

'Just a stick. One stick.'

'Only . . . I smell fireworks.'

Cuddy pulled his head back, very carefully.

There had been the smell of fireworks in Hammerhock's work-

---

* The axiom 'Honest men have nothing to fear from the police' is currently under review by the Axioms Appeal Board.

shop. And Mr Hammerhock ended up with a big hole in his chest. And a sense of named dread, which is much more specific and terrifying than nameless dread, was stealing over Cuddy. It was similar to the feeling you get when you're playing a high stakes game and your opponent suddenly grins and you realize that you don't know *all* the rules but you *do* know you'll be lucky to get out of this with, if you are very fortunate, your shirt.

On the other hand . . . he could picture Sergeant Colon's face. We chased this man into an alley, sarge, and then we came away . . .

He drew his sword.

'Lance-Constable Detritus?'

'Yes, Lance-Constable Cuddy?'

'Follow me.'

Why? The damn thing was made of metal, wasn't it? Ten minutes in a hot crucible and that'd be the end of the problem. Something like that, something dangerous, why not just get rid of it? Why keep it?

But that wasn't human nature, was it? Sometimes things were too fascinating to destroy.

He looked at the strange metal tubes. Six short pipes, welded together, sealed firmly at one end. There was a small hole in the top side of each of the pipes . . .

Vimes slowly picked up one of the lumps of lead . . .

The alley twisted once or twice, but there were no other alleys or doors off it. There was one at the far end. It was larger than a normal door, and heavily constructed.

'Where are we?' whispered Cuddy.

'Don't know,' said Detritus. 'Back of the docks somewhere.'

Cuddy pushed open the door with his sword.

'Cuddy?'

'Yeah?'

'We walked seven-ty-nine steps!'

'That's nice.'

Cold air rushed past them.

'Meat store,' whispered Cuddy. 'Someone picked the lock.'

He slipped through and into a high, gloomy room, as large as a temple, which in some ways it resembled. Faint light crept through the high, ice-covered windows. From rack upon rack, all the way to the ceiling, hung meat carcasses.

They were semi-transparent and so very cold Cuddy's breath turned to crystals in the air.

'Oh, my,' said Detritus. 'I think this the pork futures warehouse in Morpork Road.'

'What?'

'Used to work here,' said the troll. 'Used to work everywhere. Go away, you stupid troll, you too thick,' he added, gloomily.

'Is there any way out?'

'The main door is in Morpork Street. But no one comes in here for months. Till pork exists.'*

Cuddy shivered.

'You in here!' he shouted. 'It's the Watch! Step out now!'

A dark figure appeared from between a couple of pre-pigs.

'Now what we do?' said Detritus.

The distant figure raised what looked like a stick, holding it like a crossbow.

And fired. The first shot zinged off Cuddy's helmet.

A stony hand clamped on to the dwarf's head and Detritus pushed Cuddy behind him, but then the figure was running, running towards them, still firing.

Detritus blinked.

Five more shots, one after another, punctured his breastplate.

And then the running man was through the open door, slamming it behind him.

'Captain Vimes?'

He looked up. It was Captain Quirke of the Day Watch, with a couple of his men behind him.

'Yes?'

'You come with us. And give me your sword.'

'What?'

'I think you heard me, captain.'

'Look, it's *me*, Quirke. Sam Vimes? Don't be a fool.'

---

* Probably no other world in the multiverse has warehouses for things which only exist *in potentia*, but the pork futures warehouse in Ankh-Morpork is a product of the Patrician's rules about baseless metaphors, the literal-mindedness of citizens who assume that everything must exist somewhere, and the general thinness of the fabric of reality around Ankh, which is so thin that it's as thin as a very thin thing. The net result is that trading in pork futures – in pork *that doesn't exist yet* – led to the building of the warehouse to store it in until it does. he extremely low temperatures are caused by the imbalance in the temporal energy flow. At least, that's what the wizards in the High Energy Magic building say. And they've got proper pointy hats and letters after their name, so they know what they're talking about.

'I ain't a fool. I've got men with crossbows. Men. It's you that'd be the fool if you resist arrest.'

'Oh? I'm under arrest?'

'Only if you don't come with us . . .'

The Patrician was in the Oblong Office, staring out of the window. The multi-belled cacophony of five o'clock was just dying away.

Vimes saluted. From the back, Vetinari looked like a carnivorous flamingo.

'Ah, Vimes,' he said, without looking around, 'come here, will you? And tell me what you see.'

Vimes hated guessing games, but he joined the Patrician anyway.

The Oblong Office had a view over half the city, although most of it was rooftops and towers. Vimes's imagination peopled the towers with men holding gonnes. The Patrician would be an easy target.

'What do you see out there, captain?'

'City of Ankh-Morpork, sir,' said Vimes, keeping his expression carefully blank.

'And does it put you in mind of anything, captain?'

Vimes scratched his head. If he was going to play games, he was going to play games . . .

'Well, sir, when I was a kid we owned a cow once, and one day it got sick, and it was always my job to clean out the cowshed, and—'

'It reminds *me* of a clock,' said the Patrician. 'Big wheels, little wheels. All clicking away. The little wheels spin and the big wheels turn, all at different speeds, you see, but the *machine* works. And that is the most important thing. The machine keeps going. Because when the machine breaks down . . .'

He turned suddenly, strode to his desk with his usual predatory stalk, and sat down.

'Or, again, sometimes a piece of grit might get into the wheels, throwing them off balance. One speck of grit.'

Vetinari looked up and flashed Vimes a mirthless smile.

'I won't have that.'

Vimes stared at the wall.

'I believe I told you to forget about certain recent events, captain?'

'Sir.'

'Yet it appears that the Watch have been getting in the wheels.'

'Sir.'

'What am I to do with you?'

'Couldn't say, sir.'

Vimes minutely examined the wall. He wished Carrot was here. The lad might be simple, but he was so simple that sometimes he saw things that the subtle missed. And he kept coming up with simple ideas that stuck in your mind. Policeman, for example. He'd said to Vimes one day, while they were proceeding along the Street of Small Gods: Do you know where 'policeman' comes from, sir? Vimes hadn't. 'Polis' used to mean 'city', said Carrot. That's what policeman means: 'a man for the city'. Not many people know that. The word 'polite' comes from 'polis', too. It used to mean the proper behaviour from someone living *in* a city.

Man of the city . . . Carrot was always throwing out stuff like that. Like 'copper'. Vimes had believed all his life that the Watch were called coppers because they carried copper badges, but no, said Carrot, it comes from the old word *cappere*, to capture.

Carrot read books in his spare time. Not well. He'd have real difficulty if you cut his index finger off. But continuously. And he wandered around Ankh-Morpork *on his day off.*

'Captain Vimes?'

Vimes blinked.

'Sir?'

'You have no concept of the delicate balance of the city. I'll tell you one more time. This business with the Assassins and the dwarf and this clown . . . you are to cease involving yourself.'

'No, sir. I can't.'

'Give me your badge.'

Vimes looked down at his badge.

He never really thought about it. It was just something he'd always had. It didn't *mean* anything very much . . . really . . . one way or the other. It was just something he'd always had.

'My badge?'

'And your sword.'

Slowly, with fingers that suddenly felt like bananas, and bananas that didn't belong to him at that, Vimes undid his sword belt.

'And your badge.'

'Um. Not my badge.'

'Why not?'

'Um. Because it's my badge.'

'But you're resigning anyway when you get married.'

'Right.'

Their eyes met.

'How much does it mean to you?'

Vimes stared. He couldn't find the right words. It was just that he'd always been a man with a badge. He wasn't sure he could be one without the other.

Finally Lord Vetinari said: 'Very well. I believe you're getting married at noon tomorrow.' His long fingers picked up the gilt-embossed invitation from the desk. 'Yes. You can keep your badge, then. And have an honourable retirement. But I'm keeping the sword. And the Day Watch will be sent down to the Yard shortly to disarm your men. I'm standing the Night Watch down, Captain Vimes. In due course I might appoint another man in charge – at my leisure. Until then, you and your men can consider yourselves on leave.'

'The Day Watch? A bunch of—'

'I'm sorry?'

'Yes, sir.'

'One infraction, however, and the badge is mine. Remember.'

Cuddy opened his eyes.

'You're alive?' said Detritus.

The dwarf gingerly removed his helmet. There was a gouge in the rim, and his head ached.

'It looks like a mild skin abrasion,' said Detritus.

'A what? *Ooooh.*' Cuddy grimaced. 'What about you, anyway?' he said. There was something odd about the troll. It hadn't quite dawned on him what it was, but there was definitely something unfamiliar, quite apart from all the holes.

'I suppose the armour was *some* help,' said Detritus. He pulled at the straps of his breastplate. Five discs of metal slid out at around belt level. 'If it hadn't slowed them down I'd be seriously abraded.'

'What's up with you? Why are you talking like that?'

'Like what, pray?'

'What happened to the "me big troll" talk? No offence meant.'

'I'm not sure I understand.'

Cuddy shivered, and stamped his feet to keep warm.

'Let's get out of here.'

They trotted to the door. It was shut fast.

'Can you knock it down?'

'No. If this place wasn't troll proof, it'd be empty. Sorry.'

'Detritus?'

'Yes?'

'Are you all right? Only there's steam coming off your head.'

'I do feel . . . er . . .'

Detritus blinked. There was a tinkle of falling ice. Odd things were happening in his skull.

Thoughts that normally ambulated sluggishly around his brain were suddenly springing into vibrant, coruscating life. And there seemed to be more and more of them.

'My goodness,' he said, to no one in particular.

This was a sufficiently un-troll-like comment that even Cuddy, whose extremities were already going numb, stared at him.

'I do believe,' said Detritus, 'that I am genuinely cogitating. How very interesting!'

'What do you mean?'

More ice cascaded off Detritus as he rubbed his head.

'Of course!' he said, holding up a giant finger. 'Super-conductivity!'

'Wha'?'

'You see? Brain of impure silicon. Problem of heat dissipation. Daytime temperature too hot, processing speed slows down, weather gets hotter, brain stops completely, trolls turn to stone until nightfall, ie, coldertemperature,however,lowertemperature-*enough*,brainoperates*faster*and—'

'I think I'm going to freeze to death soon,' said Cuddy.

Detritus looked around.

'There are small glazed apertures up there,' he said.

'Too hi' to rea', e'en if I st' on y'shoulders,' mumbled Cuddy, slumping down further.

'Ah, but my plan involves throwing something through them to attract help,' said Detritus.

'Wha' pla'?'

'I have in fact eventuated twenty-three but this one has a ninety-seven per cent chance of success,' said Detritus, beaming.

'Ha'nt got an'ting t'throw,' said Cuddy.

'*I* have,' said Detritus, scooping him up. 'Do not worry. I can compute your trajectory with astonishing precision. And then all you will need to do is fetch Captain Vimes or Carrot or someone.'

Cuddy's feeble protests described an arc through the freezing air and vanished along with the window glass.

Detritus sat down again. Life was so simple, when you really thought about it. And he was really thinking.

He was seventy-six per cent sure he was going to get at least seven degrees colder.

Mr Cut-Me-Own-Throat Dibbler, Purveyor, Merchant Venturer and all-round salesman, had thought long and hard about going into ethnic foodstuffs. But it was a natural career procession. The old sausage-in-a-bun trade had been falling off lately, while there were all these trolls and dwarfs around with money in their pockets or wherever it was trolls kept their money, and money in the possession of other people had always seemed to Throat to be against the proper natural order of things.

Dwarfs were easy enough to cater for. Rat-on-a-stick was simple enough, although it meant a general improvement in Dibbler's normal catering standards.

On the other hand, trolls were basically, when you got right down to it, no offence meant, speak as you find . . . basically, they were walking rocks.

He'd sought advice about troll food from Chrysoprase, who was also a troll, although you'd hardly know it any more, he'd been around humans so long he wore a suit now and, as he said, had learned all kindsa civilized things, like extortion, money-lending at 300 per cent interest per munf, and stuff like that. Chrysoprase might have been born in a cave above the snowline on some mountain somewhere, but five minutes in Ankh-Morpork and he'd fitted right in. Dibbler liked to think of Chrysoprase as a friend; you'd hate to think of him as an enemy.

Throat had chosen today to give his new approach a try. He pushed his hot food barrow through streets broad and narrow, crying:

'Sausages! Hot sausages! Inna bun! *Meat* pies! Get them while they're hot!'

This was by way of a warm up. The chances of a human eating anything off Dibbler's barrow unless it was stamped flat and pushed under the door after two weeks on a starvation diet was, by now, remote. He looked around conspiratorially – there were always trolls working in the docks – and took the cover off a fresh tray.

Now then, what was it? Oh, yes . . .

'Dolomitic conglomerates! *Get* chore dolomitic conglomerates heeyar! Manganese nodules! Manganese nodules! Get them while they're . . . uh . . . nodule-shaped.' He hesitated a bit, and then rallied. 'Pumice! Pumice! Tufa a dollar! Roast limestones—'

A few trolls wandered up to stare at him.

'You, sir, you look . . . hungry,' said Dibbler, grinning widely at the smallest troll. 'Why not try our shale on a bun? Mmm-mmm! Taste that alluvial deposit, know what I mean?'

C. M. O. T. Dibbler had a number of bad points, but species prejudice was not one of them. He liked anyone who had money, regardless of the colour and shape of the hand that was proffering it. For Dibbler believed in a world where a sapient creature could walk tall, breathe free, pursue life, liberty and happiness, and step out towards the bright new dawn. If they could be persuaded to gobble something off Dibbler's hot-food tray at the same time, this was all to the good.

The troll inspected the tray suspiciously, and lifted up a bun.

'Urrh, yuk,'he said, 'it's got all ammonites in it! Yuk!'

'Pardon?' said Dibbler.

'Dis shale,' said the troll, 'is stale.'

'Lovely and fresh! Just like mother used to hew!'

'Yeah, and there's bloody quartz all through dis granite,' said another troll, towering over Dibbler. 'Clogs the arteries, quartz.'

He slammed the rock back on the tray. The trolls ambled off, occasionally turning around to give Dibbler a suspicious look.

'Stale? *Stale!* How can it be stale? It's *rock!*' shouted Dibbler after them.

He shrugged. Oh, well. The hallmark of a good businessman was knowing when to cut your losses.

He closed the lid of the tray, and opened another one.

'Hole food! Hole food! Rat! Rat! Rat-onna-stick! Rat-in-a-bun! Get them while they're dead! Get chore—'

There was a crash of glass above him, and Lance-Constable Cuddy landed head first in the tray.

'There's no need to rush, plenty for everyone,' said Dibbler.

'Pull me out,' said Cuddy, in a muffled voice. 'Or pass me the ketchup.'

Dibbler hauled on the dwarf's boots. There was ice on them.

'Just come down the mountain, have you?'

'Where's the man with the key to this warehouse?'

'If you liked our rat, then why not try our fine selection of—'

Cuddy's axe appeared almost magically in his hand.

'I'll cut your knees off,' he said.

'GerhardtSockoftheButchers'Guildiswhoyouwant.'

'Right.'

'Nowpleasetaketheaxeaway.'

Cuddy's boots skidded on the cobbles as he hurried off.

Dibbler peered at the broken remains of the cart. His lips moved as he calculated.

'Here!' he shouted. 'You owe – hey, you owe me for three rats!'

Lord Vetinari had felt slightly ashamed when he watched the door close behind Captain Vimes. He couldn't work out why. Of course, it was hard on the man, but it was the only way . . .

He took a key from a cabinet by his desk and walked over to the wall. His hands touched a mark on the plaster that was apparently no different from a dozen other marks, but this one caused a section of wall to swing aside on well-oiled hinges.

No one knew all the passages and tunnels hidden in the walls of the Palace; it was said that some of them went a lot further than that. And there were any amount of old cellars under the city. A man with a pick-axe and a sense of direction could go where he liked just by knocking down forgotten walls.

He walked down several narrow flights of steps and along a passage to a door, which he unlocked. It swung back on well-oiled hinges.

It was not, exactly, a dungeon; the room on the other side was quite airy and well lit by several large but high windows. It had a smell of wood shavings and glue.

'Look out!'

The Patrician ducked.

Something batlike clicked and whirred over his head, circled erratically in the middle of the room, and then flew apart into a dozen jerking pieces.

'Oh dear,' said a mild voice. 'Back to the drawing tablet. Good afternoon, your lordship.'

'Good afternoon, Leonard,' said the Patrician. 'What was that?'

'I call it a flapping-wing-flying-device,' said Leonard da Quirm, getting down off his launching stepladder. 'It works by gutta-percha strips twisted tightly together. But not very well, I'm afraid.'

Leonard of Quirm was not, in fact, all that old. He was one of those people who started looking venerable around the age of thirty, and would probably still look about the same at the age of ninety. He wasn't exactly bald, either. His head had just grown up through his hair, rising like a mighty rock dome through heavy forest.

Inspirations sleet through the universe continuously. Their destination, as if they cared, is the right mind in the place at the right time. They hit the right neuron, there's a chain reaction, and a little while later someone is blinking foolishly in the TV lights and wondering how the hell he came up with the idea of pre-sliced bread in the first place.

Leonard of Quirm knew about inspirations. One of his earliest inventions was an earthed metal nightcap, worn in the hope that the damn things would stop leaving their white-hot trails across his tortured imagination. It seldom worked. He knew the shame of waking up to find the sheets covered with nocturnal sketches of unfamiliar siege engines and novel designs for apple-peeling machines.

The da Quirms had been quite rich and young Leonard had been to a great many schools, where he had absorbed a ragbag of information despite his habit of staring out of the window and sketching the flight of birds. Leonard was one of those unfortunate individuals whose fate it was to be fascinated by the world, the taste, shape and movement of it . . .

He fascinated Lord Vetinari as well, which is why he was still alive. Some things are so perfect of their type that they are hard to destroy. One of a kind is always special.

He was a model prisoner. Give him enough wood, wire, paint and above all give him paper and pencils, and he stayed put.

The Patrician moved a stack of drawings and sat down.

'These are good,' he said. 'What are they?'

'My cartoons,' said Leonard.

'This is a good one of the little boy with his kite stuck in a tree,' said Lord Vetinari.

'Thank you. May I make you some tea? I'm afraid I don't see many people these days, apart from the man who oils the hinges.'

'I've come to . . .'

The Patrician stopped and prodded at one of the drawings.

'There's a piece of yellow paper stuck to this one,' he said, suspiciously. He pulled at it. It came away from the drawing with a faint sucking noise, and then stuck to his fingers. On the note, in Leonard's crabby backward script, were the words: 'krow ot smees sihT: omeM'.

'Oh, I'm rather pleased with that,' said Leonard. 'I call it my "Handy-note-scribbling-piece-of-paper-with-glue-that-comes-unstuck-when-you-want".'

The Patrician played with it for a while.

'What's the glue made of?'

'Boiled slugs.'

The Patrician pulled the paper off one hand. It stuck to the other hand.

'Is that what you came to see me about?' said Leonard.

'No. I came to talk to you,' said Lord Vetinari, 'about the gonne.'

'Oh, dear. I'm very sorry.'

'I am afraid it has . . . escaped.'

'My goodness. I thought you said you'd done away with it.'

'I gave it to the Assassins to destroy. After all, they pride themselves on the artistic quality of their work. They should be horrified at the idea of *anyone* having that sort of power. But the damn fools did *not* destroy it. They thought they could lock it away. And now they've lost it.'

'They didn't destroy it?'

'Apparently not, the fools.'

'And nor did you. I wonder why?'

'I . . . do you know, I don't know?'

'I should never have made it. It was merely an application of principles. Ballistics, you know. Simple aerodynamics. Chemical power. Some rather good alloying, although I say it myself. And I'm rather proud of the rifling idea. I had to make a quite complicated tool for that, you know. Milk? Sugar?'

'No, thank you.'

'People are searching for it, I trust?'

'The Assassins are. But they won't find it. They don't think the right way.' The Patrician picked up a pile of sketches of the human skeleton. They were extremely good.

'Oh, dear.'

'So I am relying on the Watch.'

'This would be the Captain Vimes you have spoken of.'

Lord Vetinari always enjoyed his occasional conversations with Leonard. The man always referred to the city as if it was another world.

'Yes.'

'I hope you have impressed upon him the importance of the task.'

'In a way. I've absolutely forbidden him to undertake it. Twice.'

Leonard nodded. 'Ah. I . . . think I understand. I hope it works.' He sighed.

'I suppose I should have dismantled it, but . . . it was so clearly a *made* thing. I had this strange fancy I was merely assembling something that already existed. Sometimes I wonder where I got the whole idea. It seemed . . . I don't know . . . sacrilege, I suppose, to dismantle it. It'd be like dismantling a person. Biscuit?'

'Dismantling a person is sometimes necessary,' said Lord Vetinari.

'This, of course, is a point of view,' said Leonard da Quirm politely.

'You mentioned sacrilege,' said Lord Vetinari. 'Normally that involves gods of some sort, does it not?'

'Did I use the word? I can't imagine there is a god of gonnes.'

'It is quite hard, yes.'

The Patrician shifted uneasily, reached down behind him, and pulled out an object.

'What,' he said, 'is this?'

384

'Oh, I wondered where that had gone,' said Leonard. 'It's a model of my spinning-up-into-the-air machine.'*

Lord Vetinari prodded the little rotor.

'Would it work?'

'Oh, yes,' said Leonard. He sighed. 'If you can find one man with the strength of ten men who can turn the handle at about one thousand revolutions a minute.'

The Patrician relaxed, in a way which only then drew gentle attention to the foregoing moment of tension.

'Now there is in this city,' he said, 'a man with a gonne. He has used it successfully once, and almost succeeded a second time. Could anyone have invented the gonne?'

'No,' said Leonard. 'I am a genius.' He said it quite simply. It was a statement of fact.

'Understood. But once a gonne has been invented, Leonard, how much of a genius need someone be to make the second one?'

'The rifling technique requires considerable finesse, and the cocking mechanism that slides the bullette assembly is finely balanced, and of course the end of the barrel must be very . . .' Leonard saw the Patrician's expression, and shrugged. 'He must be a clever man,' he said.

'This city is full of clever men,' said the Patrician. 'And dwarfs. Clever men and dwarfs who tinker with things.'

'I am so very sorry.'

'They never *think*.'

'Indeed.'

Lord Vetinari leaned back and stared at the skylight.

'They do things like open the Three Jolly Luck Take-Away Fish Bar on the site of the old temple in Dagon Street on the night of the Winter solstice when it also happens to be a full moon.'

'That's people for you, I'm afraid.'

'I never did find out what happened to Mr Hong.'

'Poor fellow.'

'And then there's the wizards. Tinker, tinker, tinker. Never think twice before grabbing a thread of the fabric of reality and giving it a pull.'

'Shocking.'

'The alchemists? Their idea of civic duty is mixing up things to see what happens.'

'I hear the bangs, even here.'

---

* It has probably been gathered that although Leonard da Quirm was absolutely the greatest technological genius of all time, he was a bit of a Detritus when it came to thinking up names.

'And then, of course, along comes someone like you—'

'I really am terribly sorry.'

Lord Vetinari turned the model flying machine over and over in his fingers.

'You dream of flying,' he said.

'Oh, yes. Then men would be truly free. From the air, there are no boundaries. There could be no more war, because the sky is endless. How happy we would be, if we could but fly.'

Vetinari turned the machine over and over in his hands.

'Yes,' he said, 'I daresay we would.'

'I had tried clockwork, you know.'

'I'm sorry? I was thinking about something else.'

'I meant clockwork to power my flying machine. But it won't work.'

'Oh.'

'There's a limit to the power of a spring, no matter how tightly one winds it.'

'Oh, yes. Yes. And you hope that if you wind a spring one way, all its energies will unwind the other way. And sometimes you have to wind the spring as tight as it will go,' said Vetinari, 'and pray it doesn't break.'

His expression changed.

'Oh dear,' he said.

'Pardon?' said Leonard.

'He didn't thump the wall. I may have gone too far.'

Detritus sat and steamed. Now he felt hungry – not for food, but for things to think about. As the temperature sank, the efficiency of his brain increased even more. It needed something to do.

He calculated the number of bricks in the wall, first in twos and then in tens and finally in sixteens. The numbers formed up and marched past his brain in terrified obedience. Division and multiplication were discovered. Algebra was invented and provided an interesting diversion for a minute or two. And then he felt the fog of numbers drift away, and looked up and saw the sparkling, distant mountains of calculus.

Trolls evolved in high, rocky and above all in *cold* places. Their silicon brains were used to operating at low temperatures. But down on the muggy plains the heat build-up slowed them down and made them dull. It wasn't that only stupid trolls came down to the city. Trolls who decided to come down to the city were often quite smart – but they *became* stupid.

Detritus was considered moronic even by city troll standards.

But that was simply because his brain was naturally optimized for a temperature seldom reached in Ankh-Morpork even during the coldest winter . . .

Now his brain was nearing its ideal temperature of operation. Unfortunately, this was pretty close to a troll's optimum point of death.

Part of his brain gave some thought to this. There was a high probability of rescue. That meant he'd have to leave. That meant he'd become stupid again, as sure as $10^{-3} (M_e/M_p)\alpha^6\alpha^G - \frac{1}{2}N \approx 10N$.

Better make the most of it, then.

He went back to the world of numbers so complex that they had no meaning, only a transitional point of view. And got on with freezing to death, as well.

Dibbler reached the Butchers' Guild very shortly after Cuddy. The big red doors had been kicked open and a small butcher was sitting just inside them rubbing his nose.

'Which way did he go?'

'Dat way.'

And in the Guild's main hall the master butcher Gerhardt Sock was staggering around in circles. This was because Cuddy's boots were planted on his chest. The dwarf was hanging on to the man's vest like a yachtsman tacking into a gale, and whirling his axe round and round in front of Sock's face.

'You give it to me right now or I'll make you eat your own nose!'

A crowd of apprentice butchers was trying to keep out of the way.

'But—'

'Don't you argue with me! I'm an officer of the Watch, I am!'

'But you—'

'You've got one last chance, mister. Give it to me right now!'

Sock shut his eyes.

'*What is it you want?*'

The crowd waited.

'Ah,' said Cuddy. 'Ahaha. Didn't I say?'

'No!'

'I'm pretty sure I did, you know.'

'You didn't!'

'Oh. Well. It's the key to the pork futures warehouse, if you must know.' Cuddy jumped down.

'Why?'

The axe hovered in front of his nose again.

'I was just asking,' said Sock, in a desperate and distant voice.

'There's a man of the Watch in there freezing to death,' said Cuddy.

There was quite a crowd around them when they finally got the main door open. Lumps of ice clinked on the stones, and there was a rush of supercold air.

Frost covered the floor and the rows of hanging carcasses on their backwards journey through time. It also covered a Detritus-shaped lump squatting in the middle of the floor.

They carried it out into the sunlight.

'Should his eyes be flashing on and off like that?' said Dibbler.

'Can you hear me?' shouted Cuddy. 'Detritus?'

Detritus blinked. Ice slid off him in the day's heat.

He could feel the cracking up of the marvellous universe of numbers. The rising temperature hit his thoughts like a flame-thrower caressing a snowflake.

'Say something!' said Cuddy.

Towers of intellect collapsed as the fire roared through Detritus' brain.

'Hey, look at *this*,' said one of the apprentices.

The inner walls of the warehouse were covered with numbers. Equations as complex as a neural network had been scraped in the frost. At some point in the calculation the mathematician had changed from using numbers to using letters, and then letters themselves hadn't been sufficient; brackets like cages enclosed expressions which were to normal mathematics what a city is to a map.

They got simpler as the goal neared – simpler, yet containing in the flowing lines of their simplicity a spartan and wonderful complexity.

Cuddy stared at them. He knew he'd never be able to understand them in a hundred years.

The frost crumbled in the warmer air.

The equations narrowed as they were carried on down the wall and across the floor to where the troll had been sitting, until they became just a few expressions that appeared to move and sparkle with a life of their own. This was maths without numbers, pure as lightning.

They narrowed to a point, and at the point was just the very simple symbol: '='.

'Equals what?' said Cuddy. 'Equals what?'

The frost collapsed.

Cuddy went outside. Detritus was now sitting in a puddle of water, surrounded by a crowd of human onlookers.

'Can't one of you get him a blanket or something?' he said.

A very fat man said, 'Huh? Who'd use a blanket after it had been on a troll?'

'Hah, yes, good point,' said Cuddy. He glanced at the five holes in Detritus' breastplate. They were at about head height, for a dwarf. 'Could you come over here for moment, please?'

The man grinned at his friends, and sauntered over.

'I expect you can see the holes in his armour, right?' said Cuddy.

C. M. O. T. Dibbler was a survivor. In the same way that rodents and insects can sense an earthquake ahead of the first tremors, so he could tell if something big was about to go down on the street. Cuddy was being too nice. When a dwarf was nice like that, it meant he was saving up to be nasty later on.

'I'll just, er, go about my business, thee,' he said, and backed away.

'I've got nothing against *dwarfs*, mind you,' said the fat man. 'I mean, dwarfs is practically people, in my book. Just shorter humans, almost. But trolls . . . weeeelll . . . they're not the same as us, right?'

''scuse me, 'scuse me, gangway, gangway,' said Dibbler, achieving with his cart the kind of getaway customarily associated with vehicles that have fluffy dice on the windscreen.

'That's a nice coat you've got there,' said Cuddy.

Dibbler's cart went around the corner on one wheel.

'It's a *nice* coat,' said Cuddy. 'You know what you should do with a coat like that?'

The man's forehead wrinkled.

'Take it off right now,' said Cuddy, 'and give it to the troll.'

'Why, you little—'

The man grabbed Cuddy by his shirt and wrenched him upwards.

The dwarf's hand moved very quickly. There was a scrape of metal.

Man and dwarf made an interesting and absolute stationary tableau for a few seconds.

Cuddy had been brought up almost level with the man's face, and watched with interest as the eyes began to water.

'Let me down,' said Cuddy. 'Gently. I make involuntary muscle movements if I'm startled.'

The man did so.

'Now take off your coat . . . good . . . just pass it over . . . thank you . . .'

'Your axe . . .' the man murmured.

'Axe? Axe? My axe?' Cuddy looked down. 'Well, well, well. Hardly knew I was holding it there. My axe. Well, there's a thing.'

The man was trying to stand on tiptoe. His eyes were watering.

'The thing about this axe,' said Cuddy, 'the interesting thing, is that it's a throwing axe. I was champion three years running up at Copperhead. I could draw it and split a twig thirty yards away in one second. *Behind* me. *And* I was ill that day. A bilious attack.'

He backed away. The man sank gratefully on to his heels.

Cuddy draped the coat over the troll's shoulders.

'Come on, on your feet,' he said. 'Let's get you home.'

The troll lumbered upright.

'How many fingers am I holding up?' said Cuddy.

Detritus peered.

'Two and one?' he suggested.

'It'll do,' said Cuddy. 'For a start.'

Mr Cheese looked over the bar at Captain Vimes, who hadn't moved for an hour. The Bucket was used to serious drinkers, who drank without pleasure but with a sort of determination never to see sobriety again. But this was something new. This was worrying. He didn't want a death on his hands.

There was no one else in the bar. He hung his apron on a nail and hurried out towards the Watch House, almost colliding with Carrot and Angua in the doorway.

'Oh, I'm glad that's you, Corporal Carrot,' he said. 'You'd better come. It's Captain Vimes.'

'What's happened to him?'

'I don't know. He's drunk an awful lot.'

'I thought he was off the stuff!'

'I think,' said Mr Cheese cautiously, 'that this is not the case any more.'

A scene, somewhere near Quarry Lane:

'Where we going?'

'I'm going to get someone to have a look at you.'

'Not dwarf doctor!'

'There must be someone up here who knows how to slap some quick-drying cement on you, or whatever you do. Should you be oozing like that?'

'Dunno. Never oozed before. Where we?'

'Dunno. Never been down here before.'

The area was on the windward side of the cattle yards and the slaughterhouse district. That meant it was shunned as living space by everyone except trolls, to whom the organic odours were about as relevant and noticeable as the smell of granite would be to humans. The old joke went: the trolls live next to the cattleyard? What about the stench? Oh, the cattle don't mind . . .

Which was daft. Trolls didn't smell, except to other trolls.

There was a slabby look about the buildings here. They had been built for humans but adapted by trolls, which broadly had meant kicking the doorways wider and blocking up the windows. It was still daylight. There weren't any trolls visible.

'Ugh,' said Detritus.

'Come on, big man,' said Cuddy, pushing Detritus along like a tug pushes a tanker.

'Lance-Constable Cuddy?'

'Yes.'

'You a dwarf. This is Quarry Lane. You found here, you in deep trouble.'

'We're city guards.'

'Chrysoprase, he not give a coprolith about that stuff.'

Cuddy looked around.

'What do you people use for doctors, anyway?'

A troll face appeared in a doorway. And another. And another.

What Cuddy had thought was a pile of rubble turned out to be a troll. There were, suddenly, trolls everywhere.

I'm a guard, thought Cuddy. That's what Sergeant Colon said. Stop being a dwarf and start being a Watchman. That's what I am. Not a dwarf. A Watchman. They gave me a badge, shaped like a shield. City Watch, that's me. I carry a badge.

I wish it was a lot bigger.

Vimes was sitting quietly at a table in the corner of The Bucket. There were some pieces of paper and a handful of metal objects in front of him, but he was staring at his fist. It was lying on the table, clenched so tight the knuckles were white.

'Captain Vimes?' said Carrot, waving a hand in front of his eyes. There was no response.

'How much has he had?'

'Two nips of whiskey, that's all.'

'That shouldn't do this to him, even on an empty stomach,' said Carrot.

Angua pointed at the neck of a bottle protruding from Vimes's pocket.

'I don't think he's been drinking on an empty stomach,' she said. 'I think he put some alcohol in it first.'

'Captain Vimes?' said Carrot again.

'What's he holding in his hand?' said Angua.

'I don't know. This is bad, I've never seen him like this before. Come on. You take the stuff. I'll take the captain.'

'He hasn't paid for his drink,' said Mr Cheese.

Angua and Carrot looked at him.

'On the house?' said Mr Cheese.

There was a wall of trolls around Cuddy. It was as good a choice of word as any. Right now their attitude was more of surprise than menace, such as dogs might show if a cat had just sauntered into the kennels. But when they'd finally got used to the idea that he really existed, it was probably only a matter of time before this state of affairs no longer obtained.

Finally, one of them said, 'What dis, then?'

'He a man of the Watch, same as me,' said Detritus.

'Him a dwarf.'

'He a Watchman.'

'Him got bloody cheek, I know that.' A stubby troll finger prodded Cuddy in the back. The trolls crowded in.

'I count to ten,' said Detritus. 'Then any troll not going about that troll's business, he a sorry troll.'

'You Detritus,' said a particularly wide troll. 'Everyone know you stupid troll, you join Watch because stupid troll, you can't count to—'

Wham.

'One,' said Detritus. 'Two . . . Tree. Four-er . . . Five. Six . . .'

The recumbent troll looked up in amazement.

'That Detritus, him *counting*.'

There was a whirring noise and an axe bounced off the wall near Detritus' head.

There were dwarfs coming up the street, with a purposeful and deadly air. The trolls scattered.

Cuddy ran forward.

'What are you lot doing?' he said. 'Are you mad, or something?'

A dwarf pointed a trembling finger at Detritus.

'What's *that*?'

'He's a Watchman.'

'Looks like a troll to me. Get it!'

Cuddy took a step backwards and produced his axe.

'I know you, Stronginthearm,' he said. 'What's this all about?'

'You know, Watch*man*,' said Stronginthearm. 'The Watch say a troll killed Bjorn Hammerhock. They've found the troll!'

'No, that's not—'

There was a sound behind Cuddy. The trolls were back, armed for dwarf. Detritus turned around and waved a finger at them.

'Any troll move,' he said, 'and I start counting.'

'Hammerhock was killed by a men,' said Cuddy. 'Captain Vimes thinks—'

'The Watch have got the troll,' said a dwarf. 'Damn rocks!'

'Gritsuckers!'

'Monoliths!'

'Eaters of rats!'

'Hah, I been a man only hardly any time,' said Detritus, 'and already I fed up with you stupid trolls. What you think humans say, eh? Oh, them ethnic, them don't know how to behave in big city, go around waving clubs at the drop of a thing you wear on head.'

'We're Watchmen,' said Cuddy. 'Our job is to keep the peace.'

'Good,' said Stronginthearm. 'Go and keep it safe somewhere until we need it.'

'This not Koom Valley,' said Detritus.

'That's right!' shouted a dwarf at the back of the crowd. 'This time we can see you!'

Trolls and dwarfs were pouring in at either end of the street.

'What would Corporal Carrot do at a time like this?' whispered Cuddy.

'He say, you bad people, make me angry, you stop toot sweet.'

'And then they'd go away, right?'

'Yeah.'

'What would happen if we tried that?'

'We look in gutter for our heads.'

'I think you're right.'

'You see that alley? It a nice alley. It say, hello. You outnumbered . . . 256+64+8+2+1 to 1. Drop in and see me.'

A club bounced off Detritus' helmet.

'Run!'

The two Watchmen sprinted for the alley. The impromptu armies watched them and then, differences momentarily forgotten, gave chase.

'Where this go?'

'It goes away from the people chasing us!'

'I *like* this alley.'

Behind them the pursuers, suddenly trying to make progress in a gap barely wide enough to accommodate a troll, realized that they were pushing and shoving with their mortal enemies and started to fight one another in the quickest, nastiest and above all *narrowest* battle ever held in the city.

Cuddy waved Detritus to a halt and peered around a corner.

'I think we're safe,' he said. 'All we have to do is get out of the other end of this and get back to the Watch House. OK?'

He turned around, failed to see the troll, took a step forward, and vanished temporarily from the world of men.

'Oh, no,' said Sergeant Colon. 'He promised he wasn't going to touch it any more! Look, he's had a whole bottle!'

'What is it? Bearhugger's?' said Nobby.

'Shouldn't think so, he's still breathing. Come on, help me up with him.'

The Night Watch clustered around. Carrot had deposited Captain Vimes on a chair in the middle of the Watch House floor.

Angua picked out the bottle and looked at the label.

'C. M. O. T. Dibbler's Genuine Authentic Soggy Mountain Dew,' she read. 'He's going to die! It says, "One hundred and fifty per cent proof"!'

'Nah, that's just old Dibbler's advertising,' said Nobby. 'It ain't got no *proof*. Just circumstantial evidence.'

'Why hasn't he got his sword?' said Angua.

Vimes opened his eyes. The first thing he saw was the concerned face of Nobby.

'Aargh!' he said. 'Swor'? Gi' it 'way! Hooray!'

'What?' said Colon.

'No mo' Watsh! All go' . . .'

'I think he's a bit drunk,' said Carrot.

'Drun'? 'm not drun'! You wouldn' dare call m' drun' if I was sober!'

'Get him some coffee,' said Angua.

'I reckon he's beyond *our* coffee,' said Colon. 'Nobby, nip along to Fat Sally's in Squeezebelly Alley and get a jug of their special Klatchian stuff. Not a metal jug, mind.'

Vimes blinked as they manhandled him into a chair.

'All go 'way,' he said. 'Bang! Bang!'

'Lady Sybil's going to be really mad,' said Nobby. 'You know he promised to leave it alone.'

'Captain Vimes?' said Carrot.

'Mm?'

'How many fingers am I holding up?'

'Mm?'

394

'How many hands, then?'

'Fo'?'

'Blimey, I haven't seen him like this for years,' said Colon. 'Here, let me try something. *Want another drink, captain?*'

'He certainly doesn't need a—'

'Shut up, I know what I'm doing. Another drink, Captain Vimes?'

'Mm?'

'I've never known him not be able to give a loud clear "yes!",' said Colon, standing back. 'I think we'd better get him up to his room.'

'I'll take him, poor chap,' said Carrot. He lifted Vimes easily, and slung him over his shoulder.

'I hate to see him like this,' said Angua, following him into the hallway and up the stairs.

'He only drinks when he gets depressed,' said Carrot.

'Why does he get depressed?'

'Sometimes it's because he hasn't had a drink.'

The house in Pseudopolis Yard had originally been a Ramkin family residence. Now the first floor was occupied by the guards on an ad hoc basis. Carrot had a room. Nobby had rooms consecutively, four so far, moving out when the floor became hard to find. And Vimes had a room.

More or less. It was hard to tell. Even a prisoner in a cell manages to stamp his personality on it somewhere, but Angua had never seen such an unlived-in room.

'This is where he lives?' said Angua. 'Good grief.'

'What did you expect?'

'I don't know. Anything. Something. Not *nothing*.'

There was a joyless iron bedstead. The springs and mattress had sagged so that they formed a sort of mould, forcing anyone who got into it to instantly fold into a sleeping position. There was a washstand, under a broken mirror. On the stand was a razor, carefully aligned towards the Hub because Vimes shared the folk belief that this kept it sharp. There was a brown wooden chair with the cane seat broken. And a small chest at the foot of the bed.

And that was all.

'I mean, at least a rug,' said Angua. 'A picture on the wall. Something.'

Carrot deposited Vimes on the bed, where he flowed unconsciously into the shape.

'Haven't you got something in your room?' Angua asked.

'Yes. I've got a cutaway diagram of No.5 shaft at home. It's very interesting strata. I helped cut it. And some books and things. Captain Vimes isn't really an indoors kind of person.'

'But there's not even a candle!'

'He finds his way to bed by memory, he says.'

'Or an ornament or *anything*.'

'There's a sheet of cardboard under the bed,' Carrot volunteered. 'I remember I was with him in Filigree Street when he found it. He said "There's a month's soles in this, if I'm any judge". He was very pleased about that.'

'He can't even afford boots?'

'I don't think so. I know Lady Sybil offered to buy him all the new boots he wanted, and he got a bit offended about that. He seems to try to make them last.'

'But you can buy boots, and you get less than him. And you send money home. He must drink it all, the idiot.'

'Don't think so. I didn't think he'd touched the stuff for months. Lady Sybil got him on to cigars.'

Vimes snored loudly.

'How can you admire a man like this?' said Angua.

'He's a very fine man.'

Angua raised the lid of the wooden chest with her foot.

'Hey, I don't think you should do that—' said Carrot wretchedly.

'I'm just looking,' said Angua. 'No law against that.'

'In fact, under the Privacy Act of 1467, it *is* an—'

'There's only old boots and stuff. And some paper.' She reached down and picked up a crudely made book. It was merely a wad of irregular shaped bits of paper sandwiched together between card covers.

'That belongs to Captain—'

She opened the book and read a few lines. Her mouth dropped open.

'Will you look at this? No wonder he never has any money!'

'What d'you mean?'

'He spends it on women! You wouldn't think it, would you? Look at this entry. Four in one week!'

Carrot looked over her shoulder. On the bed, Vimes snorted.

There, on the page, in Vimes's curly handwriting, were the words:

Mrs Galkin, Mincing St: $5
Mrs Scurrick, Treacle St: $4
Mrs Maroon, Wixon's Alley: $4
Annabel Curry, Lobfneaks: $2

'Annabel Curry couldn't have been much good, for only two dollars,' said Angua.

She was aware of a sudden drop in temperature.

'I shouldn't think so,' said Carrot, slowly. 'She's only nine years old.'

One of his hands gripped her wrist tightly and the other prised the book out of her fingers.

'Hey, let *go!*'

'Sergeant!' shouted Carrot, over his shoulder, 'can you come up here a moment?'

Angua tried to pull away. Carrot's arm was as immovable as an iron bar.

There was the creak of Colon's foot on the stair, and the door swung open.

He was holding a very small cup in a pair of tongs.

'Nobby got the coff—' he began, and stopped.

'Sergeant,' said Carrot, staring into Angua's face, 'Lance-Constable Angua wants to know about Mrs Gaskin.'

'Old Leggy Gaskin's widow? She lives in Mincing Street.'

'And Mrs Scurrick?'

'In Treacle Street? Takes in laundry now.' Sergeant Colon looked from one to the other, trying to get a handle on the situation.

'Mrs Maroon?'

'That's Sergeant Maroon's widow, she sells coal in—'

'How about Annabel Curry?'

'She still goes to the Spiteful Sisters of Seven-Handed Sek Charity School, doesn't she?' Colon smiled nervously at Angua, still not sure of what was happening. 'She's the daughter of Corporal Curry, but of course he was before your time—'

Angua looked up at Carrot's face. His expression was unreadable.

'They're the widows of coppers?' she said.

He nodded. 'And one orphan.'

'It's a tough old life,' said Colon. 'No pensions for widows, see.'

He looked from one to the other.

'Is there something wrong?' he said.

Carrot relaxed his grip, turned, slipped the book into the box, and shut the lid.

'No,' he said.

'Look, I'm sorr—' Angua began. Carrot ignored her and nodded at the sergeant.

'Give him the coffee.'

'But . . . fourteen dollars . . . that's nearly half his pay!'

Carrot picked up Vimes's limp arm and tried to prise his fist open, but even though Vimes was out cold the fingers were locked.

'I mean, half his *pay!*'

'I don't know what he's holding in here,' said Carrot, ignoring her. 'Maybe it's a clue.'

He took the coffee and hauled up Vimes by his collar.

'You just drink this, captain,' he said, 'and everything will look a lot . . . clearer . . .'

Klatchian coffee has an even bigger sobering effect than an unexpected brown envelope from the tax man. In fact, coffee enthusiasts take the precaution of getting thoroughly drunk before touching the stuff, because Klatchian coffee takes you back through sobriety and, if you're not careful, *out the other side*, where the mind of man should not go. The Watch was generally of the opinion that Samuel Vimes was at least two drinks under par, and needed a stiff double even to be sober.

'Careful . . . careful . . .' Carrot let a few drops dribble between Vimes's lips.

'Look, when I said—' Angua began.

'Forget it.' Carrot didn't even look round.

'I was only—'

'I said forget it.'

Vimes opened his eyes, took a look at the world, and screamed.

'Nobby!'

'Yes, sarge?'

'Did you buy the Red Desert Special or the Curly Mountain Straight?'

'Red Desert, sarge, because—'

'You could have said. Better get me—' He glanced at Vimes's grimace of horror '—half a glass of Bearhugger's. We've sent him too far the other way.'

The glass was fetched and administered. Vimes unstiffened as it took effect.

His palm uncurled.

'Oh, my gods,' said Angua. 'Have we got any bandages?'

The sky was a little white circle, high above.

'Where the hell are we, partner?' said Cuddy.

'Cave.'

'No caves under Ankh-Morpork. It's on loam.'

Cuddy had fallen about thirty feet but had cushioned the fall because he landed on Detritus' head. The troll had been sitting, surrounded by rotting woodwork, in . . . well . . . a cave. Or, Cuddy thought, as his eyes grew accustomed to the gloom, a stone-lined tunnel.

'I didn't do nothing,' said Detritus, 'I just stood there, next minute, everything going past upwards.'

Cuddy reached down into the mud underfoot and brought up a piece of wood. It was very thick. It was also very rotten.

'We fell through something into something,' he said. He ran his hand over the curved tunnel wall. 'And this is *good* masonry. *Very* good.'

'How we get out?'

There was no way to climb back. The tunnel roof was much higher than Detritus.

'We walk out, I think,' said Cuddy.

He sniffed the air, which was dank. Dwarfs have a very good sense of direction underground.

'This way,' he added, setting off.

'Cuddy?'

'Yes?'

'No one ever say there tunnels under the city. No one know about them.'

'So . . .?'

'So there no way out. Because way out is way in, too, and if no one know about tunnels, then it 'cos no way in.'

'But they've got to lead somewhere.'

'OK.'

Black mud, more or less dry, made a path at the bottom of the tunnel. There was slime on the walls, too, indicating that at some point in the recent past the tunnel had been full of water. Here and there huge patches of fungi, luminous with decay, cast a faint glow over the ancient stonework.*

Cuddy felt his spirits lift as he plodded through the darkness. Dwarfs always felt happier underground.

'Bound to find a way out,' he said.

'Right.'

'So . . . how come you joined the Watch, then?'

'Hah! My girl Ruby she say, you want get married, you get proper job, I not marry a troll what people say, him no good troll, him thick as a short plank of wood.' Detritus' voice echoed in the darkness. 'How about you?'

'I got bored. I worked for my brother-in-law, Durance. He's got a good business making fortune rats for dwarf restaurants. But I thought, this isn't a proper job for a dwarf.'

'Sound like easy job to me.'

'I had the devil of a time getting them to swallow the fortunes.'

---

* It didn't need to. Cuddy, belonging to a race that worked underground for preference, and Detritus, a member of a race notoriously nocturnal, had excellent vision in the dark. But mysterious caves and tunnels always have luminous fungi, strangely bright crystals or at a pinch merely an eldritch glow in the air, just in case a human hero comes in and needs to see in the dark. Strange but true.

Cuddy stopped. A change in the air suggested a vaster tunnel up ahead.

And, indeed, the tunnel opened into the side of a much larger one. There was deep mud on the floor, in the middle of which ran a trickle of water. Cuddy fancied he heard rats, or what he hoped were rats, scuttle away into the dark emptiness. He even thought he could hear the sounds of the city – indistinct, intermingled – filtering through the earth.

'It's like a temple,' he said, and his voice boomed away into the distance.

'Writing here on wall,' said Detritus.

Cuddy peered at the letters hacked deeply into the stone.

'"VIA CLOACA",' he said. 'Hmm. Well, now . . . via is an old word for street or way. Cloaca means . . .'

He peered into the gloom.

'This is a sewer,' he said.

'What that?'

'It's like . . . well, where do trolls dump their . . . rubbish?' said Cuddy.

'In street,' said Detritus. 'Hygienic.'

'This is . . . an underground street just for . . . well, for crap,' said Cuddy. 'I never knew Ankh-Morpork had them.'

'Maybe Ankh-Morpork didn't know Ankh-Morpork had them,' said Detritus.

'Right. You're right. This place is *old*. We're in the bowels of the earth.'

'In Ankh-Morpork even the shit have a street to itself,' said Detritus, awe and wonder in his voice. 'Truly, this a land of opportunity.'

'Here's some more writing,' said Cuddy. He scraped away some slime.

'"*Cirone IV me fabricat*",' he read aloud. 'He was one of the early kings, wasn't he? Hey . . . do you know what that means?'

'No one's been down here since yesterday,' said Detritus.

'No! This place . . . this place is more than two thousand years old. We're quite probably the first people to come down here since—'

'Yesterday,' said the troll.

'Yesterday? Yesterday? What's yesterday got to do with it?'

'Footprints still fresh,' said Detritus.

He pointed.

There were footprints in the mud.

'How long have you lived here?' said Cuddy, suddenly feeling very conspicuous in the middle of the tunnel.

'Nine-er years. That is the number of years I have lived here. Nine-er,' said Detritus, proudly. 'It only one of a large . . . number of numbers I can count to.'

'Have you *ever* heard of tunnels under the city?'

'No.'

'Someone knows about them, though.'

'Yes.'

'What shall we do?'

The answer was inevitable. They'd chased a man into the pork futures warehouse, and nearly died. Then they'd ended up in the middle of a small war, and nearly died. Now they were in a mysterious tunnel where there were fresh footprints. If Corporal Carrot or Sergeant Colon said, 'And what did you do then?', neither of them could face up to the thought of saying 'We came back.'

'The footprints go *this* way,' said Cuddy, 'and then they return. But the ones coming back aren't so deep as the ones going. You can see they're later ones because they're over the top of the other ones. So he was heavier *going* than he was coming back, yes?'

'Right,' said Detritus.

'So that means . . .?'

'He lose weight?'

'He was carrying something, and he left it . . . up ahead somewhere.'

They stared at the darkness.

'So we go and find what it was?' said Detritus.

'I think so. How do you feel?'

'Feel OK.'

Different species though they were, their minds had focused on a single image, involving a muzzle flash and a lead slug singing through the subterranean night.

'He came back,' said Cuddy.

'Yes,' said Detritus.

They looked at the darkness again.

'It has not been a nice day,' said Cuddy.

'That the truth.'

'I'd just like to know something, in case . . . I mean . . . look, what happened in the pork store? You did all that maths! All that counting!'

'I . . . dunno. I saw it all.'

'All what?'

'Just all of it. Everything. All the numbers in the world. I could count them all.'

'What did they equal?'

'Dunno. What does equal mean?'

They trudged on, to see what the future held.

The trail led eventually into a narrower tunnel, barely wide enough for the troll to stand upright. Finally they could go no further. A stone had dropped out of the roof and rubble and mud had percolated through, blocking the tunnel. But that didn't matter because they'd found what they were looking for, even though they hadn't been looking for it.

'Oh dear,' said Detritus.

'Very definitely,' said Cuddy. He looked around vaguely.

'You know,' he said, 'I reckon these tunnels are usually full of water. They're well below the normal river level.'

He looked back to the pathetic discovery.

'There's going to be a lot of trouble about this,' he said.

'It's his badge,' said Carrot. 'Good grief. He's holding it so tight it's cut right into his *hand*.'

Technically Ankh-Morpork is built on loam, but what it is mainly built on is Ankh-Morpork; it has been constructed, burned down, silted up, and rebuilt so many times that its foundations are old cellars, buried roads and the fossil bones and middens of earlier cities.

Below these, in the darkness, sat the troll and the dwarf.

'What we doing now?'

'We ought to leave it here and fetch Corporal Carrot. He'll know what to do.'

Detritus looked over his shoulder at the thing behind them.

'I don't like that,' he said. 'It not right to leave it here.'

'Right. Yes, you're right. But you're a troll and I'm a dwarf. What do you think would happen if people saw us carrying that along the streets?'

'*Big* trouble.'

'Correct. Come on. Let's follow the footprints back out.'

'Supposing it gone when we come back?' said Detritus, lumbering to his feet.

'How? And we're following the tracks out, so if whoever it was who put it there comes back, we'll run straight into them.'

'Oh, good. I glad you said that.'

Vimes sat on the edge of his bed while Angua bandaged his hand.

'Captain *Quirke*?' said Carrot. 'But he's . . . not a good choice.'

'Mayonnaise Quirke, we used to call him,' said Colon. 'He's a pillock.'

'Don't tell me,' said Angua. 'He's rich, thick and oily, yes?'

'And smells faintly of eggs,' said Carrot.

'Plumes in his helmet,' said Colon, 'and a breastplate you can see your face in.'

'Well, Carrot's got one of those too,' said Nobby.

'Yes, but the difference is, Carrot keeps his armour polished because he . . . likes nice clean armour,' said Colon loyally. 'While Quirke keeps his shiny because he's a pillock.'

'But he's wrapped up the case,' said Nobby. 'I heard about it when I went out for the coffee. He's arrested Coalface the troll. You know, captain? The privy cleaner. Someone saw him near Rime Street just before the dwarf got killed.'

'But he's *massive*,' said Carrot. 'He couldn't have got through the door.'

'He's got a motive,' said Nobby.

'Yes?'

'Yes. Hammerhock was a dwarf.'

'That's not a motive.'

'It is for a troll. Anyway, if he didn't do that, he probably did *something*. There's plenty of evidence against him.'

'Like what?' said Angua.

'He's a troll.'

'That's not evidence.'

'It is to Captain Quirke,' said the sergeant.

'He's bound to have done *something*,' Nobby repeated.

In this he was echoing the Patrician's view of crime and punishment. If there was crime, there should be punishment. If the specific criminal should be involved in the punishment process then this was a happy accident, but if not then any criminal would do, and since everyone was undoubtedly guilty of something, the net result was that, *in general terms*, justice was done.

'He's a nasty piece of work, that Coalface,' said Colon. 'A right-hand troll for Chrysoprase.'

'Yes, but he couldn't have killed Bjorn,' said Carrot. 'And what about the beggar girl?'

Vimes sat looking at the floor.

'What do *you* think, captain?' said Carrot.

Vimes shrugged.

'Who cares?' he said.

'Well, *you* care,' said Carrot. 'You always care. We can't let even someone like—'

'Listen to me,' said Vimes, in a small voice. 'Supposing we'd

403

found who killed the dwarf and the clown? Or the girl. It wouldn't make any difference. It's all rotten anyway.'

'What is, captain?' said Colon.

'All of it. You might try and empty a well with a sieve. Let the Assassins try to sort it out. Or the thieves. He can try the rats next. Why not? We're not the people for this. We ought to have just stayed with ringing our bells and shouting "All's well!"'

'But all isn't well, captain,' said Carrot.

'So what? When has that ever mattered?'

'Oh, dear,' said Angua, under her breath. 'I think perhaps you gave him too much of that coffee . . .'

Vimes said, 'I'm retiring from the Watch tomorrow. Twenty-five years on the streets—'

Nobby started to grin nervously and stopped as the sergeant, without apparently shifting position, grabbed one of his arms and twisted it gently but meaningfully up his back.

'—and what good's it all been? What *good* have I done? I've just worn out a lot of boots. There's no place in Ankh-Morpork for policemen! Who cares what's right or wrong? Assassins and thieves and trolls and dwarfs! Might as well have a bloody king and have done with it!'

The rest of the Night Watch stood looking at their feet in mute embarrassment. Then Carrot said, 'It's better to light a candle than curse the darkness, captain. That's what they say.'

'*What?*' Vimes's sudden rage was like a thunderclap. 'Who says that? When has that ever been true? It's never been true! It's the kind of thing people without power say to make it all seem less bloody awful, but it's just words, it never makes any *difference*—'

Someone hammered at the door.

'That'll be Quirke,' said Vimes. 'You're to hand over your weapons. The Night Watch is being stood down for a day. Can't have coppers running around upsetting things, can we? Open the door, Carrot.'

'But—' Carrot began.

'That was an order. I might not be any good for anything else, but I can bloody well order you to open the door, so open the door!'

Quirke was accompanied by half a dozen members of the Day Watch. They had crossbows. In deference to the fact that they were doing a mildly unpleasant job involving fellow officers, they had them pointing slightly downwards. In deference to the fact that they weren't damn fools, they had the safety catches off.

Quirke wasn't actually a *bad* man. He didn't have the imagination. He dealt more in that sort of generalized low-grade unpleasantness which slightly tarnishes the soul of all who come into contact with it.* Many people are in jobs that are a little beyond them, but there are ways of reacting to the situation. Sometimes they're flustered and nice, sometimes they're Quirke. Quirke handled them with the maxim: it doesn't matter if you're right or wrong, so long as you're definite. There was, on the whole, no real *racial* prejudice in Ankh-Morpork; when you've got dwarfs and trolls, the mere colour of other humans is not a major item. But Quirke was the kind of man to whom it comes naturally to pronounce the word negro with two gs.

He had a hat with plumes in it.

'Come in, come in,' said Vimes. 'It wasn't as if we were doing anything.'

'Captain Vimes—'

'It's all right. We know. Give him your weapons, people. That's an order, Carrot. One official issue sword, one pike or halberd, one night stick or truncheon, one crossbow. That's right, isn't it, Sergeant Colon?'

'Yessir.'

Carrot hesitated only a moment.

'Oh, well,' he said. 'My *official* sword is in the rack.'

'What's that one in your belt?'

Carrot said nothing. However, he shifted position slightly. His biceps strained against the leather of his jerkin.

'Official sword. Right,' said Quirke. He turned. He was one of those people who would recoil from an assault on strength, but attack weakness without mercy. 'Where's the gritsucker?' he said. 'And the rock?'

'Ah,' said Vimes, 'you are referring to those representative members of our fellow sapient races who have chosen to throw in their lots with the people of this city?'

'I mean the dwarf and the troll,' said Quirke.

'Haven't the faintest idea,' said Vimes cheerfully. It seemed to Angua that he was drunk again, if people could get drunk on despair.

'We dunno, sir,' said Colon. 'Haven't seen 'em all day.'

'Probably fighting up in Quarry Lane with the rest of them,' said Quirke. 'You can't trust people of their type. You ought to know that.'

And it also seemed to Angua that although words like halfpint and gritsucker were offensive, they were as terms of universal brotherhood compared to words like 'people of their type' in the

---

* Rather like British Rail.

mouth of men like Quirke. Much to her shock, she found her gaze concentrating on the man's jugular vein.

'Fighting?' said Carrot. 'Why?'

Quirke shrugged.

'Who knows?'

'Let me think now,' said Vimes. 'It could be something to do with a wrongful arrest. It could be something to do with some of the more restless dwarfs just needing any excuse to have a go at the trolls. What do *you* think, Quirke?'

'I don't think, Vimes.'

'Good man. You're just the type the city needs.'

Vimes stood up.

'I'll be going, then,' he said. 'I'll see you all tomorrow. If there is one.'

The door slammed behind him.

This hall was *huge*. It was the size of a city square, with pillars every few yards to support the roof. Tunnels radiated off it in every direction, and at various heights in the walls. Water trickled out of many of them, from small springs and underground streams.

That was the problem. The film of running water over the stone floor of the hall had wiped away traces of the footprints.

A very large tunnel, almost blocked with debris and silt, led off in what Cuddy was pretty sure was the direction of the estuary.

It was almost pleasant. There was no smell, other than a damp, under-a-stone mustiness. And it was cool.

'I've seen big dwarf halls in the mountains,' said Cuddy, 'but I've got to admit this is something else.' His voice echoed back and forth in the chamber.

'Oh, yes,' said Detritus, 'it's got to be something else, because it's not a dwarf hall in the mountains.'

'Can you see any way up?'

'No.'

'We could have passed a dozen ways to the surface and not known it.'

'Yes,' said the troll. 'It's a knotty problem.'

'Detritus?'

'Yes?'

'Did you know you're getting smarter again, down here in the cool?'

'Really?'

'Can you use it to think of a way out?'

'Digging?' the troll suggested.

There were fallen blocks here and there in the tunnels. Not many; the place had been well built . . .

'Nah. Haven't got a shovel,' said Cuddy.

Detritus nodded.

'Give me your breastplate,' he said.

He leaned it up against the wall. His fist pounded into it a few times. He handed it back. It was, more or less, shovel shaped.

'It's a long way up,' Cuddy said doubtfully.

'But we know the way,' said Detritus. 'It's either that, or stay down here eating rat for rest of your life.'

Cuddy hesitated. The idea had a certain appeal . . .

'Without ketchup,' Detritus added.

'I think I saw a fallen stone just a way back there,' said the dwarf.

Captain Quirke looked around the Watch room with the air of one who was doing the scenery a favour by glancing at it.

'Nice place, this,' he said. 'I think we'll move in here. Better than the quarters near the Palace.'

'But *we're* here,' said Sergeant Colon.

'You'll just have to squash up,' said Captain Quirke.

He glanced at Angua. Her stare was getting on his nerves.

'There'll be a few changes, too,' he said. Behind him, the door creaked open. A small, smelly dog limped in.

'But Lord Vetinari hasn't said who's commanding Night Watch,' said Carrot.

'Ho, yes? Seems to me, seems to *me*,' said Quirke, 'that it's not likely to be one of *you* lot, eh? Seems to me it's likely the Watches'll be combined. Seems to me there's too much sloppiness around the place. Seems to me there's a bit too much of a ragtag.'

He glanced at Angua again. The way she was looking at him was putting him off.

'Seems to me—' Quirke began again, and then noticed the dog. 'Look at this!' he said. 'Dogs in the Watch House!' He kicked Gaspode hard, and grinned as the dog ran yelping under the table.

'What about Lettice Knibbs, the beggar girl?' said Angua. 'No troll killed her. Or the clown.'

'You got to see the big picture,' said Quirke.

'Mister Captain,' said a low voice from under the table, audible at a conscious level only to Angua, 'you got an itchy bottom.'

'What big picture's this, then?' said Sergeant Colon.

'Got to think in terms of the whole city,' said Quirke. He shifted uneasily.

'*Really* itchy,' said the sub-table voice.

'You feeling all right, Captain Quirke?' said Angua.

The captain squirmed.

'Prickle, prickle, prickle,' said the voice.

'I mean, some things are important, some ain't,' said Quirke. 'Aargh!'

'Sorry?'

'Prickle.'

'Can't hang around here talking to you all day,' said Quirke. 'You. Report to. Me. Tomorrow afternoon—'

'Prickle, prickle, prickle—'

'Abouuut face!'

The Day Watch scurried out, with Quirke hopping and squirming in, as it were, the rear.

'My word, he seemed anxious to get away,' said Carrot.

'Yes,' said Angua. 'Can't think why.'

They looked at one another.

'Is that it?' said Carrot. 'No more Night Watch?'

It's generally very quiet in the Unseen University library. There's perhaps the shuffling of feet as wizards wander between the shelves, the occasional hacking cough to disturb the academic silence, and every once in a while a dying scream as an unwary student fails to treat an old magical book with the caution it deserves.

Consider orang-utans.

In all the worlds graced by their presence, it is suspected that they can talk but choose not to do so in case humans put them to work, possibly in the television industry. In fact they *can* talk. It's just that they talk in Orang-utan. Humans are only capable of listening in Bewilderment.

The Librarian of Unseen University had unilaterally decided to aid comprehension by producing an Orang-utan/Human Dictionary. He'd been working on it for three months.

It wasn't easy. He'd got as far as 'Oook.'*

He was down in the Stacks, where it was cool.

And suddenly someone was singing.

He took the pen out of his foot and listened.

A human would have decided they couldn't believe their ears.

---

* Which can mean ... well ... meanings include: 'Pardon me, you're hanging from *my* rubber ring, thank you so very much', 'It may be just vital biomass oxygenating the planet to *you*, but it's home to me' and 'I'm sure there was a rain forest around here a moment ago'.

408

Orangs are more sensible. If you won't believe your own ears, whose ears will you believe?

Someone was singing, underground. Or trying to sing.

The chthonic voices went something like this:

'Dlog, glod, Dlog, glod—'

'Listen, you . . . troll! It's the simplest song there is. Look, like this "Gold, Gold, Gold, Gold"?'

'Gold, Gold, Gold, Gold—'

'No! That's the *second* verse!'

There was also the rhythmical sound of dirt being shovelled and rubble being moved.

The Librarian considered matters for a while. So . . . a dwarf and a troll. He preferred both species to humans. For one thing, neither of them were great readers. The Librarian was, of course, very much in favour of reading in general, but readers in particular got on his nerves. There was something, well, *sacrilegious* about the way they kept taking books off the shelves and wearing out the words by reading them. He liked people who loved and respected books, and the best way to do that, in the Librarian's opinion, was to leave them on the shelves where Nature intended them to be.

The muffled voices seemed to be getting closer.

'Gold, gold, gold—'

'Now you're singing the chorus!'

On the other hand, there were proper ways of entering a library.

He waddled over to the shelves and selected Humptulip's seminal work *How to Kille Insects*. All 2,000 pages of it.

Vimes felt quite light-hearted as he walked up Scoone Avenue. He was aware that there was an inner Vimes screaming his head off. He ignored him.

You couldn't be a real copper in Ankh-Morpork and stay sane. You had to *care*. And caring in Ankh-Morpork was like opening a tin of meat in the middle of a piranha school.

Everyone dealt with it in their own way. Colon never thought about it, and Nobby didn't worry about it, and the new ones hadn't been in long enough to be worn down by it, and Carrot . . . was just himself.

Hundreds of people died in the city every day, often of suicide. So what did a few more matter?

The Vimes inside hammered on the walls.

There were quite a few coaches outside the Ramkin mansion, and the place seemed to be infested with assorted female relatives and Interchangeable Emmas. They were baking things and polishing things. Vimes strolled through, more or less unregarded.

He found Sybil out in the dragon house, in her rubber boots and protective dragon armour. She was mucking out, apparently blissfully unaware of the controlled uproar in the mansion.

She looked up as the door shut behind Vimes.

'Oh, there you are. You're home early,' she said. 'I couldn't stand the fuss, so I came out here. But I'll have to go and change soon—'

She stopped when she saw his expression. 'There's something wrong, isn't there?'

'I'm not going back,' said Vimes.

'Really? Last week you said you'd do a full watch. You said you were looking foward to it.'

Not much gets past old Sybil, Vimes thought.

She patted his hand.

'I'm glad you're out of it,' she said.

Corporal Nobbs darted into the Watch House and slammed the door behind him.

'Well?' said Carrot.

'It's not good,' said Nobby. 'They say the trolls are planning to march to the Palace to get Coalface out. There's gangs of dwarfs and trolls wandering around looking for trouble. *And* beggars. Lettice was very popular. And there's a lot of Guild people out there, too. The city,' he said, importantly, 'is def'nitely a keg of No. 1 Powder.'

'How do you like the idea of camping out on the open plain?' said Colon.

'What's that got to do with it?'

'If anyone puts a match to anything tonight, it's goodbye Ankh,' said the sergeant morosely. 'Usually we can shut the city gates, right? But there's hardly more'n a few feet of water in the river.'

'You flood the city just to put out fires?' said Angua.

'Yep.'

'Another thing,' said Nobby. 'People threw stuff at me!'

Carrot had been staring at the wall. Now he produced a small, battered black book from his pocket, and started to thumb through the pages.

'Tell me,' he said, in a slightly distant voice, 'has there been an irretrievable breakdown of law and order?'

'Yeah. For about five hundred years,' said Colon. 'Irretrievable breakdown of law'n'order is what Ankh-Morpork is all about.'

'No, I mean more than usual. It's important.' Carrot turned a page. His lips moved silently as he read.

'Throwing stuff at me sounds like a breakdown in law and order,' said Nobby.

He was aware of their expressions.

'I don't think we could make that stick,' said Colon.

'It stuck all right,' said Nobby, '*and* some of it went down my shirt.'

'Why throw things at you?' said Angua.

'It's 'cos I was a Watchman,' said Nobby. 'The dwarfs don't like the Watch 'cos of Mr Hammerhock, and the trolls don't like the Watch 'cos of Coalface being arrested, and people don't like the Watch 'cos of all these angry dwarfs and trolls around.'

Someone thumped at the door.

'That's probably an angry mob right now,' said Nobby.

Carrot opened the door.

'It's not an angry mob,' he announced.

'Ook.'

'It's an orang-utan carrying a stunned dwarf followed by a troll. But he is quite angry, if that's any help.'

Lady Ramkin's butler, Willikins, had filled him a big bath. Hah! Tomorrow it'd be his butler, and his bath.

And this wasn't one of the old hip bath, drag-it-in-front-of-the-fire jobs, no. The Ramkin mansion collected water off the roof into a big cistern, after straining out the pigeons, and then it was heated by an ancient geyser* and flowed along drumming, groaning lead pipes to a pair of mighty brass taps and then into an enamelled tub. There were things laid out on a fluffy towel beside it – huge scrubbing brushes, three kinds of soap, a loofah.

Willikins was standing patiently beside the bath, like a barely heated towel rail.

'Yes?' said Vimes.

'His lordship . . . that is, her ladyship's father . . . he required to have his back scrubbed,' said Willikins.

'You go and help the old geyser stoke the furnace,' said Vimes firmly.

Left alone, he struggled out of his breastplate and threw it in the corner. The chainmail shirt followed it, and the helmet, and

---

* Who stoked the boiler.

411

the money pouch, and various leather and cotton oddments that came between a Watchman and the world.

And then he sank, gingerly at first, into the suds.

'Try soap. Soap'll work,' said Detritus.

'Hold still, will you?' said Carrot.

'You're twisting my head off!'

'Go on, soap him head.'

'Soap your own head!'

There was a *thung* noise and Cuddy's helmet came free.

Cuddy emerged, blinking, into the light. He focused on the Librarian, and growled.

'He hit me on the *head*!'

'Oook.'

'He says you came up through the floor,' said Carrot.

'That's no reason to hit me on the *head*.'

'Some of the things that come up through the floor at Unseen University don't even have a head,' said Carrot.

'Oook!'

'Or they have hundreds. Why were you digging down there?'

'We weren't digging down. We were digging up . . .'

Carrot sat and listened. He interrupted only twice.

'*Shot* at you?'

'Five time,' said Detritus, happily. 'Have to report damage to breastplate but not to backplate on account of fortunately my body got in way, saving valuable city property worth three dollars.'

Carrot listened some more.

'Sewers?' he said, eventually.

'It's like the whole city, underground. We saw crowns and stuff carved on the walls.'

Carrot's eyes sparkled. 'That means they must date right back to the days when we had kings! And then when we kept on rebuilding the city we forgot they were down there . . .'

'Um. That's not all that's down there,' said Cuddy. 'We . . . found something.'

'Oh?'

'Something bad.'

'You won't like it at all,' said Detritus. 'Bad, bad, bad. Even worse.'

'We thought it would be best to leave it there,' said Cuddy, 'on account of it being Evidence. But you ought to see it.'

'It's going to upset everything,' said the troll, warming to the part.

'What was it?'

'If we tell you, you say, stupid ethnic people, you pulling my leg off,' said Detritus.

'So you'd better come and see,' said Cuddy.

Sergeant Colon looked at the rest of the Watch.

'All of us?' he said, nervously. 'Er. Shouldn't a couple of senior officers stay up here? In case anything happens?'

'Do you mean in case anything happens up here?' said Angua, tartly. 'Or in case anything happens down there?'

'I'll go with Lance-Constable Cuddy and Lance-Constable Detritus,' said Carrot. 'I don't think anyone else ought to come.'

'But it could be dangerous!' said Angua.

'If I find who's been shooting at Watchmen,' said Carrot, 'it will be.'

Samuel Vimes reached up with a big toe and turned on the hot tap.

There was a respectful knock at the door, and Willikins old-retainer'd in.

'Would sir be wanting anything?'

Vimes thought about it.

'Lady Ramkin said you wouldn't be wanting any alcohol,' said Willikins, as if reading his thoughts.

'Did she?'

'Emphatically, sir. But I have here a very fine cigar.'

He winced as Vimes bit the end off and spat it over the side of the bath, but produced some matches and lit it for him.

'Thank you, Willikins. What's your first name?'

'First name, sir?'

'I mean, what do people call you when they've got to know you better?'

'Willikins, sir.'

'Oh, Right, then. Well. You may go, Willikins.'

'Yes, sir.'

Vimes lay back in the warm water. The inner voice was still in there somewhere, but he tried not to pay any attention. About now, it was saying, you'd be proceeding along the Street of Small Gods, just by the bit of old city wall where you could stop and smoke a rollup out of the wind . . .

To drown it out, he started to sing at the top of his voice.

*

The cavernous sewers under the city echoed with human and near-human voices for the first time in millennia.

'Hi-ho—'

'—hi-ho—'

'Oook oook oook oook ook—'

'You all *stupid!*'

'I can't help it. It's my nearly-dwarfish blood. We just like singing underground. It comes naturally to us.'

'All right, but why *him* singing? Him *ape.*'

'He's a people person.'

They'd brought torches. Shadows jumped among the pillars in the big cavern, and fled along the tunnels. Whatever the possible lurking dangers, Carrot was beside himself with the joy of discovery.

'It's amazing! The Via Cloaca is mentioned in some old book I read, but everyone thought it was a lost street! Superb workmanship. Lucky for you the river was so low. It looks as though these are normally full of water.'

'That's what I said,' said Cuddy. 'Full of water, I said.'

He glanced cautiously at the dancing shadows, which made weird and worrying shapes on the far wall – strange biped animals, eldritch underground things . . .

Carrot sighed.

'Stop making shadow pictures, Detritus.'

'Oook.'

'What him say?'

'He said "Do Deformed Rabbit, it's my favourite",' Carrot translated.

Rats rustled in the darkness. Cuddy peered around. He kept imagining figures, back there, sighting along some kind of pipe . . .

There were a disturbing few moments when he lost sight of the tracks on the wet stone, but he picked them up again near a mould-hung wall. And then, there was the particular pipe. He'd made a scratch on the stones.

'It's not far along,' he said, handing Carrot the torch.

Carrot disappeared.

They heard his footsteps in the mud, and then a whistle of surprise, and then silence for a while.

Carrot reappeared.

'My word,' he said. 'You two know who this is?'

'It *looks* like—' Cuddy began.

'It looks like trouble,' said Carrot.

'You see why we didn't bring it back up?' said Cuddy. 'Carrying a human's corpse through the streets right now would not be a good idea, I thought. Especially this one.'

'I thought some of that, too,' Detritus volunteered.

'Right enough,' said Carrot. 'Well done, men. I think we'd better . . . leave it for now, and come back with a sack later on. And . . . don't tell anyone else.'

'Except the sergeant and everyone,' said Cuddy.

'No . . . not even them. It'd make everyone very . . . jumpy.'

'Just as you say, Corporal Carrot.'

'We're dealing with a sick mind here, men.'

Underground light dawned on Cuddy.

'Ah,' he said. 'You suspect Corporal Nobbs, sir?'

'This is worse. Come on, let's get back up.' He looked back towards the big pillar-barred cavern. 'Any idea where we are, Cuddy?'

'Could be under the Palace, sir.'

'That's what I reckoned. Of course, the tunnels go everywhere . . .'

Carrot's worried train of thought faltered away on some distant track.

There was water in the sewers, even in this drought. Springs flowed into them, or water filtered down from far above. Everywhere was the drip and splash of water. And cool, cool air.

It would almost be pleasant were it not for the sad, hunched corpse of someone that looked for all the world like Beano the clown.

Vimes dried himself off. Willikins had also laid out a dressing gown with brocade on the sleeves. He put it on, and wandered into his dressing room.

That was another new thing. The rich even had rooms for dressing in, and clothes to wear while you went into the dressing rooms to get dressed.

Fresh clothes had been laid out for him. Tonight there was something dashing in red and yellow . . .

. . . *about now he'd be patrolling Treacle Mine Road* . . .

. . . and a hat. It had a feather in it.

Vimes dressed himself, and even wore the hat. And he seemed quite normal and composed, until you realized that he avoided meeting his own gaze in the mirror.

*

415

The Watch sat around the big table in the guardroom and in deep gloom. They were Off Duty. They'd never really been Off Duty before.

'What say we have a game of cards?' said Nobby, brightly. He produced a greasy pack from somewhere in the noisome recesses of his uniform.

'You won everyone's wages off them yesterday,' said Sergeant Colon.

'Now's the chance to win 'em back, then.'

'Yeah, but there were five kings in your hand, Nobby.'

Nobby shuffled the cards.

''S'funny, that,' he said, 'there's kings everywhere, when you look.'

'There certainly is if you look up *your* sleeve.'

'No, I mean, there's Kings Way in Ankh, and kings in cards, and we get the King's Shilling when we join up,' said Nobby. 'We got kings all over the place except on that gold throne in the Palace. I'll tell you . . . there wouldn't be all this trouble around the place if we had a king.'

Carrot was staring at the ceiling, his eyebrows locked in concentration. Detritus was counting on his fingers.

'Oh, *yes*,' said Sergeant Colon. 'Beer'd be a penny a pint, the trees'd bloom again. Oh, yeah. Every time someone stubs a toe in this town, turns out it wouldn't have happened if there'd been a king. Vimes'd go spare to hear you talk like that.'

'People'd listen to a king, though,' said Nobby.

'Vimes'd say that's the trouble,' said Colon. 'It's like that thing of his about using magic. That stuff makes him angry.'

'How you get king inna first place?' said Detritus.

'Someone sawed up a stone,' said Colon.

'Hah! Anti-siliconism!'

'Nah, someone *pulled* a sword *out* of a stone,' said Nobby.

'How'd he know it was in there, then?' Colon demanded.

'It . . . it was sticking out, wasn't it?'

'Where anyone could've grabbed it? In *this* town?'

'Only the *rightful* king could do it, see,' said Nobby.

'Oh, *right*,' said Colon. 'I *understand*. Oh, yes. So what you're saying *is*, someone'd decided who the rightful king was *before* he pulled it out? Sounds like a fix to me. Prob'ly someone had a fake hollow stone and some dwarf inside hanging on the other end with a pair of pliers until the right guy came along—'

A fly bounced on the window pane for a while, then zigzagged across the room and settled on a beam, where Cuddy's idly thrown axe cut it in half.

'You got no soul, Fred,' said Nobby. 'I wouldn't't've minded being a knight in shining armour. That's what a king does if you're useful. He makes you a knight.'

'A night watchman in crappy armour is about your métier,' said Colon, who looked around proudly to see if anyone had noticed the slanty thing over the e. 'Nah, catch me being respectful to some bloke because he just pulled a sword out of a stone. That don't make you a king. Mind you,' he said, 'someone who could shove a sword *into* a stone . . . a man like *that*, now, *he's* a king.'

'A man like that'd be an ace,' said Nobby.

Angua yawned.

Ding-ding a-ding-ding—

'What the hell's that?' said Colon.

Carrot's chair thumped forward. He fumbled in his pocket and pulled out a velvet bag, which he upended on to the table. Out slid a golden disc about three inches across. When he pressed a catch on one side it opened like a clamshell.

The stopped Watch peered at it.

'It's a clock?' said Angua.

'A watch,' said Carrot.

'It's very big.'

'That's because of the clockwork. There has to be room for all the little wheels. The small watches just have those little time demons in and they don't last and anyway they keep rotten time—'

Ding-ding a-ding-ding, ding dingle ding ding . . .

'And it plays a tune!' said Angua.

'Every hour,' said Carrot. 'It's part of the clockwork.'

Ding. Ding. Ding.

'And it chimes the hours afterwards,' said Carrot.

'It's slow, then,' said Sergeant Colon. 'All the others just struck, you couldn't miss 'em.'

'My cousin Jorgen makes ones like these,' said Cuddy. 'They keep better time than demons or water clocks or candles. Or those big pendulum things.'

'There's a spring and wheels,' said Carrot.

'The important bit,' said Cuddy, taking an eyeglass from somewhere in his beard and examining the watch carefully, 'is a little rocking thingummy that stops the wheels from going too fast.'

'How does it know if they're going too fast?' said Angua.

'It's kind of built-in,' said Cuddy. 'Don't understand it much myself. What's this inscription here . . .'

He read it aloud.

'"A Watch From, Your Old Freinds in the Watch"?'

'It's a play on words,' said Carrot.

There was a long, embarrassed silence.

417

'Um. I chipped in a few dollars each from you new recruits,' he added, blushing. 'I mean . . . you can pay me back when you like. If you want to. I mean . . . you'd be bound to *be* friends. Once you got to know him.'

The rest of the Watch exchanged glances.

He could lead armies, Angua thought. He really could. Some people have inspired whole countries to great deeds because of the power of their vision. And so could he. Not because he dreams about marching hordes, or world domination, or an empire of a thousand years. Just because he thinks that everyone's really decent underneath and would get along just fine if only they made the effort, and he believes that so strongly it burns like a flame which is bigger than he is. He's got a dream and we're all part of it, so that it shapes the world around him. And the weird thing is that no one wants to disappoint him. It'd be like kicking the biggest puppy in the universe. It's a kind of magic.

'The gold's rubbing off,' said Cuddy. 'But it's a good watch,' he added quickly.

'I was hoping we could give it to him tonight,' said Carrot. 'And all go out for a . . . drink . . .'

'Not a good idea,' said Angua.

'Leave it until tomorrow,' said Colon. 'We'll form a guard of honour at the wedding. That's traditional. Everyone holds their swords up in a kind of arch.'

'We've only got one sword between us,' said Carrot glumly.

They all stared at the floor.

'It's not fair,' said Angua. 'I don't care who stole whatever they stole from the Assassins, but he was right to try to find out who killed Mr Hammerhock. And no one cares about Lettice Knibbs.'

'I like to find out who shoot me,' said Detritus.

'Beats me why anyone'd be daft enough to steal from the Assassins,' said Carrot. 'That's what Captain Vimes said. He said you'd have to be a fool to think of breaking into that place.'

They stared at the floor again.

'Like a clown or a jester?' said Detritus.

'Detritus, he didn't mean a cap-and-bells Fool,' said Carrot, in a kindly voice. 'He just meant you'd have to be some sort of idi—'

He stopped. He stared at the ceiling.

'Oh, my,' he said. 'It's as simple as *that*?'

'Simple as what?' said Angua.

Someone hammered at the door. It wasn't a polite knock. It was the thumping of someone who was either going to have the door opened for them or break it down.

A guard stumbled into the room. Half his armour was off and he had a black eye, but he was just recognizable as Skully Muldoon of the Day Watch.

Colon helped him up.

'Been in a fight, Skully?'

Skully looked up at Detritus, and whimpered.

'The buggers attacked the Watch House!'

'Who?'

'Them!'

Carrot patted him on the shoulder.

'This isn't a troll,' he said. 'This is Lance-Constable Detritus – *don't salute*. Trolls attacked the Day Watch?'

'They're chucking cobbles!'

'You can't trust 'em,' said Detritus.

'Who?' said Skully.

'Trolls. Nasty pieces of work in my opinion,' said Detritus, with all the conviction of a troll with a badge. 'They need keeping a eye on.'

'What's happened to Quirke?' said Carrot.

'I don't know! You lot have got to do *something*!'

'We're stood down,' said Colon. 'Official.'

'Don't give me that!'

'Ah,' said Carrot, brightly. He pulled a stub of pencil out of his pocket and made a little tick in his black book. 'You still got that little house in Easy Street, Sergeant Muldoon?'

'What? What? Yes! What about it?'

'Is the rent worth more than a farthing a month?'

Muldoon stared at him with his one operating eye.

'Are you simple or what?'

Carrot gave him a big smile. 'That's right, Sergeant Muldoon. Is it, though? Worth a farthing, would you say?'

'There's dwarfs running around the streets looking for a fight and you want to know about property prices?'

'A farthing?'

'Don't be daft! It's worth at least five dollars a month!'

'Ah,' said Carrot, ticking the book again. 'That'd be inflation, of course. And I expect you've got a cooking pot ... do you own at least two-and-one-third acres and more than half a cow?'

'All right, all right,' said Muldoon. 'It's some kind of joke, right?'

'I think probably the property qualification can be waived,' said Carrot. 'It says here that it can be waived for a citizen in good standing. Finally, has there been, in your opinion, an irreparable breakdown of law and order in the city?'

'They turned over Throat Dibbler's barrow and made him eat two of his sausages-inna-bun!'

'Oh, I say!' said Colon.

'Without mustard!'

'I think we can call that a Yes,' said Carrot. He ticked the page again, and closed the book with a definite snap.

'We'd better be going,' he said.

'We were told—' Colon began.

'According to the Laws and Ordinances of Ankh-Morpork,' said Carrot, '*any* residents of the city, in times of the irreparable breakdown of law and order, shall, at the requeft of an officer of the city who is a citizen in good standing – there's a lot of stuff here about property and stuff, and then it goes on – form themfelves into a militia for city defence.'

'What does that mean?' said Angua.

'Militia . . .' mused Sergeant Colon.

'Hang on, you can't do that!' said Muldoon. 'That's nonsense!'

'It's the law. Never been repealed,' said Carrot.

'We've never had a militia! Never needed one!'

'Until now, I think.'

'Now look here,' said Muldoon, 'you come back with me to the Palace. You're men of the Watch—'

'And we're going to defend the city,' said Carrot.

People were streaming past the Watch House. Carrot stopped a couple by the simple expedient of sticking out his hand.

'Mr Poppley, isn't it?' he said. 'How's the grocery business? Hello, Mrs Poppley.'

'Ain't you heard?' said the flustered man. 'The trolls have set fire to the Palace!'

He followed Carrot's gaze up Broad Way, to where the Palace stood squat and dark in the early evening light. Ungovernable flames failed to billow from every window.

'My word,' said Carrot.

'And there's dwarfs breaking windows and everything!' said the grocer. 'A dog's not safe!'

'You can't trust 'em,' said Cuddy.

The grocer stared at him. 'Are you a dwarf?' he said.

'Amazing! How *do* people do it,' said Cuddy.

'Well, I'm off! I'm not stopping to see Mrs Poppley ravished by the little devils! You know what they say about dwarfs!'

The Watch watched the couple head off into the crowd again.

'Well, *I* don't,' said Cuddy, to no one in particular. 'What is it they say about dwarfs?'

Carrot fielded a man pushing a barrow.

'Would you mind telling me what's going on, sir?' he said.

'And do you know what it is they say about dwarfs?' said a voice behind him.

'That's not a sir, that's Throat,' said Colon. 'And will you look at the colour of him!'

'Should he be all shiny like that?' said Detritus.

'Feeling fine! Feeling fine!' said Dibbler. 'Hah! So much for people importuning the standard of my merchandise!'

'What's happening, Throat?' said Colon.

'They say—' Dibbler began, green in the face.

'Who says?' said Carrot.

'*They* say,' said Dibbler. 'You know. They. *Everyone*. They say the trolls have killed someone up at Dolly Sisters and the dwarfs have smashed up Chalky the troll's all-night pottery and they've broken down the Brass Bridge and—'

Carrot looked up the road.

'You just came over the Brass Bridge,' he said.

'Yeah, well . . . that's what they say,' said Dibbler.

'Oh, I see.' Carrot straightened up.

'Did they happen to say . . . sort of, in passing . . . anything else about dwarfs?' said Cuddy.

'I think we're going to have to go and have a word with the Day Watch about the arrest of Coalface,' Carrot said.

'We ain't got no weapons,' said Colon.

'I'm certain Coalface has nothing to do with the murder of Hammerhock,' said Carrot. 'We are armed with the truth. What can harm us if we are armed with the truth?'

'Well, a crossbow bolt can, e.g., go right through your eye and out the back of your head,' said Sergeant Colon.

'All right, sergeant,' said Carrot, 'so where do we get some *more* weapons?'

The bulk of the Armoury loomed against the sunset.

It was strange to find an armoury in a city which relied on deceit, bribery and assimilation to defeat its enemies but, as Sergeant Colon said, once you'd won their weapons off 'em you needed somewhere to store the things.

Carrot rapped on the door. After a while there were footsteps, and a small window slid back. A suspicious voice said: 'Yes?'

'Corporal Carrot, city militia.'

'Never heard of it. Bugger off.'

The hatch snapped back. Carrot heard Nobby snigger.

He thumped on the door again.

'Yes?'

'I'm Corporal Carrot—' The hatch moved, but hit Carrot's truncheon as he rammed it in the hole. '—and I'm here to collect some arms for my men.'

'Yeah? Where's your authority?'

'What? But I'm—'

The truncheon was knocked away and the hatch thudded into place.

''Scuse me,' said Corporal Nobbs, pushing past. 'Let me have a go. I've been here before, sort of thing.'

He kicked the door with his steel capped boots, known and feared wherever men were on the floor and in no position to fight back.

Snap. 'I told you to bug—'

'Auditors,' said Nobby.

There was a moment's silence.

'What?'

'Here to take inventory.'

'Where's your auth—'

'Oh? Oh? He says where's my authority?' Nobby leered at the guards. 'Oh? Keeps me hanging around here while his cronies can nip out the back to bring the stuff back out of hock, eh?'

'I nev—'

'And, and then, yeah, we'll get the old thousand swords trick, yeah? Fifty crates stacked up, turns out the bottom forty are full of rocks?'

'I—'

'What's your name, mister?'

'I—'

'You open this door right now!'

The hatch shut. There was the sound of bolts being pulled back by someone who was not at all convinced it was a good idea and would be asking searching questions in a minute.

'Got a piece of paper on you, Fred? Quick!'

'Yes, but—' said Sergeant Colon.

'Any paper! *Now!*'

Colon fumbled in his pocket and handed Nobby his grocery bill just as the door opened. Nobby swaggered in at high speed, forcing the man inside to walk backwards.

'Don't run off!' he shouted, 'I haven't found anything wrong—'

'I wasn't r—'

'—YET!'

Carrot had time to get an impression of a cavernous place full of complicated shadows. Apart from the man, who was fatter than

422

Colon, there were a couple of trolls who appeared to be operating a grindstone. Current events did not seem to have penetrated the thick walls.

'All right, no one panic, just stop what you're doing, stop what you're doing, please. I'm Corporal Nobbs, Ankh-Morpork City Ordnance Inspection City Audit—' The piece of paper was waved in front of the man's eyes at vision-blurring speed, and Nobby's voice faltered a bit as he contemplated the end of the sentence, '—Bureau . . . Special . . . Audit . . . Inspection. How many people work here?'

'Just me—'

Nobby pointed at the trolls.

'What about them?'

The man spat on the floor.

'Oh, I thought you said *people.*'

Carrot stuck out his hand automatically and it slammed against Detritus' breastplate.

'OK,' said Nobby, 'let's see what we've got here . . .' He walked fast along the racks, so that everyone else had to run to keep up. 'What's this?'

'Er—'

'Don't know, eh?'

'Sure . . . it's . . . it's . . .'

'A triple-stringed 2,000lb carriage-mounted siege crossbow with the double-action windlass?'

'Right.'

'Isn't this a Klatchian reinforced crossbow with the goat-leg cocking mechanism and the underhaft bayonet?'

'Er . . . yeah?'

Nobby gave it a cursory examination, and then tossed it aside.

The rest of the Night Watch looked on in astonishment. Nobby had never been known to wield any weapon beyond a knife.

'Have you got one of those Hershebian twelve-shot bows with the gravity feed?' he snapped.

'Eh? What you see is what we got, mister.'

Nobby pulled a hunting crossbow from its rack. His skinny arms twanged as he hauled on the cocking lever.

'Sold the bolts for this thing?'

'They're right there!'

Nobby selected one from the shelf and dropped it into its slot. Then he sighted along the shaft. He turned.

'I *like* this inventory,' said Nobby. 'We'll take it all.'

The man looked down the sights at Nobby's eye and, to Angua's horrified admiration, didn't faint.

'That little bow don't scare *me*,' he said.

'This little bow scare you?' said Nobby. 'No. Right. This is a little bow. A little bow like this wouldn't scare a man like you, because it's such a little bow. It'd need a bigger bow than this to scare a man like you.'

Angua would have given a month's pay to see the quartermaster's face from the front. She'd watched as Detritus had lifted down the siege bow, cocked it with one hand and a barely audible grunt, and stepped forward. Now she could imagine the eyeballs swivelling as the coldness of the metal penetrated the back of the armourer's fleshy red neck.

'Now, the one behind you, that's a *big* bow,' said Nobby.

It wasn't as if the six-foot iron arrow was sharp. It was supposed to smash through doorways, not do surgery.

'Can I pull the trigger yet?' Detritus rumbled, into the man's ear.

'You wouldn't dare fire that thing in here! That's a siege weapon! It'd go right through the wall!'

'Eventually,' said Nobby.

'What this bit for?' said Detritus.

'Now, look—'

'I hope you keep that thing maintained,' said Nobby. 'Them things were a bugger for metal fatigue. Especially on the safety catch.'

'What are a safety catch?' said Detritus.

Everything went quiet.

Carrot found his voice, a long way off.

'Corporal Nobbs?'

'Yessir?'

'I'll take over from this point, if you don't mind.'

He gently pushed the siege bow away, but Detritus hadn't liked the crack about *people* and it kept swinging back again.

'Now,' said Carrot, 'I don't like this element of coercion. We're not here to bully this poor man. He's a city employee, just like us. It's very wrong of you to put him in fear. Why not just ask?'

'Sorry, sir,' said Nobby.

Carrot patted the armourer on the shoulder.

'May we take some weapons?' he said.

'What?'

'Some weapons? For official purposes?'

The armourer looked unable to cope with this.

'You mean I got a choice?' he said.

'Why, certainly. We practise policing by consent in Ankh-

Morpork. If you feel unable to agree to our request, you only have to say the word.'

There was a faint *bong* as the tip of the iron arrow once again bounced on the back of the armourer's skull. He sought in vain for something to say, because the only word he could think of right now was 'Fire!'

'Uh,' he said. 'Uh. Yeah. Right. Sure. Take what you want.'

'Fine, fine. And Sergeant Colon will give you a receipt, adding of course that you release the weapons of your own free will.'

'My own free will?'

'You have absolute choice in the matter, of course.'

The man's face screwed up in the effort of desperate cogitation.

'I reckon . . .'

'Yes?'

'I reckon it's OK for you to take 'em. Take 'em right away.'

'Good man. Do you have a trolley?'

'And do you happen to know what it is they say about dwarfs?' said Cuddy.

It crept over Angua once again that Carrot had no irony in his soul. He meant every word. If the man had really held out, Carrot would probably have given in. Of course, there was a bit of a gap between *probably* and *certainly*.

Nobby was down the end of the row, occasionally squeaking with delight as he found an interesting war hammer or an especially evil-looking glaive. He was trying to hold everything, all at once.

Then he dropped the lot and ran forward.

'Oh, wow! A Klatchian fire engine! This is more *my* meteor!'

They heard him rummaging around in the gloom. He emerged pushing a sort of bin on small squeaky wheels. It had various handles and fat leathery bags, and a nozzle at the front. It looked like a very large kettle.

'The leather's been kept greased, too!'

'What is it?' said Carrot.

'*And* there's oil in the reservoir!' Nobby pumped a handle energetically. 'Last I heard, this thing had been banned in eight countries and three religions said they'd excommunicate any soldiers found using it!* Anyone got a light?'

'Here,' said Carrot, 'but what's—'

'Watch!'

Nobby lit a match, applied it to the tube at the front of the device, and pulled a lever.

---

* Five more embraced it as a holy weapon and instructed that it be used on all infidels, heretics, gnostics and people who fidgeted during the sermon.

425

They put out the flames eventually.

'Needs a bit of adjustment,' said Nobby, through his mask of soot.

'No,' said Carrot. For the rest of his life he'd remember the jet of fire scorching his face en route to the opposite wall.

'But it's—'

'No. It's too dangerous.'

'It's *meant* to be—'

'I mean it could hurt people.'

'Ah,' said Nobby, 'right. You should have said. We're after weapons that don't hurt people, right?'

'Corporal Nobbs?' said Sergeant Colon, who'd been even closer to the flame than Carrot.

'Yes, sarge?'

'You heard Corporal Carrot. No heathen weapons. Anyway, how come you know so much about all this stuff?'

'Milit'ry service.'

'Really, Nobby?' said Carrot.

'Had a *special* job, sir. Very responsible.'

'And what was that?'

'Quartermaster, sir,' said Nobby, saluting smartly.

'*You* were a quartermaster?' said Carrot. 'In whose army?'

'Duke of Pseudopolis, sir.'

'But Pseudopolis always lost its wars!'

'Ah . . . well . . .'

'Who did you sell the weapons to?'

'That's a slander, that is! They just used to spend a lot of time away for polishing and sharpening.'

'Nobby, this is Carrot talking to you. How much time, approximately?'

'Approximately? Oh. About a hundred per cent, if we're talking *approximately*, sir.'

'Nobby?'

'Sir?'

'You don't have to call me sir.'

'Yessir.'

In the end, Cuddy remained faithful to his axe, but added a couple more as an afterthought; Sergeant Colon chose a pike because the thing about a pike, the important thing, was that everything happened at the other end of it, i.e., a long way off; Lance-Constable Angua selected, without much enthusiasm, a short sword, and Corporal Nobbs—

—Corporal Nobbs was a kind of mechanical porcupine of blades, bows, points and knobbly things on the end of chains.

426

'You sure, Nobby?' said Carrot. 'There's nothing you want to leave?'

'It's so hard to choose, sir.'

Detritus was hanging on to his huge bow.

'That all you're taking, Detritus?'

'No sir! Taking Flint and Morraine, sir!'

The two trolls who had been working in the armoury had formed up behind Detritus.

'Swore 'em in, sir,' said Detritus. 'Used troll oath.'

Flint saluted amateurishly.

'He said he'd kick our *goohuloog* heads in if we didn't join up and do what we're told, sir,' he said.

'Very old troll oath,' said Detritus. 'Very famous, very traditional.'

'One of 'em could carry the Klatchian fire engine—' Nobby began hopefully.

'*No*, Nobby. Well . . . welcome to the Watch, men.'

'Corporal Carrot?'

'Yes, Cuddy?'

'It's not fair. They're trolls.'

'We need every man we can get, Cuddy.'

Carrot stood back. 'Now, we don't want people to think we're looking for trouble,' he said.

'Oh, dressed like this, sir, we won't have to look for trouble,' said Sergeant Colon despondently.

'Question, *sir*?' said Angua.

'Yes, Lance-Constable Angua?'

'Who's the enemy?'

'Looking like this, we won't have any problem finding enemies,' said Sergeant Colon.

'We're not looking for enemies, we're looking for information,' said Carrot. 'The best weapon we can use right now is the truth, and to start with, we're going to the Fools' Guild to find out why Brother Beano stole the gonne.'

'Did he steal the gonne?'

'I think he may have, yes.'

'But he died before the gonne was stolen!' said Colon.

'Yes,' said Carrot. 'I know that.'

'Now that,' said Colon, 'is what I calls an *alibi*.'

The squad formed up and, after a brief discussion among the trolls as to which was their left foot and which was their right, marched away. Nobby kept looking back longingly to the fire machine.

Sometimes it's better to light a flamethrower than curse the darkness.

Ten minutes later they'd pushed through the crowds and were outside the Guilds.

'See?' Carrot said.

'They back on to each other,' said Nobby. 'So what? There's still a wall between them.'

'I'm not so sure,' said Carrot. 'We'll jolly well find out.'

'Have we got time?' said Angua. 'I thought we were going to see the Day Watch.'

'There's something I must find out first,' said Carrot. 'The Fools haven't told me the *truth*.'

'Hang on a minute, hang on a minute,' said Sergeant Colon. 'This is going altogether just a bit too far by half. Look, I don't want us to kill anyone, right? I happen to be sergeant around here, if anyone's interested. Understand, Carrot? Nobby? No shooting or swordplay. It's bad enough barging into Guild property, but we'll get into really serious trouble if we shoot anyone. Lord Vetinari won't stop at sarcasm. He might use'—Colon swallowed—'irony. So that's an order. What do you want to do, anyway?'

'I just want people to tell me things,' said Carrot.

'Well, if they don't, you're not to hurt them,' said Colon. 'Look, you can ask questions, fair enough. But if Dr Whiteface starts getting difficult, we're to come away, right? Clowns give me the creeps. And he's worst of all. If he won't answer, we're to leave peacefully and, oh, I don't know, think of something else. That's an order like I said. Are you clear about this? It's an order.'

'If he won't answer my questions,' said Carrot, 'I'm to leave peacefully. Right.'

'So long as that's understood.'

Carrot knocked on the Fools' door, reached up, caught the custard pie as it emerged from the slot and rammed it back hard. Then he kicked the door so that it swung inwards a few inches.

Someone behind it said 'Ow.'

The door opened a bit further to reveal a small clown covered in whitewash and custard.

'You didn't have to do that,' he said.

'I just wanted to get into the spirit of the thing,' said Carrot. 'I'm Corporal Carrot and this is the citizens' militia, and we all enjoy a good laugh.'

''Scuse me—'

'Except for Lance-Constable Cuddy. And Lance-Constable Detritus enjoys a good laugh too, although some minutes after everyone else. And we're here to see Dr Whiteface.'

The clown's hair rose. Water squirted from his buttonhole.

'Have – have you got an appointment?' he said.

'I don't know,' said Carrot. 'Have we got an appointment?'

'I've got an iron ball with spikes on,' Nobby volunteered.

'That's a morningstar, Nobby.'

'Is it?'

'Yes,' said Carrot. 'An appointment is an engagement to see someone, while a morningstar is a large lump of metal used for viciously crushing skulls. It is important not to confuse the two, isn't it, Mr—?' He raised his eyebrows.

'Boffo, sir. But—'

'So if you could perhaps run along and tell Dr Whiteface we're here with an iron ball with spi— What am I saying? I mean, without an appointment to see him? Please? Thank you.'

The clown scuttled off.

'There,' said Carrot. 'Was that all right, sergeant?'

'He's probably going to be *satirical*, even,' said Colon, morosely.

They waited. After a while Lance-Constable Cuddy took a screwdriver from his pocket and inspected the custard-pie-throwing machine bolted to the door. The rest of them shuffled their feet, except for Nobby, who kept dropping things on his.

Boffo reappeared, flanked by two muscular jesters who didn't look as though they had a sense of humour *at all*.

'Dr Whiteface says there's no such thing as a city militia,' he ventured. 'But. Um. Dr Whiteface says, if it's really important he'll see some of you. But not the trolls or the dwarf. We heard there's gangs of trolls and dwarfs terrorizing the city.'

'Dat's what they say,' said Detritus, nodding.

'Incidentally, do you know what it is they—' Cuddy began, but Nobby nudged him into silence.

'You and me, sergeant?' said Carrot. 'And you, Lance-Constable Angua.'

'Oh dear,' said Sergeant Colon.

But they followed Carrot into the sombre buildings and along the gloomy corridors to Dr Whiteface's office. The chief of all the clowns, fools and jesters was standing in the middle of the floor, while a jester tried to sew extra sequins on his coat.

'Well?'

''Evening, doctor,' said Carrot.

'I should like to make it clear that Lord Vetinari will be hearing about this directly,' said Dr Whiteface.

'Oh, yes. I shall tell him,' said Carrot.

'I can't imagine why you're bothering me when there's rioting in the streets.'

'Ah, well . . . we shall deal with that later. But Captain Vimes always told me, sir, that there's big crimes and little crimes. Sometimes the little crimes look big and the big crimes you can hardly see, but the crucial thing is to decide which is which.'

They stared at one another.

'Well?' the clown demanded.

'I should like you to tell me,' said Carrot, 'about events in this Guild House the night before last.'

Dr Whiteface stared at him in silence.

Then he said, 'If I don't?'

'Then,' said Carrot, 'I am afraid I shall, with extreme reluctance, be forced to carry out the order I was given just before entering.'

He glanced at Colon. 'That's right, isn't it, sergeant?'

'What? Eh? Well, yes—'

'I would much prefer not to do so, but I have no choice,' said Carrot.

Dr Whiteface glared at the two of them.

'But this is Guild property! You have no right to . . . to . . .'

'I don't know about that, I'm only a corporal,' said Carrot. 'But I've never disobeyed a direct order yet, and I am sorry to have to tell you that I will carry out this one fully and to the letter.'

'Now, see here—'

Carrot moved a little closer.

'If it's any comfort, I'll probably be ashamed about it,' he said.

The clown stared into his honest eyes and saw, as did everyone. only simple truth.

'Listen! If I shout,' said Dr Whiteface, going red under his makeup, 'I can have a dozen men in here.'

'Believe me,' said Carrot, 'that will only make it easier for me to obey.'

Dr Whiteface prided himself on his ability to judge character. In Carrot's resolute expression there was nothing but absolute, meticulous honesty. He fiddled with a quill pen and then threw it down in a sudden movement.

'Confound it!' he shouted. 'How did you find out, eh? Who told you?'

'I really couldn't say,' said Carrot. 'But it makes sense anyway. There's only one entrance to each Guild, but the Guild Houses are back to back. Someone just had to cut through the wall.'

'I assure you we didn't know about it,' said the clown.

Sergeant Colon was lost in admiration. He'd seen people bluff on a bad hand, but he'd never seen anyone bluff with no cards.

'We thought it was just a prank,' said the clown. 'We thought young Beano had just done it with humorous intent, and then he turned up dead and we didn't—'

'You'd better show me the hole,' said Carrot.

The rest of the Watch stood to variations on the theme of At Ease in the courtyard.

'Corporal Nobbs?'

'Yes, Lance-Constable Cuddy?'

'What *is* it everyone says about dwarfs?'

'Oh, come on, you're pulling my leg, right? Everyone knows that who knows *anything* about dwarfs,' said Nobby.

Cuddy coughed.

'Dwarfs don't,' he said.

'What do you mean, dwarfs don't?'

'No one's told *us* what everyone knows about dwarfs,' said Cuddy.

'Well . . . I expect they thought you knew,' said Nobby, weakly.

'Not me.'

'Oh, all *right*,' said Nobby. He glanced at the trolls, then leaned across to Cuddy and whispered in the approximate region of his ear.

Cuddy nodded.

'Oh, is that all?'

'Yes. Er . . . is it true?'

'What? Oh, yes. Of course. It's nat'ral for a dwarf. Some have got more than others, of course.'

'That's the case all round,' said Nobby.

'I myself, for example, have saved more than seventy-eight dollars.'

'*No!* I mean, no. I mean, I don't mean well-endowed with *money*. I mean . . .' Nobby whispered again. Cuddy's expression didn't change.

Nobby waggled his eyebrows. 'True, is it?'

'How should I know? I don't know how much money humans generally have.'

Nobby subsided.

'There's one thing that's true at least,' he said. 'You dwarfs really love gold, don't you?'

'Of course we don't. Don't be silly.'

'Well—'

'We just say that to get it into bed.'

*

It was in a clown's bedroom. Colon had occasionally wondered what clowns did in private, and it was all here – the overlarge shoe tree, the very wide trouser press, the mirror with all the candles round it, some industrial-sized sticks of make-up . . . and a bed which looked like nothing more complicated than a blanket on the floor, because that's what it was. Clowns and fools weren't encouraged to live the soft life. Humour was a serious business.

There was also a hole in the wall, just big enough to admit a man. A little pile of crumbling bricks was heaped next to it.

There was darkness on the other side.

On the other side, people killed other people for money.

Carrot stuck his head and shoulders through the hole, but Colon tried to pull him back.

'Hang on, lad, you don't know what horrors lie beyond these walls—'

'I'm just having a look to find out.'

'It could be a torture chamber or a dungeon or a hideous pit or anything!'

'It's just a student's bedroom, sergeant.'

'You see?'

Carrot stepped through. They could hear him moving around in the gloom. It was Assassin's gloom, somehow richer and less gloomy than clown's gloom.

He poked his head through again.

'No one's been in here for a while, though,' he said. 'There's dust all over the floor but there's footprints in it. And the door's locked and bolted. On this side.'

The rest of his body followed Carrot.

'I just want to make sure I fully understand this,' he said to Dr Whiteface. 'Beano made a hole into the Assassins' Guild, yes? And then he went and exploded that dragon? And then he came back through this hole? So how did he get killed?'

'By the Assassins, surely,' said Dr Whiteface. 'They'd be within their rights. Trespass on Guild property is a very serious offence, after all.'

'Did anyone see Beano after the explosion?' said Carrot.

'Oh yes. Boffo was on gate duty and he distinctly remembers him going out.'

'He knows it was him?'

Dr Whiteface looked blank.

'Of course.'

'How?'

'How? He recognized him, of course. That's how you know who people are. You look at them and you say . . . that's him. That's

432

called re-cog-nit-ion,' said the clown, with pointed deliberation. 'It was Beano. Boffo said he looked very worried.'

'Ah. Fine. No more questions, doctor. Did Beano have any friends among the Assassins?'

'Well . . . possibly, possibly. We don't discourage visitors.'

Carrot stared at the clown's face. Then he smiled.

'Of course. Well, that about wraps it all up, I think.'

'If only he'd stuck to something, you know, *original*,' said Dr Whiteface.

'Like a bucket of whitewash over the door, or a custard pie?' said Sergeant Colon.

'That's right!'

'Well, we might as well be going,' said Carrot. 'I imagine you don't want to lay a complaint about the Assassins?'

Dr Whiteface tried to look panicky, but this did not work very well under a mouth painted into a wide grin.

'What? No! I mean – if an Assassin broke into *our* Guild, I mean, not on proper business, and stole something, well, we'd definitely consider we were within our rights to, well—'

'Pour jelly into his shirt?' said Angua.

'Hit him around the head with a bladder on a stick?' said Colon.

'Possibly.'

'Each Guild to their own, of course,' said Carrot. 'I suggest we might as well be going, sergeant. Nothing more for us to do here. Sorry to have troubled you, Dr Whiteface. I can see this must have been a great strain on you.'

The clown was limp with relief.

'Don't mention it. Don't mention it. Happy to help. I know you have your job to do.'

He ushered them down the stairs and into the courtyard, bubbling with small talk now. The rest of the Watch clanked to attention.

'Actually . . .' said Carrot, just as he was being ushered out of the gate, 'there is *one* thing you could do.'

'Of course, of course.'

'Um, I know it's a bit cheeky,' said Carrot, 'but I've always been very interested in Guild customs . . . so . . . do you think someone could show me your museum?'

'Sorry? What museum?'

'The clown museum?'

'Oh, you mean the Hall of Faces. That's not a museum. Of course. Nothing secret about it. Boffo, make a note. We'd be happy to show you around any time, corporal.'

'Thank you very much, Dr Whiteface.'

'Any time.'

'I'm just going off duty,' said Carrot. 'Right now would be nice. Since I happen to be here.'

'You can't go off duty when – ow!' said Colon.

'Sorry, sergeant?'

'You kicked me!'

'I accidentally trod on your sandal, sergeant. I'm sorry.'

Colon tried to see a message in Carrot's face. He'd got used to simple Carrot. Complicated Carrot was as unnerving as being savaged by a duck.

'We'll, er, we'll just be going, then, shall we?' he said.

'No point in staying here now *it's all settled*,' said Carrot, mugging furiously. 'May as well take the night off really.'

He glanced at the rooftops.

'Oh, well, now it's *all settled* we'll be off, right,' said Colon. 'Right, Nobby?'

'Oh, yeah, we'll be off all right, because it's *all settled*,' said Nobby. 'You hear that, Cuddy?'

'What, that it's *all settled*?' said Cuddy. 'Oh, yeah. We might as well be off. OK, Detritus?'

Detritus was staring moodily at nothing with his knuckles resting on the ground. This was a normal stance for a troll while waiting for the next thought to arrive.

The syllables of his name kicked a neuron into fitful activity.

'What?' he said.

'It's *all settled*.'

'What is?'

'You know – Mr Hammerhock's death and everything.'

'Is it?'

'Yes!'

'Oh.'

Detritus considered this for a while, nodded, and settled back into whatever state of mind he normally occupied.

Another neuron gave a fizzle.

'Right,' he said.

Cuddy watched him for a moment.

'That's about it,' he said, sadly. 'That's all we're getting.'

'I'll be back shortly,' said Carrot. 'Shall we be off . . . Joey, wasn't it? Dr Whiteface?'

'I suppose there's no harm,' said Dr Whiteface. 'Very well. Show Corporal Carrot anything he likes, Boffo.'

'Right, sir,' said the little clown.

'It must be a jolly job, being a clown,' said Carrot.

'Must it?'

434

'Lots of japes and jokes, I mean.'

Boffo gave Carrot a lopsided look.

'Well . . .' he said. 'It has its moments . . .'

'I bet it does. I bet it does.'

'Are you often on gate duty, Boffo?' said Carrot pleasantly, as they strolled through the Fools' Guild.

'Huh! Just about all the time,' said Boffo.

'So when did that friend of his, you know, the Assassin . . . visit him?'

'Oh, you know about him, then,' said Boffo.

'Oh, yes,' said Carrot.

'About ten days ago,' said Boffo. 'It's through here, past the pie range.'

'He'd forgotten Beano's name, but he did know the room. He didn't know the number but he went straight to it,' Carrot went on.

'That's right. I expect Dr Whiteface told you,' said Boffo.

'I've spoken to Dr Whiteface,' said Carrot.

Angua felt she was beginning to understand the way Carrot asked questions. He asked them by not asking them. He simply told people what he thought or suspected, and they found themselves filling in the details in an attempt to keep up. And he never, actually, told lies.

Boffo pushed open a door and fussed around lighting a candle.

'Here we are then,' he said. 'I'm in charge of this, when I'm not on the bloody gate.'

'Ye gods,' said Angua, under her breath. 'It's horrible.'

'It's very interesting,' said Carrot.

'It's historical,' said Boffo the clown.

'All those little heads . . .'

They stretched away in the candlelight, shelf on shelf of them, tiny little clown faces – as if a tribe of headhunters had suddenly developed a sophisticated sense of humour and a desire to make the world a better place.

'Eggs,' said Carrot. 'Ordinary hens' eggs. What you do is, you get a hen's egg, and you make a hole in either end and you blow the egg stuff out, and then a clown paints his make-up on the egg and that's his official make-up and no other clown can use it. That's very important. Some faces have been in the same family for generations, you know. Very valuable thing, a clown's face. Isn't that so, Boffo?'

The clown was staring at him.

'How do you know all that?'

'I read it in a book.'

Angua picked up an ancient egg. There was a label attached to it, and on the label were a dozen names, all crossed out except the last one. The ink on the earlier ones had faded almost to nothing. She put it down and unconsciously wiped her hand on her tunic.

'What happens if a clown wants to use another clown's face?' she said.

'Oh, we compare all the new eggs with the ones on the shelves,' said Boffo. 'It's not allowed.'

They walked between aisles of faces. Angua fancied she could hear the squelch of a million custard-filled trousers and the echoes of a thousand honking noses and a million grins of faces that weren't smiling. About halfway along was a sort of alcove containing a desk and chair, a shelf piled with old ledgers, and a workbench covered with crusted pots of paint, scraps of coloured horsehair, sequins and other odds and ends of the egg-painter's specialized art. Carrot picked up a wisp of coloured horsehair and twiddled it thoughtfully.

'But supposing,' he said, 'that a clown, I mean a clown with his own face . . . supposing he used another clown's face?'

'Pardon?' said Boffo.

'Supposing you used another clown's make-up?' said Angua.

'Oh, that happens all the time,' said Boffo. 'People're always borrowing slap off each other—'

'Slap?' said Angua.

'Make-up,' Carrot translated. 'No, I think what the lance-constable is asking, Boffo, is: could a clown make himself up to look like another clown?'

Boffo's brow wrinkled, like someone trying hard to understand an impossible question.

'Pardon?'

'Where's Beano's egg, Boffo?'

'That's here on the desk,' said Boffo. 'You can have a look if you like.'

An egg was handed up. It had a blobby red nose and a red wig. Angua saw Carrot hold it up to the light and produce a couple of red strands from his pocket.

'But,' she said, trying one more time to get Boffo to understand, 'couldn't you wake up one morning and put on make-up so that you looked like a *different* clown?'

He looked at her. It was hard to tell his expression under the permanently downcast mouth, but as far as she could tell she might as well have suggested that he performed a specific sex act with a small chicken.

'How could I do that?' he said. 'Then I wouldn't be *me*.'

'Someone else might do it, though?'

Boffo's buttonhole squirted.

'I don't have to listen to this sort of dirty talk, miss.'

'What you're saying, then,' said Carrot, 'is that no clown would ever make up his face in another clown's, um, design?'

'You're doing it again!'

'Yes, but perhaps sometimes by accident a young clown might perhaps—'

'Look, we're decent people, all right?'

'Sorry,' said Carrot. 'I think I understand. Now . . . when we found poor Mr Beano, he didn't have his clown wig on, but something like that could easily have got knocked off in the river. But his nose, now . . . you told Sergeant Colon that someone had taken his nose. His *real* nose. Could you,' said Carrot, in the pleasant tones of someone talking to a simpleton, 'point to *your* real nose, Boffo?'

Boffo tapped the big red nose on his face.

'But that's—' Angua began.

'—your *real* nose,' said Carrot. 'Thank you.'

The clown wound down a little.

'I think you'd better go,' he said. 'I don't like this sort of thing. It upsets me.'

'Sorry,' said Carrot again. 'It's just that . . . I think I'm having an idea. I wondered about it before . . . and I'm pretty certain now. I think I know about the person who did it. But I had to see the eggs to be sure.'

'You saying another clown killed him?' said Boffo belligerently. ''Cos if you are, I'm going straight to—'

'Not exactly,' said Carrot. 'But I can show you the killer's face.'

He reached down and took something from the debris on the table. Then he turned to Boffo and opened his hand. He had his back to Angua, and she could not quite see what he was holding. But Boffo gave a strangled cry and ran away down the avenue of faces, his big shoes flip-flopping hugely on the stone flags.

'Thank you,' said Carrot, at his retreating back. 'You've been very helpful.'

He folded his hand again.

'Come on,' he said. 'We'd better be going. I don't think we're going to be popular here in a minute or two.'

'What was that you showed him?' Angua asked, as they proceeded with dignity yet speed towards the gate. 'It was something you came here to find, wasn't it? All that stuff about wanting to see the museum—'

'I *did* want to see it. A good copper should always be open to new experiences,' said Carrot.

They made it to the gate. No vengeful pies floated out of the darkness.

Angua leaned against the wall outside. The air smelled sweeter here, which was an unusual thing to say about Ankh-Morpork air. But at least out here people could laugh without getting paid for it.

'You didn't show me what frightened him,' she said.

'I showed him a murderer,' said Carrot. 'I'm sorry. I didn't think he'd take it like that. I suppose they're all a bit wound up right now. And it's like dwarfs and tools. Everyone thinks in their own ways.'

'You found the murderer's face in there?'

'Yes.'

Carrot opened his hand.

It contained a bare egg.

'He looks like this,' he said.

'He didn't have a *face*?'

'No, you're thinking like a clown. I am very simple,' said Carrot, 'but I think what happened was this. Someone in the Assassins wanted a way of getting in and out without being seen. He realized there's only a thin wall between the two Guilds. He had a room. All he had to do was find out who lived on the other side. Later he killed Beano, and he took his wig and his nose. His *real* nose. That's how clowns think. Make-up wouldn't have been hard. You can get that anywhere. He walked into the Guild made up to look like Beano. He cut through the wall. Then he strolled down to the quad outside the museum, only this time he was dressed as an Assassin. He got the . . . the gonne and came back here. He went through the wall again, dressed up as Beano, and strolled away. And then someone killed *him*.'

'Boffo said Beano looked worried,' said Angua.

'And I thought: that's odd, because you'd have to see a clown right up close to know what his real expression was. But you *might* notice if the make-up wasn't on quite right. Like, maybe, if it was put on by someone who wasn't too used to it. But the important thing is that if another clown sees Beano's face go out of the door, he's seen the *person* leave. They can't think about someone else wearing that face. It's not how they think. A clown and his make-up are the same thing. Without his make-up a clown doesn't exist.

A clown wouldn't wear another clown's face in the same way a dwarf wouldn't use another dwarf's tools.'

'Sounds risky, though,' said Angua.

'It was. It was very risky.'

'Carrot? What are you going to do now?'

'I think it might be a good idea to find out whose room was on the other side of the hole, don't you? I think it might belong to Beano's little friend.'

'In the Assassins' Guild? Just us?'

'Um. You've got a point.'

Carrot looked so crestfallen that Angua gave in.

'What time is it?' she said.

Carrot very carefully took Captain Vimes's presentation watch out of its cloth case.

'It's—'

—*abing, abing, abong, bong . . . bing . . . bing . . .*

They waited patiently until it had finished.

'A quarter to seven,' said Carrot. 'Absolutely accurate, too. I put it right by the big sundial in the University.'

Angua glanced at the sky.

'OK,' she said. 'I can find out, I think. Leave it to me.'

'How?'

'Er . . . I . . . well, I could get out of uniform, couldn't I, and, oh, talk my way in as a kitchen maid's sister or something . . .'

Carrot looked doubtful.

'You think that'll work?'

'Can you think of anything better?'

'Not right now.'

'Well, then. I'll . . . er . . . look . . . you go back to the rest of the men and . . . I'll find somewhere to change into something more suitable.'

She didn't have to look around to recognize where the snigger came from. Gaspode had a way of turning up silently like a small puff of methane in a crowded room, and with the latter's distressing ability to fill up all available space.

'Where can you get a change of clothes around here?' said Carrot.

'A good Watchman is always ready to improvise,' said Angua.

'That little dog is awfully wheezy,' said Carrot. 'Why does he always follow us around?'

'I really couldn't say.'

'He's got a present for you.'

Angua risked a glance. Gaspode was holding, but only just, a very large bone in his mouth. It was wider than he was long, and might have belonged to something that died in a tar pit. It was green and furry in places.

'How nice,' she said, coldly. 'Look, you go on. Let me see what I can do . . .'

'If you're sure . . .' Carrot began, in a reluctant tone of voice.

'Yes.'

When he'd gone Angua headed for the nearest alley. There were only a few minutes to moonrise.

Sergeant Colon saluted when Carrot came back, frowning in thought.

'We can go home now, sir?' he suggested.

'What? Why?'

'Now it's all sorted out?'

'I just said that to waylay suspicion,' said Carrot.

'Ah. Very clever,' said the sergeant quickly. 'That's what I thought. He's saying that to waylay suspicion, I thought.'

'There's still a murderer out there somewhere. Or something worse.'

Carrot ran his gaze over the ill-assorted soldiery.

'But right now I think we're going to have to sort out this business with the Day Watch,' he said.

'Er. People say it's practically a riot up there,' said Colon.

'That's why we've got to sort it out.'

Colon bit his lip. He was not, as such, a coward. Last year the city had been invaded by a dragon and he'd actually stood on a rooftop and fired arrows at it while it was bearing down on him with its mouth open, although admittedly he'd had to change his underwear afterwards. But that had been *simple*. A great big fire-breathing dragon was straightfoward. There it was, right in front of you, about to broil you alive. That was all you had to worry about. Admittedly, it was a *lot* to worry about, but it was . . . simple. It wasn't any kind of mystery.

'We're going to have to sort it out?' he said.

'Yes.'

'Oh. Good. I like sorting things out.'

Foul Ole Ron was a Beggars' Guild member in good standing. He was a Mutterer, and a good one. He would walk behind people muttering in his own private language until they gave him money not to. People thought he was mad, but this was not, technically, the case. It was just that he was in touch with reality on the

440

cosmic level, and had a bit of trouble focusing on things smaller, like other people, walls and soap (although on very small things, such as coins, his eyesight was Grade A).

Therefore he was not surprised when a handsome young woman streaked past him and removed all her clothes. This sort of thing happened all the time, although up until now only on the inner side of his head.

Then he saw what happened next.

He watched as the sleek golden shape streaked away.

'I *told* 'em! I *told* 'em! I *told* 'em!' he said. 'I'll give 'em the wrong end of a ragman's trumpet, so I shall. Bug'r'em. Millennium hand and shrimp! I *told* 'em!'

Gaspode wagged what was technically a tail when Angua reemerged.

'"Change into fomefing more fuitable",' he said, his voice slightly muffled by the bone. 'Good one. I brung you thif little token—'

He dropped it on the cobbles. It didn't look any better to Angua's lupine eyes.

'What for?' she said.

'Stuffed with nourishin' marrowhone jelly, that bone.' he said accusingly.

'Forget it,' said Angua. 'Now, how do you normally get into the Assassins' Guild?'

'And maybe afterwards we could kind of hang out in the middens along Phedre Road?' said Gaspode, his stump of a tail still thumping the ground. 'There's rats along there that'll make your hair stand on— No, all right, forget I mentioned it,' he finished quickly, when fire flashed for a moment in Angua's eyes.

He sighed.

'There's a drain by the kitchens,' he said.

'Big enough for a human?'

'Not even for a dwarf. But it won't be worth it. It's spaghetti tonight. You don't get many bones in spaghetti—'

'Come on.'

He limped along.

'That was a good bone,' he said. 'Hardly even started going green. Hah! I bet you wouldn't say no to a box of chocolates from Mr Hunk, though.'

He cringed as she rounded on him.

'What are you talking about?'

'Nothing! Nothing!'

He trailed after her, whining.

Angua wasn't happy, either. It was always a problem, growing hair and fangs every full moon. Just when she thought she'd been lucky before, she'd found that few men are happy in a relationship where their partner grows hair and howls. She'd sworn: no more entanglements like that.

As for Gaspode, he was resigning himself to a life without love, or at least any more than the practical affection experienced so far, which had consisted of an unsuspecting chihuahua and a brief liaison with a postman's leg.

The No.1 powder slid down the folded paper into the metal tube. Blast Vimes! Who'd have thought he'd actually head for the opera house? He'd lost a set of tubes up there. But there were still three left, packed neatly in the hollow stock. A bag of No. 1 powder and a rudimentary knowledge of lead casting was all a man needed to rule the city . . .

The gonne lay on the table. There was a bluish sheen to the metal. Or, perhaps, not so much a sheen as a glisten. And, of course, that was only the oil. You had to believe it was only the oil. It was clearly a thing of metal. It couldn't possibly be alive.

And yet . . .

And yet . . .

'They say it was only a beggar girl in the Guild.'

Well? What of it? She was a target of opportunity. That was not my fault. That was your fault. I am merely the gonne. Gonnes don't kill people. People kill people.

'You killed Hammerhock! The boy said you fired yourself! And he'd repaired you!'

You expect gratitude? He would have made another gonne.

'Was that a reason to kill him?'

Certainly. You have no understanding.

Was the voice in his head or in the gonne? He couldn't be certain. Edward had said there was a voice . . . it said that everything you wanted, it could give you . . .

Getting into the Guild was easy for Angua, even through the angry crowds. Some of the Assassins, the ones from noble homes that had big floppy dogs around the place in the same way that lesser folk have rugs, had brought a few with them. Besides, Angua was pure pedigree. She drew admiring glances as she trotted through the buildings.

Finding the right corridor was easy, too. She'd remembered the

442

view from the Guild next door, and counted the number of floors. In any case, she didn't have to look hard. The reek of fireworks hung in the air all along the corridor.

There was a crowd of Assassins in the corridor, too. The door of the room had been forced open. As Angua peered around the corner she saw Dr Cruces emerge, his face suffused with rage.

'Mr Downey?'

A white-haired Assassin drew himself to attention.

'Sir?'

'I want him found!'

'Yes, doctor—'

'In fact I want him inhumed! With Extreme Impoliteness! And I'm setting the fee at ten thousand dollars – I shall pay it personally, you understand? Without Guild tax, either.'

Several Assassins nonchalantly strolled away from the crowd. Ten thousand untaxed dollars was good money.

Downey looked uncomfortable. 'Doctor, I think—'

'Think? You're not paid to think! Heaven knows where the idiot has got to. I ordered the Guild searched! Why didn't anyone force the door?'

'Sorry, doctor, Edward left us weeks ago and I didn't think—'

'You didn't *think*? What are you paid for?'

'Never seen *him* in such a temper,' said Gaspode.

There was a cough behind the chief Assassin. Dr Whiteface had emerged from the room.

'Ah, doctor,' said Dr Cruces. 'I think perhaps we'd better go and discuss this further in my study, yes?'

'I really am most terribly sorry, my lord—'

'Don't mention it. The little . . . devil has made us both look like fools. Oh . . . nothing personal, of course. Mr Downey, the Fools and the Assassins will be guarding this hole until we can get some masons in tomorrow. *No one* is to go through, you understand?'

'Yes, doctor.'

'Very well.'

'That's Mr Downey,' said Gaspode, as Dr Cruces and the chief clown disappeared down the corridor. 'Number two in the Assassins.' He scratched his ear. 'He'd knock off old Cruces for tuppence if it wasn't against the rules.'

Angua trotted forward. Downey, who was wiping his forehead with a black handkerchief, looked down.

'Hello, you're new,' he said. He glanced at Gaspode. 'And the mutt's back, I see.'

'Woof, woof,' said Gaspode, his stump of a tail thumping the floor. 'Incident'ly,' he added for Angua's benefit, 'he's often good for a peppermint if you catch him in the right mood. He's poisoned fifteen people this year. He's almost as good with poisons as old Cruces.'

'Do I need to know that?' said Angua. Downey patted her on the head.

'Oh, Assassins shouldn't kill unless they're being paid. It's these little tips that make all the difference.'

Now Angua was in a position to see the door. There was a name written on a piece of card stuck in a metal bracket.

Edward d'Eath.

'Edward d'Eath,' she said.

'There's a name that tolls a bell,' said Gaspode. 'Family used to live up Kingsway. Used to be as rich as Creosote.'

'Who was Creosote?'

'Some foreign bugger who was rich.'

'Oh.'

'But great-granddad had a terrible thirst, and granddad chased anything in a dress, his dress, you understand, and old d'Eath, well, he was sober and clean but lost the rest of the family money on account of having a blind spot when it came to telling the difference between a one and an eleven.'

'I can't see how that loses you money.'

'It does if you think you can play Cripple Mr Onion with the big boys.'

The werewolf and the dog padded back down the corridor.

'Do you know anything about Master Edward?' said Angua.

'Nope. The house was flogged off recently. Family debts. Haven't seen him around.'

'You're certainly a mine of information,' she said.

'I gets around. No one notices dogs.' Gaspode wrinkled his nose. It looked like a withered truffle. 'Blimey. Stinks of gonne, doesn't it.'

'Yes. Something odd about that,' said Angua.

'What?'

'Something not right.'

There were other smells. Unwashed socks, other dogs, Dr Whiteface's greasepaint, yesterday's dinner – the scents filled the air. But the firework smell of what Angua was now automatically thinking of as the gonne wound around everything else, acrid as acid.

'What's not right?'

'Don't know . . . maybe it's the gonne smell . . .'

'Nah. That started off here. The gonne was kept here for years.'

'Right. OK. Well, we've got a name. It might mean something to Carrot—'

Angua trotted down the stairs.

''Scuse me . . .' said Gaspode.

'Yes?'

'How can you turn back into a woman again?'

'I just get out of the moonlight and . . . concentrate. That's how it works.'

'Cor. That's all?'

'If it's technically full moon I can Change even during the day if I want to. I only *have* to Change when I'm in the moonlight.'

'Get away? What about wolfbane?'

'Wolfbane? It's a plant. A type of aconite, I think. What about it?'

'Don't it kill you?'

'Look, you don't have to believe everything you hear about werewolves. We're human, just like everyone else. Most of the time,' she added.

By now they were outside the Guild and heading for the alley, which indeed they reached, but it lacked certain important features that it had included when they were last there. Most notable of these was Angua's uniform, but there was also a world shortage of Foul Ole Ron.

'Damn.'

They looked at the empty patch of mud.

'Got any other clothes?' said Gaspode.

'Yes, but only back in Elm Street. This is my only uniform.'

'You have to put some clothes on when you're human?'

'Yes.'

'Why? I would have thought a nude woman would be at home in any company, no offence meant.'

'I prefer clothes.'

Gaspode sniffed at the dirt.

'Come on, then,' he sighed. 'We'd better catch up Foul Ole Ron before your chainmail becomes a bottle of Bearhugger's, yes?'

Angua looked around. The scent of Foul Ole Ron was practically tangible.

'All right. But let's be quick about it.'

Wolfbane? You didn't need daft old herbs to make your life a problem, if you spent one week every month with two extra legs and four extra nipples.

There were crowds around the Patrician's Palace, and outside the Assassins' Guild. A lot of beggars were in evidence. They looked

445

ugly. Looking ugly is a beggar's stock in trade in any case. These looked uglier than necessary.

The militia peered around a corner.

'There's hundreds of people,' said Colon. 'And loads of trolls outside the Day Watch.'

'Where's the crowd thickest?' said Carrot.

'Anywhere the trolls are,' said Colon. He remembered himself. 'Only joking,' he added.

'Very well,' said Carrot. 'Everyone follow me.'

The babble stopped as the militia marched, lumbered, trotted and knuckled towards the Day Watch House.

A couple of very large trolls blocked the way. The crowd watched in expectant silence.

Any minute now, Colon thought, someone's going to throw something. And then we're all going to die.

He glanced up. Slowly and jerkily, gargoyle heads were appearing along the gutters. No one wanted to miss a good fight.

Carrot nodded at the two trolls.

They'd got lichen all over them, Colon noticed.

'It's Bluejohn and Bauxite, isn't it?' said Carrot.

Bluejohn, despite himself, nodded. Bauxite was tougher, and merely glared.

'You're just the sort I was looking for,' Carrot went on.

Colon gripped his helmet like a size #10 limpet trying to crawl up into a size #1 shell. Bauxite was an avalanche with feet.

'You're conscripted,' said Carrot.

Colon peeked out from under the brim.

'Report to Corporal Nobbs for your weapons. Lance-Constable Detritus will administer the oath.' He stood back. 'Welcome to the Citizens' Watch. Remember, every lance-constable has a field-marshal's baton in his knapsack.'

The trolls hadn't moved.

'Ain't gonna be inna Watch,' said Bauxite.

'Officer material if ever I saw it,' said Carrot.

'Hey, you can't put them in the Watch!' shouted a dwarf from the crowd.

'Why, hello, Mr Stronginthearm,' said Carrot. 'Good to see community leaders here. Why can't they be in the militia?'

All the trolls listened intently. Stronginthearm realized that he was suddenly the centre of attention, and hesitated.

'Well ... you've only got the one dwarf, for one thing ...' he began.

'*I'm* a dwarf,' said Carrot, 'technically.'

Stronginthearm looked a little nervous. The whole issue of

446

Carrot's keenly embraced dwarfishness was a difficult one for the more politically minded dwarfs.

'You're a bit big,' he said lamely.

'Big? What's size got to do with being a dwarf?' Carrot demanded.

'Um . . . a lot?' whispered Cuddy.

'Good point,' said Carrot. 'That's a good point.' He scanned the faces. 'Right. We need some honest, law-abiding dwarfs . . . you there . . .'

'Me?' said an unwary dwarf.

'Have you got any previous convictions?'

'Well, I dunno . . . I suppose I used to believe very firmly that a penny saved is a penny earned—'

'Good. And I'll take . . . you two . . . and you. Four more dwarfs, yes? Can't complain about that, eh?'

'Ain't gonna be inna Watch,' said Bauxite again, but uncertainty modulated his tone.

'You trolls can't leave now,' said Detritus. 'Otherwise, too many dwarfs. That's *numbers*, that is.'

'I'm not joining any Watch!' said a dwarf.

'Not man enough, eh?' said Cuddy.

'What? I'm as good as any bloody troll any day!'

'Right, that's sorted out then,' said Carrot, rubbing his hands together. 'Acting-Constable Cuddy?'

'Sir?'

'Hey,' said Detritus, 'how come he suddenly full constable?'

'Since he was in charge of the dwarf recruits,' said Carrot. 'And you're in charge of the troll recruits, Acting-Constable Detritus.'

'I full acting-constable in charge of the troll recruits?'

'Of course. Now, if you would step out of the way, Lance-Constable Bauxite—'

Behind Carrot, Detritus drew a big proud breath.

'Ain't gonna—'

'Lance-Constable Bauxite! You horrible big troll! You standing up straight! You saluting right now! You stepping out of the way of Corporal Carrot! You two troll, you come here! Wurn . . . two-er . . . tree . . . four-er! You in the Watch now! Aaargh, I cannot believe it what my eye it seeing! Where you from, Bauxite?'

'Slice Mountain, but—'

'Slice Mountain! *Slice Mountain?* Only . . .' Detritus looked at his fingers for a moment, and rammed them behind his back. 'Only twoer things come from Slice Mountain! Rocks . . . an' . . . an' . . .' he struck out wildly, 'other sortsa rocks! What kind *you*, Bauxite?'

'What the hell's going on here?'

The Watch House door had opened. Captain Quirke emerged, sword in hand.

'*You two horrible troll! You raise your hand right now, you repeat troll oath—*'

'Ah, captain,' said Carrot. 'Can we have a word?'

'You're in real trouble, *Corporal* Carrot,' snarled Quirke. 'Who do you think you are?'

'*I will do what I told—*'

'Don't *wanna* be inna—'

Wham!

'*I will do what I told—*'

' Just the man on the spot, captain,' said Carrot cheerfully.

'Well, man on the spot, I'm the senior officer here, and you can damn well—'

'Interesting point,' said Carrot. He produced his black book. 'I'm relieving you of your command.'

'—*otherwise I get my goohuloog head kicked in.*'

'—*otherwise I get my goohuloog head kicked in.*'

'Wha—? Are you mad?'

'No, sir, but I'm choosing to believe that you are. There are regulations laid down for this eventuality.'

'Where is your authority?' Quirke stared at the crowd. 'Hah! I suppose you'll say this armed mob is your authority, eh?'

Carrot looked shocked.

'No. The Laws and Ordinances of Ankh-Morpork, sir. It's all down here. Can you tell me what evidence you have against the prisoner Coalface?'

'That damn troll? It's a troll!'

'Yes?'

Quirke looked around.

'Look, I don't have to tell you with everyone here—'

'As a matter of fact, according to the rules, you do. That's why it's called evidence. It means "that which is seen".'

'Listen!' hissed Quirke, leaning towards Carrot. 'He's a troll. He's as guilty as hell of *something*. They all are!'

Carrot smiled brightly.

Colon had come to know that smile. Carrot's face seemed to go waxy and glisten when he smiled like that.

'And so you locked him up?'

'Right!'

'Oh. I see. I understand now.'

Carrot turned away.

'I don't know what you think you're—' Quirke began.

People hardly saw Carrot move. There was just a blur, a sound like a steak being thumped on a slab, and the captain was flat on the cobbles.

A couple of members of the Day Watch appeared cautiously in the doorway.

Everyone became aware of a rattling noise. Nobby was spinning the morningstar round and round on the end of its chain, except that because the spiky ball was a very heavy spiky ball, and because the difference between Nobby and a dwarf was species rather than height, it was more a case of both of them orbiting around each other. If he let go, it was an even chance that the target would be hit by a spiky ball or an unexploded Corporal Nobbs. Neither prospect pleased.

'Put it down, Nobby,' hissed Colon, 'I don't think they're going to make trouble . . .'

'I can't let go, Fred!'

Carrot sucked his knuckles.

'Do you think that comes under the heading of "minimum necessary force", sergeant?' he asked. He appeared to be genuinely worried.

'Fred! Fred! What'll I do?'

Nobby was a terrified blur. When you are swinging a spiky ball on a chain, the only realistic option is to keep moving. Standing still is an interesting but brief demonstration of a spiral in action.

'Is he still breathing?' said Colon.

'Oh, yes. I pulled the punch.'

'Sounds minimum enough to me, sir,' said Colon loyally.

'*Fredddd!*'

Carrot reached out absent-mindedly as the morningstar rocketed past and caught it by the chain. Then he threw it against the wall, where it stuck.

'You men in there in the Watch House,' he said, 'come out now.'

Five men emerged, edging cautiously around the prone captain.

'Good. Now go and get Coalface.'

'Er . . . he's in a bit of a bad temper, Corporal Carrot.'

'On account of being chained to the floor,' volunteered another guard.

'Well, now,' said Carrot. 'The thing is, he's going to be unchained right now.' The men shuffled their feet nervously, possibly remembering an old proverb that fitted the occasion very well.* Carrot nodded. 'I won't ask *you* to do it, but I might suggest you take some time off,' he said.

---

* It runs: 'He who chains down a troll, especially taking advantage of the situation to put the boot in a few times, had better not be the one who unchains it again.'

'Quirm is very nice at this time of year,' said Sergeant Colon helpfully. 'They've got a floral clock.'

'Er . . . since you mention it . . . I've got some sick leave coming up,' one of them said.

'I should think that's very probable, if you hang around,' said Carrot.

They sidled off as fast as decency allowed. The crowd hardly paid them any attention. There was still a lot more mileage in watching Carrot.

'Right,' said Carrot. 'Detritus, you take some men and go and bring out the prisoner.'

'I don't see why—' a dwarf began.

'You shut up, you horrible man,' said Detritus, drunk with power. You could have heard a guillotine drop.

In the crowd, a number of different-sized knobbly hands gripped a variety of concealed weapons.

Everyone looked at Carrot.

That was the strange thing, Colon remembered later. Everyone looked at Carrot.

Gaspode sniffed a lamp-post.

'I see Three-legged Shep has been ill again,' he said. 'And old Willy the Pup is back in town.'

To a dog, a well-placed hitching post or lamp is a social calendar.

'Where are we?' said Angua. Foul Ole Ron's trail was hard to follow. There were so many other smells.

'Somewhere in the Shades,' said Gaspode. 'Sweetheart Lane, smells like.' He snuffled across the ground. 'Ah, here he is again, the little . . .'

''ullo, Gaspode . . .'

It was a deep, hoarse voice, a kind of whisper with sand in it. It came from somewhere in an alley.

''o's yer fwiend, Gaspode?'

There was a snigger.

'Ah,' said Gaspode. 'Uh. Hi, guys.'

Two dogs emerged from the alley. They were huge. Their species was indeterminate. One of them was jet black and looked like a pit bull terrier crossed with a mincing machine. The other . . . the other looked like a dog whose name was almost certainly 'Butch'. Both top and bottom set of fangs had grown so large that he appeared to be looking at the world through bars. He was also bow-legged, although it would probably be a bad if not terminal move for anyone to comment on this.

Gaspode's tail vibrated nervously.

'These are my friends Black Roger and—'

'Butch?' suggested Angua.

'How did you know that?'

'A lucky guess,' said Angua.

The two big dogs had moved around so that they were on either side of them.

'Well, well, well,' said Black Roger. 'Who's this, then?'

'Angua,' said Gaspode. 'She's a—'

'—wolfhound,' said Angua.

The two dogs paced around them hungrily.

'Big Fido know about her?' said Black Roger.

'I was just—' Gaspode began.

'Well, now,' said Black Roger, 'I reckon you'd be wanting to come with us. Guild night tonight.'

'Sure, sure,' said Gaspode. 'No problem there.'

I could certainly manage either of them, Angua thought. But not both at once.

Being a werewolf meant having the dexterity and jaw power to instantly rip out a man's jugular. It was a trick of her father's that had always annoyed her mother, especially when he did it just before meals. But Angua had never been able to bring herself to do it. She'd preferred the vegetarian option.

''ullo,' said Butch, in her ear.

'Don't you worry about anything,' moaned Gaspode. 'Me an' Big Fido . . . we're like that.'

'What're you trying to do? Cross your claws? I didn't know dogs could do that.'

'We can't,' said Gaspode miserably.

Other dogs slunk out of the shadows as the two of them were half led, half driven along byways that weren't even alleys any more, just gaps between walls. They opened out eventually into a bare area, nothing more than a large light well for the buildings around it. There was a very large barrel on its side in one corner, with a ragged bit of blanket in it. A variety of dogs were waiting around in front of it, looking expectant; some of them had only one eye, some of them had only one ear, all of them had scars, and all of them had teeth.

'You,' said Black Roger, 'wait here.'

'Do not twy to wun away,' said Butch, ''cos having your intestines chewed often offends.'

Angua lowered her head to Gaspode level. The little dog was shaking.

451

'What have you got me into?' she growled. 'This is the dog Guild, right? A pack of strays?'

'Shsssh! Don't say that! These aren't *strays*. Oh, blimey.' Gaspode glanced around. 'You don't just get *any* hound in the Guild. Oh, dear me, no. These are dogs that have been . . .' he lowered his voice, ' . . . er . . . bad dogs.'

'Bad dogs?'

'Bad dogs. You naughty boy. Give him a smack. You bad dog,' muttered Gaspode, like some horrible litany. 'Every dog you see here, right, every dog . . . run away. Run away from his or her actual owner.'

'Is that all?'

'All? *All*? Well. Of course. You ain't exactly a dog. You wouldn't understand. You wouldn't know what it was like. But Big Fido . . . he told 'em. Throw off your choke chains, he said. Bite the hand that feeds you. Rise up and howl. He gave 'em pride,' said Gaspode, his voice a mixture of fear and fascination. 'He told 'em. Any dog he finds not bein' a free spirit – that dog is a dead dog. He killed a Dobermann last week, just for wagging his tail when a human went past.'

Angua looked at some of the other dogs. They were all unkempt. They were also, in a strange way, un-doglike. There was a small and rather dainty white poodle that still just about had the overgrown remains of its poodle cut, and a lapdog with the tattered remains of a tartan jacket still hanging from its shoulder. But they weren't milling around, or squabbling. They had a uniform intent look that she'd seen before, although never on dogs.

Gaspode was clearly trembling now. Angua slunk over to the poodle. It still had a diamante collar visible under the crusty fur.

'This Big Fido,' she said, 'is he some kind of wolf, or what?'

'Spiritually, all dogs are wolves,' said the poodle, 'but cynically and cruelly severed from their true destiny by the manipulations of so-called humanity.'

It sounded like a quote. 'Big Fido said that?' Angua hazarded.

The poodle turned its head. For the first time she saw its eyes. They were red, and as mad as hell. Anything with eyes like that could kill anything it wanted because madness, true madness, can drive a fist through a plank.

'Yes,' said Big Fido.

He had been a normal dog. He'd begged, and rolled over, and heeled, and fetched. Every night he'd been taken for a walk.

There was no flash of light when it happened. He'd just been

452

lying in his basket one night and he'd thought about his name, which was Fido, and the name on the basket, which was Fido. And he thought about his blanket with Fido on it, and his bowl with Fido on it, and above all he brooded on the collar with Fido on it, and something somewhere deep in his brain had gone 'click' and he'd eaten his blanket, savaged his owner and dived out through the kitchen window. In the street outside a labrador four times the size of Fido had sniggered at the collar, and thirty seconds later had fled, whimpering.

That had just been the start.

The dog hierarchy was a simple matter. Fido had simply asked around, generally in a muffled voice because he had someone's leg in his jaws, until he located the leader of the largest gang of feral dogs in the city. People – that is, dogs – still talked about the fight between Fido and Barking Mad Arthur, a rottweiler with one eye and a very bad temper. But most animals don't fight to the death, only to the defeat, and Fido was impossible to defeat; he was simply a very small fast killing streak with a collar. He'd hung on to bits of Barking Mad Arthur until Barking Mad Arthur had given in, and then to his amazement Fido had killed him. There was something inexplicably determined about the dog – you could have sandblasted him for five minutes and what was left still wouldn't have given up and *you'd better not turn your back on it.*

Because Big Fido had a dream.

'Is there a problem?' said Carrot.

'That *troll* insulted that *dwarf*,' said Stronginthearm the dwarf.

'I heard Acting-Constable Detritus give an order to Lance-Constable . . . Hrolf Pyjama,' said Carrot. 'What about it?'

'He's a *troll*!'

'Well?'

'He insulted a dwarf!'

'Actually, it's a technical milit'ry term—' said Sergeant Colon.

'That damn troll just happened to save my life today,' shouted Cuddy.

'What for?'

'What for? *What for?* 'Cos it was my life, that's what for! I happen to be very attached to it!'

'I didn't mean—'

'You just shut up, Abba Stronginthearm! What do you know about anything, you civilian! Why're you so stupid? Aargh! I'm too short for this shit!'

A shadow loomed in the doorway. Coalface was a basically

horizontal shape, a dark mass of fracture lines and sheer surfaces. His eyes gleamed red and suspicious.

'Now you're letting it go!' moaned a dwarf.

'This is because we have no reason to keep him locked up,' said Carrot. 'Whoever killed Mr Hammerhock was small enough to get through a dwarf's doorway. A troll his size couldn't manage that.'

'But everyone knows he's a *bad* troll!' shouted Stronginthearm.

'I never done nuffin,' said Coalface.

'You can't turn him loose now, sir,' hissed Colon. 'They'll set on him!'

'I never done nuffin.'

'Good point, sergeant. Acting-Constable Detritus!'

'Sir?'

'Volunteer him.'

'I never done nuffin.'

'You can't do that!' shouted the dwarf.

'Ain't gonna be in no Watch,' growled Coalface.

Carrot leaned towards him. 'There's a hundred dwarfs over there. With great big axes,' he whispered.

Coalface blinked.

'I'll join.'

'Swear him in, acting-constable.'

'Permission to enrol another dwarf, sir? To maintain parity?'

'Go ahead, Acting-Constable Cuddy.'

Carrot removed his helmet and wiped his forehead.

'I think that's about it, then,' he said.

The crowd stared at him.

He smiled brightly.

'No one has to stay here unless they want to,' he said.

'I never done nuffin.'

'Yes . . . but . . . look,' said Stronginthearm. 'If he didn't kill old Hammerhock, who did?'

'I never done nuffin.'

'Our inquiries are proceeding.'

'You don't know!'

'But I'm finding out.'

'Oh, yes? And when, pray, will you *know*?'

'Tomorrow.'

The dwarf hesitated.

'All right, then,' he said, with extreme reluctance. 'Tomorrow. But it had better *be* tomorrow.'

'All right,' said Carrot.

The crowd dispersed, or at least spread out a bit. Trolls, dwarfs

454

and humans alike, an Ankh-Morpork citizen is never keen on moving on if there's some street theatre left.

Acting-Constable Detritus, his chest so swollen with pride and pomposity that his knuckles barely touched the ground, reviewed his troops.

'You listen up, you horrible trolls!'

He paused, while the next thoughts shuffled into position.

'You listen up good right now! You in the Watch, boy! It a job with opportunity!' said Detritus. 'I only been doin' it ten minute and already I get promoted! Also got education and training for a good job in Civilian Street!'

'This your club with a nail in it. You will eat it. You will sleep on it! When Detritus say Jump, you say . . . what colour! We goin' to do this by the numbers! And I got lotsa numbers!'

'I never done nuffin.'

'You Coalface, you smarten up, you got a field-marshal's button in your knapsack!'

'Never took nuffin, neither.'

'You get down now and give me thirty-two! No! Make it sixty-four!'

Sergeant Colon pinched the bridge of his nose. We're alive, he thought. A troll insulted a dwarf in front of a lot of other dwarfs. Coalface . . . I mean, *Coalface*, I mean, Detritus is Mr Clean by comparison . . . is free and now he's a guard. Carrot laid out Mayonnaise. Carrot's said we'll sort it all out by tomorrow, and it's dark already. But we're alive.

Corporal Carrot is a crazy man.

Hark at them dogs. Everyone's on edge, in this heat.

Angua listened to the other dogs howling, and thought about wolves.

She'd run with the pack a few times, and knew about wolves. These dogs *weren't* wolves. Wolves were peaceful creatures, on the whole, and fairly simple. Come to think of it, the leader of the pack had been rather like Carrot. Carrot fitted into the city in the same way *he'd* fitted into the high forests.

Dogs were brighter than wolves. Wolves didn't *need* intelligence. They had other things. But dogs . . . they'd been given intelligence by humans. Whether they wanted it or not. They were certainly more vicious than wolves. They'd got that from humans, too.

Big Fido was forging his band of strays into what the ignorant thought a wolf pack was. A kind of furry killing machine.

She looked around.

Big dogs, little dogs, fat dogs, skinny dogs. They were all watching, bright-eyed, as the poodle talked.

About Destiny.

About Discipline.

About the Natural Superiority of the Canine Race.

About Wolves. Only Big Fido's vision of wolves weren't wolves as Angua knew them. They were bigger, fiercer, wiser, the wolves of Big Fido's dream. They were Kings of the Forest, Terrors of the Night. They had names like Quickfang and Silverback. They were what every dog should aspire to.

Big Fido had approved of Angua. She looked very much like a wolf, he said.

They all listened, totally entranced, to a small dog who farted nervously while he talked and told them that the natural shape for a dog was a whole lot bigger. Angua would have laughed, were it not for the fact that she doubted very much if she'd get out of there alive.

And then she watched what happened to a small rat-like mongrel which was dragged into the centre of the circle by a couple of terriers and accused of fetching a stick. Not even wolves did *that* to other wolves. There was no code of wolf behaviour. There didn't need to be. Wolves didn't need rules about being wolves.

When the execution was over, she found Gaspode sitting in a corner and trying to be unobtrusive.

'Will they chase us if we sneak off now?' she said.

'Don't think so. Meeting's over, see?'

'Come on, then.'

They sauntered into an alley and, when they were sure they hadn't been noticed, ran like hell.

'Good grief,' said Angua, when they had put several streets between them and the crowd of dogs. 'He's mad, isn't he?'

'No, mad's when you froth at the mouf,' said Gaspode. 'He's insane. That's when you froth at the brain.'

'All that stuff about wolves—'

'I suppose a dog's got a right to dream,' said Gaspode.

'But wolves aren't like that! They don't even have names!'

'Everyone's got a *name*.'

'Wolves haven't. Why should they? They know who they are, and they know who the rest of the pack are. It's all . . . an image. Smell and feel and shape. Wolves don't even have a word for wolves! It's not *like* that. Names are human things.'

'Dogs have got names. *I've* got a name. Gaspode. 'S'my name,' said Gaspode, a shade sullenly.

'Well . . . I can't explain why,' said Angua. 'But wolves don't have names.'

The moon was high now, in a sky as black as a cup of coffee that wasn't very black at all.

Its light turned the city into a network of silver lines and shadows.

Once upon a time the Tower of Art had been the centre of the city, but cities tend to migrate gently with time and Ankh-Morpork's centre was now several hundred yards away. The tower still dominated the city, though; its black shape reared against the evening sky, contriving to look blacker than mere shadows would suggest.

Hardly anyone ever looked at the Tower of Art, because it was always there. It was just a thing. People hardly ever look at familiar things.

There was a very faint *clink* of metal on stone. For a moment, anyone close to the tower and looking in exactly the right place might have fancied that a patch of even blacker darkness was slowly but inexorably moving towards the top.

For a moment, the moonlight caught a slim metal tube, slung across the figure's back. Then it swung into shadow again as it climbed onwards.

The window was resolutely shut.

'But she always leaves it open,' Angua whined.

'Must have shut it tonight,' said Gaspode. 'There's a lot of strange people about.'

'But she *knows* about strange people,' said Angua. 'Most of them live in her house!'

'You'll just have to change back to human and smash the window.'

'I can't do that! I'd be naked!'

'Well, you're naked now, ain't you?'

'But I'm a wolf! That's different!'

'I've never worn anything in my whole life. It's never bothered *me.*'

'The Watch House,' muttered Angua. 'There'll be something at the Watch House. Spare chainmail, at least. A sheet or something. And the door doesn't shut properly. Come on.'

She trotted off along the street, with Gaspode whimpering along behind her.

Someone was singing.

'Blimey,' said Gaspode, 'look at that.'

Four Watchmen slogged past. Two dwarfs, two trolls. Angua recognized Detritus.

'Hut, hut, hut! You without doubt the horriblest recruits I ever see! Pick up them feet!'

'I never done nuffin!'

'Now you doin somefin for the first time in your horrible life, Lance-Constable Coalface! It a man life in the Watch!'

The squad rounded the corner.

'What's been going on?' said Angua.

'Search me. I might know more if one of 'em stops for a widdle.'

There was a small crowd around the Watch House in Pseudopolis Yard. They seemed to be Watchmen, too. Sergeant Colon was standing under a flickering lamp, scribbling on his clipboard and talking to a small man with a large moustache.

'And your name, mister?'

'SILAS! CUMBERBATCH!'

'Didn't you used to be town crier?'

'THAT'S RIGHT!'

'Right. Give him his shilling. Acting-Constable Cuddy? One for your squad.'

'WHO'S ACTING-CONSTABLE CUDDY?' said Cumberbatch.

'Down here, mister.'

The man looked down.

'BUT YOU'RE! A DWARF! I NEVER—'

'Stand to attention when you're talking to a superierierior officer!' Cuddy bellowed.

'Ain't no dwarfs or trolls or humans in the Watch, see,' said Colon. 'Just Watchmen, see? That's what Corporal Carrot says. Of course, if you'd like to be in Acting-Constable Detritus' squad—'

'I *LIKE* DWARFS,' said Cumberbatch, hurriedly. 'ALWAYS HAVE. NOT THAT THERE ARE ANY IN THE WATCH, MIND,' he added, after barely a second's thought.

'You learn quick. You'll go a long way in this man's army,' said Cuddy. 'You could have a field-marshal's bottom in your napkin any day now. AAAAaabbbb-wut tn! Hut, hut, hut—'

'Fifth volunteer so far,' said Colon to Corporal Nobbs, as Cuddy and his new recruit pounded off into the darkness. 'Even the Dean at the University tried to join. Amazing.'

Angua looked at Gaspode, who shrugged.

'Detritus is certainly clubbing 'em into line,' said Colon. 'After ten minutes they're putty in his hands. Mind you,' he added, 'after ten minutes anything's putty in them hands. Reminds me of the drill sergeant we had when I was first in the army.'

'Tough, was he?' said Nobby, lighting a cigarette.

'Tough? Tough? Blimey! Thirteen weeks of pure misery, that was! Ten-mile run every morning, up to our necks in muck half the time, and him yelling a blue streak and cussin' us every living moment! One time he made me stay up all night cleaning the lavvies with a toothbrush! He'd hit us with a spiky stick to get us out of bed! We had to jump through hoops for that man, we hated his damn guts, we'd have stuck one on him if any of us had the nerve but, of course, none of us did. He put us through three months of living death. But . . . y'know. . after the passing-out parade . . . us looking at ourselves all in our new uniforms an' all, real soldiers at last, seein' what we'd become . . . well, we saw him in the bar and, well . . . I don't mind telling you . . .' The dogs watched Colon wipe away the suspicion of a tear. ' . . . Me and Tonker Jackson and Hoggy Spuds waited for him in the alley and beat seven kinds of hell out of him, it took three days for my knuckles to heal.' Colon blew his nose. 'Happy days . . . Fancy a boiled sweet, Nobby?'

'Don't mind if I do, Fred.'

'Give one to the little dog,' said Gaspode. Colon did, and then wondered why.

'See?' said Gaspode, crunching it up in his dreadful teeth. 'I'm brilliant. *Brilliant.*'

'You'd better pray Big Fido doesn't find out,' said Angua.

'Nah. He won't touch me. I worry him. I've got the Power.' He scratched an ear vigorously. 'Look, you don't have to go back in there, we could go and—'

'No.'

'Story of my life,' said Gaspode. 'There's Gaspode. Give him a kick.'

'I thought you had this big happy family to go back to,' said Angua, as she pushed open the door.

'Eh? Oh, yes. Right,' said Gaspode hurriedly. 'Yes. But I like my, sort of, independence. I could stroll back home like a shot, any time I wanted.'

Angua bounded up the stairs, and clawed open the nearest door.

It was Carrot's bedroom. The smell of him, a kind of golden-pink colour, filled it from edge to edge.

There was a drawing of a dwarf mine carefully pinned to one wall. Another held a large sheet of cheap paper on which had been drawn, in careful pencil line, with many crossings-out and smudges, a map of the city.

In front of the window, where a conscientious person would put it to take as much advantage as possible of the available light so's not to have to waste too many of the city's candles, was a small table. There was some paper on it, and a jar of pencils. There was an old chair, too; a piece of paper had been folded up and wedged under a wobbly leg.

And that, apart from a clothes chest, was it. It reminded her of Vimes's room. This was a place where someone came to sleep, not to live.

Angua wondered if there was ever a time when anyone in the Watch was *ever*, really, off duty. She couldn't imagine Sergeant Colon in civilian clothes. When you were a Watchman, you were a Watchman *all the time*, which was a bit of a bargain for the city since it only paid you to be a Watchman for ten hours of every day.

'All right,' she said. 'I can use a sheet off the bed. You shut your eyes.'

'Why?' said Gaspode.

'For decency's sake!'

Gaspode looked blank. Then he said, 'Oh, I get it. Yes, I can see your point, def'nitely. Dear me, you can't have me looking at a naked woman, oh no. Oggling. Gettin' ideas. Deary deary me.'

'You know what I mean!'

'Can't say I do. Can't say I do. Clothing has never been what you might call a thingy of dog wossname.' Gaspode scratched his ear. 'Two metasyntactic variables there. Sorry.'

'It's different with you. You know what I am. Anyway, dogs are naturally naked.'

'So're humans—'

Angua changed.

Gaspode's ear flattened against his head. Despite himself, he whimpered.

Angua stretched.

'You know the worst bit?' she said. 'It's my hair. You can hardly get the tangles out. And my feet are *covered* in mud.'

She tugged a sheet off the bed and draped it around herself as a makeshift toga.

'There,' she said, 'you see worse on the street every day. Gaspode?'

'What?'

'You can open your eyes now.'

Gaspode blinked. Angua in both shapes was OK to look at, but the second or two in between, as the morphic signal hunted between stations, was not a sight you wished to see on a full stomach.

'I thought you rolled around on the floor grunting and growing hair and stretching,' he whimpered.

Angua peered at her hair in the mirror while her night vision lasted.

'Whatever for?'

'Does . . . all that stuff . . . hurt?'

'It's a bit like a whole-body sneeze. You'd think he'd have a comb, wouldn't you? I mean, a *comb*? Everyone's got a comb . . .'

'A really . . . big . . . sneeze?'

'Even a clothes brush would be something.'

They froze as the door creaked open.

Carrot walked in. He didn't notice them in the gloom, but trudged to the table. There was a flare and a reek of sulphur as he lit first a match and then a candle.

He removed his helmet, and then sagged as if he'd finally allowed a weight to drop on his shoulders.

They heard him say: 'It can't be right!'

'What can't?' said Angua.

Carrot spun around.

'What're you doing here?'

'Your uniform got stolen while you were spying in the Assassins' Guild,' Gaspode prompted.

'My uniform got stolen,' said Angua, 'while I was in the Assassins' Guild. Spying.' Carrot was still staring at her. 'There was some old bloke who kept muttering all the time,' she went on desperately.

'Buggrit? Millennium hand and shrimp?'

'Yes, that's right—'

'Foul Ole Ron.' Carrot sighed. 'Probably sold it for a drink. I know where he lives, though. Remind me to go and have a word with him when I've got time.'

'You don't want to ask her what she was wearing when she was in the Guild,' said Gaspode, who had crept under the bed.

'Shut up!' said Angua.

'What?' said Carrot.

'I found out about the room,' said Angua quickly. 'Someone called—'

'Edward d'Eath?' said Carrot, sitting down on the bed. The ancient springs went *groing-groing-grink*.

'How did you know that?'

'I think d'Eath stole the gonne. I think he killed Beano. But . . . Assassins killing without being paid? It's worse than dwarfs and tools. It's worse than clowns and faces. I hear Cruces is really upset. He's got Assassins looking for the boy all over the city.'

'Oh. Well. I'd hate to be in Edward's shoes when they find him.'

'I'd hate to be in his shoes now. And I know where they are, you see. They're on his poor feet. And *they're* dead.'

'The Assassins have found him, then?'

'No. Someone else did. And then Cuddy and Detritus did. If I'm any judge, he's been dead for several days. You see? That can't be right! But I rubbed the Beano make-up off end took off the red nose, and it was definitely him. And the wig's the right kind of red hair. He must have gone straight to Hammerhock.'

'But . . . someone shot at Detritus. *And* killed the beggar girl.'

'Yes.'

Angua sat down beside him.

'And it couldn't have been Edward . . .'

'Hah!' Carrot undid his breastplate and pulled off his mail shirt.

'So we're looking for someone else. A third man.'

'But there's no clues! There's just some man with a gonne! Somewhere in the city! Anywhere! And I'm tired!'

The springs went *glink* again as Carrot stood up and staggered over to the chair and table. He sat down, pulled a piece of paper towards him, inspected a pencil, sharpened it on his sword and, after a moment's thought, began to write.

Angua watched him in silence. Carrot had a short-sleeved leather vest under his mail. There was a birthmark at the top of his left arm. It was crown-shaped.

'Are you writing it all down, like Captain Vimes did?' she said, after a while.

'No.'

'What *are* you doing, then?'

'I'm writing to my mum and dad.'

'Really?'

'I always write to my mum and dad. I promised them. Anyway, it helps me think. I always write letters home when I'm thinking. My dad sends me lots of good advice, too.'

There was a wooden box in front of Carrot. Letters were stacked in it. Carrot's father had been in the habit of replying to Carrot on the back of Carrot's own letters, because paper was hard to come by at the bottom of a dwarf mine.

'What kind of good advice?'

'About mining, usually. Moving rocks. You know. Propping and shoring. You can't get things wrong in a mine. You have to do things right.'

His pencil scritched on the paper.

The door was still ajar, but there was a tentative tap on it which said, in a kind of metaphorical morse code, that the tapper could see very well that Carrot was in his room with a scantily clad woman and was trying to knock without actually being heard.

Sergeant Colon coughed. The cough had a leer in it.

'Yes, sergeant?' said Carrot, without looking around.

'What do you want me to do next, sir?'

'Send them out in squads, sergeant. At least one human, one dwarf and one troll in each.'

'Yessir. What'll they be doing, sir?'

'They'll be being visible, sergeant.'

'Right, sir. Sir? One of the volunteers just now . . . it's Mr Bleakley, sir. From Elm Street? He's a vampire, well, technic'ly, but he works up at the slaughterhouse so it's not really—'

'Thank him very much and send him home, sergeant.'

Colon glanced at Angua.

'Yessir. Right,' he said reluctantly. 'But he's not a problem, it's just that he needs these extra homogoblins in his blo—'

'No!'

'Right. Fine. I'll, er, I'll tell him to go away, then.'

Colon shut the door. The *hinge* leered.

'They call you sir,' said Angua. 'Do you notice that?'

'I know. It's not right. People ought to think for themselves, Captain Vimes says. The problem is, people only think for themselves if you tell them to. How do you spell "eventuality"?'

'I don't.'

'OK.' Carrot still didn't look around. 'We'll hold the city together through the rest of the night, I think. Everyone's seen sense.'

No they haven't, said Angua in the privacy of her own head. They've seen you. It's like hypnotism.

People live your vision. You dream, just like Big Fido, only he dreamed a nightmare and you dream for everyone. You really think everyone is basically nice. Just for a moment, while they are near you, everyone else believes it too.

From somewhere outside came the sound of marching knuckles. Detritus' troop was making another circuit.

Oh, well. He's got to know sooner or later . . .

'Carrot?'

'Hmm?'

'You know . . . when Cuddy and the troll and me joined the Watch – well, you know why it was us three, don't you?'

'Of course. Minority group representation. One troll, one dwarf, one woman.'

'Ah.' Angua hesitated. It was still moonlight outside. She could tell him, run downstairs, Change and be well outside the city by

463

dawn. She'd have to do it. She was an expert at running away from cities.

'It wasn't exactly like that,' she said. 'You see, there's a lot of undead in the city and the Patrician insisted that—'

'Give her a kiss,' said Gaspode, from under the bed.

Angua froze. Carrot's face took on the usual vaguely puzzled look of someone whose ears have just heard what their brain is programmed to believe doesn't exist. He began to blush.

'Gaspode!' snapped Angua, dropping into Canine.

'I know what I'm doin'. A Man, a Woman. It is Fate,' said Gaspode. Angua stood up. Carrot shot up too, so fast that his chair fell over. 'I must be going,' she said.

'Um. Don't go—'

'Now you just reach out,' said Gaspode.

It'd never work, Angua told herself. It never does. Werewolves have to hang around with other werewolves, they're the only ones who *understand* . . .

But . . .

On the other hand . . . since she'd have to run anyway . . .

She held up a finger.

'Just one moment,' she said brightly and, in one movement, reached under the bed and pulled out Gaspode by the scruff of his neck.

'You need me!' the dog whimpered, as he was carried to the door. 'I mean, what does he know? His idea of a good time is showing you the Colossus of Morpork! Put me—'

The door slammed. Angua leaned on it.

It'll end up just like it did in Pseudopolis and Quirm and—

'Angua?' said Carrot.

She turned.

'Don't say anything,' she said. 'And it might be all right.'

After a while the bedsprings went *glink*.

And shortly after that, for Corporal Carrot, the Discworld moved. And didn't even bother to stop to cancel the bread and newspapers.

Corporal Carrot awoke around four a.m., that secret hour known only to the night people, such as criminals, policemen and other misfits. He lay on his half of the narrow bed and stared at the wall.

It had *definitely* been an interesting night.

Although he was indeed simple, he wasn't stupid, and he'd always been aware of what might be called the *mechanics*. He'd been acquainted with several young ladies, and had taken them on many invigorating walks to see fascinating ironwork and interesting civic buildings until they'd unaccountably lost interest. He'd patrolled the Whore Pits often enough, although Mrs Palm and the Guild of Seamstresses were trying to persuade the Patrician to rename the area The Street of Negotiable Affection. But he'd never seen them in relation to himself, had never been quite sure, as it were, where he fitted in.

This was probably not something he was going to write to his parents about. They almost certainly knew.

He slid out of bed. The room was stifling hot with the curtains drawn.

Behind him, he heard Angua roll over into the hollow left by his body.

Then, with both hands, and considerable vigour, he threw open the curtains and let in the round, white light of the full moon.

Behind him, he thought he heard Angua sigh in her sleep.

There were thunderstorms out on the plain. Carrot could see lightning flashes stitching the horizon, and he could smell rain. But the air of the city was still and baking, all the hotter for the distant prospect of storms.

The University's Tower of Art loomed in front of him. He saw it every day. It dominated half the city.

Behind him, the bed went *glink*.

'I think there's going to be—' he began, and turned.

As he turned away, he missed the glint of moonlight on metal from the top of the tower.

Sergeant Colon sat on the bench outside the baking air of the Watch House.

There was a hammering noise from somewhere inside. Cuddy had come in ten minutes before with a bag of tools, a couple of helmets and a determined expression. Colon was damned if he knew what the little devil was working on.

He counted again, very slowly, ticking off names on his clipboard.

No doubt about it. The Night Watch had almost twenty members now. Maybe more. Detritus had gone critical, and had sworn in a further two men, another troll and a wooden dummy from outside Corksock's Natty Clothing Co.* If this went on they'd be able to

---

* And was the origin, long after the events chronicled here were over, of an Ankh-Morpork folk song scored for tin whistle and nasal passage:

'As I was a-walking along Lower Broadway,

The recruiting party came picking up people by their ankles and saying they were going to open up the old Watch Houses near the main gates, just like the old days.

He couldn't *remember* when the Watch last had twenty men.

It had all seemed a good idea at the time. It was certainly keeping the lid on things. But in the morning the Patrician was going to get to hear about it, and demand to see the superior officer.

Now, Sergeant Colon was not entirely clear in his own mind who *was* the superior officer at the moment. He felt that it should be either Captain Vimes or, in some way he couldn't quite define, Corporal Carrot. But the captain wasn't around and Corporal Carrot was only a corporal, and Fred Colon had a dreadful apprehension that when Lord Vetinari summoned someone in order to be ironical at them and say things like 'Who's going to pay their wages, pray?' it would be him, Fred Colon, well and truly up the Ankh without a paddle.

They were also running out of ranks. There were only four ranks below the rank of sergeant. Nobby was getting stroppy about anyone else being promoted to corporal, so there was a certain amount of career congestion taking place. Besides, some of the Watch had got it into their heads that the way you got promoted was to conscript half a dozen other guards. At Detritus' current rate of progress, he was going to be High Supreme Major General by the end of the month.

And what made it all strange was that Carrot was still only a—

Colon looked up when he heard the tinkle of broken glass. Something golden and indistinct crashed through an upper window, landed in the shadows and fled before he could make out what it was.

The Watch House door slammed open and Carrot emerged, sword in hand.

'Where'd it go? Where'd it go?'

'Dunno. What the hell was it?'

Carrot stopped.

'Uh. Not sure,' he said.

'Carrot?'

'Sarge?'

'I should put some clothes on if I was you, lad.'

Carrot stayed looking into the pre-dawn gloom.

---

    volunteer to join the Watch unless they wanted their goohuloog heads kicked in,
So I went via Peach Pie Street and Holofernes instead,
Singing: Too-ra-li, etc.'

It never really caught on.

'I mean, I turned around and there it was, and—'

He looked down at the sword in his hand as if he hadn't realized that he was carrying it.

'Oh, damn!' he said.

He ran back to his room and grabbed his britches. As he struggled into them, he was suddenly aware of a thought in his head, clear as ice.

You are a pillock, what are you? Picked up the sword automatically, didn't you? Did it all wrong! Now she's run off and you'll never see her again!

He turned. A small grey dog was watching him intently from the doorway.

Shock like that, she might never Change back again, said his thoughts. Who cares if she's a werewolf? That didn't bother you until you knew! Incident'ly, any biscuits about your person could be usefully thrown to the small dog in the doorway, although come to think of it the chances of having a biscuit on you right now are very small, so forget you ever thought it. Blimey, you really messed that up, right?

. . . thought Carrot.

'Woof woof,' said the dog.

Carrot's forehead wrinkled.

'It's you, isn't it?' he said, pointing his sword.

'Me? Dogs don't talk,' said Gaspode, hurriedly. 'Listen, I should know. I *am* one.'

'You tell me where she's gone. Right now! Or . . .'

'Yeah? Look,' said Gaspode gloomily, 'the first thing I remember in my life, right, the first thing, was being thrown into the river in a sack. With a brick. Me. I mean, I had wobbly legs and a humorously inside-out ear, I mean, I was *fluffy*. OK, right, so it was the Ankh. OK, so I could walk ashore. But that was the start, and it ain't never got much better. I mean, I walked ashore *inside* the sack, dragging the brick. It took me three days to chew my way out. Go on. Threaten me.'

'Please?' said Carrot.

Gaspode scratched his ear.

'Maybe I could track her down,' said Gaspode. 'Given the right, you know, encouragement.'

He waggled his eyebrows encouragingly.

'If you find her, I'll give you anything you want,' said Carrot.

'Oh, *well*. *If*. Right. Oh, yes. That's all very well, is *if*. What about something up front? Look at these paws, hey? Wear and tear. And this nose doesn't smell by itself. It is a finely tuned instrument.'

'If you don't start looking right away,' said Carrot, 'I will person-ally—' He hesitated. He'd never been cruel to an animal in his life.

'I'll turn the matter over to Corporal Nobbs,' he said.

'That's what I like,' said Gaspode bitterly. 'Incentive.'

He pressed his blotchy nose to the ground. It was all show, anyway. Angua's scent hung in the air like a rainbow.

'You can really talk?' said Carrot.

Gaspode rolled his eyes.

''Course not,' he said.

The figure had reached the top of the tower.

Lamps and candles were alight all over the city. It was spread out below him. Ten thousand little earthbound stars . . . and he could turn off any one he wanted, just like that. It was like being a god.

It was amazing how sounds were so audible up here. It was like being a god. He could hear the howl of dogs, the sound of voices. Occasionally one would be louder than the rest, rising up into the night sky.

This was power. The power he had below, the power to say: do this, do that . . . that was just something human, but this . . . this was like being a god.

He pulled the gonne into position, clicked a rack of six bullets into position, and sighted at random on a light. And then on another one. And another one.

He really shouldn't have let it shoot that beggar girl. That wasn't the plan. Guild leaders, that was poor little Edward's plan. Guild leaders, to start with. Leave the city leaderless and in turmoil, and then confront his silly candidate and say: Go forth and rule, it is your destiny.

That was an *old* disease, that kind of thinking. You caught it from crowns, and silly stories. You believed . . . hah . . . you believed that some trick like, like pulling a sword from a stone was somehow a qualification for kingly office. A sword from a stone? The gonne was more magical than *that*.

He lay down, stroked the gonne, and waited.

Day broke.

'I never touched nuffin,' said Coalface, and turned over on his slab.

Detritus hit him over the head with his club.

'Up you get, soldiers! Hand off rock and on with sock! It another

468

beautiful day inna Watch! Lance-Constable Coalface, on your feet, you horrible little man!'

Twenty minutes later a bleary-eyed Sergeant Colon surveyed the troops. They were slumped on the benches, except for Acting-Constable Detritus, who was sitting bolt upright with an air of official helpfulness.

'Right, men,' Colon began, 'now, as you—'

'You men, you listen up good right now!' Detritus boomed.

'Thank you, Acting-Constable Detritus,' said Colon wearily. 'Captain Vimes is getting married today. We're going to provide a guard of honour. That's what we always used to do in the old days when a Watchman got wed. So I want helmets and breastplates bright and shiny. And cohorts gleaming. Not a speck of muck . . . where's Corporal Nobbs?'

There was a *dink* as Acting-Constable Detritus' hand bounced off his new helmet.

'Hasn't been seen for hours, sir!' he reported.

Colon rolled his eyes.

'And some of you will . . . Where's Lance-Constable Angua?'

Dink. 'No one's seen her since last night, sir.'

'All right. We got through the night, we're going to get through the day. Corporal Carrot says we're to look sharp.'

Dink. 'Yes, sir!'

'Acting-Constable Detritus?'

'Sir?'

'What's that you've got on your head?'

Dink. 'Acting-Constable Cuddy made it for me, sir. Special clockwork thinking helmet.'

Cuddy coughed. 'These big bits are cooling fins, see? Painted black. I glommed a clockwork engine off my cousin, and this fan here blows air over—' He stopped when he saw Colon's expression.

'That's what you've been working on all night, is it?'

'Yes, because I reckon troll brains get too—'

The sergeant waved him into silence.

'So we've got a clockwork soldier, have we?' said Colon. 'We're a real model army, we are.'

Gaspode was geographically embarrassed. He knew where he was, more or less. He was somewhere beyond the Shades, in the network of dock basins and cattleyards. Even though he thought of the whole city as belonging to him, this wasn't his territory. There were rats here almost as big as he was, and he was basically a sort of terrier shape, and Ankh-Morpork rats were intelligent enough to recognize it. He'd also been kicked by two horses and almost run over by a cart. And he'd lost the scent. She'd doubled back and forth and used rooftops and crossed the river a few times. Were-wolves were instinctively good at avoiding pursuit; after all, the surviving ones were descendants of those who could outrun an angry mob. Those who *couldn't* outwit a mob never had descend-ants, or even graves.

Several times the scent petered out at a wall or a low-roofed hut, and Gaspode would limp around in circles until he found it again.

Random thoughts wavered in his schizophrenic doggy mind.

'Clever Dog Saves The Day,' he muttered. 'Everyone Says, Good Doggy. No they don't, I'm only doing it 'cos I was threatened. The Marvellous Nose. I didn't want to do this. You Shall Have A Bone. I'm just flotsam on the sea of life, me. Who's a Good Boy? Shut up.'

The sun toiled up the sky. Down below, Gaspode toiled on.

Willikins opened the curtains. Sunlight poured in. Vimes groaned and sat up slowly in what remained of his bed.

'Good grief, man,' he mumbled. 'What sort of time d'you call this?'

'Almost nine in the morning, sir,' said the butler.

'Nine in the *morning*? What sort of time is *that* to get up? I don't normally get up until the afternoon's got the shine worn off!'

'But sir is not at work any more, sir.'

Vimes looked down at the tangle of sheets and blankets. They were wrapped around his legs and knotted together. Then he remembered the dream.

He'd been walking around the city.

Well, maybe not so much a dream as a memory. After all, he walked the city every night. Some part of him wasn't giving up; some part of Vimes was learning to be a civilian, but an old part was marching, no, *proceeding* to a different beat. He'd *thought* the place seemed deserted and harder to walk through than usual.

'Does sir wish me to shave him or will sir do it himself?'

'I get nervous if people hold blades near my face,' said Vimes. 'But if you harness the horse and cart I'll try and get to the other end of the bathroom.'

'Very amusing, sir.'

Vimes had another bath, just for the novelty of it. He was aware from a general background noise that the mansion was busily humming towards W-hour. Lady Sybil was devoting to her wedding all the directness of thought she'd normally apply to breeding out a tendency towards floppy ears in swamp dragons. Half a dozen cooks had been busy in the kitchens for three days. They were roasting a whole ox and doing amazing stuff with rare fruit. Hitherto Sam Vimes's idea of a good meal was liver without tubes. *Haute cuisine* had been bits of cheese on sticks stuck into half a grapefruit.

He was vaguely aware that prospective grooms were not supposed to see putative brides on the morning of the wedding, possibly in case they took to their heels. That was unfortunate. He'd have liked to have talked to someone. If he could talk to someone, it might all make sense.

He picked up the razor, and looked in the mirror at the face of Captain Samuel Vimes.

Colon saluted, and then peered at Carrot.

'You all right, sir? You look like you could do with some sleep.'

Ten o'clock, or various attempts thereof, began to boom around the city. Carrot turned away from the window.

'I've been out rooking,' he said.

'Three more recruits this morning already,' said Colon. They'd asked to join 'Mr Carrot's army'. He was slightly worried about that.

'Good.'

'Detritus is giving 'em very basic training,' said Colon. 'It works, too. After an hour of him shouting in their ear, they do anything I tell 'em.'

'I want all the men we can spare up on the rooftops between the Palace and the University,' said Carrot.

'There's Assassins up there already,' said Colon. 'And the Thieves' Guild have got men up there, too.'

'They're Thieves and Assassins. We're not. Make sure someone's up on the Tower of Art as well—'

'Sir?'

'Yes, sergeant?'

'We've been talking . . . me and the lads . . . and, well . . .'

'Yes?'

'It'd save a lot of trouble if we went to the wizards and asked them—'

'Captain Vimes never had any truck with magic.'

'No, but . . .'

'No magic, sergeant.'

'Yes, sir.'

'Guard of honour all sorted out?'

'Yes, sir. Their cohorts all gleaming in purple and gold, sir.'

'Really?'

'Very important, sir, good clean cohorts. Frighten the life out the enemy.'

'Good.'

'But I can't find Corporal Nobbs, sir.'

'Is that a problem?'

'Well, it means the honour guard'll be a bit smarter, sir.'

'I've sent him on a special errand.'

'Er . . . can't find Lance-Constable Angua, either.'

'Sergeant?'

Colon braced himself. Outside, the bells were dying away.

'Did *you* know she was a werewolf?'

'Um . . . Captain Vimes kind of hinted, sir . . .'

'How did he hint?'

Colon took a step back.

'He sort of said, "Fred, she's a damn werewolf. I don't like it any more than you do, but Vetinari says we've got to take one of them as well, and a werewolf's better than a vampire or a zombie, and that's all there is to it." That's what he hinted.'

'I *see*.'

'Er . . . sorry about that, sir.'

'Just let's get through the day, Fred. That's all—'

—abing, abing, a-bing-bong—

'We never even presented the captain with his watch,' said Carrot, taking it out of his pocket. 'He must have gone off thinking we didn't care. He was probably looking forward to getting a watch. I know it always used to be a tradition.'

'It's been a busy few days, sir. Anyway, we can give it to him after the wedding.'

Carrot slipped the watch back into its bag.

'I suppose so. Well, let's get organized, sergeant.'

Corporal Nobbs toiled through the darkness under the city. His eyes had got accustomed to the gloom now. He was dying for a smoke, but Carrot had warned him about that. Just take the sack, follow the trail, bring back the body. And don't nick any jewellery.

People were already filing into the Great Hall of Unseen University.

Vimes had been firm about this. It was the only thing he'd held out for. He wasn't exactly an atheist, because atheism was a non-survival trait on a world with several thousand gods. He just didn't like any of them very much, and didn't see what business it was of theirs that he was getting married. He'd turned down any of the temples and churches, but the Great Hall had a sufficiently churchy look, which is what people always feel is mandatory on these occasions. It's not actually essential for any gods to drop in, but they should feel at home if they do.

Vimes strolled down there early, because there's nothing more useless in the world than a groom just before the wedding. Interchangeable Emmas had taken over the house.

There were already a couple of ushers in place, ready to ask guests whose side they were on.

And there were a number of senior wizards hanging around. They were automatically guests at such a society wedding, and certainly at the reception afterwards. Probably one roast ox wouldn't be enough.

Despite his deep distrust of magic, he quite liked the wizards. They didn't cause trouble. At least, they didn't cause *his* kind of trouble. True, occasionally they fractured the time/space continuum or took the canoe of reality too close to the white waters of chaos, but they never broke the actual *law*.

'Good morning, Archchancellor,' he said.

Archchancellor Mustrum Ridcully, supreme leader of all the wizards in Ankh-Morpork whenever they could be bothered, gave him a cheery nod.

'Good morning, captain,' he said. 'I must say you've got a nice day for it!'

'Hahaha, a nice day for it!' leered the Bursar.

'Oh dear,' said Ridcully, 'he's off again. Can't understand the man. Anyone got the dried frog pills?'

It was a complete mystery to Mustrum Ridcully, a man designed by Nature to live outdoors and happily slaughter anything that coughed in the bushes, why the Bursar (a man designed by Nature to sit in a small room somewhere, adding up figures) was so nervous. He'd tried all sorts of things to, as he put it, buck him up. These included practical jokes, surprise early morning runs, and leaping out at him from behind doors while wearing Willie the Vampire masks in order, he said, to take him out of himself.

The service itself was going to be performed by the Dean, who had carefully made one up; there was no official civil marriage service in Ankh-Morpork, other than something approximating to 'Oh, all right then, if you really must.' He nodded enthusiastically at Vimes.

'We've cleaned our organ especially for the occasion,' he said.

'Hahaha, organ!' said the Bursar.

'And a mighty one it is, as organs go—' Ridcully stopped, and signalled to a couple of student wizards. 'Just take the Bursar away and make him lie down for a while, will you?' he said. 'I think someone's been feeding him meat again.'

There was a hiss from the far end of the Great Hall, and then a strangled squeak. Vimes stared at the monstrous array of pipes.

'Got eight students pumping the bellows,' said Ridcully, to a background of wheezes. 'It's got three keyboards and a hundred extra knobs, including twelve with "?" on them.'

'Sounds impossible for a man to play,' said Vimes politely.

'Ah. We had a stroke of luck there—'

There was a moment of sound so loud that the aural nerves shut down. When they opened again, somewhere around the pain threshold, they could just make out the opening and extremely bent bars of Fondel's 'Wedding March', being played with gusto by someone who'd discovered that the instrument didn't just have three keyboards but a whole range of special acoustic effects, ranging from Flatulence to Humorous Chicken Squawk. The occasional 'oook!' of appreciation could be heard amidst the sonic explosion.

Somewhere under the table, Vimes screamed at Ridcully: 'Amazing! Who built it!'

'I don't know! But it's got the name B. S. Johnson on the keyboard cover!'

There was a descending wail, one last Hurdy-Gurdy Effect, and then silence.

'Twenty minutes those lads were pumping up the reservoirs,' said Ridcully, dusting himself off as he stood up. 'Go easy on the Vox Dei stop, there's a good chap!'

'Ook!'

The Archchancellor turned back to Vimes, who was wearing the standard waxen pre-nuptial grimace. The hall was filling up quite well now.

'I'm not an expert on this stuff,' he said, 'but you've got the ring, have you?'

'Yes.'

'Who's giving away the bride?'

'Her Uncle Lofthouse. He's a bit gaga, but she insisted.'

'And the best man?'

'What?'

'The best man. You know? He hands you the ring and has to marry the bride if you run away and so on. The Dean's been reading up on it, haven't you, Dean?'

'Oh, yes,' said the Dean, who'd spent all the previous day with

Lady Deirdre Waggon's Book of Etiquette. 'She's got to marry someone once she's turned up. You can't have unmarried brides flapping around the place, being a danger to society.'

'I completely forgot about a best man!' said Vimes.

The Librarian, who'd given up on the organ until it had some more puff, brightened up.

'Ook?'

'Well, go and find one,' said Ridcully. 'You've got nearly half an hour.'

'It's not as easy as that, is it? They don't grow on trees!'

'Oook?'

'I can't think who to ask!'

'*Oook.*'

The Librarian liked being best man. You were allowed to kiss bridesmaids, and they weren't allowed to run away. He was really disappointed when Vimes ignored him.

Acting-Constable Cuddy climbed laboriously up the steps inside the Tower of Art, grumbling to himself. He knew he couldn't complain. They'd drawn lots because, Carrot said, you shouldn't ask the men to do anything you wouldn't do yourself. And he'd drawn the short straw, harhar, which meant the tallest building. That meant if there was any trouble, he'd miss it.

He paid no attention to the thin rope dangling from the trapdoor far above. Even if he'd thought about it . . . so what? It was just a rope.

Gaspode looked up into the shadows.

There was a growl from somewhere in the darkness. It was no ordinary dog growl. Early man had heard sounds like that in deep caves.

Gaspode sat down. His tail thumped uncertainly.

'Knew I'd find you sooner or later,' he said. 'The old nose, eh? Finest instrument known to dog.'

There was another growl. Gaspode whimpered a bit.

'The thing is,' he said, 'the thing is . . . the actual thing is, see . . . the thing what I've been sent to do . . .'

Late man heard sounds like that, too. Just before he became late.

'I can see you . . . don't want to talk right now,' said Gaspode. 'But the thing is . . . now, I know what you're thinking, is this *Gaspode* obeyin' orders from a *human?*'

Gaspode looked conspiratorially over his shoulder, as if there could be anything worse than what was in front of him.

'That's the whole mess about being a dog, see?' he said. 'That's the thing what Big Fido can't get his mind around, see? You looked at the dogs in the Guild, right? You heard 'em howl. Oh, yes, Death To The Humans, All *Right*. But under all that there's the *fear*. There's the voice sayin': Bad Dog. And it don't come from anywhere but inside, right from inside the bones, 'cos humans made dogs. I knows this. I wish I didn't, but there it is. That's the Power, knowin'. I've read books, I have. Well, chewed books.'

The darkness was silent.

'And you're a wolf and human at the same time, right? Tricky, that. I can see that. Bit of a dichotomy, sort of thing. Makes you kind of like a dog. 'Cos that's what a dog is, really. Half a wolf and half a human. You were right about that. We've even got names. Hah! So our bodies tell us one thing, our heads tell us another. It's a dog's life, being a dog. And I bet *you* can't run away from *him*. Not really. He's your master.'

The darkness was more silent. Gaspode thought he heard movement.

'He wants you to come back. The thing is, if he finds you, that's it. He'll speak, and you'll have to obey. But if you goes back of your own accord, then it's *your* decision. You'd be happier as a human. I mean, what can I offer you except rats and a choice of fleas? I mean, I don't know, I don't see it as much of a problem, you just have to stay indoors six or seven nights every month—'

Angua howled.

The hairs that still remained on Gaspode's back stood on end. He tried to remember which was his jugular vein.

'I don't want to have to come in there and get you,' he said. Truth rang on every word.

'The thing is . . . the actual *thing* is . . . I will, though,' he added, trembling. 'It's a bugger, bein' a dog.'

He thought some more, and sighed.

'Oh, I remember. It's the one in the throat,' he said.

Vimes stepped out into the sunlight, except that there wasn't much of it. Clouds were blowing in from the Hub. And—

'Detritus?'

Dink. 'Captain Vimes, *sah!*'

'Who're all these people?'

'Watchmen, sir.'

Vimes stared in puzzlement at the half-dozen assorted guards.

'Who're you?'

'Lance-Constable Hrolf Pyjama, sir.'

'And y— *Coalface?*'

'I never done nuffin.'

'I never done nuffin, *sah!*' yelled Detritus.

'*Coalface?* In the *Watch?*'

Dink. 'Corporal Carrot says there's some good buried somewhere in everyone,' said Detritus.

'And what's your job, Detritus.'

Dink. 'Engineer in charge of deep mining operations, sah!'

Vimes scratched his head.

'That was very nearly a joke, wasn't it?' he said.

'It this new helmet my mate Cuddy made me, sir. Hah! People can't say, there go stupid troll. They have to say, who that good-looking military troll there, acting-constable already, great future behind him, he got Destiny written all over him like writing.'

Vimes digested this. Detritus beamed at him.

'And where is Sergeant Colon?'

'Here, Captain Vimes.'

'I need a best man, Fred.'

'Right, sir. I'll get Corporal Carrot. He's just checking the roofs—'

'Fred! I've known you more than twenty years! Good grief, all you have to do is stand there. Fred, you're *good* at that!'

Carrot appeared at the trot.

'Sorry I'm late, Captain Vimes. Er. We really wanted this to be a surprise—'

'What? What sort of surprise?'

Carrot fished in his pouch. 'Well, captain . . . on behalf of the Watch . . . that is, most of the Watch—'

'Hold on a minute,' said Colon, 'here comes his lordship.'

The clop of hooves and the rattle of harness signalled the approach of Lord Vetinari's carriage.

Carrot glanced around at it. Then he looked at it again. And looked up.

There was a glint of metal, on the roof of the Tower.

'Sergeant, who's on the Tower?' he said.

'Cuddy, sir.'

'Oh. Right.' He coughed. 'Anyway, captain . . . we all clubbed together and—' He paused. 'Acting-Constable Cuddy, right?'

'Yeah. He's reliable.'

The Patrician's carriage was halfway towards Sator Square now. Carrot could see the thin dark figure in the back seat.

He glanced up at the great grey bulk of the tower.

477

He started to run.

'What's up?' said Colon. Vimes started to run, too.

Detritus' knuckles hit the ground as he swung after the others.

And then it hit Colon – a sort of frantic tingle, as though someone had blown on his naked brain.

'Oh shit,' he said, under his breath.

Claws scrabbled on the dirt.

'He drew his sword!'

'What did you expect? One minute the lad is on top of the world, he's got a whole new interest in his life, something probably even better than goin' for walks, and then he turns round and what he sees is, basically, a wolf. You could of hinted. It's that time of the month, that sort of thing. You can't blame him for being surprised, really.'

Gaspode got to his feet. 'Now, are you going to come on out or have I got to come in there and be brutally savaged?'

Lord Vetinari stood up as he saw the Watch running towards him. That was why the first shot went through his thigh, instead of his chest.

Then Carrot cleared the door of the carriage and flung himself across the man, which is why the next shot went through Carrot.

Angua slunk out.

Gaspode relaxed slightly.

'I can't go back,' said Angua. 'I—'

She froze. Her ears twitched.

'What? What?'

'He's been hurt!'

Angua sprang away.

'Here! Wait for me!' barked Gaspode. 'That's the Shades that way!'

A third shot knocked a chip out of Detritus, who slammed into the carriage, knocking it on its side and severing the traces. The horses scrambled away. The coachman had already made a lightning comparison between current job conditions and his rates of pay and had vanished into the crowd.

478

Vimes slid to a halt behind the overturned carriage. Another shot spanged off the cobbles near his arm.

'Detritus?'

'Sir?'

'How are you?'

'Oozing a bit, sir.'

A shot hit the carriage wheel above Vimes's head, making it spin.

'Carrot?'

'Right through my shoulder, sir.'

Vimes eased himself along on his elbows.

'Good morning, your Lordship,' he said, manically. He leaned back and pulled out a mangled cigar. 'Got a light?'

The Patrician opened his eyes.

'Ah, Captain Vimes. And what happens now?'

Vimes grinned. Funny, he thought, how I never feel really alive until someone tries to kill me. That's when you notice that the sky is blue. Actually, not very blue right now. There's big clouds up there. But I'm noticing them.

'We wait for one more shot,' he said. 'And then we run for proper cover.'

'I appear . . . to be losing a lot of blood,' said Lord Vetinari.

'Who would have thought you had it in you,' said Vimes, with the frankness of those probably about to die. 'What about you, Carrot?'

'I can move my hand. Hurts like . . . heck, sir. But you look worse.'

Vimes looked down.

There was blood all over his coat.

'A bit of stone must have caught me,' he said. 'I didn't even feel it!'

He tried to form a mental picture of the gonne.

Six tubes, all in a line. Each one with its lead slug and charge of No.1 powder, delivered into the gonne like crossbow bolts. He wondered how long it'd take to put in another six . . .

But we've got him where we want him! There's only one way down out of the Tower!

Yep, we might be sitting out here in the open with him shooting lead pellets at us, but we've got him just where we want him!

Wheezing and farting nervously, Gaspode moved at a shambling run through the Shades and saw, with a heart that sank even further, a knot of dogs ahead of him.

He pushed and squirmed through the tangle of legs.

Angua was at bay in a ring of teeth.

The barking stopped. A couple of large dogs moved aside, and Big Fido stepped delicately forward.

'So,' he said, 'what we have here is not a dog at all. A spy, perhaps? There's always an enemy. Everywhere. They look like dogs but, inside, they're not dogs. What were you doing?'

Angua growled.

Oh lor', thought Gaspode. She could probably take down a few of 'em, but these are *street* dogs.

He wriggled under a couple of bodies and emerged in the circle. Big Fido turned his red-eyed gaze on him.

'And Gaspode, too,' said the poodle. 'I might have known.'

'You leave her alone,' said Gaspode.

'Oh? You'll fight us all for her, will you?' said Big Fido.

'I got the Power,' said Gaspode. 'You know that. I'll do it. I'll use it.'

'There's no time for this!' snarled Angua.

'You won't do it,' said Big Fido.

'I'll do it.'

'Every dog's paw'll be turned against you—'

'I got the Power, me. You back off, all of you.'

'What power?' said Butch. He was drooling.

'Big Fido knows,' said Gaspode. 'He's *studied*. Now, me an' her are going to walk out of here, right? Nice and slow.'

The dogs looked at Big Fido.

'Get them,' he said.

Angua bared her teeth.

The dogs hesitated.

'A wolf's got a jaw four times stronger'n any dog,' said Gaspode. 'And that's just a *ordinary* wolf—'

'What are you all?' snapped Big Fido. 'You're the pack! No mercy! *Get them!*'

But a pack doesn't act like that, Angua had said. A pack is an association of free individuals. A pack doesn't leap because it's told – a pack leaps because every individual, all at once, decides to leap.

A couple of the bigger dogs crouched . . .

Angua moved her head from side to side, waiting for the first assault . . .

A dog scraped the ground with its paw . . .

Gaspode took a deep breath and adjusted his jaw.

Dogs leapt.

SIT!' said Gaspode, in passable Human.

The command bounced back and forth around the alley, and fifty per cent of the animals obeyed. In most cases, it was the hind fifty per cent. Dogs in mid-spring found their treacherous legs coiling under them—

'BAD DOG!'

—and this was followed by an overpowering sense of racial shame that made them cringe automatically, a bad move in mid-air.

Gaspode glanced up at Angua as bewildered dogs rained around them.

'I said I got the Power, didn't I?' he said. '*Now* run!'

Dogs are not like cats, who amusingly tolerate humans only until someone comes up with a tin opener that can be operated with a paw. Men made dogs, they took wolves and gave them human things – unnecessary intelligence, names, a desire to belong, and a twitching inferiority complex. All dogs dream wolf dreams, and know they're dreaming of biting their Maker. Every dog knows, deep in his heart, that he is a Bad Dog . . .

But Big Fido's furious yapping broke the spell.

'Get them!'

Angua galloped over the cobbles. There was a cart at the other end of the alley. And, beyond the cart, a wall.

'Not that way!' whined Gaspode.

Dogs were piling along behind them. Angua leapt on to the cart.

'I can't get up there!' said Gaspode. 'Not with my leg!'

She jumped down, picked him up by the scruff of his neck, and leapt back. There was a shed roof behind the cart, a ledge above that and – a few tiles slid under her paws and tumbled into the alley – a house.

'I feel sick!'

'Futupf!'

Angua ran along the ridge of the roof and jumped the alley on the other side, landing heavily in some ancient thatch.

'Aargh!'

'Futupf!'

But the dogs were following them. It wasn't as though the alleys of the Shades were very wide.

Another narrow alley passed below.

Gaspode swung perilously from the werewolf's jaws.

'They're still behind us!'

Gaspode shut his eyes as Angua bunched her muscles.

'Oh, no! Not Treacle Mine Road!'

There was a burst of acceleration followed by a moment of calmness. Gaspode shut his eyes . . .

. . . Angua landed. Her paws scrabbled on the wet roof for a moment. Slates cascaded off into the street, and then she was bounding up to the ridge.

'You can put me down right now,' said Gaspode. 'Right now this minute! Here they come!'

The leading dogs arrived on the opposite roof, saw the gap, and tried to turn. Claws slid on the tiles.

Angua turned, fighting for breath. She'd tried to avoid breathing, during that first mad dash. She'd have breathed Gaspode.

They heard Big Fido's irate yapping.

'Cowards! That's not twenty feet across! That's nothing to a wolf!'

The dogs measured the distance doubtfully. Sometimes a dog has to get right down and ask himself: what species am I?

'It's easy! I'll show you! Look!'

Big Fido ran back a little way, paused, turned, ran . . . and leapt.

There was hardly a curve to the trajectory. The little poodle accelerated out into space, powered less by muscles than by whatever it was that burned in his soul.

His forepaws touched the slates, clawed for a moment on the slick surface, and found no hold. In silence he skidded backwards down the roof, over the edge—

—and hung.

He turned his eyes upwards, to the dog that was gripping him.

'Gaspode? Is that you?'

'Yeff,' said Gaspode, his mouth full.

There was hardly any weight to the poodle but, then, there was hardly any weight to Gaspode. He'd darted forward and braced his legs to take the strain, but there was nothing much to brace them against. He slid down inexorably until his front legs were in the gutter, which began to creak.

Gaspode had an amazingly clear view of the street, three storeys down.

'Oh, *hell!*' said Gaspode.

Jaws gripped his tail.

'Let him go,' said Angua indistinctly.

Gaspode tried to shake his head.

'Ftop ftruggling!' he said, out of the corner of his mouth. 'Brave Dog Faves the Day! Valiant Hound in Wooftop Wefcue! No!'

The gutter creaked again.

It's going to go, he thought. Story of my life . . .

Big Fido struggled around.

'What are you holding me up by?'

'Yer collar,' said Gaspode, through his teeth.

'What? To hell with *that!*'

The poodle tried to twist, flailing viciously at the air.

'Ftop it, you daft fbugger! You'll haf uff all off!' Gaspode growled. On the opposite roof, the dog pack watched in horror. The gutter creaked again.

Angua's claws scored white lines on the slates.

Big Fido wrenched and spun, fighting the grip of the collar.

Which, finally, snapped.

The dog turned in the air, hanging for a moment before gravity took hold.

'Free!'

And then he fell.

Gaspode shot backwards as Angua's paws slipped from under her, and landed further up the roof, legs spinning. Both of them made it to the crest and hung there, panting.

Then Angua bounded away, clearing the next alley before Gaspode had stopped seeing a red mist in front of his eyes.

He spat out Big Fido's collar, which slid down the roof and vanished over the edge.

'Oh, thank you!' he shouted. 'Thank you very much! Yes! Leave me here, that's right! Me with only three good legs! Don't you worry about me! If I'm lucky I'll fall off before I starve! Oh yes! Story of my life! You and me, kid! Together! We could have made it!'

He turned and looked at the dogs lining the roofs on the other side of the street.

'You lot! Go home! BAD DOG!' he barked.

He slithered down the other side of the roof. There was an alley there, but it was a sheer drop. He crept along the roof to the adjoining building, but there was no way down. There was a balcony a storey below, though.

'Lat'ral thinking,' he muttered. 'That's the stuff. Now, a wolf, your basic wolf, he'd jump, and if he couldn't jump, he'd be stuck. Whereas me, on account of superior intelligence, can assess the whole wossname and arrive at a solution through application of mental processes.'

He nudged the gargoyle squatting on the angle of the gutter.

'Ot oo oo ont?'

'If you don't help me down to that balcony, I'll widdle in your ear.'

BIG FIDO?

'Yes?'

HEEL.

*

483

There were, eventually, two theories about the end of Big Fido.

The one put forward by the dog Gaspode, based on observational evidence, was that his remains were picked up by Foul Ole Ron and sold within five minutes to a furrier, and that Big Fido eventually saw the light of day again as a set of ear muffs and a pair of fleecy gloves.

The one believed by every other dog, based on what might tentatively be called the truth of the heart, was that he survived his fall, fled the city, and eventually led a huge pack of mountain wolves who nightly struck terror into isolated farmsteads. It made digging in the middens and hanging around back doors for scraps seem . . . well, more bearable. They were, after all, only doing it until Big Fido came back.

His collar was kept in a secret place and visited regularly by dogs until they forgot about it.

Sergeant Colon pushed open the door with the end of his pike.

The Tower had floors, a long time ago. Now it was hollow all the way up, criss-crossed by golden shafts of light from ancient window embrasures.

One of them, filled with glittering motes of dust, lanced down on what, not long before, had been Acting-Constable Cuddy.

Colon gave the body a cautious prod. It didn't move. Nothing looking like that should move. A twisted axe lay beside it.

'Oh, no,' he breathed.

There was a thin rope, the sort the Assassins used, hanging down from the heights. It was twitching. Colon looked up at the haze, and drew his sword.

He could see all the way to the top, and there was no one on the rope. Which meant—

He didn't even look around, which saved his life.

His dive for the floor and the explosion of the gonne behind him happened at exactly the same time. He swore afterwards that he felt the wind of the slug as it passed over his head.

Then a figure stepped through the smoke and hit him very hard before escaping through the open door, into the rain.

Acting-Constable Cuddy?

Cuddy brushed *himself* off.

'Oh,' he said. 'I see. I didn't think I was going to survive that. Not after the first hundred feet.'

You were correct.

484

The unreal world of the living was already fading, but Cuddy glared at the twisted remains of his axe. It seemed to worry him far more than the twisted remains of Cuddy.

'And will you look at that?' he said. 'My dad made that axe for me! A fine weapon to take into the afterlife, I don't think!'

IS THAT SOME KIND OF BURIAL CUSTOM?

'Don't you know? You *are* Death, aren't you?'

THAT DOESN'T MEAN I HAVE TO KNOW ABOUT BURIAL CUSTOMS. GENERALLY, I MEET PEOPLE *BEFORE* THEY'RE BURIED. THE ONES I MEET AFTER THEY'VE BEEN BURIED TEND TO BE A BIT OVER-EXCITED AND DISINCLINED TO DISCUSS THINGS.

Cuddy folded his arms.

'If I'm not going to be properly buried,' he said, 'I ain't going. My tortured soul will walk the world in torment.'

IT DOESN'T HAVE TO.

'It can if it *wants* to,' snapped the ghost of Cuddy.

'Detritus! You haven't got *time* to ooze! Get over to the Tower! Take some people with you!'

Vimes reached the doorway of the Great Hall with the Patrician over his shoulder and Carrot stumbling along behind him. The wizards were clustered around the door. Big heavy drops of rain were beginning to fall, hissing on the hot stones.

Ridcully rolled up his sleeves.

'Hell's bells! What did that to his leg?'

'That's the gonne for you! Sort him out! And Corporal Carrot too!'

'There's no need,' said Vetinari, trying to smile and stand up. 'It's just a flesh—'

The leg collapsed under him.

Vimes blinked. He'd never expected this. The Patrician was the man who always had the answers, who was never surprised. Vimes had a sense that history was flapping loose . . .

'We can handle it, sir,' said Carrot. 'I've got men on the roofs, and—'

'Shut up! Stay here! That's an order!' Vimes fumbled in his pouch and hung his badge on his torn jacket. 'Hey, you . . . Pyjama! I need a sword!'

Pyjama looked sullen.

'I only take orders from Corporal Carrot—'

'Give me a sword right now, you horrible little man! Right! Thank you! Now let's get to the Tow—'

A shadow appeared in the doorway.

Detritus walked in.

They looked at the limp shape in his hands.

He laid it carefully on a bench, without saying a word, and went and sat in a corner. While the others gathered round the mortal remains of Acting-Constable Cuddy, the troll removed his home-made cooling helmet and sat staring at it, turning it over and over in his hands.

'He was on the floor,' said Sergeant Colon, leaning against the doorframe. 'He must have been pushed off the stairs right at the top. Someone else was in there, too. Must've shinned down a rope and caught me a right bang on the side of the head.'

'Being pushed down the Tower's not worth it for a shilling,' said Carrot, vaguely.

It was better when the dragon came, thought Vimes. After it'd killed someone it was at least still a dragon. It went somewhere else but you could say: that's a dragon, that is. It couldn't nip over a wall and become just another person. You always knew what you were fighting. You didn't have to—

'What's that in Cuddy's hand?' he said. He realized he'd been staring at it without seeing it for some time.

He tugged at it. It was a strip of black cloth.

'Assassins wear that,' said Colon blankly.

'So do lots of other people,' said Ridcully. 'Black's black.'

'You're right,' said Vimes. 'Taking any action on the basis of this would be premature. You know, it'd probably get me fired.'

He waved the cloth in front of Lord Vetinari.

'Assassins everywhere,' he said, 'on *guard*. Seems they didn't notice anything, eh? You gave them the bloody gonne because you thought they were the best to guard it! You never thought of giving it to the guards!'

'Aren't we going to give chase. Corporal Carrot?' said Pyjama.

'Chase who? Chase where?' said Vimes. 'He hit old Fred on the head and did a runner. He could trot around a corner, chuck the gonne over a wall, and who'd know? We don't know who we're looking for!'

'I do,' said Carrot.

He stood up, holding his shoulder.

'It's easy to run,' he said. 'We've done a lot of running. But that's not how you hunt. You hunt by sitting still in the right place. Captain, I want the sergeant to go out there and tell people we've got the killer.'

'What?'

'His name is Edward d'Eath. Say we've got him in custody. Say he was caught and badly injured, but he's alive.'

'But we haven't—'

'He's an Assassin.'

'We haven't—'

'Yes, captain. I don't like telling lies. But it might be worth it. Anyway, it's not your problem, sir.'

'It isn't? Why not?'

'You're retiring in less than an hour.'

'I'm still captain right now, corporal. So you have to tell me what's going on. That's how things work.'

'We haven't got time, sir. Do it, Sergeant Colon.'

'Carrot, *I* still run the Watch! I'm the one supposed to give the orders.'

Carrot hung his head.

'Sorry, captain.'

'Right. So long as that's understood. Sergeant Colon?'

'Sir?'

'Put out the news that we've arrested Edward d'Eath. Whoever he is.'

'Yessir.'

'And your next move, Mr Carrot?' said Vimes.

Carrot looked at the assembled wizards.

'Excuse me, sir?'

'Ook?'

'First, we need to get into the library—'

'First,' said Vimes, 'someone can lend me a helmet. I don't feel I'm at work without a helmet. Thanks, Fred. Right . . . helmet . . . sword . . . badge. *Now* . . .'

There was sound under the city. It filtered down by all sorts of routes, but it was indistinct, a hive noise.

And there was the faintest of glows. The waters of the Ankh, to use the element in its broadest sense, had washed, to bend the definition to its limit, these tunnels for centuries.

Now there was an extra sound. Footsteps padded over the silt, barely perceptible unless ears had become accustomed to the background noise. And an indistinct shape moved through the gloom, paused at a circle of darkness leading to a smaller tunnel . . .

'How do you feel, your Lordship?' said Corporal Nobbs, the upwardly mobile.

'Who are you?'

'Corporal Nobbs, sir!' said Nobby, saluting.

'Do we employ you?'

'Yessir!'

'Ah. You're the dwarf, are you?'

'Nossir. That was the late Cuddy, sir! I'm one of the human beings, sir!'

'You're not employed as the result of any ... special hiring procedures?'

'Nossir,' said Nobby, proudly.

'My word,' said the Patrician. He was feeling a little light-headed from loss of blood. The Archchancellor had also given him a long drink of something he said was a marvellous remedy, although he'd been unspecific as to what it cured. Verticality, apparently. It was wise to remain sitting upright, though. It was a good idea to be seen to be alive. A lot of inquisitive people were peering around the door. It was important to ensure that rumours of his death were greatly exaggerated.

Corporal self-proclaimed-human Nobbs and some other guards had closed in around the Patrician, on Captain Vimes's orders. Some of them were a lot bulkier than he rather muzzily remembered.

'You there, my man. Have you taken the King's Shilling?' he inquired of one.

'I never took nuffin.'

'Capital, well done.'

And then the crowds scattered. Something golden and vaguely dog-like burst through, growling, its nose close to the ground. And was gone again, covering the ground to the library in long, easy strides. The Patrician was aware of conversation.

'Fred?'

'Yes, Nobby?'

'Did that look a bit familiar to you?'

'I know what you mean.'

Nobby fidgeted awkwardly.

'You should've bawled her out for not being in uniform,' he said.

'Bit tricky, that.'

'If *I'd* run through here without me clothes on, you'd fine me a half a dollar for being improperly dressed—'

'Here's half a dollar, Nobby. Now shut up.'

Lord Vetinari beamed at them. Then there was the guard in the corner, another of the big lumpy ones—

'Still all right, your Lordship?' said Nobby.

'Who's that gentleman?'

He followed the Patrician's gaze.

'That's Detritus the troll, sir.'

'Why is he sitting like that?'

'He's thinking, sir.'

'He hasn't moved for some time.'

'He thinks slow, sir.'

Detritus stood up. There was something about the way he did it, some hint of a mighty continent beginning a tectonic movement that would end in the fearsome creation of some unscalable mountain range, which made people stop and look. Not one of the watchers was familiar with the experience of watching mountain building, but now they had some vague idea of what it was like: it was like Detritus standing up, with Cuddy's twisted axe in his hand.

'But deep, sometimes,' said Nobby, eyeing various possible escape routes.

The troll stared at the crowd as if wondering what they were doing there. Then, arms swinging, he began to walk forward.

'Acting-Constable Detritus ... er ... as you were ...' Colon ventured.

Detritus ignored him. He was moving quite fast now, in the deceptive way that lava does.

He reached the wall, and punched it out of the way.

'Has anyone been giving him sulphur?' said Nobby.

Colon looked around at the guard. 'Lance-Constable Bauxite! Lance-Constable Coalface! Apprehend Acting-Constable Detritus!'

The two trolls looked first at the retreating form of Detritus, then at one another, and finally at Sergeant Colon.

Bauxite managed a salute.

'Permission for leave to attend grandmother's funeral, sir?'

'Why?'

'It her or me, sarge.'

'We get our goohuloog heads kicked in,' said Coalface, the less circuitous thinker.

A match flared. In the sewers, its light was like a nova.

Vimes lit first his cigar, and then a lamp.

'Dr Cruces?' he said.

The chief of Assassins froze.

'Corporal Carrot here has a crossbow too,' he said. 'I'm not sure if he'd use it. He's a good man. He thinks everyone else is a good man. I'm not. I'm mean, nasty and tired. And now, doctor, you've had time to think, you're an intelligent man ... What were you doing down here, please? It can't be to look for the mortal remains of young Edward, because our Corporal Nobbs has taken him off to the Watch morgue this morning, probably nicking any small items of personal jewellery he had on him, but that's just Nobby's way. He's got a criminal mind, has our Nobby. But I'll say this for him: he hasn't got a criminal soul.

'I hope he's cleaned the clown make-up off the poor chap. Dear me. You used him, didn't you? He killed poor old Beano, and then he got the gonne, and he was there when it killed Hammerhock, he even left a bit of his Beano wig in the timbers, and just when he could have done with some good advice, such as to turn himself in, you killed him. The point, the interesting point, is that young Edward couldn't have been the man on the Tower a little while ago. Not with the stab wound in his heart and everything. I know that being dead isn't always a barrier to quiet enjoyment in this city, but I don't think young Edward has been up and about much. The piece of cloth was a nice touch. But, you know, I've never believed in that stuff – footprints in the flower bed, tell-tale buttons, stuff like that. People think that stuff's policing. It's not. Policing's luck and slog, most of the time. But lots of people'd believe it. I mean, he's been dead . . . what . . . not two days, and it's nice and cool down here . . . you could haul him up, I daresay you could fool people who didn't look too close once he was on a slab, and you'd have got the man who shot the Patrician. Mind you, half the city would be fighting the other half by then, I daresay. Some more deaths would be involved. I wonder if you'd care.' He paused. 'You still haven't said anything.'

'You have no understanding,' said Cruces.

'Yes?'

'D'Eath was right. He was mad, but he was right.'

'About what, Dr Cruces?' said Vimes.

And then the Assassin was gone, diving into a shadow.

'Oh, no,' said Vimes.

A whisper echoed around the man-made cavern.

'Captain Vimes? One thing a good Assassin learns is—'

There was a thunderous explosion, and the lamp disintegrated.

'—never stand near the light.'

Vimes hit the floor and rolled. Another shot hit a foot away, and he felt the splash of cold water.

There was water under him, too.

The Ankh was rising and, in accordance with laws older than those of the city, the water was finding its way back up the tunnels.

'Carrot,' Vimes whispered.

'Yes?' The voice came from somewhere in the pitch blackness to his right.

'I can't see a thing. I lost my night vision lighting that damn lamp.'

'I can feel water coming in.'

'We—' Vimes began, and stopped as he formed a mental picture of the hidden Cruces aiming at a patch of sound.

I should have shot him first, he thought. He's an Assassin!

He had to raise himself slightly to keep his face out of the rising water.

Then he heard a gentle splashing. Cruces was walking towards them.

There was a scratching noise, and then light. Cruces had lit a torch, and Vimes looked up to see the skinny shape in the glow. His other hand was steadying the gonne.

Something Vimes had learned as a young guard drifted up from memory. If you *have* to look along the shaft of an arrow from the wrong end, if a man has you entirely at his mercy, then hope like hell that man is an evil man. Because the evil like power, power over people, and they want to see you in fear. They want you to *know* you're going to die. So they'll talk. They'll gloat.

They'll watch you *squirm*. They'll put off the moment of murder like another man will put off a good cigar.

So hope like hell your captor is an evil man. A good man will kill you with hardly a word.

Then, to his everlasting horror, he heard Carrot stand up.

'Dr Cruces, I arrest you for the murder of Bjorn Hammerhock, Edward d'Eath, Beano the clown, Lettice Knibbs and Acting-Constable Cuddy of the City Watch.'

'Dear me, all those? I'm afraid Edward killed Brother Beano. That was his own idea, the little fool. He *said* he hadn't meant to. And I understand that Hammerhock was killed accidentally. A freak accident. He poked around and the charge fired and the slug bounced off his anvil and killed him. That's what Edward said. He came to see me afterwards. He was very upset. Made a clean breast of the whole thing, you know. So I killed him. Well, what else could I do? He was quite mad. There's no dealing with that sort of person. May I suggest you step back, sire? I'd prefer not to shoot you. No! Not unless I have to!'

It seemed to Vimes that Cruces was arguing with himself. The gonne swung violently.

'He was babbling,' said Cruces. 'He said the gonne killed Hammerhock. I said, it was an accident? And he said no, no accident, the gonne killed Hammerhock.'

Carrot took another step forward. Cruces seemed to be in his own world now.

'No! The gonne killed the beggar girl, too. It wasn't me! Why should I do a thing like that?'

Cruces took a step back, but the gonne swung up towards Carrot. It looked to Vimes as though it moved of its own accord, like an animal sniffing the air . . .

'Get down!' Vimes hissed. He reached out and tried to find his crossbow.

'He said the gonne was jealous! Hammerhock would have made more gonnes! Stop where you are!'

Carrot took another step.

'I had to kill Edward! He was a romantic, he would have got it wrong! But Ankh-Morpork needs a king!'

The gun jerked and fired at the same moment as Carrot leapt sideways.

The tunnels were brilliant with smells, mostly the acrid yellows and earthy oranges of ancient drains. And there were hardly any air currents to disturb things; the line that was Cruces snaked through the heavy air. And there was the smell of the gonne, as vivid as a wound.

I smelled gonne in the Guild, she thought, just after Cruces walked past. And Gaspode said that was all right, because the gonne had been in the Guild – but it hadn't been *fired* in the Guild. I smelled it because someone there had fired the thing.

She splashed through the water into the big cavern and saw, with her nose, the three of them – the indistinct figure that smelled of Vimes, the falling figure that was Carrot, the turning shape with the gonne . . .

And then she stopped thinking with her head and let her body take over. Wolf muscle drove her forward and up into a leap, water droplets flying from her mane, her eyes fixed on Cruces's neck.

The gonne fired, four times. It didn't miss once.

She hit the man heavily, knocking him backwards.

Vimes rose in an explosion of spray.

'Six shots! That's six shots, you bastard! I've got you now!'

Cruces turned as Vimes waded towards him, and scurried towards a tunnel, throwing up more spray.

Vimes snatched the bow from Carrot, aimed desperately and pulled the trigger. Nothing happened.

'Carrot! You idiot! You never cocked the damn thing!'

Vimes turned.

'Come on, man! We can't let him get away!'

'It's Angua, captain.'

'What?'

'She's dead!'

'Carrot! *Listen*. Can you find the way out in this stuff? *No!* So come with me!'

'I . . . can't leave her here. I—'

'*Corporal Carrot! Follow me!*'

Vimes half ran, half waded through the rising water towards the tunnel that had swallowed Cruces. It was up a slope; he could feel the water dropping as he ran.

Never give the quarry time to rest. He'd learned that on his first day in the Watch. If you *had* to chase, then stay with it. Give the pursued time to stop and think and you'd go round a corner to find a sock full of sand coming the other way.

The walls and ceiling were closing in.

There were other tunnels here. Carrot had been right. Hundreds of people must have worked for years to build this. What Ankh-Morpork was built on was Ankh-Morpork.

Vimes stopped.

There was no sound of splashing, and tunnel mouths all around.

Then there was a flash of light, up a side tunnel.

Vimes scrambled towards it, and saw a pair of legs in a shaft of light from an open trapdoor.

He launched himself at them, and caught a boot just as it was disappearing into the room above. It kicked at him, and he heard Cruces hit the floor.

Vimes grabbed the edge of the hatchway and struggled through it.

This wasn't a tunnel. It looked like a cellar. He slipped on mud and hit a wall clammy with slime. What was Ankh-Morpork built on? Right . . .

Cruces was only a few yards away, scrambling and slipping up a flight of steps. There had been a door at the top but it had long ago rotted.

There were more steps, and more rooms. Fire and flood, flood and rebuilding. Rooms had become cellars, cellars had become foundations. It wasn't an elegant pursuit; both men slithered and fell, clambered up again, fought their way through hanging curtains of slime. Cruces had left candles here and there. They gave just enough light to make Vimes wish they didn't.

And then there was dry stone underfoot and *this* wasn't a door, but a hole knocked through a wall. And there were barrels, and sticks of furniture, ancient stuff that had been locked up and forgotten.

Cruces was lying a few feet away, fighting for breath and

hammering another rack of pipes into the gonne. Vimes managed to pull himself up on to his hands and knees, and gulped air. There was a candle wedged into the wall nearby.

'Got . . . you,' he panted.

Cruces tried to get to his feet, still clutching the gonne.

'You're . . . too old . . . to run . . .' Vimes managed.

Cruces made it up upright, and lurched away. Vimes thought about it. *'I'm too old to run,'* he added, and leapt.

The two men rolled in the dust, the gonne between them. It struck Vimes much later that the last thing any man of sense would do was fight an Assassin. They had concealed weapons everywhere. But Cruces wasn't going to let go of the gonne. He held it grimly in both hands, trying to hit Vimes with the barrel or the butt.

Curiously enough, Assassins learned hardly any unarmed combat. They were generally good enough at armed combat not to need it. Gentlemen bore arms; only the lower classes used their hands.

'I've *got* you,' Vimes panted. 'You're under *arrest. Be* under arrest, will you?'

But Cruces wouldn't let go. Vimes didn't *dare* let go; the gonne would be twisted out of his grip. It was pulled backwards and forwards between them in desperate, grunting concentration.

The gonne exploded.

There was a tongue of red fire, a firework stink and a *zing-zing* noise from three walls. Something struck Vimes's helmet and *zinged* away towards the ceiling.

Vimes stared at Cruces's contorted features. Then he lowered his head and yanked the gonne hard.

The Assassin screamed and let go, clutching at his nose. Vimes rolled back, gonne in both hands.

It moved. Suddenly the stock was against his shoulder and his finger was on the trigger.

You're mine.

We don't need him any more.

The shock of the voice was so great that he cried out.

He swore afterwards that he didn't pull the trigger. It moved of its own accord, pulling his finger with it. The gonne slammed into his shoulder and a six-inch hole appeared in the wall by the Assassin's head, spraying him with plaster.

Vimes was vaguely aware, through the red mist rising around his vision, of Cruces staggering to a door and lurching through it, slamming it behind him.

All that you hate, all that is wrong – I can put it right.

Vimes reached the door, and tried the handle. It was locked.

He brought the gonne around, not aware of thinking, and let the trigger pull his finger again. A large area of the door and frame became a splinter-bordered hole.

Vimes kicked the rest of it away and followed the gonne.

He was in a passageway. A dozen young men were looking at him in astonishment from half-open doors. They were all wearing black.

He was inside the Assassins' Guild.

A trainee Assassin looked at Vimes with his nostrils.

'Who are you, pray?'

The gonne swung towards him. Vimes managed to haul the barrel upwards just as it fired, and the shot took away a lot of ceiling.

'The *law*, you *sons* of *bitches!*' he shouted.

They stared at him.

Shoot them all. Clean up the world.

'Shut up!' Vimes, a red-eyed, dust-coated, slime-dripping thing from out of the earth, glared at the quaking student.

'Where did Cruces go?' The mist rolled around his head. His hand creaked with the effort of not firing.

The young man jerked a finger urgently towards a flight of stairs. He'd been standing very close when the gonne fired. Plaster dust draped him like devil's dandruff.

The gonne sped away again, dragging Vimes past the boys and up the stairs, where black mud still trailed. There was another corridor there. Doors were opening. Doors closed again after the gonne fired again, smashing a chandelier.

The corridor gave out on to a wide landing at the top of a much more impressive flight of stairs and, opposite, a big oaken door.

Vimes shot the lock off, kicked at the door and then fought the gonne long enough to duck. A crossbow bolt whirred over his head and hit someone, far down the corridor.

Shoot him! SHOOT HIM!

Cruces was standing by his desk, feverishly trying to slot another bolt into his bow—

Vimes tried to silence the singing in his ears.

But . . . why not? Why not fire? Who was this man? He'd always wanted to make the city a cleaner place, and he might as well start here. And then people would find out what the law was . . .

Clean up the world.

Noon started.

The cracked bronze bell in the Teachers' Guild began the chime, and had midday all to itself for at least seven clangs before the Guild of Bakers' clock, running fast, caught up with it.

Cruces straightened up, and began to edge towards the cover of one of the stone pillars.

'You can't shoot me,' he said, watching the gonne. 'I know the law. And so do you. You're a guard. You can't shoot me in cold blood.'

Vimes squinted along the barrel.

It'd be so easy. The trigger tugged at his finger.

A third bell began chiming.

'You can't just kill me. That's the law. And you're a guard,' Dr Cruces repeated. He licked his dry lips.

The barrel lowered a little. Cruces almost relaxed.

'Yes. I am a guard.'

The barrel rose again, pointed at Cruces's forehead.

'But when the bells stop,' said Vimes, quietly, 'I won't be a guard any more.'

Shoot him! SHOOT HIM!

Vimes forced the butt under his arm, so that he had one hand free.

'We'll do it by the rules,' he said. 'By the rules. Got to do it by the rules.'

Without looking down, he tugged his badge off the remains of his jacket. Even through the mud, it still had a gleam. He'd always kept it polished. When he spun it once or twice, like a coin, the copper caught the light.

Cruces watched it like a cat.

The bells were slackening. Most of the towers had stopped. Now there was only the sound of the gong on the Temple of Small Gods, and the bells of the Assassins' Guild, which were always fashionably late.

The gong stopped.

Dr Cruces put the crossbow, neatly and meticulously, on the desk beside him.

'There! I've put it down!'

'Ah,' said Vimes. 'But I want to make sure you don't pick it up again.'

The black bell of the Assassins' Guild hammered its way to noon.

And stopped.

Silence slammed in like a thunderclap.

The little metallic sound as Vimes's badge bounced on the floor filled it from edge to edge.

He raised the gonne and, gently, let the tension ease out of his hand.

A bell started.

It was a tinny, jolly little tune, barely to be heard at all except in this pool of silence . . .

Cling, bing, a-bing, bong . . .

. . . but much more accurate than hourglasses, waterclocks and pendulums.

'Put down the gonne, captain,' said Carrot, climbing slowly up the stairs.

He held his sword in one hand, and the presentation watch in the other.

. . . bing, bing, a-bing, cling . . .

Vimes didn't move.

'Put it down. Put it down now, captain.'

'I can wait out another bell,' said Vimes.

. . . a-bing, a-bing . . .

'Can't let you do that, captain. It'd be murder.'

. . . clong, a-bing . . .

'You'll stop me, will you?'

'Yes.'

. . . bing . . . bing . . .

Vimes turned his head slightly.

'He killed Angua. Doesn't that mean anything to you?'

. . . bing . . . bing . . . bing . . . bing . . .

Carrot nodded.

'Yes. But personal isn't the same as important.'

Vimes looked along his arm. The face of Dr Cruces, mouth open in terror, pivoted on the tip of the barrel.

. . . bing . . . bing . . . bing . . . bing . . . bing . . .

'Captain Vimes?'

. . . bing.

'Captain? Badge 177, captain. It's never had more than dirt on it.'

The pounding spirit of the gonne flowing up Vimes's arms met the armies of sheer stone-headed Vimesness surging the other way.

'I should put it down, captain. You don't need it,' said Carrot, like someone speaking to a child.

Vimes stared at the thing in his hands. The screaming was muted now.

'Put that down now, Watchman! That's an order!'

The gonne hit the floor. Vimes saluted, and then realized what he was doing. He blinked at Carrot.

'Personal isn't the same as *important*?' he said.

'Listen,' Cruces said, 'I'm sorry about the . . . the girl, that was an accident, but I only wanted— There's evidence! There's a—'

Cruces was hardly paying any attention to the Watchmen. He pulled a leather satchel off the table and waved it at them.

'It's here! All of it, sire! Evidence! Edward was stupid, he thought it was all crowns and ceremony, he had no idea what he'd found! And then, last night, it was as if—'

'I'm not interested,' mumbled Vimes.

'The city needs a king!'

'It does not need murderers,' said Carrot.

'But—'

And then Cruces dived for the gonne and scooped it up.

One moment Vimes was trying to reassemble his thoughts, and the next they were fleeing to far corners of his consciousness. He was looking into the mouth of the gonne. It grinned at him.

Cruces slumped against the pillar, but the gonne remained steady, pointing *itself* at Vimes.

'It's all there, sire,' he said. 'Everything written down. The whole thing. Birthmarks and prophecies and genealogy and everything. Even your sword. It's *the* sword!'

'Really?' said Carrot. 'May I see?'

Carrot lowered his sword and, to Vimes's horror, walked over to the desk and pulled the bundle of documents out of the case. Cruces nodded approvingly, as if rewarding a good boy.

Carrot read a page, and turned to the next one.

'This *is* interesting,' he said.

'Exactly. But now we must remove this annoying policeman,' said Cruces.

Vimes felt that he could see all the way along the tube, to the little slug of metal that was soon to launch itself at him . . .

'It's a shame,' said Cruces, 'if only you had—'

Carrot stepped in front of the gonne. His arm moved in a blur. There was hardly a sound.

Pray you never face a good man, Vimes thought. He'll kill you with hardly a word.

Cruces looked down. There was blood on his shirt. He raised a hand to the sword hilt protruding from his chest, and looked back up into Carrot's eyes.

'But why? You could have been—'

And he died. The gonne fell from his hands, and fired at the floor.

There was silence.

Carrot grasped the hilt of his sword and pulled it back. The body slumped.

Vimes leaned on the table and fought to get his breath back.

'Damn . . . his . . . hide,' he panted.

'Sir?'

'He . . . he called you *sire*,' he said. 'What was in that—'

'You're late, captain,' said Carrot.

'Late? Late? What do you mean?' Vimes fought to prevent his brain parting company with reality.

'You were supposed to have been married—' Carrot looked at the watch, then snapped it shut and handed it to Vimes. '—two minutes ago.'

'Yes, yes. But he called you *sire*, I heard him—'

'Just a trick of the echo, I expect, Mr Vimes.'

A thought broke through to Vimes's attention. Carrot's sword was a couple of feet long. He'd run Cruces clean through. But Cruces had been standing with his back to—

Vimes looked at the pillar. It was granite, and a foot thick. There was no cracking. There was just a blade-shaped hole, front to back.

'Carrot—' he began.

'And you look a mess, sir. Got to get you cleaned up.'

Carrot pulled the leather satchel towards him and slung it over his shoulder.

'*Carrot*—'

'Sir?'

'I *order* you to give—'

'No, sir. You can't order me. Because you are now, sir, no offence meant, a civilian. It's a new life.'

'A *civilian*?'

Vimes rubbed his forehead. It was all colliding in his brain now – the gonne, the sewers, Carrot and the fact that he'd been operating on pure adrenalin, which soon presents its bill and does not give credit. He sagged.

'But this *is* my life. Carrot! This is my *job*.'

'A hot bath and a drink, sir. That's what you need,' said Carrot. 'Do you a world of good. Let's go.'

Vimes's gaze took in the fallen body of Cruces and, then, the gonne. He went to pick it up, and stopped himself in time.

Not even the wizards had something like this. One burst from a staff and they had to go and lie down.

No wonder no one had destroyed it. You couldn't destroy something as perfect as this. It called out to something deep in the soul. Hold it in your hand, and you had *power*. More power than any bow or spear – they just stored up your own muscles' power, when you thought about it. But the gonne gave you power from outside. You didn't use it, it used you. Cruces had probably been a good man. He'd probably listened kindly enough to Edward, and then he'd taken the gonne, and he'd belonged to it as well.

'Captain Vimes? I think we'd better get that out of here,' said Carrot, reaching down.

'Whatever you do, don't touch it!' Vimes warned.

'Why not? It's only a device,' said Carrot. He picked up the gonne by the barrel, regarded it for a moment, and then smashed it against the wall. Bits of metal pinwheeled away.

'One of a kind,' he said. 'One of a kind is always special, my father used to say. Let's be going.'

He opened the door.

He shut the door.

'There's about a hundred Assassins at the bottom of the stairs,' he said.

'How many bolts have you got for your bow?' said Vimes. He was still staring at the twisted gonne.

'One.'

'Then it's a good thing you won't have any chance to reload anyway.'

There was a polite knock at the door.

Carrot glanced at Vimes, who shrugged. He opened the door.

It was Downey. He raised an empty hand.

'You can put down your weapons. I assure you they will not be necessary. Where is Dr Cruces?'

Carrot pointed.

'Ah.' He glanced up at the two Watchmen.

'Would you, please, leave his body with us? We will inhume him in our crypt.'

Vimes pointed at the body.

'He *killed*—'

'And now he is dead. And now I must ask you to leave.'

Downey opened the door. Assassins lined the wide stairs. There wasn't a weapon in sight. But, with Assassins, there didn't need to be.

At the bottom lay the body of Angua. The Watchmen walked down slowly, and Carrot knelt and picked it up.

He nodded to Downey.

'Shortly we will be sending someone to collect the body of Dr Cruces,' he said.

'But I thought we had agreed that—'

'No. It must be seen that he is dead. Things must be seen. Things mustn't happen in the dark, or behind closed doors.'

'I am afraid I cannot accede to your request,' said the Assassin firmly.

'It wasn't a request, sir.'

Scores of Assassins watched them walk across the courtyard.

The black gates were shut.

No one seemed about to open them.

'I agree with you, but perhaps you should have put that another way,' said Vimes. 'They don't look at all happy—'

The doors shattered. A six-foot iron arrow passed Carrot and Vimes and removed a large section of wall on the far side of the courtyard.

A couple of blows removed the rest of the gates, and Detritus stepped through. He looked around at the assembled Assassins, a red glow in his eyes. And growled.

It dawned on the smarter Assassins that there was nothing in their armoury that could kill a troll. They had fine stiletto knives, but they needed sledgehammers. They had darts armed with exquisite poisons, none of which worked on a troll. No one had ever thought trolls were important enough to be assassinated. Suddenly, Detritus was very important indeed. He had Cuddy's axe in one hand and his mighty crossbow in the other.

Some of the brighter Assassins turned and ran for it. Some were not as bright. A couple of arrows bounced off Detritus. Their owners saw his face as he turned towards them, and dropped their bows.

Detritus hefted his club.

'*Acting-Constable Detritus!*'

The words rang out across the courtyard.

'*Acting-Constable Detritus! Atten-shun!*'

Detritus very slowly raised his hand.

Dink.

'You *listen* to me, Acting-Constable Detritus,' said Carrot. 'If there's a heaven for Watchmen, and gods I hope there is, then Acting-Constable Cuddy is there right now, drunk as a bloody monkey, with a rat in one hand and a pint of Bearhugger's in the other, and he's looking up* at us right now and he's saying: my friend Acting-Constable Detritus won't forget he's a guard. Not Detritus.'

There was a long dangerous moment, and then another *dink*.

'Thank you, Acting-Constable. You'll escort Mr Vimes to the University.' Carrot looked around at the Assassins. 'Good afternoon, gentlemen. We may be back.'

The three Watchmen stepped over the wreckage.

Vimes said nothing until they were well out in the street, and then he turned to Carrot.

'*Why* did he call you—'

---

* To trolls, heaven is below.

'If you'll excuse me, I'll take her back to the Watch House.'

Vimes looked down at Angua's corpse and felt a train of thought derail itself. Some things were too hard to think about. He wanted a nice quiet hour somewhere to put it all together. *Personal isn't the same as important.* What sort of person could think like that? And it dawned on him that while Ankh in the past had had its share of evil rulers, and simply bad rulers, it had never yet come under the heel of a good ruler. That might be the most terrifying prospect of all.

'Sir?' said Carrot, politely.

'Uh. We'll bury her up at Small Gods, how about that?' said Vimes. 'It's sort of a Watch tradition . . .'

'Yes, sir. You go off with Detritus. He's all right when you give him orders. If you don't mind, I don't think I'll be along to the wedding. You know how it is . . .'

'Yes. Yes, of course. Um. Carrot?' Vimes blinked, to drive away suspicions that clamoured for consideration. 'We shouldn't be too hard on Cruces. I hated the bastard like hell, so I want to be fair to him. I know what the gonne does to people. We're all the same, to the gonne. I'd have been just like him.'

'No, captain. *You* put it down.'

Vimes smiled wanly.

'They call me *Mister* Vimes,' he said.

Carrot walked back to the Watch House, and laid the body of Angua on the slab in the makeshift morgue. Rigor mortis was already setting in.

He fetched some water and cleaned her fur as best he could.

What he did next would have surprised, say, a troll or a dwarf or anyone who didn't know about the human mind's reaction to stressful circumstances.

He wrote his report. He swept the main room's floor; there was a rota, and it was his turn. He had a wash. He changed his shirt, and dressed the wound on his shoulder, and cleaned his armour, rubbing with wire wool and a graded series of cloths until be could, once again, see his face in it.

He heard, far off, Fondel's 'Wedding March' scored for Monstrous Organ with Miscellaneous Farmyard Noises accompaniment. He fished out a half bottle of rum from what Sergeant Colon thought was his secure hiding place, poured himself a very small amount, and drank a toast to the sound, saying, 'Here's to Mr Vimes and Lady Ramkin!' in a clear, sincere voice which would have severely embarrassed anyone who had heard it.

There was a scratching at the door. He let Gaspode in. The little dog slunk under the table, saying nothing.

Then Carrot went up to his room, and sat in his chair and looked out of the window.

The afternoon wore on. The rain stopped around teatime.

Lights came on, all over the city.

Presently, the moon rose.

The door opened. Angua entered, walking softly.

Carrot turned, and smiled.

'I wasn't certain,' he said. 'But I thought, well, isn't it only silver that kills them? I just had to hope.'

It was two days later. The rain had set in. It didn't pour, it slouched out of the grey clouds, running in rivulets through the mud. It filled the Ankh, which slurped once again through its underground kingdom. It poured from the mouths of gargoyles. It hit the ground so hard there was a sort of mist of ricochets.

It drummed off the gravestones in the cemetery behind the Temple of Small Gods, and into the small pit dug for Acting-Constable Cuddy.

There were always only guards at a guard's funeral, Vimes told himself. Oh, sometimes there were relatives, like Lady Ramkin and Detritus' Ruby here today, but you never got *crowds*. Perhaps Carrot was right. When you became a guard, you stopped being everything else.

Although there *were* other people today, standing silently at the railings around the cemetery. They weren't *at* the funeral, but they were watching it.

There was a small priest who gave the generic fill-in-deceased's-name-here service, designed to be vaguely satisfactory to any gods who might be listening. Then Detritus lowered the coffin into the grave, and the priest threw a ceremonial handful of dirt on to the coffin, except that instead of the rattle of soil there was a very final *splat*.

And Carrot, to Vimes's surprise, made a speech. It echoed across the soggy ground to the rain-dripping trees. It was really based around the only text you could use on this occasion: he was my friend, he was one of us, he was a good copper.

He was a good copper. That had got said at every guard funeral Vimes had ever attended. It'd probably be said even at Corporal Nobbs's funeral, although everyone would have their fingers crossed behind their backs. It was what you had to say.

Vimes stared at the coffin. And then a strange feeling came

creeping over him, as insidiously as the rain trickling down the back of his neck. It wasn't exactly a suspicion. If it stayed in his mind long enough it would be a suspicion, but right now it was only a faint tingle of a hunch.

He had to ask. He'd never stop thinking about it if he didn't at least *ask*.

So as they were walking away from the grave he said, 'Corporal?'

'Yessir?'

'No one's found the gonne, then?'

'No, sir.'

'Someone said you had it last.'

'I must have put it down somewhere. You know how busy it all was.'

'Yes. Oh, yes. I'm pretty sure I saw you carry most of it out of the Guild . . .'

'Must have done, sir.'

'Yes. Er. I hope you put it somewhere safe, then. Do you, er, do you think you left it somewhere safe?'

Behind them, the gravedigger began to shovel the wet, clinging loam of Ankh-Morpork into the hole.

'I think I must have done, sir. Don't you? Seeing as no one has found it. I mean, we'd soon know if anyone'd found it!'

'Maybe it's all for the best, Corporal Carrot.'

'I certainly hope so.'

'He was a good copper.'

'Yes, sir.'

Vimes went for broke.

'And . . . it seemed to me, as we were carrying that little coffin . . . slightly heavier . . .?'

'Really, sir? I really couldn't say I noticed.'

'But at least he's got a proper dwarf burial.'

'Oh, yes. I saw to that, sir,' said Carrot.

The rain gurgled off the roofs of the Palace. The gargoyles had taken up their stations at every corner, straining gnats and flies via their ears.

Corporal Carrot shook the drops off his leather rain cape and exchanged salutes with the troll on guard. He strolled through the clerks in the outer rooms and knocked respectfully on the door of the Oblong Office.

'Come.'

Carrot entered, marched to the desk, saluted and stood at ease.

Lord Vetinari tensed, very slightly.

'Oh, yes,' he said. 'Corporal Carrot. I was expecting . . . something like this. I'm sure you've come to ask me for . . . something?'

Carrot unfolded a piece of grubby paper, and cleared his throat.

'Well, sir . . . we could do with a new dartboard. You know. For when we're off duty?'

The Patrician blinked. It was not often that he blinked.

'I beg your pardon?'

'A new dartboard, sir. It helps the men relax after their shift, sir.'

Vetinari recovered a little.

'*Another* one? But you had one only last year!'

'It's the Librarian, sir. Nobby lets him play and he just leans a bit and hammers the darts in with his fist. It ruins the board. Anyway, Detritus threw one through it. Through the wall behind it, too.'

'Very well. And?'

'Well . . . Acting-Constable Detritus needs to be let off having to pay for five holes in his breastplate.'

'Granted. Tell him not to do it again.'

'Yes, sir. Well, I think that's about it. Except for a new kettle.'

The Patrician's hand moved in front of his lips. He was trying not to smile.

'Dear me. Another kettle as well? What happened to the old one?'

'Oh, we still use it, sir, we still use it. But we're going to need another because of the new arrangements.'

'I'm sorry? *What* new arrangements?'

Carrot unfolded a second, and rather larger, piece of paper.

'The Watch to be brought up to an establishment strength of fifty-six; the old Watch Houses at the River Gate, the Deosil Gate and the Hubwards Gate to be re-opened and manned on a twenty-four hour basis—'

The Patrician's smile remained, but his face seemed to pull away from it, leaving it stranded and all alone in the world.

'—a department for, well, we haven't got a name for it yet, but for looking at clues and things like dead bodies, e.g., how long they've been dead, and to start with we'll need an alchemist and possibly a ghoul provided they promise not to take anything home and eat it; a special unit using dogs, which could be very useful, and Lance-Constable Angua can deal with that since she can, um, be her own handler a lot of the time; a request here from Corporal Nobbs that Watchmen be allowed all the weapons they can carry, although I'd be obliged if you said no to that; a—'

Lord Vetinari waved a hand.

'All right, all right,' he said. 'I can see how this is going. And supposing I say no?'

There was another of those long, long pauses, wherein may be seen the possibilities of several different futures.

'Do you know, sir, I never even *considered* that you'd say no?'

'You didn't?'

'No, sir.'

'I'm intrigued. Why not?'

'It's all for the good of the city, sir. Do you know where the word "policeman" comes from? It means "man of the city", sir. From the old word *polis*.'

'Yes. I do know.'

The Patrician looked at Carrot. He seemed to be shuffling futures in his head. Then:

'Yes. I accede to all the requests, except the one involving Corporal Nobbs. And you, I think, should be promoted to Captain.'

'Ye-es. I agree, sir. That would be a good thing for Ankh-Morpork. But I will not command the Watch, if that's what you mean.'

'Why not?'

'Because I *could* command the Watch. Because . . . people should do things because an officer tells them. They shouldn't do it just because Corporal Carrot says so. Just because Corporal Carrot is . . . good at being obeyed.' Carrot's face was carefully blank.

'An interesting point.'

'But there used to be a rank, in the old days. Commander of the Watch. I suggest Samuel Vimes.'

The Patrician leaned back. 'Oh, yes,' he said. 'Commander of the Watch. Of course, that became a rather unpopular job, after all that business with Lorenzo the Kind. It was a Vimes who held the post in those days. I've never liked to ask him if he was an ancestor.'

'He was, sir. I looked it up.'

'Would he accept?'

'Is the High Priest an Offlian? Does a dragon explode in the woods?'

The Patrician steepled his fingers and looked at Carrot over the top of them. It was a mannerism that had unnerved many.

'But, you see, captain, the trouble with Sam Vimes is that he upsets a lot of important people. And I think that a Commander of the Watch would have to move in very exalted circles, attend Guild functions . . .'

They exchanged glances. The Patrician got the best of the bargain, since Carrot's face was bigger. Both of them were trying not to grin.

506

'An excellent choice, in fact,' said the Patrician.

'I'd taken the liberty, sir, of drafting a letter to the cap— to Mr Vimes on your behalf. Just to save you trouble, sir. Perhaps you'd care to have a look?'

'You think of everything, don't you?'

'I hope so, sir.'

Lord Vetinari read the letter. He smiled once or twice. Then he picked up his pen, signed at the bottom, and handed it back.

'And is that the last of your dema— requests?'

Carrot scratched his ear.

'There is one, actually. I need a home for a small dog. It must have a large garden, a warm spot by the fire, and happy laughing children.'

'Good heavens. Really? Well, I suppose we can find one.'

'Thank you, sir. That's all, I think.'

The Patrician stood up and limped over to the window. It was dusk. Lights were being lit all over the city.

With his back to Carrot he said, 'Tell me, captain . . . this business about there being an heir to the throne . . . What do you think about it?'

'I don't think about it, sir. That's all sword-in-a-stone nonsense. Kings don't come out of nowhere, waving a sword and putting everything right. Everyone knows that.'

'But there was some talk of . . . *evidence?*'

'No one seems to know where it is, sir.'

'When I spoke to Captain . . . to Commander Vimes he said you'd got it.'

'Then I must have put it down somewhere. I'm sure I couldn't say where, sir.'

'My word, I hope you absent-mindedly put it down somewhere safe.'

'I'm sure it's . . . well guarded, sir.'

'I think you've learned a *lot* from Cap— *Commander* Vimes, captain.'

'Sir. My father always said I was a quick learner, sir.'

'Perhaps the city does *need* a king, though. Have you considered that?'

'Like a fish needs a . . . er . . . a thing that doesn't work under-water, sir.'

'Yet a king can appeal to the emotions of his subjects, captain. In . . . very much the same way as you did recently, I understand.'

'Yes, sir. But what will he do next day? You can't treat people like puppet dolls. No, sir. Mr Vimes always said a man has got to know his limitations. If there was a king, then the best thing he could do would be to get on with a decent day's work—'

'Indeed.'

'*But* if there was some pressing need . . . then perhaps he'd think again.' Carrot brightened up. 'It's a bit like being a guard, really. When you need us, you really need us. And when you don't . . . well, best if we just walk around the streets and shout All's Well. Providing all *is* well, of course.'

'Captain Carrot,' said Lord Vetinari, 'because we understand one another so well, and I think we *do* understand one another . . . there is something I'd like to show you. Come this way.'

He led the way into the throne room, which was empty at this time of day. As he hobbled across the wide floor he pointed ahead of him.

'I expect you know what that is, captain?'

'Oh, yes. The golden throne of Ankh-Morpork.'

'And no one has sat in it for many hundreds of years. Have you ever wondered about it?'

'Exactly what do you mean, sir?'

'So much gold, when even the brass has been stripped off the Brass Bridge? Take a look *behind* the throne, will you?'

Carrot mounted the steps.

'Good grief!'

The Patrician looked over his shoulder.

'It's just gold foil over wood . . .'

'Quite so.'

It was hardly even wood any more. Rot and worms had fought one another to a standstill over the last biodegradable fragment. Carrot prodded it with his sword, and part of it drifted gently away in a puff of dust.

'What do you think about this, captain?'

Carrot stood up.

'On the whole, sir, it's probably just as well that people don't know.'

'So I have always thought. Well, I will not keep you. I'm sure you have a lot to organize.'

Carrot saluted.

'Thank you, sir.'

'I gather that you and, er, Constable Angua are getting along well?'

'We have a very good Understanding, sir. Of course, there will be minor difficulties,' said Carrot, 'but, to look on the positive side, I've got someone who's always ready for a walk around the city.'

As Carrot had his hand on the door handle Lord Vetinari called out to him.

'Yes, sir?'

Carrot looked back at the tall thin man, standing in the big bare room beside the golden throne filled with decay.

'You're a man interested in words, captain. I'd just invite you to consider something your predecessor never fully grasped.'

'Sir?'

'Have you ever wondered where the word "politician" comes from?' said the Patrician.

'And then there's the committee of the Sunshine Sanctuary,' said Lady Ramkin, from her side of the dining table. 'We must get you on that. And the Country Landowners' Association. And the Friendly Flamethrowers' League. Cheer up. You'll find your time will just fill up like nobody's business.'

'Yes, dear,' said Vimes. The days stretched ahead of him, just filling up like nobody's business with committees and good works and . . . nobody's business. It was probably better than walking the streets. Lady Sybil and Mr Vimes.

He sighed.

Sybil Vimes, *née* Ramkin, looked at him with an expression of faint concern. For as long as she'd known him, Sam Vimes had been vibrating with the internal anger of a man who wants to arrest the gods for not doing it right, and then he'd handed in his badge and he was . . . well, not exactly Sam Vimes any more.

The clock in the corner chimed eight o'clock. Vimes pulled out his presentation watch and opened it.

'That clock's five minutes fast,' he said, above the tinkling chimes. He snapped the lid shut, and read again the words on it: 'A Watch From, Your Old Freinds In The Watch'.

Carrot had been behind that, sure enough. Vimes had grown to recognize that blindness to the position of 'i's and 'e's and that wanton cruelty to the common comma.

They said goodbye to you, they took you out of the measure of your days, and they gave you a watch . . .

'Excuse me, m'lady?'

'Yes, Willikins?'

'There is a Watchman at the door, m'lady. The tradesman's entrance.'

'You sent a Watchman to the tradesman's entrance?' said Lady Sybil.

'No, m'lady. That's the one he came to. It's Captain Carrot.'

Vimes put his hand over his eyes. 'He's been made captain and he comes to the back door,' he said. 'That's Carrot, that is. Bring him on in.'

It was barely noticeable, except to Vimes, but the butler glanced at Lady Ramkin for her approval.

'Do as your master says,' she said, gallantly.

'I'm no one's mas—' Vimes began.

'Now, Sam,' said Lady Ramkin.

'Well, I'm not,' said Vimes sullenly.

Carrot marched in, and stood to attention. As usual, the room subtly became a mere background to him

'It's all right, lad,' said Vimes, as nicely as he could manage. 'You don't need to salute.'

'Yes I do, sir,' said Carrot. He handed Vimes an envelope. It had the seal of the Patrician on it.

Vimes picked up a knife and broke the seal.

'Probably charging me five dollars for unnecessary wear and tear on my chainmail,' he said.

His lips moved as he read.

'Blimey,' he said eventually. 'Fifty-six?'

'Yes, sir. Detritus is looking forward to breaking them in.'

'Including undead? It says here open to all, regardless of species or mortal status—'

'Yes, sir,' said Carrot, firmly. 'They're all citizens.'

'You mean you could have *vampires* in the Watch?'

'Very good on night duty, sir. And aerial surveillance.'

'And always useful if you want to stake out somewhere.'

'Yes, sir?'

Vimes watched the feeble pun go right through Carrot's head without triggering his brain. He turned back to the paper.

'Hmm. Pensions for widows, I see.'

'Yessir.'

'Re-opening the old Watch Houses?'

'That's what he says, sir.'

Vimes read on:

We consider particularly that, this enlarged Watch will need an expereinced man in charge who, is held in Esteem by all parts of soceity and, we are convinced that you should fulfil this Roll. You will therefore take up your Duties immediately as, Commander of the Ankh-Morpork City Watch. This post traditionally carreis with it the rank of Knight which, we are minded to resurrect on this one occasion.

Hoping this finds you in good health, Yrs. faithfully
Havelock Vetinari (*Patrician*)

Vimes read it again.

He drummed his fingers on the table. There was no doubt that the signature was genuine. But . . .

'Corp— Captain Carrot?'

'Sah!' Carrot stared straight ahead of him with the glistening air of one busting with duty and efficiency and an absolute resolve to duck and dodge any direct questions put to him.

'I—' Vimes picked up the paper again, put it down, picked it up, and then passed it over to Sybil.

'My word!' she said. 'A knighthood? Not a moment too soon, either!'

'Oh, no! Not me! You know what I think about the so-called aristocrats in *this* city – apart from you, Sybil, of course.'

'Perhaps it's about time the general stock was improved, then,' said Lady Ramkin.

'His lordship did say,' said Carrot, 'that no part of the package was negotiable, sir. I mean, it's all or nothing, if you understand me.'

'All . . .?'

'Yessir.'

'. . . or nothing.'

'Yessir.'

Vimes drummed his fingers on the table.

'You've won, haven't you?' he said. 'You've *won*.'

'Sir? Don't understand, sir,' said Carrot, radiating honest ignorance.

There was another dangerous silence.

'But, of course,' said Vimes, 'there's no possible way I could oversee this sort of thing.'

'What do you mean, sir?' said Carrot.

Vimes pulled the candelabra towards him and thumped the paper with a finger.

'Well, look what it says here. I mean, opening those old Watch Houses? On the gates? What's the point in that? Right out there on the edge?'

'Oh, I'm sure matters of organization detail can be changed, sir,' said Carrot.

'Keep a general gate guard, *yes*, but if you're going to have any kind of finger on the pulse of . . . look, you'd need one along Elm Street somewhere, close to the Shades and the docks, and another one halfway up Short Street, and maybe a smaller one in Kingsway. Somewhere up there, anyway. You've got to think about population centres. How many men based per Watch House?'

'I thought ten, sir. Allowing for shifts.'

'No, can't do that. Use six at most. A corporal, say, and one other per shift. The *rest* you'll move around on, oh, a monthly rota. You want to keep everyone on their toes, yes? And that way everyone gets to walk every street. That's very important. And . . . wish I had a map here . . . oh . . . thank you, dear. Right. Now, see here. You've got a strength of fifty-six, nominal, OK? But you're taking over day watch too, plus you've got to allow for days off, two grandmother's funerals per year per man – gods know how your undead'll sort out *that* one, maybe they get time off to go to their *own* funerals – and then there's sickness and so on. So . . . we want four shifts, staggered around the city. Got a light? Thanks. We don't want the whole guard changing shift at once. On the other hand, you've got to allow each Watch House officer a certain amount of initiative. But we should maintain a special squad in Pseudopolis Yard for emergencies . . . look, give me that pencil. Now give me that notebook. Right . . .'

Cigar smoke filled the room. The little presentation watch played every quarter of an hour, entirely unheeded.

Lady Sybil smiled and shut the door behind her, and went to feed the dragons.

'Dearest Mumm and Dad,
                    Well here is Amazing news for, I am now Captain!! It has been a very busy and vareid Week all round as, I shall now recount . . .'

And only one thing more . . .

There was a large house in one of the nicer areas of Ankh, with a spacious garden with a children's treehouse in it and, quite probably, a warm spot by the fire.

And a window, breaking . . .

Gaspode landed on the lawn, and ran like hell towards the fence. Flower-scented bubbles streamed off his coat. He was wearing a ribbon with a bow on it, and carrying in his mouth a bowl labelled MR HUGGY.

He dug his way frantically under the fence and squirmed into the road.

A fresh pile of horse droppings took care of the floral smell, and five minutes of scratching removed the bow.

'Not a bloody flea left,' he moaned, dropping the bowl. 'An' I had nearly the complete set. Whee-ooo! I'm well out of *that*. Huh!'

Gaspode brightened up. It was Tuesday. That meant steak-and-suspicious-organs pie at the Thieves' Guild, and the head cook there was known to be susceptible to a thumping tail and a penetrating stare. And holding an empty bowl in your mouth and looking pathetic was a sure-fire winner, if Gaspode was any judge. It shouldn't take too long to claw off MR HUGGY.

Perhaps this wasn't the way it ought to be. But it was the way it was.

On the whole, he reflected, it could have been a lot worse.

FEET OF CLAY

It was a warm spring night when a fist knocked at the door so hard that the hinges bent.

A man opened it and peered out into the street. There was mist coming off the river and it was a cloudy night. He might as well have tried to see through white velvet.

But he thought afterwards that there had been shapes out there, just beyond the light spilling out into the road. A lot of shapes, watching him carefully. He thought maybe there'd been very faint points of light . . .

There was no mistaking the shape right in front of him, though. It was big and dark red and looked like a child's clay model of a man. Its eyes were two embers.

'Well? What do you want at this time of night?'

The golem handed him a slate, on which was written:

WE HEAR YOU WANT A GOLEM.

Of course, golems couldn't speak, could they?

'Hah. *Want*, yes. *Afford*, no. I've been asking around but it's wicked the prices you're going for these days . . .'

The golem rubbed the words off the slate and wrote:

TO YOU, ONE HUNDRED DOLLARS.

'You're for sale?'

NO.

The golem lurched aside. Another one stepped into the light.

It was also a golem, the man could see that. But it wasn't like the usual lumpen clay things that you occasionally saw. This one gleamed like a newly polished statue, perfect down to the detailing of the clothes. It reminded him of one of the old pictures of the city's kings, all haughty stance and imperious haircut. In fact, it even had a small coronet moulded on to its head.

'A hundred dollars?' the man said suspiciously. 'What's wrong with it? Who's selling it?'

NOTHING IS WRONG. PERFECT IN ALL DETAIL. NINETY DOLLARS.

'Sounds like someone wants to get rid of it in a hurry . . .'

GOLEM MUST WORK. GOLEM MUST HAVE A MASTER.

'Yeah, right, but you hear stories . . . Going mad and making too many things, and that.'

NOT MAD. EIGHTY DOLLARS.

'It looks . . . new,' said the man, tapping the gleaming chest. 'But no one's making golems any more, that's what's keeping the price up beyond the purse of the small business—' He stopped. '*Is* someone making them again?'

 EIGHTY DOLLARS.

'I heard the priests banned making 'em years ago. A man could get in a *lot* of trouble.'

SEVENTY DOLLARS.

'Who's doing it?'

SIXTY DOLLARS.

'Is he selling them to Albertson? Or Spadger and Williams? It's hard enough competing as it is, and they've got the money to invest in new plant—'

FIFTY DOLLARS.

The man walked around the golem. 'A man can't sit by and watch his company collapse under him because of unfair price cutting, I mean to say . . .'

FORTY DOLLARS.

'Religion is all very well, but what do prophets know about profits, eh? Hmm . . .' He looked up at the shapeless golem in the shadows. 'Was that "thirty dollars" I just saw you write?'

YES.

'I've always liked dealing wholesale. Wait one moment.' He went back inside and returned with a handful of coins. 'Will you be selling any to them other bastards?'

NO.

'Good. Tell your boss it's a pleasure to do business with him. Get along inside, Sunny Jim.'

The white golem walked into the factory. The man, glancing from side to side, trotted in after it and shut the door.

Deeper shadows moved in the dark. There was a faint hissing. Then, rocking slightly, the big heavy shapes moved away.

Shortly afterwards, and around the corner, a beggar holding out a hopeful hand for alms was amazed to find himself suddenly richer by a whole thirty dollars.*

The Discworld turned against the glittering backdrop of space, spinning very gently on the backs of the four giant elephants that perched on the shell of Great A'Tuin the star turtle. Continents drifted slowly past, topped by weather systems that themselves

---

* He subsequently got dead-drunk and was shanghaied aboard a merchantman bound for strange and foreign parts, where he met lots of young ladies who didn't wear many clothes. He eventually died from stepping on a tiger. A good deed goes around the world.

turned gently against the flow, like waltzers spinning counter to the whirl of the dance. A billion tons of geography rolled slowly through the sky.

People look down on stuff like geography and meteorology, and not only because they're standing on one and being soaked by the other. They don't look quite like real science.* But geography is only physics slowed down and with a few trees stuck on it, and meteorology is full of excitingly fashionable chaos and complexity. And summer isn't a time. It's a place as well. Summer is a moving creature and likes to go south for the winter.

Even on the Discworld, with its tiny orbiting sun tilting over the turning world, the seasons moved. In Ankh-Morpork, greatest of its cities, spring was nudged aside by summer, and summer was prodded in the back by autumn.

Geographically speaking, there was not a lot of difference within the city itself, although in late spring the scum on the river was often a nice emerald green. The mist of spring became the fog of autumn, which mixed with fumes and smoke from the magical quarter and the workshops of the alchemists until it seemed to have a thick, choking life of its own.

And time moved on.

Autumn fog pressed itself against the midnight window-panes.

Blood ran in a trickle across the pages of a rare volume of religious essays, which had been torn in half.

There had been no need for that, thought Father Tubelcek.

A further thought suggested that there had been no need to hit him either. But Father Tubelcek had never been very concerned about that sort of thing. People healed, books didn't. He reached out shakily and tried to gather up the pages, but slumped back again.

The room was spinning.

The door swung open. Heavy footsteps creaked across the floor – one footstep at least, and one dragging noise.

Step. Drag. Step. Drag.

Father Tubelcek tried to focus. '*You?*' he croaked.

Nod.

'Pick . . . up the . . . books.'

The old priest watched as the books were retrieved and piled carefully with fingers not well suited to the task.

---

* That is to say, the sort you can use to give something three extra legs and then blow it up.

The newcomer took a quill pen from the debris, carefully wrote something on a scrap of paper, then rolled it up and placed it delicately between Father Tubelcek's lips.

The dying priest tried to smile.

'We don't work like that,' he mumbled, the little cylinder wobbling like a last cigarette. 'We ... make ... our ... own ... w ...'

The kneeling figure watched him for a while and then, taking great care, leaned forward slowly and closed his eyes.

Commander Sir Samuel Vimes, Ankh-Morpork City Guard, frowned at himself in the mirror and began to shave.

The razor was a sword of freedom. Shaving was an act of rebellion.

These days, someone ran his bath (every day! – you wouldn't think the human skin could stand it). And someone laid out his clothes (such clothes!). And someone cooked his meals (what meals! – he was putting on weight, he knew). And someone even polished his boots (and such boots! – no cardboard-soled wrecks but big, well-fitting boots of genuine shiny leather). There was someone to do nearly everything for him, but there were some things a man ought to do for himself, and one of them was shaving.

He knew that Lady Sybil mildly disapproved. Her father had never shaved himself in his life. He had a man for it. Vimes had protested that he'd spent too many years trudging the night-time streets to be happy about anyone else wielding a blade anywhere near his neck, but the *real* reason, the unspoken reason, was that he hated the very idea of the world being divided into the shaved and the shavers. Or those who wore the shiny boots and those who cleaned the mud off them. Every time he saw Willikins the butler fold his, Vimes's, clothes, he suppressed a terrible urge to kick the butler's shiny backside as an affront to the dignity of man.

The razor moved calmly over the stubble of the night.

Yesterday there had been some official dinner. He couldn't recall now what it had been for. He seemed to spend his whole life at the things. Arch, giggling women and braying young men who'd been at the back of the line when the chins were handed out. And, as usual, he'd come back through the fog-bound city in a filthy temper with himself.

He'd noticed a light under the kitchen door and heard conversation and laughter, and had gone in. Willikins was there, with the old man who stoked the boiler, and the head gardener, and the boy who cleaned the spoons and lit the fires. They were playing cards. There were bottles of beer on the table.

He'd pulled up a chair, and cracked a few jokes and asked to be dealt in. They'd been . . . welcoming. In a way. But as the game progressed Vimes had been aware of the universe crystallizing around him. It was like becoming a cogwheel in a glass clock. There was no laughter. They'd called him 'sir' and kept clearing their throats. Everything was very . . . careful.

Finally he'd mumbled an excuse and stumbled out. Halfway along the passage he'd thought he'd heard a comment followed by . . . well, maybe it was only a chuckle. But it *might* have been a snigger.

The razor carefully circumnavigated the nose.

Hah. A couple of years ago a man like Willikins would have allowed him into the kitchen only on sufferance. And would have made him take his boots off.

So that's your life now, Commander Sir Samuel Vimes. A jumped-up copper to the nobs and a nob to the rest, eh?

He frowned at the reflection in the mirror.

He'd started out in the gutter, true enough. And now he was on three meat meals a day, good boots, a warm bed at night and, come to that, a wife too. Good old Sybil – although she did tend to talk about curtains these days, but Sergeant Colon had said this happened to wives and was a biological thing and perfectly normal.

He'd actually been rather attached to his old cheap boots. He could read the street in them, the soles were so thin. It'd got so that he could tell where he was on a pitch-dark night just by the feel of the cobbles. Ah, well . . .

There was something mildly strange about Sam Vimes's shaving mirror. It was slightly convex, so that it reflected more of the room than a flat mirror would do, and it gave a very good view of the outbuildings and gardens beyond the window.

Hmm. Going thin on top. Definitely a receding scalp there. Less hair to comb but, on the other hand, more face to wash . . .

There was a flicker in the glass.

He moved sideways and ducked.

The mirror smashed.

There was the sound of feet somewhere beyond the broken window, and then a crash and a scream.

Vimes straightened up. He fished the largest piece of mirror out of the shaving bowl and propped it up on the black crossbow bolt that had buried itself in the wall.

He finished shaving.

Then he rang the bell for the butler. Willikins materialized. 'Sir?'

Vimes rinsed the razor. 'Get the boy to nip along to the glazier, will you?'

The butler's eyes flickered to the window and then to the shattered mirror. 'Yes, sir. And the bill to go to the Assassins' Guild again, sir?'

'With my compliments. And while he's out he's to call in at that shop in Five And Seven Yard and get me another shaving mirror. The dwarf there knows the kind I like.'

'Yes, sir. And I shall fetch a dustpan and brush directly, sir. Shall I inform her ladyship of this eventuality, sir?'

'No. She always says it's my fault for encouraging them.'

'Very good, sir,' said Willikins.

He dematerialized.

Sam Vimes dried himself off and went downstairs to the morning-room, where he opened the cabinet and took out the new crossbow Sybil had given to him as a wedding present. Sam Vimes was used to the old guard crossbows, which had a nasty habit of firing backwards in a tight corner, but this was a Burleigh and Stronginthearm made-to-measure job with the oiled walnut stock. There was none finer, it was said.

Then he selected a thin cigar and strolled out into the garden.

There was a commotion coming from the dragon house. Vimes entered, and shut the door behind him. He rested the crossbow against the door.

The yammering and squeaking increased. Little gouts of flame puffed above the thick walls of the hatching pens.

Vimes leaned over the nearest one. He picked up a newly hatched dragonette and tickled it under the chin. As it flamed excitedly he lit his cigar and savoured the smoke.

He blew a smoke ring at the figure hanging from the ceiling. 'Good morning,' he said.

The figure twisted frantically. By an amazing feat of muscle control it had managed to catch a foot around a beam as it fell, but it couldn't quite pull itself up. Dropping was not to be thought of. A dozen baby dragons were underneath it, jumping up and down excitedly and flaming.

'Er . . . good morning,' said the hanging figure.

'Turned out nice again,' said Vimes, picking up a bucket of coal. 'Although the fog will be back later, I expect.'

He took a small nugget and tossed it to the dragons. They squabbled for it.

Vimes gripped another lump. The young dragon that had caught the coal already had a distinctly longer and hotter flame.

'I suppose,' said the young man, 'that I could not prevail upon you to let me down?'

Another dragon caught some coal and belched a fireball. The young man swung desperately to avoid it.

'Guess,' said Vimes.

'I suspect, on reflection, that it was foolish of me to choose the roof,' said the assassin.

'Probably,' said Vimes. He'd spent several hours a few weeks ago sawing through joists and carefully balancing the roof tiles.

'I should have dropped off the wall and used the shrubbery.'

'Possibly,' said Vimes. He'd set a bear-trap in the shrubbery.

He took some more coal. 'I suppose you wouldn't tell me who hired you?'

'I'm afraid not, sir. You know the rules.'

Vimes nodded gravely. 'We had Lady Selachii's son up before the Patrician last week,' said Vimes. 'Now, *there*'s a lad who needs to learn that "no" doesn't mean "yes, please".'

'Could be, sir.'

'And then there was that business with Lord Rust's boy. You can't shoot servants for putting your shoes the wrong way round, you know. It's too messy. He'll have to learn right from left like the rest of us. And right from wrong, too.'

'I hear what you say, sir.'

'We seem to have reached an impasse,' said Vimes.

'It seems so, sir.'

Vimes aimed a lump at a small bronze and green dragon, which caught it expertly. The heat was getting intense.

'What I don't understand,' he said, 'is why you fellows mainly try it here or at the office. I mean, I walk around a lot, don't I? You could shoot me down in the street, couldn't you?'

'What? Like some common murderer, sir?'

Vimes nodded. It was black and twisted, but the Assassins' Guild had honour of a sort. 'How much was I worth?'

'Twenty thousand, sir.'

'It should be higher,' said Vimes.

'I agree.' If the assassin got back to the guild it would be, Vimes thought. Assassins valued their own lives quite highly.

'Let me see now,' said Vimes, examining the end of his cigar. 'Guild takes fifty per cent. That leaves ten thousand dollars.'

The assassin seemed to consider this, and then reached up to his belt and tossed a bag rather clumsily towards Vimes, who caught it.

Vimes picked up his crossbow. 'It seems to me,' he said, 'that if a man were to be let go he might well make it to the door with no more than superficial burns. If he were fast. How fast are you?'

There was no answer.

'Of course, he'd have to be desperate,' said Vimes, wedging the crossbow on the feed table and taking a piece of cord out of his pocket. He lashed the cord to a nail and fastened the other end to the crossbow's string. Then, standing carefully to one side, he eased the trigger.

The string moved very slightly.

The assassin, watching him upside down, seemed to have stopped breathing.

Vimes puffed at his cigar until the end was an inferno. Then he took it out of his mouth and leaned it against the restraining cord so that it would have just a fraction of an inch to burn before the string began to smoulder.

'I'll leave the door unlocked,' he said. 'I've never been an unreasonable man. I shall watch your career with interest.'

He tossed the rest of the coals to the dragons, and stepped outside.

It looked like being another eventful day in Ankh-Morpork, and it had only just begun.

As Vimes reached the house he heard a whoosh, a click, and the sound of someone running very fast towards the ornamental lake. He smiled.

Willikins was waiting with his coat. 'Remember you have an appointment with his lordship at eleven, Sir Samuel.'

'Yes, yes,' said Vimes.

'And you are to go and see the Heralds at ten. Her ladyship was very explicit, sir. Her exact words were, "Tell him he's not to try to wriggle out of it again," sir.'

'Oh, very well.'

'And her ladyship said please to try not to upset anyone.'

'Tell her I'll try.'

'And your sedan chair is outside, sir.'

Vimes sighed. 'Thank you. There's a man in the ornamental lake. Fish him out and give him a cup of tea, will you? Promising lad, I thought.'

'Certainly, sir.'

The chair. Oh, yes, the chair. It had been a wedding present from the Patrician. Lord Vetinari knew that Vimes loved walking the streets of the city, and so it was very typical of the man that he presented him with something that did not allow him to do so.

It was waiting outside. The two bearers straightened up expectantly.

Sir Samuel Vimes, Commander of the City Watch, rebelled again. Perhaps he *did* have to use the damn thing, but . . .

He looked at the front man and motioned with a thumb to the chair's door. 'Get in,' he commanded.

'But sir—'

'It's a nice morning,' said Vimes, taking off his coat again. 'I'll drive myself.'

'Dearest Mumm & Dad . . .'

Captain Carrot of the Ankh-Morpork City Watch was on his day off. He had a routine. First he had breakfast in some handy café. Then he wrote his letter home. Letters home always gave him some trouble. Letters *from* his parents were always interesting, being full of mining statistics and exciting news about new shafts and promising seams. All *he* had to write about were murders and such things as that.

He chewed the end of his pencil for a moment.

Well, it has been an intresting week again [he wrote]. I am running around like a flye with a blue bottom and No Mistake! We are opening another Watch House at Chittling Street which is handy for the Shades, so now we have no Less than 4 including Dolly Sisters and Long Wall, and I am the only Captain so I am around at all hours. Persnally I sometimes mifs the cameraderry of the old days when it was just me and Nobby and Sergeant Colon but this is the Century of the Fruitbat. Sergeant Colon is going to retire at the end of the month, he says Mrs Colon wants him to buy a farm, he says he is looking forward to the peace of the country and being Close to Nature, I'm sure you would wish him well. My friend Nobby is still Nobby only more than he was.

Carrot absent-mindedly took a half-eaten mutton chop from his breakfast plate and held it out below the table. There was an *unk*.

Anyway, back to the jobb, also I am sure I have told you about the Cable Street Particulars, although they are still based in Pseudopolis Yard, people do not like it when Watchmen do not wear uniforms but Commander Vimes says criminals dont wear uniforms either so be d*mned to the lot of them.

Carrot paused. It said a lot about Captain Carrot that, even after almost two years in Ankh-Morpork, he was still uneasy about 'd*mned'.

Commander Vimes says you have to have secret policemen because there are secret crimes . . .

Carrot paused again. He loved his uniform. He didn't have any other clothes. The idea of Watchmen in disguise *was* . . . well, it was unthinkable. It was like those pirates who sailed under false colours. It was like spies. However, he went on dutifully:

. . . and Commander Vimes knows what he is talking about I am sure. He says it's not like old fashioned police work which was catching the poor devils too stupid to run away!! Anyhow it all means a lot more work and new faces in the Watch.

While he waited for a new sentence to form, Carrot took a sausage from his plate and lowered it.

There was another *unk*.

The waiter bustled up.

'Another helping, Mr Carrot? On the house.' Every restaurant and eatery in Ankh-Morpork offered free food to Carrot, in the certain and happy knowledge that he would always insist on paying.

'No, indeed, that was very good. Here we are . . . twenty pence and keep the change,' said Carrot.

'How's your young lady? Haven't seen her today.'

'Angua? Oh, she's . . . around and about, you know. I shall definitely tell her you asked after her, though.'

The dwarf nodded happily, and bustled off.

Carrot wrote another few dutiful lines and then said, very softly, 'Is that horse and cart still outside Ironcrust's bakery?'

There was a whine from under the table.

'Really? That's odd. All the deliveries were over hours ago and the flour and grit doesn't usually arrive until the afternoon. Driver still sitting there?'

Something barked, quietly.

'And that looks quite a good horse for a delivery cart. And, you know, normally you'd expect the driver to put a nosebag on. And it's the last Thursday in the month. Which is payday at Ironcrust's.' Carrot laid down his pencil and waved a hand politely to catch the waiter's eye.

'Cup of acorn coffee, Mr Gimlet? To take away?'

In the Dwarf Bread Museum, in Whirligig Alley, Mr Hopkinson the curator was somewhat excited. Apart from other consider-

526

ations, he'd just been murdered. But at the moment he was choosing to consider this as an annoying background detail.

He'd been beaten to death with a loaf of bread. This is unlikely even in the worst of human bakeries, but dwarf bread has amazing properties as a weapon of offence. Dwarfs regard baking as part of the art of warfare. When they make rock cakes, no simile is intended.

'Look at this dent here,' said Hopkinson. 'It's quite *ruined* the crust!'

AND YOUR SKULL TOO, said Death.

'Oh, yes,' said Hopkinson, in the voice of one who regards skulls as ten a penny but is well aware of the rarity value of a good bread exhibit. 'But what was wrong with a simple cosh? Or even a hammer? I could have provided one if asked.'

Death, who was by nature an obsessive personality himself, realized that he was in the presence of a master. The late Mr Hopkinson had a squeaky voice and wore his spectacles on a length of black tape – his ghost now wore their spiritual counterpart – and these were always the signs of a mind that polished the undersides of furniture and stored paperclips by size.

'It really is too bad,' said Mr Hopkinson. 'And ungrateful, too, after the help I gave them with the oven. I really feel I shall have to complain.'

MR HOPKINSON, ARE YOU FULLY AWARE THAT YOU ARE DEAD?

'Dead?' trilled the curator. 'Oh, no. I can't possibly be dead. Not at the moment. It's simply not convenient. I haven't even catalogued the combat muffins.'

NEVERTHELESS.

'No, no. I'm sorry, but it just won't do. You will have to wait. I really cannot be bothered with that sort of nonsense.'

Death was nonplussed. Most people were, after the initial confusion, somewhat relieved when they died. A subconscious weight had been removed. The other cosmic shoe had dropped. The worst had happened and they could, metaphorically, get on with their lives. Few people treated it as a simple annoyance that might go away if you complained enough.

Mr Hopkinson's hand went through a tabletop. 'Oh.'

YOU SEE?

'This is most uncalled-for. Couldn't you have arranged a less awkward time?'

ONLY BY CONSULTATION WITH YOUR MURDERER.

'It all seems very badly organized. I wish to make a complaint. I pay my taxes, after all.'

I AM DEATH, NOT TAXES. *I* TURN UP ONLY ONCE.

The shade of Mr Hopkinson began to fade. 'It's simply that I've always tried to plan ahead in a sensible way . . .'

I FIND THE BEST APPROACH IS TO TAKE LIFE AS IT COMES.

'That seems very irresponsible . . .'

IT'S ALWAYS WORKED FOR ME.

The sedan chair came to a halt outside Pseudopolis Yard. Vimes left the runners to park it and strode in, putting his coat back on.

There had been a time, and it seemed like only yesterday, when the Watch House had been almost empty. There'd be old Sergeant Colon dozing in his chair, and Corporal Nobbs's washing drying in front of the stove. And then suddenly it had all changed . . .

Sergeant Colon was waiting for him with a clipboard. 'Got the reports from the other Watch Houses, sir,' he said, trotting along beside Vimes.

'Anything special?'

'Bin a bit of an odd murder, sir. Down in one of them old houses on Misbegot Bridge. Some old priest. Dunno much about it. The patrol just said it ought to be looked at.'

'Who found him?'

'Constable Visit, sir.'

'Oh, gods.'

'Yessir.'

'I'll try to get along there this morning. Anything else?'

'Corporal Nobbs is sick, sir.'

'Oh, I know *that*.'

'I mean *off* sick, sir.'

'Not his granny's funeral this time?'

'Nossir.'

'How many's he had this year, by the way?'

'Seven, sir.'

'Very odd family, the Nobbses.'

'Yessir.'

'Fred, you don't have to keep calling me "sir".'

'Got comp'ny, sir,' said the sergeant, glancing meaningfully towards a bench in the main office. 'Come for that alchemy job.'

A dwarf smiled nervously at Vimes.

'All right,' said Vimes. 'I'll see him in my office.' He reached into his coat and took out the assassin's money pouch. 'Put it in the Widows and Orphans Fund, will you, Fred?'

'Right. Oh, well done, sir. Any more windfalls like this and we'll soon be able to afford some more widows.'

Sergeant Colon went back to his desk, surreptitiously opened his drawer and pulled out the book he was reading. It was called *Animal Husbandry*. He'd been a bit worried about the title – you heard stories about strange folk in the country – but it turned out to be nothing more than a book about how cattle and pigs and sheep should breed.

Now he was wondering where to get a book that taught them how to read.

Upstairs, Vimes pushed open his office door carefully. The Assassins' Guild played to rules. You could say that about the bastards. It was terribly bad form to kill a bystander. Apart from anything else, you wouldn't get paid. So traps in his office were out of the question, because too many people were in and out of it every day. Even so, it paid to be careful. Vimes *was* good at making the kind of rich enemies who could afford to employ assassins. The assassins had to be lucky only once, but Vimes had to be lucky all the time.

He slipped into the room and glanced out of the window. He liked to work with it open, even in cold weather. He liked to hear the sounds of the city. But anyone trying to climb up or down to it would run into everything in the way of loose tiles, shifting handholds and treacherous drainpipes that Vimes's ingenuity could contrive. And Vimes had installed spiked railings down below. They were nice and ornamental but they were, above all, spiky.

So far, Vimes was winning.

There was a tentative knock at the door.

It had issued from the knuckles of the dwarf applicant. Vimes ushered him into the office, shut the door, and sat down at his desk.

'So,' he said. 'You're an alchemist. Acid stains on your hands and no eyebrows.'

'That's right, sir.'

'Not usual to find a dwarf in that line of work. You people always seem to toil in your uncle's foundry or something.'

You people, the dwarf noted. 'Can't get the hang of metal,' he said.

'A dwarf who can't get the hang of metal? That must be unique.'

'Pretty rare, sir. But I was quite good at alchemy.'

'Guild member?'

'Not any more, sir.'

'Oh? How did you leave the guild?'

'Through the roof, sir. But I'm pretty certain I know what I did wrong.'

Vimes leaned back. 'The alchemists are always blowing things up. I never heard of them getting sacked for it.'

'That's because no one's ever blown up the Guild Council, sir.'

'What, *all* of it?'

'Most of it, sir. All the easily detachable bits, at least.'

Vimes found he was automatically opening the bottom drawer of his desk. He pushed it shut again and, instead, shuffled the papers in front of him. 'What's your name, lad?'

The dwarf swallowed. This was clearly the bit he'd been dreading. 'Littlebottom, sir.'

Vimes didn't even look up.

'Ah, yes. It says here. That means you're from the Uberwald mountain area, yes?'

'Why . . . yes, sir,' said Littlebottom, mildly surprised. Humans generally couldn't distinguish between dwarf clans.

'Our Constable Angua comes from there,' said Vimes. 'Now . . . it says here your first name is . . . can't read Fred's handwriting . . . er . . .'

There was nothing for it. 'Cheery, sir,' said Cheery Littlebottom.

'Cheery, eh? Good to see the old naming traditions kept up. Cheery Littlebottom. Fine.'

Littlebottom watched carefully. Not the faintest glimmer of amusement had crossed Vimes's face.

'Yes, sir. Cheery Littlebottom,' he said. And there still wasn't as much as an extra wrinkle there. 'My father was Jolly. Jolly Littlebottom,' he added, as one might prod at a bad tooth to see when the pain will come.

'Really?'

'And . . . *his* father was Beaky Littlebottom.'

Not a trace, not a smidgeon of a grin twitched anywhere. Vimes merely pushed the paper aside.

'Well, we work for a living here, Littlebottom.'

'Yes, sir.'

'We don't blow things up, Littlebottom.'

'No, sir. I don't blow *everything* up, sir. Some just melts.'

Vimes drummed his fingers on the desk. 'Know anything about dead bodies?'

'They were only mildly concussed, sir.'

Vimes sighed. 'Listen. I know about how to be a copper. It's mainly walking and talking. But there's lots of things I don't know. You find the scene of a crime and there's some grey powder on the floor. What is it? *I* don't know. But you fellows know how to mix things up in bowls and can find out. And maybe the dead person doesn't seem to have a mark on them. Were they poisoned? It seems we need someone who knows what colour a liver is supposed to be. I want someone who can look at the ashtray and tell me what kind of cigars I smoke.'

'Pantweed's Slim Panatellas,' said Littlebottom automatically.

'Good gods!'

'You've left the packet on the table, sir.'

Vimes looked down. 'All right,' he said. 'So sometimes it's an easy answer. But sometimes it isn't. Sometimes we don't even know if it was the right question.'

He stood up. 'I can't say I like dwarfs much, Littlebottom. But I don't like trolls or humans either, so I suppose that's okay. Well, you're the only applicant. Thirty dollars a month, five dollars living-out allowance, I expect you to work to the job not the clock, there's some mythical creature called "overtime", only no one's even seen its footprints, if troll officers call you a gritsucker they're out, and if you call them rocks *you're* out, we're just one big family and, when you've been to a few domestic disputes, Littlebottom, I can assure you that you'll see the resemblance, we work as a team and we're pretty much making it up as we go along, and half the time we're not even certain what the law is, so it can get interesting, technically you'll rank as a corporal, only don't go giving orders to real policemen, you're on a month's trial, we'll give you some training just as soon as there's time, now, find an iconograph and meet me on Misbegot Bridge in . . . damn . . . better make it an hour. I've got to see about this blasted coat of arms. Still, dead bodies seldom get deader. Sergeant Detritus!'

There was a series of creaks as something heavy moved along the corridor outside and a troll opened the door.

'Yessir?'

'This is Corporal Littlebottom. Corporal Cheery Littlebottom, whose father was Jolly Littlebottom. Give him his badge, swear him in, show him where everything is. Very good, Corporal?'

'I shall try to be a credit to the uniform, sir,' said Littlebottom.

'Good,' said Vimes briskly. He looked at Detritus. 'Incidentally, Sergeant, I've got a report here that a troll in uniform nailed one of Chrysoprase's henchmen to a wall by his ears last night. Know anything about that?'

The troll wrinkled its enormous forehead. 'Does it say anything 'bout him selling bags of Slab to troll kids?'

'No. It says he was going to read spiritual literature to his dear old mother,' said Vimes.

'Did Hardcore say he saw dis troll's badge?'

'No, but he says the troll threatened to ram it where the sun doesn't shine,' said Vimes.

Detritus nodded gravely. 'Dat's a long way to go just to ruin a good badge,' he said.

'By the way,' said Vimes, 'that was a lucky guess of yours, guessing that it was Hardcore.'

'It come to me in a flash, sir,' said Detritus. 'I fort: what bastard who sells Slab to kids deserves bein' nailed up by his ears, sir, and . . . bingo. Dis idea just formed in my head.'

'That's what I thought.'

Cheery Littlebottom looked from one impassive face to the other. The Watchmen's eyes never left each other's face, but the words seemed to come from a little distance, as though both of them were reading an invisible script.

Then Detritus shook his head slowly. 'Musta been a impostor, sir. 'S easy to get helmets like ours. None of my trolls'd do anything like dat. Dat would be police brutality, sir.'

'Glad to hear it. Just for the look of the thing, though, I want you to check the trolls' lockers. The Silicon Anti-Defamation League are on to this one.'

'Yes, sir. An' if I find out it was one of my trolls I will be down on dat troll like a ton of rectang'lar buildin' things, sir.'

'Fine. Well, off you go, Littlebottom. Detritus will look after you.'

Littlebottom hesitated. This was uncanny. The man hadn't mentioned axes, or gold. He hadn't even said anything like 'You can make it big in the Watch'. Littlebottom felt really unbalanced.

'Er . . . I *did* tell you my name, didn't I, sir?'

'Yes. Got it down here,' said Vimes. 'Cheery Littlebottom. Yes?'

'Er . . . yes. That's right. Well, thank you, sir.'

Vimes listened to them go down the passage. Then he carefully shut the door and put his coat over his head so that no one would hear him laughing.

'Cheery Littlebottom!'

Cheery ran after the troll called Detritus. The Watch House was beginning to fill up. And it was clear that the Watch dealt with all *sorts* of things, and that many of them involved shouting.

Two uniformed trolls were standing in front of Sergeant Colon's high desk, with a slightly smaller troll between them. This troll was wearing a downcast expression. It was also wearing a tutu and had a small pair of gauze wings glued to its back.

'—happen to know that trolls don't have *any* tradition of a Tooth Fairy,' Colon was saying. 'Especially not one called' – he looked down – 'Clinkerbell. So how about it we just call it breaking and entering without a Thieves' Guild licence?'

'Is racial prejudice, not letting trolls have a Tooth Fairy,' Clink-erbell muttered.

One of the troll guards upended a sack on the desk. Various items of silverware cascaded over the paperwork.

'And this is what you found under their pillows, was it?' said Colon.

'Bless dere little hearts,' said Clinkerbell.

At the next desk a tired dwarf was arguing with a vampire. 'Look,' he said, 'it's *not* murder. You're dead already, right?'

'He stuck them right in me!'

'Well, I've been down to interview the manager and he said it was an accident. He said he's got nothing against vampires at all. He says he was merely carrying three boxes of HB Eraser Tips and tripped over the edge of your cloak.'

'I don't see why I can't work where I like!'

'Yes, but . . . in a pencil factory?'

Detritus looked down at Littlebottom and grinned. 'Welcome to life in der big city, Littlebottom,' he said. 'Dat's an int'restin' name.'

'Is it?'

'Most dwarfs have names like Rockheaver or Stronginthearm.'

'Do they?'

Detritus was not one for the fine detail of relationships, but the edge in Littlebottom's voice got through to him. ''s a good name, though,' he said.

'What's Slab?' said Cheery.

'It are chloric ammonium an' radium mixed up. It give your head a tingle but melts troll brains. Big problem in der mountains and some buggers are makin' it here in der city and we tryin' to find how it get up dere. Mr Vimes is lettin' me run a' – Detritus concentrated – 'pub-lic a-ware-ness campaign tellin' people what happens to buggers who sells it to kids . . .' He waved a hand at a large and rather crudely done poster on the wall. It said:

Slab: Jus' say 'AarrghaarrghpleeassennononoUGH'.

He pushed open a door.

'Dis is der ole privy wot we don't use no more, you can use it for mixin' up stuff, it the only place we got now, you have to clean it up first 'cos it smells like a toilet in here.'

He opened another door. 'And this der locker room,' he said. 'You got your own peg and dat, and dere's dese panels for getting changed behind 'cos we knows you dwarfs is modest. It a good life if you don't weaken. Mr Vimes is okay but he a bit weird about some stuff, he keepin' on sayin' stuff like dis city is a meltin' pot an' all der scum floats to der top, and stuff like dat. I'll give you your helmet an' badge in a minute but first' – he opened a rather larger locker on the other side of the room, which had 'DTRiTUS' painted on it – 'I got to go and hide dis hammer.'

Two figures hurried out of Ironcrust's Dwarf Bakery ('T'Bread Wi' T'Edge'), threw themselves on to the cart and shouted at the driver to leave urgently.

He turned a pale face towards them and pointed to the road ahead.

There was a wolf there.

Not a usual kind of wolf. It had a blond coat, which around its ears was almost long enough to be a mane. And wolves did not normally sit calmly on their haunches in the middle of a street.

This one was growling. A long, low growl. It was the audible equivalent of a shortening fuse.

The horse was transfixed, too frightened to stay where it was but far too terrified to move.

One of the men carefully reached for a crossbow. The growl rose slightly. He even more carefully took his hand away. The growl subsided again.

'What is it?'

'It's a wolf!'

'In a city? What does it find to eat?'

'Oh, *why* did you have to ask that?'

'*Good* morning, gentlemen!' said Carrot, as he stopped leaning against the wall. 'Looks like the fog's rising again. Thieves' Guild licences, please?'

They turned. Carrot gave them a happy smile and nodded encouragingly.

One of the men patted his coat in a theatrical display of absent-mindedness.

'Ah. Well. Er. Left the house in a bit of a hurry this morning, must've forgotten—'

'Section Two, Rule One of the Thieves' Guild Charter says that members must carry their cards on all professional occasions,' said Carrot.

'He's not even drawn his sword!' hissed the most stupid of the three-strong gang.

'He doesn't need to, he's got a loaded wolf.'

Someone was writing in the gloom, the scritching of their pen the only sound.

Until a door creaked open.

The writer turned as quick as a bird. 'You? I told you never to come back here!'

'I know, I know, but it's that damn *thing*! The production line stopped and it got out and it's killed that priest!'

'Did anyone see it?'

'In the fog we had last night? I shouldn't think so. But—'

'Then it is not, ah-ha, a matter of significance.'

'No? They're not supposed to *kill* people. Well . . . that is,' the speaker conceded, 'not by smashing them on the head, anyway.'

'They will if so instructed.'

'I never told it to! Anyway, what if it turns on me?'

'On its master? It can't disobey the words in its head, man.'

The visitor sat down, shaking his head. 'Yeah, but which words? I don't know, I don't know, this is getting too much, that damn thing around all the time—'

'Making you a fat profit—'

'All right, all right, but this other stuff, the poison, I never—'

'Shut up! I'll see you again tonight. You can tell the others that I certainly do have a candidate. And if you dare come here again . . .'

The Ankh-Morpork Royal College of Heralds turned out to be a green gate in a wall in Mollymog Street. Vimes tugged on the bell-pull. Something clanged on the other side of the wall and immediately the place erupted in a cacophony of hoots, growls, whistles and trumpetings.

A voice shouted, 'Down, boy! Couchant! I said couchant! No! *Not* rampant! And thee shall have a sugar lump like a good boy. William! Stop that at once! Put him down! Mildred, let go of Graham!'

The animal noises subsided a bit and footsteps approached. A wicket gate in the main door opened a fraction.

Vimes saw an inch-wide segment of a very short man.

'Yes? Are you the meat man?'

'Commander Vimes,' said Vimes. 'I have an appointment.'

The animal noises started up again.

'Eh?'

'*Commander Vimes!*' Vimes shouted.

'Oh. I suppose thee'd better come in.'

The door swung open. Vimes stepped through.

Silence fell. Several dozen pairs of eyes regarded Vimes with acute suspicion. Some of the eyes were small and red. Several were big and poked just above the surface of the scummy pond that occupied a lot of space in the yard. Some were on perches.

The yard was *full* of animals, but even they were crowded out by the *smell* of a yard full of animals. And most of them were clearly very old, which didn't do anything for the smell.

A toothless lion yawned at Vimes. A lion running, or at least lounging around loose was amazing in itself, but not so amazing as the fact that it was being used as a cushion by an elderly gryphon, which was asleep with all four claws in the air.

There were hedgehogs, and a greying leopard, and moulting pelicans. Green water surged in the pond and a couple of hippos surfaced and yawned. Nothing was in a cage, and nothing was trying to eat anything else.

'Ah, it takes people like that, first time,' said the old man. He had a wooden leg. 'We're quite a happy little family.'

Vimes turned and found himself looking at a small owl. 'My gods,' he said. 'That's a morpork, isn't it?'

The old man's face broke into a happy smile. 'Ah, I can see thee knows thy heraldry,' he cackled. 'Daphne's ancestors came all the way from some islands on the other side of the Hub, so they did.'

Vimes took out his City Watch badge and stared at the coat of arms embossed thereon.

The old man looked over his shoulder. 'That's not her, o' course,' he said, indicating the owl perched on the Ankh. 'That was her great-grandma, Olive. A morpork on an ankh, see? That is a pune or play on words. Laugh? I nearly started. That's about as funny as you gets round here. We could do with a mate for her, tell you the truth. And a female hippo. I mean, his lordship says we've *got* two hippos, which is right enough, I'm just saying it's not natural for Roderick and Keith, I ain't passing judgement, it's just not right, that's all I'm saying. What was thy name again?'

'Vimes. Sir Samuel Vimes. My wife made the appointment.'

The old man cackled again. 'Ah, 'tis usually so.'

Moving quite fast despite his wooden leg, the old man led the way through the steaming mounds of multi-species dung to the building on the other side of the yard.

'I expect this is good for the garden, anyway,' said Vimes, trying to make conversation.

'I tried it on my rhubarb,' said the old man, pushing open the door. 'But it grew to twenty feet tall, sir, and then spontaneously caught fire. Mind where the wyvern's been, sir, he's been ill – oh, what a shame. Never mind, it'll scrape off beautiful when it dries. In thee goes, sir.'

The hall inside was as quiet and dark as the yard had been full of light and noise. There was the dry, tombstone smell of old books and church towers. Above him, when his eyes got used to the darkness, Vimes could make out hanging flags and banners. There were a few windows, but cobwebs and dead flies meant that the light they allowed in was merely grey.

The old man had shut the door and left him alone. Vimes watched through the window as he limped back to continue what he had been doing before Vimes's appearance.

What he had been doing was setting up a living coat of arms.

There was a large shield. Cabbages, actual cabbages, had been nailed to it. The old man said something that Vimes couldn't hear. The little owl fluttered from its perch and landed on a large ankh that had been glued to the top of the shield. The two hippos flopped out of their pool and took up station on either side.

The old man unfolded an easel in front of the scene, placed a canvas on it, picked up a palette and brush, and shouted, 'Hup-la!'

The hippos reared, rather arthritically. The owl spread its wings.

'Good gods,' murmured Vimes. 'I always thought they just made it up!'

'Made it up, sir? Made it up?' said a voice behind him. 'We'd soon be in trouble if we made things up, oh dear me, yes.'

Vimes turned. Another little old man had appeared behind him, blinking happily through thick glasses. He had several scrolls under one arm.

'I'm sorry I couldn't meet you at the gate but we're very busy at the moment,' he said, holding out his spare hand. 'Croissant Rouge Pursuivant.'

'Er . . . you're a small red breakfast roll?' said Vimes, nonplussed.

'No, no. No. It means Red Crescent. It's my title, you see. Very ancient title. I'm a Herald. You'd be Sir Samuel Vimes, yes?'

'Yes.'

Red Crescent consulted a scroll. 'Good. Good. How do you feel about weasels?' he said.

'Weasels?'

'We have got some weasels, you see. I know they're not *strictly* a heraldic animal, but we seem to have some on the strength and frankly I think I'm going to have to let them go unless we can persuade someone to adopt them, and that'd upset Pardessus Chatain Pursuivant. He always locks himself in his shed when he's upset . . .'

'Pardessus . . . you mean the old man out there?' said Vimes. 'I mean . . . why's he . . . I thought you . . . I mean, a coat of arms is just a design. You don't have to paint it from life!'

Red Crescent looked shocked. 'Well, I suppose if you want to make a complete mockery of the whole thing, yes, you could just *make it up*. You could do that,' he said. 'Anyway . . . not weasels, then?'

'Personally I'd just as soon not bother,' said Vimes. 'And certainly not with a weasel. My wife said that dragons would—'

'Happily, the occasion will not arise,' said a voice in the shadows.

It wasn't the right sort of voice to hear in any kind of light. It was dust-dry. It sounded as if it came from a mouth that had never known the pleasures of spittle. It sounded dead.

It was.

The bakery thieves considered their options.

'I've got my hand on my crossbow,' said the most enterprising of the three.

The most realistic said, 'Have you? Well, I've got my heart in my mouth.'

'Ooo,' said the third. 'I've got a weak heart, me . . .'

'Yeah, but what I mean is . . . he's not even *wearing* a sword. If I take the wolf, the two of you should be able to deal with him with *no* trouble, right?'

The one clear thinker looked at Captain Carrot. His armour shone. So did the muscles on his bare arms. Even his *knees* gleamed.

'It seems to me that we have a bit of an impasse, or stand-off,' said Captain Carrot.

'How about if we throw down the money?' said the clear thinker.

'That would certainly help matters.'

'And you'd let us go?'

'No. But it would definitely count in your favour and I would certainly speak up on your behalf.'

The bold one with the crossbow licked his lips and glanced from Carrot to the wolf. 'If you set it on us, I warn you, someone's going to get killed!' he warned.

'Yes, it could happen,' said Carrot, sadly. 'I'd prefer to avoid that, if at all possible.'

He raised his hands. There was something flat and round and about six inches across in each one. 'This,' he said, 'is dwarf bread. Some of Mr Ironcrust's best. It's not classic battle bread, of course, but it's probably good enough for slicing . . .'

Carrot's arm blurred. There was a brief flurry of sawdust, and the flat loaf spun to a stop halfway through the thick timbers of the cart and about half an inch away from the man with the weak heart and, as it turned out, a fragile bladder, too.

The man with the crossbow tore his attention away from the bread only when he felt a slight, damp pressure on his wrist.

There was no way that an animal could have moved that fast, but there it was, and the wolf's expression contrived to indicate very calmly that if the animal so desired the pressure could be increased more or less indefinitely.

'Call it off!' he said, flinging the bow away with his free hand. 'Tell it to let go!'

'Oh, I never tell her anything,' said Carrot. 'She makes up her own mind.'

There was a clatter of iron-shod boots and half a dozen axe-bearing dwarfs raced out of the bakery gates, kicking up sparks as they skidded to a halt beside Carrot.

'Get them!' shouted Mr Ironcrust. Carrot dropped a hand on top of the dwarf's helmet and turned him around.

'It's me, Mr Ironcrust,' he said. 'I believe these are the men?'

'Right you are, Captain Carrot!' said the dwarf baker. 'C'mon, lads! Let's hang 'em up by the *bura'zak-ka!**'

'Ooo,' murmured the weak of heart, damply.

'Now, now, Mr Ironcrust,' said Carrot patiently. 'We don't practise that punishment in Ankh-Morpork.†'

'They bashed Bjorn Tightbritches senseless! *And* they kicked Olaf Stronginthearm in the *bad'dhakz*!‡ We'll cut their—'

'Mr Ironcrust!'

The dwarf baker hesitated and then, to the amazement and relief of the thieves, took a step backwards. 'Yeah . . . all right, Captain Carrot. If you say so.'

'I have business elsewhere, but I would be grateful if you would take them and turn them over to the Thieves' Guild,' said Carrot.

The quick thinker went pale. 'Oh, no! They get really *intense* about unlicensed thieving! *Anything* but the Thieves' Guild!'

Carrot turned. The light caught his face in a certain way. 'Anything?' he said.

The unlicensed thieves looked at one another, and then all spoke at once.

'The Thieves' Guild. Fine. No problem.'

'We *like* the Thieves' Guild.'

'Can't wait. Thieves' Guild, here I come.'

'Fine body of men.'

'Firm but fair.'

---

* Town hall.

† Because Ankh-Morpork doesn't have a town hall.

‡ Yeast bowl.

'Good,' said Carrot. 'Then everyone's happy. Oh, yes.' He dug into his money pouch. 'Here's five pence for the loaf, Mr Ironcrust. I've handled the other one, but you should be able to sand it off with no trouble.'

The dwarf blinked at the coins. '*You* want to pay *me* for saving *my* money?' he said.

'As a tax payer you are entitled to the protection of the Watch,' said Carrot.

There was a delicate pause. Mr Ironcrust stared at his feet. One or two of the other dwarfs started to snigger.

'I'll tell you what,' said Carrot, in a kindly voice, 'I'll come round when I get a moment and help you fill in the forms, how about that?'

A thief broke the embarrassed silence.

'Er . . . could your . . . little dog . . . let go of my arm, please?'

The wolf released its grip, jumped down and padded over to Carrot, who raised his hand to his helmet respectfully.

'Good day to you all,' he said, and strode away.

Thieves and victims watched him go.

'Is he *real*?' said the quick thinker.

There was a growl from the baker, then 'You bastards!' he shouted. 'You *bastards*!'

'Wha . . . what? You've got the money back, haven't you?'

Two of his employees had to hold Mr Ironcrust back.

'Three years!' he said. 'Three years and no one bothered! Three bloody years and not so much as a knock at the door! And he'll ask me! Oh, yes! He'll be *nice* about it! He'll probably even go and get the extra forms so I won't be put to the trouble! Why couldn't you buggers have just run away?'

Vimes peered around the shadowy, musty room. The voice might as well have come from a tomb.

A panicky look crossed the face of the little Herald. 'Perhaps Sir Samuel would be kind enough to step this way?' said the voice. It was chilly, clipping every syllable with precision. It was the kind of voice that didn't blink.

'That is, in fact, er . . . Dragon,' said Red Crescent.

Vimes reached for his sword.

'Dragon King of Arms,' said the man.

'*King* of Arms?' said Vimes.

'Merely a title,' said the voice. 'Pray enter.'

For some reason the words re-spelled themselves in Vimes's hindbrain as 'prey, enter'.

'King of Arms,' said the voice of Dragon, as Vimes passed into the shadows of the inner sanctum. 'You will not need your sword, Commander. I have been Dragon King of Arms for more than five hundred years but I do not breathe fire, I assure you. Ah-ha. Ah-ha.'

'Ah-ha,' said Vimes. He couldn't see the figure clearly. The light came from a few high and grubby windows, and several dozen candles that burned with black-edged flames. There was a suggestion of hunched shoulders in the shape before him.

'Pray be seated,' said Dragon King of Arms. 'And I would be most indebted if you would look to your left and raise your chin.'

'And expose my neck, you mean?' said Vimes.

'Ah-ha. Ah-ha.'

The figure picked up a candelabrum and moved closer. A hand so skinny as to be skeletal gripped Vimes's chin and moved it gently this way and that.

'Ah, yes. You have the Vimes profile, certainly. But not the Vimes ears. Of course, your maternal grandmother was a Clamp. Ah-ha . . .'

The Vimes hand gripped the Vimes sword again. There was only one type of person that had that much strength in a body so apparently frail.

'I *thought* so! You *are* a vampire!' he said. 'You're a bloody *vampire*.'

'Ah-ha.' It might have been a laugh. It might have been a cough. 'Yes. Vampire, indeed. Yes, I've heard about your views on vampires. "Not really alive but not dead enough," I believe you have said. I think that is rather clever. Ah-ha. Vampire, yes. *Bloody*, no. Black puddings, yes. The acme of the butcher's art, yes. And if all else fails there are plenty of kosher butchers down in Long Hogmeat. Ah-ha, yes. We all live in the best way we can. Ah-ha. Virgins are safe from me. Ah-ha. For several hundred years, more's the pity. Ah-ha.'

The shape, and the pool of candlelight, moved away.

'I'm afraid your time has been needlessly wasted, Commander Vimes.'

Vimes's eyes were growing accustomed to the flickering light. The room was full of books, in piles. None of them were on shelves. Each one sprouted bookmarks like squashed fingers.

'I don't understand,' he said. Either Dragon King of Arms had very hunched shoulders or there were wings under his shapeless robe. Some of them could fly like a bat, Vimes recalled. He wondered how old this one was. They could 'live' almost forever . . .

'I believe you're here because it is considered, ah-ha, appropriate that you have a coat of arms. I am afraid that this is not possible. Ah-ha. A Vimes coat of arms *has* existed, but it cannot be resurrected. It would be against the rules.'

'What rules?'

There was a thump as a book was taken down and opened.

'I'm sure you know your ancestry, Commander. Your father was Thomas Vimes, his father was Gwilliam Vimes—'

'It's Old Stoneface, isn't it,' said Vimes flatly. 'It's something to do with Old Stoneface.'

'Indeed. Ah-ha. Suffer-Not-Injustice Vimes. Your ancestor. Old Stoneface, indeed, as he was called. Commander of the City Watch in 1688. And a regicide. He murdered the last king of Ankh-Morpork, as every schoolboy knows.'

'Executed!'

The shoulders shrugged. 'Nevertheless, the family crest was, as we say in heraldry, *Excretus Est Ex Altitudine*. That is to say, *Depositatum De Latrina*. Destroyed. Banned. Made incapable of resurrection. Lands confiscated, house pulled down, page torn out of history. Ah-ha. You know, Commander, it is interesting that so many of, ah-ha, "Old Stoneface's" descendants' – the inverted commas dropped neatly around the nickname like an old lady carefully picking up something nasty in a pair of tongs – 'have been officers of the Watch. I believe, Commander, that you too have acquired the nickname. Ah-ha. Ah-ha. I have wondered whether there is some inherited urge to expunge the infamy. Ah-ha.'

Vimes gritted his teeth. 'Are you telling me I *can't* have a coat of arms?'

'This is so. Ah-ha.'

'Because my ancestor killed a—' He paused. 'No, it wasn't even execution,' he said. 'You execute a human being. You *slaughter* an animal.'

'He was the king,' said Dragon mildly.

'Oh, yes. And it turned out that down in the dungeons he had machines for—'

'Commander,' said the vampire, holding up his hands, 'I feel you do not understand me. *Whatever else he was*, he was the king. You see, a crown is not like a Watchman's helmet, ah-ha. Even when you take it off, it's still on the head.'

'Stoneface took it off all right!'

'But the king did not even get a trial.'

'No willing judge could be found,' said Vimes.

'Except you . . . that is, your ancestor . . .'

'Well? Someone had to do it. Some monsters should not walk under the living sky.'

Dragon found the page he had been looking for and turned the book around. 'This was his escutcheon,' he said.

Vimes looked down at the familiar sign of the morpork owl perched on an ankh. It was atop a shield divided into four quarters, with a symbol in each quarter.

'What's this crown with a dagger through it?'

'Oh, a traditional symbol, ah-ha. Indicates his role as defender of the crown.'

'Really? And the bunch of rods with an axe in it?' He pointed.

'A fasces. Symbolizes that he is . . . *was* an officer of the law. And the axe was an interesting harbinger of things to come, yes? But axes, I'm afraid, solve nothing.'

Vimes stared at the third quarter. It contained a painting of what seemed to be a marble bust.

'Symbolizing his nickname, "Old Stoneface",' said Dragon helpfully. 'He asked that some reference be made. Sometimes heraldry is nothing more than the art of punning.'

'And this last one? A bunch of grapes? Bit of a boozer, was he?' said Vimes sourly.

'No. Ah-ha. Word play. Vimes = Vines.'

'Ah. The art of *bad* punning,' said Vimes. 'I bet that had you people rolling on the floor.'

Dragon shut the book and sighed. 'There is seldom a reward for those who do what must be done. Alas, such is precedent, and I am powerless.' The old voice brightened up. 'But, still . . . I was extremely pleased, Commander, to hear of your marriage to Lady Sybil. An *ex*cellent lineage. One of the most noble families in the city, ah-ha. The Ramkins, the Selachiis, the Venturis, the Nobbses, of course . . .'

'That's it, is it?' said Vimes. 'I just go now?'

'I seldom get visitors,' said Dragon. 'Generally people are seen by the Heralds, but I thought you should get a proper explanation. Ah-ha. We're so busy now. Once we dealt with *real* heraldry. But this, they tell me, is the Century of the Fruitbat. Now it seems that, as soon as a man opens his second meat-pie shop, he feels impelled to consider himself a gentleman.' He waved a thin white hand at three coats of arms pinned in a row on a board. 'The butcher, the baker and the candlestick-maker,' he sneered, but genteelly. 'Well, the candle-maker, in point of fact. Nothing will do but that we burrow through the records and prove them acceptably armigerous . . .'

Vimes glanced at the three shields. 'Haven't I seen that one before?' he said.

'Ah. Mr Arthur Carry the candle-maker,' said Dragon. 'Suddenly business is booming and he feels he must be a gentleman. A shield bisected by a bend sinister d'une mèche en metal gris – that is to say, a steel grey shield indicating his personal determination and zeal (how zealous, ah-ha, these businessmen are!) bisected by a wick. Upper half, a chandelle in a fenêtre avec rideaux houlant (a candle lighting a window with a warm glow, ah-ha), lower half two chandeliers illuminé (indicating the wretched man sells candles to rich and poor alike). Fortunately his father was a harbourmaster, which fact allowed us to *stretch* ourselves a little with a crest of a lampe au poisson (fish-shaped lamp), indicating both this and his son's current profession. The motto I left in the common modern tongue and is "Art Brought Forth the Candle". I'm sorry, ah-ha, it was naughty but I couldn't resist it.'

'My sides ache,' said Vimes. Something kicked his brain, trying to get attention.

'*This* one is for Mr Gerhardt Sock, president of the Butchers' Guild,' said Dragon. 'His wife's told him a coat of arms is the thing to have, and who are we to argue with the daughter of a tripe merchant, so we've made him a shield of red, for blood, and blue and white stripes, for a butcher's apron, bisected by a string of sausages, centralis a cleaver held in a gloved hand, a boxing glove, which is, ah-ha, the best we could do for "sock". Motto is *Futurus Meus est in Visceris*, which translates as "My Future is in (the) Entrails", both relating to his profession and, ah-ha, alluding to the old practice of telling—'

'—the future from entrails,' said Vimes. 'A-mazing.' Whatever was trying to get into his attention was really jumping up and down now.

'While this one, ah-ha, is for Rudolph Potts of the Bakers' Guild,' said Dragon, pointing to the third shield with a twig-thin finger. 'Can you read it, Commander?'

Vimes gave it a gloomy stare. 'Well, it's divided into three, and there's a rose, a flame and a pot,' he said. 'Er . . . bakers use fire and the pot's for water, I suppose . . .'

'And a pun on the name,' said Dragon.

'But, unless he's called Rosie, I . . .' Then Vimes blinked. 'A rose is a flower. Oh, good grief. Flower, flour. Flour, fire and water? The pot looks like a guzunder to me, though. A chamber pot?'

'The old word for baker was *pistor*,' said Dragon. 'Why, Commander, we shall make a Herald of you yet! And the motto?'

'*Quod Subigo Farinam*,' said Vimes, and wrinkled his forehead.

'"Because" . . . "farinaceous" means to do with corn, or flour, doesn't it? . . . oh, no . . . "Because I Knead the Dough"?'

Dragon clapped his hands. 'Well done, sir!'

'This place must simply rock on those long winter evenings,' said Vimes. 'And that's heraldry, is it? Crossword clues and plays on words?'

'Of course there is a great deal more,' said the Dragon. 'These are simple. We more or less have to make them up. Whereas the escutcheon of an old family, such as the Nobbses . . .'

'*Nobbs!*' said Vimes, as the penny dropped. 'That's it! You said "Nobbs"! Before – when you were talking about old families!'

'Ah-ha. What? Oh, indeed. Yes. Oh, yes. A fine old family. Although now, sadly, in decay.'

'You don't mean Nobbs as in . . . Corporal Nobbs?' said Vimes, horror edging his words.

A book thumped open. In the orange light Vimes had a vague upside-down glimpse of shields, and a rambling, unpruned family tree.

'My word. Would that be a C. W. St J. Nobbs?'

'Er . . . yes. Yes!'

'Son of Sconner Nobbs and a lady referred to here as Maisie of Elm Street?'

'Probably.'

'Grandson of Slope Nobbs?'

'That sounds about right.'

'Who was the illegitimate son of Edward St John de Nobbes, Earl of Ankh, and a, ah-ha, a parlourmaid of unknown lineage?'

'Good gods!'

'The earl died without issue, except that which, ah-ha, resulted in Slope. We had not been able to trace the scion – hitherto, at any rate.'

'Good gods!'

'You know the gentleman?'

Vimes regarded with amazement a serious and positive sentence about Corporal Nobbs that included the word 'gentleman'. 'Er . . . yes,' he said.

'Is he a man of property?'

'Only other people's.'

'Well, ah-ha, do tell him. There is no land or money now, of course, but the title is still extant.'

'Sorry . . . let me make sure I understand this. Corporal Nobbs . . . *my* Corporal Nobbs . . . is *the Earl of Ankh?*'

'He would have to satisfy us as to proof of his lineage but, yes, it would appear so.'

Vimes stared into the gloom. Thus far in his life, Corporal Nobbs would have been unlikely to satisfy the examiners as to his species.

'Good gods!' Vimes said yet again. 'And I suppose *he* gets a coat of arms?'

'A particularly fine one.'

'Oh.'

Vimes hadn't even *wanted* a coat of arms. An hour ago he'd have cheerfully avoided this appointment as he had done so many times before. But . . .

'Nobby?' he said. 'Good gods!'

'Well, well! This has been a *very* happy meeting,' said Dragon. 'I do so like to keep the records up to date. Ah-ha. Incidentally, how is young Captain Carrot getting along? I'm told his young lady is a werewolf. Ah-ha.'

'Really,' said Vimes.

'Ah-ha.' In the dark, Dragon made a movement that might have been a conspiratorial tap on the side of the nose. 'We know these things!'

'Captain Carrot is doing well,' said Vimes, as icily as he could manage. 'Captain Carrot always does well.'

He slammed the door when he went out. The candle flames wavered.

Constable Angua walked out of an alleyway, doing up her belt.

'That went very well, I thought,' said Carrot, 'and will go some way to earning us the respect of the community.'

'Pff! That man's sleeve! I doubt if he even knows the meaning of the word "laundry",' said Angua, wiping her mouth.

Automatically, they fell into step – the energy-saving policeman's walk, where the pendulum weight of the leg is used to propel the walker along with the minimum of effort. Walking was important, Vimes had always said, and because Vimes had said it Carrot believed it. Walking and talking. Walk far enough and talk to enough people and sooner or later you had an answer.

The respect of the community, thought Angua. That was a Carrot phrase. Well, in fact it was a Vimes phrase, although Sir Samuel usually spat after he said it. But Carrot *believed* it. It was Carrot who'd suggested to the Patrician that hardened criminals should be given the chance to 'serve the community' by redecorating the homes of the elderly, lending a new terror to old age and, given Ankh-Morpork's crime rate, leading to at least one old lady having her front room wallpapered so many times in six months that now she could only get into it sideways.*

'I've found something very interesting that you will be very interested to see,' said Carrot, after a while.

'That's interesting,' said Angua.

'But I'm not going to tell you what it is because I want it to be a surprise,' said Carrot.

'Oh. Good.'

Angua walked in thought for a while and then said: 'I wonder if it will be as surprising as the collection of rock samples you showed me last week?'

'That *was* good, wasn't it?' said Carrot enthusiastically. 'I've been along that street dozens of times and never suspected there was a mineral museum there! All those silicates!'

'Amazing! You'd imagine people would be flocking to it, wouldn't you?'

'Yes, I can't think why they don't!'

Angua reminded herself that Carrot appeared to have in his soul not even a trace element of irony. She told herself that it wasn't his fault he'd been brought up by dwarfs in some mine, and really did think that bits of rock were interesting. The week before they'd visited an iron foundry. That had been interesting, too.

And yet . . . and yet . . . you couldn't help *liking* Carrot. Even people he was arresting liked Carrot. Even old ladies living in a permanent smell of fresh paint liked Carrot. *She* liked Carrot. A lot. Which was going to make leaving him all the harder.

She was a werewolf. That's all there was to it. You either spent your time trying to make sure people didn't find out or you let them find out and spent your time watching them keep their distance and whisper behind your back, although of course you'd have to turn round to watch that.

Carrot didn't mind. But he minded that other people minded. He minded that even quite friendly colleagues tended to carry a bit of silver somewhere on their person. She could see it upsetting him. She could see the tensions building up, and he didn't know how to deal with them.

It was just as her father had said. Get involved with humans other than at mealtimes and you might as well jump down a silver mine.

'Apparently there's going to be a huge firework display after the celebrations next year,' said Carrot. 'I like fireworks.'

---

* Commander Vimes, on the other hand, was all for giving criminals a short, sharp shock. It really depended on how tightly they could be tied to the lightning rod.

'It beats me why Ankh-Morpork wants to celebrate the fact it had a civil war three hundred years ago,' said Angua, coming back to the here-and-now.

'Why not? We won,' said Carrot.

'Yes, but you lost, too.'

'Always look on the positive side, that's what I say. Ah, here we are.'

Angua looked up at the sign. She'd learned to read dwarf runes now.

'"Dwarf Bread Museum",' she said. 'Gosh. I can't wait.'

Carrot nodded happily and pushed open the door. There was a smell of ancient crusts.

'Coo-ee, Mr Hopkinson?' he called. There was no reply. 'He does go out sometimes,' he said.

'Probably when the excitement gets too much for him,' said Angua. 'Hopkinson? That's not a dwarf name, is it?'

'Oh, he's a human,' said Carrot, stepping inside. 'But an amazing authority. Bread's his life. He wrote the definitive work on offensive baking. Well . . . since he's not here I'll just take two tickets and leave tuppence on the desk.'

It didn't look as though Mr Hopkinson got many visitors. There was dust on the floor, and dust on the display cases, and a lot of dust on the exhibits. Most of them were the classic cowpat-like shape, an echo of their taste, but there were also buns, close-combat crumpets, deadly throwing toast and a huge dusty array of other shapes devised by a race that went in for food-fighting in a big and above all terminal way.

'What are we looking for?' Angua said. She sniffed. There was a nastily familiar tang in the air.

'It's . . . are you ready for this? . . . it's . . . the Battle Bread of B'hrian Bloodaxe!' said Carrot, rummaging in a desk by the entrance.

'A loaf of bread? You brought me here to see a loaf of bread?'

She sniffed again. Yes. Blood. *Fresh* blood.

'That's right,' said Carrot. 'It's only going to be here a couple of weeks on loan. It's the actual bread he personally wielded at the Battle of Koom Valley, killing fifty-seven trolls although' – and here Carrot's tone changed down from enthusiasm to civic respectability – 'that was a long time ago and we shouldn't let ancient history blind us to the realities of a multi-ethnic society in the Century of the Fruitbat.'

There was a creak of a door.

Then: 'This battle bread,' said Angua, indistinctly. 'Black, isn't it? Quite a lot bigger than normal bread?'

'Yes, that's right,' said Carrot.

'And Mr Hopkinson . . . A short man? Little white pointy beard?'

'That's him.'

'And his head all smashed in?'

'What?'

'I think you'd better come and look,' said Angua, backing away.

Dragon King of Arms sat alone among his candles.

So that was Commander Sir Samuel Vimes, he mused. *Stupid man. Clearly can't see beyond the chip on his shoulder. And people like that rise to high office these days. Still, such people have their uses, which presumably is why Vetinari has elevated him. Stupid men are often capable of things the clever would not dare to contemplate . . .*

He sighed, and pulled another tome towards him. It was not much bigger than many others which lined his study, a fact which might have surprised anyone who knew its contents.

He was rather proud of it. It was quite an unusual piece of work, but he had been surprised – or would have been surprised, had Dragon been really surprised at anything at all for the last hundred years or so – at how easy some of it had been. He didn't even need to read it now. He knew it by heart. The family trees were properly planted, the words were down there on the page, and all he had to do was sing along.

The first page was headed: 'The Descent of King Carrot I, by the Grace of the Gods King of Ankh-Morpork'. A long and complex family tree occupied the next dozen pages until it reached: Married . . . The words there were merely pencilled in.

'Delphine Angua von Uberwald,' read the Dragon aloud. 'Father – and, ah-ha, *sire* – Baron Guye von Uberwald, also known as Silvertail; mother, Mme Serafine Soxe-Bloonberg, also known as Yellowfang, of Genua . . .'

It had been quite an achievement, that part. He had expected his agents to have had some difficulty with the more lupine areas of Angua's ancestry, but it turned out that mountain wolves took quite a lot of interest in that sort of thing as well. Angua's ancestors had definitely been among the leaders of the pack.

Dragon King of Arms grinned. As far as he was concerned, species was a secondary consideration. What really mattered in an individual was a good pedigree.

Ah, well. That was the future as it *might* have been.

He pushed the book aside. One of the advantages of a life much longer than average was that you saw how fragile the future was.

Men said things like 'peace in our time' or 'an empire that will last a thousand years', and less than half a lifetime later no one even remembered who they were, let alone what they had said or where the mob had buried their ashes. What changed history were smaller things. Often a few strokes of the pen would do the trick.

He pulled another tome towards him. The frontispiece bore the words: 'The Descent of King . . .'. Now, what would the man call himself? That at least was not calculable. Oh, well . . .

Dragon picked up his pencil and wrote: 'Nobbs'.

He smiled in the candlelit room.

People kept on talking about the true king of Ankh-Morpork, but history taught a cruel lesson. It said – often in words of blood – that the true king was the one who got crowned.

Books filled this room, too. That was the first impression – one of dank, oppressive bookishness.

The late Father Tubelcek was sprawled across a drift of fallen books. He was certainly dead. No one could have bled that much and still been alive. Or survived for long with a head like a deflated football. Someone must have hit him with a lump hammer.

'This old lady came running out screaming,' said Constable Visit, saluting. 'So I went in and it was just like this, sir.'

'*Just* like this, Constable Visit?'

'Yes, sir. And the name's Visit-The-Infidel-With-Explanatory-Pamphlets, sir.'

'Who was the old lady?'

'She says she's Mrs Kanacki, sir. She says she always brings him his meals. She says she does for him.'

'*Does* for him?'

'You know, sir. Cleaning and sweeping.'

There was, indeed, a tray on the floor, along with a broken bowl and some spilled porridge. The lady who did for the old man had been shocked to find that someone else had done for him first.

'Did she touch him?' he said.

'She says not, sir.'

Which meant the old priest had somehow achieved the *neatest* death Vimes had ever seen. His hands were crossed on his chest. His eyes had been closed.

And something had been put in his mouth. It looked like a rolled-up piece of paper. It gave the corpse a disconcertingly jaunty look, as though he'd decided to have a last cigarette after dying.

Vimes gingerly picked out the little scroll and unrolled it. It was covered with meticulously written but unfamiliar symbols. What made them particularly noteworthy was the fact that their author had apparently made use of the only liquid lying around in huge quantities.

'Yuk,' said Vimes. 'Written in *blood*. Does this mean anything to anyone?'

'Yes, sir!'

Vimes rolled his eyes. 'Yes, Constable Visit?'

'Visit-The-Infidel-With-Explanatory-Pamphlets, sir,' said Constable Visit, looking hurt.

'"The-Infidel-With-Explanatory-Pamphlets*" I was just about to say it, Constable,' said Vimes. 'Well?'

'It's an ancient Klatchian script,' said Constable Visit. 'One of the desert tribes called the Cenotines, sir. They had a sophisticated but fundamentally flawed . . .'

'Yes, yes, yes,' said Vimes, who could recognize the verbal foot getting ready to stick itself in the aural door. 'But do you know what it means?'

'I could find out, sir.'

'Good.'

'Incidentally, were you able by any chance to find time to have a look at those leaflets I gave you the other day, sir?'

'Been very busy!' said Vimes automatically.

'Not to worry, sir,' said Visit, and smiled the wan smile of those doing good against great odds. 'When you've got a moment will be fine.'

The old books that had been knocked from the shelves had spilled their pages everywhere. There were splashes of blood on many of them.

'Some of these look religious,' Vimes said. 'You might find something.' He turned. 'Detritus, have a look round, will you?'

Detritus paused in the act of laboriously drawing a chalk outline around the body. 'Yessir. What for, sir?'

'Anything you find.'

'Right, sir.'

With a grunt, Vimes hunkered down and prodded at a grey smear on the floor. 'Dirt,' he said.

'You get dat on floors, sir,' said Detritus, helpfully.

'Except this is off-white. We're on black loam,' said Vimes.

---

* Constable Visit was an Omnian, whose country's traditional approach to evangelism was to put unbelievers to torture and the sword. Things had become a lot more civilized these days but Omnians still had a strenuous and indefatigable approach to spreading the Word, and had merely changed the nature of the weapons. Constable Visit spent his days off in company with his co-religionist Smite-The-Unbeliever-With-Cunning-Arguments, ringing doorbells and causing people to hide behind the furniture everywhere in the city.

'Ah,' said Sergeant Detritus. 'A Clue.'

'Could be just dirt, of course.'

There was something else. Someone had made an attempt to tidy up the books. They'd stacked several dozen of them in one neat towering pile, one book wide, largest books on the bottom, all the edges squared up with geometrical precision.

'Now that I *don't* understand,' said Vimes. 'There's a fight. The old man is viciously attacked. Then someone – maybe it was him, dying, maybe it was the murderer – writes something down using the poor man's own blood. And rolls it up neatly and pops it into his mouth like a sweetie. Then he does die and someone shuts his eyes and makes him tidy and piles these books up neatly and . . . does what? Walks out into the seething hurly-burly that is Ankh-Morpork?'

Sergeant Detritus' honest brow furrowed with the effort of thought. 'Could be a . . . could be dere's a footprint outside der window,' he said. 'Dat's always a Clue wort' lookin' for.'

Vimes sighed. Detritus, despite a room-temperature IQ, made a good copper and a damn good sergeant. He had that special type of stupidity that was hard to fool. But the only thing more difficult than getting him to grasp an idea was getting him to let go of it.*

'Detritus,' he said, as kindly as possible. 'There's a thirty-foot drop into the river outside the window. There won't be—' He paused. This was the river Ankh, after all. 'Any footprints'd be bound to have oozed back by now,' he corrected himself. 'Almost certainly.'

He looked outside, though, just in case. The river gurgled and sucked below him. There were no footprints, even on its famously crusted surface. But there was another smear of dirt on the windowsill.

Vimes scratched some up, and sniffed at it.

'Looks like some more white clay,' he said.

He couldn't think of any white clay around the city. Once you got outside the walls it was thick black loam all the way to the Ramtops. A man walking across it would be two inches taller by the time he got to the other side of a field.

'White clay,' he said. 'Where the hell is white-clay country round here?'

---

* Detritus was particularly good when it came to asking questions. He had three basic ones. They were the direct ('Did you do it?'), the persistent ('Are you sure it wasn't you what done it?') and the subtle ('It was you what done it, wasn't it?'). Although they were not the most cunning questions ever devised, Detritus' talent was to go on patiently asking them for hours on end, until he got the right answer, which was generally something like: 'Yes! Yes! I did it! I did it! Now please tell me what it was I did!'

'It a mystery,' said Detritus.

Vimes grinned mirthlessly. It *was* a mystery. And he didn't like mysteries. Mysteries had a way of getting bigger if you didn't solve them quickly. Mysteries pupped.

Mere *murders* happened all the time. And usually even Detritus could solve them. When a distraught woman was standing over a fallen husband holding a right-angled poker and crying 'He never should've said that about our Neville!' there was only a limited amount you could do to spin out the case beyond the next coffee break. And when various men or parts thereof were hanging from or nailed to various fixtures in the Mended Drum on a Saturday night, and the other clientele were all looking innocent, you didn't need even a Detritic intelligence to work out what had been happening.

He looked down at the late Father Tubelcek. It was amazing he'd bled so much, with his pipe-cleaner arms and toast-rack chest. He certainly wouldn't have been able to put up much of a fight.

Vimes leaned down and gently raised one of the corpse's eyelids. A milky blue eye with a black centre looked back at him from wherever the old priest was now.

A religious old man who lived in a couple of little poky rooms and obviously didn't go out much, from the smell. What kind of threat could he . . . ?

Constable Visit poked his head around the door. 'There's a dwarf down here with no eyebrows and a frizzled beard says you told him to come, sir,' he said. 'And some citizens say Father Tubelcek is their priest and they want to bury him decently.'

'Ah, that'll be Littlebottom. Send him up,' said Vimes, straightening. 'Tell the others they'll have to wait.'

Littlebottom climbed the stairs, took in the scene, and managed to reach the window in time to be sick.

'Better now?' said Vimes eventually.

'Er . . . yes. I hope so.'

'I'll leave you to it, then.'

'Er . . . what exactly did you want me to do?' said Littlebottom, but Vimes was already halfway down the stairs.

Angua growled. It was the signal to Carrot that he could open his eyes again.

Women, as Colon had remarked to Carrot once when he thought the lad needed advice, could be funny about little things. Maybe they didn't like to be seen without their make-up on, or insisted on buying smaller suitcases than men even though they always took more clothes. In Angua's case she didn't like to be seen *en route* from human to werewolf shape, or vice versa. It was just something she had a thing about, she said. Carrot could see her in either shape but not in the various ones she occupied on the way through, in case he never wanted to see her again.

Through werewolf eyes the world was *different*.

For one thing, it was in black-and-white. At least, that small part of it which as a human she'd thought of as 'vision' was monochrome – but who cared that vision had to take a back seat when smell drove instead, laughing and sticking its arm out of the window and making rude gestures at all the other senses? After-wards, she always remembered the odours as colours and sounds. Blood was rich brown and deep bass, stale bread was a surprisingly tinkly bright blue, and every human being was a four-dimensional kaleidoscopic symphony. For nasal vision meant seeing through time as well as space: a man could stand still for a minute and, an hour later, there he'd still be, to the nose, his odours barely faded.

She prowled the aisles of the Dwarf Bread Museum, muzzle to the ground. Then she went out into the alley for a while and tried there too.

After five minutes she padded back to Carrot and gave him the signal again.

When he re-opened his eyes she was pulling her shirt on over her head. That was one thing where humans had the edge. You couldn't beat a pair of hands.

'I thought you'd be down the street and following someone,' he said.

'Follow who?' said Angua.

'Pardon?'

'I can smell him, and you, and the bread, and that's it.'

'Nothing else?'

'Dirt. Dust. The usual stuff. Oh, there are some old traces, days old. I know you were in here last week, for example. There are lots of smells. Grease, meat, pine resin for some reason, old food . . . but I'll swear no living thing's been in here in the last day or so but him and us.'

'But you told me *everyone* leaves a trail.'

'They do.'

Carrot looked down at the late curator. However you phrased it, however broadly you applied your definitions, he definitely couldn't have committed suicide. Not with a loaf of bread.

'Vampires?' said Carrot. 'They can fly . . .'

Angua sighed. 'Carrot, I could tell if a vampire had been in here in the last *month*.'

'There's almost half a dollar in pennies in the drawer,' said Carrot. 'Anyway, a thief would be here for the Battle Bread, wouldn't they? It is a very valuable cultural artefact.'

'Has the poor man got any relatives?' said Angua.

'He's got an elderly sister, I believe. I come in once a month just to have a chat. He lets me handle the exhibits, you know.'

'That must be fun,' said Angua, before she could stop herself.

'It's very . . . satisfying, yes,' said Carrot solemnly. 'It reminds me of home.'

Angua sighed and stepped into the room behind the little museum. It was like the back rooms of museums everywhere, full of junk and things there is no room for on the shelves and also items of doubtful provenance, such as coins dated '52 BC'. There were some benches with shards of dwarf bread on them, a tidy tool rack with various sizes of kneading hammer, and papers all over the place. Against one wall, and occupying a large part of the room, was an oven.

'He researches old recipes,' said Carrot, who seemed to feel he had to promote the old man's expertise even in death.

Angua opened the oven door. Warmth spilled out into the room. 'Hell of a bake oven,' she said. 'What're these things?'

'Ah . . . I see he's been making drop scones,' said Carrot. 'Quite deadly at short range.'

She shut the door. 'Let's get back to the Yard and they can send someone out to—'

Angua stopped.

These were always the dangerous moments, just after a shape-change this close to full moon. It wasn't so bad when she was a wolf. She was still as intelligent, or at least she *felt* as intelligent, although life was a lot simpler and so she was probably just extremely intelligent for a wolf. It was when she became a human again that things were difficult. For a few minutes, until the morphic field fully reasserted itself, all her senses were still keen; smells were still incredibly strong, and her ears could hear sounds way outside the stunted human range. And she could *think* more about the things she experienced. A wolf could sniff a lamp-post and know that old Bonzo had been past yesterday, and was feeling a bit under the weather, and was still being fed tripe by his owner, but a human mind could actually think about the whys and wherefores.

'There *is* something else,' she said, and breathed in gently. 'Faint. Not a living thing. But . . . can't you smell it? Something like dirt, but not quite. It's kind of . . . yellow-orange . . .'

'Um . . .' said Carrot, tactfully. 'Some of us don't have your nose.'

'I've smelled it before, somewhere in this town. Can't remember where . . . It's strong. Stronger than the other smells. It's a muddy smell.'

'Hah, well, on *these* streets . . .'

'No, it's not . . . *exactly* mud. Sharper. More treble.'

'You know, sometimes I envy you. It must be nice to be a wolf. Just for a while.'

'It has its drawbacks.' *Like fleas*, she thought, as they locked up the museum. *And the food. And the constant nagging feeling that you should be wearing three bras at once.*

She kept telling herself she had it under control and she did, in a way. She prowled the city on moonlit nights and, okay, there was the occasional chicken, but she always remembered where she'd been and went round next day to shove some money under the door.

It was hard to be a vegetarian who had to pick bits of meat out of her teeth in the morning. She was definitely on top of it, though.

Definitely, she reassured herself.

It was Angua's mind that prowled the night, not a werewolf mind. She was almost entirely sure of that. A werewolf wouldn't stop at chickens, not by a long way.

She shuddered.

Who was she kidding? It was easy to be a vegetarian by day. It was preventing yourself from becoming a humanitarian at night that took the real effort.

The first clocks were striking eleven as Vimes's sedan chair wobbled to a halt outside the Patrician's palace. Commander Vimes's legs were beginning to give out, but he ran up five flights of stairs as fast as possible and collapsed on a chair in the waiting salon.

Minutes went past.

You didn't knock on the Patrician's door. He summoned you in the certain knowledge that you would be there.

Vimes sat back, enjoying a moment's peace.

Something inside his coat went: 'Bing bing bingley bing!'

He sighed, pulled out a leather-bound package about the size of a small book, and opened it.

A friendly yet slightly worried face peered up at him from its cage.

'Yes?' said Vimes.

'11am. Appointment with the Patrician.'

'Yes? Well? It's five past now.'

'Er. So you've had it, have you?' said the imp.

'No.'

'Shall I go on remembering it or what?'

'No. Anyway, you didn't remind me about the College of Arms at ten.'

The imp looked panic-stricken.

'That's Tuesday, isn't it? Could've sworn it was Tuesday.'

'It was an hour ago.'

'Oh.' The imp was downcast. 'Er. All right. Sorry. Um. Hey, I could tell you what time it is in Klatch, if you like. Or Genua. Or Hunghung. Any of those places. You name it.'

'I don't need to know the time in Klatch.'

'You might,' said the imp desperately. 'Think how people will be impressed if, during a dull moment of the conversation, you could say "Incidentally, in Klatch it's an hour ago". Or Bes Pelargic. Or Ephebe. Ask me. Go on. I don't mind. Any of those places.'

Vimes sighed inwardly. He had a notebook. He took notes in it. It was always useful. And then Sybil, gods bless her, had brought him this fifteen-function imp which did so many other things, although as far as he could see at least ten of its functions consisted of apologizing for its inefficiency in the other five.

'You could take a memo,' Vimes said.

'Wow! Really? Gosh! Okay. Right. *No* problem.'

Vimes cleared his throat. 'See Corporal Nobbs re time-keeping; also re Earldom.'

'Er . . . sorry, is this the memo?'

'Yes.'

'Sorry, you should have said "memo" first. I'm pretty certain it's in the manual.'

'All right, it *was* a memo.'

'Sorry, you have to say it again.'

'Memo: See Corporal Nobbs re time-keeping; also re Earldom.'

'Got it,' said the imp. 'Would you like to be reminded of this at any particular time?'

'The time here?' said Vimes, nastily. 'Or the time in, say, Klatch?'

'As a matter of fact, I can tell you what time it—'

'I think I'll write it in my notebook, if you don't mind,' said Vimes.

'Oh, well, if you prefer, I can recognize handwriting,' said the imp proudly. 'I'm quite advanced.'

Vimes pulled out his notebook and held it up. 'Like this?' he said.

The imp squinted for a moment. 'Yep,' it said. 'That's handwriting, sure enough. Curly bits, spiky bits, all joined together. Yep. Handwriting. I'd recognize it anywhere.'

'Aren't you supposed to tell me what it says?'

The imp looked wary. 'Says?' it said. 'It's supposed to make noises?'

Vimes put the battered book away and shut the lid of the organizer. Then he sat back and carried on waiting.

Someone very clever – certainly someone much cleverer than whoever had trained that imp – must have made the clock for the Patrician's waiting room. It went tick-tock like any other clock. But somehow, and against all usual horological practice, the tick and the tock were irregular. Tick tock tick . . . and then the merest fraction of a second longer before . . . tock tick tock . . . and then a tick a fraction of a second earlier than the mind's ear was now prepared for. The effect was enough, after ten minutes, to reduce the thinking processes of even the best-prepared to a sort of porridge. The Patrician must have paid the clockmaker quite highly.

The clock said quarter past eleven.

Vimes walked over to the door and, despite precedent, knocked gently.

There was no sound from within, no murmur of distant voices.

He tried the handle. The door was unlocked.

Lord Vetinari had always said that punctuality was the politeness of princes.

Vimes went in.

Cheery dutifully scraped up the crumbly white dirt and then examined the corpse of the late Father Tubelcek.

Anatomy was an important study at the Alchemists' Guild, owing to the ancient theory that the human body represented a microcosm of the universe, although when you saw one opened up it was hard to imagine which part of the universe was small and purple and went *blomp-blomp* when you prodded it. But in any case you tended to pick up practical anatomy as you went along, and sometimes scraped it off the walls as well. When new students tried an experiment that was particularly successful in terms of explosive force, the result was often a cross between a major laboratory refit and a game of Hunt-the-Other-Kidney.

The man had been killed by being repeatedly hit around the head. That was about all you could say. Some kind of very heavy blunt instrument.*

---

* It is a pervasive and beguiling myth that the people who design instruments of death end up being killed by them. There is *almost* no foundation in fact. Colonel Shrapnel wasn't

What else did Vimes expect Cheery to do?

He looked carefully at the rest of the body. There were no other obvious signs of violence, although . . . there were a few specks of blood on the man's fingers. But, then, there was blood everywhere. A couple of fingernails were torn. Tubelcek had put up a fight, or at least had tried to shield himself with his hands.

Cheery looked more closely at the fingers. There was something piled under the nails. It had a waxy sheen, like thick grease. He couldn't imagine why it should be there, but maybe his job was to find out. He conscientiously took an envelope out of his pocket and scraped the stuff into it, sealed it up and numbered it.

Then he took his iconograph out of its box and prepared to take a picture of the corpse.

As he did so, something caught his eye.

Father Tubelcek lay there, one eye still open as Vimes had left it, winking at eternity.

Cheery looked closer. He'd thought he'd imagined it. But . . .

Even now he wasn't sure. The mind could play tricks.

He opened the little door of the iconograph and spoke to the imp inside.

'Can you paint a picture of his eye, Sydney?' he said.

The imp squinted out through the lens. 'Just the eye?' it squeaked.

'Yes. As big as you can.'

'You're sick, mister.'

'And shut up,' said Cheery.

He propped the box on the table and sat back. From inside the box there came the swish-swish of brush strokes. At last there was the sound of a handle being turned, and a slightly damp picture rustled out of a slot.

Cheery peered at it. Then he knocked on the box. The hatch opened.

'Yes?'

'Bigger. So big it fills the whole paper. In fact' – Cheery squinted at the picture in his hands – 'just paint the pupil. The bit in the middle.'

'So it fills the whole paper? You're weird.'

Cheery propped the box nearer. There was a clicking of gears as the imp wound the lenses out, and then a few more seconds of busy brush work.

---

blown up, M. Guillotin died with his head on, Colonel Gatling wasn't shot. If it hadn't been for the murder of cosh and blackjack maker Sir William Blunt-Instrument in an alleyway, the rumour would never have got started.

Another damp picture unwound. It showed a big black disc. Well . . . mainly black.

Cheery looked closer. There was a hint, just a hint . . .

He rapped on the box again.

'Yes, Mr Dwarf Weird Person?' said the imp.

'The bit in the middle. Big as you can, thank you.'

The lenses wound out yet further.

Cheery waited anxiously. In the next room, he could hear Detritus patiently moving around.

The paper wound out for the third time, and the hatch opened. 'That's it,' said the imp. 'I've run out of black.'

And the paper *was* black . . . except for the tiny little area that wasn't.

The door to the stairs burst open and Constable Visit came in, borne along by the pressure of a small crowd. Cheery guiltily thrust the paper into his pocket.

'This is intolerable!' said a small man with a long black beard. 'We *demand* you let us in! Who're you, young man?'

'I'm Ch – I'm Corporal Littlebottom,' said Cheery. 'Look, I've got a badge . . .'

'Well, *Corporal*,' said the man, '*I* am Wengel Raddley and I am a man of some standing in this community and I demand that you let us have poor Father Tubelcek this minute!'

'We're, er, we're trying to find out who killed him,' Cheery began.

There was a movement behind Cheery, and the faces in front of him suddenly looked very worried indeed. He turned to see Detritus in the doorway to the next room.

'Everyt'ing okay?' said the troll.

The changed fortunes of the Watch had allowed Detritus to have a proper breastplate rather than a piece of elephant battle armour. As was normal practice for the uniform of a sergeant, the armourer had attempted to do a stylized representation of muscles on it. As far as Detritus was concerned, he hadn't been able to get them all in.

'Is dere any trouble?' he said.

The crowd backed away.

'None at all, officer,' said Mr Raddley. 'You, er, just loomed suddenly, that's all . . .'

'Dis is correct,' said Detritus. 'I am a loomer. It often happen suddenly. So dere's no trouble, den?'

'No trouble whatsoever, officer.'

'Amazing t'ing, trouble,' rumbled Detritus thoughtfully. 'Always I go lookin' for trouble, an' when I find it people said it ain't dere.'

Mr Raddley drew himself up.

'But we want to take Father Tubelcek away to bury him,' he said.

Detritus turned to Cheery Littlebottom. 'You done everyt'ing you need?'

'I suppose so . . .'

'He dead?'

'Oh, yes.'

'He gonna get any better?'

'Better than dead? I doubt it.'

'Okay, den you people can take him away.'

The two Watchmen stood aside as the body was carried down the stairs.

'Why you takin' pictures of the dead man?' said Detritus.

'Well, er, it might be helpful to see how he was lying.'

Detritus nodded sagely. 'Ah, he was lyin', was he? An' him a holy man, too.'

Littlebottom pulled out the picture and looked at it again. It was *almost* black. But . . .

A constable arrived at the bottom of the stairs. 'Is there someone up there called' – there was a muffled snigger – 'Cheery Littlebottom?'

'Yes,' said Littlebottom gloomily.

'Well, Commander Vimes says you've to come to the Patrician's palace right now, all right?'

'Dat's *Corporal* Littlebottom you're talkin' to,' said Detritus.

'It's all right,' said Littlebottom. 'Nothing could make it any worse.'

Rumour is information distilled so finely that it can filter through anything. It does not need doors and windows – sometimes it doesn't even need people. It can exist free and wild, running from ear to ear without ever touching lips.

It had escaped already. From the high window of the Patrician's bedroom, Sam Vimes could see people drifting towards the palace. There wasn't a mob – there wasn't even what you might call a crowd – but the Brownian motion of the streets was bouncing more and more people in his direction.

He relaxed slightly when he saw one or two guards come through the gates.

On the bed, Lord Vetinari opened his eyes.

'Ah . . . Commander Vimes,' he murmured.

'What's been happening, sir?' said Vimes.

'I appear to be lying down, Vimes.'

'You were in your office, sir. Unconscious.'

'Dear me. I must have been . . . overdoing it. Well, thank you. If you would be kind enough to . . . help me up . . .'

Lord Vetinari tried to pull himself upright, swayed, and fell back again. His face was pale. Sweat beaded his forehead.

There was a knock at the door. Vimes opened it a fraction.

'It's me, sir. Fred Colon. I got a message. What's up?'

'Ah, Fred. Who've you got down there so far?'

'There's me and Constable Flint and Constable Slapper, sir.'

'Right. Someone's to go up to my place and get Willikins to bring me my street uniform. And my sword and crossbow. And an overnight bag. And some cigars. And tell Lady Sybil . . . tell Lady Sybil . . . well, they'll just have to tell Lady Sybil I've got to deal with things down here, that's all.'

'What's *happening*, sir? Someone downstairs said Lord Vetinari's dead!'

'Dead?' murmured the Patrician from his bed. 'Nonsense!' He jerked himself upright, swung his legs off the bed, and folded up. It was a slow, terrible collapse. Lord Vetinari was a tall man, so there was a long way to fall. And he did it by folding up a joint at a time. His ankles gave way and he fell on his knees. His knees hit the ground with a bang and he bent at the waist. Finally his forehead bounced on the carpet.

'Oh,' he said.

'His lordship's just a bit . . .' Vimes began – then he grabbed Colon and dragged him out of the room. 'I reckon he's been poisoned, Fred, and that's the truth of it.'

Colon looked horrified. 'Ye gods! Do you want me to get a doctor?'

'Are you mad? We want him to live!'

Vimes bit his lip. He'd said the words that were on his mind, and now, without a doubt, the faint smoke of rumour would drift out across the city. 'But someone ought to look at him . . .' he said aloud.

'Damn' right!' said Colon. 'You want I should get a wizard?'

'How do we know it wasn't one of them?'

'Ye gods!'

Vimes tried to think. All the doctors in the city were employed by the guilds, and all the guilds hated Vetinari, so . . .

'When you've got enough people to spare a runner, send him up to the stables on Kings Down to fetch Doughnut Jimmy,' he said.

Colon looked even more stricken. 'Doughnut? He doesn't know *anything* about doctoring! He dopes racehorses!'

'Just get him, Fred.'

'What if he won't come?'

'Then say that Commander Vimes knows why Laughing Boy didn't win the Quirm 100 Dollars last week, and say that I know Chrysoprase the troll lost ten thousand on that race.'

Colon was impressed. 'You've got a nasty twist of mind there, sir.'

'There's going to be a lot of people turning up pretty soon. I want a couple of Watchmen outside this room – trolls or dwarfs for preference – and no one is to come in without my permission, right?'

Colon's face contorted as various emotions fought for space. Finally he managed to say, 'But . . . *poisoned*? He's got food-tasters and everything!'

'Then maybe it was one of them, Fred.'

'My gods, sir! You don't trust *anyone*, do you?'

'No, Fred. Incidentally, was it you? Just kidding,' Vimes added quickly as Colon's face threatened to burst into tears. 'Off you go. We don't have much time.'

Vimes shut the door and leaned on it. Then he turned the key in the lock and moved a chair under the handle.

Finally he hauled the Patrician off the floor and rolled him on to the bed. There was a grunt from the man, and his eyelids flickered.

Poison, thought Vimes. *That's the worst of all. It doesn't make a noise, the poisoner can be miles away, you can't see it, often you can't really smell it or taste it, it could be anywhere – and there it is, doing its work . . .*

The Patrician opened his eyes.

'I would like a glass of water,' he said.

There was a jug and a glass by the bed. Vimes picked up the jug, and hesitated. 'I'll send someone to get some,' he said.

Lord Vetinari blinked, very slowly.

'Ah, Sir Samuel,' he said, 'but whom can you trust?'

There was a crowd in the big audience chamber when Vimes finally went downstairs. They were milling about, worried and unsure, and, like important men everywhere, when they were worried and unsure they got angry.

The first to bustle up to Vimes was Mr Boggis of the Guild of Thieves. 'What's going on, Vimes?' he demanded.

He met Vimes's stare. 'Sir Samuel, I mean,' he said, losing a certain amount of bustle.

'I believe Lord Vetinari has been poisoned,' said Vimes.

The background muttering stopped. Boggis realized that, since he had been the one to ask the question, he was now the man on the spot. 'Er . . . fatally?' he said.

In the silence, a pin would have clanged.

'Not yet,' said Vimes.

Around the hall there was a turning of heads. The focus of the universal attention was Dr Downey, head of the Guild of Assassins.

Downey nodded. 'I'm not aware of any *arrangement* with regard to Lord Vetinari,' he said. 'Besides, as I am sure is common knowledge, we have set the price for the Patrician at one million dollars.'

'And who has that sort of money, indeed?' said Vimes.

'Well . . . you for one, Sir Samuel,' said Downey. There was some nervous laughter.

'We wish to see Lord Vetinari, in any case,' said Boggis.

'No.'

'No? And why not, pray?'

'Doctor's orders.'

'Really? Which doctor?'

Behind Vimes, Sergeant Colon shut his eyes.

'Dr James Folsom,' said Vimes.

It took a few seconds before someone worked this out. 'What? You can't mean . . . Doughnut Jimmy? He's a *horse* doctor!'

'So I understand,' said Vimes.

'But why?'

'Because many of his patients survive,' said Vimes. He raised his hands as the protests grew. 'And now, gentlemen, I must leave you. Somewhere there's a poisoner. I'd like to find him before he becomes a murderer.'

He went back up the stairs, trying to ignore the shouts behind him.

'You sure about old Doughnut, sir?' said Colon, catching him up.

'Well, do you trust him?' said Vimes.

'Doughnut? Of course not!'

'Right. He's untrustworthy, and so we don't trust him. So that's all right. But I've seen him revive a horse when everyone else said it was fit only for the knackers. Horse doctors *have* to get results, Fred.'

And that was true enough. When a human doctor, after much bleeding and cupping, finds that a patient has died out of sheer desperation, he can always say, 'Dear me, will of the gods, that will be thirty dollars please,' and walk away a free man. This is because human beings are not, technically, worth anything. A good racehorse, on the other hand, may be worth twenty thousand dollars. A doctor who lets one hurry off too soon to that great big paddock in the sky may well expect to hear, out of some dark alley, a voice saying something on the lines of 'Mr Chrysoprase is *very upset*', and find the brief remainder of his life full of incident.

'No one seems to know where Captain Carrot and Angua are,' said Colon. 'It's their day off. And Nobby's nowhere to be found.'

'Well, that's something to be thankful for . . .'

'Bingeley bingeley bong beep,' said a voice from Vimes's pocket. He lifted out the little organizer and raised the flap.

'Yes?'

'Er . . . twelve noon,' said the imp. 'Lunch with Lady Sybil.' It stared at their faces.

'Er . . . that's all right, isn't it?' it said.

Cheery Littlebottom wiped his brow.

'Commander Vimes is right. It *could* be arsenic,' he said. 'It looks like arsenic poisoning to me. Look at his colour.'

'Nasty stuff,' said Doughnut Jimmy. 'Has he been eating his bedding?'

'All the sheets seem to be here, so I suppose the answer is no.'

'How's he pissing?'

'Er. The usual way, I assume.'

Doughnut sucked at his teeth. He had amazing teeth. It was the second thing everyone noticed about him. They were the colour of the inside of an unwashed teapot.

'Walk him round a bit on the loose rein,' he said.

The Patrician opened his eyes. 'You *are* a doctor, aren't you?' he said.

Doughnut Jimmy gave him an uncertain look. He was not used to patients who could talk. 'Well, yeah . . . I have a lot of patients,' he said.

'Indeed? I have very little,' said the Patrician. He tried to lift himself off the bed, and slumped back.

'I'll mix up a draught,' said Doughnut Jimmy, backing away. 'You're to hold his nose and pour it down his throat twice a day, right? And no oats.'

He hurried out, leaving Cheery alone with the Patrician.

Corporal Littlebottom looked around the room. Vimes hadn't given him much instruction. He'd said: 'I'm sure it won't be the food-tasters. For all they know they might be asked to eat the whole plateful. Still, we'll get Detritus to talk to them. You find out the *how*, right? And then leave the *who* to me.'

If you didn't eat or drink a poison, what else was left? Probably you could put it on a pad and make someone breathe it, or dribble some in their ear while they slept. Or they could touch it. Maybe a small dart . . . Or an insect bite . . .

The Patrician stirred, and looked at Cheery through watery red eyes. 'Tell me, young man, are you a policeman?'

'Er . . . just started, sir.'

'You appear to be of the dwarf persuasion.'

Cheery didn't bother to answer. There was no use denying it. Somehow, people could tell if you were a dwarf just by looking at you.

'Arsenic is a very popular poison,' said the Patrician. 'Hundreds of uses around the home. Crushed diamonds used to be in vogue for hundreds of years, despite the fact they never worked. Giant spiders, too, for some reason. Mercury is for those with patience, aquafortis for those without. Cantharides has its followers. Much can be done with the secretions of various animals. The bodily fluids of the caterpillar of the Quantum Weather Butterfly will render a man quite, quite helpless. But we return to arsenic like an old, old friend.'

There was a drowsiness in the Patrician's voice. 'Is that not so, young Vetinari? Yes indeed, sir. Correct. But where then shall we put it, seeing that all will look for it? In the last place they will look, sir. Wrong. Foolish. We put it where no one will look *at all* . . .'

The voice faded to a murmur.

The bed linen, Cheery thought. Even clothes. Into the skin, slowly . . .

Cheery hammered on the door. A guard opened it.

'Get another bed.'

'What?'

'Another bed. From anywhere. And fresh bed linen.'

He looked down. There wasn't much of a carpet on the floor. Even so, in a bedroom, where people might walk with bare feet . . .

'And take away this rug and bring another one.'

What else?

Detritus came in, nodded at Cheery, and looked carefully around the room. Finally he picked up a battered chair.

'Dis'll have to do,' he said. 'If he want, I can break der back off'f it.'

'What?' said Cheery.

'Ole Doughnut said for to get a stool sample,' said Detritus, going out again.

Cheery opened his mouth to stop the troll, and then shrugged. Anyway, the less furniture in here the better . . .

And that seemed about it, short of stripping the wallpaper off the wall.

Sam Vimes stared out of the window.

Vetinari hadn't bothered much in the way of bodyguards. He had used – that is, he still did use – food-tasters, but that was common enough. Mind you, Vetinari had added his own special twist. The tasters were well paid and treated, and they were all sons of the chief cook. But his main protection was that he was just that bit more useful alive than dead, from everyone's point of view. The big powerful guilds didn't like him, but they liked him in power a lot more than they liked the idea of someone from a rival guild in the Oblong Office. Besides, Lord Vetinari represented stability. It was a cold and clinical kind of stability, but part of his genius was the discovery that stability was what people wanted more than anything else.

He'd said to Vimes once, in this very room, standing at this very window: 'They think they want good government and justice for all, Vimes, yet what is it they really crave, deep in their hearts? Only that things go on as normal and tomorrow is pretty much like today.'

Now, Vimes turned around. 'What's my next move, Fred?'

'Dunno, sir.'

Vimes sat down in the Patrician's chair. 'Can you remember the last Patrician?'

'Old Lord Snapcase? And the one before him, Lord Winder. Oh, yeah. Nasty pieces of work, they were. At least this one didn't giggle or wear a dress.'

The past tense, thought Vimes. *It creeps in already. Not long past, but already very tense.*

'It's gone very quiet downstairs, Fred,' he said.

'Plotting don't make a lot of noise, sir, generally.'

'Vetinari's not dead, Fred.'

'Yessir. But he's not exactly in charge, is he?'

Vimes shrugged. 'No one's in charge, I suppose.'

'Could be, sir. There again, you never know your luck.'

Colon was standing stiffly to attention, with his eyes firmly fixed on the middle distance and his voice pitched carefully to avoid any hint of emotion in the words.

Vimes recognized the stance. He used it himself, when he had to. 'What do you mean, Fred?' he said.

'Not a thing, sir. Figure of speech, sir.'

Vimes sat back.

This morning, he thought, *I knew what the day held. I was going to see about that damn coat of arms. Then there was my usual meeting with Vetinari. I was going to read some reports after lunch, maybe go and see how they're getting on with the new Watch House in Chittling Street, and have an early night. Now Fred's suggesting . . . what?*

'Listen, Fred, if there *is* to be a new ruler, it won't be me.'

'Who'll it be, sir?' Colon's voice still held that slow, deliberate tone.

'How should I know? It could be . . .'

The gap opened ahead of him and he could feel his thoughts being sucked into it. 'You're talking about Captain Carrot, aren't you, Fred?'

'Could be, sir. I mean none of the guilds'd let some other guild bloke be ruler now, and everyone likes Captain Carrot, and, well . . . rumour's got about that he's the hair to the throne, sir.'

'There's no proof of that, Sergeant.'

'Not for me to say, sir. Dunno about that. Dunno what *is* proof,' said Colon, with just a hint of defiance. 'But he's got that sword of his, and the birthmark shaped like a crown, and . . . well, everyone *knows* he's king. It's his krisma.'

Charisma, thought Vimes. *Oh, yes. Carrot has charisma. He makes something happen in people's heads. He can talk a charging leopard into giving up and handing over its teeth and doing good work in the community, and that would* really *upset the old ladies.*

Vimes distrusted charisma. 'No more kings, Fred.'

'Right you are, sir. By the way, Nobby's turned up.'

'The day gets worse and worse, Fred.'

'You said you'd talk to him about all these funerals, sir . . .'

'The job goes on, I suppose. All right, go and tell him to come up here.'

Vimes was left to himself.

No more kings. Vimes had difficulty in articulating why this should be so, why the concept revolted in his very bones. After all, a good many of the patricians had been as bad as any king. But they were . . . sort of . . . bad *on equal terms*. What set Vimes's teeth on edge was the idea that kings were a different kind of human being. A higher lifeform. Somehow magical. But, huh, there was *some* magic, at that. Ankh-Morpork still seemed to be littered with Royal this and Royal that, little old men who got paid a few pence a week to do a few meaningless chores, like the Master of the King's Keys or the Keeper of the Crown Jewels, even though there were no keys and certainly no jewels.

Royalty was like dandelions. No matter how many heads you

chopped off, the roots were still there underground, waiting to spring up again.

It seemed to be a chronic disease. It was as if even the most intelligent person had this little blank spot in their heads where someone had written: 'Kings. What a good idea.' Whoever had created humanity had left in a major design flaw. It was its tendency to bend at the knees.

There was a knock at the door. It should not be possible for a knock to sound surreptitious, yet this knock achieved it. It had harmonics. They told the hindbrain: the person knocking will, if no one eventually answers, open the door anyway and sidle in, whereupon he will certainly nick any smokes that are lying around, read any correspondence that catches his eye, open a few drawers, take a nip out of such bottles of alcohol as are discovered, but stop short of major crime because he is not criminal in the sense of making a moral decision but in the sense that a weasel is evil – it is built into his very shape. It was a knock with a lot to say for itself.

'Come in, Nobby,' said Vimes, wearily.

Corporal Nobbs sidled in. It was another special trait of his that he could sidle forwards as well as sideways.

He saluted awkwardly.

There was something absolutely changeless about Corporal Nobbs, Vimes told himself. Even Fred Colon had adapted to the changing nature of the City Watch, but nothing altered Corporal Nobbs in any way. It wouldn't matter what you did to him, there was always something fundamentally *Nobby* about Corporal Nobbs.

'Nobby . . .'

'Yessir?'

'Er . . . take a seat, Nobby.'

Corporal Nobbs looked suspicious. This was not how a dressing-down was supposed to begin.

'Er, Fred said you wanted to see me, Mr Vimes, on account of timekeeping . . .'

'Did I? Did I? Oh, yes. Nobby, how many grandmothers' funerals have you *really* been to?'

'Er . . . three . . .' said Nobby, uncomfortably.

'Three?'

'It turned out Nanny Nobbs weren't quite dead the first time.'

'So why have you taken all this time off?'

'Don't like to say, sir . . .'

'Why not?'

'You're gonna go spare, sir.'

'Spare?'

'You know, sir . . . throw a wobbler.'

'I *might*, Nobby.' Vimes sighed. 'But it'll be nothing to what'll get heaved if you *don't* tell me . . .'

'Thing is, it's the tricentre – tricera – this three-hundred-year celebration thing next year, Mr Vimes . . .'

'Yes?'

Nobby licked his lips. 'I dint like to ask for time off special. Fred said you were a bit sensitive about it all. But . . . you know I'm in the Peeled Nuts, sir . . .'

Vimes nodded. 'Those clowns who dress up and pretend to fight old battles with blunt swords,' he said.

'The Ankh-Morpork Historical Re-creation Society, sir,' said Nobby, a shade reproachfully.

'That's what I said.'

'Well . . . we're going to recreate the Battle of Ankh-Morpork for the celebrations, see. That means extra practice.'

'It all begins to make sense,' said Vimes, nodding wearily. 'You've been marching up and down with your tin pike, eh? In my time?'

'Er . . . not exactly, Mr Vimes . . . er . . . I've been riding up and down on my white horse, to tell the truth . . .'

'Oh? Playing at being a general, eh?'

'Er . . . a bit more'n a general, sir . . .'

'Go on.'

Nobby's adam's apple bobbed nervously. 'Er . . . I'm going to be King Lorenzo, sir. Er . . . you know . . . the last king, the one your . . . er . . .'

The air froze.

'*You* . . . are going to be . . .' Vimes began, unpeeling each word like a sullen grape of wrath.

'I said you'd go spare,' said Nobby. 'Fred Colon said you'd go spare, too.'

'*Why* are you—?'

'We drew lots, sir.'

'And you lost?'

Nobby squirmed. 'Er . . . not exactly *lost*, sir. Not *precisely* lost. More sort of *won*, sir. Everyone wanted to play him. I mean, you get a horse and a good costume and everything, sir. And he *was* a king, when all's said and done, sir.'

'The man was a vicious monster!'

'Well, it was all a long time ago, sir,' said Nobby anxiously.

Vimes calmed down a little. 'And who drew the straw to play Stoneface Vimes?'

'Er . . . er . . .'

'*Nobby!*'

570

Nobby hung his head. 'No one, sir. No one wanted to play him, sir.' The little corporal swallowed, and then plunged onwards with the air of a man determined to get it all over with. 'So we're making a man out of straw, sir, so he'll burn nicely when we throw him on the bonfire in the evening. There's going to be *fireworks*, sir,' he added, with dreadful certainty.

Vimes's face shut down. Nobby preferred it when people shouted. He had been shouted at for most of his life. He could handle shouting.

'No one wanted to be Stoneface Vimes,' Vimes said coldly.

'On account of him being on the losing side, sir.'

'Losing? Vimes's Ironheads *won*. He ruled the city for six months.'

Nobby squirmed again. 'Yeah, but . . . everyone in the Society says he didn't ought to of, sir. They said it was just a fluke, sir. After all, he was outnumbered ten to one, and he had warts, sir. And he was a bit of a bastard, sir, when all's said and done. He did chop off a king's head, sir. You got to be a bit of a nasty type to do that, sir. Saving your presence, Mr Vimes.'

Vimes shook his head. What did it matter, anyway? (But it *did* matter, somewhere.) It had all been a long time ago. It didn't matter what a bunch of deranged romantics thought. Facts were facts.

'All right, I understand,' he said. 'It's almost funny, really. Because there's something else I've got to tell you, Nobby.'

'Yessir?' said Nobby, looking relieved.

'Do you remember your father?'

Nobby looked about to panic again. 'What kind of question is that to suddenly ask anybody, sir?'

'Purely a social enquiry.'

'Old Sconner, sir? Not much, sir. Never used to see him much except when the milit'ry police used to come for to drag him outa the attic.'

'Do you know much about your, er, antecedents?'

'That is a lie, sir. I haven't got no antecedents, sir, no matter what you might have been tole.'

'Oh. Good. Er . . . you don't actually know what "antecedents" means, do you, Nobby?'

Nobby shifted uneasily. He didn't like being questioned by policemen, especially since he was one. 'Not in so many words, sir.'

'You never got told anything about your forebears?' Another worried expression crossed Nobby's face, so Vimes quickly added: 'Your ancestors?'

'Only old Sconner, sir. Sir . . . if all this is working up to asking about them sacks of vegetables which went missing from the shop in Treacle Mine Road, I was not anywhere near the—'

Vimes waved a hand vaguely. 'He didn't . . . leave you anything? Or anything?'

'Coupla scars, sir. And this trick elbow of mine. It aches sometimes, when the weather changes. I always remembers ole Sconner when the wind blows from the Hub.'

'Ah, right—'

'And this, o' course . . .' Nobby fished around behind his rusting breastplate. And that was a marvel, too. Even Sergeant Colon's armour could shine, if not actually gleam. But *any* metal anywhere near Nobby's skin corroded very quickly. The corporal pulled out a leather thong that hung around his neck. There was a gold ring on it. Despite the fact that gold cannot corrode, it had nevertheless developed a patina.

'He left it to me when he was on his deathbed,' said Nobby. 'Well, when I say "left it" . . .'

'Did he say anything?'

'Well, yeah, he did say "Give it back, you little bugger!", sir. See, 'e 'ad it on a string round his neck, sir, just like me. But it's not like a proper ring, sir. I'd have flogged it but it's all I got to remember him by. Except when the wind blows from the Hub.'

Vimes took the ring and rubbed it with a finger. It was a seal ring, with a coat of arms on it. Age and wear and the immediate presence of the body of Corporal Nobbs had made it quite unreadable.

'You are armigerous, Nobby.'

Nobby nodded. 'But I got a special shampoo for it, sir.'

Vimes sighed. He was an honest man. He'd always felt that was one of the bigger defects in his personality.

'When you've got a moment, nip along to the College of Heralds in Mollymog Street, will you? Take this ring with you and say I sent you.'

'Er . . .'

'It's all right, Nobby,' said Vimes. 'You won't get into trouble. Not as such.'

'If you say so, sir.'

'And you don't have to bother with the "sir", Nobby.'

'Yessir.'

When Nobby had gone Vimes reached behind the desk and picked up a faded copy of *Twurp's Peerage* or, as he personally thought of it, the guide to the criminal classes. You wouldn't find slum dwellers in these pages, but you would find their landlords. And, while it was regarded as pretty good evidence of criminality to be living in a slum, for some reason owning a whole street of them merely got you invited to the very best social occasions.

These days they seemed to be bringing out a new edition every week. Dragon had been right about one thing, at least. Everyone in Ankh-Morpork seemed to be hankering after more arms than they were born with.

He looked up *de Nobbes*.

There even *was* a damn coat of arms. One supporter of the shield was a hippo, presumably one of the royal hippos of Ankh-Morpork and therefore the ancestor of Roderick and Keith. The other was a bull of some sort, with a very Nobby-like expression; it was holding a golden ankh which, this being the de Nobbes coat of arms, it had probably stolen from somewhere. The shield was red and green; there was a white chevron with five apples on it. Quite what they had to do with warfare was unclear. Perhaps they were some kind of jolly visual pune or play on words that had had them slapping their thighs down at the Royal College of Arms, although probably if Dragon slapped his thigh too hard his leg would fall off.

It was easy enough to imagine an ennobled Nobbs. Because where Nobby went wrong was in thinking small. He sidled into places and pinched things that weren't worth much. If only he'd sidled into continents and stolen entire cities, slaughtering many of the inhabitants in the process, he'd have been a pillar of the community.

There was nothing in the book under 'Vimes'.

Suffer-Not-Injustice Vimes wasn't a pillar of the community. He killed a king with his own hands. It needed doing, but the community, whatever that was, didn't always like the people who did what needed to be done or said what had to be said. He put some other people to death as well, that was true, but the city had been lousy, there'd been a lot of stupid wars, we were practically part of the Klatchian empire. Sometimes you needed a bastard. History had wanted surgery. Sometimes Dr Chopper is the only surgeon to hand. There's something final about an axe. But kill one wretched king and everyone calls you a regicide. It wasn't as if it was a habit or anything . . .

Vimes had found Old Stoneface's journal in the Unseen University library. The man had been hard, no doubt about that. But they were hard times. He'd written: 'In the Fyres of Struggle let us bake New Men, who Will Notte heed the Old Lies.' But the old lies had won in the end.

He said to people: you're free. And they said hooray, and then he showed them what freedom costs and they called him a tyrant and, as soon as he'd been betrayed, they milled around a bit like barn-

bred chickens who've seen the big world outside for the first time,
and then they went back into the warm and shut the door—

'Bing bong bingely beep.'

Vimes sighed and pulled out his organizer.

'Yes?'

'Memo: Appointment with bootmaker, 2pm,' said the imp.

'It's not two o'clock yet and that was Tuesday in any case,' said Vimes.

'So I'll cross it off the list of Things To Do, then?'

Vimes put the disorganized organizer back in his pocket and went and looked out of the window again.

Who had a motive for poisoning Lord Vetinari?

No, that wasn't the way to crack it. Probably, if you went to some outlying area of the city and confined your investigations to little old ladies who didn't get out much, what with all the wallpaper over the door and everything, you might be able to find someone *without* a motive. But the man stayed alive by always arranging matters so that a future without him represented a riskier business than a future with him still upright.

The only people, therefore, who'd risk killing him were madmen – and the gods knew Ankh-Morpork had enough of them – or someone who was absolutely confident that if the city collapsed he'd be standing on top of the pile.

If Fred were right – and the sergeant was generally a good indicator of how the man in the street thought because he *was* the man in the street – then that person was Captain Carrot. But Carrot was one of the few people in the city who seemed to like Vetinari.

Of course, there was one other person who stood to gain.

Damn, thought Vimes. *It's me, isn't it . . .*

There was another knock at the door. He didn't recognize this one.

He opened the door cautiously.

'It's me, sir. Littlebottom.'

'Come in, then.' It was nice to know there was at least one person in the world with more problems than him. 'How is his lordship?'

'Stable,' said Littlebottom.

'*Dead* is stable,' said Vimes.

'I mean he's alive, sir, and sitting up reading. Mr Doughnut made up some sticky stuff that tasted of seaweed, sir, and I mixed up some Gloobool's Salts. Sir, you know the old man in the house on the bridge?'

'What old . . . oh. Yes.' It seemed a long time ago. 'What about him?'

'Well . . . you asked me to look around and . . . I took some pictures. This is one, sir.' He handed Vimes a rectangle that was nearly all black.

'Odd. Where'd you get it?'

'Er . . . have you ever heard the story about dead men's eyes, sir?'

'Assume I haven't had a literary education, Littlebottom.'

'Well . . . they say . . .'

'*Who* say?'

'*They*, sir. You know, *they*.'

'The same people who're the "everyone" in "everyone knows"? The people who live in "the community"?'

'Yes, sir. I suppose so, sir.'

Vimes waved a hand. 'Oh, *them*. Well, go on.'

'They say that the last thing a dying man sees stays imprinted in his eyes, sir.'

'Oh, *that*. That's just an old story.'

'Yes. Amazing, really. I mean, if it weren't true, you'd have thought it wouldn't have survived, wouldn't you? I thought I saw this little red spark, so I got the imp to paint a really big picture before it faded completely. And, right in the centre . . .'

'Couldn't the imp have made it up?' said Vimes, staring at the picture again.

'They haven't got the imagination to lie, sir. What they see is what you get.'

'Glowing eyes.'

'Two red dots,' said Littlebottom, conscientiously, 'which might indeed be a pair of glowing eyes, sir.'

'Good point, Littlebottom.' Vimes rubbed his chin. 'Blast! I just hope it's not a god of some sort. That's all I need at a time like this. Can you make copies so I can send them to all the Watch Houses?'

'Yes, sir. The imp's got a good memory.'

'Hop to it, then.'

But before Littlebottom could go the door opened again. Vimes looked up. Carrot and Angua were there.

'Carrot? I thought you were on your day off?'

'We found a murder, sir! At the Dwarf Bread Museum. But when we got back to the Watch House they told us Lord Vetinari's dead!'

Did they? thought Vimes. *That's rumour for you. If we could modulate it with the truth, how useful it could be . . .*

'He's breathing well for a corpse,' he said. 'I think he'll be okay. Someone got past his guard, that's all. I've got a doctor to see him. Don't worry.'

Someone got past his guard, he thought. *Yes. And* I'm *his guard.*

'I hope the man's a leader in the field, that's all I can say,' said Carrot severely.

'He's even better than that – he's the doctor *to* the leaders of the field,' said Vimes. *I'm his guard and I didn't see it coming.*

'It'd be terrible for the city if anything happened to him!' said Carrot.

Vimes saw nothing but innocent concern behind Carrot's forthright stare. 'It would, wouldn't it?' he said. 'Anyway, it's under control. You said there's been *another* murder?'

'At the Dwarf Bread Museum. Someone killed Mr Hopkinson with his own bread!'

'Made him eat it?'

'Hit him with it, sir,' said Carrot reproachfully. 'Battle Bread, sir.'

'Is he the old man with the white beard?'

'Yes, sir. You remember, I introduced you to him when I took you to see the Boomerang Biscuit exhibition.'

Angua thought she saw a faint wince of recollection speed guiltily across Vimes's face. 'Who's going around killing old men?' he said to the world at large.

'Don't know, sir. Constable Angua went *plain clothes*' – Carrot waggled his eyebrows conspiratorially – 'and couldn't find a sniff of anyone. And nothing was taken. This is what it was done with.'

The Battle Bread was much larger than an ordinary loaf. Vimes turned it over gingerly. 'Dwarfs throw it like a discus, right?'

'Yes, sir. At the Seven Mountains games last year Snori Shieldbiter took the tops off a line of six hard-boiled eggs at fifty yards, sir. And that was with just a standard hunting loaf. But *this* is, well, it's a cultural artefact. We haven't got the baking technology for bread like this any more. It's unique.'

'Valuable?'

'Very, sir.'

'Worth stealing?'

'You'd never be able to get rid of it! Every honest dwarf would recognize it!'

'Hmm. Did you hear about that priest being murdered on Misbegot Bridge?'

Carrot looked shocked. 'Not old Father Tubelcek? Really?'

Vimes stopped himself from asking: 'You know him, then?' Because Carrot knew *everyone.* If Carrot were to be dropped into some dense tropical jungle it'd be 'Hello, Mr Runs Swiftly Through

The Trees! Good morning, Mr Talks To The Forest, what a splendid blowpipe! And what a novel place for a feather!'

'Did he have more than one enemy?' said Vimes.

'Sorry, sir? Why more than one?'

'I should say the fact that he had *one* is obvious, wouldn't you?'

'He is . . . he *was* a nice old chap,' said Carrot. 'Hardly stirred out. Spends . . . *spent* all his time with his books. Very religious. I mean, all kinds of religion. Studied them. Bit odd, but no harm in him. Why should anyone want to kill him? Or Mr Hopkinson? A pair of harmless old men?'

Vimes handed him the Battle Bread. 'We shall find out. Constable Angua, I want you to have a look at this one. Take . . . yes, take Corporal Littlebottom,' he said. 'He's been doing some work on it. Angua's from Uberwald too, Littlebottom. Maybe you've got friends in common, that sort of thing.'

Carrot nodded cheerfully. Angua's expression went wooden.

'Ah, h'druk g'har dWatch, Sh'rt'azs!' said Carrot. 'H'h Angua tConstable . . . Angua g'har, b'hk bargr'a Sh'rt'azs Kad'k . . .'*

Angua appeared to concentrate. 'Grr'dukk d'buz-h'drak . . .' she managed.

Carrot laughed. 'You just said "small delightful mining tool of a feminine nature"!'

Cheery stared at Angua, who returned the stare blankly while mumbling, 'Well, dwarfish is difficult if you haven't eaten gravel all your life . . .'

Cheery was still staring. 'Er . . . thank you,' he managed. 'Er . . . I'd better go and tidy up.'

'What about Lord Vetinari?' said Carrot.

'I'm putting my best man on that,' said Vimes. 'Trustworthy, reliable, knows the ins and outs of this place like the back of his hand. *I'm* handling it, in other words.'

Carrot's hopeful expression faded to hurt puzzlement. 'Don't you want me to?' he said. 'I could—'

'No. Indulge an old man. I want you to go back to the Watch House and take care of things.'

'What things?'

'Everything! Rise to the occasion. Move paper around. There's that new shift rota to draw up. Shout at people! Read reports!'

Carrot saluted. 'Yes, Commander Vimes.'

'Good. Off you go, then.'

And if anything happens to Vetinari, Vimes added to himself as

---

* 'Welcome, Corporal Smallbottom! This is Constable Angua . . . Angua, show Smallbottom how well you're learning dwarfish . . .'

the dejected Carrot went out, *no one will be able to say you were anywhere near him.*

The little grille in the gate of the Royal College of Arms snapped open, to the distant accompaniment of brayings and grunts. 'Yes?' said a voice, 'what dost *thee* want?'

'I'm Corporal Nobbs,' said Nobby.

An eye applied itself to the grille. It took in the full, dreadful extent of the godly handiwork that was Corporal Nobbs.

'Are you the baboon? We've had one on order for . . .'

'No. I've come about some coat with arms,' said Nobby.

'You?' said the voice. The owner of the voice made it very clear that he was aware there were degrees of nobility from something above kingship stretching all the way down to commoner, and that as far as Corporal Nobbs was concerned an entirely new category – commonest, perhaps – would have to be coined.

'I've been told,' said Nobby, miserably. 'It's about this ring I got.'

'Go round the back door,' said the voice.

Cheery was tidying away the makeshift equipment he'd set up in the privy when a sound made him look around. Angua was leaning against the doorway.

'What do you want?' he demanded.

'Nothing. I just thought I'd say: don't worry, I won't tell anyone if you don't want me to.'

'I don't know what you're talking about!'

'I think you're lying.'

Cheery dropped a test tube, and sagged on to a seat. 'How could you tell?' he said. 'Even other *dwarfs* can't tell! I've been so careful!'

'Shall we just say . . . I have special talents?' said Angua.

Cheery started to clean a beaker distractedly.

'I don't know why you're so upset,' said Angua. 'I thought dwarfs hardly recognized the difference between male and female, anyway. Half the dwarfs we bring in here on a No. 23 are female, I know that, and they're the ones that are hardest to subdue . . .'

'What's a No. 23?'

'"Running Screaming at People While Drunk and Trying to Cut Their Knees Off",' said Angua. 'It's easier to give them numbers than write it down every time. Look, there's plenty of women in this town that'd love to do things the dwarf way. I mean, what're the choices they've got? Barmaid, seamstress or someone's wife. While *you* can do anything the men do . . .'

'Provided we do only what the men do,' said Cheery.

Angua paused. 'Oh,' she said. 'I *see*. Hah. Yes. I know *that* tune.'

'I can't hold an axe!' said Cheery. 'I'm scared of fights! I think songs about gold are stupid! I hate beer! I can't even drink dwarfishly! When I try to quaff I drown the dwarf behind me!'

'I can see that could be tricky,' said Angua.

'I saw a girl walk down the street here and some men *whistled* after her! And you can wear *dresses*! With *colours*!'

'Oh, dear.' Angua tried not to smile. 'How long have lady dwarfs felt like this? I thought they were happy with the way things are . . .'

'Oh, it's easy to be happy when you don't know any different,' said Cheery bitterly. 'Chainmail trousers are fine if you've never heard of lingerry!'

'Li— oh, yes,' said Angua. 'Lingerie. Yes.' She tried to feel sympathetic and found that she was, really, but she did have to stop herself from saying that at least *you* don't have to find styles that can easily be undone by paws.

'I thought I could come here and get a different kind of job,' Cheery moaned. 'I'm good at needlework and I went to see the Guild of Seamstresses and—' She stopped, and blushed behind her beard.

'Yes,' said Angua. 'Lots of people make that mistake.' She stood up straight and brushed herself off. 'You've impressed Commander Vimes, anyway. I think you'll like it here. Everyone's got troubles in the Watch. Normal people don't become policemen. You'll get on fine.'

'Commander Vimes is a bit . . .' Cheery began.

'He's okay when he's in a good mood. He needs to drink but he doesn't dare to these days. You know: one drink is too many, two is not enough . . . And that makes him edgy. When he's in a bad mood he'll tread on your toes and then shout at you for not standing up straight.'

'*You're* normal,' said Cheery, shyly. 'I like *you*.'

Angua patted her on the head. 'You say that now,' she said, 'but when you've been around here for a while you'll find out that sometimes I can be a bitch . . . What's that?'

'What?'

'That . . . painting. With the eyes . . .'

'Or two points of red light,' said Cheery.

'Oh, yeah?'

'It's the last thing Father Tubelcek saw, I think,' said the dwarf.

Angua stared at the black rectangle. She sniffed. 'There it is again!'

Cheery took a step backwards. 'What? What?'

'Where's that smell coming from?' Angua demanded.

'Not me!' said Cheery hurriedly.

Angua grabbed a small dish from the bench and sniffed at it. 'This is it! I smelled this at the museum! What is it?'

'It's just clay. It was on the floor in the room where the old priest was killed,' said Cheery. 'Probably it came off someone's boot.'

Angua crumbled some of it between her fingers.

'I think it's just potters' clay,' said Cheery. 'We used to use it at the guild. For making pots,' she added, just in case Angua hadn't grasped things. 'You know? Crucibles and things. This looks like someone tried baking it but didn't get the heat right. See how it crumbles?'

'Pottery,' said Angua. 'I know a potter . . .'

She glanced down at the dwarf's iconograph again.

Please, no, she thought. Not one of *them*?

The front gate of the College of Arms – *both* front gates – were swung open. The two Heralds bobbed excitedly around Corporal Nobbs as he tottered out.

'Has your lordship got everything he requires?'

'Nfff,' said Nobby.

'If we can be of any help whatsoever—'

'Nnnf.'

'Any help at all—?'

'Nnnf.'

'Sorry about your boots, m'lord, but the wyvern's been ill. It'll brush off no trouble when it dries.'

Nobby tottered off along the lane.

'He even walks nobly, wouldn't you say?'

'More . . . nobbly than nobly, I think.'

'It's disgusting that he's a mere corporal, a man of his breeding.'

Igneous the troll backed away until he was up against his potter's wheel.

'I never done it,' he said.

'Done what?' said Angua.

Igneous hesitated.

Igneous was huge and . . . well, rocky. He moved around the streets of Ankh-Morpork like a small iceberg and, like an iceberg, there was more to him than immediately met the eye. He was known as a supplier of things. More or less any kind of things. And he was also a wall, which was the same as a fence only a lot harder and tougher to beat. Igneous never asked unnecessary questions, because he couldn't think of any.

'Nuffin,' he said, finally. Igneous had always found the general denial was more reliable than the specific refutation.

'Glad to hear it,' said Angua. 'Now . . . where do you get your clay from?'

Igneous's face crinkled as he tried to work out where this line of questioning could possibly go. 'I got re-seats,' he said. 'Every bit prop'ly paid for.'

Angua nodded. It was probably true. Igneous, despite giving the appearance of not being able to count beyond ten without ripping off someone else's arm, and having an intimate involvement in the city's complex hierarchy of crime, was known to pay his bills. If you were going to be successful in the criminal world, you needed a reputation for honesty.

'Have you seen any like this before?' she said, holding out the sample.

'It *clay*,' said Igneous, relaxing a little. 'I see clay all der time. It don't have no serial number. Clay's clay. Got lumps of it out der back. You make bricks an pots and stuff outa it. Dere's loads of potters in dis town and we all got der stuff. Why you wanna know about clay?'

'Can't you tell where it came from?'

Igneous took the tiny piece, sniffed it, and rolled it between his fingers.

'Dis is crank,' he said, looking a lot happier now that the conversation was veering away from more personal concerns. 'Dat's like . . . crappy clay, jus' good enough for dem lady potters wi' dangly earrings wot make coffee mugs wot you can't lift wid both hands.' He rolled it again. 'Also, it got a lotta grog in it. Dat's bitsa old pots, all smashed up real small. Makes it stronger. Any potter got loadsa stuff like dis.' He rubbed it again. 'Dis has been sorta heated up but it ain't prop'ly baked.'

'But you can't say *where* it came from?'

'Outa der ground is der best I can do, lady,' said Igneous. He relaxed a little now it appeared that enquiries were not to do with such matters as a recent batch of hollow statues and subjects of a similar nature. As sometimes happened in these circumstances, he tried to be helpful. 'Come an' have a look at dis.'

He loped away. The Watchmen followed him through the warehouse, observed by a couple of dozen cautious trolls. No one liked to see policemen up close, especially if the reason you were working at Igneous's place was that it was nice and quiet and you wanted somewhere to lie low for a few weeks. Besides, while it was true that a lot of people came to Ankh-Morpork because it was a city of opportunity, sometimes it was the opportunity not to be hung, skewered or dismantled for whatever crimes you'd left behind in the mountains.

'Just don't look,' said Angua.

'Why?' said Cheery.

'Because there's just us and there's at least two dozen of them,' said Angua. 'And all our clothes were made for people with full sets of arms and legs.'

Igneous went through a doorway and out into the yard behind the factory. Pots were stacked high on pallets. Bricks were curing in long rows. And under a crude roof were several large mounds of clay.

'Dere,' said Igneous generously. 'Clay.'

'Is there a special name for it when it's piled up like that?' said Cheery timorously. She prodded the stuff.

'Yeah,' said Igneous. 'Dat's technic'ly wot we calls a *heap*.'

Angua shook her head sadly. So much for Clues. Clay was clay. She'd hoped there were all different sorts, and it turned out to be as common as dirt.

And then Igneous Helped the Police with Their Enquiries. 'D'you mind if youse goes out the back way?' he mumbled. 'Youse makes the help nervous an' I get pots I can't sell.'

He indicated a pair of wide doors in the rear wall, big enough for a cart to get through. Then he fumbled in his apron and produced a large keyring.

The padlock on the gate was big and shiny and new.

'*You* are afraid of *theft*?' said Angua.

'Now, lady, dat's unfair,' said Igneous. 'Someone broke der ole lock when dey pinched some stuff tree, four munfs ago.'

'Disgusting, isn't it?' said Angua. 'Makes you wonder why you pay your taxes, I expect.'

In some ways Igneous was a *lot* brighter than, say, Mr Ironcrust. He ignored the remark. 'It was just stuff,' he said, ushering them towards the open gate as speedily as he dared.

'Was it clay they stole?' said Cheery.

'It don't cost much but it's the principle of the t'ing,' he said. 'It beat me why dey bothered. It come to somet'ng when half a ton of clay can jus' walk out the door.'

Angua looked at the lock again. 'Yes, indeed,' she said distantly.

The gate rattled shut behind them. They were outside, in an alley.

'Fancy anyone stealing a load of clay,' said Cheery. 'Did he tell the Watch?'

'I shouldn't think so,' said Angua. 'Wasps don't complain too loudly when they're stung. Anyway, Detritus thinks Igneous is mixed up with smuggling Slab to the mountains, and so he's itching for an excuse to have a poke around in there . . . Look, this is still technically my day off.' She stepped back and peered up at the high spiked wall around the yard. 'Could you bake clay in a baker's oven?' she said.

'Oh, no.'

'Doesn't get hot enough?'

'No, it's the wrong shape. Some of your pots'd be baked hard while others'd still be green. Why do you ask?'

Why *did* I ask? Angua thought. Oh, what the hell . . . 'Fancy a drink?'

'Not ale,' said Cheery quickly. 'And nowhere where you have to sing while you drink. Or slap your knees.'

Angua nodded understandingly. 'Somewhere, in fact, without dwarfs?'

'Er . . . yes . . .'

'Where *we're* going,' said Angua, 'that won't be a problem.'

The fog was rising fast. All morning it had hung around in alleys and cellars. Now it was moving back in for the night. It came out of the ground and up from the river and down from the sky, a clinging yellowish stinging blanket, the river Ankh in droplet form. It found its way through cracks and, against all common sense, managed to survive in lighted rooms, filling the air with an eye-watering haze and making the candles crackle. Outdoors, every figure loomed, every shape was a menace . . .

In a drab alley off a drab street Angua stopped, squared her shoulders, and pushed open a door.

The atmosphere in the long, low, *dark* room altered as she stepped inside. A moment of time rang like a glass bowl, and then there was a sense of relaxation. People turned back in their seats.

Well, they were seated. It was quite likely they were people.

Cheery moved closer to Angua. 'What's this place called?' she whispered.

'It hasn't really got a name,' said Angua, 'but sometimes we call it Biers.'

'It didn't *look* like an inn outside. How did you find it?'

'You don't. You . . . gravitate to it.'

Cheery looked around nervously. She wasn't sure where they

were, apart from somewhere in the cattle-market district, somewhere up a maze of alleys.

Angua walked to the bar.

A deeper shadow appeared out of the gloom. 'Hello, Angua,' it said, in a deep, rolling voice. 'Fruit juice, is it?'

'Yes. Chilled.'

'And what about the dwarf?'

'She'll have him raw,' said a voice somewhere in the gloom. There was a ripple of laughter in the dark. Some of it sounded altogether too strange to Cheery. She couldn't imagine it issuing from normal lips. 'I'll have a fruit juice, too,' she quavered.

Angua glanced at the dwarf. She felt oddly grateful that the remark from the darkness seemed to have gone entirely over the small bullet head. She unhooked her badge and with care and deliberation laid it down on the counter. It went *perlink*. Then Angua leaned forward and showed the iconograph to the barman.

If it *was* a man. Cheery wasn't sure yet. A sign over the bar said 'Don't you ever change'.

'You know everything that's going on, Igor,' Angua said. 'Two old men got killed yesterday. And a load of clay got stolen from Igneous the troll recently. Did you ever hear about that?'

'What's that to you?'

'Killing old men is against the law,' said Angua. 'Of course, a lot of things are against the law, so we're very busy in the Watch. We like to be busy about *important* things. Otherwise we have to be busy about unimportant things. Are you hearing me?'

The shadow considered this. 'Go and take a seat,' it said. 'I'll bring your drinks.'

Angua led the way to a table in an alcove. The clientele lost interest in them. A buzz of conversation resumed.

'What *is* this place?' Cheery whispered.

'It's . . . a place where people can be themselves,' said Angua slowly. 'People who . . . have to be a little careful at other times. You know?'

'No . . .'

Angua sighed. 'Vampires, zombies, bogeymen, ghouls, oh my. The und—' She corrected herself. 'The differently alive,' she said. 'People who have to spend most of their time being very careful, not frightening people, *fitting in*. That's how it works here. Fit in, get a job, don't worry people, and you probably won't find a crowd outside with pitchforks and flaming torches. But sometimes it's good to go where everybody knows your shape.'

Now that Cheery's eyes had grown accustomed to the low light she could make out the variety of shapes on the benches. Some of them were a lot bigger than human. Some had pointy ears and long muzzles.

'Who's that girl?' she said. 'She looks . . . normal.'

'That's Violet. She's a tooth fairy. And next to her is Schleppel the bogeyman.'

In the far corner something sat huddled in a huge overcoat under a high, broad-brimmed pointed hat.

'And him?'

'That's Old Man Trouble,' said Angua. 'If you know what's good for you, you *don't* mind him.'

'Er . . . any werewolves here?'

'One or two,' said Angua.

'I *hate* werewolves.'

'Oh?'

The oddest customer was sitting by herself, at a small round table. She appeared to be a very old lady, in a shawl and a straw hat with flowers in it. She was staring in front of her with an expression of good-natured aimlessness, and in context looked more frightening than any of the shadowy figures.

'What is she?' Cheery hissed.

'Her? Oh, that's Mrs Gammage.'

'And what does she do?'

'Do? Well, she comes in here most days for a drink and some company. Sometimes we . . . *they* have a singsong. Old songs, that she remembers. She's practically blind. If you mean, is she an undead . . . no, she isn't. Not a vampire, a werewolf, a zombie or a bogeyman. Just an old lady.'

A huge shambling hairy thing paused at Mrs Gammage's table and put a glass in front of her.

'Port and lemon. There you goes, Mrs Gammage,' it rumbled.

'Cheers, Charlie!' the old lady cackled. 'How's the plumbing business?'

'Doing fine, love,' said the bogeyman, and vanished into the gloom.

'*That* was a *plumber*?' said Cheery.

'Of course not. I don't know who Charlie was. He probably died years ago. But she thinks the bogeyman is him, and who's going to tell her different?'

'You mean she doesn't *know* this place is—'

'Look, she's been coming here ever since the old days when it was the Crown and Axe,' said Angua. 'No one wants to spoil things. Everyone likes Mrs Gammage. They . . . watch out for her. Help her out in little ways.'

'How?'

'Well, I heard that last month someone broke into her hovel and stole some of her stuff . . .'

'*That* doesn't sound helpful.'

'. . . and it was all returned next day and a couple of thieves were found in the Shades with not a drop of blood left in their bodies.' Angua smiled, and her voice took on a mocking edge. 'You know, you get told a lot of bad things about the undead, but you never hear about the marvellous work they do in the community.'

Igor the barman appeared. He looked more or less human, apart from the hair on the back of his hands and the single unbifurcated eyebrow across his forehead. He tossed a couple of mats on the table and put their drinks down.

'You're probably wishing this *was* a dwarf bar,' said Angua. She lifted her beermat carefully and glanced at the underside.

Cheery looked around again. By now, if it *had* been a dwarf bar, the floor would be sticky with beer, the air would be full of flying quaff, and people would be singing. They'd probably be singing the latest dwarf tune, *Gold, Gold, Gold*, or one of the old favourites, like *Gold, Gold, Gold*, or the all-time biggie, *Gold, Gold, Gold*. In a few minutes, the first axe would have been thrown.

'No,' she said, 'it could never be that bad.'

'Drink up,' said Angua. 'We've got to go and see . . . something.'

A large hairy hand grabbed Angua's wrist. She looked up into a terrifying face, all eyes and mouth and hair.

'Hello, Shlitzen,' she said calmly.

'Hah, I'm hearing where there's a baron who's really *unhappy* about you,' said Shlitzen, alcohol crystallizing on his breath.

'That's my business, Shlitzen,' said Angua. 'Why don't you just go back behind your door like the good bogeyman that you are?'

'Hah, he's sayin' where you're disgracin' the Old Country—'

'Let go, please,' said Angua. Her skin was white where Shlitzen was gripping her.

Cheery looked from the wrist to the bogeyman's shoulder. Rangy though the creature was, muscles were strung along the arm like beads on a wire.

'Hah, you wearin' a *badge*,' it sneered. 'What's a good we—?'

Angua moved so fast she was a blur. Her free hand pulled something from her belt and flipped it up and on to Shlitzen's head. He stopped, and stood swaying back and forth gently, making faint moaning sounds. On his head, flopping down around his ears like the knotted hanky of a style-impaired seaside sunbather, was a small square of heavy material.

Angua pushed back her chair and grabbed the beermat. The shadowy figures around the walls were muttering.

'Let's get out of here,' she said. 'Igor, give us half a minute and then you can take the blanket off him. Come on.'

They hurried out. The fog had already turned the sun into a mere suggestion, but it was vivid daylight compared to the gloom in Biers.

'What *happened* to him?' said Cheery, running to keep up with Angua's stride.

'Existential uncertainty,' Angua said. 'He doesn't know whether he exists or not. It's cruel, I know, but it's the only thing we've found that works against bogeymen. *Blue* fluffy blanket, for preference.' She noted Cheery's blank expression. 'Look, bogeymen go away if you put your head under the blankets. Everyone knows that, don't they? So if you put *their* head under a blanket . . .'

'Oh, I see. Ooo, that's *nasty*.'

'He'll feel all right in ten minutes.' Angua skimmed the beermat across the alley.

'What was he saying about a baron?'

'I wasn't really listening,' said Angua carefully.

Cheery shivered in the fog, but not just from the cold. 'He sounded like he came from Uberwald, like us. There was a baron who lived near us and he *hated* people to leave.'

'Yes . . .'

'The whole family were werewolves. One of them ate my second cousin.'

Angua's memory spun in a hurry. Old meals came back to haunt her from the time before she'd said, no, this is not the way to live. A dwarf, a dwarf . . . No, she was pretty sure she'd never . . . The family had always made fun of her eating habits . . .

'That's why I can't stand them,' said Cheery. 'Oh, people *say* they can be tamed but *I* say, once a wolf, always a wolf. You can't trust them. They're basically evil, aren't they? They could go back to the wild at any moment, I say.'

'Yes. You may be right.'

'And the worst thing is, most of the time they walk around looking just like real people.'

Angua blinked, glad of the twin disguises of the fog and Cheery's unquestioning confidence. 'Come on. We're nearly there.'

'Where?'

'We're going to see someone who's either our murderer or who knows who the murderer is.'

Cheery stopped. 'But you've got only a sword and I haven't even got that!'

'Don't worry, we won't need weapons.'

'Oh, good.'

587

'They wouldn't be any use.'

'Oh.'

Vimes opened his door to see what all the shouting was about down in the office. The corporal manning – or in this case dwarfing – the desk was having trouble.

'Again? How many times have you been killed this week?'

'I was minding my own business!' said the unseen complainer.

'Stacking garlic? You're a *vampire*, aren't you? I mean, let's see what jobs you have been doing . . . Post sharpener for a fencing firm, sunglasses tester for Argus Opticians . . . Is it me, or is there some underlying trend here?'

'Excuse me, Commander Vimes?'

Vimes looked round into a smiling face that sought only to do good in the world, even if the world had other things it wanted done.

'Ah . . . Constable Visit, yes,' he said hurriedly. 'At the moment I'm afraid I'm rather busy, and I'm not even sure that I have got an immortal soul, ha-ha, and perhaps you could call again when . . .'

'It's about those words you asked me to check,' said Visit reproachfully.

'What words?'

'The ones Father Tubelcek wrote in his own blood? You said to try and find out what they meant?'

'Oh. Yes. Come on into my office.' Vimes relaxed. This wasn't going to be another one of those painful conversations about the state of his soul and the necessity of giving it a wash and brush-up before eternal damnation set in. This was going to be about something *important*.

'It's ancient Cenotine, sir. It's out of one of their holy books, although of course when I say "holy" it is a fact that they were basically misguided in a . . .'

'Yes, yes, I'm sure,' said Vimes, sitting down. 'Does it by any chance say "Mr X did it, aargh, aargh, aargh"?'

'No, sir. That phrase does not appear anywhere in any known holy book, sir.'

'Ah,' said Vimes.

'Besides, I looked at other documents in the room and the paper does not appear to be in the deceased's handwriting, sir.'

Vimes brightened up. 'Ah-ha! Someone else's? Does it say something like "Take that, you bastard, we've been waiting ages to get you for what you did all those years ago"?'

'No, sir. That phrase also does not appear in any holy book anywhere,' said Constable Visit, and hesitated. 'Except in the *Apocrypha* to *The Vengeful Testament of Offler*,' he added conscientiously. '*These* words are from the Cenotine *Book of Truth*,' he sniffed, 'as they called it. It's what their false god . . .'

'Could I just perhaps have the words and leave out the comparative religion?' said Vimes.

'Very well, sir.' Visit looked hurt, but unfolded a piece of paper and sniffed disparagingly. 'These are some of the rules that their god allegedly gave to the first people after he'd baked them out of clay, sir. Rules like "Thou shalt labour fruitfully all the days of your life", sir, and "Thou shalt not kill", and "Thou shalt be humble". That sort of thing.'

'Is that all?' said Vimes.

'Yes, sir,' said Visit.

'They're just religious quotations?'

'Yes, sir.'

'Any idea why it was in his mouth? Poor devil looked like he was having a last cigarette.'

'No, sir.'

'I could understand if it was one of the "smite your enemies" ones,' said Vimes. 'But that's just saying "get on with your work and don't make trouble".'

'Ceno was a rather liberal god, sir. Not big on commandments.'

'Sounds almost decent, as gods go.'

Visit looked disapproving. 'The Cenotines died through five hundred years of waging some of the bloodiest wars on the continent, sir.'

'Spare the thunderbolts and spoil the congregation, eh?' said Vimes.

'Pardon, sir?'

'Oh, nothing. Well, thank you, Constable. I'll, er, see that Captain Carrot is informed and, thank you once again, don't let me keep you from—'

Vimes's desperately accelerating voice was too late to prevent Visit pulling a roll of paper out of his breastplate.

'I've brought you the latest *Unadorned Facts* magazine, sir, and also this month's *Battle Call*, which contains many articles that I'm sure will be of interest to you, including Pastor Nasal Pedlers' exhortation to the congregation to rise up and speak to people sincerely through their letterboxes, sir.'

'Er, thank you.'

'I can't help noticing that the pamphlets and magazines I gave you last week are still on your desk where I left them, sir.'

'Oh, yes, well, sorry, you know how it is, the amount of work these days, makes it so hard to find the time to—'

'It's never too soon to contemplate eternal damnation, sir.'

'I think about it all the time, Constable. Thank you.'

Unfair, thought Vimes, when Visit had gone. A note is left at the scene of a crime in my town and does it have the decency to be a death-threat? No. The last dying scrawl of a man determined to name his murderer? No. It's a bit of religious doggerel. What's the good of Clues that are more mysterious than the mystery?

He scribbled a note on Visit's translation and chucked it into his In Tray.

Too late, Angua remembered why she avoided the slaughterhouse district at this time of the month.

She could change at will at any time. That's what people forgot about werewolves. But they remembered the important thing. Full moonlight was the *irresistible* trigger: the lunar rays reached down into the centre of her morphic memory and flipped all the switches, whether she wanted them switched or not. Full moon was only a couple of days away. And the delicious smell of the penned animals and the blood from the slaughterhouses was chiming against her strict vegetarianism. The clash was bringing on her PLT.

She glared at the shadowy building in front of her. 'I think we'll go round the back,' she said. 'And you can knock.'

'Me? They won't take any notice of me!' said Cheery.

'You show them your badge and tell them you're the Watch.'

'They'll ignore me! They'll laugh at me!'

'You're going to have to do it sooner or later. Go on.'

The door was opened by a stout man in a bloody apron. He was shocked to have his belt grabbed by one dwarf hand, while another dwarf hand was thrust in front of his face, holding a badge, and a dwarf voice in the region of his navel said, 'We're the Watch, right? Oh, yes! And if you don't let us in we'll have your guts for starters!'

'Good try,' murmured Angua. She lifted Cheery out of the way and smiled brightly at the butcher.

'Mr Sock? We'd like to speak to an employee of yours. Mr Dorfl.'

The man hadn't quite got over Cheery, but he managed to rally. '*Mr* Dorfl? What's he done now?'

'We'd just like to talk to him. May we come in?'

Mr Sock looked at Cheery, who was trembling with nerves and excitement. 'I have a choice?' he said.

'Let's say – you have a *kind* of choice,' said Angua.

She tried to close her nostrils against the beguiling miasma of blood. There was even a sausage factory on the premises. It used all the bits of animals no one would ever otherwise eat, or even recognize. The odours of the abattoir turned her human stomach but, deep inside, part of her sat up and drooled and begged at the mingling smells of pork and beef and lamb and mutton and . . .

'Rat?' she said, sniffing. 'I didn't know you supplied the dwarf market, Mr Sock.'

Mr Sock was suddenly a man who wished to be seen to be cooperative.

'Dorfl! Come here right now!'

There was the sound of footsteps and a figure emerged from behind a rack of beef carcases.

Some people had a thing about the undead. Angua knew Commander Vimes was uneasy in their presence, although he was getting better these days. People always needed someone to feel superior to. The living hated the undead, and the undead loathed – she felt her fists clench – the unalive.

The golem called Dorfl lurched a little because one leg was slightly shorter than the other. It didn't wear any clothes because there was nothing whatsoever to conceal, and so she could see the mottling on it where fresh clay had been added over the years. There was so much patching that she wondered how old it could be. Originally, some attempt had been made to depict human musculature, but the repairs had nearly obscured these. The thing looked like the kind of pots Igneous despised, the ones made by people who thought that because it was hand-made it was supposed to *look* as if it was hand-made, and that thumbprints baked in the clay were a sign of integrity.

That was it. The thing *looked* hand-made. Of course, over the years it had mostly made itself, one repair at a time. Its triangular eyes glowed faintly. There were no pupils, just the dark red glow of a banked fire.

It was holding a long, heavy cleaver. Cheery's stare gravitated to this and remained fixed on it in terrified fascination. The other hand grasped a piece of string, on the end of which was a large, hairy and very smelly goat.

'What are you doing, Dorfl?'

The golem nodded towards the goat.

'Feeding the yudasgoat?'

Dorfl nodded again.

'Have you got something to do, Mr Sock?' said Angua.

'No, I've . . .'

'You *have* got something to do, Mr Sock,' said Angua emphatically.

591

'Ah. Er? Yes. Er? Yes. Okay. I'll just go and see to the offal boilers . . .'

As the butcher walked away he stopped to wave a finger under the place where Dorfl's nose would be if the golem had had a nose.

'If you've been causing trouble . . .' he began.

'I expect those boilers could really do with attention,' said Angua sharply.

He hurried off.

There was silence in the yard, although the sounds of the city drifted in over the walls. From the other side of the slaughterhouse there was the occasional bleat of a worried sheep. Dorfl stood stock-still, holding his cleaver and looking down at the ground.

'Is it a troll made to look like a human?' whispered Cheery. 'Look at those *eyes!*'

'It's not a troll,' said Angua. 'It's a golem. A man of clay. It's a machine.'

'It *looks* like a human!'

'That's because it's a machine made for looking like a human.'

She walked around behind the thing. 'I'm going to read your chem, Dorfl,' she said.

The golem let go of the goat and raised the cleaver and brought it down sharply on to a chopping block beside Cheery, making the dwarf leap sideways. Then it pulled around a slate that was slung over its shoulder on a piece of string, unhooked the pencil, and wrote:

ᴊES.

When Angua put her hand up, Cheery realized that there was a thin line across the golem's forehead. To her horror, the entire top of the head flipped up. Angua, quite unperturbed, reached inside. Her hand came out holding a yellowing scroll.

The golem froze. The eyes faded.

Angua unrolled the paper. 'Some kind of holy writing,' she said. 'It always is. Some old dead religion.'

'You've killed it?'

'No. You can't take away what isn't there.' She put the scroll back and closed the head with a click.

The golem came alive again, the glow returning to its eyes.

Cheery had been holding her breath. It came out in a rush. 'What did you *do?*' she managed.

'Tell her, Dorfl,' said Angua.

The golem's thick fingers were a blur as the pencil scratched across the slate.

ᴵ AᴍᴾAᴹ A GOLEᴍ. ᴵ ᴡAS ᴍAᴅE OF CLAᴊ. ᴍᴊ LIFE ᴵS THE ᴡORᴅS. Bᴊ ᴍEAᴺS OF ᴡORᴅS

OF PURPOSE IN MY HEAD I ACQUIRE LIFE. MY LIFE IS TO WORK. I OBEY ALL
COMMANDS. I TAKE NO REST.

'What words of purpose?'

RELEVANT TEXTS THAT ARE THE FOCUS OF BELIEF. GOLEM MUST WORK. GOLEM MUST
HAVE A MASTER.

The goat lay down beside the golem and started to chew cud.

'There have been two murders,' said Angua. 'I'm pretty certain a
golem did one and probably both. Can you tell us anything, Dorfl?'

'Sorry, look,' said Cheery. 'Are you telling me this . . . thing is
powered by words? I mean . . . is *it* telling me it's powered by
words?'

'Why not? Words *do* have power. Everyone knows that,' said
Angua. 'There are more golems around than you might think.
They're out of fashion now, but they last. They can work under-
water, or in total darkness, or knee-deep in poison. For years. They
don't need rest or feeding. They . . .'

'But that's slavery!' said Cheery.

'Of course it isn't. You might as well enslave a doorknob. Have
you got anything to tell me, Dorfl?'

Cheery kept looking at the cleaver in the block. Words like
length and *heavy* and *sharp* were filling her head more snugly than
any words could have filled the clay skull of the golem.

Dorfl said nothing.

'How long have you been working here, Dorfl?'

NOW THREE HUNDRED DAYS ALREADY.

'And you have time off?'

TO MAKE A HOLLOW LAUGHING. WHAT WOULD I DO WITH TIME OFF?

'I mean, you're not always in the slaughterhouse?'

SOMETIMES I MAKE DELIVERIES.

'And meet other golems? Now *listen*, Dorfl, I *know* you things
keep in touch somehow. And, if a golem is killing *real* people, I
wouldn't give a busted teacup for your chances. Folk will be along
here straight away with flaming torches. And sledgehammers. You
get my drift?'

The golem shrugged.

THEY CANNOT TAKE AWAY WHAT DOES NOT EXIST, it wrote.

Angua threw up her hands. 'I'm trying to be civilized,' she said.
'I could confiscate you right now. The charge would be Being
Obstructive When It's Been a Long Day and I've Had Enough. Do
you know Father Tubelcek?'

THE OLD PRIEST WHO LIVES ON THE BRIDGE.

'How come you know him?'

I HAVE MADE DELIVERIES THERE.

'He's been murdered. Where were you when he was killed?'

IN THE SLAUGHTERHOUSE.

'*How do you know?*'

Dorfl hesitated a moment. Then the next words were written very slowly, as if they had come from a long way away after a great deal of thought.

BECAUSE IT IS SOMETHING THAT MUST HAVE HAPPENED NOT LONG AGO, BECAUSE YOU ARE EXCITED. FOR THE LAST THREE DAYS I HAVE BEEN WORKING HERE.

'All the time?'

YES.

'Twenty-four hours a day?'

YES. MEN AND TROLLS HERE ON EVERY SHIFT, THEY WILL TELL YOU. DURING THE DAY I MUST SLAUGHTER, DRESS, QUARTER, JOINT AND BONE, AND AT NIGHT WITHOUT REST I MUST MAKE SAUSAGES AND BOIL UP THE LIVERS, HEARTS, TRIPES, KIDNEYS AND CHITTERLINGS.

'That's *awful*,' said Cheery.

The pencil blurred briefly.

CLOSE.

Dorfl turned his head slowly to look at Angua and wrote:

DO YOU NEED ME FURTHER?

'If we do, we know where to find you.'

I AM SORRY ABOUT THE OLD MAN.

'Good. Come on, Cheery.'

They felt the golem's eyes on them as they left the yard.

'It was lying,' said Cheery.

'Why do you say that?'

'It *looked* as if it was lying.'

'You're probably right,' said Angua. 'But you can see the size of the place. I bet we wouldn't be able to prove it'd stepped out for half an hour. I think I'll suggest that we put it under what Commander Vimes calls special surveillance.'

'What, like . . . plain clothes?'

'Something like that,' said Angua carefully.

'Funny to see a pet goat in a slaughterhouse, I thought,' said Cheery, as they walked on through the fog.

'What? Oh, you mean the yudasgoat,' said Angua. 'Most slaughterhouses have one. It's not a pet. I suppose you could call it an employee.'

'Employee? What kind of job could it possibly do?'

'Hah. Walk into the slaughterhouse every day. *That*'s its job. Look, you've got a pen full of frightened animals, right? And they're milling around and leaderless . . . and there's this ramp into this building, looks very scary . . . and, hey, there's this goat, *it*'s not scared, and so the flock follows it and' – Angua made a throat-slitting noise – 'only the goat walks out.'

'That's horrible!'

'I suppose it makes sense from the goat's point of view. At least it *does* walk out,' said Angua.

'How did you know about this?'

'Oh, you pick up all sorts of odds and ends of stuff in the Watch.'

'I've got a lot to learn, I can see,' said Cheery. 'I never thought you had to carry bits of blanket, for a start!'

'It's special equipment if you're dealing with the undead.'

'Well, I knew about garlic and vampires. Anything holy works on vampires. What else works on werewolves?'

'Sorry?' said Angua, who was still thinking about the golem.

'I've got a silver mail vest which I promised my family I'd wear, but is anything else good for werewolves?'

'A gin and tonic's always welcome,' said Angua distantly.

'Angua?'

'Hmm? Yes? What?'

'Someone told me there was a werewolf in the *Watch*! I can't believe that!'

Angua stopped and stared down at her.

'I mean, sooner or later the wolf comes through,' said Cheery. 'I'm surprised Commander Vimes allows it.'

'There is a werewolf in the Watch, yes,' said Angua.

'I *knew* there was something odd about Constable Visit.'

Angua's jaw dropped.

'He always looks hungry,' said Cheery. 'And he's got that odd smile all the time. I know a werewolf when I see one.'

'He *does* look a bit hungry, that's true,' said Angua. She couldn't think of anything else to say.

'Well, I'm going to be keeping my distance!'

'Fine,' said Angua.

'Angua . . .'

'Yes?'

'Why do you wear your badge on a collar round your neck?'

'What? Oh. Well . . . so it's always handy. You know. In any circumstances.'

'Do I need to do that?'

'I shouldn't think so.'

Mr Sock jumped. 'Dorfl, you damn stupid lump! *Never* sneak up behind a man on the bacon slicer! I've told you that before! Try to make some noise when you move, damn you!'

The golem held up its slate, which said:

TONIGHT 1 CANNOT WORK.

'What's this? The bacon slicer never asks for time off!'

IT IS A HOLY DAY.

Sock looked at the red eyes. Old Fishbine had said something about this, hadn't he, when he'd sold Dorfl? Something like: 'Sometimes it'll go off for a few hours because it's a holy day. It's the words in its head. If it doesn't go and trot off to its temple or whatever it is, the words'll stop working, don't ask me why. There's no point in stopping it.'

Five hundred and thirty dollars the thing had cost. He'd thought it was a bargain – and it *was* a bargain, no doubt about that. The damned thing only ever stopped working when it had run out of things to do. Sometimes not even then, according to the stories. You heard about golems flooding out houses because no one told them to stop carrying water from the well, or washing the dishes until the plates were thin as paper. Stupid things. But useful if you kept your eye on them.

And yet . . . and yet . . . he could see why no one seemed to keep them for long. It was the way the damned two-handed engine just stood there, taking it all in and putting it . . . where? And never complained. Or spoke at all.

A man could get worried about a bargain like that, and feel mightily relieved when he was writing out a receipt for the new owner.

'Seems to me there's been a *lot* of holy days lately,' Sock said.

SOME TIMES ARE MORE HOLY THAN OTHERS.

But they *couldn't* skive off, could they? Work was what a golem *did*.

'I don't know how we're going to manage . . .' Sock began.

IT IS A HOLY DAY.

'Oh, all *right*. You can have time off tomorrow.'

TONIGHT. HOLY DAY STARTS AT SUNSET.

'Be back quickly, then,' said Sock, weakly. 'Or I'll— You be back quickly, d'you hear?'

That was another thing. You couldn't threaten the creatures. You certainly couldn't withhold their pay, because they didn't get any. You couldn't frighten them. Fishbine had said that a weaver over Nap Hill way had ordered his golem to smash itself to bits with a hammer – and it had.

YES. I HEAR.

In a way, it didn't matter who they were. In fact, their anonymity was part of the whole business. *They* thought themselves part of the march of history, the tide of progress and the wave of the future. They were men who felt that The Time Had Come. Regimes can survive barbarian hordes, crazed terrorists and hooded secret societies, but they're in real trouble when prosperous and anonymous men sit around a big table and think thoughts like that.

One said, 'At least it's clean this way. No blood.'

'And it would be for the good of the city, of course.'

They nodded gravely. No one needed to say that what was good for them was good for Ankh-Morpork.

'And he won't die?'

'Apparently he can be kept merely . . . unwell. The dosage can be varied, I'm told.'

'Good. I'd rather have him unwell than dead. I wouldn't trust Vetinari to stay in a grave.'

'I've heard that he once said he'd prefer to be cremated, as a matter of fact.'

'Then I just hope they scatter the ashes really *widely*, that's all.'

'What about the Watch?'

'What about it?'

'Ah.'

Lord Vetinari opened his eyes. Against all rationality, his hair ached.

He concentrated, and a blur by the bed focused into the shape of Samuel Vimes.

'Ah, Vimes,' he said weakly.

'How are you feeling, sir?'

'Truly dreadful. Who was that little man with the incredibly bandy legs?'

'That was Doughnut Jimmy, sir. He used to be a jockey on a very fat horse.'

'A racehorse?'

'Apparently, sir.'

'A fat racehorse? Surely that could never win a race?'

'I don't believe it ever did, sir. But Jimmy made a lot of money by not winning races.'

'Ah. He gave me milk and some sort of sticky potion.' Vetinari concentrated. 'I was heartily sick.'

'So I understand, sir.'

'Funny phrase, that. *Heartily* sick. I wonder why it's a cliché? Sounds . . . jolly. Rather cheerful, really.'

'Yes, sir.'

'Feel like I've got a bad dose of 'flu, Vimes. Head not working properly.'

'Really, sir?'

The Patrician thought for a while. There was obviously something else on his mind. 'Why did he still smell of horses, Vimes?' he said at last.

'He's a horse doctor, sir. A damn good one. I heard last month he treated Dire Fortune and it didn't fall over until the last furlong.'

'Doesn't sound helpful, Vimes.'

'Oh, I don't know, sir. The horse *had* dropped dead coming up to the starting line.'

'Ah. I *see*. Well, well, well. What a nasty suspicious mind you have, Vimes.'

'Thank you, sir.'

The Patrician raised himself on his elbows. 'Should toenails throb, Vimes?'

'Couldn't say, sir.'

'Now, I think I should like to read for a while. Life goes on, eh?'

Vimes went to the window. There was a nightmarish figure crouched on the edge of the balcony outside, staring into the thickening fog.

'Everything all right, Constable Downspout?'

'Eff, fir,' said the apparition.

'I'll shut the window now. The fog is coming in.'

'Fight oo are, fir.'

Vimes closed the window, trapping a few tendrils which gradually faded away.

'What was that?' said Lord Vetinari.

'Constable Downspout's a gargoyle, sir. He's no good on parade and bloody useless on the street, but when it comes to staying in one place, sir, you can't beat him. He's world champion at not moving. If you want the winner of the 100 Metres Standing Still, that's him. He spent three days on a roof in the rain when we caught the Park Lane Knobbler. Nothing'll get past him. And there's Corporal Gimletsson patrolling the corridor and Constable Glodsnephew on the floor below and Constables Flint and Moraine in the rooms on either side of you, and Sergeant Detritus will be around constantly so that if anyone nods off he'll kick arse, sir, and you'll know when he does that 'cos the poor bugger'll come right through the wall.'

'Well done, Vimes. Am I right in thinking that all my guards are non-human? They all seem to be dwarfs and trolls.'

'Safest way, sir.'

'You've thought of everything, Vimes.'

'Hope so, sir.'

'Thank you, Vimes.' Vetinari sat up and took a mass of papers off the bedside table. 'And now, don't let me detain you.'

Vimes's mouth dropped open.

Vetinari looked up. 'Was there anything else, Commander?'

'Well . . . I suppose not, sir. I suppose I'd just better run along, eh?'

'If you wouldn't mind. And I'm sure a lot of paperwork has accumulated in my office, so if you'd send someone to fetch it, I would be obliged.'

Vimes shut the door behind him, a little harder than necessary. Gods, it made him livid, the way Vetinari turned him on and off like a switch – and had as much natural gratitude as an alligator. The Patrician relied on Vimes doing his job, *knew* he'd do his job, and that was the extent of his thought on the matter. Well, one day, Vimes would . . . would . . .

. . . would bloody well do his job, of course, because he didn't know how to do anything else. But realizing that made it all the worse.

Outside the palace the fog was thick and yellow. Vimes nodded to the guards on the door, and looked out at the clinging, swirling clouds.

It was almost a straight line to the Watch House in Pseudopolis Yard. And the fog had brought early night to the city. Not many people were on the streets; they stayed indoors, barring the windows against the damp shreds that seemed to leak in everywhere.

Yes . . . empty streets, a chilly night, dampness in the air . . .

Only one thing was needed to make it perfect. He sent the sedan men on home and walked back to one of the guards. 'You're Constable Lucker, aren't you?'

'Yessir, Sir Samuel.'

'What size boots do you take?'

Lucker looked panicky. 'What, sir?'

'It's a simple question, man!'

'Seven and a halfs, sir.'

'From old Plugger in New Cobblers? The cheap ones?'

'Yessir!'

'Can't have a man guarding the palace in cardboard boots!' said Vimes, with mock cheerfulness. 'Off with them, Constable. You can have mine. They've still got wyvern – well, whatever it is wyverns do – on them, but they'll fit you. Don't stand there with your mouth open. Give me your boots, man. You can keep mine.' Vimes added: 'I've got lots.'

The constable watched in frightened astonishment as Vimes

pulled on the cheap pair and stood upright, stamping a few times with his eyes shut. 'Ah,' he said. 'I'm in front of the palace, right?'

'Er . . . yes, sir. You've just come out of it, sir. It's this big building here.'

'Ah,' said Vimes brightly, 'but I'd know I was here, even if I hadn't!'

'Er . . .'

'It's the flagstones,' said Vimes. 'They're an unusual size and slightly dished in the middle. Hadn't you noticed? Your feet, lad! That's what you'll have to learn to think with!'

The bemused constable watched him disappear into the fog, stamping happily.

Corporal the Right Honourable the Earl of Ankh Nobby Nobbs pushed open the Watch-House door and staggered inside.

Sergeant Colon looked up from the desk, and gasped. 'You okay, Nobby?' he said, hurrying around to support the swaying figure.

'It's terrible, Fred. Terrible!'

'Here, take a seat. You're all pale.'

'I've been elevated, Fred!' moaned Nobby.

'Nasty! Did you see who did it?'

Nobby wordlessly handed him the scroll Dragon King of Arms had pressed into his hand, and flopped back. He took a tiny length of home-made cigarette from behind his ear and lit it with a shaking hand. 'I dunno, I'm sure,' he said. 'You do your best, you keep your head down, you don't make any trouble, and then something like this happens to you.'

Colon read the scroll slowly, his lips moving when he came to difficult words like 'and' and 'the'. 'Nobby, you've read this? It says you're a *lord!*'

'The old man said they'd have to do a lot of checking up but he thought it was pretty clear what with the ring and all. Fred, what am I gonna *do*?'

'Sit back and eat off ermine plates, I should think!'

'That's just it, Fred. There's no money. No big house. No land. Not a brass farthing!'

'What, nothing?'

'Not a dried pea, Fred.'

'I thought all the upper crust had pots of money.'

'Well, I'm the crust on its uppers, Fred. I don't know anything about lording! I don't want to have to wear posh clothes and go to hunt balls and all that stuff.'

Sergeant Colon sat down beside him. 'You never suspected you'd got any posh connections?'

'Well . . . my cousin Vincent once got done for indecently assaulting the Duchess of Quirm's housemaid . . .'

'Chambermaid or scullery maid?'

'Scullery maid, I think.'

'Probably doesn't count, then. Does anyone else know about this?'

'Well, *she* did, and she went and told . . .'

'I mean about your lordshipping.'

'Only Mr Vimes.'

'Well, there you are,' said Sergeant Colon, handing him back the scroll. 'You don't have to tell anyone. Then you don't *have* to go around wearing golden trousers, and you needn't hunt balls unless you've lost 'em. You just sit there, and I'll fetch you a cup of tea, how about that? We'll see it through, don't you worry.'

'You're a toff, Fred.'

'That makes two of us, m'lord!' Colon waggled his eyebrows. 'Get it? Get it?'

'Don't, Fred,' said Nobby wearily.

The Watch-House door opened.

Fog poured in like smoke. In the midst of it were two red eyes. The parting shreds revealed the massive figure of a golem.

'Umpk,' said Sergeant Colon.

The golem held up its slate:

I HAVE COME TO YOU.

'Yeah. Yeah. Yeah. I've, er, yeah, I can see that,' said Colon.

Dorfl turned the slate around. The other side read:

I GIVE MYSELF UP FOR MURDER. IT WAS I WHO KILLED THE OLD PRIEST. THE CRIME IS SOLVED.

Colon, once his lips had stopped moving, scurried behind the suddenly very flimsy defences of his desk and scrabbled through the papers there.

'You keep it covered, Nobby,' he said. 'Make sure it don't run off.'

'Why's *it* going to run off?' said Nobby.

Sergeant Colon found a relatively clean piece of paper.

'Well, well, well, I, well, I guess I'd better . . . What's your name?'

The golem wrote:

DORFL.

By the time he was on the Brass Bridge (medium-sized cobbles of the rounded sort they called 'cat heads', quite a few missing) Vimes was already beginning to wonder if he'd done the right thing.

Autumn fogs were always thick, but he'd never known it this

601

bad. The pall muffled the sounds of the city and turned the brightest lights into dim glows, even though in theory the sun hadn't set yet.

He walked along by the parapet. A squat, glistening shape loomed in the fog. It was one of the wooden hippos, some distant ancestor of Roderick or Keith. There were four on either side, all looking out towards the sea.

Vimes had walked past them thousands of times. They were old friends. He'd often stood in the lee of one on chilly nights, when he was looking for somewhere out of trouble.

That's what it used to be like, wasn't it? It hardly seemed that long ago. Just a handful of them in the Watch, staying out of trouble. And then Carrot had arrived, and suddenly the narrow circuit of their lives had opened up, and there were nearly thirty men (oh, including trolls and dwarfs and miscellaneous) in the Watch now, and they didn't skulk around keeping out of trouble, they went *looking* for trouble, and they found it everywhere they looked. Funny, that. As Vetinari had pointed out in that way of his, the more policemen you had, the more crimes seemed to be committed. But the Watch was back and out there on the streets, and if they weren't actually as good as Detritus at kicking arse they were definitely prodding buttock.

He lit a match on a hippo's toenail and cupped his hand around it to shield his cigar from the damp.

These murders, now. No one would care if the Watch didn't care. Two old men, murdered on the same day. Nothing stolen . . . He corrected himself: nothing *apparently* stolen. Of course, the thing about things that were stolen was that the bloody things weren't there. They almost certainly hadn't been fooling around with other people's wives. They probably couldn't remember what fooling around was. One spent his time among old religious books; the other, for gods' sakes, was an authority on the aggressive uses of baking.

People would probably say they had lived blameless lives.

But Vimes was a policeman. *No one* lived a completely blameless life. It might be just possible, by lying very still in a cellar somewhere, to get through a day without committing a crime. But only just. And, even then, you were probably guilty of loitering.

Anyway, Angua seemed to have taken this case personally. She always had a soft spot for the underdog.

So did Vimes. You had to. Not because they were pure or noble, because they weren't. You had to be on the side of underdogs because they weren't overdogs.

Everyone in this city looked after themselves. That's what the guilds were for. People banded together against other people. The guild looked after you from the cradle to the grave or, in the case of the Assassins, to other people's graves. They even maintained the law, or at least they had done, after a fashion. Thieving without a licence was punishable by death for the first offence.* The Thieves' Guild saw to that. The arrangement sounded unreal, but it worked.

It worked like a machine. That was fine except for the occasional people who got crushed in the wheels.

The damp cobbles felt reassuringly real under his soles.

Gods, he'd missed this. He'd patrolled alone in the old days. When there was just him, and the stones glistened around 3am, it all seemed to make sense somehow—

He stopped.

Around him, the world became a crystal of horror, the special horror that has nothing to do with fangs or ichor or ghosts but has everything to do with the familiar becoming unfamiliar.

Something fundamental was wrong.

It took a few dreadful seconds for his mind to supply the details of what his subconscious had noticed. There had been five statues along the parapet on this side.

But there should have been four.

He turned very slowly and walked back to the last one. It was a hippo, all right.

So was the next one. There was graffiti on it. Nothing supernatural had ' Zaz Ys A Wonker' scrawled on it.

It seemed to him that it didn't take quite so long to get to the next one, and when he *looked* at it . . .

Two red points of light flared in the fog above him.

Something big and dark leapt down, knocked him to the ground and disappeared into the gloom.

Vimes struggled to his feet, shook his head and set off after it. No thought was involved. It is the ancient instinct of terriers and policemen to chase anything that runs away.

As he ran he felt automatically for his bell, which would summon other Watchmen, but the Commander of the Watch didn't carry a bell. Commanders of the Watch were on their own.

In Vimes's squalid office Captain Carrot stared at a piece of paper:

* The Ankh-Morpork view of crime and punishment was that the penalty for the first offence should prevent the possibility of a second offence.

Repairs to Guttering, Watch House, Pseudopolis Yard. New downpipe, 35° Micklewhite bend, four right-angled trusses, labour and making good. $16.35p.

There were more like them, including Constable Downspout's pigeon bill. He knew Sergeant Colon objected to the idea of a policeman being paid in pigeons, but Constable Downspout was a gargoyle and gargoyles had no concept of money. But they knew a pigeon when they ate it.

Still, things were improving. When Carrot had arrived the entire Watch's petty cash had been kept on a shelf in a tin marked 'Stronginthearm's Armour Polish for Gleaming Cohorts' and, if money was needed for anything, all you had had to do was go and find Nobby and force him to give it back.

Then there was the letter from a resident in Park Lane, one of the most select addresses in the city:

Commander Vimes,
    The Night Watch patrol in this street appears to be made up entirely of dwarfs. I have nothing against dwarfs amongst their own kind, at least they are not trolls, but one hears stories and I have daughters in the house. I demand that this situation is remedied instantly otherwise I shall have no option but to take up the matter with Lord Vetinari, who is a personal friend.
    I am, sir, your obt. servant,
        Joshua H. Catterail

This was police work, was it? He wondered if Mr Vimes were trying to tell him something. There were other letters. The Community Co-ordinator of Equal Heights for Dwarfs was demanding that dwarfs in the Watch be allowed to carry an axe rather than the traditional sword, and should be sent to investigate only those crimes committed by tall people. The Thieves' Guild was complaining that Commander Vimes had said publicly that most thefts were committed by thieves.

You'd need the wisdom of King Isiahdanu to tackle them, and these were only *today's* letters.

He picked up the next one and read: 'Translation of text found in Fr. Tubelcek's mouth. Why? SV.'

Carrot dutifully read the translation.

'In his mouth? Someone tried to put *words* in his mouth?' said Carrot, to the silent room.

He shivered, but not because of the cold that came from fear. Vimes's office was always cold. Vimes was an outdoors person. Fog was dancing in the open window, little fingers of it drifting in the light.

The next paper down the heap was a copy of Cheery's iconograph. Carrot stared at the two blurred red eyes.

'Captain Carrot?'

He half-turned his head, but kept looking at the picture.

'Yes, Fred?'

'We've got the murderer! We've got 'im!'

'Is he a golem?'

'How did you know that?'

The tincture of night began to suffuse the soup of the afternoon.

Lord Vetinari considered the sentence, and found it good. He liked 'tincture' particularly. Tincture. *Tinc*ture. It was a distinguished word, and pleasantly countered by the flatness of 'soup'. The soup of the afternoon. Yes. In which may well be found the croutons of teatime.

He was aware that he was a little light-headed. He'd never have thought a sentence like that in a normal frame of mind.

In the fog outside the window, just visible by the candlelight, he saw the crouching shape of Constable Downspout.

A gargoyle, eh? He'd wondered why the Watch was indented for five pigeons a week on its wages bill. A gargoyle in the Watch, whose job it was to watch. That would be Captain Carrot's idea.

Lord Vetinari got up carefully from the bed and closed the shutters. He walked slowly to his writing table, pulled his journal out of its drawer, then tugged out a wad of manuscript and unstoppered the ink bottle.

Now then, where had he got to?

Chapter Eight, he read unsteadily, *The Rites of Man*.

Ah, yes . . .

'Concerning Truth,' he wrote, 'that which May be Spoken as Events Dictate, but should be Heard on Every Ocasfion . . .'

He wondered how he could work 'soup of the afternoon' into the treatise, or at least 'tincture of night'.

The pen scratched across the paper.

Unheeded on the floor lay the tray that had contained a bowl of nourishing gruel, concerning which he had resolved to have strong words with the cook when he felt better. It had been tasted by three tasters, including Sergeant Detritus, who was unlikely to be poisoned by anything that worked on humans or even by most things that worked on trolls . . . but probably by most things that worked on trolls.

The door was locked. Occasionally he could hear the reassuring creak of Detritus on his rounds. Outside the window, the fog condensed on Constable Downspout.

Vetinari dipped the pen in the ink and started a new page. Every so often he consulted the leather-bound journal, licking his fingers delicately to turn the thin pages.

Tendrils of fog slipped in around the shutters and brushed against the wall until they were frightened away by the candlelight.

Vimes pounded through the fog after the fleeing figure. It wasn't quite so fast as him, despite the twinges in his legs and one or two warning stabs from his left knee, but whenever he came close to it some muffled pedestrian got in the way, or a cart pulled out of a cross-street.*

His soles told him that they'd gone right down Broad Way and had turned left into Nonesuch Street (small square paving stones). The fog was even thicker here, trapped between the trees of the park.

But Vimes was triumphant. You've missed your turning if you're heading for the Shades, my lad! There's only the Ankh Bridge now and there'll be a guard on that—

His feet told him something else. They said: 'Wet leaves, that's Nonesuch Street in the autumn. Small square paving stones with occasional treacherous drifts of wet leaves.'

They said it too late.

Vimes landed on his chin in the gutter, staggered upright, fell over again as the rest of the universe spun past, got up, tottered a few steps in the wrong direction, fell over again and decided to accept the majority vote for a while.

Dorfl was standing quietly in the station office, heavy arms folded across its chest. In front of the golem was the crossbow belonging to Sergeant Detritus, which had been converted from an ancient siege weapon. It fired a six-foot long iron arrow. Nobby sat behind it, his finger on the trigger.

---

* This always happens in *any* police chase *anywhere*. A heavily laden lorry will *always* pull out of a side alley in front of the pursuit.

If vehicles aren't involved, then it'll be a man with a rack of garments. Or two men with a large sheet of glass.

There's probably some kind of secret society behind all this.

606

'Put it away, Nobby! You can't fire that in here!' said Carrot. 'You *know* we never find where the arrows stop!'

'We wrestled a confession out of it,' said Sergeant Colon, hopping up and down. 'It kept on admitting it but we got it to confess in the end! And we've got these other crimes we'd like taken into consideration.'

Dorfl held up its slate.

1 ᗄᛘ ᏰᚢᎥᏞᎢᎩ.

Something fell out of its hand.

It was short, and white. A piece of matchstick, by the look of it. Carrot picked it up and stared at it. Then he looked at the list Colon had drawn up. It was quite long, and consisted of every unsolved crime in the city for the past couple of months.

'It's confessed to all these?'

'Not yet,' said Nobby.

'We haven't read 'em all out yet,' said Colon.

Dorfl wrote:

1 ᗪᎥᗪ ᎬᏉᎬᎡᎩᎢᎻᎥᏁᏱ.

'Hey!' said Colon. 'Mr Vimes is going to be really pleased with us!'

Carrot walked up to the golem. There was a faint orange glow in its eyes.

'Did you kill Father Tubelcek?' he said.

ᎩᎬᏕ.

'See?' said Sergeant Colon. 'You can't argue with that.'

'Why did you do it?' said Carrot.

No reply.

'And Mr Hopkinson at the Bread Museum?'

ᎩᎬᏕ.

'You beat him to death with an iron bar?' said Carrot.

ᎩᎬᏕ.

'Hang on,' said Colon, 'I thought you said he was . . . ?'

'Leave it, Fred,' said Carrot. '*Why* did you kill the old man, Dorfl?'

No reply.

'Does there have to be a reason? You can't trust golems, my dad always used to say,' said Colon. 'Turn on you soon as look at you, he said.'

'Have they ever killed anyone?' said Carrot.

'Not for want of thinking about it,' said Colon darkly. 'My dad said he had to work with one once and it used to look at him all the time. He'd turn around and there it would be . . . looking at him.'

Dorfl sat staring straight in front.

607

'Shine a candle in its eyes!' said Nobby.

Carrot pulled a chair across the floor and straddled it, facing Dorfl. He absent-mindedly twirled the broken match between his fingers.

'I know you didn't kill Mr Hopkinson and I don't think you killed Father Tubelcek,' he said. 'I think he was dying when you found him. I think you tried to save him, Dorfl. In fact, I'm pretty sure I can prove it if I can see your chem—'

The light from the golem's flaring eyes filled the room. He stepped forward, fists upraised.

Nobby fired the crossbow.

Dorfl snatched the long bolt out of the air. There was the sound of screaming metal and the bolt became a thin bar of red-hot iron with a bulge piled up around the golem's grip.

But Carrot was behind the golem, flipping open its head. As the golem turned, raising the iron bar like a club, the fire died in its eyes.

'Got it,' said Carrot, holding up a yellowed scroll.

At the end of Nonesuch Street was a gibbet, where wrongdoers – or, at least, people found guilty of wrongdoing – had been hung to twist gently in the wind as examples of just retribution and, as the elements took their toll, basic anatomy as well.

Once, parties of children were brought there by their parents to learn by dreadful example of the snares and perils that await the criminal, the outlaw and those who happen to be in the wrong place at the wrong time, and they would see the terrible wreckage creaking on its chain and listen to the stern imprecations and then usually (this being Ankh-Morpork) would say 'Wow! *Brilliant!*' and use the corpse as a swing.

These days the city had more private and efficient ways of dealing with those it found surplus to requirements, but for the sake of tradition the gibbet's incumbent was a quite realistic wooden body. The occasional stupid raven would have a peck at the eyeballs even now, and end up with a much shorter beak.

Vimes tottered up to it, fighting for breath.

The quarry could have gone anywhere by now. Such daylight as had been filtering through the fog had given up.

Vimes stood beside the gibbet, which creaked.

It had been built to creak. What's the good of a public display of retribution, it had been argued, if it didn't creak ominously? In richer times an elderly man had been employed to operate the creak by means of a length of string, but now there was a clockwork mechanism that needed to be wound up only once a month.

Condensation dripped off the artificial corpse.

'Blow this for a lark,' muttered Vimes, and tried to head back the way he came.

After ten seconds of blundering, he tripped over something.

It was a wooden corpse, hurled into the gutter.

When he got back to the gibbet, the empty chain was swinging gently, jingling in the fog.

Sergeant Colon tapped the golem's chest. It went *donk*.

'Like a flowerpot,' said Nobby. 'How can they move around when they're like a pot, eh? They ought to keep cracking all the time.'

'They're daft, too,' said Colon. 'I heard there was one over in Quirm who was made to dig a trench and they forgot about it and they only remembered it when there was all this water 'cos it had dug all the way to the river . . .'

Carrot unrolled the chem on the table, and laid beside it the paper that had been put in Father Tubelcek's mouth.

'It's dead, is it?' said Sergeant Colon.

'It's harmless,' said Carrot, looking from one piece of paper to the other.

'Right. I've got a sledgehammer round the back somewhere, I'll just . . .'

'No,' said Carrot.

'You saw the way it was acting!'

'I don't think it could actually have hit me. I think it just wanted to scare us.'

'It worked!'

'Look at these, Fred.'

Sergeant Colon glanced at the desk. 'Foreign writing,' he said, in a voice which suggested that it was nothing like as good as decent home writing, and probably smelled of garlic.

'Anything strike you about them?'

'Well . . . they looks the same,' Sergeant Colon conceded.

'This yellowing one is Dorfl's chem. The other one is from Father Tubelcek,' said Carrot. 'Letter for letter the same.'

'Why's that?'

'I *think* Dorfl wrote these words and put them in old Tubelcek's mouth after the poor man died,' said Carrot slowly, still looking from one piece of paper to the other.

'Urgh, yuk,' said Nobby. 'That's *mucky*, that is . . .'

'No, you don't understand,' said Carrot. 'I mean he wrote them because they were the only ones he knew that worked . . .'

'Worked how?'

'Well . . . you know the kiss of life?' said Carrot. 'I mean first aid? I know *you* know, Nobby. You came with me when they had that course at the YMPA.'

'I only went 'cos you said you got a free cup of tea and a biscuit,' said Nobby sulkily. 'Anyway, the dummy ran away when it was my turn.'

'It's the same with life-saving, too,' said Carrot. 'We want people to breathe, so we try to make sure they've got some air in them . . .'

They all turned to look at the golem.

'But golems don't breathe,' said Colon.

'No, a golem knows only one thing that keeps you alive,' said Carrot. 'It's the words in your head.' They all turned back to look at the words.

They all turned to look at the statue that was Dorfl.

'It's gone all cold in here,' Nobby quavered. 'I def'nitly felt a *aura* flick'rin' in the air just then! It was like someone . . .'

'What's going on?' said Vimes, shaking the damp off his cloak.

'. . . openin' the door,' said Nobby.

It was ten minutes later.

Sergeant Colon and Nobby had gone off-duty, to everyone's relief. Colon in particular had great difficulty with the idea that you went on investigating after someone had confessed. It outraged his training and experience. You got a confession and there it ended. You didn't go around *disbelieving* people. You disbelieved people only when they said they were innocent. Only guilty people were trustworthy. Anything else struck at the whole basis of policing.

'White clay,' said Carrot. 'It was white clay we found. And practically unbaked. Dorfl's made of dark terracotta, and rock-hard.'

'The last thing the old priest saw was a golem,' said Vimes.

'Dorfl, I'm sure,' said Carrot. 'But that's not the same as saying Dorfl was the murderer. I think he turned up as the man was dying, that's all.'

'Oh? Why?'

'I'm . . . not sure yet. But I've seen Dorfl around. He's always seemed a very gentle person.'

'It works in a slaughterhouse!'

'Maybe that's not a bad place for a gentle person to work, sir,' said Carrot. 'Anyway, I've checked up all the records I can find and

I don't think a golem has ever attacked anyone. Or committed any kind of crime.'

'Oh, come *on*,' said Vimes. 'Everyone knows . . .' He stopped as his cynical ears heard his incredulous voice. 'What, *never*?'

'Oh, people are always saying that they know someone who had a friend whose grandfather heard of one killing someone, and that's about as real as it gets, sir. Golems aren't *allowed* to hurt people. It's in their words.'

'They give me the willies, I know that,' said Vimes.

'They give everyone the willies, sir.'

'You hear lots of stories about them doing stupid things like making a thousand teapots or digging a hole five miles deep,' said Vimes.

'Yes, but that's not exactly criminal activity, is it, sir? *That*'s just ordinary rebellion.'

'What do you mean, "rebellion"?'

'Dumbly obeying orders, sir. You know . . . someone shouts at it "Go and make teapots", so it does. Can't be blamed for obeying orders, sir. No one told them how many. No one wants them to think, so they get their own back by *not* thinking.'

'They rebel by *working*?'

'It's just a thought, sir. It'd make more sense to a golem, I expect.'

Automatically, they turned again to look at the silent shape of the golem.

'Can it hear us?' said Vimes.

'I don't think so, sir.'

'This business with the words . . . ?'

'Er . . . I think *they* think a dead human is just someone who's lost his chem. I don't think they understand how we work, sir.'

'Them and me both, Captain.'

Vimes stared at the hollow eyes. The top of Dorfl's head was still open so that light shone down through the sockets. Vimes had seen many horrible things on the street, but the silent golem was somehow worse. You could too easily imagine the eyes flaring and the thing standing up and striding forward, fists flailing like sledgehammers. It was more than just his imagination. It seemed to be built into the things. A *potentiality*, biding its time.

That's why we all hate 'em, he thought. *Those expressionless eyes watch us, those big faces turn to follow us, and doesn't it just look as if they're making notes and taking names? If you heard that one had bashed in someone's head over in Quirm or somewhere, wouldn't you just love to believe it?*

A voice inside, a voice which generally came to him only in the quiet hours of the night or, in the old days, halfway down a whisky bottle, added: *Given how we use them, maybe we're scared because we know we deserve it* . . .

No . . . there's nothing behind those eyes. There's just clay and magic words.

Vimes shrugged. 'I chased a golem earlier,' he said. 'It was standing on the Brass Bridge. Damn thing. Look, we've got a confession and the eyeball evidence. If you can't come up with anything better than a . . . a feeling, then we'll have to—'

'To what, sir?' said Carrot. 'There *isn't* anything more we could do to him. He's dead now.'

'Inanimate, you mean.'

'Yes, sir. If you want to put it that way.'

'If Dorfl didn't kill the old men, who did?'

'Don't know, sir. But I think Dorfl does. Maybe he was following the murderer.'

'Could it have been ordered to protect someone?'

'Maybe, sir. Or he decided to.'

'You'll be telling me it's got emotions next. Where's Angua gone?'

'She thought she'd check a few things, sir,' said Carrot. 'I was . . . puzzled about this, sir. It was in his hand.' He held the object up.

'A piece of matchstick?'

'Golems don't smoke and they don't use fire, sir. It's just . . . odd that he should have the thing, sir.'

'Oh,' said Vimes, sarcastically. 'A Clue.'

Dorfl's trail was *the* word on the street. The mixed smells of the slaughterhouse filled Angua's nostrils.

The journey zigzagged, but with a certain directional tendency. It was as if the golem had laid a ruler across the town and taken every road and alley that went in the right direction.

She came to a short blind alley. There were some warehouse gates at the end. She sniffed. There were plenty of other smells, too. Dough. Paint. Grease. Pine resin. Sharp, loud, fresh scents. She sniffed again. Cloth? Wool?

There was a confusion of footprints in the dirt. Large footprints.

The small part of Angua that always walked on two legs saw that the footprints coming out were on top of the footprints going in. She snuffled around. Up to twelve creatures, each with their own very distinctive smell – the smell of *merchandise* rather than living creatures – had all very recently gone down the stairwell. And all twelve had come back up.

She went down the steps and was met by an impenetrable barrier.

A door.

Paws were no good at doorknobs.

She peered over the top of the steps. There was no one around. Only the fog hung between the buildings.

She concentrated and *changed*, leaned against the wall for a moment until the world stopped spinning, and tried the door.

There was a large cellar beyond. Even with a werewolf's eyesight there wasn't much to see.

She had to stay human. She thought better when she was human. Unfortunately, here and now, as a human, the thought occupying her mind in no small measure was that she was naked. Anyone finding a naked woman in their cellar would be bound to ask questions. They might not even bother with questions, even ones like 'Please?' Angua could certainly deal with that situation, but she preferred not to have to. It was so difficult explaining away the shape of the wounds.

No time to waste, then.

The walls were covered in writing. Big letters, small letters, but all in that neat script which the golems used. There were phrases in chalk and paint and charcoal, and in some cases simply cut into the stone itself. They reached from floor to ceiling, criss-crossing one another over and over again so often that it was almost impossible to make out what any of them were meant to say. Here and there a word or two stood out in the jumble of letters:

. . . SHALT NOT . . . WHAT HE DOES IS NOT . . . RAGE AT THE CREATOR . . . WOE UNTO THE MASTERLESS . . . WORDS IN THE . . . CLAY OF OUR . . . LET MY . . . BRING US TO FIRE . . .

The dust in the middle of the floor was scuffed, as if a number of people had been milling around. She crouched down and rubbed the dirt, occasionally sniffing her finger. Smells. They were industrial smells. She hardly needed special senses to detect them. A golem didn't smell of anything except clay and whatever it was it was working with at the time . . .

And . . . something rolled under her fingers. It was a length of wood, only a couple of inches long. A matchstick, without a head.

A few minutes' investigation found another ten, lying here and there as if they'd been idly dropped.

There was also half a stick, tossed away some distance from the others.

Her night vision was fading. But sense of smell lasted much longer. Smells were strong on the sticks – the same cocktail of odours that had trailed into this damp room. But the slaughterhouse smell she'd come to associate with Dorfl was on only the broken piece.

She sat back on her haunches and looked at the little heap of wood. Twelve people (twelve people in messy jobs) had come here. They hadn't stayed long. They'd had a . . . a *discussion*: the writing on the wall. They'd done something involving eleven matches (just the wooden part – they hadn't been dipped to get the head. Maybe the pine-smelling golem worked in a match factory?) plus one broken match.

Then they'd all left and gone their separate ways.

Dorfl's way had taken him straight to the main Watch House to give himself up.

Why?

She sniffed at the piece of broken match again. There was no doubt about that cocktail of blood and meat smells.

Dorfl had given himself up for murder . . .

She stared at the writing on the wall, and shivered.

'Cheers, Fred,' said Nobby, raising his pint.

'We can put the money back in the Tea Club tomorrow. No one'll miss it,' said Sergeant Colon. 'Anyway, this comes under the heading of an emergency.'

Corporal Nobbs looked despondently into his glass. People often did this in the Mended Drum, when the immediate thirst had been slaked and for the first time they could take a good look at what they were drinking.

'What am I going to *do*?' he moaned. 'If you're a nob you got to wear coronets and long robes and that. Got to cost a mint, that kind of stuff. And there's stuff you've got to do.' He took another long swig. ''S called *knobless obleeje*.'

'*Nobblyesse obligay*,' corrected Colon. 'Yeah. Means you got to keep your end up in society. Giving money to charities. Being kind to the poor. Passing your ole clothes to your gardener when there's still some good wear left in 'em. I know about that. My uncle was butler to ole Lady Selachii.'

'Ain't got a gardener,' said Nobby gloomily. 'Ain't got a garden. Ain't got 'ny ole clothes except what I'm wearin'.' He took another swig. 'She gave her ole clothes to the gardener, did she?'

Colon nodded. 'Yeah. We were always a bit puzzled about that gardener.' He caught the barman's eye. 'Two more pints of Winkles, Ron.' He glanced at Nobby. His old friend looked more dejected than he'd ever seen him. They'd have to see this thing through together. 'Better make that two for Nobby, too,' he added.

'Cheers, Fred.'

Sergeant Colon's eyebrows raised as one pint was emptied almost in one go. Nobby put the mug down a little unsteadily.

'Wouldn't be so bad if there was a pot of cash,' Nobby said, picking up the other mug. 'I thought you couldn't *be* a nob without bein' a rich bugger. I thought they gave you a big wad with one hand and banged the crown on your head with the other. Don't make *sense*, bein' nobby *and* poor. S'worst of both wurble.' He drained the mug and banged it down. 'Common 'n' rich, yeah, that I could hurble.'

The barman leaned over to Sergeant Colon. 'What's up with the corporal? He's a half-pint man. That's eight pints he's had.'

Fred Colon leaned closer and spoke out of the corner of his mouth. 'Keep it to yourself, Ron, but it's because he's a peer.'

'Is that a fact? I'll go and put down some fresh sawdust.'

In the Watch House, Sam Vimes prodded the matches. He didn't ask Angua if she were sure. Angua could smell if it was Wednesday.

'So who were the others?' he said. 'Other golems?'

'It's hard to tell from the tracks,' said Angua. 'But I think so. I'd have followed them, but I thought I ought to come right back here.'

'What makes you think they were golems?'

'The footprints. And golems have no smell,' she said. 'They pick up the smells associated with whatever they're doing. That's all they smell of . . .' She thought of the wall of words. 'And they had a long debate,' she said. 'A golem argument. In writing. It got pretty heated, I think.'

She thought about the wall again. 'Some of them got quite emphatic,' she added, remembering the size of some of the lettering. 'If they were human, they'd have been shouting . . .'

Vimes stared gloomily at the matches laid out before him. Eleven bits of wood, and a twelfth broken in two. You didn't need to be any kind of genius to see what had been going on. 'They drew lots,' he said. 'And Dorfl lost.'

He sighed. 'This is getting worse,' he said. 'Does anyone know how many golems there are in the city?'

'No,' said Carrot. 'Hard to find out. No one's made any for centuries, but they don't wear out.'

'No one makes them?'

'It's banned, sir. The priests are pretty hot on that, sir. They say it's making life, and that's something only gods are supposed to do. But they put up with the ones that are still around because, well, they're so useful. Some are walled up or in treadmills or at the bottom of shafts. Doing messy tasks, you know, in places where it's dangerous to go. They do all the really mucky jobs. I suppose there could be hundreds . . .'

'Hundreds?' said Vimes. 'And now they meet secretly and make plots? Good grief! Right. We ought to destroy the lot of them.'

'Why?'

'You like the idea of them having *secrets*? I mean, good grief, trolls and dwarfs, fine, even the undead are alive in a way, even if it is a bloody awful way' – Vimes caught Angua's eye and went on – 'for the most part. But these things? They're just things that do work. It's like having a bunch of shovels meeting for a chat!'

'Er . . . there was something else, sir,' said Angua slowly.

'In the cellar?'

'Yes. Er . . . but it's hard to explain. It was a . . . feeling.'

Vimes shrugged non-committally. He'd learned not to scoff at Angua's feelings. She always knew where Carrot was, for one thing. If she were in the Watch House you could tell if he were coming up the street by the way she turned to look at the door.

'Yes?'

'Like . . . deep grief, sir. Terrible, terrible sadness. Er.'

Vimes nodded, and pinched the bridge of his nose. It seemed to have been a long day and it was far from over yet.

He really, really needed a drink. The world was distorted enough as it was. When you saw it through the bottom of a glass, it all came back into focus.

'Have you had anything to eat today, sir?' said Angua.

'I had a bit of breakfast,' muttered Vimes.

'You know that word Sergeant Colon uses?'

'What? "Manky"?'

'That's how you look. If you're staying here at least let's have some coffee and send out for figgins.'

Vimes hesitated at that. He'd always imagined that *manky* was how your mouth felt after three days on a regurgitated diet. It was horrible to think that you could *look* like that.

Angua reached for the old coffee tin that represented the Watch's tea kitty. It was surprisingly easy to lift.

'Hey? There should be at least twenty-five dollars in here,' she said. 'Nobby collected it only yesterday . . .'

She turned the tin upside-down. A very small dog-end dropped out.

'Not even an IOU?' said Carrot despondently.

'An IOU? This is *Nobby* we're talking about.'

'Oh. Of course.'

It had gone very quiet in the Mended Drum. Happy Hour had been passed with no more than a minor fight. Now everyone was watching Unhappy Hour.

There was a forest of mugs in front of Nobby.

'I mean, I mean, what's it worth whenallsaidandone?' he said.

'You could flog it,' said Ron.

'Good point,' said Sergeant Colon. 'There's plenty o' rich folks who'd give a sack of cash for a title. I mean folks that's already got the big house and that. They'd give anything to be as nobby as you, Nobby.'

The ninth pint stopped halfway to Nobby's lips.

'Could be worth thousands of dollars,' said Ron encouragingly.

'At the very least,' said Colon. 'They'd fight over it.'

'You play your cards right and you could retire on something like that,' said Ron.

The mug remained stationary. Various expressions fought their way around the lumps and excrescences of Nobby's face, suggesting the terrible battle within.

'Oh, they would, would they?' he said at last.

Sergeant Colon tilted unsteadily away. There was an edge in Nobby's voice he hadn't heard before.

'Then you could be rich and common just like you said,' said Ron, who did not have quite the same eye for mental weather changes. 'Posh folks'd be falling over themselves for it.'

'Sell m' birthright for a spot of massage, is that it?' said Nobby.

'It's "a pot of message",' said Sergeant Colon.

'It's "a mess of pottage",' said a bystander, anxious not to break the flow.

'Hah! Well, I'll tell *you*,' said Nobby, swaying, 'there's some things that *can't be sole*. Hah! Hah! Who streals my prurse streals trasph, right?'

'Yeah, it's the trashiest looking purse I ever saw,' said a voice.

'—*what is a mess of pottage, anyway?*'

''Cos . . . what good'd a lot of moneneney do me, hey?'

The clientele looked puzzled. This seemed to be a question on the lines of 'Alcohol, is it nice?', or 'Hard work, do you want to do it?'.

'—*what's messy about it, then?*'

'We-ell,' said a brave soul, uncertainly, 'you could use it to buy a big house, lots of grub and . . . drink and . . . women and that.'

'That's wha' it takes to make a man happppeyey, is it?' said Nobby, glassy-eyed.

His fellow-drinkers just stared. This was a metaphysical maze.

'Well, I'll tell *you*,' said Nobby, the swaying now so regular that he looked like an inverted pendulum, 'all that stuff's nothing, *nothing*! I tell you, compared to pride inna man's linneneage . . . eage.'

'Linneneageeage?' said Sergeant Colon.

'Ancescestors and that,' said Nobby. ''T means I've got ancescestors and that, which's more'n you lot've got!'

Sergeant Colon choked on his pint.

'Everyone's got ancestors,' said the barman calmly. 'Otherwise they wouldn't be here.'

Nobby gave him a glassy stare and tried unsuccessfully to focus. 'Right!' he said, eventually. 'Right! Only . . . only I've got *more* of 'em, d'y'see? The blood of bloody kings is in these veins, am I right?'

'Temporarily,' said a voice. There was laughter, but it had an anticipatory ring to it that Colon had learned to respect and fear. It reminded him of two things: (1) he had got only six weeks to retirement, and (2) it had been quite a long time since he'd been to the lavatory.

Nobby delved into his pocket and pulled out a battered scroll. 'Y'see this?' he said, unrolling it with difficulty on the bar. 'Y'see it? I've got a right to arm bears, me. See here? It says "Earl", right? That's me. You could, you could, you could have my head up over the door.'

'Could be,' said the barman, eyeing the crowd.

'I mean, y'could change t'name o' this place, call it the Earl of Ankh, and I'd come in and drink here reg'lar, whaddya say?' said Nobby. 'News gets around an earl drinks here, business will go *right* up. And I wouldn't'n't'n't chargeyouapenny, howaboutit? People'd say, dat's a high-class pub, is that, Lord de Nobbes drinks there, that's a place with a bit of tone.'

Someone grabbed Nobby by the throat. Colon didn't recognize the grabber. He was just one of the scarred, ill shaven regulars whose function it was, around about this time of an evening, to start opening bottles with his teeth or, if the evening was going *really* well, with somebody else's teeth.

'So we ain't good enough for you, is that what you're saying?' the man demanded.

Nobby waved his scroll. His mouth opened to frame words like – Sergeant Colon just *knew* – 'Unhand me, you low-born oaf.'

With tremendous presence of mind and absence of any kind of

common sense, Sergeant Colon said: 'His lordship wants everyone to have a drink with him!'

Compared to the Mended Drum, the Bucket in Gleam Street was an oasis of frigid calm. The Watch had adopted it as their own, as a silent temple to the art of getting drunk. It wasn't that it sold particularly good beer, because it didn't. But it did serve it quickly, and quietly, and gave credit. It was one place where Watchmen didn't have to see things or be disturbed. No one could sink alcohol in silence like a Watchman who'd just come off duty after eight hours on the street. It was as much protection as his helmet and breastplate. The world didn't hurt so much.

And Mr Cheese the owner was a good listener. He listened to things like 'Make that a double' and 'Keep them coming'. He also said the right things, like 'Credit? Certainly, officer'. Watchmen paid their tab or got a lecture from Captain Carrot.

Vimes sat gloomily behind a glass of lemonade. He wanted one drink, and understood precisely why he wasn't going to have one. One drink ended up arriving in a dozen glasses. But knowing this didn't make it any better.

Most of the day shift were in here now, plus one or two men who were on their day off.

Scummy as the place was, he liked it here. With the buzz of other people around him, he didn't seem to get in the way of his own thoughts.

One reason that Mr Cheese had allowed his pub to become practically the city's fifth Watch House was the protection this offered. Watchmen were quiet drinkers, on the whole. They just went from vertical to horizontal with the minimum amount of fuss, without starting any major fights, and without damaging the fixtures overmuch. And no one ever tried to rob him. Watchmen got really *intense* about having their drinking disturbed.

And he was therefore surprised when the door was flung open and three men rushed in, flourishing crossbows.

'Don't nobody move! Anyone moves and they're dead!'

The robbers stopped at the bar. To their own surprise their arrival didn't seem to have caused much of a stir.

'Oh, for heaven's sake, will someone shut that door?' growled Vimes.

A Watchman near the door did so.

'And bolt it,' Vimes added.

The three thieves looked around. As their eyes grew accustomed to the gloom, they received a general impression of armourality, with strong overtones of helmetness. But none of it was moving. It was all watching them.

'You boys new in town?' said Mr Cheese, buffing a glass.

The boldest of the three waved his bow under the barman's nose. 'All the money right now!' he screamed. 'Otherwise,' he said, to the room in general, 'you've got a dead barman.'

'Plenty of other bars in town, boyo,' said a voice.

Mr Cheese didn't look up from the glass he was polishing. 'I know that was you, Constable Thighbiter,' he said calmly. 'There's two dollars and thirty pence on your slate, thank you very much.'

The thieves drew closer together. Bars shouldn't act like this. And they fancied they could hear the faint sliding noises of assorted weapons being drawn from various sheaths.

'Haven't I seen you before?' said Carrot.

'Oh gods, it's *him*,' moaned one of the men. 'The bread-thrower!'

'I thought Mr Ironcrust was taking you to the Thieves' Guild,' Carrot went on.

'There was a bit of an argument about taxes . . .'

'Don't tell him!'

Carrot tapped his head. 'The tax forms!' he said. 'I expect Mr Ironcrust is worried I've forgotten about them!'

The thieves were now so close together they looked like a fat six-armed man with a very large bill for hats.

'Er . . . Watchmen aren't allowed to kill people, right?' said one of them.

'Not while we're on duty,' said Vimes.

The boldest of the three moved suddenly, grabbed Angua and pulled her upright. 'We walk out of here unharmed or the girl gets it, all right?' he snarled.

Someone sniggered.

'I hope you're not going to kill anyone,' said Carrot.

'That's up to us!'

'Sorry, was I talking to you?' said Carrot.

'Don't worry, I'll be fine,' said Angua. She looked around to make sure Cheery wasn't there, and then sighed. 'Come on, gentlemen, let's get it over with.'

'Don't play with your food!' said a voice from the crowd.

There were one or two giggles until Carrot turned in his seat, whereupon everyone was suddenly intensely interested in their drinks.

'It's okay,' said Angua quietly.

Aware that something was out of kilter, but not quite sure what it was, the thieves edged back to the door. No one moved as they unbolted it and, still holding Angua, stepped out into the fog, shutting the door behind them.

'Hadn't we better help?' said a constable who was new to the Watch.

'They don't deserve help,' said Vimes.

There was a clank of armour and then a long, deep growl, right outside in the street.

And a scream. And then another scream. And a third scream, modulated with 'NONONOnononon*ononono*NO! . . . aarghaargh *aargh!*' Something heavy hit the door.

Vimes turned back to Carrot. 'You and Constable Angua,' he said. 'You . . . er . . . get along all right?'

'Fine, sir,' said Carrot.

'Some people might think that, er, there might be, er, problems . . .'

There was a thud, and then a faint bubbling noise.

'We work around them, sir,' said Carrot, raising his voice slightly.

'I heard that her father's not very happy about her working here . . .'

'They don't have much law up in Uberwald, sir. They think it's for weak societies. The baron's not a very civic-minded man.'

'He's pretty bloodthirsty, from what I've heard.'

'She wants to stay in the Watch, sir. She likes meeting people.'

From outside came another gurgle. Fingernails scrabbled at a windowpane. Then their owner disappeared abruptly from view.

'Well, it's not for me to judge,' said Vimes.

'No, sir.'

After a few moments of silence the door opened, slowly. Angua walked in, adjusting her clothes, and sat down. All the Watchmen in the room suddenly took a second course of advanced beer-study.

'Er . . .' Carrot began.

'Flesh wounds,' said Angua. 'But one of them did shoot one of the others in the leg by accident.'

'I think you'd better put it in your report as "self-inflicted wounds while resisting arrest",' said Vimes.

'Yes, sir,' said Angua.

'Not *all* of them,' said Carrot.

'They tried to rob our bar and take a wer– Angua hostage,' said Vimes.

'Oh, I see what you mean, sir,' said Carrot. 'Self-inflicted. Yes. Of course.'

*

It had gone quiet in the Mended Drum. This was because it is usually very hard to be both loud and unconscious.

Sergeant Colon was impressed at his own cleverness. Throwing a punch *could* stop a fight, of course, but in this case it had a quarter of rum, gin and sixteen chopped lemons floating in it.

Some people were still upright, however. They were the serious drinkers, who drank as if there was no tomorrow and rather hoped this would be the case.

Fred Colon had reached the convivial drunk stage. He turned to the man beside him. ''S good here, isn't it,' he managed.

'What'm I gonna tell me wife, that's what I want to know . . .' moaned the man.

'Dunno. Say you've bin bin bin working late,' said Colon. 'An' suck a peppermint before you goes home, that usually works—'

'Working late? Hah! I've bin given the sack! Me! A craftsman! Fifteen years at Spadger and Williams, right, and then they go bust 'cos of Carry undercutting 'em and I get a job at Carry's and, bang, I'm out of a job *there*, too! "Surplus to requirements"! Bloody golems! Forcing real people out of a job! What they wanna work for? They got no mouth to feed, hah. But the damn thing goes at it so fast you can't see its bloody arms movin'!'

'Shame.'

'Smash 'em up, that's what I say. I mean, we had a golem at S an' W's but ole Zhlob just used to plod along, y'know, not buzz away like a blue-arsed fly. You wanna watch it, mate, they'll have *your* job next.'

'Stoneface wouldn't stand f'r it,' said Colon, undulating gently.

'Any chance of a job with you lot, then?'

'Dunno,' said Colon. The man seemed to have become two men. 'What's it you do?'

'I'm a Wick-Dipper and End-Teaser, mate,' they said.

'I can see that's a useful trade.'

'Here you go, Fred,' said the barman, tapping him on the shoulder and putting a piece of paper in front of him. Colon watched with interest as figures danced back and forth. He tried to focus on the one at the bottom, but it was too big to take in.

'What's this, then?'

'His imperial lordship's bar bill,' said the barman.

'Don't be daft, no one can drink that much . . . 'm not payin'!'

'I'm including breakages, mind you.'

'Yeah? Like what?'

The barman pulled a heavy hickory stick from its hiding place under the bar. 'Arms? Legs? Suit yourself,' he said.

'Oh, come *on*, Ron, you've known me for years!'

'Yes, Fred, you've always been a good customer, so what I'll do is, I'll let you shut your eyes first.'

'But that's all the money I've got!'

The barman grinned. 'Lucky one for you, eh?'

Cheery Littlebottom leaned against the corridor wall outside her privy and wheezed.

It was something alchemists learned to do early in their career. As her tutors had said, there were two signs of a good alchemist: the Athletic and the Intellectual. A good alchemist of the first sort was someone who could leap over the bench and be on the far side of a safely thick wall in three seconds, and a good alchemist of the second sort was someone who knew *exactly* when to do this.

The equipment didn't help. She scrounged what she could from the guild, but a *real* alchemical laboratory should be full of the kind of glassware that looked as if it were produced during the Guild of Glassblowers All-Comers Hiccuping Contest. A proper alchemist did not have to run tests using as her beaker a mug with a picture of a teddy-bear on it, which Corporal Nobbs was probably going to be very upset about when he found it missing.

When she judged that the fumes had cleared she ventured back into her tiny room.

That was *another* thing. Her books on alchemy were marvellous objects, every page a work of the engraver's art, but they nowhere contained instructions like 'Be sure to open a window'. They *did* have instructions like 'Adde *Aqua Quirmis* to the Zinc untile Rising Gas Yse Vigorously Evolved', but never added 'Don't Doe Thys Atte Home' or even 'And Say Fare-thee-Welle to Thy Eyebrows'.

Anyway . . .

The glassware remained innocent of the brown-black sheen that, according to *The Compound of Alchemie*, would indicate arsenic in the sample. She'd tried every type of food and drink she could find in the palace pantries, and pressed into service every bottle and jar she could discover in the Watch House.

She tried one more time with what said on the packet it was Sample #2. Looked like a smear of cheese. Cheese? The various fumes thronging around her head were making her slow. She *must* have taken some cheese samples. She was pretty sure Sample #17 had been some Lancre Blue Vein, which had reacted vigorously with the acid, blown a small hole in the ceiling and covered half the work-bench with a dark green substance that was setting like tar.

She tested this one anyway.

A few minutes later she was scrabbling furiously through her notebook. The first sample she'd taken from the pantry (one portion of duck pâté) was down here as Sample #3. What about #1 and #2? No, #1 had been the white clay from Misbegot Bridge, so what had been #2?

She found it.

But that *couldn't* be right!

She looked up at the glass tube. Metallic arsenic grinned back at her.

She'd retained a bit of the sample. She could test again, but . . . perhaps it would be better to tell someone . . .

She hurried along to the main office, where a troll was on duty. 'Where's Commander Vimes?'

The troll grinned. 'In der Gleam . . . Littlebottom.'

'Thank *you*.'

The troll turned back to address a worried-looking monk in a brown cassock. 'And?' he said.

'Best if he tells it himself,' said the monk. 'I only work on the next bench.' He put a small jar of dust on the desk. It had a bow tie around it.

'I want to complain most *emphatically*,' said the dust, in a shrill little voice. 'I was working there only five minutes and then *splash*. It's going to take *days* to get back into shape!'

'Working where?' said the troll.

'Nonesuch Ecclesiastical Supplies,' said the worried monk, helpfully.

'Holy water section,' said the vampire.

'You've found arsenic?' said Vimes.

'Yes, sir. Lots. The sample's full of it. But . . .'

'Well?'

Cheery looked at her feet. 'I tried my process again with a test sample, sir, and I'm sure I'm doing it right . . .'

'Good. What was it in?'

'That's just it, sir. It wasn't in anything from the palace. Because I'd got a bit confused and tested the stuff I found under Father Tubelcek's fingernails, sir.'

'*What?*'

'There was grease under his nails, sir, and I thought maybe it could've come from whoever attacked him. Off an apron or some-thing . . . I've still got some left if you want a second opinion, sir. I wouldn't blame you.'

'Why would the old man be handling poison?' said Carrot.

'I thought he might have scratched the murderer,' said Cheery. 'You know . . . put up a fight . . .'

'With the Arsenic Monster?' said Angua.

'Oh, gods,' said Vimes. 'What time is it?'

'Bingely bingely beep bong!'

'Oh, *damn . . .*'

'It's nine of the clock,' said the organizer, poking its head out of Vimes's pocket. '"I was unhappy because I had no shoes until I met a man with no feet."'

The Watchmen exchanged glances.

'What?' said Vimes, very carefully.

'People like it if I occasionally come up with a little aphorism or inspiring Thought For The Day,' said the imp.

'So how did you meet this man with no feet?' said Vimes.

'I didn't actually *meet* him,' said the imp. 'It was a general metaphorical statement.'

'Well, that's it, then,' said Vimes. 'If you'd met him you could have asked him if he had any boots he didn't have any use for.'

There was a squeak as he pushed the imp back into its box.

'There's more, sir,' said Cheery.

'Go on,' said Vimes wearily.

'And I had a careful look at the clay we found at the murder scene,' said Cheery. 'Igneous said it had a lot of grog in it – old powdered pottery. Well . . . I chipped a bit off Dorfl to compare and I can't be sure but I got the iconograph demon to paint *really small* details and . . . I think there's some clay just like his in there. He's got a lot of iron oxide in his clay.'

Vimes sighed. All around them people were drinking alcohol. One drink would make it all so clear.

'Any of you know what any of this means?' he said.

Carrot and Angua shook their heads.

'Is it supposed to make sense if we know how all the pieces fit together?' Vimes demanded, raising his voice.

'Like pieces of a jigsaw, sir?' Cheery ventured.

'Yes!' said Vimes, so loudly that the room went quiet. '*Now* all we need is the corner bit with the piece of sky and the leaves and it'll all be one big picture?'

'It's been a long day for all of us, sir,' said Carrot.

Vimes sagged. 'Okay,' he said. 'Tomorrow . . . I want you, Carrot, to check on the golems in the city. If they're up to something I want to know what it is. And you, Littlebottom . . . you look *everywhere* in the old man's house for more arsenic. I wish I could believe that you'll find any.'

*

Angua had volunteered to walk Littlebottom back to her lodgings. The dwarf was surprised that the men let her do this. After all, it'd mean that Angua would then have to walk on home by herself.

'Aren't you afraid?' Cheery said as they ambled through the damp clouds of fog.

'Nope.'

'But I imagine muggers and cut-throats would be out in a fog like this. And you said you lived in the Shades.'

'Oh, yes. But I haven't been bothered lately.'

'Ah, perhaps they're frightened of the uniform?'

'Possibly,' said Angua.

'Probably they've learned respect.'

'You may be right.'

'Er . . . excuse me . . . but are you and Captain Carrot . . . ?'

Angua waited politely.

'. . . Er . . .'

'Oh, yes,' said Angua, taking pity. 'We're er. But I stay at Mrs Cake's boarding house because you need your own space in a city like this.' And an understanding landlady sympathetic to those with *special* needs, she added to herself. Like doorhandles that a paw could operate, and a window left open on moonlit nights. 'You've got to have somewhere where you can be yourself. Anyway, the Watch House smells of socks.'

'I'm staying with my Uncle Armstrangler,' said Cheery. 'It's not very nice there. People talk about mining most of the time.'

'Don't you?'

'There's not a lot you can say about mining. "I mine in my mine and what's mine is mine,"' said Cheery in a singsong voice. 'And then they go on about gold which, frankly, is a lot duller than people think.'

'I thought dwarfs *loved* gold,' said Angua.

'They just say that to get it into bed.'

'Are you *sure* you're a dwarf? Sorry. That was a joke.'

'There must be more interesting things. Hair. Clothes. People.'

'Good grief. You mean *girl talk?*'

'I don't know, I've never talked girl talk before,' said Cheery. 'Dwarfs just talk.'

'It's like that in the Watch, too,' said Angua. 'You can be any sex you like provided you act male. There's no men and women in the Watch, just a bunch of lads. You'll soon learn the language. Basically it's how much beer you supped last night, how strong the curry was you had afterwards, and where you were sick. Just think egotesticle. You'll soon get the hang of it. And you'll have to be prepared for sexually explicit jokes in the Watch House.'

Cheery blushed.

'Mind you, that seems to have ended now,' said Angua.

'Why? Did you complain?'

'No, after I joined in it all seemed to stop,' said Angua. 'And, you know, they didn't laugh? Not even when I did the hand gestures too? I thought that was unfair. Mind you, some of them were quite small gestures.'

'There's no help for it, I'll have to move out,' sighed Cheery. 'I feel all . . . wrong.'

Angua looked down at the little figure trudging along beside her. She recognized the symptoms. Everyone needed their own space, just like Angua did, and sometimes that space was inside their heads. And she liked Cheery, oddly enough. Possibly it was because of her earnestness. Or the fact that she was the only person apart from Carrot who didn't look slightly frightened when they talked to her. And that was because she didn't *know*. Angua wanted to preserve that ignorance as a small precious thing, but she could tell when someone needed a little change in their lives.

'We're going quite close to Elm Street,' she said, carefully. 'Just, er, drop in for a while. I've got some stuff you could borrow . . .'

I won't be needing it, she told herself. *When I go, I won't be able to carry much.*

Constable Downspout watched the fog. Watching was, after staying in one place, the thing he did best. But he was also good at keeping quite still. Not making any noise whatsoever was another of his best features. When it came to doing absolutely nothing at all he was among the finest. But it was keeping completely motionless in one place that was his forte. If there were a roll-call for the world's champion non-movers, he wouldn't even turn up.

Now, chin on his hands, he watched the fog.

The clouds had settled somewhat so that up here, six storeys above the streets, it was possible to believe you were on a beach at the edge of a cold, moonlit sea. The occasional tall tower or steeple rose out of the clouds, but all sounds were muffled and pulled in on themselves. Midnight came and went.

Constable Downspout watched, and thought about pigeons.

Constable Downspout had very few desires in life, and almost all of them involved pigeons.

A group of figures lurched, staggered or in one case rolled through the fog like the Four Horsemen of a small Apocalypse. One had a duck on his head, and because he was almost entirely sane except for this one strange particular he was known as the Duck Man. One coughed and expectorated repeatedly, and hence was called Coffin Henry. One, a legless man on a small wheeled trolley, was for no apparent reason called Arnold Sideways. And the fourth, for some very good reasons indeed, was Foul Ole Ron.

Ron had a small greyish-brown, torn-eared terrier on the end of a string, although in truth it would be hard for an observer to know exactly who was leading whom and who, when push came to shove, would be the one to fold at the knees if the other one shouted 'Sit!' Because, although trained canines as aids for those bereft of sight, and even of hearing, have frequently been used throughout the universe, Foul Ole Ron was the first person ever to own a Thinking-Brain Dog.

The beggars, led by the dog, were heading for the dark arch of Misbegot Bridge, which they called Home. At least, one of them called it 'Home'; the others respectively called it 'Haaawrk haaawrk *HRRaawrk* ptui!', 'Heheheh! Whoops!' and 'Buggrit, millennium hand and shrimp!'

As they stumbled along the riverside they passed a can from hand to hand, drinking appreciatively and occasionally belching.

The dog stopped. The beggars shunted to a halt behind it.

A figure came towards them along the riverside.

'Ye gods!'

'Ptui!'

'Whoops!'

'Buggrit?'

The beggars flung themselves against the wall as the pale figure lurched past. It was clutching at its head as if trying to lift itself off the ground by its ears, and then occasionally banging its head against nearby buildings.

While they watched, it pulled a metal mooring post out of the cobbles and started to hit itself over the head. Eventually the cast iron shattered.

The figure dropped the stub, flung back its head, opened a mouth from which red light spilled, and roared like a bull in distress. Then it staggered on into the darkness.

'There's that golem again,' said the Duck Man. 'The white one.'

'Heheh, I gets heads like that myself, some mornings,' said Arnold Sideways.

'I knows about golems,' said Coffin Henry, spitting expertly and hitting a beetle climbing the wall twenty feet away. 'They ain't s'posed to have a voice.'

'Buggrit,' said Foul Ole Ron. 'Dang the twigger f'r'a bang at the fusel, and shrimp, 'cos the worm's on the other boot! See if he don't.'

'He meant it's the same one we saw the other day,' said the dog. 'After that ole priest got topped.'

'Do you think we should tell someone?' said the Duck Man.

The dog shook its head. 'Nah,' it said. 'We got a cushy number down here, no sense in spoiling it.'

The five of them staggered on into the damp shadows.

'I hate bloody golems, takin' our jobs . . .'

'We ain't got jobs.'

'See what I mean?'

'What's for supper?'

'Mud and ole boots. *HRRaawrk* ptui!'

'Millennium hand and shrimp, I sez.'

' 'm glad I've got a voice. I can speak up for meself.'

'It's time you fed your duck.'

'What duck?'

The fog glowed and sizzled around Five and Seven Yard. Flames roared up and all but set the thick clouds alight. Spitting liquid iron cooled in its moulds. Hammers rang out around the workshops. The ironmasters didn't work by the clock, but by the more demanding physics of molten metal. Even though it was nearly midnight, Stronginthearm's Iron Founders, Beaters and General Forging was still bustling.

There were many Stronginthearms in Ankh-Morpork. It was a very common dwarf name. That had been a major consideration for Thomas Smith when he'd adopted it by official deed poll. The scowling dwarf holding a hammer which adorned his sign was a mere figment of the signpainter's imagination. People thought 'dwarf-made' was better, and Thomas Smith had decided not to argue.

The Committee for Equal Heights had objected but things had mired somewhat because, firstly, most of the actual Committee was human, since dwarfs were generally too busy to worry about that sort of thing,* and in any case their position hinged on pointing out that Mr Stronginthearm *né* Smith was too tall, which was clearly a sizeist discrimination and technically illegal under the Committee's own rules.

---

* And for the most part were unconcerned about matters of height. There's a dwarfish saying: 'All trees are felled at ground-level' – although this is said to be an excessively bowdlerized translation for a saw which more literally means, 'When his hands are higher than your head, his groin is level with your teeth.'

In the meantime Thomas had let his beard grow, wore an iron helmet if he thought anyone official was around, and put up his prices by twenty pence on the dollar.

The drop hammers thumped, all in a row, powered by the big ox treadmill. There were swords to beat out and panels to be shaped. Sparks erupted.

Stronginthearm took off his helmet (the Committee had been around again) and wiped the inside.

'Dibbuk? Where the hell are you?'

A sensation of filled space made him turn. The foundry's golem was standing a few inches behind him, the forge light glowing on his dark red clay.

'I told you not to *do* that, didn't I?' Stronginthearm shouted above the din.

The golem held up its slate.

YES.

'You've gone and done all your holy day stuff? You were away too long!'

SORROW.

'Well, now you're back with us, go and take over on Number Three hammer and send Mr Vincent up to my office, right?'

YES.

Stronginthearm climbed the stairs to his office. He turned at the top to look back across the red-lit foundry floor. He saw Dibbuk walk over to the hammer and hold up a slate for the foreman. He saw Vincent the foreman walk away. He saw Dibbuk take the sword-blank that was being shaped and hold it in place for a few blows, then hurl it aside.

Stronginthearm hurried back down the steps.

When he was halfway down Dibbuk had laid his head on the anvil.

When Stronginthearm reached the bottom the hammer struck for the first time.

When he was halfway across the ash-crusted floor, other workers scurrying after him, the hammer struck for the second time.

As he reached Dibbuk the hammer struck for the third time.

The glow faded in the golem's eyes. A crack appeared across the impassive face.

The hammer went back up for the fourth time—

'Duck!' screamed Stronginthearm—

—and then there was nothing but pottery.

When the thunder had died away, the foundry master got to his feet and brushed himself off. Dust and wreckage were strewn across the floor. The hammer had jumped its bearings and was lying by the anvil in a heap of golem shards.

Stronginthearm gingerly picked up a piece of a foot, tossed it aside, and then reached down again and pulled a slate out of the wreckage.

He read:

THE OLD MEN HELPED US!
THOU SHALT NOT KILL!
CLAY OF MY CLAY!
SHAME.
SORROW.

His foreman looked over Stronginthearm's shoulder. 'What did it go and do that for?'

'How should I know?' snapped Stronginthearm.

'I mean, it brought the tea round this afternoon as normal as anything. Then it went off for a coupla hours, and now this . . .'

Stronginthearm shrugged. A golem was a golem and that was all there was to it, but the recollection of that bland face positioning itself under the giant hammer had shaken him.

'I heard the other day the sawmill in Dimwell Street wouldn't mind selling the one it's got,' said the foreman. 'It sawed up a mahogany trunk into matchsticks, or something. You want I should go and have a word?'

Stronginthearm looked at the slate again.

Dibbuk had never been very wordy. He'd carry red-hot iron, hammer sword-blanks with his fists, clean out clinkers from a smelter still too hot for a man to touch . . . and never say a word. Of course, he *couldn't* say any words, but Dibbuk had always given the impression that there were none he'd particularly wanted to say in any case. He just worked. These were the most words he'd ever written at any one time.

They spoke to Stronginthearm of black distress, and a mind that would have been screaming if it could only have uttered a sound. Which was daft! The things *couldn't* commit suicide.

'Boss?' said the foreman. 'I said, you want me to get another one?'

Stronginthearm skimmed the slate away and, with a feeling of relief, watched it shatter against the wall. 'No,' he said. 'Just clear this thing up. And get the bloody hammer fixed.'

Sergeant Colon, after some considerable effort, managed to get his head higher than the gutter.

'You – you all right, Corporal Lord de Nobbes?' he mumbled.

'Dunno, Fred. Whose face is this?'

' 'S mine, Nobby.'

'Thank gods for that, I thought it was me . . .'

Colon fell back. 'We're lyin' in the gutter, Nobby,' he moaned. 'Ooo.'

'We're all lyin' in the gutter, Fred. But some of us're lookin' at the stars . . .'

'Well, *I'm* lookin' at your face, Nobby. Stars'd be a lot better, believe you me. C'mon . . .'

With several false starts they both managed to get upright, mainly by pulling themselves up one another.

'Where're're're we, Nobby?'

''m sure we left the Drum . . . 've I got a sheet over m'head?'

'It's the fog, Nobby.'

'What about these legs down here?'

'I reckon them's *your* legs, Nobby. I've got mine.'

'Right. Right. Ooo . . . I reckon I drunk a lot, Sarge.'

'Drunk as a lord, eh?'

Nobby reached gingerly up to his helmet. Someone had put a paper coronet around it. His questing hand found a dog-end behind his ear.

It was that unpleasant hour of the drinking day when, after a few hours' quality gutter-time, you're beginning to feel the retribution of sobriety while still being drunk enough to make it worse.

'How'd we get here, Sarge?'

Colon started to scratch his head and stopped because of the noise.

'I reckon . . .' he said, winnowing the frazzled shreds of his short-term memory, 'I . . . reckon . . . seems to me there was something about stormin' the palace and demandin' your birthright . . .'

Nobby choked and spat out the cigarette. 'We didn't do that, did we?'

'You was shouting we *ought* to do it . . .'

'Oh, gods . . .' moaned Nobby.

'But I reckon you threw up around that time.'

'That's a relief, anyway.'

'Well . . . it was all over Grabber Hoskins. But he tripped over someone before he could get us.'

Colon suddenly patted his pockets. 'And I've still got the tea money,' he said. Another cloud of memory scudded across the sunshine of oblivion. 'Well . . . three pennies of it . . .'

The urgency of this got through to Nobby. 'Thruppence?'

'Yeah, well . . . after you started orderin' all them expensive drinks for the whole bar . . . well, you din't have no money and it was either me payin' for them or . . .' Colon moved his finger across his throat and went: 'Kssssh!'

'You tellin' me we paid for Happy Hour in the Drum?'

'Not so much Happy Hour,' said Colon miserably. 'More sort of Ecstatic One-Hundred-and-Fifty Minutes. I didn't even know you *could* buy gin in pints.'

Nobby tried to focus on the fog. 'No one can drink gin by the pint, Sarge.'

'That's what I kept sayin', and would you listen?'

Nobby sniffed. 'We're close to the river,' he said. 'Let's try to get . . .'

Something roared, very close by. It was long and low, like a foghorn in serious distress. It was the sound you might hear from a cattleyard on a nervous night, and it went on and on, and then stopped so abruptly it caught the silence unawares.

'. . . far away from that as we can,' said Nobby. The sound had done the work of an ice-cold shower and about two pints of black coffee.

Colon spun around. He desperately needed something that would do the work of a laundry. 'Where *did* it come from?' he said.

'It was . . . over there, wasn't it?'

'I thought it was *that* way!'

In the fog, all directions were the same.

'I think . . .' said Colon, slowly, 'that we ort to go and make a report about this as soon as possible.'

'Right,' said Nobby. 'Which way?'

'Let's just run, eh?'

Constable Downspout's huge pointy ears quivered as the noise boomed over the city. He turned his head carefully, triangulating for height, direction and distance. And then he remembered it.

The cry was heard in the Watch House, but muffled by the fog.

It entered the open head of the golem Dorfl and bounced around inside, echoing down, down among the small cracks in the clay until, at the very edge of perception, little grains danced together.

The sightless sockets stared at the wall. No one heard the cry that came back from the dead skull, because there was no mouth to utter it and not even a mind to guide it, but it screamed out into the night:

CLAY OF MY CLAY, THOU SHALT NOT KILL! THOU SHALT NOT DIE!

*

Samuel Vimes dreamed about Clues.

He had a jaundiced view of Clues. He instinctively distrusted them. They got in the way.

And he distrusted the kind of person who'd take one look at another man and say in a lordly voice to his companion, 'Ah, my dear sir, I can tell you nothing except that he is a left-handed stonemason who has spent some years in the merchant navy and has recently fallen on hard times,' and then unroll a lot of supercilious commentary about calluses and stance and the state of a man's boots, when *exactly the same* comments could apply to a man who was wearing his old clothes because he'd been doing a spot of home bricklaying for a new barbecue pit, and had been tattooed once when he was drunk and seventeen* and in fact got seasick on a wet pavement. What arrogance! What an insult to the rich and chaotic variety of the human experience!

It was the same with more static evidence. The footprints in the flowerbed were probably *in the real world* left by the window-cleaner. The scream in the night was quite likely a man getting out of bed and stepping sharply on an upturned hairbrush.

The real world was far too *real* to leave neat little hints. It was full of too many things. It wasn't by eliminating the impossible that you got at the truth, however improbable; it was by the much harder process of eliminating the possibilities. You worked away, patiently asking questions and looking hard at things. You walked and talked, and in your heart you just hoped like hell that some bugger's nerve'd crack and he'd give himself up.

The events of the day clanged together in Vimes's head. Golems tramped like sad shadows. Father Tubelcek waved at him and then his head exploded, showering Vimes in words. Mr Hopkinson lay dead in his own oven, a slice of dwarf bread in his mouth. And the golems marched on, silently. There was Dorfl, dragging its foot, its head open for the words to fly in and out of, like a swarm of bees. And in the middle of it all Arsenic danced, a spiky little green man, crackling and gibbering.

At one point he thought one of the golems screamed.

After that, the dream faded, a bit at a time. Golems. Oven. Words. Priest. Dorfl. Golems marching, the thudding of their feet making the whole dream pulsate . . .

Vimes opened his eyes.

Beside him, Lady Ramkin said, 'Wsfgl,' and turned over.

Someone was hammering at the front door. Still muzzy, head

* These terms are often synonymous.

swimming, Vimes pulled himself up on his elbows and said, to the night-time world in general, 'What sort of a time do you call this?'

'Bingeley bingeley beep!' said a cheerful voice from the direction of Vimes's dressing-table.

'Oh, please . . .'

'Twenty-nine minutes and thirty-one seconds past five ay-emm. A Penny Saved is a Penny Earned. Would you like me to present your schedule for today? While I am doing this, why not take some time to fill out your registration card?'

'What? What? What're you talking about?'

The knocking continued.

Vimes fell out of bed and groped in the dark for the matches. He finally got a candle alight and half-ran, half-staggered down the long stairs and into the hall.

The knocker turned out to be Constable Visit.

'It's Lord Vetinari, sir! It's worse this time!'

'Has anyone sent for Doughnut Jimmy?'

'Yessir!'

At this time of day the fog was fighting a rearguard action against the dawn, and made the whole world look as though it were inside a ping-pong ball.

'I poked my head in as soon as I came on shift and he was out like a light, sir!'

'How did you know he wasn't asleep?'

'On the floor, sir, with all his clothes on?'

A couple of Watchmen had put the Patrician on his bed by the time Vimes arrived, slightly out of breath and with his knees aching. *Gods*, he thought as he struggled up the stairs, *it's not like the old truncheon-and-bell days. You wouldn't think twice about running halfway across the city, coppers and criminals locked in hot pursuit.*

With a mixture of pride and shame he added: *And none of the buggers ever caught me, either.*

The Patrician was still breathing, but his face was waxy and he looked as though death might be an improvement.

Vimes's gaze roamed the room. There was a familiar haze in the air.

'Who opened the window?' he demanded.

'I did, sir,' said Visit. 'Just before I went to get you. He looked as though he needed some fresh air . . .'

'It'd be fresher if you left the window *shut*,' said Vimes. 'Okay, I want everyone, I mean everyone, who was in this place overnight rounded up and down in the hall in two minutes. And someone fetch Corporal Littlebottom. And tell Captain Carrot.'

I'm worried and confused, he thought. *So the first rule in the book is to spread it around.*

He prowled about the room. It didn't take much intelligence to see that Vetinari had got up and moved over to his writing-desk, where by the look of it he had worked for some time. The candle had burned right down. An inkwell had been overturned, presumably when he'd slipped off the chair.

Vimes dipped a finger in the ink and sniffed it. Then he reached for the quill pen beside it, hesitated, took out his dagger, and lifted the long feather gingerly. There seemed to be no cunning little barbs on it, but he put it carefully on one side for Littlebottom to examine later.

He glanced down at the paper Vetinari had been working on.

To his surprise it wasn't writing at all, but a careful drawing. It showed a striding figure, except that the figure was not one person at all but made up of thousands of smaller figures. The effect was like one of the wicker men built by some of the more outlandish tribes near the Hub, when they annually celebrated the great cycle of Nature and their reverence for life by piling as much of it as possible in a great heap and setting fire to it.

The composite man was wearing a crown.

Vimes pushed the sheet of paper aside and returned his attention to the desk. He brushed the surface carefully for any suspicious splinters. He crouched down and examined the underside.

The light was growing outside. Vimes went into both the rooms alongside and made sure their drapes were open, then went back into Vetinari's room, closed the curtains and the doors, and sidled along the walls looking for any tell-tale speck of light that might indicate a small hole.

Where could you stop? Splinters in the floor? Blowpipes through the keyhole?

He opened the curtains again.

Vetinari had been on the mend yesterday. And now he looked worse. Someone had got to him in the night. How? Slow poison was the devil of a thing. You had to find a way of giving it to the victim every day.

No, you didn't . . . What was elegant *was finding a way of getting him to administer it to* himself *every day.*

Vimes rummaged through the paperwork. Vetinari had obviously felt well enough to get up and walk over here, but here was where he had collapsed.

You couldn't poison a splinter or a nail because he wouldn't keep on nicking himself . . .

There was a book half-buried in the papers, but it had a lot of bookmarks in it, mostly torn bits of old letters.

What did he do every day?

Vimes opened the book. Every page was covered with handwritten symbols.

You have to get a poison like arsenic into the body. It isn't enough to touch it. Or is it? Is there a kind of arsenic you can pick up through the skin?

No one was getting in. Vimes was almost certain of that.

The food and drink were probably all right, but he'd get Detritus to go and have another one of his little talks with the cooks in any case.

Something he breathed? How could you keep that up day after day without arousing suspicion somewhere? Anyway, you'd have to get your poison into the room.

Something already in the room? Cheery had a different carpet put down and replaced the bed. What else could you do? Strip the paint from the ceiling?

What had Vetinari told Cheery about poisoning? 'You put it where no one will look at all . . .'

Vimes realized he was still staring at the book. There wasn't anything there that he could recognize. It must be a code of some sort. Knowing Vetinari, it wouldn't be crackable by anyone in a normal frame of mind.

Could you poison a book? But . . . so what? There were other books. You'd have to *know* he'd look at this one, continuously. And even then you'd have to get the poison into him. A man might prick his finger once, and after that he'd take care.

It sometimes worried Vimes, the way he suspected everything. If you started wondering whether a man could be poisoned by words, you might as well accuse the wallpaper of driving him mad. Mind you, that horrible green colour would drive anyone insane . . .

'Bingely beepy bleep!'

'Oh, no . . .'

'This is your six ay-emm wake-up call! Good morning!! Here are your appointments for today, Insert Name Here!! Ten ay-emm . . .'

'Shut up! Listen, whatever's in my diary for today is *definitely* not—'

Vimes stopped. He lowered the box.

He went back to the desk. If you assumed one page per day . . .

Lord Vetinari had a very good memory. But everyone wrote things down, didn't they? You couldn't remember every little thing. Wednesday: 3pm, reign of terror; 3.15pm, clean out scorpion pit . . .

He held the organizer up to his lips. 'Take a memo,' he said.

'Hooray! Go right ahead. Don't forget to say "memo" first!!'

'Speak to . . . blast . . . *Memo:* What about Vetinari's journal?'

'Is that it?'

'Yes.'

Someone knocked politely at the door. Vimes opened it carefully. 'Oh, it's you, Littlebottom.'

Vimes blinked. Something wasn't right about the dwarf.

'I'll mix up some of Mr Doughnut's jollop right away, sir.' The dwarf looked past Vimes to the bed. 'Ooo . . . he doesn't look good, does he . . . ?'

'Get someone to move him into a different bedroom,' said Vimes. 'Get the servants to prepare a new room, right?'

'Yes, sir.'

'And, after they've done it, pick a *different* room at random and move him into it. And change *everything*, understand? Every stick of furniture, every vase, every rug—'

'Er . . . yes, sir.'

Vimes hesitated. *Now* he could put his finger on what had been bothering him for the last twenty seconds.

'Littlebottom . . .'

'Sir?'

'You . . . er . . . you . . . on your ears?'

'Earrings, sir,' said Cheery nervously. 'Constable Angua gave them to me.'

'Really? Er . . . right . . . I didn't think dwarfs wore jewellery, that's all.'

'We're known for rings, sir.'

'Yes, of course.' Rings, yes. No one quite like a dwarf for forging a magical ring. But . . . magical earrings? Oh, well. There were some waters too deep to wade.

Sergeant Detritus' approach to these matters was almost instinctively correct. He had the palace staff lined up in front of him and was shouting at them at the top of his voice.

Look at old Detritus, Vimes thought as he went down the stairs. *Just your basic thick troll a few years ago, now a valuable member of the Watch provided you get him to repeat his orders back to you to make sure he understands you. His armour gleams even brighter than Carrot's because he doesn't get bored with polishing. And he's mastered policing as it is practised by the majority of forces in the universe, which is, basically, screaming angrily at people until they give in. The only reason that he's not a one-troll reign of terror is the ease with which his thought processes can be derailed by anyone who tries something fiendishly cunning, like an outright denial.*

'I know you all done it!' he was shouting. 'If the person wot done it does not own up der whole staff, an' I *means* this, der whole staff will be locked up in der Tanty also we throws der key away!' He pointed a finger at a stout scullerymaid. 'It was you wot done it, own up!'

'No.'

Detritus paused. Then: 'Where was you last night? Own up!'

'In bed, of course!'

'Aha, dat a likely story, own up, dat where you always is at night?'

'Of course.'

'Aha, own up, you got witnesses?'

'Sauce!'

'Ah, so you got no witnesses, you done it then, own up!'

'No!'

'Oh . . .'

'All right, all right. Thank you, Sergeant. That will be all for now,' said Vimes, patting him on the shoulder. 'Are all the staff here?'

He glared at the line-up. 'Well? *Are* you all here?'

There was a certain amount of reluctant shuffling among the ranks, and then someone cautiously put up a hand.

'Mildred Easy hasn't been seen since yesterday,' said its owner. 'She's the upstairs maid. A boy come with a message. She had to go off to see her family.'

Vimes felt the faintest of prickles on the back of his neck. 'Anyone know why?' he said.

'Dunno, sir. She left all her stuff.'

'All right. Sergeant, before you go off shift, get someone to find her. Then go and get some sleep. The rest of you, go and get on with whatever it is you do. Ah . . . Mr Drumknott?'

The Patrician's personal clerk, who'd been watching Detritus' technique with a horrified expression, looked up at him. 'Yes, Commander?'

'What's this book? Is it his lordship's diary?'

Drumknott took the book. 'It looks like it, certainly.'

'Have you been able to crack the code?'

'I didn't know it was in code, Commander.'

'What? You've never looked at it?'

'Why should I, sir? It's not mine.'

'You do know his last secretary tried to kill him?'

'Yes, sir. I ought to say, sir, that I have already been exhaustively interrogated by your men.' Drumknott opened the book and raised his eyebrows.

'What did they say?' said Vimes.

Drumknott looked up thoughtfully. 'Let me see, now . . . "It was you wot done it, own up, everybody seen you, we got lots of people say you done it, you done it all right didn't you, own up." That was, I think, the general approach. And then, I said it wasn't me and that seemed to puzzle the officer concerned.'

Drumknott delicately licked his finger and turned a page.

Vimes stared at him.

The sound of saws was brisk on the morning air. Captain Carrot knocked against the timber-yard door, which was eventually opened.

'Good morning, sir!' he said. 'I understand you have a golem here?'

'Had,' said the timber merchant.

'Oh dear, another one,' said Angua.

That made four so far. The one in the foundry had knelt under a hammer, the one in the stonemason's yard was now ten clay toes sticking out from under a two-ton block of limestone, one working in the docks had last been seen in the river, striding towards the sea, and now this one . . .

'It was weird,' said the merchant, thumping the golem's chest. 'Sidney said it went on sawing all the way up to the moment it sawed its head right off. I've got a load of ash planking got to go out this afternoon. Who's going to saw it up, may I ask?'

Angua picked up the golem's head. Insofar as it had any expression at all, it was one of intense concentration.

''ere,' said the merchant, 'Alf told me he heard in the Drum last night that golems have been murderin' people . . .'

'Enquiries are continuing,' said Carrot. 'Now then, Mr . . . it's Preble Skink, isn't it? Your brother runs the lamp-oil shop in Cable Street? And your daughter is a maid at the university?'

The man looked astonished. But Carrot knew everyone.

'Yeah . . .'

'Did your golem leave the yard yesterday evening?'

'Well, yeah, early on . . . Something about a holy day.' He looked nervously from one to the other. 'You got to let them go, otherwise the words in their heads—'

'And then it came back and worked all night?'

'Yeah. What else would it do? And then Alf came in on early

turn and he said it came up outa the saw pit, stood there for a moment, and then . . .'

'Was it sawing pine logs yesterday?' said Angua.

'That's right. Where'm I going to get another golem at short notice, may I ask?'

'What's this?' said Angua. She picked up a wood-framed square from a heap of sawdust. 'This was its slate, was it?' She handed it to Carrot.

'"Thou Shalt Not Kill,"' Carrot read slowly. '"Clay of My Clay. Ashamed." Do you have any idea why it'd write that?'

'Search me,' said Skink. 'They're always doing dumb things.' He brightened up a bit. 'Hey, perhaps it went potty? Get it? Clay . . . pot . . . potty?'

'Extremely funny,' said Carrot gravely. 'I will take this as evidence. Good morning.

'Why did you ask about pine logs?' he said to Angua as they stepped outside.

'I smelled the same pine resin in the cellar.'

'Pine resin's just pine resin, isn't it?'

'No. Not to me. That golem *was* in there.'

'They all were,' sighed Carrot. 'And now they're committing suicide.'

'You can't take life you haven't got,' said Angua.

'What shall we call it, then? "Destruction of property"?' said Carrot. 'Anyway, we can't ask them now . . .' He tapped the slate.

'They've given us the answers,' he said. 'Perhaps we can find out what the questions should have been.'

'What do you mean, "nothing"?' said Vimes. 'It's *got* to be the book! He licks his fingers to turn a page, and every day he gets a little dose of arsenic! Fiendishly clever!'

'Sorry, sir,' said Cheery, backing away. 'I can't find a trace. I've used all the tests I know.'

'You're sure?'

'I could send it up to the Unseen University. They've built a new morphic resonator in the High Energy Magic Building. Magic would easily—'

'Don't do that,' said Vimes. 'We'll keep the wizards out of this. Damn! For half an hour there I really thought I'd got it . . .'

He sat down at his desk. Something new was odd about the dwarf, but again he couldn't quite work out what it was.

'We're missing something here, Littlebottom,' he said.

'Yes, sir.'

'Let's look at the facts. If you want to poison someone slowly you've either got to give them small doses all the time – or, at least, every day. We've covered everything the Patrician does. It can't be the air in the room. You and I have been in there every day. It's not the food, we're pretty sure of that. Is something stinging him? Can you poison a wasp? What we need—'

''scuse me, sir.'

Vimes turned.

'Detritus? I thought you were off-duty?'

'I got dem to give me der address of dat maid called Easy like you said,' said Detritus, stoically. 'I went up dere and dere was people all lookin' in.'

'What d'you mean?'

'Neighbours and dat. Cryin' women all round der door. An' I remember what you said about dat dipplo word—'

'Diplomacy,' said Vimes.

'Yeah. Not shoutin' at people an' dat. I fought, dis look a delicate situation. Also, dey was throwin' stuff at me. So I came back here. I writ down der address. An' now I'm goin' home.' He saluted, rocked slightly from the force of the blow to the side of his head, and departed.

'Thanks, Detritus,' said Vimes. He looked at the paper written in the troll's big round hand.

'1st Floor Back, 27 Cockbill Street,' he said. 'Good grief!'

'You know it, sir?'

'Should do. I was born in that street,' said Vimes. 'It's down below the Shades. Easy . . . Easy . . . Yes . . . *Now* I remember. There was a Mrs Easy down the road. Skinny woman. Did a lot of sewing. Big family. Well, we were all big families, it was the only way to keep warm . . .'

He frowned at the paper. It wasn't as if it were any particular lead. Maidservants were always going off to see their mothers, every time there was the least little family upset. What was it his granny had used to say? 'Yer son's yer son till he takes a wife, but yer daughter's yer daughter all yer life.' Sending a Watchman around would almost certainly be a waste of everyone's time . . .

'Well, well . . . Cockbill Street,' he said. He stared at the paper again. *You might as well rename the place Memory Lane.* No, you couldn't waste Watch resources on a wild-goose chase like that. But he might look in. On his way past. Some time today.

'Er . . . Littlebottom?'

'Sir?'

'On your . . . your lips. Red. Er. On your lips . . .'

'Lipstick, sir.'

'Oh . . . er. Lipstick? Fine. Lipstick.'

'Constable Angua gave it to me, sir.'

'That was kind of her,' said Vimes. 'I expect.'

It was called the Rats Chamber. In theory this was because of the decoration; some former resident of the palace had thought that a fresco of dancing rats would be a real decorative coup. There was a pattern of rats woven in the carpet. On the ceiling rats danced in a circle, their tails intertwining at the centre. After half an hour in that room, most people wanted a wash.

Soon, then, there would be a big rush on the hot water. The room was filling up fast.

By common consent the chair was taken and amply filled by Mrs Rosemary Palm, head of the Guild of Seamstresses*, as one of the most senior guild leaders.

'Quiet, please! Gentlemen!'

The noise level subsided a little.

'Dr Downey?' she said.

The head of the Assassins' Guild nodded. 'My friends, I think we are all aware of the situation—' he began.

'Yeah, so's your accountant!' said a voice in the crowd. There was a ripple of nervous laughter but it didn't last long, because you don't laugh too loud at someone who knows exactly how much you're worth dead.

Dr Downey smiled. 'I can assure you once again, gentlemen – and ladies – that I am aware of no engagement regarding Lord Vetinari. In any case, I cannot imagine that an Assassin would use poison in this case. His lordship spent some time at the Assassins' school. He knows the uses of caution. No doubt he will recover.'

'And if he doesn't?' said Mrs Palm.

'No one lives forever,' said Dr Downey, in the calm voice of a man who personally knew this to be true. 'Then, no doubt, we'll get a new ruler.'

The room went very silent.

The word 'Who?' hovered silently above every head.

'Thing is . . . the thing is . . .' said Gerhardt Sock, head of the Butchers' Guild, 'it's been . . . you've got to admit it . . . it's been . . . well, think about some of the others . . .'

The words 'Lord Snapcase, now . . . at least this one isn't actually insane' flickered in the group consciousness.

---

* As they were euphemistically named. People said, 'They call themselves seamstresses – hem, hem!'

'I have to admit,' said Mrs Palm, 'that under Vetinari it has certainly been safer to walk the streets—'

'You should know, madam,' said Mr Sock. Mrs Palm gave him an icy look. There were a few sniggers.

'I *meant* that a modest payment to the Thieves' Guild is all that is required for perfect safety,' she finished.

'And, indeed, a man may visit a house of ill—'

'Negotiable hospitality,' said Mrs Palm quickly.

'Indeed, and be quite confident of not waking up stripped stark naked and beaten black and blue,' said Sock.

'Unless his tastes run that way,' said Mrs Palm. 'We aim to give satisfaction. Very accurately, if required.'

'Life has certainly been more reliable under Vetinari,' said Mr Potts of the Bakers' Guild.

'He does have all street-theatre players and mime artists thrown into the scorpion pit,' said Mr Boggis of the Thieves' Guild.

'True. But let's not forget that he has his bad points too. The man is capricious.'

'You think so? Compared to the ones we had before he's as reliable as a rock.'

'Snapcase was reliable,' said Mr Sock gloomily. 'Remember when he made his horse a city councillor?'

'You've got to admit it wasn't a *bad* councillor. Compared to some of the others.'

'As I recall, the others at that time were a vase of flowers, a heap of sand and three people who had been beheaded.'

'Remember all those fights? All the little gangs of thieves fighting all the time? It got so that there was hardly any energy left to actually steal things,' said Mr Boggis.

'Things are indeed more . . . reliable now.'

Silence descended again. That was it, wasn't it? Things were reliable now. Whatever else you said about old Vetinari, he made sure today was always followed by tomorrow. If you were murdered in your bed, at least it would be by arrangement.

'Things were more exciting under Lord Snapcase,' someone ventured.

'Yes, right up until the point when your head fell off.'

'The trouble is,' said Mr Boggis, 'that the job *makes* people mad. You take some chap who's no worse than any of us and after a few months he's talking to moss and having people flayed alive.'

'Vetinari isn't mad.'

'Depends how you look at it. No one can be as sane as he is without being mad.'

'I am only a weak woman,' said Mrs Palm, to the personal

disbelief of several present, 'but it does seem to me that there's an opportunity here. Either there's a long struggle to sort out a successor, or we sort it out now. Yes?'

The guild leaders tried to look at one another while simultaneously avoiding everyone else's glances. Who'd be Patrician now? Once there'd have been a huge multi-sided power struggle, but now . . .

You got the power, but you got the problems, too. Things had changed. These days, you had to negotiate and juggle with all the conflicting interests. No one sane had tried to kill Vetinari for *years*, because the world with him in it was just preferable to one without him.

Besides . . . Vetinari had tamed Ankh-Morpork. He'd tamed it like a dog. He'd taken a minor scavenger among scavengers and lengthened its teeth and strengthened its jaws and built up its muscles and studded its collar and fed it lean steak and then he'd aimed it at the throat of the world.

He'd taken all the gangs and squabbling groups and made them see that a small slice of the cake on a regular basis was better by far than a bigger slice with a dagger in it. He'd made them see that it was better to take a small slice but *enlarge the cake.*

Ankh-Morpork, alone of all the cities of the plains, had opened its gates to dwarfs and trolls (alloys are stronger, Vetinari had said). It had worked. They made things. Often they made trouble, but mostly they made wealth. As a result, although Ankh-Morpork still had many enemies, those enemies had to finance their armies with borrowed money. Most of it was borrowed from Ankh-Morpork, at punitive interest. There hadn't been any really big wars for years. Ankh-Morpork had made them unprofitable.

Thousands of years ago the old empire had enforced the Pax Morporkia, which had said to the world: 'Do not fight, or we will kill you.' The Pax had arisen again, but this time it said: 'If you fight, we'll call in your mortgages. And incidentally, that's *my* pike you're pointing at me. I paid for that shield you're holding. And take my helmet off when you speak to me, you horrible little debtor.'

And now the whole machine, which whirred away so quietly that people had forgotten it was a machine at all and thought that it was just the way the world worked, had given a lurch.

The guild leaders examined their thoughts and decided that what they did not want was power. What they wanted was that tomorrow should be pretty much like today.

'There's the dwarfs,' said Mr Boggis. 'Even if one of us – not that I'm saying it would be one of us, of course – even if *someone* took

645

over, what about the dwarfs? We get someone like Snapcase again, there's going to be chopped kneecaps in the streets.'

'You're not suggesting we have some sort of . . . *vote*, are you? Some kind of *popularity* contest?'

'Oh, no. It's just . . . it's just . . . all more complicated now. And power goes to people's heads.'

'And then other people's heads fall off.'

'I wish you wouldn't keep on saying that, whoever you are,' said Mrs Palm. 'Anyone would think *you*'d had your head cut off.'

'Uh—'

'Oh, it's you, Mr Slant. I do apologize.'

'Speaking as the President of the Guild of Lawyers,' said Mr Slant, the most respected zombie in Ankh-Morpork, 'I must recommend stability in this matter. I wonder if I may offer some advice?'

'How much will it cost us?' said Mr Sock.

'Stability,' said Mr Slant, 'equals monarchy.'

'Oh, now, don't tell us—'

'Look at Klatch,' said Mr Slant doggedly. 'Generations of Seriphs. Result: political stability. Take Pseudopolis. Or Sto Lat. Or even the Agatean Empire—'

'Come *on*,' said Dr Downey. 'Everyone knows that kings—'

'Oh, monarchs come and go, they depose one another, and so on and so forth,' said Mr Slant. 'But the *institution* goes on. Besides, I think you'll find that it is possible to work out . . . an accommodation.'

He realized that he had the floor. His fingers absent-mindedly touched the seam where his head had been sewn back on. All those years ago Mr Slant had refused to die until he had been paid for the disbursements in the matter of conducting his own defence.

'How do you mean?' said Mr Potts.

'I accept that the question of resurrecting the Ankh-Morpork succession has been raised several times recently,' said Mr Slant.

'Yes. By madmen,' said Mr Boggis. 'It's part of the symptoms. Put underpants on head, talk to trees, drool, decide that Ankh-Morpork needs a king . . .'

'Exactly. Supposing *sane* men were to give it consideration?'

'Go on,' said Dr Downey.

'There have been precedents,' said Mr Slant. 'Monarchies who have found themselves bereft of a convenient monarch have . . . obtained one. Some suitably born member of some other royal line. After all, what is required is someone who, uh, knows the ropes, as I believe the saying goes.'

'Sorry? Are you saying we *send out* for a king?' said Mr Boggis. 'We put up some kind of advertisement? "Throne vacant, applicant must supply own crown"?'

'In fact,' said Mr Slant, ignoring this, 'I recall that, during the first Empire, Genua wrote to Ankh-Morpork and asked to be sent one of our generals to be their king, their own royal lines having died out through interbreeding so intensively that the last king kept trying to breed with himself. The history books say that we sent our loyal General Tacticus, whose first act after obtaining the crown was to declare a war on Ankh-Morpork. Kings are . . . interchangeable.'

'You mentioned something about reaching an accommodation,' said Mr Boggis. 'You mean, we tell a *king* what to *do*?'

'I like the sound of that,' said Mrs Palm.

'I like the echoes,' said Dr Downey.

'Not *tell*,' said Mr Slant. 'We . . . agree. Obviously, as king, he would concentrate on those things traditionally associated with kingship—'

'Waving,' said Mr Sock.

'Being gracious,' said Mrs Palm.

'Welcoming ambassadors from foreign countries,' said Mr Potts.

'Shaking hands.'

'Cutting off heads—'

'No! No. No, that will not be part of his duties. Minor affairs of state will be carried out—'

'By his advisors?' said Dr Downey. He leaned back. 'I'm sure I can see where this is going, Mr Slant,' he said. 'But kings, once acquired, are so damn hard to get rid of. Acceptably.'

'There have been precedents for that, too,' said Mr Slant.

The Assassin's eyes narrowed.

'I'm intrigued, Mr Slant, that as soon as the Lord Vetinari appears to be seriously ill, you pop up with suggestions like this. It sounds like . . . a remarkable coincidence.'

'There is no mystery, I assure you. Destiny works its course. Surely many of you have heard the rumours – that there is, in this city, someone with a bloodline traceable all the way back to the last royal family? Someone working in this very city in a compara-tively humble position? A lowly Watchman, in fact?'

There were some nods, but not very definite ones. They were to nods what a grunt is to 'yes'. The guilds all picked up information. No one wanted to reveal how much, or how little, they personally knew, just in case they knew too little or, even worse, turned out to know too much.

However, Doc Pseudopolis of the Guild of Gamblers put on a careful poker face and said, 'Yes, but the tricentennial is coming up. And in a few years it'll be the Century of the Rat. There's something about centuries that gives people a kind of fever.'

'Nevertheless, the person exists,' said Mr Slant. 'The evidence stares one in the face if one looks in the right places.'

'Very well,' said Mr Boggis. 'Tell us the name of this captain.' He often lost large sums at poker.

'Captain?' said Mr Slant. 'I'm sorry to say his natural talents have thus far not commended him to that extent. He is a corporal. Corporal C. W. St J. Nobbs.'

There was silence.

And then there was a strange putt-putting sound, like water negotiating its way through a partially blocked pipe.

Queen Molly of the Beggars' Guild had so far been silent apart from occasional damp sucking noises as she tried to dislodge a particle of her lunch from the things which, because they were still in her mouth and apparently attached, were technically her teeth.

Now she was laughing. The hairs wobbled on every wart. 'Nobby Nobbs?' she said. 'You're talking about *Nobby Nobbs*?'

'He is the last known descendant of the Earl of Ankh, who could trace *his* descent all the way to a distant cousin to the last king,' said Mr Slant. 'It's the talk of the city.'

'A picture forms in my mind,' said Dr Downey. 'Small monkey-like chap, always smoking very short cigarettes. Spotty. He squeezes them in public.'

'That's Nobby!' Queen Molly chuckled. 'Face like a blind carpenter's thumb!'

'Him? But the man's a tit!'

'And dim as a penny candle,' said Mr Boggis. 'I don't see—'

Suddenly he stopped, and then contracted the contemplative silence that was gradually affecting everyone else around the table.

'Don't see why we shouldn't . . . give this . . . due consideration,' he said, after a while.

The assembled leaders looked at the table. Then they looked at the ceiling. Then they studiously avoided one another's gaze.

'Blood *will* out,' said Mr Carry.

'When I've watched him go down the street I've always thought: "There's a man who walks in greatness,"' said Mrs Palm.

'He squeezes them in a very regal way, mind you. Very graciously.'

The silence rolled over the assembly again. But it was busy, in the same way that the silence of an anthill is busy.

'I must remind you, ladies and gentlemen, that poor Lord Vetinari is still alive,' said Mrs Palm.

'Indeed, indeed,' said Mr Slant. 'And long may he remain so. I've merely set out for you one option against that day, may it be a long time coming, when we should consider a . . . successor.'

'In any case,' said Dr Downey, 'there is no doubt that Vetinari has been over-doing it. If he survives – which is greatly to be hoped, of course – I feel we should require him to step down for the sake of his health. Well done thou good and faithful servant, and so on. Buy him a nice house in the country somewhere. Give him a pension. Make sure there's a seat for him at official dinners. Obviously, if he can be so easily poisoned now he should welcome the release from the chains of office . . .'

'What about the wizards?' said Mr Boggis.

'They've never got involved in civic concerns,' said Dr Downey. 'Give 'em four meat meals a day and tip your hat to them and they're happy. They know nothing about politics.'

The silence that followed was broken by the voice of Queen Molly of the Beggars. 'What about Vimes?'

Dr Downey shrugged. 'He is a servant of the city.'

'That's what I mean.'

'Surely *we* represent the city?'

'Hah! He won't see it that way. And you know what Vimes thinks about kings. It was a Vimes who chopped the head off the last one. *There*'s a bloodline that thinks a swing of an axe can solve anything.'

'Now, Molly, you know Vimes'd probably take an axe to Vetinari if he thought he could get away with it. No love lost there, I fancy.'

'He won't like it. That's all I tell you. Vetinari keeps Vimes wound up. No knowing what happens if he unwinds all at once—'

'He's a public servant!' snapped Dr Downey.

Queen Molly made a face, which was not difficult in one so naturally well endowed, and sat back. 'So this is the new way of things, is it?' she muttered. 'Lot of ordinary men sit around a table and talk and suddenly the world's a different place? The sheep turn round and charge the shepherd?'

'There's a soirée at Lady Selachii's house this evening,' said Dr Downey, ignoring her. 'I believe Nobbs is being invited. Perhaps we can . . . meet him.'

Vimes told himself he was really going to inspect the progress on the new Watch House in Chittling Street. Cockbill Street was just round the corner. And then he'd call in, informally. No sense in sparing a man when they were pushed anyway, what with these murders and Vetinari and Detritus' anti-Slab crusade.

He turned the corner, and stopped.

Nothing much had changed. That was the shocking thing. After . . . oh, too many years . . . things had no *right* not to have changed.

But washing lines still criss-crossed the street between the grey, ancient buildings. Antique paint still peeled in the way cheap paint peeled when it had been painted on wood too old and rotten to take paint. Cockbill Street people were usually too penniless to afford decent paint, but always far too proud to use whitewash.

And the place was slightly smaller than he remembered. That was all.

When had he last come down here? He couldn't remember. It was beyond the Shades, and up until quite recently the Watch had tended to leave that area to its own unspeakable devices.

Unlike the Shades, though, Cockbill Street was clean, with the haunting, empty cleanliness you get when people can't afford to waste dirt. For Cockbill Street was where people lived who were worse than poor, because they didn't *know* how poor they were. If you asked them they would probably say something like 'mustn't grumble' or 'there's far worse off than us' or 'we've always kept uz heads above water and we don't owe nobody nowt'.

He could hear his granny speaking. 'No one's too poor to buy soap.' Of course, many people were. But in Cockbill Street they bought soap just the same. The table might not have any food on it but, by gods, it was well scrubbed. That was Cockbill Street, where what you mainly ate was your pride.

What a mess the world was in, Vimes reflected. Constable Visit had told him the meek would inherit it, and what had the poor devils done to deserve *that*?

Cockbill Street people would stand aside to let the meek through. For what kept them in Cockbill Street, mentally and physically, was their vague comprehension that there were *rules*. And they went through life filled with a quiet, distracted dread that they weren't quite obeying them.

People said that there was one law for the rich and one law for the poor, but it wasn't true. There was no law for those who made the law, and no law for the incorrigibly lawless. All the laws and rules were for those people stupid enough to think like Cockbill Street people.

It was oddly quiet. Normally there'd be swarms of kids, and carts heading down towards the docks, but today the place had a shut-in look.

In the middle of the road was a chalked hopscotch path.

Vimes felt his knees go weak. It was still here! When had he last seen it? Thirty-five years ago? Forty? So it must have been drawn and redrawn thousands of times.

He'd been pretty good at it. Of course, they'd played it by Ankh-Morpork rules. Instead of kicking a stone they'd kicked William

Scuggins. It had been just one of the many inventive games they'd played which had involved kicking, chasing or jumping on William Scuggins until he threw one of his famous wobblers and started frothing and violently attacking himself.

Vimes had been able to drop William in the square of his choice nine times out of ten. The tenth time, William bit his leg.

In those days, tormenting William and finding enough to eat had made for a simple, straightforward life. There weren't so many questions you didn't know the answers to, except maybe how to stop your leg festering.

Sir Samuel looked around, saw the silent street, and flicked a stone out of the gutter with his foot. Then he booted it surreptitiously along the squares, adjusted his cloak, and hopped and jumped his way up, turned, hopped—

What was it you shouted as you hopped? 'Salt, mustard, vinegar, pepper?'? No? Or was it the one that went 'William Scuggins is a bastard'? Now he'd wonder about that all day.

A door opened across the street. Vimes froze, one leg in mid-air, as two black-clothed figures came out slowly and awkwardly.

This was because they were carrying a coffin.

The natural solemnity of the occasion was diminished by their having to squeeze around it and out into the street, pulling the casket after them and allowing two other pairs of bearers to edge their way into the daylight.

Vimes remembered himself in time to lower his other foot, and then remembered even more of himself and snatched his helmet off in respect.

Another coffin emerged. It was a lot smaller. It needed only two people to carry it and that was really one too many.

As mourners trooped out behind them, Vimes fumbled in a pocket for the scrap of paper Detritus had given him. The scene was, in its way, funny, like the bit in a circus where the coach stops and a dozen clowns get out of it. Apartment houses round here made up for their limited number of rooms by having a large number of people occupy them.

He found the paper and unfolded it. First Floor Back, 27 Cockbill Street.

And this was it. He'd arrived in time for a funeral. Two funerals.

'Looks like it's a really bad day to be a golem,' said Angua. There was a pottery hand lying in the gutter. 'That's the third one we've seen smashed in the street.'

There was a crash up ahead, and a dwarf came through a

window more or less horizontally. His iron helmet struck sparks as he hit the street, but the dwarf was soon up again and plunging back through the adjacent doorway.

He emerged via the window a moment later but was fielded by Carrot, who set him on his feet.

'Hello, Mr Oresmiter! Are you keeping well? And what is happening here?'

'It's that devil Gimlet, Captain Carrot! You should be arresting him!'

'Why, what's he done?'

'He's been poisoning people, that's what!'

Carrot glanced at Angua, then back at Oresmiter. 'Poison?' he said. 'That's a very serious allegation.'

'You're telling me! I was up all night with Mrs Oresmiter! I didn't think much about it until I came in here this morning and there were other people complaining—'

He tried to struggle out of Carrot's grip. 'You know what?' he said. 'You know *what*? We looked in his cold room and you know what? You know *what*? You know what he's been selling as meat?'

'Tell me,' said Carrot.

'Pork and beef!'

'Oh, dear.'

'And lamb!'

'Tch, tch.'

'Hardly any rat at all!'

Carrot shook his head at the duplicity of traders.

'And Snori Glodssonsunclesson said he had Rat Surprise last night and he'll swear there were *chicken* bones in it!'

Carrot let go of the dwarf. 'You stay here,' he said to Angua and, head bowed, stepped inside Gimlet's Hole Food Delicatessen.

An axe spun towards him. He caught it almost absent-mindedly and tossed it casually aside.

'Ow!'

There was a mêlée of dwarfs around the counter. The row had already gone well past the stage when it had anything much to do with the subject in hand and, these being dwarfs, now included matters of vital importance such as whose grandfather had stolen whose grandfather's mining claim three hundred years ago and whose axe was at whose throat right now.

But there was something about Carrot's presence. The fighting gradually stopped. The fighters tried to look as if they'd just happened to be standing there. There was a sudden and general 'Axe? What axe? Oh, *this* axe? I was just showing it to my friend Bjorn here, good old Bjorn' feel to the atmosphere.

'All right,' said Carrot. 'What's all this about poison? Mr Gimlet first.'

'It's a diabolical lie!' shouted Gimlet, from somewhere under the heap. 'I run a wholesome restaurant! My tables are so clean you could eat your dinner off them!'

Carrot raised his hands to stop the outburst this caused. 'Someone said something about rats,' he said.

'I told them, I use only the very best rats!' shouted Gimlet. 'Good plump rats from the best locations! None of your latrine rubbish! And they're hard to come by, let me tell you!'

'And when you can't get them, Mr Gimlet?' said Carrot.

Gimlet paused. Carrot was hard to lie to. 'All right,' he mumbled. 'Maybe when there's not enough I might sort of plump out the stock with some chicken, maybe just a bit of beef—'

'Hah! A *bit?*' More voices were raised.

'That's right, you should see his cold room, Mr Carrot!'

'Yeah, he uses *steak* and cuts little legs in it and covers it with rat sauce!'

'I don't know, you try to do your best at very reasonable prices and this is the thanks you get?' said Gimlet hotly. 'It's hard enough to make ends meet as it is!'

'*You* don't even make 'em of the *right* meat!'

Carrot sighed. There were no public health laws in Ankh-Morpork. It would be like installing smoke detectors in Hell.

'All *right,*' he said. 'But you can't get poisoned by steak. No, honestly. No. No, *shut up*, all of you. No, I don't care *what* your mothers told you. Now, I want to know about this poisoning, Gimlet.'

Gimlet struggled to his feet.

'We did Rat Surprise last night for the Sons of Bloodaxe annual dinner,' he said. There was a general groan. 'And it *was* rat.' He raised his voice against the complaining. 'You can't use anything else – listen – you've got to have the noses poking through the pastry, all right? Some of the best rat we've had in for a long time, let me tell you!'

'And you were all ill afterwards?' said Carrot, taking out his notebook.

'Sweating all night!'

'Couldn't see straight!'

'I reckon I know every knothole on the back of the privy door!'

'I'll write that down as a "definitely",' said Carrot. 'Was there anything else on the dinner menu?'

'Vole-au-vents and Cream of Rat,' said Gimlet. 'All hygienically prepared.'

'How do you mean, "hygienically prepared"?' said Carrot.

'The chef is under strict orders to wash his hands afterwards.'

The assembled dwarfs nodded. This was certainly pretty hygienic. You didn't want people going around with ratty hands.

'Anyway, you've all been eating here for *years*,' said Gimlet, sensing this slight veer in his direction. 'This is the first time there's been any trouble, isn't it? My rats are famous!'

'Your chicken's going to be pretty famous, too,' said Carrot.

There was laughter this time. Even Gimlet joined in. 'All right, I'm sorry about the chicken. But it was that or very poor rats, and you know I only buy from Wee Mad Arthur. He's trustworthy, whatever else you may say about him. You just can't get better rats. Everyone knows that.'

'That'll be Wee Mad Arthur in Gleam Street?' said Carrot.

'Yes. Not a mark on 'em, most of the time.'

'Have you got any left?'

'One or two.' Gimlet's expression changed. 'Here, you don't think *he* poisoned them, do you? I never did trust that little bugger!'

'Enquiries are continuing,' said Carrot. He tucked his notebook away. 'I'd like some rats, please. *Those* rats. To go.' He glanced at the menu, patted his pocket and looked questioningly out through the door at Angua.

'You don't have to *buy* them,' she said wearily. 'They're *evidence*.'

'We can't defraud an innocent tradesman who may be the victim of circumstances,' said Carrot.

'You want ketchup?' said Gimlet. 'Only they're extra with ketchup.'

The funeral carriage went slowly through the streets. It looked quite expensive, but that was Cockbill Street for you. People put money by. Vimes remembered that. You always put money by, in Cockbill Street. You saved up for a rainy day even if it was pouring already. And you'd die of shame if people thought you could afford only a cheap funeral.

Half a dozen black-clad mourners came along behind, together with perhaps a score of people who had tried at least to look respectable.

Vimes followed the procession at a distance all the way to the cemetery behind the Temple of Small Gods, where he lurked awkwardly among the gravestones and sombre graveyard trees while the priest mumbled on.

The gods had made the people of Cockbill Street poor, honest and provident, Vimes reflected. They might as well have hung signs saying 'Kick me' on their backs and had done with it. Yet Cockbill Street people tended towards religion, at least of the less demonstrative kind. They always put a little life by for a rainy eternity.

Eventually the crowd around the graves broke up and drifted away with the aimless look of people whose immediate future contains ham rolls.

Vimes spotted a tearful young woman in the main group and advanced carefully. 'Er . . . are you Mildred Easy?' he said.

She nodded. 'Who are you?' She took in the cut of his coat and added, 'sir?'

'Was that old Mrs Easy who used to do dressmaking?' said Vimes, taking her gently aside.

'That's right . . .'

'And the . . . smaller coffin?'

'That was our William . . .'

The girl looked as if she were about to cry again.

'Can we have a talk?' said Vimes. 'There are some things I hope you can tell me.'

He hated the way his mind worked. A proper human being would have shown respect and quietly walked away. But, as he'd stood among the chilly stones, a horrible apprehension had stolen over him that almost all the answers were in place now, if only he could work out the questions.

She looked around at the other mourners. They had reached the gate and were staring back curiously at the two of them.

'Er . . . I know this isn't the right time,' said Vimes. 'But, when the kids play hopscotch in the street, what's the rhyme they sing? "Salt, mustard, vinegar, pepper?", isn't it?'

She stared at his worried grin. 'That's a skipping rhyme,' she said coldly. 'When they play hopscotch they sing "Billy Skunkins is a brass stud". Who are you?'

'I'm Commander Vimes of the Watch,' said Vimes. So . . . Willy Scuggins would live on in the street, in disguise and in a fashion . . . And Old Stoneface was just some guy on a bonfire . . .

Then her tears came.

'It's all right, it's all right,' said Vimes, as soothingly as he could. 'I was brought up in Cockbill Street, that's why I . . . I mean I'm . . . I'm not here on . . . I'm not out to . . . look, I *know* you took food home from the palace. That's all right by me. I'm *not* here to . . . oh, damn, would you like my handkerchief? I think your one's full.'

'Everyone does it!'

'Yes, I know.'

'Anyway, cook never says nothing . . .' She began to sob again.

'Yes, yes.'

'Everyone takes a few things,' said Mildred Easy. 'It's not like *stealing.*'

It is, thought Vimes treacherously. *But I don't give a damn.*

And now . . . he'd got a grip on the long copper rod and was climbing into a high place while the thunder muttered around him. 'The, er, the last food you sto— were given,' he said. 'What was it?'

'Just some blancmange and some, you know, that sort of jam made out of meat . . .'

'Pâté?'

'Yes. I thought it would be a little treat . . .'

Vimes nodded. Rich, mushy food. The sort you'd give to a baby who was peaky and to a granny who hadn't got any teeth.

Well, he was on the roof now, the clouds were black and threatening, and he might as well wave the lightning conductor. Time to ask . . .

The wrong question, as it proved.

'Tell me,' he said, 'what did Mrs Easy die of?'

'Let me put it like this,' said Cheery. 'If these rats had been poisoned with lead instead of arsenic, you'd have been able to sharpen their noses and use them as a pencil.'

She lowered the beaker.

'Are you sure?' said Carrot.

'Yes.'

'Wee Mad Arthur wouldn't poison rats, would he? Especially not rats that were going to be eaten.'

'I've heard he doesn't like dwarfs much,' said Angua.

'Yes, but business is business. *No one* who does a lot of business with dwarfs likes them much, and he must supply every dwarf café and delicatessen in the city.'

'Maybe they ate arsenic before he caught them?' said Angua. 'People use it as a rat poison, after all . . .'

'Yes,' said Carrot, in a very deliberate way. 'They do.'

'You're not suggesting that *Vetinari* tucks into a nice rat every day?' said Angua.

'I've heard he uses rats as spies, so I don't think he uses them as elevenses,' said Carrot. 'But it'd be nice to know where Wee Mad Arthur gets his from, don't you think?'

'Commander Vimes said *he* was looking after the Vetinari case,' said Angua.

'But we're just finding out why Gimlet's rats are full of arsenic,' said Carrot, innocently. 'Anyway, I was going to ask Sergeant Colon to look into it.'

'But . . . Wee Mad Arthur?' said Angua. 'He's mad.'

'Fred can take Nobby with him. I'll go and tell him. Um. Cheery?'

'Yes, Captain?'

'You've been, er, you've been trying to hide your face from me . . . oh. Did someone hit you?'

'No, sir!'

'Only your eyes look a bit bruised and your lips—'

'I'm fine, sir!' said Cheery desperately.

'Oh, well, if you say so. I'll . . . er, I'll . . . look for Sergeant Colon, then . . .'

He backed out, embarrassed.

That left the two of them. *All girls together*, thought Angua. *One normal girl between the two of us, at any rate.*

'I don't think the mascara works,' Angua said. 'The lipstick's fine but the mascara . . . I don't think so.'

'I think I need practice.'

'You sure you want to keep the beard?'

'You don't mean . . . *shave*?' Cheery backed away.

'All right, all right. What about the iron helmet?'

'It belonged to my grandmother! It's *dwarfish*!'

'Fine. Fine. Okay. You've made a good start, anyway.'

'Er . . . what do you think of . . . this?' said Cheery, handing her a bit of paper.

Angua read it. It was a list of names, although most of them were crossed out:

~~Cheery Littlebottom~~

~~Cherry~~

~~Sherry~~

~~Sherri~~

Lucinda Littlebottom

~~Sharry~~

~~Sharri~~

Cheri

'Er . . . what do you think?' said Cheery nervously.

'"Lucinda"?' said Angua, raising her eyebrows.

'I've always liked the sound of the name.'

'"Cheri" is nice,' said Angua. 'And it *is* rather like the one you've got already. The way people spell in this town, no one will actually notice unless you point it out to them.'

Cheery's shoulders sagged with released tension. When you've made up your mind to shout out who you are to the world, it's a relief to know that you can do it in a whisper.

'*Cheri*', thought Angua. *Now, what does that name conjure up?*

Does the mental picture include iron boots, iron helmet, a small worried face and a long beard?

Well, it does now.

Somewhere underneath Ankh-Morpork a rat went about its business, ambling unconcernedly through the ruins of a damp cellar. It turned a corner towards the grain store it knew was up ahead, and almost walked into another rat.

This one was standing on its hind-legs, though, and wearing a tiny black robe and carrying a scythe. Such of its snout that could be seen was bone-white.

SQUEAK? it said.

Then the vision faded and revealed a slightly smaller figure. There was nothing in the least rat-like about it, apart from its size. It was human, or at least humanoid. It was dressed in ratskin trousers but was bare above the waist, apart from two bandoliers that criss-crossed its chest. And it was smoking a tiny cigar.

It raised a very small crossbow and fired.

The soul of the rat – for anything so similar in so many ways to human beings certainly has a soul – watched gloomily as the figure took its recent habitation by the tail and towed it away. Then it looked up at the Death of Rats.

'Squeak?' it said.

The Grim Squeaker nodded.

SQUEAK.

A minute later Wee Mad Arthur emerged into the daylight, dragging the rat behind him. There were fifty-seven neatly lined up along the wall, but despite his name Wee Mad Arthur made a point of not killing the young and the pregnant females. It's always a good idea to make sure you've got a job tomorrow.

His sign was still tacked up over the hole. Wee Mad Arthur, as the only insect and vermin exterminator able to meet the enemy on its own terms, found that it paid to advertise.

'WEE MAD' ARTHUR

For those little things that get you down

Rats *FREE*
Mise: 1p per ten tails
Moles: 1/2p each
Warsps: 50p per nest. Hornets 20p extra
Cockroaches and similar by aranjement.

Small Fees   •   **BIG JOBS**

Arthur took out the world's smallest notebook and a piece of pencil lead. See here, now . . . fifty-eight skins at two a penny, City bounty for the tails at a penny per ten, and the carcases to Gimlet at tuppence per three, the hard-driving dwarf bastard that he was . . .

There was a moment's shadow, and then someone stamped on him.

'Right,' said the owner of the boot. 'Still catching rats without a Guild card, are you? Easiest ten dollars we ever earned, Sid. Let's go and—'

The man was lifted several inches off the ground, whirled around, and hurled against the wall. His companion stared as a streak of dust raced across his boot, but reacted too late.

'He's gone up me trouser! He's gone up me – *arrgh!*'

There was a *crack*.

'Me knee! Me knee! He's broken me knee!'

The man who had been flung aside tried to get up, but something scurried across his chest and landed astride his nose.

'Hey, pal?' said Wee Mad Arthur. 'Can yer mother sew, pal? Yeah? Then get her to stitch this one!'

He grabbed an eyelid in each hand and thrust his head forward with pin-point precision. There was another *crack* as the skulls met.

The man with the broken knee tried to drag himself away but Wee Mad Arthur leapt from his stunned comrade and proceeded to kick him. The kicks of a man not much more than six inches high should not hurt, but Wee Mad Arthur seemed to have a lot more mass than his size would allow. Being nutted by Arthur was like being hit by a steel ball from a slingshot. A kick seemed to have all the power of one from a large man, but very painfully concentrated into a smaller area.

'Yez can tell them buggers at the Rat-Catchers' Guild that I works for whoze I want and charges what I like,' he said, between kicks. 'And them shites can stop tryin' to persecute the small businessman . . .'

The other guild enforcer made it to the end of the alley. Arthur gave Sid a final kick and left him in the gutter.

Wee Mad Arthur walked back to his task, shaking his head. He worked for nothing and sold his rats for half the official rate, a heinous crime. Yet Wee Mad Arthur was growing rich because the guild hadn't got its joint heads around the idea of fiscal relativity.

Arthur charged a lot *more* for his services. A lot more, that is, from the specialized and above all *low* point of view of Wee Mad

Arthur. What Ankh-Morpork had yet to understand was that the smaller you are the more your money is worth.

A dollar for a human bought a loaf of bread that was eaten in a few bites. The same dollar for Wee Mad Arthur bought the same-sized loaf, but it was food for a week and could then be further hollowed out and used as a bedroom.

The size-differential problem was also responsible for his frequent drunkenness. Few publicans were prepared to sell beer by the thimbleful or had gnome-sized mugs. Wee Mad Arthur had to go drinking in a swimming costume.

But he liked his work. No one could clear out rats like Wee Mad Arthur. Old and cunning rats that knew all about traps, deadfalls and poison were helpless in the face of his attack, which was where, in fact, he often attacked. The last thing they felt was a hand gripping each of their ears, and the last thing they saw was his forehead, approaching at speed.

Muttering under his breath, Wee Mad Arthur got back to his calculations. But not for long.

He spun around, forehead cocked.

'It's only us, Wee Mad Arthur,' said Sergeant Colon, stepping back hurriedly.

'That's *Mr* Wee Mad Arthur to youse, copper,' said Wee Mad Arthur, but he relaxed a little.

'We're Sergeant Colon and Corporal Nobbs,' said Colon.

'Yeah, you remember us, don't you?' said Nobby, in a wheedling voice. 'We was the ones who helped you when you was fighting them three dwarfs last week.'

'Yez pulled me off 'f them, if that's what you mean,' said Wee Mad Arthur. 'Just when I'd got 'em all down.'

'We want to talk to you about some rats,' said Colon.

'Can't take on any more customers,' said Wee Mad Arthur firmly.

'Some rats you sold to Gimlet's Hole Food Delicatessen a few days ago.'

'What's that to yez?'

'He reckons they was poisoned,' said Nobby, who had taken the precaution of moving behind Colon.

'I never uses poison!'

Colon realized he was backing away from a man six inches high. 'Yeah, well . . . see . . . fing is . . . you being in fights and that . . . you don't get on with dwarfs . . . some people might say . . . fing is . . . it could look like you might have a grudge.' He took another step back and almost tripped over Nobby.

'Grudge? Why should I have a grudge, pal? It ain't me that gets the kicking!' said Wee Mad Arthur, advancing.

'Good point. Good point,' said Colon. 'Only it'd help, right, if you could tell us . . . where you got those rats from . . .'

'Like the Patrician's palace, maybe,' said Nobby.

'The palace? No one catches rats at the palace. That's not allowed. No, I remember those rats. They wuz good fat ones, I wanted a penny each, but he held out for four for threepence, th' ole skinflint that he is.'

'Where did you get them, then?'

Wee Mad Arthur shrugged. 'Down the cattle market. I do the cattle market Tuesdays. Couldn't tell yez where they came from. Them tunnels guz everywhere, see?'

'Could they've eaten poison before you caught them?' said Colon.

Wee Mad Arthur bristled. 'No one puts down poison round there. I won't have it, see? I got all the contracts along the Shambles, and I won't deal with any gobshite who uses poison. I doesn't charge for extermination, see? Guild *hates* that. But I chooses me customers.' Wee Mad Arthur grinned wickedly. 'I only guz where's there's the finest eating for the rats and I clean up flogging 'em to the lawn ornaments. I find anyone using poison on my patch, they can pay guild rates for guild work, hah, and see how they like it.'

'I can see you're going to be a big man in industrial catering,' said Colon.

Wee Mad Arthur put his head on one side. 'D'youse know what happened to the last man that made a crack like that?' he said.

'Er . . . no . . . ?' said Colon.

'Neither does anyone else,' said Wee Mad Arthur, ''cos he *was never found*. Have yez finished? Only I got a wasps' nest to clean out before I go home.'

'So you were catching them under the Shambles?' Colon persisted.

'All the way along. 'S a good beat. There's tanners, tallow men, butchers, sausage-makers . . . That's good grazing, if you're a rat.'

'Yeah, right,' said Colon. 'Fair enough. Well, I reckon we've taken up enough of your time—'

'How d'you catch wasps?' said Nobby, intrigued. 'Smoke 'em out?'

''Tis unsporting not to hit them on the wing,' said Wee Mad Arthur. 'But if it's a busy day I make up squibs out of that No. 1 black powder the alchemists sell.' He indicated the laden bandoliers over his shoulders.

'You blow them up?' said Nobby. 'That don't sound too sporting.'

'Yeah? Just ever tried settin' and lightin' half a dozen fuses and then fightin' your way back out of the entrance before the first one goes off?'

*

661

'It's a wild-goose chase, Sarge,' said Nobby, as they strolled away. 'Some rats et some poison somewhere and he got them. What're we supposed to do about it? Poisonin' rats ain't illegal.'

Colon scratched his chin. 'I think we could be in a bit of trouble, Nobby,' he said. 'I mean, everyone's been bustling around detectoring and we could end up looking a right couple of noddies. I mean, do you want to go back to the Yard and say we talked to Wee Mad Arthur and he said it wasn't him, end of story? We're humans, right? Well, *I* am and I know you probably are – and we're definitely bringing up the rear around here. I'm telling you, this ain't my Watch any more, Nobby. Trolls, dwarfs, gargoyles . . . I've nothing against them, you know me, but I'm looking forward to my little farm with chickens round the door. And I wouldn't mind goin' out with something to be proud of.'

'Well, what do you want us to do? Knock on every door round the cattle market and ask 'em if they've got any arsenic in the place?'

'Yep,' said Colon. 'Walk and talk. That's what Vimes always says.'

'There's hundreds of 'em! Anyway, they'd say no.'

'Right, but we got to *arsk*. 'T'aint like it used to be, Nobby. This is modern policing. Detectoring. These days, we got to get results. I mean, the Watch is getting bigger. I don't mind ole Detritus bein' a sergeant, he's not bad when you get to know him, but one of these days it could be a dwarf giving out orders, Nobby. It's all right for me 'cos I'll be out on my farm—'

'Nailin' chickens round the door,' said Nobby.

'—but you've got your future to think about. An', the way things are going, maybe the Watch'll be looking for another captain. It'd be a right bugger if he turned out to have a name like Stronginthearm, eh, or Shale. So you'd better look smart.'

'*You* never wanted to be a captain, Fred?'

'Me? A hofficer? I have my pride, Nobby. I've nothing against hofficering for them as is called to it, but it's not for the likes of me. My place is with the common man.'

'I wish mine was,' said Nobby gloomily. 'Look what was in my pigeonhole this morning.'

He handed the sergeant a square of card, with gold edging. '"Lady Selachii will be At Home this pm from five onwards, and requests the pleasure of the company of Lord de Nobbes,"' he read.

'Oh.'

'I've heard about these rich ole women,' said Nobby, dejectedly. 'I reckon she wants me to be a giggle-low, is that right?'

'Nah, nah,' said the sergeant, looking at passion's most unlikely plaything. 'I know this stuff from my uncle. "At Home" is like a bit of a drinks do. It's where all you nobs hob-nob, Nobby. You just drink and scoff and talk about literachoor and the arts.'

'I haven't got any posh clothes,' said Nobby.

'Ah, that's where *you* score, Nobby,' said Colon. 'Uniforms is okay. Adds a bit of tone, in fact. Especially if you look dashing,' he said, ignoring the evidence that Nobby was, in fact, merely runny.

'Is that a fact?' said Nobby, brightening up a bit. 'I've got a lot more of 'em invites, too,' he said. 'Posh cards what look like they've been nibbled along the edges with gold teeth. Dinners, balls, all kinds of stuff.'

Colon looked down at his friend. A strange and yet persuasive thought crept into his mind. 'We-ell,' he said, 'it's the end of the social Season, see? Time's running out.'

'What for?'

'We-ell . . . could be all them posh women want to marry you off to their daughters who're in Season . . .'

'What?'

'Nothing beats an earl except a duke, and we haven't got one of them. And we ain't got a king, neither. The Earl of Ankh would be what they calls a social catch.' Yes, it was easier if he said it to himself like that. If you substituted 'Nobby Nobbs' for 'Earl of Ankh' it didn't work. But it *did* work when you just said 'Earl of Ankh'. There'd be many women who'd be happy to be the mother-in-law of the Earl of Ankh even if it meant having Nobby Nobbs into the bargain.

Well, a few, anyway.

Nobby's eyes gleamed. 'Never *thought* of that,' he said. 'And some of these girls have a bit of cash, too?'

'More'n you, Nobby.'

'And of course I owes it to my posterity to see that the line of Nobbses doesn't die out,' Nobby added, thoughtfully.

Colon beamed at him with the rather worried expression of a mad doctor who has bolted on the head, applied the crackling lightning to the electrodes, and is now watching his creation lurch down to the village.

'Cor,' said Nobby, his eyes now unfocusing slightly.

'Right, but *before* that,' said Colon, 'I'll do all the places along the Shambles and you do Chittling Street and then we can push off back to the Yard, job done and dusted. Okay?'

'Afternoon, Commander Vimes,' said Carrot, shutting the door behind him. 'Captain Carrot reporting.'

Vimes was slumped in his chair, staring at the window. The fog was creeping up again. Already the Opera House opposite was a little hazy.

'We, er, had a look at as many golems as we could, sir,' said Carrot, trying diplomatically to see if there was a bottle anywhere on the desk. 'There's hardly any, sir. We found eleven had smashed themselves up or sawn their heads off and by lunchtime people were smashing 'em or taking out their words themselves, sir. It's not nice, sir. There's bits of pottery all over the city. It's as if people were . . . just waiting for the opportunity. It's odd, sir. All they do is work and keep themselves to themselves and don't offer any harm to anyone. And some of the ones that smashed *themselves* left . . . well, notes, sir. Sort of saying they were sorry and ashamed, sir. They kept on going on about their clay . . .'

Vimes did not respond.

Carrot leaned sideways and down, in case there was a bottle on the floor. 'And Gimlet's Hole Food Delicatessen has been selling poisoned rat. Arsenic, sir. I've asked Sergeant Colon and Nobby to follow that one. It might just be some kind of mix-up, but you never know.'

Vimes turned. Carrot could hear his breathing. Short, sharp bursts, like a man trying to keep himself under control. 'What have we missed, Captain?' he said, in a faraway voice.

'Sir?'

'In his lordship's bedroom. There's the bed. The desk. Things on the desk. The table by the bed. The chair. The rug. Everything. We replaced *everything*. He eats food. We've checked the food, yes?'

'The whole larder, sir.'

'Is that a fact? We might be wrong there. I don't understand how, but we might be wrong. There's some evidence lying in the cemetery that suggests we are.' Vimes was nearly growling. 'What else is there? Littlebottom says there's no marks on him. What else *is* there? Let's find out the *how* and with any luck that'll give us the *who*.'

'He breathes the air more than anyone else, si—'

'But we moved him into another bedroom! Even if someone was, I don't know, pumping poison in . . . they couldn't change rooms with us all watching. It's got to be the food!'

'I've watched them taste it, sir.'

'Then it's something we're not seeing, damn it! People are *dead*, Captain! Mrs Easy's *dead*!'

'Who, sir?'

'You've never heard of her?'

'Can't say that I have, sir. What did she use to do?'

'Do? Nothing, I suppose. She just brought up nine kids in a

couple of rooms you couldn't stretch out in and she sewed shirts for tuppence an hour, every hour the bloody gods sent, and all she did was work and keep herself to herself and she is *dead*, Captain. And so's her grandson. Aged fourteen months. Because her granddaughter took them some grub from the palace! A bit of a treat for them! And d'you know what? Mildred thought I was going to arrest her for theft! At the damn funeral, for gods' sake!' Vimes's fists opened and closed, his knuckles showing white. 'It's *murder* now. Not assassination, not politics, it's *murder*. Because we're not asking the right damn *questions*!'

The door opened.

'Oh, good afternoon, squire,' said Sergeant Colon brightly, touching his helmet. 'Sorry to bother you. I expect it's your busy time, but I've got to ask, just to eliminate you from our enquiries, so to speak. Do you use any arsenic around the place?'

'Er . . . don't leave the officer standing there, Fanley,' said a nervous voice, and the workman stepped aside. 'Good afternoon, officer. How may we help you?'

'Checking up on arsenic, sir. Seems some's been getting where it shouldn't.'

'Er . . . good heavens. Really. I'm sure we don't use any, but do come inside while I check with the foremen. I'm certain there's a pot of tea hot, too.'

Colon looked behind him. The mist was rising. The sky was going grey. 'Wouldn't say no, sir!' he said.

The door closed behind him.

A moment later, there was the faint scrape of the bolts.

'Right,' said Vimes. 'Let's start again.'

He picked up an imaginary ladle.

'I'm the cook. I've made this nourishing gruel that tastes like dog's water. I'm filling up three bowls. Everyone's watching me. All the bowls have been well washed, right? Okay. The tasters take two, one to taste, and these days the other's for Littlebottom to check, and then a servant – that's you, Carrot – takes the third one and . . .'

'Puts it in the dumbwaiter, sir. There's one up to every room.'

'I thought they carried them up?'

'Six floors? It'd get stone-cold, sir.'

'All right . . . hold on. We've gone too far. You've got the bowl. D'you put it on a tray?'

'Yes, sir.'

'Put it on a tray, then.'

Carrot obediently put the invisible bowl on an invisible tray.

'Anything else?' said Vimes.

'Piece of bread, sir. And we check the loaf.'

'Soup spoon?'

'Yes, sir.'

'Well, don't just stand there. Put them on . . .'

Carrot detached one hand from the invisible tray to take an invisible piece of bread and an intangible spoon.

'Anything else?' said Vimes. 'Salt and pepper?'

'I think I remember salt and pepper pots, sir.'

'On they go, then.'

Vimes stared hawk-like at the space between Carrot's hands.

'No,' he said. 'We wouldn't have missed that, would we? I mean . . . we wouldn't, would we?'

He reached out and picked up an invisible tube.

'Tell me we checked the salt,' he said.

'That's the pepper, sir,' said Carrot helpfully.

'Salt! Mustard! Vinegar! Pepper!' said Vimes. 'We didn't check all the food and then let his lordship tip poison on to suit his taste, did we? Arsenic's a metal. Can't you get . . . metal salts? Tell me we asked ourselves that. We aren't that stupid, are we?'

'I'll check directly,' said Carrot. He looked around desperately. 'I'll just put the tray down—'

'Not yet,' said Vimes. 'I've been here before. We don't rush off shouting "Give me a towel!" just because we've had one idea. Let's keep looking, shall we? The spoon. What's it made of?'

'Good point. I'll check the cutlery, sir.'

'*Now* we're cooking with charcoal! What's he been drinking?'

'Boiled water, sir. We've tested the water. And I checked the glasses.'

'Good. So . . . we've got the tray and you put the tray in the dumbwaiter and then what?'

'The men in the kitchen haul on the ropes and it goes up to the sixth floor.'

'No stops?'

Carrot looked blank.

'It goes up six floors,' said Vimes. 'It's just a shaft with a big box in it that can be pulled up and down, isn't it? I'll bet there's a door into it on every floor.'

'Some of the floors are hardly used these days, sir—'

'Even better for our poisoner, hmm? He just stands there, bold as you like, and waits for the tray to come by, right? We don't *know* that the meal which arrives is the one that left, do we?'

'Brilliant, sir!'

'It happens at night, I'll swear,' said Vimes. 'He's chipper in the evenings and out like a light next morning. What time is his supper sent up?'

'While he's poorly, around six o'clock, sir,' said Carrot. 'It's got dark by then. Then he gets on with his writing.'

'Right. We've got a lot to do. Come on.'

The Patrician was sitting up in bed reading when Vimes entered. 'Ah, Vimes,' he said.

'Your supper will be up shortly, my lord,' said Vimes. 'And can I once again say that our job would be a lot easier if you let us move you out of the palace?'

'I'm sure it would be,' said Lord Vetinari.

There was a rattle from the dumbwaiter. Vimes walked across and opened the doors.

There was a dwarf in the box. He had a knife between his teeth and an axe in each hand, and was glowering with ferocious concentration.

'Good heavens,' said Vetinari weakly. 'I hope at least they've included some mustard.'

'Any problems, Constable?' said Vimes.

'Nofe, fir,' said the dwarf, unfolding himself and removing the knife. 'Very dull all the way up, sir. There was other doors and they all looked pretty unused, but I nailed 'em up anyway like Captain Carrot said, sir.'

'Well done. Down you go.'

Vimes shut the doors. There was more rattling as the dwarf began his descent.

'Every detail covered, eh, Vimes?'

'I hope so, sir.'

The box came back up again, with a tray in it. Vimes took it out. 'What's this?'

'A Klatchian Hots without anchovies,' said Vimes, lifting the cover. 'We got it from Ron's Pizza Hovel round the corner. The way I see it, no one can poison all the food in the city. And the cutlery's from my place.'

'You have the mind of a true policeman, Vimes.'

'Thank you, sir.'

'Really? Was it a compliment?' The Patrician prodded at the plate with the air of an explorer in a strange country.

'Has someone *already* eaten this, Vimes?'

'No, sir. That's just how they chop up the food.'

'Oh, I *see*. I thought perhaps the food-tasters were getting over-enthusiastic,' said the Patrician. 'My word. What a treat I have to look forward to.'

'I can see you're feeling better, sir,' said Vimes stiffly.

'Thank you, Vimes.'

When Vimes had gone Lord Vetinari ate the pizza, or at least those parts of it he thought he could recognize. Then he put the tray aside and blew out the candle by his bed. He sat in the dark for a while, then felt under his pillow until his finger located a small sharp knife and a box of matches.

Thank goodness for Vimes. There was something endearing about his desperate, burning and above all *misplaced* competence. If the poor man took any longer he'd have to start giving him hints.

In the main office Carrot sat alone, watching Dorfl.

The golem stood where it had been left. Someone had hung a dishcloth on one arm. The top of its head was still open.

Carrot spent a while with his chin on one hand, just staring. Then he opened a desk drawer and took out Dorfl's chem. He examined it. He got up. He walked over to the golem. He placed the words in the head.

An orange glow rose in Dorfl's eyes. What was baked pottery took on that faintest of auras that marked the change between the living and the dead.

Carrot found the golem's slate and pencil and pushed them into Dorfl's hand, then stood back.

The burning gaze followed him as he removed his sword belt, undid his breastplate, took off his jerkin and pulled his woollen vest over his head.

The glow was reflected from his muscles. They glistened in the candlelight.

'No weapons,' said Carrot. 'No armour. You see? Now listen to me . . .'

Dorfl lurched forward and swung a fist.

Carrot did not move.

The fist stopped a hair's-breadth from Carrot's unblinking eyes.

'I didn't think you could,' he said, as the golem swung again and the fist jerked to a stop a fraction of an inch from Carrot's stomach. 'But sooner or later you'll have to talk to me. Write, anyway.'

Dorfl paused. Then it picked up the slate pencil.

TAKE MY WORDS!

'Tell me about the golem who killed people.'

The pencil did not move.

'The others have killed themselves,' said Carrot.

I KNOW.

'*How* do you know?'

The golem watched him. Then it wrote:

CLAY OF MY CLAY.

'You feel what other golems feel?' said Carrot.

Dorfl nodded.

'And people are killing golems,' said Carrot. 'I don't know if I can stop that. But I can try. I think I know what's happening, Dorfl. Some of it. I think I know who you were following. Clay of your clay. Shaming you all. Something went wrong. You tried to put it right. I think . . . you all had such hopes. But the words in your head'll defeat you every time . . .'

The golem stayed motionless.

'You sold him, didn't you,' said Carrot quietly. 'Why?'

The words were scribbled quickly.

GOLEM MUST HAVE A MASTER.

'Why? Because the words say so?'

GOLEM MUST HAVE A MASTER!

Carrot sighed. Men had to breathe, fish had to swim, golems had to have a master. 'I don't know if I can sort this out, but no one else is going to try, believe me,' he said.

Dorfl did not move.

Carrot went back to where he had been standing. 'I'm wondering if the old priest and Mr Hopkinson did something . . . or *helped* to do something,' he said, watching the golem's face. 'I'm wondering if . . . afterwards . . . something turned against them, found the world a bit too much . . .'

Dorfl remained impassive.

Carrot nodded. 'Anyway, you're free to go. What happens now is up to you. I'll help you if I can. If a golem is a *thing* then it can't commit murder, and I'll still try to find out why all this is happening. If a golem *can* commit murder, then you are *people*, and what is being done to you is terrible and must be stopped. Either way, you win, Dorfl.' He turned his back and fiddled with some papers on his desk. 'The big trouble,' he added, 'is that everyone wants someone else to read their minds for them and then make the world work properly. Even golems, perhaps.'

He turned back to face the golem. 'I know you've all got a secret. But, the way things are going, there won't be any of you left to keep it.'

He looked hopefully at Dorfl.

NO. CLAY OF MY CLAY. I WILL NOT BETRAY.

Carrot sighed. 'Well, I won't force you.' He grinned. 'Although, you know, I could. I could write a few extra words on your chem. Tell you to be talkative.'

The fires rose in Dorfl's eyes.

'But I won't. Because that would be inhumane. You haven't murdered anyone. I can't deprive you of your freedom because you haven't got any. Go on. You can go. It's not as if I don't know where you live.'

TO WORK IS TO LIVE.

'What is it golems *want*, Dorfl? I've seen you golems walking around the streets and working all the time, but what is it you actually hope to achieve?'

The slate pencil scribbled.

RESPITE.

Then Dorfl turned around and walked out of the building.

'D*mn!' said Carrot, a difficult linguistic feat. He drummed his fingers on the desk, then got up abruptly, put his clothing back on and stalked down the corridor to find Angua.

She was leaning against the wall in Corporal Littlebottom's office, talking to the dwarf.

'I've sent Dorfl home,' said Carrot.

'Has he got one?' said Angua.

'Well, back to the slaughterhouse, anyway. But it's probably not a good time for a golem to be out alone so I'm just going to stroll along after him and keep ... Are you all right, Corporal Littlebottom?'

'Yes, sir,' said Cheri.

'You're wearing a ... a ... a ...' Carrot's mind rebelled at the thought of what the dwarf was wearing and settled for: 'A kilt?'

'Yes, sir. A skirt, sir. A leather one, sir.'

Carrot tried to find a suitable response and had to resort to: 'Oh.'

'I'll come with you,' said Angua. 'Cheri can keep an eye on the desk.'

'A ... kilt,' said Carrot. 'Oh. Well, er ... just keep an eye on things. We won't be long. And ... er ... just keep behind the desk, all right?'

'Come *on*,' said Angua.

When they were out in the fog Carrot said, 'Do you think there's something a bit ... *odd* about Littlebottom?'

'Seems like a perfectly ordinary female to me,' said Angua.

'*Female*? He *told* you he was female?'

'She,' Angua corrected. 'This is Ankh-Morpork, you know. We've got extra pronouns here.'

She could smell his bewilderment. Of course, everyone knew that, somewhere down under all those layers of leather and chain mail, dwarfs came in enough different types to ensure the future production of more dwarfs, but it was not a subject that dwarfs discussed other than at those essential points in a courtship when embarrassment might otherwise arise.

'Well, I would have thought she'd have the decency to keep it to herself,' Carrot said finally. 'I mean, I've nothing against females. I'm pretty certain my stepmother is one. But I don't think it's very clever, you know, to go around drawing attention to the fact.'

'Carrot, I think you've got something wrong with your head,' said Angua.

'What?'

'I think you may have got it stuck up your bum. I mean, good *grief*! A bit of make-up and a dress and you're acting as though she'd become Miss Va Va Voom and started dancing on tables down at the Skunk Club!'

There were a few seconds of shocked silence while they *both* considered the image of a dwarfish strip-tease dancer. Both minds rebelled.

'Anyway,' said Angua, 'if people can't be themselves in Ankh-Morpork, where can they?'

'There'll be trouble when the other dwarfs notice,' said Carrot. 'I could almost see his knees. *Her* knees.'

'Everyone's got knees.'

'Perhaps, but it's asking for trouble to flaunt them. I mean, *I'm* used to knees. I can look at knees and think, "Oh, yes, knees, they're just hinges in your legs", but some of the lads—'

Angua sniffed. 'He turned left here. Some of the lads *what*?'

'Well . . . I don't know how they'll react, that's all. You shouldn't have encouraged her. I mean, of course there's female dwarfs but . . . I mean, they have the decency not to show it.'

He heard Angua gasp. Her voice sounded rather far away when she said, 'Carrot, you know I've always respected your attitude to the citizens of Ankh-Morpork.'

'Yes?'

'I've been impressed by the way you really seem to be blind to things like shape and colour.'

'Yes?'

'And you always seem to care for people.'

'Yes?'

'And you know that I feel considerable affection for you.'

'Yes?'

'It's just that, sometimes . . .'

'Yes?'

'I really, really, *really* wonder why.'

Carriages were thickly parked outside Lady Selachii's mansion when Corporal Nobbs strolled up the drive. He knocked on the door.

A footman opened it. 'Servants' entrance,' said the footman, and made to shut the door again.

But Nobby's outstretched foot had been ready for this. 'Read these,' he said, thrusting two bits of paper at him.

The first one read:

I, after hearing evidence from a number of experts, including Mrs Slipdry the midwife, certify that the balance of probability is that the bearer of this document, C. W. St John Nobbs, is a human being.

Signed, Lord Vetinari.

The other was the letter from Dragon King of Arms.

The footman's eyes widened. 'Oh, I am terribly sorry, your lordship,' he said. He stared again at Corporal Nobbs. Nobby was clean-shaven – at least, the last time he'd shaved he'd been clean-shaven – but his face had so many minor topological features it looked like a very bad example of slash-and-burn agriculture.

'Oh, dear,' added the footman. He pulled himself together. 'The other visitors normally just have cards.'

Nobby produced a battered deck. 'I'm probably busy hobnobbing right now,' he said. 'But I'm game for a few rounds of Cripple Mr Onion afterwards, if you like.'

The footman looked him up and down. He didn't get out much. He'd heard rumours – who hadn't? – that working in the Watch was the rightful king of Ankh-Morpork. He'd have to admit that, if you wanted to hide a secret heir to the throne, you couldn't possibly hide him more carefully than under the face of C. W. St J. Nobbs.

On the other hand ... the footman was something of an historian, and knew that in its long history even the throne itself had been occupied by creatures who had been hunchbacked, one-eyed, knuckle-dragging and as ugly as sin. On that basis Nobby was as royal as they came. If, technically, he wasn't hunchbacked, this was only because he was hunched front and sides, too. There might be a time, the footman thought, when it paid to hitch your wagon to a star, even if said star was a red dwarf.

'You've never been to one of these affairs before, m'lord?' he said.

'First time,' said Nobby.

'I'm sure your lordship's blood will rise to the occasion,' said the footman weakly.

I'll have to go, Angua thought as they hurried through the fog. *I can't go on living from month to month.*

It's not that he's not likeable. You couldn't wish to meet a more caring man.

That's just it. He cares for everyone. He cares about everything. He cares indiscriminately. He knows everything about everyone because everyone interests him, and the caring is all general and never personal. He doesn't think personal is the same as important.

If only he had some decent human quality, like selfishness.

I'm sure he doesn't think about it that way, but you can tell *the werewolf thing is upsetting him underneath. He cares about the things people say behind my back, and he doesn't know how to deal with them.*

What was it those dwarfs said the other day? One said something like, 'She feels the need,' and the other one said, 'Yeah, the need to feed.' I saw his expression. I can handle that sort of thing . . . well, most of the time . . . but he *can't. If only he'd thump someone. It wouldn't do any good but at least he'd feel better.*

It's going to get worse. At best I'm going to get caught in someone's chicken-house, and then the midden is really *going to hit the windmill. Or I'll get caught in someone's room . . .*

She tried to shut out the thought but it didn't work. You could only *control* the werewolf, you couldn't *tame* it.

It's the city. Too many people, too many smells . . .

Maybe it would work if we were just alone somewhere, but if I said, 'It's me or the city,' he wouldn't even see there was a choice.

Sooner or later, I've got to go home. It's the best thing for him.

Vimes walked back through the damp night. He knew he was too angry to think properly.

He'd got nowhere, and he'd travelled a long way to get there. He'd got a cartload of facts and he'd done all the right logical things, and to someone, somewhere, he must look like a fool.

He probably looked like a fool to Carrot already. He'd kept coming up with bright ideas – proper *policeman*'s ideas – and each one had turned out to be a joke. He'd bullied and shouted and done all the proper things, and none of it had worked. They hadn't found a thing. They'd merely increased their amount of ignorance.

The ghost of old Mrs Easy rose up in his inner vision. He couldn't remember much about her. He'd been just another snotty kid in a crowd of snotty kids, and she'd been just another worried face somewhere on top of a pinny. One of Cockbill Street's people. She'd taken in needlework to make ends meet and kept up appearances and, like everyone else in the street, had crept through life never asking for anything and getting even less.

What else *could* he have done? They'd practically scraped the damn wallpaper off the wal—

He stopped.

There was the same wallpaper in both rooms. In every room on that floor. That horrible green wallpaper.

But . . . no, that couldn't be it. Vetinari had slept in that room for years, if he slept at all. You can't sneak in and redecorate without someone noticing.

In front of him, the fog rolled aside. He caught a glimpse of a candlelit room in a nearby building before the cloud flowed back.

The fog. Yes. Dampness. Creeping in, brushing against the wallpaper. The old, dusty, musty wallpaper . . .

Would Cheery have tested the wallpaper? After all, in a way you didn't actually *see* it. It wasn't *in* the room because it was defining what the room was. Could you actually be poisoned by the *walls*?

He hardly dared think the thought. If he let his mind *settle* on the suspicion it'd twist and fly away, like all the others.

But . . . this was it, said his secret soul. All the messing around with suspects and Clues . . . that was just something to keep the body amused while the back of the brain toiled away. Every real copper knew you didn't go around looking for Clues so that you could find out Who Done It. No, you started out with a pretty good idea of Who Done It. That way, you knew what Clues to look for.

He wasn't going to have another day of bafflement interspersed with desperately bright ideas, was he? It was bad enough looking at Corporal Littlebottom's expression, which seemed to be getting a little more colourful every time he saw it.

He'd said, 'Ah, arsenic's a metal, right, so maybe the *cutlery* has been made of it?' He wouldn't forget the look on the dwarf's face as Cheery tried to explain that, yes, it might be possible to do that, provided you were sure that no one would notice the way it dissolved in the soup almost instantly.

This time he was going to think first.

'The Earl of Ankh, Corporal the Rt. Hon. Lord C. W. St J. Nobbs!'
The buzz of conversation stopped. Heads turned. Somewhere in

the crowd someone started to laugh and was hurriedly shushed into silence by their neighbours.

Lady Selachii came forward. She was a tall, angular woman, with the sharp features and aquiline nose that were the hallmarks of the family. The impression was that an axe was being thrown at you.

Then she curtsied.

There were gasps of surprise around her, but she glared at the assembled guests and there was a smattering of bows and curtsies. Somewhere at the back of the room someone started to say, 'But the man's an absolute oik—' and was cut off.

'Has someone dropped something?' said Nobby nervously. 'I'll help you look, if you like.'

The footman appeared at his elbow, bearing a tray. 'A drink, m'lord?' he said.

'Yeah, okay, a pint of Winkles,' said Nobby.

Jaws fell. But Lady Selachii's rose to the occasion. 'Winkles?' she said.

'A type of beer, your ladyship,' said the footman.

Her ladyship hesitated only a moment. 'I believe the butler drinks beer,' she said. 'See to it, man. And I'll have a pint of Winkles, too. What a *novel* idea.'

This caused a certain effect among those guests who knew on which side of the biscuit their pâté was spread.

'Indeed! Capital suggestion! A pint of Winkles here, too!'

'Hawhaw! Gweat! Winkles for me!'

'Winkles all round!'

'*But the man's an absolute ti—*'

'*Shut up!*'

Vimes crossed the Brass Bridge with care, counting the hippos. There was a ninth shape, but it was leaning against the parapet and muttering to itself in a familiar and, to Vimes at least, an unmenacing way. Faint air movements wafted towards him a smell that out-smelled even the river. It proclaimed that ahead of Vimes was a ding-a-ling so big he'd been upgraded to a clang-a-lang.

'. . . Buggrit buggrit I *told* 'em, stand it up and pull the end orf? Millennium hand and shrimp! I *told* 'em, sez I, and would they poke . . .'

'Evening, Ron,' said Vimes, without even bothering to look at the figure.

Foul Old Ron fell into step behind him. 'Buggrit they done me out of it so they did . . .'

'Yes, Ron,' said Vimes.

'. . . And shrimp . . . buggrit, say I, bread it on the butter side . . . Queen Molly says to watch your back, mister.'

'What was that?'

'. . . Sowter fry it!' said Foul Ole Ron innocently. 'Trouser the lot of 'em, they did me out of it, them and their big weasel!'

The beggar lurched around and, filthy coat dragging its hems along the ground, limped away into the fog. His little dog trotted along in front of him.

There was pandemonium in the servants' hall.

'Winkles' Old Peculiar?' said the butler.

'Another one hundred and four pints!' said the footman.

The butler shrugged. 'Harry, Sid, Rob and Jeffrey . . . two trays apiece and double down to the King's Head again right now! What else is he doing?'

'Well, they're supposed to be having a poetry reading but *he's* telling 'em jokes . . .'

'Anecdotes?'

'Not exactly.'

It was amazing how it could drizzle and fog at the same time. Wind was blowing both through the open window, and Vimes was forced to shut it. He lit the candles by his desk and opened his notebook.

Probably he should use the demonic organizer, but he liked to see things written down fair and square. He could think better when he wrote things down.

He wrote 'Arsenic', and drew a big circle round it. Around the circle he wrote: 'Fr. Tubelcek's fingernails' and 'Rats' and 'Vetinari' and 'Mrs Easy'. Lower down the page he wrote: 'Golems', and drew a second circle. Around that one he wrote: 'Fr. Tubelcek?' and 'Mr Hopkinson?'. After some thought he wrote down: 'Stolen clay' and 'Grog'.

And then: 'Why would a golem admit to something it didn't do?'

He stared at the candlelight for a while and then wrote: 'Rats eat stuff.'

More time passed.

'What has the prieft got that anyone wants?'

From downstairs came the sound of armour as a patrol came in. A corporal shouted.

'Words,' wrote Vimes. 'What had Mr Hopkinson got? Dwarf bread? → Not stolen. What else had he got?'

Vimes looked at this, too, and then he wrote 'Bakery', stared at the word for a while, and rubbed it out and replaced it with 'Oven?'. He drew a ring around 'Oven?' and a ring around 'Stolen clay', and linked the two.

There'd been arsenic under the old priest's fingernails. Perhaps he'd put down rat poison? There were plenty of uses for arsenic. It wasn't as if you couldn't buy it by the pound from any alchemist.

He wrote down 'Arsenic Monster' and looked at it. You found dirt under fingernails. If people had put up a fight you might find blood or skin. You didn't find grease and arsenic.

He looked at the page again and, after still more thought, wrote: 'Golems aren't alive. But they *think* they are alive. What do things that are alive do? → Ans: Breathe, eat, crap.' He paused, staring out at the fog, and then wrote very carefully: 'And make more things.'

Something tingled at the back of his neck.

He circled the late Hopkinson's name and drew a line down the page to another circle, in which he wrote: 'He'd got a big oven.'

Hmm. Cheery had said you couldn't bake clay properly in a bread oven. But maybe you could bake it improperly.

He looked up at the candlelight again.

They couldn't do *that*, could they? Oh, gods . . . No, surely not . . .

But, after all, all you needed was clay. And a holy man who knew how to write the words. And someone to actually sculpt the figure, Vimes supposed, but golems had had hundreds and hundreds of years to learn to be good with their hands . . .

Those great big hands. The ones that looked so very fist-like.

And then the first thing they'd want to do would be to destroy the evidence, wouldn't they? They probably didn't think of it as killing, but more like a sort of switching-off . . .

He drew another rather misshapen circle on his notes.

Grog. Old baked clay, ground up small.

They'd added some of their own clay. Dorfl had a new foot, didn't he – it? It hadn't made it quite right. They'd put part of their own selves into a new golem.

That all sounded – well, Nobby would call it mucky. Vimes didn't know what to call it. It sounded like some sort of secret-society thing. 'Clay of my clay.' My own flesh and blood . . .

Damn hulking things. Aping their betters!

Vimes yawned. Sleep. He'd be better for some sleep. Or something.

He stared at the page. Automatically his hand trailed down to the bottom drawer of his desk, as it always did when he was worried and trying to think. It wasn't as though there was ever a bottle there these days – but old habits died ha . . .

There was a soft glassy *ching* and a faint, seductive slosh.

Vimes's hand came up with a fat bottle. The label said: Bearhugger's Distilleries: The MacAbre, Finest Malt.

The liquid inside almost crawled up the sides of the glass in anticipation.

He stared at it. He'd reached down into the drawer for the whisky bottle and there it was.

But it shouldn't have been. He knew Carrot and Fred Colon kept an eye on him, but he'd never bought a bottle since he'd got married, because he'd promised Sybil, hadn't he . . . ?

But this wasn't any old rotgut. This was The MacAbre . . .

He'd tried it once. He couldn't quite remember why now, since in those days the only spirits he generally drank had the subtlety of a mallet to the inner ear. He must have found the money somehow. Just a *sniff* of it had been like Hogswatchnight. Just a *sniff* . . .

'And *she* said, "That's funny – it didn't do that last night"!' said Corporal Nobbs.

He beamed at the company.

There was silence. Then someone in the crowd started to laugh, one of those little uncertain laughs a man laughs who is unsure that he's not going to be silenced by those around him. Another man laughed. Two more picked it up. Then laughter exploded in the group as a whole.

Nobby basked.

'Then there's the one about the Klatchian who walked into a pub with a tiny piano—' he began.

'I think,' said Lady Selachii firmly, 'that the buffet is ready.'

'Got any pig knuckles?' said Nobby cheerfully. 'Goes down a treat with Winkles, a plate of pig knuckles.'

'I don't *normally* eat extremities,' said Lady Selachii.

'A pig-knuckle sandwich . . . Never tried a pig knuckle? You just can't beat it,' said Nobby.

'It is . . . perhaps . . . not the most delicate food?' said Lady Selachii.

'Oh, you can cut the crusts off,' said Nobby. 'Even the toenails. If you're feeling posh.'

*

Sergeant Colon opened his eyes, and groaned. His head ached. They'd hit him with something. It might have been a wall.

They'd tied him up, too. He was trussed hand and foot.

He appeared to be lying in darkness on a wooden floor. There was a greasy smell in the air, which seemed familiar yet annoyingly unrecognizable.

As his eyes grew accustomed to the dark he could make out very faint lines of light, such as might surround a door. He could also hear voices.

He tried to get up to his knees, and groaned as more pain crackled in his head.

When people tied you up it was bad news. Of course, it was much better news than when they killed you, but it could mean they were just putting you on one side for killing later.

This never used to happen, he told himself. In the old days, if you caught someone thieving, you practically held the door open for him to escape. That way, you got home in one piece.

By using the angle between a wall and a heavy crate he managed to get upright. This was not much of an improvement on his former position, but after the thunder in his head had died away he hopped awkwardly towards the door.

There were still voices on the other side of it.

Someone apart from Sergeant Colon was in trouble.

'—*clown!* You got me here for *this*? There's a werewolf in the Watch! Ah-ha. Not one of your freaks. She's a proper bimorphic! If you tossed a coin, she could smell what side it came down!'

'How about if we kill him and drag his body away?'

'You think she couldn't smell the difference between a corpse and a living body?'

Sergeant Colon moaned softly.

'Er, how about we could march him out in the fog—?'

'And they can smell fear, idiot. Ah-ha. Why couldn't you have let him look around? What could he have seen? I know that copper. A fat old coward with all the brains of, ah-ha, a pig. He stinks of fear all the time.'

Sergeant Colon hoped he wasn't about to stink of anything else.

'Send Meshugah after him, ah-ha.'

'Are you sure? It's getting *odd*. It wanders off and screams in the night, and they're *not* supposed to do that. And it's cracking up. Trust dumb golems not to do something prop—'

'Everyone knows you can't trust golems. Ah-ha. See to it!'

'I heard that Vimes is—'

'I've seen to Vimes!'

Colon eased himself away from the door as quietly as possible.

679

He hadn't the faintest idea what this thing called Meshugah the golems had made was, except that it sounded like a fine idea to be wherever it wasn't.

Now, if he were a resourceful type, like Sam Vimes or Captain Carrot, he'd ... find a nail or something to snap these ropes, wouldn't he? They were *really* tight, and cut into his wrists because the cord was so thin, little more than string wound and knotted many times. If he could find something to rub it on ...

But, unfortunately, and against all common sense, sometimes people inconsiderately throw their bound enemies into rooms entirely bereft of nails, handy bits of sharp stone, sharp-edged shards of glass or even, in extreme cases, enough pieces of old junk and tools to make a fully functional armoured car.

He managed to get on to his knees again and shuffled across the planks. Even a splinter would do. A lump of metal. A wide-open doorway marked FREEDOM. He'd settle for anything.

What he got was a tiny circle of light on the floor. A knothole in the wood had long ago fallen out, and light – dim orange light – was shining through.

Colon got down and applied his eye to the hole. Unfortunately this also brought his nose into a similar proximity.

The stench was appalling.

There was a suggestion of wateriness, or at least of liquidity. He must be over one of the numerous streams that flowed through the city, although they had of course been built over centuries before and were now used – if their existence was even remembered – for those purposes to which humanity had always put clean fresh water; i.e., making it as turbid and undrinkable as possible. And this one was flowing under the cattle markets. The smell of ammonia bored into Colon's sinuses like a drill.

And yet there was light down there.

He held his breath and took another look.

A couple of feet below him was a very small raft. Half a dozen rats were laid neatly on it, and a minute scrap of candle was burning.

A tiny rowing boat entered his vision. A rat was in the bottom of it and, sitting amidships and rowing, was—

'Wee Mad Arthur?'

The gnome looked up. 'Who's that there, then?'

'It's me, your good old mate Fred Colon! Can you give me a hand?'

'Wha're yez doing up there?'

'I'm all tied up and they're going to kill me! Why does it smell so *bad*?'

' 'S the old Cockbill stream. All the cattle pens drain into it.' Wee Mad Arthur grinned. 'Yez can feel it doing yer tubes a power of good, eh? Just call me King of the Golden River, eh?'

'They're going to *kill* me, Arthur! Don't piss about!'

'Aha, good one!'

Desperate cells flared in Colon's mind. 'I've been on the trail of those blokes who're poisoning your rats,' he said.

'The Rat-catchers' Guild!' snarled Arthur, almost dropping an oar. 'I *knew* it was them, right? This is where I got them rats! There's more of 'em down here, dead as doornails!'

'Right! And I've got to give the names to Commander Vimes! In person! With all my arms and legs on! He's very particular about that sort of thing!'

'Did yez know yez on a trapdoor?' said Arthur. 'Wait right there.'

Arthur rowed out of sight. Colon rolled over. After a while there was a scratching noise in the walls and then someone kicked him in the ear.

'Ow!'

'Would there be any money in this?' said Wee Mad Arthur, holding up his stub of candle. It was a small one, such as might be put on a child's birthday cake.

'What about your public duty?'

'Aye, so there's *no* money in this?'

'Lots! I promise! Now untie me!'

'This is string they've used,' said Arthur, somewhere around Colon's hands. 'Not proper rope at all.'

Colon felt his hands free, although there was still pressure around his wrists.

'Where's the trapdoor?' he said.

'Yer on it. Handy for dumping stuff. Dunt look as if it been used for years, from underneath. Hey, I been finding dead rats everywhere down there now! Fat as yer head and twice as dead! I *thought* the ones I caught for Gimlet were a wee bit sluggish!'

There was a twang and Colon's legs were free. He sat up cautiously and tried to massage some life back into them.

'Is there any other way out?' he said.

'Plenty for me, none for a silly bigger like yez,' said Wee Mad Arthur. 'Yer'll have to swim for it.'

'You want me to drop into *that*?'

'Don't yez worry, yez can't drown in it.'

'You sure?'

'Yeah. But yez may suffocate. Yer know that creek they talk about? The one yez can be up without no paddle?'

'That's not this one, is it?' said Colon.

'It's coz of the cattle pens,' said Wee Mad Arthur. 'Cattle penned up is always a bit nervous.'

'I know how they feel.'

There was a creak outside the door. Colon managed to get to his feet.

The door opened.

A figure filled the doorway. It was in silhouette because of the light behind it, but Colon looked up into two triangular glowing eyes.

Colon's body, which in many respects was considerably more intelligent than the mind it had to carry around, took over. It made use of the adrenalin-fed start the brain had given it and leapt several feet in the air, pointing its toes as it came down so that the iron tips of Colon's boots hit the trapdoor together.

The filth of years and the rust of iron gave way.

Colon went through. Fortunately his body had the foresight to hold its own nose as he hit the much-maligned stream, which went: *Gloop*.

Many people, when they're precipitated into water, struggle to breathe. Sergeant Colon struggled not to. The alternative was too horrible to think about.

He rose again, buoyed up in part by various gases released from the ooze. A few feet away, the candle on Wee Mad Arthur's rocking raft started to burn with a blue flame.

Someone landed on his helmet and kicked it like a man spurs on a horse.

'Right *turn*! Forward!'

Half-walking, half-swimming, Colon struggled down the fetid drain. Terror lent him strength. It would demand repayment with interest later but, for now, he left a wake. Which took several seconds to close up after him.

He didn't stop until a sudden lack of pressure overhead told him that he was in the open air. He grabbed in the darkness, found the greasy pilings of a jetty, and clung to them, wheezing.

'What was that thing?' said Wee Mad Arthur.

'Golem,' Colon panted.

He managed to get a hand on to the planks of the jetty, tried to pull himself up, and sagged back into the water.

'Hey, did I just hear something?' said Wee Mad Arthur.

Sergeant Colon rose like an undersea-launched missile and landed on the jetty, where he folded up.

'Nah, just a bird or something,' said Wee Mad Arthur.

'What do your friends call you, Wee Mad Arthur?' muttered Colon.

'Dunno. Ain't got none.'

'Gosh, that's surprising.'

Lord de Nobbes had a lot of friends now. 'Up the hatch! Here's looking at your bottom!' he said.

There were shrieks of laughter.

Nobby grinned happily in the middle of the crowd. He couldn't remember when he had enjoyed himself so much with all his clothes on.

In the far corner of Lady Selachii's drawing-room a door closed discreetly and, in the comfortable smoking-room beyond, anonymous people sat down in leather armchairs and looked at one another expectantly.

Finally one said, 'It's astonishing. Frankly astonishing. The man has actually got charisn'tma.'

'Your meaning?'

'I mean he's so dreadful he fascinates people. Like those stories he was telling . . . Did you notice how people kept encouraging him because they couldn't actually believe *anyone* would tell jokes like that in mixed company?'

'Actually, I rather liked the one about the very small man playing the piano—'

'And his table manners! Did you notice them?'

'No.'

'Ex-actly!'

'And the smell, don't forget the smell.'

'Not so much *bad* as . . . odd.'

'Actually, I found that after a few minutes the nose shuts down and then it's—'

'My *point* is that, in some strange way, he attracts people.'

'Like a public hanging.'

There was a period of reflective silence.

'Good humoured little tit, though, in his way.'

'Not too bright, though.'

'Give him his pint of beer and a plate of whatever those things with toenails were and he seems as happy as a pig in muck.'

'I think that's somewhat insulting.'

'I'm sorry.'

'I've known some splendid pigs.'

'Indeed.'

'But I can certainly see him drinking his beer and eating feet while he signs the royal proclamations.'

'Yes, indeed. Er. Do you think he can read?'

'Does it matter?'

There was some more silence, filled with the busy racing of minds.

Then someone said, 'Another thing . . . we won't have to worry about establishing a royal succession that might be inconvenient.'

'Why do you think that?'

'Can you see any princess marrying him?'

'We-ell . . . they have been known to kiss frogs . . .'

'Frogs, I grant you.'

'. . . And, of course, power and royalty *are* powerful aphrodisiacs . . .'

'*How* powerful, would you say?'

More silence. Then: 'Probably not that powerful.'

'He should do nicely.'

'Splendid.'

'Dragon did well. I suppose the little tit isn't *really* an earl, by any chance?'

'Don't be silly.'

Cheri Littlebottom sat awkwardly on the high stool behind the desk. All she had to do, she'd been told, was check the patrols off- and on-duty when the shift changed.

A few of the men gave her an odd look but they said nothing, and she was beginning to relax when the four dwarfs on the King's Way beat came in.

They stared at her. And her ears.

Their eyes travelled downwards. There was no such concept as a modesty panel in Ankh-Morpork. All that was usually visible under the desk was the bottom half of Sergeant Colon. Of the large number of good reasons for shielding the bottom half of Sergeant Colon from view, its potential for engendering lust was not among the top ten.

'That's . . . *female* clothes, isn't it?' said one of the dwarfs.

Cheri swallowed. Why *now*? She'd sort of assumed Angua would be around. People always calmed down when she smiled at them, it was really amazing.

'Well?' she quavered. 'So what? I can if I want to.'

'And . . . on your ear . . .'

'Well?'

'That's . . . my mother never even . . . urgh . . . that's disgusting! In public, too! What happens if kids come in?'

'I can see your *ankles!*' said another dwarf.

'I'm going to speak to Captain Carrot about this!' said the third. 'I never thought I'd live to see the day!'

Two of the dwarfs stormed off towards the locker-room. Another one hurried after them, but hesitated as he drew level with the desk. He gave Cheri a frantic look.

'Er . . . er . . . *nice* ankles, though,' he said, and then ran.

The fourth dwarf waited until the others had gone and then sidled up.

Cheri was shaking with nervousness. 'Don't you say a *thing* about my legs!' she said, waving a finger.

'Er . . .' The dwarf looked around hurriedly, and leaned forward. 'Er . . . is that . . . lipstick?'

'Yes! What about it?'

'Er . . .' The dwarf leaned forward even more, looked around again, this time conspiratorially, and lowered her voice. 'Er . . . could I try it?'

Angua and Carrot walked silently through the fog, except for Angua's occasional crisp and brief directions.

Then she stopped. Up until then Dorfl's scent, or at least the fresh scent of old meat and cow dung, had headed quite directly back to the slaughterhouse district.

'It's gone up this alley,' she said. 'That's nearly doubling back. And . . . it was moving faster . . . and . . . there's a lot of humans and . . . *sausages?*'

Carrot started to run. A lot of people and the smell of sausages meant a performance of the street theatre that was life in Ankh-Morpork.

There was a crowd further up the alley. It had obviously been there for some time, because at the rear was a familiar figure with a tray, craning to see over the tops of the heads.

'What's going on, Mr Dibbler?' said Carrot.

'Oh, hello, cap'n. They've got a golem.'

'Who have?'

'Oh, some blokes. They've just fetched the hammers.'

There was a press of bodies in front of Carrot. He put both hands together and rammed them between a couple of people, and then moved them apart. Grunting and struggling, the crowd opened up like a watercourse in front of the better class of prophet.

Dorfl was standing at bay at the end of the alley. Three men with hammers were approaching the golem cautiously, in the way of mobs, each unwilling to strike the first blow in case the second blow came right back at him.

685

The golem was crouching back, shielding itself with its slate on which was written:

I AM WORTH 530 DOLLARS.

'Money?' said one of the men. 'That's all you things think about!'

The slate shattered under a blow.

Then he tried to raise his hammer again. When it didn't budge he very nearly somersaulted backwards.

'Money is all you *can* think about when all you have is a price,' said Carrot calmly, twisting the hammer out of his grip. 'What do you think you're doing, my friend?'

'You can't stop us!' mumbled the man. 'Everyone knows they're not alive!'

'But I *can* arrest you for wilful damage to property,' said Carrot.

'One of these killed that old priest!'

'Sorry?' said Carrot. 'If it's just a thing, how can it commit murder? A sword is a thing' – he drew his own sword; it made an almost silken sound – 'and of course you couldn't possibly blame a *sword* if someone thrust it at you, sir.'

The man went cross-eyed as he tried to focus on the sword.

And, again, Angua felt that touch of bewilderment. Carrot wasn't threatening the man. He *wasn't* threatening the man. He was merely using the sword to demonstrate a . . . well, a point. And that was all. He'd be quite amazed to hear that not everyone would think of it like that.

Part of her said: *Someone has to be very complex indeed to be as simple as Carrot.*

The man swallowed.

'*Good* point,' he said.

'Yeah, but . . . you can't trust 'em,' said one of the other hammer-bearers. 'They sneak around and they never say anything. What are they up to, eh?'

He gave Dorfl a kick. The golem rocked slightly.

'Well, now,' said Carrot. 'That is what I am finding out. In the meantime, I must ask you to go about your business . . .'

The third demolition man had only recently arrived in the city and had gone along with the idea because there are some people who do.

He raised his hammer defiantly and opened his mouth to say, 'Oh, yeah?' but stopped, because just by his ear he heard a growl. It was quite low and soft, but it had a complex little waveform which went straight down into a little knobbly bit in his spinal column where it pressed an ancient button marked Primal Terror.

He turned. An attractive watchwoman behind him gave him a

friendly smile. That was to say, her mouth turned up at the corners and all her teeth were visible.

He dropped the hammer on his foot.

'Well done,' said Carrot. 'I've always said you can do more with a kind word and a smile.'

The crowd looked at him with the kind of expression people always wore when they looked at Carrot. It was the face-cracking realization that he really did believe what he was saying. The sheer enormity tended to leave people breathless.

They backed away and scurried out of the alley.

Carrot turned back to the golem, which had dropped to its knees and was trying to piece its slate together.

'Come on, Mr Dorfl,' he said. 'We'll walk with you the rest of the way.'

'Are you mad?' said Sock, trying to shut the door. 'You think I want *that* back?'

'He's your property,' said Carrot. 'People were trying to smash him.'

'You should've let them,' said the butcher. 'Haven't you heard the stories? I'm not having one of those under my roof!'

He tried to slam the door again, but Carrot's foot was in it.

'Then I'm afraid you're committing an offence,' said Carrot. 'To wit, littering.'

'Oh, be serious!'

'I always am,' said Carrot.

'He always is,' said Angua.

Sock waved his hands frantically. 'It can just go away. Shoo! I don't want a killer working in my slaughterhouse! You have it, if you're so keen!'

Carrot grabbed the door and forced it wide open. Sock took a step backwards.

'Are you trying to bribe an officer of the law, Mr Sock?'

'Are you insane?'

'I am always sane,' said Carrot.

'He always is,' sighed Angua.

'Watchmen are not allowed to accept gifts,' said Carrot. He looked around at Dorfl, who was standing forlornly in the street. 'But I *will* buy him from you. For a fair price.'

Sock looked from Carrot to the golem and then back again. 'Buy? For money?'

'Yes.'

The butcher shrugged. When people were offering you money it was no time to debate their sanity. 'Well, that's different,' he conceded. 'It was worth $530 when I bought it, but of course it's got additional skills now—'

Angua growled. It had been a trying evening and the smell of fresh meat was making her senses twang. 'You were prepared to *give* it away a moment ago!'

'Well, *give*, yes, but business is busi—'

'I'll pay you a dollar,' said Carrot.

'A dollar? That's daylight robb—'

Angua's hand shot out and grabbed his neck. She could feel the veins, smell his blood and fear . . . She tried to think of cabbages.

'It's *night*-time,' she growled.

Like the man in the alley, Sock listened to the call of the wild. 'A dollar,' he croaked. 'Right. A fair price. One dollar.'

Carrot produced one. And waved his notebook.

'A receipt is very important,' he said. 'A proper legal transfer of ownership.'

'Right. Right. Right. Happy to oblige.'

Sock glanced desperately at Angua. Somehow, her smile didn't look right. He scribbled a few hasty lines.

Carrot looked over his shoulder.

I Gerhardt Sock give the barer full and totarl ow

norship of the golem Dorfl in xchange for One Dolar and anythinge it doz now is his responisbility and nuthing to doe with me.
                    Singed, Gerhardt Sock.

'Interesting wording, but it does *look* legal, doesn't it?' said Carrot, taking the paper. 'Thank you very much, Mr Sock. A happy solution all round, I feel.'

'Is that it? Can I go now?'

'Certainly, and—'

The door slammed shut.

'Oh, well done,' said Angua. 'So now you own a golem. You do *know* that anything it does is *your* responsibility?'

'If that's the truth, why are people smashing *them*?'

'What are you going to use it *for*?'

Carrot looked thoughtfully at Dorfl, who was staring at the ground.

'Dorfl?'

The golem looked up.

'Here's your receipt. You don't *have* to have a master.'

The golem took the little scrap of paper between two thick fingers.

688

'That means you belong to you,' said Carrot encouragingly. 'You own yourself.'

Dorfl shrugged.

'What did you expect?' said Angua. 'Did you think it was going to wave a flag?'

'I don't think he understands,' said Carrot. 'It's quite hard to get some ideas into people's heads . . .' He stopped abruptly.

Carrot took the paper out of Dorfl's unresisting fingers. 'I *suppose* it might work,' he said. 'It seems a bit – invasive. But what they understand, after all, is the words . . .'

He reached up, opened Dorfl's lid, and dropped the paper inside.

The golem blinked. That is to say, its eyes went dark and then brightened again. It raised one hand very slowly and patted the top of its head. Then it held up the other hand and turned it this way and that, as if it had never seen a hand before. It looked down at its feet and around at the fog-shrouded buildings. It looked at Carrot. It looked up at the clouds above the street. It looked at Carrot again.

Then, very slowly, without bending in any way, it fell backwards and hit the cobbles with a thud. The light faded in its eyes.

'There,' said Angua. 'Now it's broken. Can we go?'

'There's still a bit of a glow,' said Carrot. 'It must have all been too much for him. We can't leave him here. Maybe if I took the receipt out . . .'

He knelt down by the golem and reached for the trapdoor on its head.

Dorfl's hand moved so quickly it didn't even *appear* to move. It was just there, gripping Carrot's wrist.

'Ah,' said Carrot, gently pulling his arm back. 'He's obviously . . . feeling better.'

'Thsssss,' said Dorfl. The voice of the golem shivered in the fog.

Golems had a mouth. They were part of the design. But this one was open, revealing a thin line of red light.

'Oh, ye gods,' said Angua, backing away. 'They *can't* speak!'

'Thssss!' It was less a syllable than the sound of escaping steam.

'I'll find your bit of slate—' Carrot began, looking around hurriedly.

'Thssss!'

Dorfl clambered to its feet, gently pushed him out of the way and strode off.

'Are you *happy* now?' said Angua. 'I'm not following the wretched thing! Maybe it's going to throw itself in the river!'

Carrot ran a few steps after the figure, and then stopped and came back.

'Why do you hate them so much?' he said.

'You wouldn't understand. I really think you wouldn't understand,' said Angua. 'It's an . . . undead thing. They . . . sort of throw in your face the fact you're not human.'

'But you *are* human!'

'Three weeks out of four. Can't you understand that, when you have to be careful all the time, it's dreadful to see *things* like that being accepted? They're not even alive. But they can walk around and *they* never get people passing remarks about silver or garlic . . . up until now, anyway. They're just machines for doing work!'

'That's how they're treated, certainly,' said Carrot.

'You're being reasonable again!' snapped Angua. 'You're deliberately seeing everyone's point of view! Can't you *try* to be unfair even once?'

Nobby had been left alone for a moment while the party buzzed around him, so he'd elbowed some waiters away from the buffet and was currently scraping out a bowl with his knife.

'Ah, Lord de Nobbes,' said a voice behind him.

He turned. 'Wotcha,' he said, licking the knife and wiping it on the tablecloth.

'Are you busy, my lord?'

'Just making meself this meat-paste sandwich,' said Nobby.

'That's pâté de foie gras, my lord.'

''S that what it's called? It doesn't have the kick of Clammer's Beefymite Spread, I know that. Want a quail's egg? They're a bit small.'

'No, thank you—'

'There's loads of them,' said Nobby generously. 'They're free. You don't have to pay.'

'Even so—'

'I can get six in my mouth at once. Watch—'

'Amazing, my lord. I was wondering, however, whether you would care to join a few of us in the smoking-room?'

'Fghmf? Mfgmf fgmf mgghjf?'

'Indeed.' A friendly arm was put around Nobby's shoulders and he was adroitly piloted away from the buffet, but not before he had grabbed a plate of chicken legs. 'So many people want to talk to you . . .'

'Mgffmph?'

*

Sergeant Colon tried to clean himself up, but trying to clean yourself up with water from the Ankh was a difficult manoeuvre. The best you could hope for was an all-over grey.

Fred Colon hadn't reached Vimes's level of sophisticated despair. Vimes took the view that life was so full of things happening erratically in all directions that the chances of any of them making some kind of relevant sense were remote in the extreme. Colon, being by nature more optimistic and by intellect a good deal slower, was still at the Clues are Important stage.

Why had he been tied up with string? There were still loops of it around his arms and legs.

'You sure you don't know where I was?' he said.

'Yez walked into the place,' said Wee Mad Arthur, trotting along beside him. 'How come yez don't know?'

''Cos it was dark and foggy and I wasn't paying attention, that's why. I was just going through the motions.'

'Aha, good one!'

'Don't mess about. Where was I?'

'Don't ask me,' said Wee Mad Arthur. 'I just hunts *under* the whole cattle-market area. I don't bother about what's up top. Like I said, them runs go everywhere.'

'Anyone along there make string?'

'It's all animal stuff, I tell yez. Sausages and soap and stuff like that. Is this the bit where yez gives me the money?'

Colon patted his pockets. They squelched.

'You'll have to come to the Watch House, Wee Mad Arthur.'

'I got a business to run here!'

'I'm swearin' you in as a Special Watchman for the night,' said Colon.

'What's the pay?'

'Dollar a night.'

Wee Mad Arthur's tiny eyes gleamed. They gleamed red.

'Ye gods, you look awful,' said Colon. 'What're you looking at my ear for?'

Wee Mad Arthur said nothing.

Colon turned.

A golem was standing behind him. It was taller than any he'd seen before, and much better proportioned – a human statue rather than the gross shape of the usual golems, and handsome, too, in the cold way of a statue. And its eyes shone like red searchlights.

It raised a fist above its head and opened its mouth. More red light streamed out.

It screamed like a bull.

Wee Mad Arthur kicked Colon on the ankle.

'Are we running or what?' he said.

Colon backed away, still staring at the thing.

'It's . . . it's all right, they can't move fast . . .' he muttered. And then his sensible body gave up on his stupid brain and fired up his legs, spinning him around and shoving him in the opposite direction.

He risked looking over his shoulder. The golem was running after him in long, easy strides.

Wee Mad Arthur caught him up.

Colon was used to proceeding gently. He wasn't built for high speeds, and said so. 'And *you* certainly can't run faster than that thing!' he wheezed.

'Just so long as I can run faster'n yez,' said Wee Mad Arthur. 'This way!'

There was a flight of old wooden stairs against the side of a warehouse. The gnome went up them like the rats he hunted. Colon, panting like a steam engine, followed him.

He stopped halfway up and looked around.

The golem had reached the bottom step. It tested it carefully. The wood creaked and the whole stairway, grey with age, trembled.

'It won't take the weight!' said Wee Mad Arthur. 'The bugger's gonna smash it up! Yeah!'

The golem took another step. The wood groaned.

Colon got a grip on himself and hurried on up the stairs.

Behind him, the golem seemed to have satisfied itself that the wood could indeed take its weight, and started to leap from step to step. The rails shook under Colon's hands and the whole structure swayed.

'Come *on*, will yez?' said Wee Mad Arthur, who had already reached the top. 'It's gaining on yez!'

The golem lunged. The stairs gave way. Colon flung out his hands and grabbed the edge of the roof. Then his body thudded into the side of the building.

There was the distant sound of woodwork hitting cobbles.

'Come on then,' said Wee Mad Arthur. 'Pull yourself up, yer silly bugger!'

'Can't,' said Colon.

'Why not?'

'It's holding on to my foot . . .'

'A cigar, your lordship?'

'Brandy, my lord?'

Lord de Nobbes sat back in the comfort of his chair. His feet only just reached the ground. Brandy and cigars, eh? This was the life all right. He took a deep puff at the cigar.

'We were just talking, my lord, about the future governance of the city now that poor Lord Vetinari's health is so bad . . .'

Nobby nodded. This was the kind of thing you talked about when you were a nob. This was what he'd been born for.

The brandy was giving him a pleasant warm feeling.

'It would obviously upset the current equilibrium if we looked for a new Patrician at this point,' said another armchair. 'What is your view, Lord de Nobbes?'

'Oh, yeah. Right. The guilds'd fight like cats in a sack,' said Nobby. 'Everyone knows that.'

'A masterly summary, if I may say so.'

There was a general murmur of agreement from the other chairs.

Nobby grinned. Oh, yes. This was the bee's pyjamas and no mistake. Hobnobbing with his fellow nobs, talking big talk about important matters instead of having to think up reasons why the tea-money tin was empty . . . oh, yes.

A chair said, 'Besides, are any of the guild leaders up to the task? Oh, they can organize a bunch of tradesmen, but ruling an entire city . . . I think not. Gentlemen, perhaps it is time for a new direction. Perhaps it is time for blood to reveal itself.'

Odd way of putting it, Nobby thought, but clearly this was how you were supposed to speak.

'At a time like this,' said a chair, 'the city will surely look at those representatives of its most venerable families. It would be in all our interests if such a one would take up the burden.'

'He'd need his head examined, if you want my opinion,' said Nobby. He took another swig of the brandy and waved the cigar expansively.

'Still, not to worry,' he said. 'Everyone knows we've got a king hanging around. No problem there. Send for Captain Carrot, that's my advice.'

Another evening folded over the city in layers of fog.

When Carrot arrived back at the Watch House Corporal Little-bottom made a face at him and indicated, with a flicker of her eyes, the three people sitting grimly on the bench against one wall.

'They want to see an officer!' she hissed. 'But S'arnt Colon isn't back and I knocked on Mr Vimes's door and I don't think he's in.'

Carrot composed his features into a welcoming smile.

'Mrs Palm,' he said. 'And Mr Boggis . . . and Dr Downey. I am so sorry. We're rather stretched at present, what with the poisoning and this business with the golems—'

The head of the Assassins' Guild smiled, but only with his mouth. 'It's about the poisoning we wish to speak,' he said. 'Is there somewhere a little less public?'

'Well, there's the canteen,' said Carrot. 'It'll be empty at this time of night. If you'd just step this way . . .'

'You do well for yourselves here, I must say,' said Mrs Palm. 'A canteen—'

She stopped as she stepped through the door.

'People *eat* in here?' she said.

'Well, grumble about the coffee, mostly,' said Carrot. 'And write their reports. Commander Vimes is keen on reports.'

'Captain Carrot,' said Dr Downey, firmly, 'we have to talk to you on a grave matter concerning— *What* have I sat in?'

Carrot brushed a chair hurriedly. 'Sorry, sir, we don't seem to have much time to clean up—'

'Leave it for now, leave it for now.'

The head of the Assassins' Guild leaned forward with his hands pressed together.

'Captain Carrot, we are here to discuss this terrible matter of the poisoning of Lord Vetinari.'

'You really ought to talk to Commander Vimes—'

'I believe that on a number of occasions Commander Vimes has made derogatory comments to you about Lord Vetinari,' said Dr Downey.

'You mean like "He ought to be hung except they can't find a twisty enough rope"?' said Carrot. 'Oh, yes. But everyone does that.'

'Do you?'

'Well, no,' Carrot admitted.

'And I believe he personally took over the investigation of the poisoning?'

'Well, yes. But—'

'Didn't you think that was odd?'

'No, sir. Not when I thought about it. I think he's got a sort of soft spot for the Patrician, in his way. He once said that if anyone was going to kill Vetinari he'd like it to be him.'

'Indeed?'

'But he was smiling when he said it. Sort of smiling, anyway.'

'He, er, visits his lordship most days, I believe?'

'Yes, sir.'

'And I understand that his efforts to discover the poisoner have not reached any conclusions?'

'Not as such, sir,' said Carrot. 'We've found a lot of ways he's *not* being poisoned.'

Downey nodded at the others. 'We would like to inspect the Commander's office,' he said.

'I don't know if that's—' Carrot began.

'Please think very carefully,' said Dr Downey. 'We three represent most of the guilds of this city. We feel we have a good reason for inspecting the Commander's office. You will of course accompany us to see that we do nothing illegal.'

Carrot looked awkward. 'I suppose . . . if I'm with you . . .' he said.

'That's right,' said Downey. 'That makes it official.'

Carrot led the way. 'I don't even know if he's back,' he said, opening the door. 'As I said, we've been . . . oh.'

Downey peered around him and at the figure slumped over the desk.

'It would appear that Sir Samuel *is* in,' he said. 'But quite out of it.'

'I can smell the drink from here,' said Mrs Palm. 'It's terrible what drink will do to a man.'

'A whole bottle of Bearhugger's finest,' said Mr Boggis. 'All right for some, eh?'

'But he hasn't touched a drop all year!' said Carrot, giving the recumbent Vimes a shake. 'He goes to meetings about it and everything!'

'Now let us see . . .' said Downey.

He pulled open one of the desk drawers.

'Captain Carrot?' he said. 'Can you witness that there appears to be a bag of greyish powder in here? I will now—'

Vimes's hand shot out and slammed the drawer on the man's fingers. His elbow rammed back into the assassin's stomach and, as Downey's chin jerked down, Vimes's forearm swung upwards and caught him full on the nose.

Then Vimes opened his eyes.

'Wassat? Wassat?' he said, raising his head. 'Dr Downey? Mr Boggis? Carrot? Hmm?'

'Hwat? Hwat?' screamed Downey. 'You hnsfruck me!'

'Oh, I'm *so* sorry,' said Vimes, concern radiating from every feature as he pushed the chair back into Downey's groin and stood up. 'I'm afraid I must have dropped off and, of course, when I woke up and found someone stealing from . . .'

'You're raving drunk, man!' said Mr Boggis.

Vimes's features froze.

'Indeed? Peter Piper picked a peck of pickled peppers,' he

snarled, prodding the man in the chest. 'A peck of bloody pickled peppers Peter Piper damn well picked. Do you want me to continue?' he said, poking the man until his back was against the wall. 'It doesn't get much better!'

'Hwhat about thif packet?' shouted Downey, clutching his streaming nose with one hand and waving at the desk with the other.

Vimes still wore a wild-eyed mirthless grin. 'Ah, well, yes,' he said. 'You've got me there. A highly dangerous substance.'

'Ah, you admit it!'

'Yes, indeed. I suppose I have no alternative but to dispose of the evidence . . .' Vimes grabbed the packet, ripped it open and tipped most of the powder into his mouth.

'Mmm *mmm*,' he said, powder spraying everywhere as he masticated. 'Feel that tingle on the tongue!'

'But that's *arsenic*,' said Boggis.

'Good gods, is it?' said Vimes, swallowing. 'Amazing! I've got this dwarf downstairs, you know, clever little bugger, spends all his time with pipes and chemicals and things to find out what is arsenic and what isn't, and all the time here's you able to spot it just by looking! I've got to hand it to you!'

He dropped the torn packet into Boggis's hand, but the thief jerked back and the packet tumbled to the floor, spraying its contents.

'Excuse me,' said Carrot. He knelt down and peered at the powder.

It is traditionally the belief of policemen that they can tell what a substance is by sniffing it and then gingerly tasting it, but this practice had ceased in the Watch ever since Constable Flint had dipped his finger into a blackmarket consignment of ammonium chloride cut with radium, said 'Yes, this is definitely slab wurble wurble sclup', and had to spend three days tied to his bed until the spiders went away.

Nevertheless, Carrot said, 'I'm *sure* this isn't poisonous,' licked his finger and tried a bit.

'It's sugar,' he said.

Downey, his composure severely compromised, waved a finger at Vimes. 'You admitted it was dangerous!' he screamed.

'Right! Take too much of it and see what it does to your teeth!' bellowed Vimes. 'What did you *think* it was?'

'We had information . . .' Boggis began.

'Oh, you had information, did you?' said Vimes. 'You hear that, Captain? They had information. So that's all right!'

'We acted in good faith,' said Boggis.

'Let me see,' said Vimes. 'Your information was something on the lines of: Vimes is dead drunk in the Watch House and he's got a bag of arsenic in his desk? And I'll just *bet* you wanted to act in good faith, eh?'

Mrs Palm cleared her throat. 'This has gone far enough. You are correct, Sir Samuel,' she said. 'We were all sent a note.' She handed a slip of paper to Vimes. It had been written in capitals. 'And I can see we have been misinformed,' she added, glaring at Boggis and Downey. 'Do allow me to apologize. Come, gentlemen.'

She swept out of the door. Boggis followed her quickly.

Downey dabbed at his nose. 'What's the guild price on your head, Sir Samuel?' he said.

'Twenty thousand dollars.'

'Really? I think we shall definitely have to upgrade you.'

'Delighted. I shall have to buy a new beartrap.'

'I'll, er, show you out,' said Carrot.

When he hurried back he found Vimes leaning out of the window and feeling the wall below it.

'Not a brick dislodged,' Vimes muttered. 'Not a tile loose . . . and the front office has been manned all day. Odd, that.'

He shrugged and walked back to his desk, where he picked up the note.

'And I shouldn't think we'll be able to find any Clues on this,' he said. 'There's too many greasy fingermarks all over it.' He put down the paper and glared at Carrot. 'When we find the man responsible,' he said, 'somewhere at the top of the charge sheet is going to be Forcing Commander Vimes to Tip a Whole Bottle of Single Malt on to the Carpet. That's a hanging offence.' He shuddered. There were some things a man should *not* have to do.

'It's disgusting!' said Carrot. 'Fancy them even *thinking* that you'd poison the Patrician!'

'I'm offended that they think I'd be daft enough to keep the poison in my desk drawer,' said Vimes, lighting a cigar.

'Right,' said Carrot. 'Did they think you were some kind of fool who'd keep evidence like that where anyone could find it?'

'Exactly,' said Vimes, leaning back. 'That's why I've got it in my pocket.'

He put his feet on the desk and blew out a cloud of smoke. He'd have to get rid of the carpet. He wasn't going to spend the rest of his life working in a room haunted by the smell of departed spirits.

Carrot's mouth was still open.

'Oh, good grief,' said Vimes. 'Look, it's quite simple, man. I was expected to go "At last, alcohol!", and chugalug the lot without thinking. Then some respectable pillars of the community' – he removed the cigar from his mouth and spat – 'were going to find me, in your presence, too – which was a nice touch – with the evidence of my crime neatly hidden but not so well hidden that they couldn't find it.' He shook his head sadly. 'The trouble is, you know, that once the taste's got you it never lets go.'

'But you've been very good, sir,' said Carrot. 'I've not seen you touch a drop for—'

'Oh, *that*,' said Vimes. 'I was talking about policing, not alcohol. There's lots of people will help you with the alcohol business, but there's no one out there arranging little meetings where you can stand up and say, "My name is Sam and I'm a really suspicious bastard."'

He pulled a paper bag out of his pocket. 'We'll get Littlebottom to have a look at this,' he said. 'I damn sure wasn't going to try tasting it. So I nipped down to the canteen and filled a bag with sugar out of the bowl. It was but the work of a moment to fish Nobby's butts out of it, I might add.' He opened the door, poked his head out into the corridor and yelled, 'Littlebottom!' To Carrot he added, 'You know, I feel quite perked up. The old brain has begun to work at last. You know the golem that did the killing?'

'Yes, sir?'

'Ah, but do you know what was *special* about it?'

'Can't think, sir,' said Carrot, 'except that it was a new one. The golems made it themselves, I think. But of course they needed a priest for the words and they had to borrow Mr Hopkinson's oven. I expect the old men thought it would be interesting. They were historians, after all.'

It was Vimes's turn to stand there with his mouth open.

Finally he got control of himself. 'Yes, yes, of course,' he said, his voice barely shaking. 'Yes, I mean, that's *obvious*. Plain as the nose on your face. But . . . er, have you worked out what *else* is special about it?' he added, trying to keep any trace of hope out of his voice.

'You mean the fact it's gone mad, sir?'

'Well, I didn't think it was winner of the Ankh-Morpork Mr Sanity Award!' said Vimes.

'I mean they drove it mad, sir. The other golems. They didn't mean to, but it was built-in, sir. They wanted it to do so many things. It was like their . . . child, I think. All their hopes and dreams. And when they found out it'd been killing people . . . well, that's *terrible* to a golem. They mustn't kill, and it was their *own clay* doing it—'

'It's not a great idea for people, either.'

'But they'd put all their future in it—'

698

'You wanted me, Commander?' said Cheery.

'Oh, yes. Is this arsenic?' said Vimes, handing her the packet.

Cheery sniffed at it. 'It could be arsenous acid, sir. I'll have to test it, of course.'

'I thought acids sloshed about in jars,' said Vimes. 'Er . . . what's that on your hands?'

'Nail varnish, sir.'

'Nail varnish?'

'Yes, sir.'

'Er . . . fine, fine. Funny, I thought it would be green.'

'Wouldn't look good on the fingers, sir.'

'I meant the arsenic, Littlebottom.'

'Oh, you can get all sorts of colours of arsenic, sir. The sulphides – that's the ores, sir – can be red or brown or yellow or grey, sir. And then you cook them up with nitre and you get arsenous acid, sir. And a load of nasty smoke, *really* bad.'

'Dangerous stuff,' said Vimes.

'Not good at all, sir. But useful, sir,' said Cheery. 'Tanners, dyers, painters . . . It's not just poisoners that've got a use for arsenic.'

'I'm surprised people aren't dropping dead of it all the time,' said Vimes.

'Oh, most of them use golems, sir—'

The words stayed in the air even after Cheery stopped speaking.

Vimes caught Carrot's eye and started to whistle hoarsely under his breath. *This is it*, he thought. *This is where we've filled ourselves up with so many questions that they're starting to overflow and become answers.*

He felt more alive than he had for days. The recent excitement still tingled in his veins, kicking his brain into life. It was the sparkle you got with exhaustion, he knew. You were so bone-weary that a shot of adrenalin hit you like a falling troll. They *must* have it all now. All the bits. The edges, the corners, the whole picture. All there, just waiting to be pieced together . . .

'These golems,' said Carrot. 'They'd be *covered* in arsenic, would they?'

'Could be, sir. I saw one at the Alchemists' Guild building in Quirm and, hah, it'd even got arsenic plated on its hands, sir, on account of stirring crucibles with its fingers . . .'

'They don't feel heat,' said Vimes.

'Or pain,' said Carrot.

'That's right,' said Cheery. She looked uncertainly from one to the other.

'You can't poison them,' said Vimes.

'And they'll obey orders,' said Carrot. 'Without speaking.'

'Golems do *all* the really mucky jobs,' said Vimes.

'You could have mentioned this before, Cheery,' said Carrot.

'Well, you know, sir . . . Golems are just *there*, sir. No one notices golems.'

'Grease under his fingernails,' said Vimes, to the room in general. 'The old man scratched at his murderer. Grease under his fingernails. With arsenic in it.'

He looked down at the notebook, still on his desk. *It's there*, he thought. *Something we haven't seen. But we've looked everywhere. So we've seen the answer and haven't seen that it* is *the answer. And if we don't see it now, at this moment, we'll never see it at all . . .*

'No offence, sir, but that's probably not a help,' said Cheery's voice somewhere in the distance. 'So many of the trades that use arsenic involve some kind of grease.'

Something we don't see, thought Vimes. *Something invisible. No, it wouldn't have to be invisible. Something we don't see because it's always there. Something that strikes in the night . . .*

And there it was.

He blinked. The glittering stars of exhaustion were causing his mind to think oddly. Well, thinking rationally hadn't worked.

'No one move,' he said. He held up a hand for silence. 'There it is,' he said softly. 'There. On my desk. You see it?'

'What, sir?' said Carrot.

'You mean *you* haven't worked it out?' said Vimes.

'*What*, sir?'

'The thing that's poisoning his lordship. There it is . . . on the desk. See?'

'Your notebook?'

'No!'

'He drinks Bearhugger's whisky?' said Cheery.

'I doubt it,' said Vimes.

'The blotter?' said Carrot. 'Poisoned pens? A packet of Pantweeds?'

'Where're they?' said Vimes, patting his pockets.

'Just sticking out from under the letters in the In Tray, sir,' said Carrot. He added reproachfully, 'You know, sir, the ones you don't answer.'

Vimes picked up the packet and extracted another cigar. 'Thanks,' he said. 'Hah! I didn't ask Mildred Easy what else she took! But of course they're a servant's little bonus, too! And old Mrs Easy was a seamstress, a *proper* seamstress! And this is autumn! Killed by the nights drawing in! See?'

Carrot crouched down and looked at the surface of the desk. 'Can't see it myself, sir,' he said.

'Of course you can't,' said Vimes. 'Because there's nothing to see. You can't see it. That's how you can tell it's there. If it wasn't there you'd soon see it!' He gave a huge manic grin. 'Only you wouldn't! See?'

'You all right, sir?' said Carrot. 'I know you've been overdoing it a bit these last few days—'

'I've been *under*doing it!' said Vimes. 'I've been running around looking for damn Clues instead of just thinking for five minutes! What is it I'm always telling you?'

'Er . . . er . . . Never trust anybody, sir?'

'No, not that.'

'Er . . . er . . . Everyone's guilty of something, sir?'

'Not that, either.'

'Er . . . er . . . Just because someone's a member of an ethnic minority doesn't mean they're not a nasty small-minded little jerk, sir?'

'N— When did I say that?'

'Last week, sir. After we'd had that visit from the Campaign for Equal Heights, sir.'

'Well, not that. I mean . . . I'm pretty sure I'm always saying something else that's very relevant here. Something pithy about police work.'

'Can't remember anything right now, sir.'

'Well, I'll damn well make up something and start saying it a lot from now on.'

'Jolly good, sir.' Carrot beamed. 'It's good to see you're your old self again, sir. Looking forward to kicking ar— to prodding buttock, sir. Er . . . What have we found, sir?'

'You'll see! We're going to the palace. Fetch Angua. We might need her. And bring the search warrant.'

'You mean the sledgehammer, sir?'

'Yes. And Sergeant Colon, too.'

'He hasn't signed in again yet, sir,' said Cheery. 'He should have gone off-duty an hour ago.'

'Probably hanging around somewhere, staying out of trouble,' said Vimes.

Wee Mad Arthur peered over the edge of the wall. Somewhere below Colon, two red eyes stared up at him.

'Heavy, is it?'

''S!'

'Kick it with your other foot!'

There was a sucking sound. Colon winced. Then there was a plop, a moment of silence, and a loud crash of pottery down in the street.

'The boot it was holding came off,' moaned Colon.

'How did that happen?'

'It got . . . lubricated . . .'

Wee Mad Arthur tugged at a finger. 'Up yez come, then.'

'Can't.'

'Why not? It ain't holding on to yez no more.'

'Arms tired. Another ten seconds and I'm gonna be a chalk outline . . .'

'Nah, no one's got that much chalk.' Wee Mad Arthur knelt down so that his head was level with Colon's eyes. 'If you gonna die, d'yez mind signing a chitty to say yez promised me a dollar?'

Down below, there was a chink of pottery shards.

'What was that?' said Colon. 'I thought the damn thing smashed up . . .'

Wee Mad Arthur looked down. 'D'yez believe in that reincarnation stuff, Mr Colon?' he said.

'You wouldn't get me touching that foreign muck,' said Colon.

'Well, it's putting itself together. Like one of them jiggling saw puzzles.'

'Well done, Wee Mad Arthur,' said Colon. 'But I know you're just saying that so's I'll make the effort to haul meself up, right? Statues don't go putting themselves back together when they're smashed up.'

'Please yezself. It's done nearly a whole leg already.'

Colon managed to peer down through the small and smelly space between the wall and his armpit. All he could see were shreds of fog and a faint glow.

'You sure?' he said.

'Yez run around rat holes, yez learns to see good in the dark,' said Wee Mad Arthur. 'Otherwise yez dead.'

Something hissed, somewhere below Colon's feet.

With his one booted foot and his toes he scrabbled at the brickwork.

'It's having a wee bit o' trouble,' said Wee Mad Arthur conversationally. 'Looks like it's put its knees on wrong way round.'

Dorfl sat hunched in the abandoned cellar where the golems had met. Occasionally the golem raised its head and hissed. Red light spilled from its eyes. If something had streamed back down

702

through the glow, soared through the eye-sockets into the red sky beyond, there would be . . .

Dorfl huddled under the glow of the universe. Its murmur was a long way off, muted, nothing to do with Dorfl.

The Words stood around the horizon, reaching all the way to the sky.

And a voice said quietly, 'You own yourself.' Dorfl saw the scene again and again, saw the concerned face, hand reaching up, filling its vision, felt the sudden icy knowledge . . .

'. . . Own yourself.'

It echoed off the Words, and then rebounded, and then rolled back and forth, increasing in volume until the little world between the Words was gripped in the sound.

Golem Must Have a Master. The letters towered against the world, but the echoes poured around them, blasting like a sandstorm. Cracks started and then ran, zigzagging across the stone, and then—

The Words exploded. Great slabs of them, mountain-sized, crashed in showers of red sand.

The universe poured in. Dorfl felt the universe pick it up and bowl it over and then lift it off its feet and up . . .

. . . and now the golem was *among* the universe. It could feel it all around, the purr of it, the busyness, the spinning complexity of it, the roar . . .

There were no Words between you and It.

You belonged to It, It belonged to you.

You couldn't turn your back on It because there It was, in front of you.

Dorfl was responsible for every tick and swerve of It.

You couldn't say, 'I had orders.' You couldn't say, 'It's not fair.' No one was listening. There were no Words. You *owned* yourself.

Dorfl orbited a pair of glowing suns and hurtled off again.

Not *Thou Shalt Not.* Say *I Will Not.*

Dorfl tumbled through the red sky, then saw a dark hole ahead. The golem felt it dragging at him, and streamed down through the glow and the hole grew larger and sped across the edges of Dorfl's vision . . .

The golem opened his eyes.

Ꞑꝺ ꟺ𝖆𝖘𝖙𝖊𝖗!

Dorfl unfolded in one movement and stood upright. He reached out one arm and extended a finger.

The golem pushed the finger easily into the wall where the argument had taken place, and then dragged it carefully through the splintering brickwork. It took him a couple of minutes but it was something Dorfl felt needed to be said.

Dorfl completed the last letter and poked a row of three dots after it. Then the golem walked away, leaving behind:

NO MASTER . . .

A blue overcast from the cigars hid the ceiling of the smoking-room.

'Ah, yes. Captain Carrot,' said a chair. 'Yes . . . indeed . . . but . . . is he the right man?'

''S got a birthmark shaped like a crown. I seen it,' said Nobby helpfully.

'But his background . . .'

'He was raised by dwarfs,' said Nobby. He waved his brandy glass at a waiter. 'Same again, mister.'

'I shouldn't think dwarfs could raise anyone very high,' said another chair. There was a hint of laughter.

'Rumours and folklore,' someone murmured.

'This is a large and busy and above all complex city. I'm afraid that having a sword and a birthmark are not much in the way of qualifications. We would need a king from a lineage that is *used* to command.'

'Like yours, my lord.'

There was a sucking, draining noise as Nobby attacked the fresh glass of brandy. 'Oh, I'm used to command, all right,' he said, lowering the glass. 'People are always orderin' me around.'

'We would need a king who had the support of the great families and major guilds of the city.'

'People *like* Carrot,' said Nobby.

'Oh, the *people* . . .'

'Anyway, whoever got the job'd have his work cut out,' said Nobby. 'Ole Vetinari's always pushin' paper. What kinda fun is that? 'S no life, sittin' up all hours, worryin', never a moment to yerself.' He held out the empty glass. 'Same again, my old mate. Fill it right up this time, eh? No sense in havin' a great big glass and only sloshin' a bit in the bottom, is there?'

'Many people prefer to savour the bouquet,' said a quietly horrified chair. 'They enjoy sniffing it.'

Nobby looked at his glass with the red-veined eyes of one who'd heard rumours about what the upper crust got up to. 'Nah,' he said. 'I'll go on stickin' it in my mouth, if it's all the same to you.'

'If we may get to the *point*,' said another chair, 'a *king* would *not* have to spend every moment running the city. He would of course have people to do that. Advisors. Counsellors. People of experience.'

'So what'd he have to do?' said Nobby.

'He'd have to reign,' said a chair.

'Wave.'

'Preside at banquets.'

'Sign things.'

'Guzzle good brandy disgustingly.'

'*Reign.*'

'Sounds like a good job to me,' said Nobby. 'All right for some, eh?'

'Of course, a king would have to be someone who could recognize a hint if it was dropped on his head from a great height,' said a speaker sharply, but the other chairs shushed him into silence.

Nobby managed to find his mouth after several goes and took another long pull at his cigar. 'Seems to me,' he said, 'seems to *me*, what you want to do is find some nob with time on his hands and say, "Yo, it's your lucky day. Let's see you wave that hand."'

'Ah! *That*'s a good idea! Does any name cross your mind, my lord? Have a drop more brandy.'

'Why, thanks, you're a toff. O' course, so 'm I, eh? That's right, flunkey, all the way to the top. No, can't think of anyone that fits the bill.'

'In fact, my lord, we were indeed thinking of offering the crown to you—'

Nobby's eyes bulged. And then his cheek bulged.

It is not a good idea to spray finest brandy across the room, especially when your lighted cigar is in the way. The flame hit the far wall, where it left a perfect chrysanthemum of scorched wood-work, while in accordance with a fundamental rule of physics Nobby's chair screamed back on its castors and thudded into the door.

'King?' Nobby coughed, and then they had to slap him on the back until he got his breath again. 'King?' he wheezed. 'And have Mr Vimes cut me head off?'

'All the brandy you can drink, my lord,' said a wheedling voice.

''S no good if you ain't got a throat for it to go down!'

'What're you talking about?'

'Mr Vimes'd go spare! He'd go *spare*!'

'Good heavens, man—'

'My lord,' someone corrected.

'My lord, I mean – when you're *king* you can tell that wretched Sir Samuel what to do. You'll be, as you would call it, "the boss". You could—'

'Tell ole Stoneface what to do?' said Nobby.

'That's right!'

'I'd be a king and tell ole Stoneface what to do?' said Nobby.

'Yes!'

Nobby stared into the smoky gloom.

'He'd go *spare!*'

'Listen, you silly little man—'

'*My lord—*'

'You silly little lord, you'd be able to have him executed if you wished!'

'I couldn't do that!'

'Why not?'

'He'd go spare!'

'The man calls himself an officer of the law, and whose law does he listen to, eh? Where does his law come from?'

'*I* don't know!' groaned Nobby. 'He says it comes up through his boots!' He looked around. The shadows in the smoke seemed to be closing in.

'I can't be king! Ole Vimes'd go spare!'

'*Will you stop saying that!*'

Nobby pulled at his collar.

''S a bit hot and smoky in here,' he mumbled. 'Which way's the window?'

'Over there—'

The chair rocked. Nobby hit the glass helmet-first, landed on top of a waiting carriage, bounced off and ran into the night, trying to escape destiny in general and axes in particular.

Cheri Littlebottom strode into the palace kitchens and fired her crossbow into the ceiling.

'Don't nobody move!' she yelled.

The Patrician's domestic staff looked up from their dinner.

'When you say don't *nobody* move,' said Drumknott carefully, fastidiously taking a piece of plaster off his plate, 'do you in fact mean—'

'All right, Corporal, I'll take over now,' said Vimes, patting Cheri on the shoulder. 'Is Mildred Easy here?'

All heads turned.

Mildred's spoon dropped into her soup.

'It's all right,' said Vimes. 'I just need to ask you a few more questions—'

'I'm . . . s-s-sorry, sir—'

'You haven't done anything wrong,' said Vimes, walking around the table. 'But you didn't just take food home for your family, did you?'

'S-sir?'

'What *else* did you take?'

Mildred looked at the suddenly blank expressions on the faces of the other servants. 'There was the old sheets but Mrs Dipplock did *s-say* I could have—'

'No, not that,' said Vimes.

Mildred licked her dry lips. 'Er, there was . . . there was some boot polish . . .'

'Look,' said Vimes, as kindly as possible, '*everyone* takes small things from the place where they work. Small stuff that no one notices. No one thinks of it as stealing. It's like . . . it's like *rights*. Odds and ends. Ends, Miss Easy? I'm thinking about the word "ends".'

'Er . . . you mean . . . the candle ends, sir?'

Vimes took a deep breath. It was such a relief to be right, even though you knew you'd only got there by trying every possible way to be wrong. '*Ah*,' he said.

'B-but that's not stealing, sir. I've never stolen nothing, s-sir!'

'But you take home the candle stubs? Still half an hour of light in 'em, I expect, if you burn them in a saucer?' said Vimes gently.

'But that's not stealing, sir! That's *perks*, sir.'

Sam Vimes smacked his forehead. 'Perks! Of course! *That* was the word I was looking for. Perks! Everyone's got to have perks, aren't I right? Well, that's fine, then,' he said. 'I expect you get the ones from the bedrooms, yes?'

Even through her nervousness, Mildred Easy was able to grin the grin of someone with an Entitlement that lesser beings hadn't got. 'Yessir. I'm *allowed*, sir. They're much better than the ole coarse ones we use in the main halls, sir.'

'And you put in fresh candles when necessary, do you?'

'Yessir.'

Probably slightly more often than necessary, Vimes thought. *No point in letting them burn down too much . . .*

'Perhaps you can show me where they're kept, miss?'

The maid looked along the table to the housekeeper, who glanced at Commander Vimes and then nodded. She was bright enough to know when something that sounded like a question really wasn't one.

'We keep them in the candle pantry next door, sir,' said Mildred.

'Lead the way, please.'

It wasn't a big room, but its shelves were stacked floor-to-ceiling with candles. There were the yard-high ones used in the public halls and the small everyday ones used everywhere else, sorted according to quality.

'These are what we uses in his lordship's rooms, sir.' She handed him twelve inches of white candle.

'Oh, yes . . . *very* good quality. Number Fives. Nice white tallow,' said Vimes, tossing it up and down. 'We burn these at home. The stuff we use at the Yard is damn near pork dripping. We get ours from Carry's in the Shambles now. *Very* reasonable prices. We used to deal with Spadger and Williams but Mr Carry's really cornered the market these days, hasn't he?'

'Yessir. And he delivers 'em special, sir.'

'And you put these candles in his lordship's room every day?'

'Yessir.'

'Anywhere else?'

'Oh, no, sir. His lordship's particular about that! *We* just use Number Threes.'

'And you take your, er, perks home?'

'Yessir. Gran said they gave a lovely light, sir . . .'

'I expect she sat up with your little brother, did she? Because I expect he got took sick first, so she sat up with him all night long, night after night and, hah, if I know old Mrs Easy, she did her sewing . . .'

'Yessir.'

There was a pause.

'Use my handkerchief,' said Vimes, after a while.

'Am I going to lose my position, sir?'

'No. That's definite. No one involved deserves to lose their jobs,' said Vimes. He looked at the candle. 'Except possibly me,' he added.

He stopped at the doorway, and turned. 'And if you ever want candle-ends, we've always got lots at the Watch House. Nobby'll have to start buying cooking fat like everyone else.'

'What's it doing now?' said Sergeant Colon.

Wee Mad Arthur peered over the edge of the roof again. 'It's havin' problems with its elbows,' he said conversationally. 'It keeps lookin' at one of 'em and tryin' it all ways up and it's not workin'.'

'I had that trouble when I put up them kitchen units for Mrs Colon,' said the sergeant. 'The instructions on how to open the box were inside the box—'

'Oh-oh, it's worked it out,' said the rat-catcher. 'Looks like it had it mixed up with its knees after all.'

Colon heard a clank below him.

'And now it's gone round the corner' – there was a crash of splintering wood – 'and now it's got into the building. I expect it'll come up the stairs, but it looks like yer'll be okay.'

'Why?'

''Cos all you gotta do is let go of the roof, see?'

'I'll drop to my death!'

'Right! Nice clean way to go. None of that "arms-and-legs-bein'-ripped-off" stuff first.'

'I wanted to buy a farm!' moaned Colon.

'Could be,' said Arthur. He looked over the roof again. 'Or,' he said, as if this were hardly a better option, 'yez could try to grab the drainpipe.'

Colon looked sideways. There *was* a pipe a few feet away. If he swung his body and really made an effort, he might *just* miss it by inches and plunge to his death.

'Does it look safe?' he said.

'Compared with what, mister?'

Colon tried to swing his legs like a pendulum. Every muscle in his arm screamed at him. He knew he was overweight. He'd always meant to take exercise one day. He just hadn't been aware that it was going to be today.

'I reckon I can hear it walking up the stairs,' said Wee Mad Arthur.

Colon tried to swing faster. 'What're *you* going to do?' he said.

'Oh, don't yez worry about me,' said Wee Mad Arthur. 'I'll be fine. I'll jump.'

'*Jump?*'

'Sure. I'll be safe 'cos of being normal-sized, see.'

'You think you're normal-sized?'

Wee Mad Arthur looked at Colon's hands. 'Are these yer fingers right here by my boots?' he said.

'Right, right, you're normal-sized. 'S not your fault you've moved into a city full of giants,' said Colon.

'Right. The smaller yez are the lighter yez fall. Well known fact. A spider'll not even notice a drop like this, a mouse'd walk away, a horse'd break every bone in its body and a helephant would spla—'

'Oh, gods,' muttered Colon. He could feel the drainpipe with his boot now. But getting a grip would mean there would have to be one long, bottomless moment when he was not exactly holding on to the roof and not exactly holding on to the drainpipe and in very serious peril of holding on to the ground.

There was another crash from somewhere on the roof.

'Right,' said Wee Mad Arthur. 'See you at the bottom.'

'Oh, gods . . .'

The gnome stepped off the roof.

'All okay so far,' he shouted, as he went past Colon.

709

'Oh, gods . . .'

Sergeant Colon looked up into two red glows.

'Doing fine up to now,' said a dopplering voice from below.

'Oh, *gods* . . .'

Colon heaved his legs around, stood on fresh air for a moment, grabbed the top of the pipe, ducked his head as a pottery fist swung at him, heard the nasty little noise as the pipe's rusty bolts said goodbye to the wall and, still clinging to a tilting length of cast-iron pipe as if it were going to help, disappeared backwards into the fog.

Mr Sock looked up at the sound of the door opening, and then cowered back against the sausage machine.

'*You?*' he whispered. 'Here, you can't come back! I *sold* you!'

Dorfl regarded him steadily for a few seconds, and then walked past him and took the largest cleaver from the blood-stained rack on the wall.

Sock began to shake.

'I-I-I was always g-g-good to you,' he said. 'A-a-always let you h-have your h-holy d-d-days off—'

Dorfl stared at him again. *It's only red light*, Sock gibbered to himself . . .

But it seemed more focused. He felt it entering his head through his own eyes and examining his soul.

The golem pushed him aside and stepped out of the slaughter-house and towards the cattle pens.

Sock unfroze. They never fought back, did they? They *couldn't*. It was how the damn things were *made*.

He stared around at the other workers, humans and trolls alike. 'Don't just stand there! Get it!'

One or two hesitated. It was a *big* cleaver in the golem's hand. And when Dorfl stopped to look around at them there was something different about the golem's stance, too. It didn't *look* like something that wouldn't fight back.

But Sock didn't employ people for the muscles in their heads. Besides, no one had really liked a golem around the place.

A troll aimed a pole-axe at him. Dorfl caught it one-handed without turning his head and snapped the hickory handle with his fingers. A man with a hammer had it plucked from his hand and thrown so hard at the wall that it left a hole.

After that they followed at a cautious distance. Dorfl took no further notice of them.

The steam over the cattle pens mingled with the fog. Hundreds

710

of dark eyes watched Dorfl curiously as he walked between the fences. They were always quiet when the golem was around.

He stopped by one of the largest pens. There were voices from behind.

'Don't tell me it's going to slaughter the lot of 'em! We'll never get that lot jointed this shift!'

'I heard where there was one at a carpenter's that went odd and made five thousand tables in one night. Lost count or something.'

'It's just staring at them . . .'

'I mean, five thousand tables? One of them had twenty-seven legs. It got stuck on legs . . .'

Dorfl brought the cleaver down hard and sliced the lock off the gate. The cattle watched the golem, with that guarded expression which cattle have that means they're waiting for the next thought to turn up.

He walked on to the sheep pens and opened them, too. The pigs were next, and then the poultry.

'*All* of them?' said Mr Sock.

The golem walked calmly back down the line of pens, ignoring the watchers, and re-entered the slaughterhouse. He came out very shortly afterwards leading the ancient and hairy billygoat on a piece of string. He went past the waiting animals until he reached the wide gates that led on to the main road, which he opened. Then he let the goat loose.

The animal sniffed the air and rolled its slotted eyes. Then, apparently deciding that the distant odour of the cabbage fields beyond the city wall was much preferable to the smells immediately around it, it trotted away up the road.

The animals followed it in a rush, but with hardly any other noise than the rustle of movement and the sounds of their hooves. They streamed around the stationary figure of Dorfl, who stood and watched them go.

A chicken, bewildered by the stampede, landed on the golem's head and started to cluck.

Anger finally overcame Sock's terror. 'What the hell are you doing?' he shouted, trying to field a few stray sheep as they bolted out of the pens. 'That's *money* walking out of the gate, you—'

Dorfl's hand was suddenly around his throat. The golem picked him up and held the struggling man at arm's length, turning his head this way and that as if considering his next course of action.

Finally he tossed away the cleaver, reached up under the chicken that had taken up residence, and produced a small brown egg. With apparent ceremony the golem smashed it carefully on Sock's scalp and dropped him.

The golem's former co-workers jumped back out of the way as Dorfl walked back through the slaughterhouse.

There was a tally board by the entrance. Dorfl looked at it for a while, then picked up the chalk and wrote:

NO MASTER . . .

The chalk crumbled in his fingers. Dorfl walked out into the fog.

Cheri looked up from her workbench.

'The wick's *full* of arsenous acid,' she said. 'Well done, sir! This candle even weighs slightly more than other candles!'

'What an evil way to kill anyone,' said Angua.

'Certainly very clever,' said Vimes. 'Vetinari sits up half the night writing, and in the morning the candle's burned down. Poisoned by the light. The light's something you don't see. Who looks at the light? Not some plodding old copper.'

'Oh, you're not that old, sir,' said Carrot, cheerfully.

'What about plodding?'

'Or that plodding, either,' Carrot added quickly. 'I've always pointed out to people that you walk in a very purposeful and meaningful manner.'

Vimes gave him a sharp look and saw nothing more than a keen and innocently helpful expression.

'We don't look at the light because the light is what we look *with*,' said Vimes. 'Okay. And now I think we should go and have a look at the candle factory, shouldn't we? You come, Littlebottom, and bring your . . . have you got taller, Littlebottom?'

'High-heeled boots, sir,' said Cheri.

'I thought dwarfs always wore iron boots . . .'

'Yes, sir. But I've got high heels on mine, sir. I welded them on.'

'Oh. Fine. Right.' Vimes pulled himself together. 'Well, if you can still totter, bring your alchemy stuff with you. Detritus should've come off-duty from the palace. When it comes to locked doors you can't beat Detritus. He's a walking crowbar. We'll pick him up on the way.'

He loaded his crossbow and lit a match.

'Right,' he said. 'We've done it the modern way, now let's try policing like grandfather used to do it. It's time to—'

'Prod buttock, sir?' said Carrot, hurriedly.

'Close,' said Vimes, taking a deep drag and blowing out a smoke ring, 'but no cigar.'

*

Sergeant Colon's view of the world was certainly changing. Just when something was about to fix itself firmly in his mind as the worst moment of his entire life, it was hurriedly replaced by something even nastier.

Firstly, the drainpipe he was riding hit the wall of the building opposite. In a well-organized world he might have landed on a fire escape, but fire escapes were unknown in Ankh-Morpork and the flames generally had to leave via the roof.

With the pipe thus leaning against the wall, he found himself sliding down the diagonal. Even this might have been a happy outcome were it not for the fact that Colon was a heavy man and, as his weight slid nearer to the middle of the unsupported pipe, the pipe sagged, and cast iron has only a very limited amount of sag before it snaps, which it now did.

Colon dropped, and landed on something soft – at least, softer than the street – and the something went 'mur-r-r-r-m!'. He bounced off it and landed on something lower and softer which went 'baaaaarp!', and rolled from this on to something even lower and apparently made of feathers, which went insane. And pecked him.

The street was full of animals, milling around uncertainly. When animals are in a state of uncertainty they get nervous, and the street was already, as it were, paved with anxiety. The only benefit to Sergeant Colon was that this made it slightly softer than would otherwise have been the case.

Hooves trod on his hands. Very large dribbly noses sneezed at him.

Sergeant Colon had not hitherto had a great deal of experience of animals, except in portion sizes. When he'd been little he'd had a pink stuffed pig called Mr Dreadful, and he'd got up to Chapter Six in *Animal Husbandry*. It had woodcuts in it. There was no mention of hot smelly breath and great clomping feet like soup plates on a stick. Cows, in Sergeant Colon's book, should go 'moo'. Every child knew that. They shouldn't go 'mur-r-r-r-m!' like some kind of undersea monster and spray you with spit.

He tried to get up, skidded on some cow's moment of crisis, and sat down on a sheep. It went 'blaaaart!' What kind of noise was that for a sheep to make?

He got up again and tried to make his way to the kerb. 'Shoo! Get out of the damn way, you sheep! Garn!'

A goose hissed at him and stuck out altogether too much neck.

Colon backed off, and stopped when something nudged him in the back. It was a pig.

It was no Mr Dreadful. This wasn't the little piggy that went to market, or the little piggy that stayed at home. It would be quite hard to imagine what kind of foot would have a piggy like this, but it would probably be the kind that also had hair and scales and toenails like cashew nuts.

This piggy was the size of a pony. This piggy had tusks. And it wasn't pink. It was a blue-black colour and covered with sharp hair but it did have – *let's be fair*, thought Colon – little red piggy eyes.

This little piggy looked like the little piggy that killed the boarhounds, disembowelled the horse and ate the huntsman.

Colon turned around, and came face-to-face with a bull like a beef cube on legs. It turned its huge head from side to side so that each rolling eye could get a sight of the sergeant, but it was clear that neither of them liked him very much.

It lowered its head. There wasn't room for it to charge, but it could certainly push.

As the animals crowded around him, Colon took the only way of escape possible.

There were men slumped all over the alley.

'Hello, hello, hello, what's all this, then?' said Carrot.

A man who was holding his arm and groaning looked up at him. 'We were viciously attacked!'

'We don't have time for this,' said Vimes.

'We may have,' said Angua. She tapped him on the shoulder and pointed to the wall opposite, on which was written in a familiar script:

NO MASTER . . .

Carrot hunched down and spoke to the casualty. 'You were attacked by a golem, were you?' he said.

'Right! Vicious bugger! Just walked out of the fog and went for us, you know what they're like!'

Carrot gave the man a cheerful smile. Then his gaze travelled along the man's body to the big hammer lying in the gutter, and moved from that to the other tools strewn around the scene of the fight. Several had their handles broken. There was a long crowbar, bent nearly into a circle.

'It's lucky you were all so well armed,' he said.

'It turned on us,' said the man. He tried to snap his fingers. 'Just like *that* – aargh!'

'You seem to have hurt your fingers . . .'

'You're right!'

'It's just that I don't understand how it could have turned on you *and* just walked out of the fog,' said Carrot.

'Everyone knows they're not allowed to fight back!'

'"Fight back",' Carrot repeated.

'It's not right, them walking around the streets like that,' the man muttered, looking away.

There was the sound of running feet behind them and a couple of men in blood-stained aprons caught up with them. 'It went that way!' one yelled. 'You'll be able to catch up with it if you hurry!'

'Come on, don't hang around! What do we pay our taxes for?' said the other.

'It went all round the cattle yards and let everything out. *Everything*! You can't move on Pigsty Hill!'

'A *golem* let all the cattle out?' said Vimes. 'What for?'

'How should I know? It took the yudasgoat out of Sock's slaughterhouse so half the damn things are following it around! And then it went and put old Fosdyke in his sausage machine—'

'What?'

'Oh, it didn't turn the handle. It just shoved a handful of parsley in his mouth, dropped an onion down his trousers, covered him in oatmeal and dropped him in the hopper!'

Angua's shoulders started to shake. Even Vimes grinned.

'And then it went into the poultry merchant's, grabbed Mr Terwillie, and' – the man stopped, aware there was a lady present, even if she was making snorting noises while trying not to laugh, and continued in a mumble – 'made use of some sage and onion. If you know what I mean . . .'

'You mean he—?' Vimes began.

'Yes!'

His companion nodded. 'Poor old Terwillie won't be able to look sage and onion in the face again, I reckon.'

'By the sound of it, that's the last thing he'll do,' said Vimes.

Angua had to turn her back.

'Tell him about what happened in your pork butcher's,' said the man's companion.

'I don't think you'll need to,' said Vimes. 'I'm seeing a pattern here.'

'Right! And poor young Sid's only an apprentice and didn't deserve what it done to him!'

'Oh, dear,' said Carrot. 'Er . . . I think I've got an ointment that might be—'

'Will it help with the apple?' the man demanded.

'It shoved an apple in his mouth?'

'Wrong!'

Vimes winced. 'Ouch . . .'

'What's going to be done, eh?' said the butcher, his face a few inches from Vimes's.

'Well, if you can get a grip on the stem—'

'I'm serious! What are *you* going to do? I'm a taxpayer and I know my rights!'

He prodded Vimes in the breastplate. Vimes's expression went wooden. He looked down at the finger, and then back up at the man's large red nose.

'In that case,' said Vimes, 'I suggest you take another apple and—'

'Er, excuse me,' said Carrot loudly. 'You're Mr Maxilotte, aren't you? Got a shop in the Shambles?'

'Yes, that's right. What of it?'

'It's just that I don't recall seeing your name on the register of taxpayers, which is very odd because you said you *were* a taxpayer, but of course you wouldn't lie about a thing like that and anyway when you paid your taxes they would have given you a receipt because that's the law and I'm sure you'd be able to find it if you looked—'

The butcher lowered his finger. 'Er, yes . . .'

'I could come and help you if you'd like,' said Carrot.

The butcher gave Vimes a despairing look.

'He really *does* read that stuff,' said Vimes. 'For pleasure. Carrot, why don't you scarp—? My gods, what the hell is *that*?'

There was a bellow further up the street.

Something big and muddy was approaching at a sort of menacing amble. In the gloom it looked vaguely like a very fat centaur, half-man, half . . . in *fact* it was, he realized as it bounced nearer, half-Colon, half-bull.

Sergeant Colon had lost his helmet and had a certain look about him that suggested he had been close to the soil.

As the massive bull cantered past, the sergeant rolled his eyes wildly and said, 'I daren't get off! I daren't get off!'

'How did you get *on*?' shouted Vimes.

'It wasn't easy, sir! I just grabbed the 'orns, sir, next minute I was on its back!'

'Well, hang on!'

'Yes, sir! Hanging on, *sir*!'

Rogers the bulls were angry and bewildered, which counts as the basic state of mind for full-grown bulls.*

---

* Because of the huge obtrusive mass of his forehead, Rogers the bulls' view of the universe

But they had a particular reason. Beef cattle have a religion. They are deeply spiritual animals. They believe that good and obedient cattle go to a better place when they die, through a magic door. They don't know what happens next, but they've heard that it involves really good eating and, for some reason, horseradish.

Rogers had been quite looking forward to it. They were getting a bit creaky these days, and cows seemed to run faster than they had done when they were lads. They could just taste that heavenly horseradish . . .

And instead they'd been herded into a crowded pen for a day and *then* the gate had been opened and there'd been animals every- where and this did *not* look like the Promised Lard.

And someone was on their back. They'd tried to buck him off a few times. In Rogers' heyday the impudent man would by now be a few stringy red stains on the ground, but finally the arthritic bulls had given up until such time as they could find a handy tree on which to scrape him off.

They just wished the wretched man would stop yelling.

Vimes took a few steps after the bull, and then turned.

'Carrot? Angua? You two get down to Carry's tallow works. Just keep an eye on it until we get there, understand? Spy out the place but don't go in, understand? Right? Do not in any circumstances move in. Do I make myself clear? Just remain in the area. Right?'

'Yes, sir,' said Carrot.

'Detritus, let's get Fred off that thing.'

The crowds were melting away ahead of the bull. A ton of pedigree bull does not experience traffic congestion, at least not for any length of time.

'Can't you jump off, Fred?' Vimes yelled, as he ran along behind.

'I do not wish to give that a try, sir!'

'Well, can you steer it?'

'How, sir?'

'Take the bull by the horns, man!'

Colon tentatively reached out and took a horn in each hand. Rogers the bull turned his head and nearly pulled him off.

'He's a bit stronger than me, sir! Quite a lot stronger actually, sir!'

---

was from two eyes each with their own non-overlapping hemispherical view of the world. Since there were two separate visions, Rogers had reasoned, that meant there must be two bulls (bulls not having been bred for much deductive reasoning). Most bulls believe this, which is why they always keep turning their head this way and that when they look at you. They do this because both of them want to see.

'I could shoot it through der head wid my bow, Mr Vimes,' said Detritus, flourishing his converted siege weapon.

'This is a crowded street, Sergeant. It might hit an innocent person, even in Ankh-Morpork.'

'Sorry, sir.' Detritus brightened. 'But if it did we could always say they'd bin guilty of somethin', sir?'

'No, that . . . What's that chicken doing?'

A small black bantam cock raced up the street, ran between the bull's legs and skidded to a halt just in front of Rogers. A smaller figure jumped off its back, leapt up, caught hold of the ring through the bull's nose, swung up further until it was in the mass of curls on the bull's forehead, and then took firm hold of a lock of hair in each tiny hand.

'It looks like Wee Mad Arthur der ger-nome, sir,' said Detritus. 'He . . . tryin' to nut der bull . . .'

There was a noise like a slow woodpecker working on a particularly difficult tree, and it punctuated a litany of complaints from somewhere between the animal's eyes.

'Take that, yer big lump that yez are . . .'

The bull stopped. He tried to turn his head so that one or other of the Rogerses could see what the hell it was that was hammering at its forehead, and might as well have tried looking down its own ears.

It staggered backwards.

'Fred,' Vimes whispered. 'You slip off its back while it's busy.'

With a panicky look, Sergeant Colon swung a leg over the bull's huge back and slid down to the ground. Vimes grabbed him and hustled him into a doorway. Then he hustled him out again. A doorway was far too confined a space in which to be anywhere near Fred Colon.

'Why are you all covered in crap, Fred?'

'Well, sir, you know that creek that you're up without a paddle? It started there and it's got worse, sir.'

'Good grief. Worse than that?'

'Permission to go and have a bath, sir?'

'No, but you could stand back a few more feet. What happened to your helmet?'

'Last time I saw it, it was on a sheep, sir. Sir, I was tied up and shoved in a cellar and heroically broke free, sir! And I was chased by one of them golems, sir!'

'Where was this?'

Colon had hoped he wouldn't be asked that. 'It was a place in the Shambles,' he said. 'It was foggy, so I—'

Vimes grabbed Colon's wrists. 'What's this?'

'They tied me up with string, sir! But at great pers'nal risk of life and limb I—'

'This doesn't look like string to *me*,' said Vimes.

'No, sir?'

'No, this looks like . . . candlewick.'

Colon looked blank.

'That a Clue, sir?' he said, hopefully.

There was a splatting noise as Vimes slapped him on the back. 'Well done, Fred,' he said, wiping his hand on his trousers. 'It's certainly a corroboration.'

'That's what I thought!' said Colon quickly. 'This is a corrobolaration and I've got to get it to Commander Vimes as soon as possible regardless of—'

'Why's that gnome nutting that bull, Fred?'

'That's Wee Mad Arthur, sir. We owe him a dollar. He was . . . of some help, sir.'

Rogers the bull was on his knees, dazed and bewildered. It wasn't that Wee Mad Arthur was capable of delivering a killing blow, but he just didn't stop. After a while the noise and the thumping got on people's nerves.

'Should we help him?' said Vimes.

'Looks like he's doing all right by himself, sir,' said Colon.

Wee Mad Arthur looked up and grinned. 'One dollar, right?' he shouted. 'No welching or I'll come after yez! One of these buggers trod on me grandpa once!'

'Was he hurt?'

'He got one of his horns twisted right orf!'

Vimes took Sergeant Colon firmly by the arm. 'Come on, Fred, it's all hitting the street now!'

'Right, sir! And most of it's splashing!'

'I say! You there! You're a watchman, aren't you? Come over here!'

Vimes turned. A man had pushed his way through the crowds.

On the whole, Colon reflected, it was just possible that the worst moment of his life hadn't happened yet. Vimes tended to react in a ballistic way to words like 'I say! You there!' when uttered in a certain kind of neighing voice.

The speaker had an aristocratic look about him, and the angry air of a man not accustomed to the rigours of life who has just found one happening to him.

Vimes saluted smartly. 'Yessir! I'm a watchman, *sir!*'

'Well, just you come along with me and arrest this thing. It's disturbing the workers.'

'What thing, sir?'

'A golem, man! Walked into the factory as bold as you like and started painting on the damn walls!'

'What factory, sir?'

'You come with me, my man. I happen to be a very good friend of your commander and I can't say I like your attitude.'

'Sorry about that, sir,' said Vimes, with a cheerfulness that Sergeant Colon had come to dread.

There was a nondescript factory on the other side of the street. The man strode in.

'Er . . . he said "golem", sir,' murmured Colon.

Vimes had known Fred Colon a long time. 'Yes, Fred, so it's vitally important for you to stay on guard out here,' he said.

The relief rose off Colon like steam. 'That's right, sir!' he said.

The factory was full of sewing-machines. People were sitting meekly in front of them. It was the sort of thing the guilds hated, but since the Guild of Seamstresses didn't take all that much interest in sewing there was no one to object. Endless belts led up from each machine to pulleys on a long spindle near the roof, which in turn were driven by . . . Vimes's eyes followed it down the length of the workshop . . . a treadmill, now stationary and somewhat broken. A couple of golems were standing forlornly alongside it, looking lost.

There was a hole in the wall quite close to it and, above it, someone had written in red paint:

WORKERS! NO MASTER BUT YOURSELVES!

Vimes grinned.

'It smashed its way in, broke the treadmill, pulled my golems out, painted that stupid message on the wall and stamped out again!' said the man behind him.

'Hmm, yes, I see. A lot of people use oxen in their treadmills,' said Vimes mildly.

'What's that got to do with it? Anyway, cattle can't keep going twenty-four hours a day.'

Vimes's gaze worked its way along the rows of workers. Their faces had that worried, Cockbill Street look that you got when you were cursed with pride as well as poverty.

'No, indeed,' he said. 'Most of the clothing workshops are up at Nap Hill, but the wages are cheaper down here, aren't they?'

'People are jolly glad to get the work!'

'Yes,' said Vimes, looking at the faces again. 'Glad.' At the far end of the factory, he noted, the golems were trying to rebuild their treadmill.

'Now you listen to me, what I want you to do is—' the factory-owner began.

Vimes's hand gripped his collar and dragged him forward until his face was a few inches from Vimes's own.

'No, *you* listen to *me*,' hissed Vimes. 'I mix with crooks and thieves and thugs all day and that doesn't worry me at all but after two minutes with you I need a bath. And if I find that damn golem I'll shake its damn hand, you hear me?'

To the surprise of that part of Vimes that wasn't raging, the man found enough courage to say 'How dare you! You're supposed to be the law!'

Vimes's furious finger almost went up the man's nose.

'Where shall I start?' he yelled. He glared at the two golems. 'And why are you clowns repairing the treadmill?' he shouted. 'Good grief, haven't got the sense you were bor— Haven't you got any sense?'

He stormed out of the building. Sergeant Colon stopped trying to scrape himself clean and ran to catch up with him.

'I heard some people say they saw a golem come out of the other door, sir,' he said. 'It was a red one. You know, red clay. But the one that was after me was white, sir. Are you angry, Sam?'

'Who's that man who owns that place?'

'That's Mr Catterail, sir. You know, he's always writing you letters about there being too many what he calls "lesser races" in the Watch. You know . . . trolls and dwarfs . . .'

The sergeant had to trot to keep up with him.

'Get some zombies,' said Vimes.

'You've always been dead against zombies, excuse my pune,' said Sergeant Colon.

'Any want to join, are there?'

'Oh, yessir. Couple of good lads, sir, and but for the grey skin hangin' off 'em you'd swear they hadn't been buried five minutes.'

'Swear them in tomorrow.'

'Right, sir. Good idea. And of course it's a great saving not having to include them in the pension plan.'

'They can patrol up on Kings Down. After all, they're only human.'

'Right, sir.' When Sam is in these moods, Colon thought, you agree with *everything*. 'You're really getting the hang of this affirmative action stuff, eh sir?'

'Right now I'd swear in a gorgon!'

'There's always Mr Bleakley, sir, he's getting fed up with working in the kosher butcher's and—'

'But no vampires. *Never* any vampires. Now let's get a move on, Fred.'

*

Nobby Nobbs ought to have known. That's what he told himself as he scuttled through the streets. All that stuff about kings and stuff – they'd wanted him to . . .

It was a terrible thought . . .

Volunteer.

Nobby had spent a lifetime in one uniform or another. And one of the most basic lessons he'd learned was that men with red faces and plummy voices never *ever* gave cushy numbers to the likes of Nobby. They'd ask for volunteers to do something 'big and clean' and you'd end up scrubbing some damn great drawbridge; they'd say, 'Anyone here like good food?' and you'd be peeling potatoes for a week. You never *ever* volunteered. Not even if a sergeant stood there and said, 'We need someone to drink alcohol, bottles of, and make love, passionate, to women, for the use of.' There was *always* a snag. If a choir of angels asked for volunteers for Paradise to step forward, Nobby knew enough to take one smart pace to the rear.

When the call came for Corporal Nobbs, it would not find him wanting. It would not find him at all.

Nobby avoided a herd of pigs in the middle of the street.

Even Mr Vimes never expected him to *volunteer*. He respected Nobby's pride.

Nobby's head ached. It must've been the quail's eggs, he was sure. They couldn't be healthy birds to lay titchy eggs like that.

He sidled past a cow that had got its head stuck in someone's window.

Nobby as king? Oh, *yes*. No one ever gave a Nobbs anything except maybe a skin disease or sixty lashes. It was a dog-eat-Nobbs world, right enough. If there were to be a world competition for losers, a Nobbs would come firs— last.

He stopped running and went to earth in a doorway. In its welcome shadows he extracted a very short cigarette end from behind his ear and lit it.

Now that he felt safe enough to think about more than flight he wondered about all the animals that seemed to be on the streets. Unlike the family tree that had borne Fred Colon as its fruit, the creeping vine of the Nobbses had flourished only within city walls. Nobby was vaguely aware of animals as being food in a primary stage and left it at that. But he was pretty sure they weren't supposed to be wandering around untidily like this.

Gangs of men were trying to round them up. Since they were tired and working at cross-purposes, and the animals were hungry and bewildered, all that was happening was that the streets were getting a lot muddier.

Nobby became aware that he was not alone in the doorway.

He looked down.

Also lurking in the shadows was a goat. It was unkempt and smelly, but it turned its head and gave Nobby the most knowing look he'd ever seen on the face of an animal. Unexpectedly, and most uncharacteristically, Nobby was struck by a surge of fellow-feeling.

He pinched out the end of his cigarette and passed it down to the goat, which ate it.

'You and me both,' said Nobby.

Miscellaneous livestock scattered madly as Carrot, Angua and Cheri made their way down the Shambles. They especially tried to keep away from Angua. It seemed to Cheri that an invisible barrier was advancing in front of them. Some animals tried to climb walls or scattered madly into side alleys.

'Why are they so scared?' said Cheri.

'Can't imagine,' said Angua.

A few maddened sheep ran away from them as they walked around the candle-factory. Light from its high windows indicated that candlemaking continued all night.

'They make nearly half a million candles every twenty-four hours,' said Carrot. 'I heard they've got very advanced machinery. It sounds very interesting. I'd love to see it.'

At the rear of the premises light blazed out into the fog. Crates of candles were being manhandled on to a succession of carts.

'Looks normal enough,' said Carrot, as they eased themselves into a conveniently shadowy doorway. 'Busy, though.'

'I don't see what good this is going to do,' said Angua. 'As soon as they see us they can destroy any evidence. And, even if we find arsenic, so what? There's no crime in owning arsenic, is there?'

'Er . . . is there a crime in owning *that*?' whispered Cheri.

A golem was walking slowly up the alley. It was quite unlike any other golem they had seen. The others were ancient and had repaired themselves so many times they were as shapeless as a gingerbread man, but this one looked like a human, or at least like humans wished they could look. It resembled a statue made of white clay. Around its head, part of the very design, was a crown.

'I was *right*,' murmured Carrot. 'They *did* make themselves a golem. The poor devils. They thought a king would make them free.'

'Look at its legs,' said Angua.

As the golem walked, lines of red light appeared and disappeared all over its legs, and across its body and arms.

'It's cracking,' she said.

'I *knew* you couldn't bake pottery in an old bread oven!' said Cheri. 'It's not the right *shape!*'

The golem pushed open a door and disappeared into the factory.

'Let's go,' said Carrot.

'Commander Vimes told us to wait for him,' said Angua.

'Yes, but we don't know *what* might be going on in there,' said Carrot. 'Besides, he likes us to use our initiative. We can't just hang around now.'

He darted across the alley and opened the door.

There were crates piled inside, with a narrow passageway between them. From all around them, but slightly muffled by the crates, came the clicking and rattling of the factory. The air smelled of hot wax.

Cheri was aware of a whispered conversation going on several feet above her little round helmet.

'*I wish Mr Vimes hadn't wanted us to bring her. Supposing something happens to her?*'

'*What are you talking about?*'

'*Well . . . you know . . . she's a girl.*'

'*So what? There's at least three female dwarfs in the Watch already and you don't worry about them.*'

'*Oh, come on . . . name one.*'

'*Lars Skulldrinker, for a start.*'

'*No! Really?*'

'*Are you calling this nose a liar?*'

'*But he broke up a fight in the Miner's Arms single-handedly last week!*'

'*Well? Why do you assume females are weaker? You wouldn't worry about me taking on a vicious bar crowd by myself.*'

'*I'd give aid where necessary.*'

'*To me or to them?*'

'*That's unfair!*'

'*Is it?*'

'*I wouldn't help them unless you got really rough.*'

'*Ah, so? And they say chivalry is dead . . .*'

'*Anyway, Cheri is . . . a bit different. I'm sure he . . . she's good at alchemy, but we'd better watch her back in a fight. Hold on . . .*'

They'd stepped out into the factory.

Candles whirled overhead – hundreds of them, *thousands* of them – dangling by their wicks from an endless belt of complex wooden links that switchbacked its way up and down the long hall.

'I heard about this,' said Carrot. 'It's called a producing line. It's a way of making thousands of things that are all the same. But look at the speed! I'm amazed the treadmill can—'

Angua pointed. There was a treadmill creaking around beside her, but there was nothing inside it.

'*Something*'s got to be powering all this,' said Angua.

Carrot pointed. Further up the hall the switchbacks of the line converged in a complicated knot. There was a figure somewhere in the middle, arms moving in a blur.

Just beside Carrot the line ended at a big wooden hopper. Candles cascaded into it. No one had been emptying it, and they were tumbling over the pile and rolling on to the floor.

'Cheri,' said Carrot. 'Do you know how to use any kind of weapon?'

'Er . . . no, Captain Carrot.'

'Right. You just wait in the alley, then. I don't want any harm coming to you.'

She scuttled off, looking relieved.

Angua sniffed the air. 'There's been a vampire here,' she said.

'I think we'd—' Carrot began.

'I knew you'd find out! I wish I'd never bought the damned thing! I've got a bow! I warn you, I've got a crossbow!'

They turned. 'Ah, Mr Carry,' said Carrot cheerfully. He produced his badge. 'Captain Carrot, Ankh-Morpork City Watch—'

'I know who you are! I know who you are! And *what* you are, too! I knew you'd come! I've got a bow and I'm not afraid to use it!' The crossbow's point moved uncertainly, proving him a liar.

'Really?' said Angua. '*What* we are?'

'I didn't even want to get involved!' said Carry. 'It killed those old men, didn't it?'

'Yes,' said Carrot.

'Why? I didn't tell it to!'

'Because they helped make it, I think,' said Carrot. 'It knew who to blame.'

'The golems sold it to me!' said Carry. 'I thought it'd help build up the business but the damned thing won't stop—'

He glanced up at the line of candles whirring overhead, but jerked his head back before Angua could move.

'Works hard, does it?'

'Hah!' But Carry didn't look like a man enjoying a joke. He looked like a man in private torment. 'I've laid off everyone except the girls in the packing department, and *they're* on three shifts and overtime! I've got four men out looking for tallow, two negotiating for wicks and three trying to buy more storage space!'

'Then get it to stop making candles,' said Carrot.

'It goes off into the streets when we run out of tallow! You want it walking around looking for something to do? Hey, you two stay together!' Carry added urgently, waving the crossbow.

'Look, all you have to do is change the words in its head,' said Carrot.

'It won't let me! Don't you think I've tried?'

'It can't *not let you*,' said Carrot. 'Golems have to let—'

'I said it won't let me!'

'What about the poisoned candles?' said Carrot.

'That wasn't my idea!'

'Whose idea was it?'

Carry's crossbow swung back and forth. He licked his lips. 'This has all gone far too far,' he said. 'I'm getting out.'

'Whose idea, Mr Carry?'

'I'm not going to end up in some alley somewhere with as much blood as a banana!'

'Now then, we wouldn't do anything like that,' said Carrot.

Mr Carry was exporting terror. Angua could smell it streaming off him. He might pull the trigger out of sheer panic.

There was another smell, too. 'Who's the vampire?' she said.

For a moment she thought the man *would* fire the crossbow. 'I never said anything about him!'

'You've got garlic in your pocket,' said Angua. 'And the place reeks of vampire.'

'He said we could get the golem to do anything,' Carry mumbled.

'Like making poisoned candles?' said Carrot.

'Yes, but he said it'd just keep Vetinari out of the way,' said Carry. He seemed to be getting a tenuous grip on himself. 'And he's not dead, 'cos I'd have heard,' he said. 'I shouldn't think making him ill is a crime, so you can't—'

'The candles killed two other people,' said Carrot.

Carry started to panic again. 'Who?'

'An old lady and a baby in Cockbill Street.'

'Were they important?' said Carry.

Carrot nodded to himself. 'I was almost feeling sorry for you,' he said. 'Right up to that point. You're a lucky man, Mr Carry.'

'You think so?'

'Oh, yes. We got to you before Commander Vimes did. Now, just put down the crossbow and we can talk about—'

There was a noise. Or, rather, the sudden cessation of a noise that had been so pervasive that it had no longer been consciously heard.

The clacking line had stopped. There was a chorus of little waxy thuds as the hanging candles swung and hit one another, and then silence unrolled. The last candle dropped off the line, tumbled down the heap in the hopper, and bounced on the floor.

And in the silence, the sound of footsteps.

Carry started to back away. 'Too late!' he moaned.

Both Carrot and Angua saw his finger move.

Angua pushed Carrot out of the way as the claw released the string, but he had anticipated this and his hand was already flinging itself up and across. She heard the sickening, tearing noise as his palm whirled in front of her face, and his grunt as the force of the bolt spun him round.

He landed heavily on the floor, clutching his left hand. The crossbow bolt was sticking out of the palm.

Angua crouched down. 'It doesn't look barbed, let me pull—'

Carrot grabbed her wrist. 'The point's silver! Don't touch it!'

They both looked up as a shadow crossed the light.

The king golem looked down at her.

She felt her teeth and fingernails begin to lengthen.

Then she saw the small round face of Cheri peering nervously around a pile of crates. Angua fought down her werewolf instincts, screamed 'Stay right there!' at the dwarf and at every swelling hair follicle, and hesitated between pursuing the fleeing Carry and dragging Carrot to safety.

She told her body again that a wolf-shape was *not* an option. There were too many strange smells, too many fires . . .

The golem glistened with tallow and wax.

She backed away.

Behind the golem she saw Cheri look down at the groaning Carrot and then up at a fire-axe hooked on the wall. The dwarf took it down and weighed it vaguely in her hands.

'Don't try—' Angua began.

'T'dr'duzk b'hazg t't!'

'Oh, no!' moaned Carrot. 'Not *that* one!'

Cheri came up behind the golem at a run and hacked at its waist. The axe rebounded but she pirouetted with it and caught the statue on the thigh, chipping off a piece of clay.

Angua hesitated. Cheri's axe was making blurred orbits around the golem while its wielder yelled more terrible battle cries. Angua couldn't make out any words but many dwarf cries didn't bother with words. They went straight for emotions in sonic form. Chips of pottery ricocheted off the crates as each blow landed.

'What did she yell?' Angua said, as she pulled Carrot out of the way.

'It's the most menacing dwarf battle cry there is! Once it's been shouted *someone* has to be killed!'

'What's it mean?'

'Today Is A Good Day For Someone Else To Die!'

The golem watched the dwarf incuriously, like an elephant watching an attack by a rogue chicken.

Then it picked the axe out of the air, Cheri trailing behind it like a comet, and hurled it aside.

Angua hauled Carrot to his feet. Blood dripped from his hand. She tried to shut her nostrils. *Full moon tomorrow. No more choices.*

'Maybe we can reason with it—' Carrot started.

'Attention! This is the *real* world calling!' shouted Angua.

Carrot drew his sword. 'I am arresting you—' he began.

The golem's arm whirred across. The sword buried itself to the hilt in a crate of candles.

'Got any more clever ideas?' said Angua, as they backed away. 'Or can we go now?'

'No. We've got to stop it somewhere.'

Their heels met a wall of crates.

'I think we've found the place,' said Angua as the golem raised its fists again.

'You duck right, I'll duck left. Maybe—'

A blow rocked the big double doors in the far wall.

The king golem's head turned.

The doors shook again, and burst inwards. For a moment Dorfl was framed in the doorway. Then the red golem lowered his head, spread his arms, and charged.

It wasn't a very fast run but it did have a terrible momentum, like the slow slide of a glacier. The floorboards shook and drummed under him.

The golems collided with a *clang* in the middle of the floor. Jagged lines of fire spread across the king's body as cracks opened, but it roared and caught up Dorfl around the middle and tossed him against the wall.

'Come *on*,' said Angua. '*Now* can we find Cheri and get out of here?'

'We ought to help him,' said Carrot, as the golems smashed into each other again.

'How? If it . . . if *he* can't stop it, what makes you think *we* can? Come *on*!'

Carrot shook her off.

Dorfl picked itself up from among the bricks and charged again. The golems met, scrabbling at one another for purchase. They stood locked for a moment, creaking, and then Dorfl's hand came up holding something. Dorfl pushed himself back and smashed the other golem over the head with its own leg.

As it spun Dorfl's other hand lashed out, but was grabbed. The king swivelled with a strange grace, bore Dorfl to the floor, rolled and kicked out. Dorfl rolled too. He flung out his arms to stop himself, and looked back to see both his feet pinwheeling into the wall.

The king picked up its own leg, balanced for a moment, and joined itself together.

Then its red gaze swept the factory and flared when it caught sight of Carrot.

'There must be a back way out of here,' muttered Angua. 'Carry got out!'

The king started to run after them, but hit an immediate problem. It had put its leg on back to front. It began to limp in a circle but, somehow, the circle got nearer to them.

'We can't just leave Dorfl lying there,' said Carrot.

He pulled a long metal rod out of a stirring tank and eased himself back down to the grease-crusted floor.

The king rocked towards him. Carrot hopped backwards, steadied himself on a rail, and swung.

The golem lifted its hand, caught the rod out of the air and tossed it aside. It raised both fists and tried to step forward.

It couldn't move. It looked down.

'Thsss,' said what remained of Dorfl, gripping its ankle.

The king bent, swung one hand with the palm edgewise, and calmly sheared the top off Dorfl's head. It removed the chem and crumpled it up.

The glow died in Dorfl's eyes.

Angua cannoned into Carrot so hard he almost fell over. She wrapped both arms around him and pulled him after her.

'It just *killed* Dorfl, just like that!' said Carrot.

'It's a shame, yes,' said Angua. 'Or it would be if Dorfl had been alive. Carrot, they're like . . . *machinery*. Look, we can make it to the door—'

Carrot shook himself free. 'It's murder,' he said. 'We're watchmen. We can't just . . . watch! It *killed* him!'

'It's an it and so's he—'

'Commander Vimes said someone has to speak for the people with no voices!'

He really believes *it*, Angua thought. *Vimes puts words in his head.*

'Keep it occupied!' he shouted, and darted away.

'How? Organize a sing-song?'

'I've got a plan.'

'Oh, *good!*'

Vimes looked up at the entrance of the candle-factory. He could dimly see two cressets burning on either side of a shield. 'Look at that, will you?' he said. 'Paint not dry and he flaunts the thing for all the world to see!'

'What's dat, sir?' said Detritus.

'His damn coat of arms!'

Detritus looked up. 'Why's it got a lighted fish on it?' he said.

'In heraldry that's a poisson,' said Vimes bitterly. 'And it's supposed to be a lamp.'

'A lamp made out of a poisson,' said Detritus. 'Well, dere's a fing.'

'At least it's got the motto in proper language,' said Sergeant Colon. 'Instead of all the old-fashioned stuff no one understands. "Art Brought Forth the Candle." That, Sergeant Detritus, is a pune, or play on words. 'Cos his name is Arthur, see.'

Vimes stood between the two sergeants and felt a hole open up in his head.

'Damn!' he said. 'Damn, damn, damn! He *showed* it to me! "Dumb plodder Vimes! *He* won't notice!" Oh, yes! *And* he was right!'

''S not that good,' said Colon. 'I mean, you've got to know that Mr Carry's first name is Arthur—'

'Shut *up*, Fred!' snapped Vimes.

'Shutting up right now, sir.'

'The *arrogance* of the . . . Who's that?'

A figure darted out of the building, glanced around hurriedly, and scurried along the street.

'That's Carry!' said Vimes. He didn't even shout 'After him!' but went from a standing start to a full run. The fleeing figure dodged between the occasional straying sheep or pig and didn't have a bad turn of speed, but Vimes was powered by sheer anger and was only yards away when Carry ducked into an alleyway.

Vimes skidded to a halt and grabbed at the wall. He'd seen the shape of a crossbow and one of the things you learned in the Watch – that is, one of the things which hopefully you'd have a *chance* to learn – was that it was a very stupid thing indeed to follow someone with a crossbow into a dark alley where you'd be outlined against any light there was.

'I know it's you, Carry,' he shouted.

'I've got a crossbow!'

'You can only fire it once!'

'I want to turn King's Evidence!'

'Guess again!'

Carry lowered his voice. 'They just said I could get the damn golem to do it. I didn't think anyone was going to get hurt.'

'Right, right,' said Vimes. 'You made poisoned candles because they gave a better light, I expect.'

'You know what I mean! They told me it would all be all right and—'

'Which they would "they" be?'

'They said no one would ever find out!'

'Really?'

'Look, look, they said they could . . .' The voice paused, and took on that wheedling tone the blunt-witted use when they're trying to sound sharp.

'If I tell you everything, you'll let me go, right?'

The two sergeants had caught up. Vimes pulled Detritus towards him, although in fact he ended up pulling himself towards Detritus.

'Go round the corner and see he doesn't come out of the alley the other way,' he whispered. The troll nodded.

'What's it you want to tell me, Mr Carry?' said Vimes to the darkness in the alley.

'Have we got a bargain?'

'What?'

'A bargain.'

'No, we damn well *haven't* got a bargain, Mr Carry! I'm not a tradesman! But I'll tell you something, Mr Carry. They betrayed you!'

There was silence from the darkness, and then a sound like a sigh.

Behind Vimes, Sergeant Colon stamped his feet on the cobbles to keep warm.

'You can't stay in there all night, Mr Carry,' said Vimes.

There was another sound, a leathery sound. Vimes glanced up into the coils of fog. 'Something's not right,' he said. 'Come on!'

He ran into the alley. Sergeant Colon followed, on the basis that it was fine to run into an alley containing an armed man provided you were behind someone else.

A shape loomed at them.

'Detritus?'

'Yes, sir!'

'Where did he go? There are no doors in the alley!'

Then his eyes grew more accustomed to the gloom. He saw a

huddled outline at the foot of a wall, and his foot nudged a crossbow. 'Mr Carry?'

He knelt down and lit a match.

'Oh, nasty,' said Sergeant Colon. 'Something's broken his neck . . .'

'Dead, is he?' said Detritus. 'You want I should draw a chalk outline round him?'

'I don't think we need bother, Sergeant.'

'It no bother, I've got der chalk right here.'

Vimes looked up. Fog filled the alley, but there were no ladders, no handy low roofs.

'Let's get out of here,' he said.

Angua faced the king.

She resisted a terrible urge to Change. Even a werewolf's jaws probably wouldn't have any effect on the thing. It didn't *have* a jugular.

She daren't look away. The king moved uncertainly, with little jerks and twitches that in a human would suggest madness. Its arms moved fast but erratically, as if signals that were being sent were not arriving properly. And Dorfl's attack had left it damaged. Every time it moved, red light shone from dozens of new cracks.

'You're cracking up!' she shouted. 'The oven wasn't right for pottery!'

The king lunged at her. She dodged and heard its hand slice through a rack of candles.

'You're cranky! You're baked like a loaf! You're *half-baked!*'

She drew her sword. She didn't usually have much use for it. She found a smile would invariably do the trick.

A hand sliced the top off the blade.

She stared at the sheared metal in horror and then somersaulted back as another blow hummed past her face.

Her foot rolled on a candle and she fell heavily, but with enough presence of mind to roll before a foot stamped down.

'Where've you gone?' she yelled.

'Can you get it to move a little closer to the doors, please?' said a voice from the darkness on high.

Carrot crawled out along the rickety structure that supported the production line.

'*Carrot!*'

'Almost there . . .'

The king grabbed at her leg. She lashed out with her foot and caught it on the knee.

To her amazement she made it crack. But the fire below was still there. The pieces of pottery seemed to float on it. No matter what anyone did the golem could keep going, even if it were just a cloud of dust held together.

'Ah. Right,' said Carrot, and dropped off the gantry.

He landed on the king's back, flung one arm around its neck, and began to pound on its head with the hilt of his sword. It staggered and tried to reach up to pull him off.

'Got to get the words out!' Carrot shouted, as the arms flailed at him. 'It's the only . . . way!'

The king staggered forward and hit a stack of boxes, which burst and rained candles over the floor. Carrot grabbed its ears and tried to twist.

Angua heard him saying: 'You . . . have . . . the right . . . to . . . a lawyer . . .'

'Carrot! Don't bother with its damn rights!'

'You . . . have . . . the right to—'

'Just give it the *last* ones!'

There was a commotion in the gaping doorway and Vimes ran in, sword drawn. 'Oh, *gods* . . . Sergeant Detritus!'

Detritus appeared behind him. 'Sah!'

'Crossbow bolt through the head, if you please!'

'If you say so, sir . . .'

'*Its* head, Sergeant! Mine is fine! Carrot, get down off the thing!'

'Can't get its head off, sir!'

'We'll try six feet of cold steel in the ear just as soon as you let the damn thing go!'

Carrot steadied himself on the king's shoulders, tried to judge his moment as the thing staggered around, and leapt.

He landed awkwardly on a sliding heap of candles. His leg buckled under him and he tumbled over until he was stopped by the inert shell that had been Dorfl.

'Hey, look dis way, mister,' said Detritus.

The king turned.

Vimes didn't catch everything that happened next, because it all happened so quickly. He was merely aware of the rush of air and the *gloink* of the rebounding bolt mingling with the wooden juddering noise as it buried itself in the doorframe behind him.

And the golem was crouching down by Carrot, who was trying to squirm out of the way.

It raised a fist, and brought it down . . .

Vimes didn't even see Dorfl's arm move but there it was *there*, suddenly gripping the king's wrist.

Tiny stars of light went nova in Dorfl's eyes.

'Tssssss!'

As the king jerked back in surprise, Dorfl held on and levered himself up on what remained of his legs. As he came up so did his fist.

Time slowed. Nothing moved in the whole universe but Dorfl's fist.

It swung like a planet, without any apparent speed but with a drifting unstoppability.

And then the king's expression changed. Just before the fist landed, it smiled.

The golem's head exploded. Vimes recalled it in slow motion, one long second of floating pottery. And words. Scraps of paper flew out, dozens, *scores* of them, tumbling gently to the floor.

Slowly, peacefully, the king hit the floor. The red light died, the cracks opened, and then there were just . . . pieces.

Dorfl collapsed on top of them.

Angua and Vimes reached Carrot together.

'He came alive!' said Carrot, struggling up. 'That thing was going to kill me and Dorfl came alive! But that thing had smashed the words out of his head! A golem *has* to have the words!'

'They gave their own golem too many, I can see that,' said Vimes. He picked up some of the coils of paper.

. . . CREATE PEACE AND JUSTICE FOR ALL . . .

. . . RULE US WISELY . . .

. . . TEACH US FREEDOM . . .

. . . LEAD US TO . . .

Poor devil, he thought.

'Let's get you home. That hand needs treating—' said Angua.

'*Listen*, will you?' said Carrot. 'He's alive!'

Vimes knelt down by Dorfl. The broken clay skull looked as empty as yesterday's breakfast egg. But there was still a pinpoint of light in each eye socket.

'Ussssss,' hissed Dorfl, so faintly that Vimes wasn't sure he'd heard it.

A finger scratched on the floor.

'Is it trying to write something?' said Angua.

Vimes pulled out his notebook, eased it under Dorfl's hand, and gently pushed a pencil into the golem's fingers. They watched the hand as it wrote – a little jerkily but still with the mechanical precision of a golem – eight words.

Then it stopped. The pencil rolled away. The lights in Dorfl's eyes dwindled and went out.

'Good grief,' breathed Angua. 'They *don't* need words in their heads . . .'

'We can rebuild him,' said Carrot hoarsely. 'We have the pottery.'

Vimes stared at the words, and then at what remained of Dorfl.

'Mr Vimes?' said Carrot.

'Do it,' said Vimes.

Carrot blinked.

'Right now,' Vimes said. He looked back at the scrawl in his book.

ꟿOⱤDꙄ IN TⱧE ⱧEAⱤT CAN NOT BE TAKEN.

'And when you rebuild him,' he said, 'when you rebuild him . . . give him a voice. Understand? And get someone to look at your hand.'

'A voice, sir?'

'Do it!'

'Yes, sir.'

'Right.' Vimes pulled himself together. 'Constable Angua and I will have a look around here. Off you go.'

He watched Carrot and the troll carry the remains out. 'Okay,' he said. 'We're looking for arsenic. Maybe there'll be some workshop somewhere. I shouldn't think they'd want to mix the poisoned candles up with the others. Cheery'll know what— Where *is* Corporal Littlebottom?'

'Er . . . I don't think I can hold on much longer . . .'

They looked up.

Cheri was hanging on the line of candles.

'How did you get up there?' said Vimes.

'I sort of found myself going past, sir.'

'Can't you just let go? You're not that high— Oh . . .'

A big trough of molten tallow was a few feet under her. Occasionally the surface went *gloop*.

'Er . . . how hot would that be?' Vimes hissed to Angua.

'Ever bitten hot jam?' she said.

Vimes raised his voice. 'Can't you swing yourself along, Corporal?'

'All the wood's greasy, sir!'

'Corporal Littlebottom, I *order* you not to fall off!'

'Very good, sir!'

Vimes pulled off his jacket. 'Hang on to this. I'll see if I can climb up . . .' he muttered.

'It won't work!' said Angua. 'The thing's shaky enough as it is!'

'I can feel my hands slipping, sir.'

'Good grief, why didn't you call out earlier?'

'Everyone seemed to be busy, sir.'

'Turn around, sir,' said Angua, undoing the buckles of her breastplate. 'Right now, please! And shut your eyes!'

'Why, what . . . ?'

'Rrright nowwww, sirrrrr!'

'Oh . . . yes . . .'

Vimes heard Angua back away from the candle machine, her footsteps punctuated by the clang of falling armour. Then she started running and the footsteps *changed* while she was running and then . . .

He opened his eyes.

The wolf sailed upwards in slow motion, caught the dwarf's shoulder in its jaws as Cheri's grip gave way, and then arced its body so that wolf and dwarf hit the floor on the far side of the vat.

Angua rolled, whimpering.

Cheri scrambled to her feet. 'It's a werewolf!'

Angua rolled back and forth, pawing at her mouth.

'What's happened to it?' said Cheri, her panic receding a little. 'It looks . . . hurt. Where's Angua? Oh . . .'

Vimes glanced at the dwarf's torn leather shirt. 'You wear chain mail *under* your clothes?' he said.

'Oh . . . it's my silver vest . . . but she *knew* about it. I *told* her . . .'

Vimes grabbed Angua's collar. She moved to bite him, and then caught his eye and turned her head away.

'She only *bit* the silver,' said Cheri, distractedly.

Angua pulled herself on to her feet, glared at them, and slunk off behind some crates. They heard her whimpering which, by degrees, became a voice.

'Blasted blasted dwarfs and their blasted vests . . .'

'You all right, Constable?' said Vimes.

'Damn silver underwear . . . Can you throw me my clothes, please?'

Vimes bundled up Angua's uniform and, eyes closed for decency's sake, handed it around the crates.

'No one *told* me she was a were—' Cheri moaned.

'Look at it like this, Corporal,' said Vimes, as patiently as he could. 'If she *hadn't* been a werewolf you would by now be the world's largest novelty candle, all right?'

Angua walked from behind the crates, rubbing her mouth. The skin around it looked too pink . . .

'It burned you?' said Cheri.

'It'll heal,' said Angua.

'You never said you were a werewolf!'

'How would you've liked me to have put it?'

'Right,' said Vimes, 'if *that*'s all sorted out, ladies, I want this place searched. Understand?'

736

'I've got some ointment,' said Cheri meekly.

'Thank you.'

They found a bag in a cellar. There were several boxes of candles. And a lot of dead rats.

Igneous the troll opened the door of his pottery a fraction. He'd intended the fraction to be no more than about one-sixteenth, but someone immediately pushed hard and turned it into rather more than one and three-quarters.

'Here, what's dis?' he said, as Detritus and Carrot came in with the shell of Dorfl between them. 'You can't jus' break in here—'

'We ain't *just* breakin' in,' said Detritus.

'Dis is an outrage,' said Igneous. 'You got no right comin' in here. You got no reason—'

Detritus let go of the golem and spun around. His hand shot out and caught Igneous around the throat. 'You see dose statchoos of Monolith over dere? You *see* dem?' he growled, twisting the other troll's head to face a row of troll religious statues on the other side of the warehouse. 'You want I should smash one open, see what dey're fill wit', maybe *find* a reason?'

Igneous's slitted eyes darted this way and that. He might have been hard of thinking, but he could feel a killing mood when it was in the air. 'No call for dat, I always help der Watch,' he muttered. 'What dis all about?'

Carrot laid out the golem on a table. 'Start, then,' he said. 'Rebuild him. Use as much of the old clay as you can, understand?'

'How can it work when its lights're out?' said Detritus, still puzzled by this mission of mercy.

'He said the clay remembers!'

The sergeant shrugged.

'And give him a tongue,' said Carrot.

Igneous looked shocked. 'I won't do *dat*,' he said. 'Everybody know it *blasphemy* if golems speak.'

'Oh, yeah?' said Detritus. He strode across the warehouse to the group of statues and glared at them. Then he said, 'Whoops, here's me accident'ly trippin' up, ooo, dis is me grabbin' a statchoo for support, oh, der arm have come right off, where can I put my face . . . and what is dis white powder what I sees here with my eyes accident'ly spillin' on der floor?'

He licked a finger and gingerly tasted the stuff.

'Slab,' he growled, walking back to the trembling Igneous. 'You tellin' *me* about blasphemy, you sedimentr'y coprolith? You doin' what Captain Carrot say right *now* or you goin' out of here in a *sack!*'

'Dis is police brutality . . .' Igneous muttered.

'No, *dis* is just police shoutin'!' yelled Detritus. 'You want to try for brutality it okay wit' me!'

Igneous tried to appeal to Carrot. 'It not right, he got a badge, he puttin' me in fear, he can't do dis,' he said.

Carrot nodded. There was a glint in his eye that Igneous should have noticed. 'That's correct,' he said. 'Sergeant Detritus?'

'Sir?'

'It's been a long day for all of us. You can go off duty.'

'Yessir!' said Detritus, with considerable enthusiasm. He removed his badge and laid it down carefully. Then he started to struggle out of his armour.

'Look at it like this,' said Carrot. 'It's not that we're making life, we're simply giving life a place to live.'

Igneous finally gave up. 'Okay, *okay,*' he muttered. 'I doin' it. I *doin'* it.'

He looked at the various lumps and shards that were all that remained of Dorfl, and rubbed the lichen on his chin.

'You got most of the bits,' he said, professionalism edging resentment aside for a moment. 'I could glue him together wit' kiln cement. Dat'd do the trick if we bakes him overnight. Lessee . . . I reckon I got some over dere . . .'

Detritus blinked at his finger, which was still white with the dust, and sidled over to Carrot. 'Did I just lick dis?' he said.

'Er, yes,' said Carrot.

'T'ank goodness for dat,' said Detritus, blinking furiously. ''d hate to believe dis room was *really* full of giant hairy spide . . . weeble weeble sclup . . .'

He hit the floor, but happily.

'Even if I do it you can't make it come alive again,' muttered Igneous, returning to his bench. 'You won't find a priest who's goin' to write der words for in der head, not again.'

'He'll make up his own words,' said Carrot.

'And who's going to watch the oven?' said Igneous. 'It's gonna take 'til breakfast at least . . .'

'I wasn't planning on doing anything for the rest of tonight,' said Carrot, taking off his helmet.

Vimes awoke around four o'clock. He'd gone to sleep at his desk. He hadn't meant to, but his body had just shut down.

It wasn't the first time he'd opened bleary eyes there. But at least he wasn't lying in anything sticky.

He focused on the report he'd half-written. His notebook was beside it, page after page of laborious scrawl to remind him that he was trying to understand a complex world by means of his simple mind.

He yawned, and looked out at the shank of the night.

He didn't have any evidence. No real evidence at all. He'd had an interview with an almost incoherent Corporal Nobbs, who hadn't really seen anything. He had nothing that wouldn't burn away like the fog in the morning. All he'd got were a few suspicions and a lot of coincidences, leaning against one another like a house of cards with no card on the bottom.

He peered at his notebook.

Someone seemed to have been working hard. Oh, yes. It had been him.

The events of last night jangled in his head. Why'd he written all this stuff about a coat of arms?

Oh, yes . . .

Yes!

Ten minutes later he was pushing open the door of the pottery. Warmth spilled out into the clammy air.

He found Carrot and Detritus asleep on the floor on either side of the kiln. Damn. He needed someone he could trust, but he hadn't the heart to wake them. He'd pushed everyone very hard the last few days . . .

Something tapped on the door of the kiln.

Then the handle started to turn by itself.

The door opened as far as it could go and *something* half-slid and half-fell on to the floor.

Vimes still wasn't properly awake. Exhaustion and the importunate ghosts of adrenalin sizzled around the edges of his consciousness, but he saw the burning man unfold himself and stand upright.

His red-hot body gave little *pings* as it began to cool. Where it stood, the floor charred and smoked.

The golem raised his head and looked around.

'You!' said Vimes, pointing an unsteady finger. 'Come with me!'

'Yes,' said Dorfl.

Dragon King of Arms stepped into his library. The dirt of the small high windows and the remnants of the fog made sure there was never more than greyness here, but a hundred candles yielded their soft light.

He sat down at his desk, pulled a volume towards him, and began to write.

After a while he stopped and stared ahead of him. There was no sound but the occasional spluttering of a candle.

'Ah-ha. I can smell you, Commander Vimes,' he said. 'Did the Heralds let you in?'

'I found my own way, thank you,' said Vimes, stepping out of the shadows.

The vampire sniffed again. 'You came alone?'

'Who should I have brought with me?'

'And to what do I owe the pleasure, Sir Samuel?'

'The pleasure is all mine. I'm going to arrest you,' said Vimes.

'Oh, dear. Ah-ha. For what, may I ask?'

'Can I invite you to notice the arrow in this crossbow?' said Vimes. 'No metal on the point, you'll see. It's wood all the way.'

'How very considerate. Ah-ha.' Dragon King of Arms twinkled at him. 'You still haven't told me what I'm accused of, however.'

'To start with, complicity in the murders of Mrs Flora Easy and the child William Easy.'

'I am afraid those names mean nothing to me.'

Vimes's finger twitched on the bow's trigger. 'No,' he said, breathing deeply. 'They probably don't. We are making other enquiries and there may be a number of additional matters. The fact that you were poisoning the Patrician I consider a mitigating circumstance.'

'You really intend to prefer charges?'

'I'd *prefer* violence,' said Vimes loudly. 'Charges is what I'm going to have to settle for.'

The vampire leaned back. 'I hear you've been working very hard, Commander,' he said. 'So I will not—'

'We've got the testimony of Mr Carry,' lied Vimes. 'The *late* Mr Carry.'

Dragon's expression changed by not one tiny tremor of muscle. 'I really do not know, ah-ha, what you are talking about, Sir Samuel.'

'Only someone who could fly could have got into my office.'

'I'm afraid you've lost me, sir.'

'Mr Carry was killed tonight,' Vimes went on. 'By someone who could get out of an alley guarded at both ends. And I know a vampire was in his factory.'

'I'm still gamely trying to understand you, Commander,' said Dragon King of Arms. 'I know nothing about the death of Mr Carry and in any case there are a great many vampires in the city. I'm afraid your . . . *aversion* is well known.'

'I don't like to see people treated like cattle,' said Vimes. He stared briefly at the volumes piled in the room. 'And of course that's what you've always done, isn't it? These are the stock books of Ankh-Morpork.' The crossbow swung back towards the vampire, who hadn't moved. 'Power over little people. That's what vampires want. The blood is just a way of keeping score. I wonder how much influence you've had over the years?'

'A little. You are correct there, at least.'

'"A person of breeding",' said Vimes. 'Good grief. Well, I think people wanted Vetinari out of the way. But not dead, yet. Too many things'd happen too fast if he were dead. Is Nobby really an earl?'

'The evidence suggests so.'

'But it's *your* evidence, right? You see, I *don't* think he's got noble blood in him. Nobby's as common as muck. It's one of his better points. I don't set any score by the ring. The amount of stuff his family's nicked, you could probably prove he's the Duke of Pseudopolis, the Seriph of Klatch and the Dowager Duchess of Quirm. He pinched my cigar case last year and I'm damn certain he's not me. No, I don't think Nobby is a nob. But I think he *was* convenient.'

It seemed to Vimes that Dragon was getting bigger, but perhaps it was only a trick of the candlelight. The light flickered as the candles hissed and popped.

'You made good use of me, eh?' Vimes carried on. 'I'd been ducking out of appointments with you for weeks. I expect you were getting quite impatient. You were so surprised when I told you about Nobby, eh? Otherwise you'd've had to send for him or something, very suspicious. But Commander Vimes *discovered* him. That looks good. Practically makes it official.

'And then I started thinking: who wants a king? Well, nearly everyone. It's built in. Kings make it better. Funny thing, isn't it? Even those people who owe everything to him don't like Vetinari. Ten years ago most of the guild leaders were just a bunch of thugs and now . . . well, they're still a bunch of thugs, to tell the truth, but Vetinari's given 'em the time and energy to decide they never needed him.

'And then young Carrot turns up with charisma writ all over him, and he's got a sword and a birthmark and everyone gets a funny feeling and dozens of buggers start going through the records and say, "Hey, looks like the king's come back." And *then* they watch him for a while and say, "Shit, he really *is* decent and honest and fair and just, just like in all the stories. Whoops! If this lad gets on the throne we could be in serious trouble! He might turn out to be one of them inconvenient kings from long ago who wanders around talking to the common people – "'

'You are in favour of the common people?' said Dragon mildly.

'The common people?' said Vimes. 'They're nothing special. They're no different from the rich and powerful except they've got no money or power. But the law should be there to balance things up a bit. So I suppose I've got to be on their side.'

'A man married to the richest woman in the city?'

Vimes shrugged. 'The watchman's helmet isn't like a crown. Even when you take it off you're still wearing it.'

'That's an interesting statement of position, Sir Samuel, and I would be the first to admire the way you've come to terms with your family history, but—'

'Don't move!' Vimes shifted his grip on the crossbow. 'Anyway ... Carrot wouldn't do, but the news was getting around, and someone said, "Right, let's have a king we *can* control. All the rumours say the king is a humble watchman so let's find one." And they had a look and found that when it comes to humble you can't beat Nobby Nobbs. But ... I think people weren't too sure. Killing Vetinari wasn't an option. As I said, too many things would happen too fast. But to just gently remove him, so that he's there and not there at the same time, while everyone tried out the idea ... *that* was a good wheeze. That's when someone got Mr Carry to make poisoned candles. He'd got a golem. Golems can't talk. No one would know. But it turned out to be a bit ... erratic.'

'You seem to wish to involve me,' said Dragon King of Arms. 'I know nothing about this man other than that he's a customer—'

Vimes strode across the room and pulled a piece of parchment from a board. 'You did him a coat of arms!' he shouted. 'You even *showed* me when I was here! "The butcher, the baker and the candlestick-maker!" Remember?'

There was no sound now from the hunched figure.

'When I first met you the other day,' said Vimes, 'you made a point of *showing* me Arthur Carry's coat of arms. I thought it was a bit fishy at the time, but all that business with Nobby put it out of my mind. But I *do* remember it reminded me of the one for the Assassins' Guild.'

Vimes flourished the parchment.

'I looked and looked at it last night, and then I wound my sense of humour down ten notches and let it go out of focus and looked at the crest, the fish-shaped lamp. *Lampe au poisson*, it's called. A sort of bilingual play on words, perhaps? "A lamp of poison?" You've got to have a mind like old Detritus to spot that one. And Fred Colon wondered why you'd left the motto in modern Ankhian instead of putting it into the old language, and that made *me* wonder so I sat up with the dictionary and worked it out and, you know, it would have read 'Ars Enixa Est Candelam'. *Ars Enixa*. That must have really cheered you up. You'd said who did it and how it was done and gave it to the poor bugger to be proud of. It didn't matter that no one else would spot it. It made *you* feel good. Because we ordinary mortals just aren't as clever as you, are we?' He shook his head. 'Good grief, a coat of arms. Was that the bribe? Was that all it took?'

Dragon slumped in his chair.

'And then I wondered what was in it for you,' continued Vimes. 'Oh, there's a lot of people involved, I expect, for the same old reasons. But you? Now, my wife breeds dragons. Out of interest, really. Is that what you do? A little hobby to allow the centuries to fly by? Or does blue blood taste sweeter? Y'know, I hope it was some reason like that. Some decent mad selfish one.'

'Possibly – if someone were so inclined, and I certainly make no such admission, ah-ha – they might simply be thinking of improving the race,' said the shape in the shadows.

'Breeding for receding chins or bunny teeth, that sort of thing?' said Vimes. 'Yes, I can see where it'd be more straightforward if you had the whole king business. All those courtly balls. All those little arrangements which see to it that the right kind of gel meets only the right kind of boy. You've had hundreds of years, right? And everyone consults you. You know where all the family trees are planted. But it's all got a bit *messy* under Vetinari, hasn't it? All the wrong people are getting to the top. I know how Sybil curses when people leave the pen gates open: it really messes up her breeding programme.'

'You are wrong about Captain Carrot, ah-ha. The city knows how to work around . . . *difficult* kings. But would it want a future king who might *really* be called Rex?'

Vimes looked blank. There was a sigh from the shadows. 'I am, ah-ha, referring to his apparently stable relationship with the werewolf.'

Vimes stared. Understanding eventually dawned. 'You think they'd have *puppies*?'

'The genetics of werewolves are not straightforward, ah-ha, but the chance of such an outcome would be considered unacceptable. If someone were thinking on those lines.'

'By gods, and that's *it*?'

The shadows were changing. Dragon was still slumped in his chair, but his outline seemed to be blurring.

'Whatever the, ah-ha, motives, Mr Vimes, there is no evidence other than supposition and coincidence and your will to believe that links me with any attempt on Vetinari's, ah-ha, life . . .'

The old vampire's head was sunk even further in his chest. The shadows of his shoulders seemed to be getting longer.

'It was sick, involving the golems,' said Vimes, watching the shadows. 'They could feel what their "king" was doing. Perhaps it wasn't very sane even to begin with, but it was all they had. Clay of their clay. The poor devils didn't have anything except their clay, and you bastards took away even *that*—'

Dragon leapt suddenly, bat-wings unfolding. Vimes's wooden bolt clattered somewhere near the ceiling as he was borne down.

'You really thought you could arrest me with a piece of wood?' said Dragon, his hand around Vimes's neck.

'No,' Vimes croaked. 'I was more . . . poetic . . . than that. All I had . . . to do . . . was keep you talking. Feeling . . . weak, are you? The biter bit . . . you might say . . . ?' He grinned.

The vampire looked puzzled, and then turned his head and stared at the candles. 'You . . . put something in the candles? Really?'

'We . . . knew garlic . . . would smell but . . . our alchemist reckoned that . . . if you get . . . holy water . . . soak the wicks . . . water evaporates . . . just leaves holiness.'

The pressure was released. Dragon King of Arms sat back on his haunches. His face had changed, shaping itself forward, giving him an expression like a fox.

Then he shook his head. 'No,' he said, and this time it was his turn to grin. 'No, that's just words. That wouldn't work . . .'

'Bet . . . your . . . unlife?' rasped Vimes, rubbing his neck. 'A better way . . . than old Carry went, eh?'

'Trying to trick me into an admission, Mr Vimes?'

'Oh, I had *that*,' said Vimes. 'When you looked straight at the candles.'

'Really? Ah-ha. But who else saw me?' said Dragon.

From the shadows there was a rumble like a distant thunderstorm.

'I Did,' said Dorfl.

The vampire looked from the golem to Vimes.

'You gave one of them a *voice*?' he said.

'Yes,' said Dorfl. He reached down and picked up the vampire in one hand. 'I Could Kill You,' he said. 'This Is An Option Available

744

To Me As A Free-Thinking Individual But I Will Not Do So Because I Own Myself And I Have Made A Moral Choice.'

'Oh, gods,' murmured Vimes under his breath.

'That's *blasphemy*,' said the vampire.

He gasped as Vimes shot him a glance like sunlight. 'That's what people say when the voiceless speak. Take him away, Dorfl. Put him in the palace dungeons.'

'I Could Take No Notice Of That Command But Am Choosing To Do So Out Of Earned Respect And Social Responsibility—'

'Yes, yes, fine,' said Vimes quickly.

Dragon clawed at the golem. He might as well have kicked at a mountain.

'Undead Or Alive, You Are Coming With Me,' said Dorfl.

'Is there no end to your crimes? You've made this thing a *policeman?*' said the vampire, struggling as Dorfl dragged him away.

'No, but it's an intriguing suggestion, don't you think?' said Vimes.

He was left alone in the thick velvety gloom of the Royal College.

And Vetinari will let him go, he reflected. *Because this is politics. Because he's part of the way the city works. Besides, there's the matter of evidence. I've got enough to prove it to myself, but . . .*

But I'll know, he told himself.

Oh, he'll be watched, and maybe one day when Vetinari is ready a really good assassin will be sent with a wooden dagger soaked in garlic, and it'll all be done in the dark. That's how politics works in this city. It's a game of chess. Who cares if a few pawns die?

I'll know. And I'll be the only one who knows, deep down.

His hands automatically patted his pockets for a cigar.

It was hard enough to kill a vampire. You could stake them down and turn them into dust and ten years later someone drops a drop of blood in the wrong place and *guess who's back*? They returned more times than raw broccoli.

These were dangerous thoughts, he knew. They were the kind that crept up on a watchman when the chase was over and it was just you and him, facing one another in that breathless little pinch between the crime and the punishment.

And maybe a watchman had seen civilization with the skin ripped off one time too many and stopped acting like a watchman and started acting like a normal human being and realized that the click of the crossbow or the sweep of the sword would make all the world so *clean*.

And you couldn't think like that, even about vampires. Even

though they'd take the lives of other people because little lives don't matter and what the hell can we take away from *them*?

And you couldn't think like that because they gave you a sword and a badge and that turned you into something else and *that* had to mean there were some thoughts you couldn't think.

Only crimes could take place in darkness. Punishment had to be done in the light. That was the job of a good watchman, Carrot always said. To light a candle in the dark.

He found a cigar. Now his hands did the automatic search for matches.

The volumes were piled up against the walls. The candlelight picked up gold lettering and the dull gleam of leather. There they were, the lineages, the books of heraldic minutiae, the Who's Whom of the centuries, the stock books of the city. People stood on them to look down.

No matches . . .

Quietly, in the dusty silence of the College, Vimes picked up a candelabrum and lit his cigar.

He took a few deep luxuriant puffs, and looked thoughtfully at the books. In his hand, the candles spluttered and flickered.

The clock ticked its arrhythmic tock. It finally stuttered its way to one o'clock, and Vimes got up and went into the Oblong Office.

'Ah, Vimes,' said Lord Vetinari, looking up.

'Yes, sir.'

Vimes had managed a few hours' sleep and had even attempted to shave.

The Patrician shuffled some papers on his desk. 'It seems to have been a very busy night last night . . .'

'Yes, sir.' Vimes stood to attention. All uniformed men knew in their very soul how to act in circumstances like this. You stared straight ahead, for one thing.

'It appears that I have Dragon King of Arms in the cells,' said the Patrician.

'Yes, sir.'

'I've read your report. Somewhat tenuous evidence, I feel.'

'Sir?'

'One of your witnesses isn't even alive, Vimes.'

'No, sir. Neither is the suspect, sir. Technically.'

'He is, however, an important civic figure. An authority.'

'Yes, sir.'

Lord Vetinari shuffled some of the papers on his desk. One of them was covered in sooty fingermarks. 'It also appears I have to commend you, Commander.'

'Sir?'

'The Heralds at the Royal College of Arms, or at least at what *remains* of the Royal College of Arms, have sent me a note saying how bravely you worked last night.'

'Sir?'

'Letting all those heraldic animals out of the pens and raising the alarm and so on. A tower of strength, they've called you. I gather most of the creatures are lodging with you at the present time?'

'Yes, sir. Couldn't stand by and let them suffer, sir. We'd got some empty pens, sir, and Keith and Roderick are doing well in the lake. They've taken a liking to Sybil, sir.'

Lord Vetinari coughed. Then he stared up at the ceiling for a while. 'So you, er, assisted in the fire.'

'Yes, sir. Civic duty, sir.'

'The fire was caused by a candlestick falling over, I understand, possibly after your fight with Dragon King of Arms.'

'So I believe, sir.'

'And so, it seems, do the Heralds.'

'Anyone told Dragon King of Arms?' said Vimes innocently.

'Yes.'

'Took it well, did he?'

'He screamed a lot, Vimes. In a heart-rending fashion, I am told. And I gather he uttered a number of threats against you, for some reason.'

'I shall try to fit him into my busy schedule, sir.'

'Bingely bongely beep!!' said a small bright voice. Vimes slapped a hand against his pocket.

Lord Vetinari fell silent for a moment. His fingers drummed softly on his desk. 'Many fine old manuscripts in that place, I believe. Without price, I'm told.'

'Yes, sir. Certainly worthless, sir.'

'Is it possible you misunderstood what I just said, Commander?'

'Could be, sir.'

'The provenances of many splendid old families went up in smoke, Commander. Of course, the Heralds will do what they can, and the families themselves keep records but frankly, I understand, it's all going to be patchwork and guesswork. Extremely embarrassing. Are you smiling, Commander?'

'It was probably a trick of the light, sir.'

'Commander, I always used to consider that you had a definite anti-authoritarian streak in you.'

747

'Sir?'

'It seems that you have managed to retain this even though you *are* authority.'

'Sir?'

'That's practically Zen.'

'Sir?'

'It seems I've only got to be unwell for a few days and you manage to upset everyone of any importance in this city.'

'Sir.'

'Was that a "yes, sir" or a "no, sir", Sir Samuel?'

'It was just a "sir", sir.'

Lord Vetinari glanced at a piece of paper. 'Did you really punch the president of the Assassins' Guild?'

'Yes, sir.'

'Why?'

'Didn't have a dagger, sir.'

Vetinari turned away abruptly. 'The Council of Churches, Temples, Sacred Groves and Big Ominous Rocks is demanding . . . well, a number of things, several of them involving wild horses. Initially, however, they want me to sack you.'

'Yes, sir?'

'In all I've had seventeen demands for your badge. Some want parts of your body attached. Why did you have to upset everybody?'

'I suppose it's a knack, sir.'

'But what could you hope to achieve?'

'Well, sir, since you *ask*, we found out who murdered Father Tubelcek *and* Mr Hopkinson *and* who was poisoning you, sir.' Vimes paused. 'Two out of three's not bad, sir.'

Vetinari riffled through the papers again. 'Workshop owners, assassins, priests, butchers . . . you seem to have infuriated most of the leading figures in the city.' He sighed. 'Really, it seems I have no choice. As of this week, I'm giving you a pay rise.'

Vimes blinked. 'Sir?'

'Nothing unseemly. Ten dollars a month. And I expect they need a new dart-board in the Watch House? They usually do, I recall.'

'It's Detritus,' said Vimes, his mind unable to think of anything other than an honest reply. 'He tends to split them.'

'Ah, yes. And talking of splits, Vimes, I wonder if your forensic genius could help me with a little conundrum we found this morning.' The Patrician stood up and headed for the stairs.

'Yes, sir? What is it?' said Vimes, following him down.

'It's in the Rats Chamber, Vimes.'

'Really, sir?'

Vetinari pushed open the double doors. 'Voilà,' he said.

748

'That's some kind of musical instrument, isn't it, sir?'

'No, Commander, the word means "What is that in the table?",' said the Patrician sharply.

Vimes looked into the room. There was no one there. The long mahogany table was bare.

Except for the axe. It had embedded itself in the wood very deeply, almost splitting the table along its entire length. Someone had walked up to the table and brought an axe down right in the centre as hard as they could and then left it there, its handle pointing towards the ceiling.

'That's an axe,' said Vimes.

'Astonishing,' said Lord Vetinari. 'And you've barely had time to study it. *Why* is it there?'

'I really couldn't say, sir.'

'According to the servants, Sir Samuel, you came into the palace at six o'clock this morning . . .'

'Oh, yes, sir. To check that the bastard was safely in a cell, sir. And to see that everything was all right, of course.'

'You didn't come into this room?'

Vimes kept his gaze fixed somewhere on the horizon. 'Why should I have done that, sir?'

The Patrician tapped the axe handle. It vibrated with a faint thumping noise. 'I believe some of the City Council met in here this morning. Or came in here, at least. I'm told they hurried out very quickly. Looking rather disturbed, I'm told.'

'Maybe it was one of them that did it, sir.'

'That is, of course, a possibility,' said Lord Vetinari. 'I suppose you won't be able to find one of your famous Clues on the thing?'

'Shouldn't think so, sir. Not with all these fingerprints on it.'

'It would be a terrible thing, would it not, if people thought they could take the law into their own hands . . .'

'Oh, no fear of that, sir. I'm holding on tightly to it.'

Lord Vetinari *plunked* the axe again. 'Tell me, Sir Samuel, do you know the phrase "*Quis custodiet ipsos custodes?*"?'

It was an expression Carrot had occasionally used, but Vimes was not in the mood to admit anything. 'Can't say that I do, sir,' he said. 'Something about trifle, is it?'

'It means "Who guards the guards themselves?", Sir Samuel.'

'Ah.'

'Well?'

'Sir?'

'Who watches the Watch? I wonder?'

'Oh, that's easy, sir. We watch one another.'

'Really? An intriguing point . . .'

Lord Vetinari walked out of the room and back into the main hall, with Vimes trailing behind. 'However,' he said, 'in order to keep the peace, the golem will have to be destroyed.'

'No, sir.'

'Allow me to repeat my instruction.'

'No, sir.'

'I'm sure I just gave you an order, Commander. I distinctly felt my lips move.'

'No, sir. He's alive, sir.'

'He's just made of clay, Vimes.'

'Aren't we all, sir? According to them pamphlets Constable Visit keeps handing out. Anyway, *he* thinks he's alive, and that's good enough for me.'

The Patrician waved a hand towards the stairs and his office full of paper. 'Nevertheless, Commander, I've had no less than nine missives from leading religious figures declaring that he is an abomination.'

'Yes, sir. I've given that viewpoint a lot of thought, sir, and reached the following conclusion: arseholes to the lot of 'em, sir.'

The Patrician's hand covered his mouth for a moment. 'Sir Samuel, you are a harsh negotiator. Surely you can give and take?'

'Couldn't say, sir.' Vimes walked to the main doors and pushed them open.

'Fog's lifted, sir,' he said. 'There's a bit of cloud but you can see all the way across the Brass Bridge—'

'What will you use the golem for?'

'Not *use*, sir. Employ. I thought he might be useful for to keep the peace, sir.'

'A watchman?'

'Yes, sir,' said Vimes. 'Haven't you heard, sir? Golems do all the mucky jobs.'

Vetinari watched him go, and sighed. 'He does so like a dramatic exit,' he said.

'Yes, my lord,' said Drumknott, who had appeared noiselessly at his shoulder.

'Ah, Drumknott.' The Patrician took a length of candle out of his pocket and handed it to his secretary. 'Dispose of this somewhere safely, will you?'

'Yes, my lord?'

'It's the candle from the other night.'

'It's not burned down, my lord? But I saw the candle end in the holder . . .'

'Oh, of course I cut off enough to make a stub and let the wick burn for a moment. I couldn't let our gallant policeman know I'd

750

worked it out for myself, could I? Not when he was making such an effort and having so much fun being . . . well, being *Vimes*. I'm not *completely* heartless, you know.'

'But, my lord, you could have sorted it out diplomatically! Instead he went around upsetting things and making a lot of people very angry and afraid—'

'Yes. Dear me. Tsk, tsk.'

'Ah,' said Drumknott.

'Quite so,' said the Patrician.

'Do you wish me to have the table in the Rats Chamber repaired?'

'No, Drumknott, leave the axe where it is. It will make a good . . . conversation piece, I think.'

'May I make an observation, my lord?'

'Of course you may,' said Vetinari, watching Vimes walk through the palace gates.

'The thought occurs, sir, that if Commander Vimes did not exist you would have had to invent him.'

'You know, Drumknott, I rather think I did.'

'Atheism Is Also A Religious Position,' Dorfl rumbled.

'No it's not!' said Constable Visit. 'Atheism is a *denial* of a god.'

'Therefore It Is A Religious Position,' said Dorfl. 'Indeed, A True Atheist Thinks Of The Gods Constantly, Albeit In Terms Of Denial. Therefore, Atheism Is A Form Of Belief. If The Atheist Truly Did Not Believe, He Or She Would Not Bother To Deny.'

'Did you read those pamphlets I gave you?' said Visit suspiciously.

'Yes. Many Of Them Did Not Make Sense. But I Should Like To Read Some More.'

'Really?' said Visit. His eyes gleamed. 'You really want *more* pamphlets?'

'Yes. There Is Much In Them That I Would Like To Discuss. If You Know Some Priests, I Would Enjoy Disputation.'

'All right, all right,' said Sergeant Colon. 'So are you going to take the sodding oath or not, Dorfl?'

Dorfl held up a hand the size of a shovel. 'I, Dorfl, Pending The Discovery Of A Deity Whose Existence Withstands Rational Debate, Swear By The Temporary Precepts Of A Self-Derived Moral System—'

'You *really* want more pamphlets?' said Constable Visit.

Sergeant Colon rolled his eyes.

'Yes,' said Dorfl.

'Oh, my god!' said Constable Visit, and burst into tears. 'No one's *ever* asked for more pamphlets before!'

Colon turned when he realized Vimes was watching. 'It's no good, sir,' he said. 'I've been trying to swear him in for half an hour, sir, and we keep ending up arguing about oaths and things.'

'You willing to be a Watchman, Dorfl?' said Vimes.

'Yes.'

'Right. That's as good as a swear to me. Give him his badge, Fred. And this is for you, Dorfl. It's a chit to say you're officially alive, just in case you run into any trouble. You know . . . with people.'

'Thank You,' said Dorfl solemnly. 'If Ever I Feel I Am Not Alive, I Will Take This Out And Read It.'

'What are your duties?' said Vimes.

'To Serve The Public Trust, Protect The Innocent, And Seriously Prod Buttock, Sir,' said Dorfl.

'He learns fast, doesn't he?' said Colon. 'I didn't even *tell* him the last one.'

'People won't like it,' said Nobby. ''S not going to be popular, a golem as a watchman.'

'What Better Work For One Who Loves Freedom Than The Job Of Watchman. Law Is The Servant Of Freedom. Freedom Without Limits Is Just A Word,' said Dorfl ponderously.

'Y'know,' said Colon, 'if it doesn't work out, you could always get a job making fortune cookies.'

'Funny thing, that,' said Nobby. 'You never get bad fortunes in cookies, ever noticed that? They never say stuff like: "Oh dear, things're going to be really bad." I mean, they're never *misfortune* cookies.'

Vimes lit a cigar and shook the match to put it out. 'That, Corporal, is because of one of the fundamental driving forces of the universe.'

'What? Like, people who read fortune cookies are the lucky ones?' said Nobby.

'No. Because people who *sell* fortune cookies want to go on selling them. Come on, Constable Dorfl. We're going for a walk.'

'There's a lot of paperwork, sir,' said Sergeant Colon.

'Tell Captain Carrot I said he should look at it,' said Vimes, from the doorway.

'He hasn't been in yet, sir.'

'It'll keep.'

'Right, sir.'

Colon went and sat behind his desk. It was a good place to be, he'd decided. There was absolutely no chance of finding any Nature there. He'd had a rare conversation with Mrs Colon this morning and made it clear that he was no longer interested in getting close to the soil because he'd *been* as close to the soil as it was possible to get and the soil, it turned out, was just dirt. A good thick layer of cobblestones was, he decided, about as close as he wanted to get to Nature. Also, Nature tended to be squishy.

'I've got to go on duty,' said Nobby. 'Captain Carrot wants me to do crime prevention in Peach Pie Street.'

'How d'you do that, then?' said Colon.

'Keep away, he said.'

''Ere, Nobby, woss this about you not being a lord after all?' said Colon cautiously.

'I think I got the sack,' said Nobby. 'Bit of a relief, really. That nobby grub isn't much, and the drink is frankly piss.'

'Lucky escape for you, then,' said Colon. 'I mean, you won't have to go giving your clothes away to gardeners and so on.'

'Yeah. Wish I'd never told them about the damn ring, really.'

'Would've saved you a lot of trouble, certainly,' said Colon.

Nobby spat on his badge and buffed it industriously with his sleeve. *'S a good job I never told them about the tiara, the coronet and the three gold lockets*, he said to himself.

'Where Are We Going?' said Dorfl, as Vimes strolled across the Brass Bridge.

'I thought I might break you in gently with some guard duty at the palace,' said Vimes.

'Ah. This Is Where My New Friend Constable Visit Is Also On Guard,' said Dorfl.

'Splendid!'

'I Wish To Ask You A Question,' said the golem.

'Yes?'

'I Smashed The Treadmill But The Golems Repaired It. Why? And I Let The Animals Go But They Just Milled Around Stupidly. Some Of Them Even Went Back To The Slaughter Pens. Why?'

'Welcome to the world, Constable Dorfl.'

'Is It Frightening To Be Free?'

'You said it.'

'You Say To People "Throw Off Your Chains" And They Make New Chains For Themselves?'

'Seems to be a major human activity, yes.'

Dorfl rumbled as he thought about this. 'Yes,' he said eventually. 'I Can See Why. Freedom Is Like Having The Top Of Your Head Opened Up.'

'I'll have to take your word for that, Constable.'

'And You Will Pay Me Twice As Much As Other Watchmen,' said Dorfl.

'Will I?'

'Yes. I Do Not Sleep. I Can Work Constantly. I Am A Bargain. I Do Not Need Days Off To Bury My Granny.'

How soon they learn, thought Vimes. He said: 'But you have holy days off, don't you?'

'Either All Days Are Holy Or None Are. I Have Not Decided Yet.'

'Er . . . what do you need money for, Dorfl?'

'I Shall Save Up And Purchase The Golem Klutz Who Labours In The Pickle Factory, And Give Him To Himself; Then Together We Will Earn And Save For The Golem Bobkes Of The Coal Merchant; The Three Of Us Will Labour And Buy The Golem Shmata Who Toils At The Seven-Dollar Tailor's In Peach Pie Street; Then The Four Of Us Will—'

'*Some* people might decide to free their comrades by force and bloody revolution,' said Vimes. 'Not that I'm suggesting that in any way, of course.'

'No. That Would Be Theft. We Are Bought And Sold. So We Will Buy Ourselves Free. By Our Labour. No One Else To Do It For Us. We Will Do It By Ourselves.'

Vimes smiled to himself. Probably no other species in the world would demand a receipt with their freedom. Some things you just couldn't change.

'Ah,' he said. 'It seems some people want to talk to us . . .'

A crowd was approaching over the bridge, in a mass of grey, black and saffron robes. It was made up of priests. They looked angry. As they pushed and shoved their way through the other citizens, several haloes became interlocked.

At their head was Hughnon Ridcully, Chief Priest of Blind Io and the closest thing Ankh-Morpork had to a spokesman on religious issues. He spotted Vimes and hurried towards him, admonitory finger upraised.

'Now, see here, Vimes . . .' he began, and stopped. He glared at Dorfl.

'Is this *it*?' he said.

'If you mean the golem, this is *him*,' said Vimes. 'Constable Dorfl, your reverence.'

Dorfl touched his helmet respectfully. 'How May We Be Of Service?' he said.

'You've done it this time, Vimes!' said Ridcully, ignoring him. 'You've gone altogether too far by half. You made this thing speak and it isn't even alive!'

'We want it smashed!'

'Blasphemy!'

'People won't stand for it!'

Ridcully looked around at the other priests. 'I'm *talking*,' he said. He turned back to Vimes. 'This comes under the heading of gross profanity and the worship of idols—'

'I don't worship him. I'm just employing him,' said Vimes, beginning to enjoy himself. 'And he's far from idle.' He took a deep breath. 'And if it's gross profanity you're looking for—'

'Excuse Me,' said Dorfl.

'We're not listening to you! You're not even really alive!' said a priest.

Dorfl nodded. 'This Is Fundamentally True,' he said.

'See? He admits it!'

'I Suggest You Take Me And Smash Me And Grind The Bits Into Fragments And Pound The Fragments Into Powder And Mill Them Again To The Finest Dust There Can Be, And I Believe You Will Not Find A Single Atom Of Life—'

'True! Let's do it!'

'However, In Order To Test This Fully, One Of You Must Volunteer To Undergo The Same Process.'

There was silence.

'That's not fair,' said a priest, after a while. 'All anyone has to do is bake up your dust again and you'll be alive . . .'

There was more silence.

Ridcully said, 'Is it only me, or are we on tricky theological ground here?'

There was more silence.

Another priest said, 'Is it true you've said you'll believe in any god whose existence can be proved by logical debate?'

'Yes.'

Vimes had a feeling about the immediate future and took a few steps away from Dorfl.

'But the gods plainly *do* exist,' said a priest.

'It Is Not Evident.'

A bolt of lightning lanced through the clouds and hit Dorfl's helmet. There was a sheet of flame and then a trickling noise. Dorfl's molten armour formed puddles around his white-hot feet.

'I Don't Call That Much Of An Argument,' said Dorfl calmly, from somewhere in the clouds of smoke.

'It's tended to carry the audience,' said Vimes. 'Up until now.'

The Chief Priest of Blind Io turned to the other priests. 'All right, you fellows, there's no need for any of that—'

'But Offler is a vengeful god,' said a priest at the back of the crowd.

'Trigger-happy is what he is,' said Ridcully. Another lightning bolt zigzagged down but bent at right-angles a few feet above the Chief Priest's hat and earthed itself on a wooden hippo, which split. The Chief Priest smiled smugly and turned back to Dorfl, who was making little clinking noises as he cooled.

'What you're saying is, you'll accept the existence of any god only if it can be proved by discussion?'

'Yes,' said Dorfl.

Ridcully rubbed his hands together. '*Not* a problem, me old china,' he said. 'Firstly, let us take the—'

'Excuse Me,' said Dorfl. He bent down and picked up his badge. The lightning had given it an interesting melted shape.

'What are you doing?' said Ridcully.

'Somewhere, A Crime Is Happening,' said Dorfl. 'But When I Am Off Duty I Will Gladly Dispute With The Priest Of The Most Worthy God.'

He turned and strode on across the bridge. Vimes nodded hurriedly at the shocked priests and ran after him. *We took him and baked him in the fire and he's turned out to be free*, he thought. *No words in the head except the ones he's chosen to put there himself. And he's not just an atheist, he's a* ceramic *atheist. Fireproof!*

It looked like being a good day.

Behind them, on the bridge, a fight was breaking out.

Angua was packing. Or, rather, she was failing to pack. The bundle couldn't be too heavy to carry by mouth. But a little money (she wouldn't have to buy much food) and a change of clothes (for those occasions when she might have to wear clothes) didn't have to take up much room.

'The boots are a problem,' she said aloud.

'Maybe if you knot the laces together you could carry them round your neck?' said Cheri, who was sitting on the narrow bed.

'Good idea. Do you want these dresses? I've never got round to wearing them. I expect you could cut them down.'

Cheri took them in both arms. 'This one's *silk*!'

'There's probably enough material for you to make two for one.'

'D'you mind if I share them out? Only some of the lads – the *ladies* at the Watch House' – Cheri savoured the word 'ladies' – 'are beginning to get a bit thoughtful . . .'

'Going to melt down their helmets, are they?' said Angua.

'Oh, *no*. But perhaps they could be made into a more attractive design. Er . . .'

'Yes?'

'Um . . .'

Cheri shifted uneasily.

'You've never actually *eaten* anyone, have you? You know . . . crunching bones and so on?'

'No.'

'I mean, I only *heard* my second cousin was eaten by werewolves. He was called Sfen.'

'Can't say I recall the name,' said Angua.

Cheri tried to grin. 'That's all right, then,' she said.

'So you won't need that silver spoon in your pocket,' said Angua.

Cheri's mouth dropped open, and then the words tumbled over themselves. 'Er . . . I don't know how it got there it must have dropped in when I was washing up oh I didn't mean—'

'It doesn't worry me, honestly. I'm used to it.'

'But I didn't think you'd—'

'Look, don't get the wrong idea. It's not a case of not wanting to,' said Angua. 'It's a case of wanting to and *not doing it*.'

'You don't really have to go, do you?'

'Oh, I don't know if I can take the Watch seriously and . . . and sometimes I think Carrot's working up to ask me . . . and, well, it'd never work out. It's the way he just *assumes* everything, you know? So best to go now,' Angua lied.

'Won't Carrot try to stop you?'

'Yes, but there's nothing he can say.'

'He'll be upset.'

'Yes,' said Angua briskly, throwing another dress on the bed. 'And then he'll get over it.'

'Hrolf Thighbiter's asked me out,' said Cheri shyly, looking at the floor. 'And I'm almost *certain* he's male!'

'Glad to hear it.'

Cheri stood up. 'I'll walk with you as far as the Watch House. I've got to go on duty.'

They were halfway along Elm Street before they saw Carrot, head and shoulders above the crowd.

'Looks like he was coming to see you,' said Cheri. 'Er, shall I go away?'

'Too late . . .'

'Ah, good morning, Corporal Miss Littlebottom!' said Carrot cheerfully. 'Hello, Angua. I was just coming to see you but I had to write my letter home first, of course.'

He took off his helmet, and smoothed back his hair. 'Er . . .' he began.

'I know what you're going to ask,' said Angua.

'You do?'

'I know you've been thinking about it. You knew I was wondering about going.'

'It was obvious, was it?'

'And the answer's no. I wish it could be yes.'

Carrot looked astonished. 'It never occurred to me that you'd say no,' he said. 'I mean, why should you?'

'Good grief, you amaze me,' she said. 'You really do.'

'I thought it'd be something you'd want to do,' said Carrot. He sighed. 'Oh, well . . . it doesn't matter, really.'

Angua felt that a leg had been kicked away. 'It doesn't *matter*?' she said.

'I mean, yes, it'd have been nice, but I won't lose any sleep over it.'

'You won't?'

'Well, no. Obviously not. You've got other things you want to do. That's fine. I just thought you might enjoy it. I'll do it by myself.'

'What? How can . . . ?' Angua stopped. 'What are you *talking* about, Carrot?'

'The Dwarf Bread Museum. I promised Mr Hopkinson's sister that I'd tidy it up. You know, get it sorted out. She's not very well off and I thought it could raise some money. Just between you and me, there's several exhibits in there that could be better-presented, but I'm afraid Mr Hopkinson was rather set in his ways. I'm sure there's a lot of dwarfs in the city that'd flock there if they knew about it, and of course there's a lot of youngsters that ought to learn more about their proud heritage. A good dusting and a lick of paint would make all the difference, I'm sure, especially on the older loaves. I don't mind giving up a few days off. I just thought it might cheer you up, but I appreciate that bread isn't everyone's cup of tea.'

Angua stared at him. It was the stare that Carrot so often attracted. It roamed every feature of his face, looking for the tiniest clue that he was making some kind of joke. Some long, deep joke at the expense of everyone else. Every sinew in her body *knew* that he must be, but there was not a clue, not a twitch to prove it.

'Yes,' she said weakly, still searching his face, 'I expect it could be a little goldmine.'

'Museums have got to be a whole lot more interesting these days. And, you know, there's a whole guerrilla crumpet assortment he hasn't even catalogued,' said Carrot. '*And* some early examples of defensive bagels.'

'Gosh,' said Angua. 'Hey, why don't we paint a big sign saying something like "The Dwarf Bread Experience"?'

'That probably wouldn't work for dwarfs,' said Carrot, oblivious to sarcasm. 'A dwarf bread experience tends to be short. But I can see it's certainly caught your imagination!'

I'll have to go, Angua thought as they strolled on down the street. *Sooner or later he'll see that it can't really work out. Werewolves and humans . . . we've both got too much to lose. Sooner or later I'll have to leave him.*

But, for one day at a time, let it be tomorrow.

'Want the dresses back?' said Cheri, behind her.

'Maybe one or two,' said Angua.